Also by Laura Knetzger
Sea Urchin (Retrofit Comics)

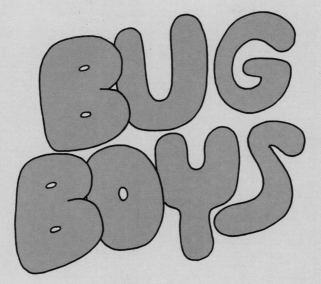

BUG BOYS

By Laura Knetzger
Colors by Lyle Lynde

RH
GRAPHIC

Bug Boys was made with pen and ink on Bristol board and Photoshop.

Cover art, text, and interior illustrations copyright © 2011, 2012, 2013, 2014, 2015, 2020 by Laura Knetzger

All rights reserved. Published in the United States by RH Graphic, an imprint of Random House Children's Books, a division of Penguin Random House LLC, New York. Originally published in the United States in black and white and in different form by Czap Books, Providence, Rhode Island, in 2015.

RH Graphic with the book design is a trademark of Penguin Random House LLC.

Visit us on the Web! RHKidsGraphic.com • @RHKidsGraphic
LauraKnetzger.com

Educators and librarians, for a variety of teaching tools, visit us at RHTeachersLibrarians.com

Library of Congress Cataloging-in-Publication Data
Names: Knetzger, Laura, author, illustrator. | Lynde, Lyle, colorist.
Title: Bug boys / by Laura Knetzger ; colored by Lyle Lynde.
Description: First RH Graphic edition. | New York : RH Graphic, [2020] |
"Originally published in the United States in black and white and in different form by Czap Books, Providence, Rhode Island, in 2015." |
Summary: Follows two bug friends, Stag-B and Rhino-B, as they explore their world and share adventures.
Identifiers: LCCN 2019018102 | ISBN 978-0-593-12522-9 (library binding) | ISBN 978-1-9848-9676-6 (hardcover) | ISBN 978-1-9848-9677-3 (ebook)
Subjects: LCSH: Graphic novels. | CYAC: Graphic novels. | Insects—Fiction. | Adventure and adventurers—Fiction. | Best friends—Fiction. | Friendship—Fiction.
Classification: LCC PZ7.7.K655 Bug 2020 | DDC 741.5/973—dc23

Designed by Patrick Crotty
Colored by Lyle Lynde

MANUFACTURED IN CHINA
10 9 8 7 6 5 4 3 2 1
First American Edition

A comic on every bookshelf.

To Bob and Deb

Special thanks to:
Kevin Czap
Mark Friedman
Stuart Solomon
Christopher Wessel

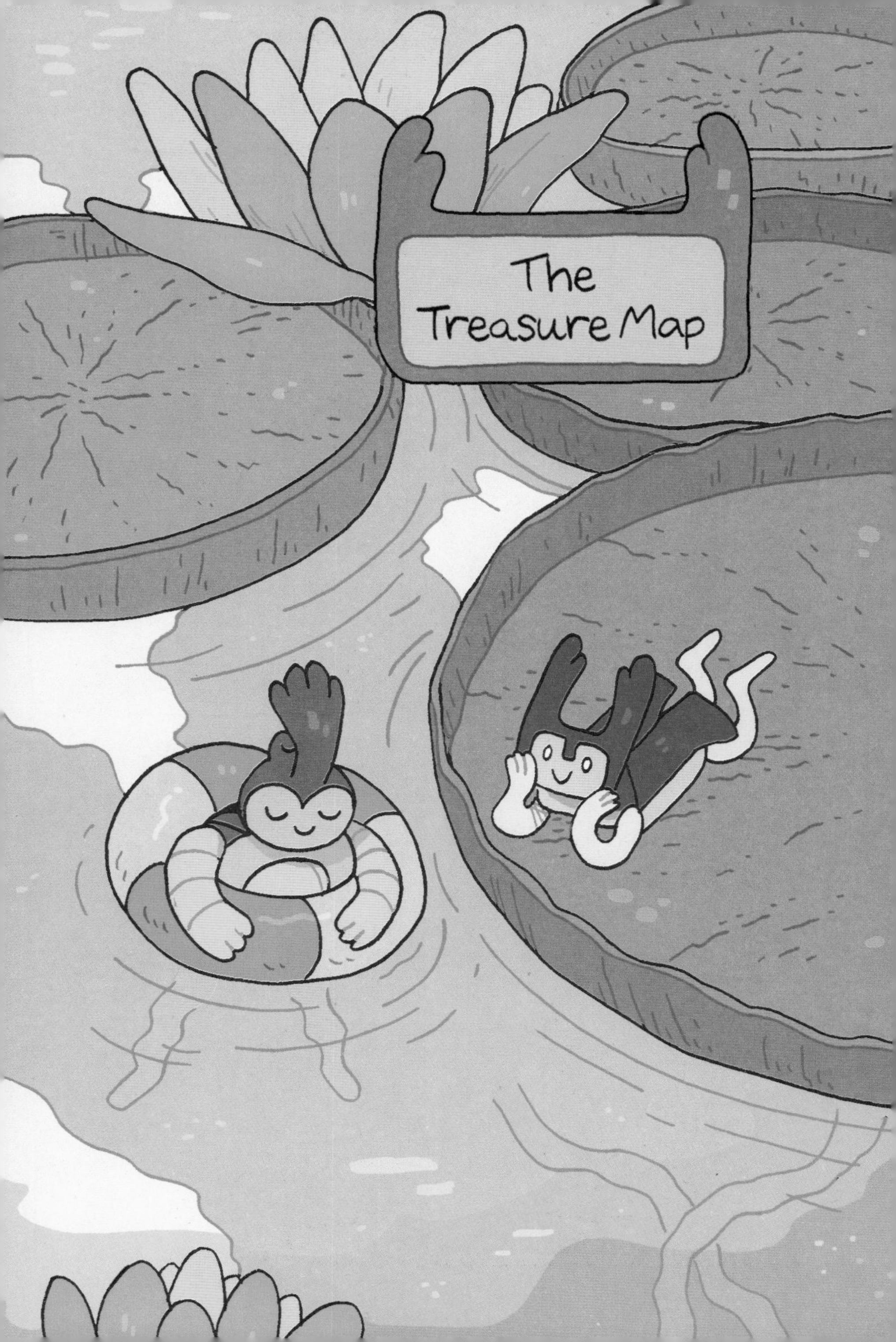
The
Treasure Map

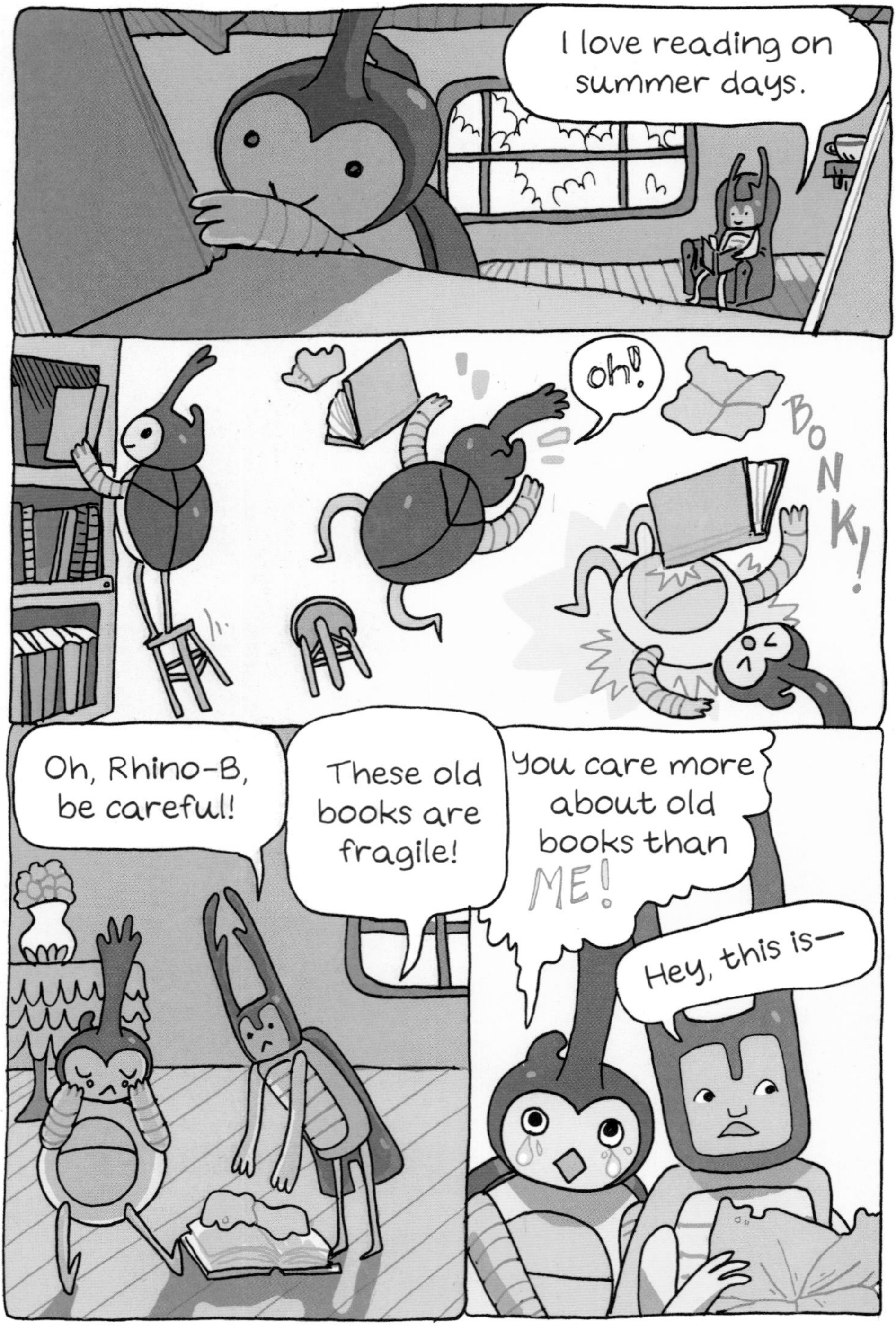
I love reading on summer days.
oh!
BONK!
Oh, Rhino-B, be careful!
These old books are fragile!
You care more about old books than ME!
Hey, this is—

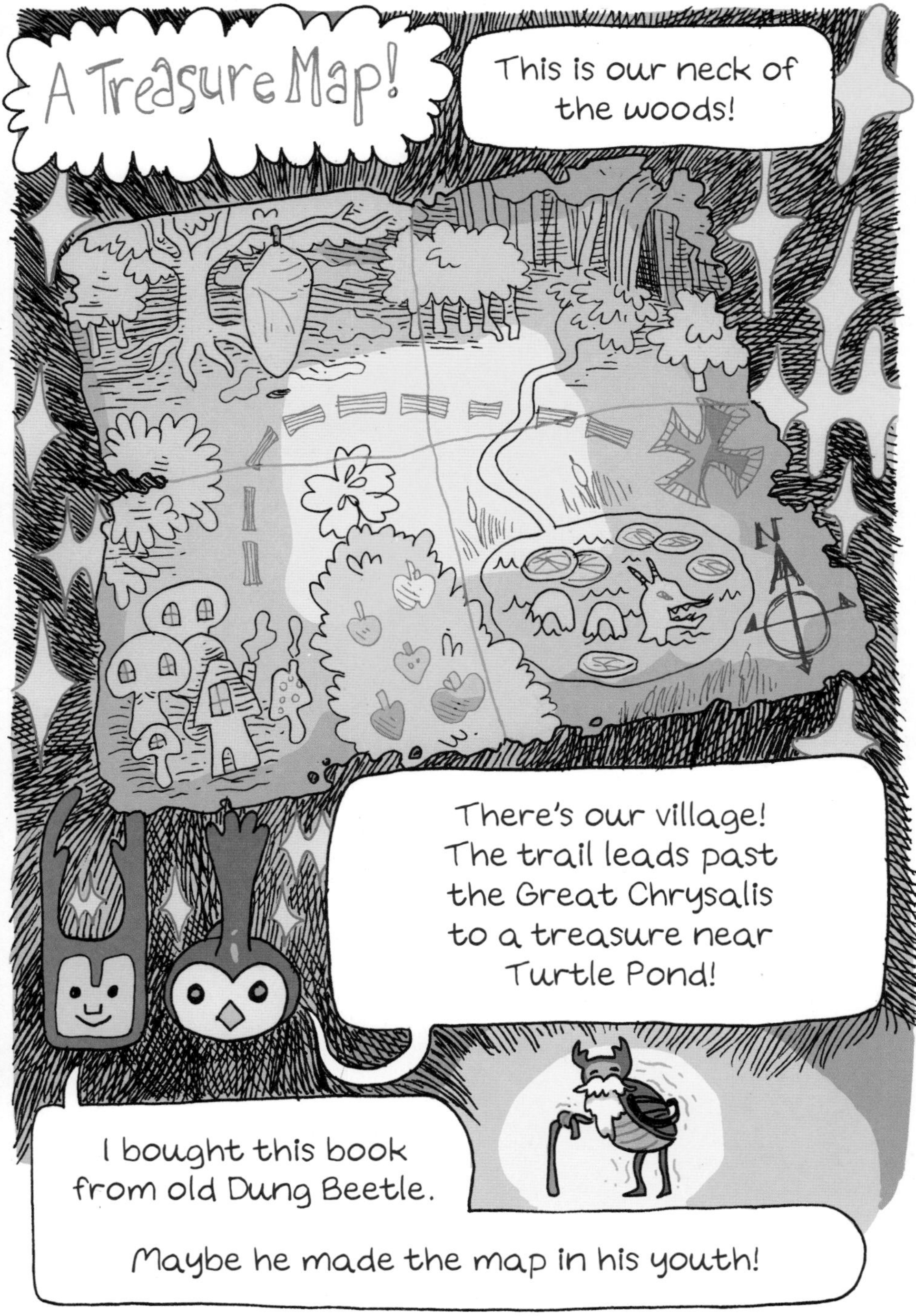
A Treasure Map!
This is our neck of the woods!
There's our village! The trail leads past the Great Chrysalis to a treasure near Turtle Pond!
I bought this book from old Dung Beetle.
Maybe he made the map in his youth!

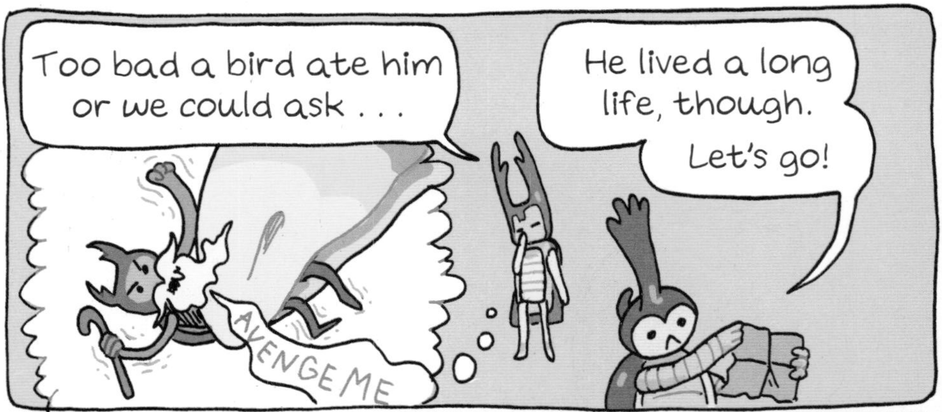
Too bad a bird ate him or we could ask . . .
AVENGE ME
He lived a long life, though.
Let's go!

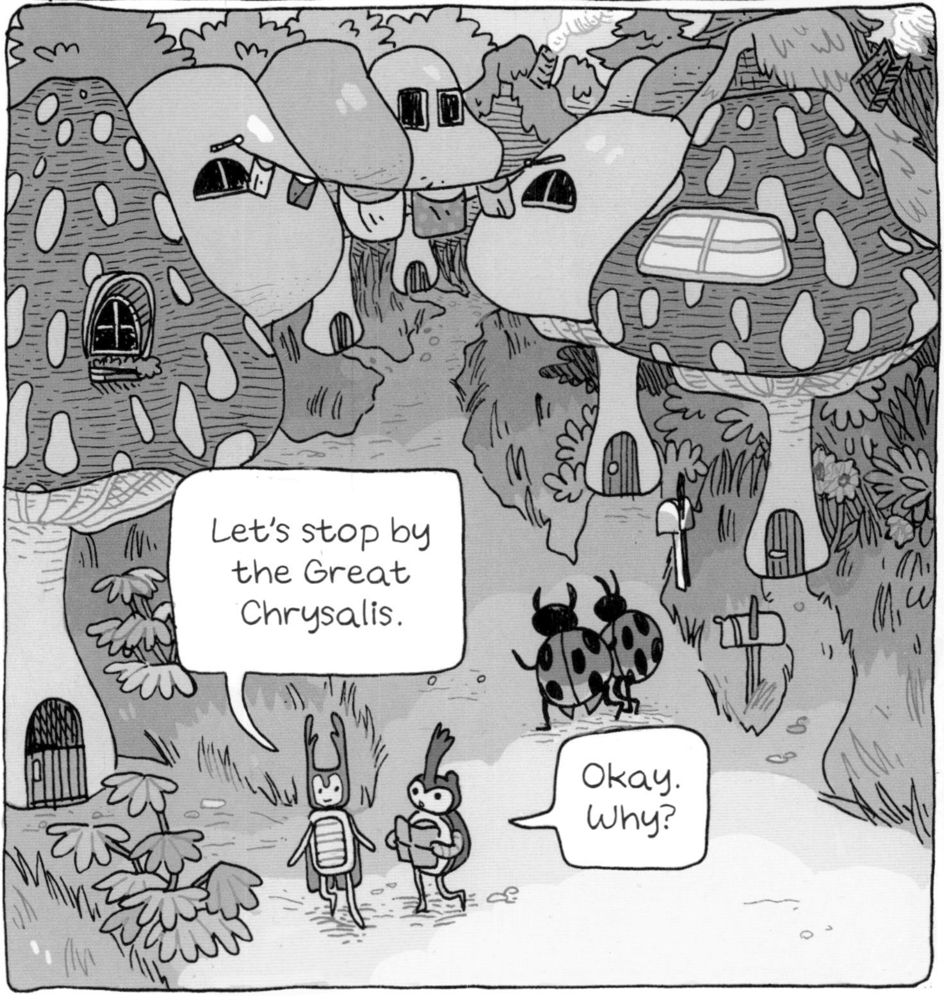
Let's stop by the Great Chrysalis.
Okay. Why?

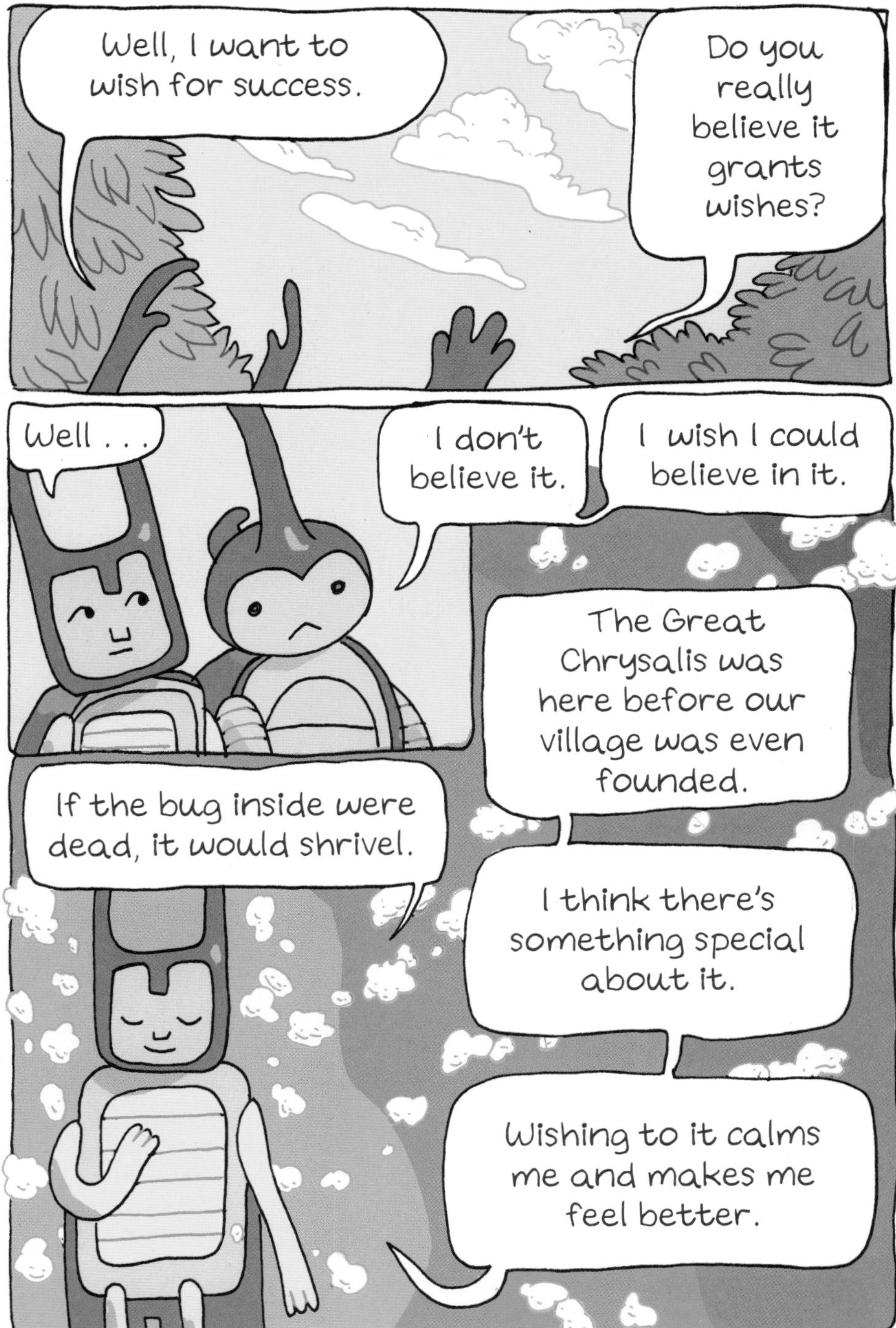
Well, I want to wish for success.
Do you really believe it grants wishes?
Well . . .
I don't believe it.
I wish I could believe in it.
The Great Chrysalis was here before our village was even founded.
If the bug inside were dead, it would shrivel.
I think there's something special about it.
Wishing to it calms me and makes me feel better.

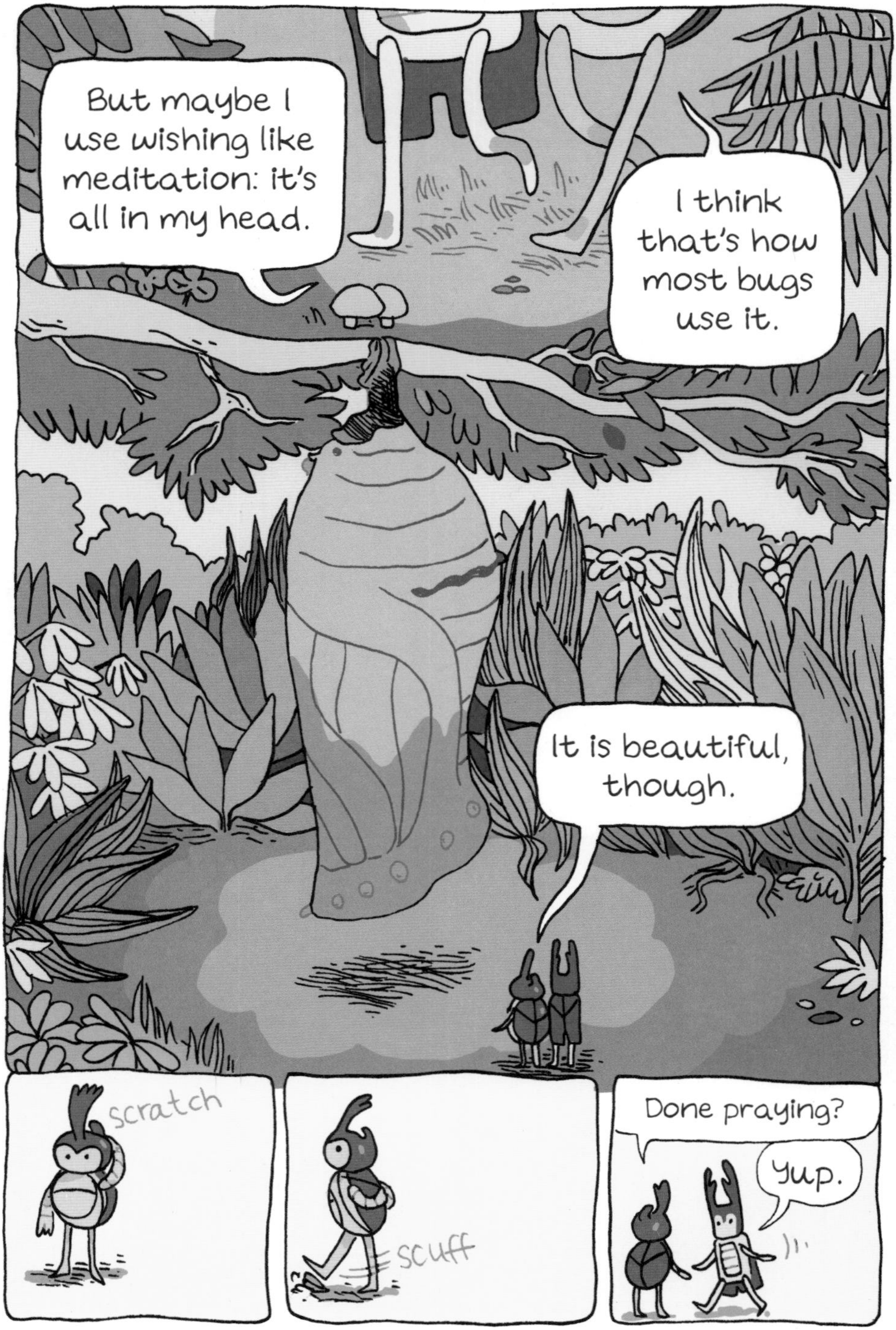
But maybe I use wishing like meditation: it's all in my head.
I think that's how most bugs use it.
It is beautiful, though.
scratch
scuff
Done praying?
Yup.

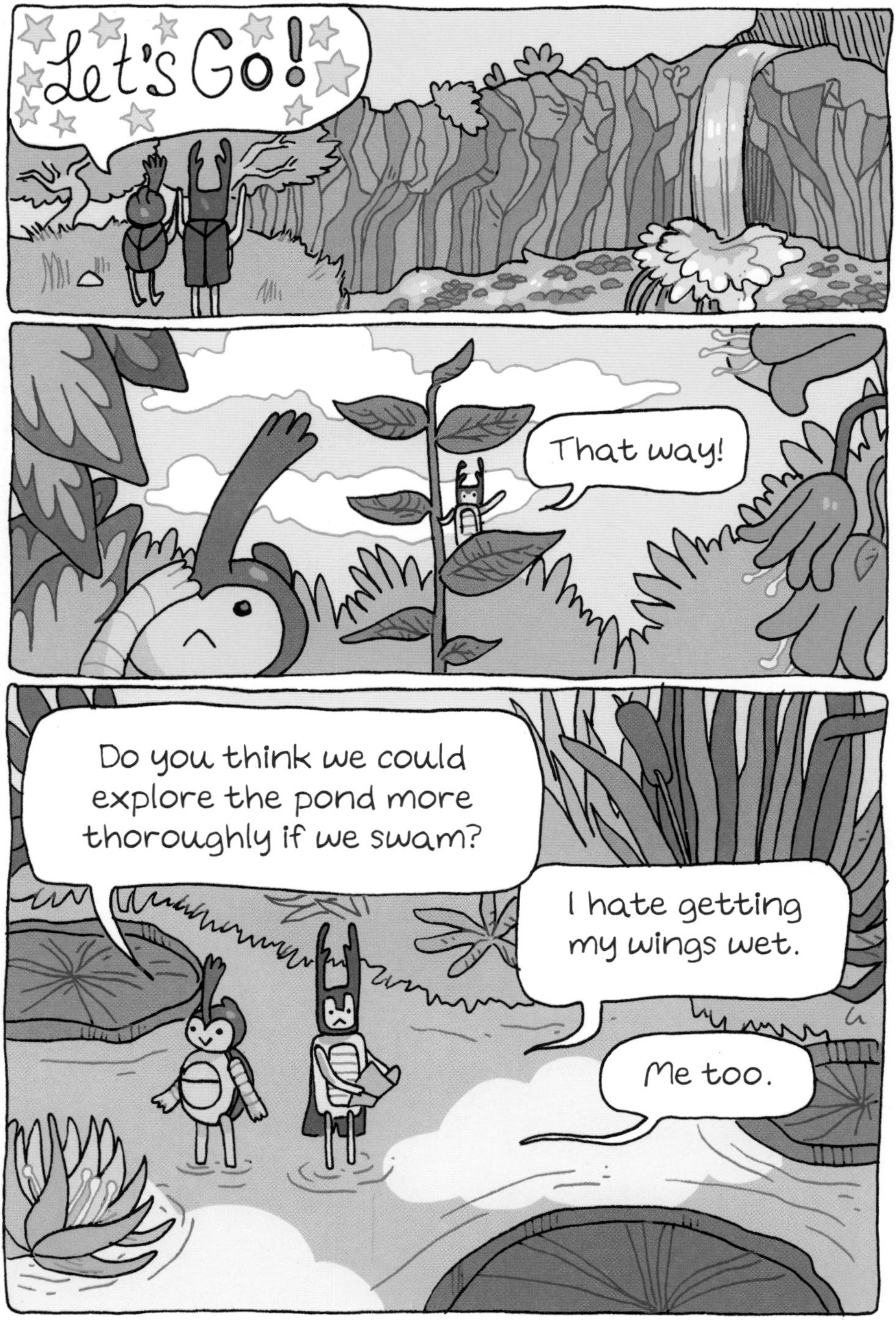
Let's Go!
That way!
Do you think we could explore the pond more thoroughly if we swam?
I hate getting my wings wet.
Me too.

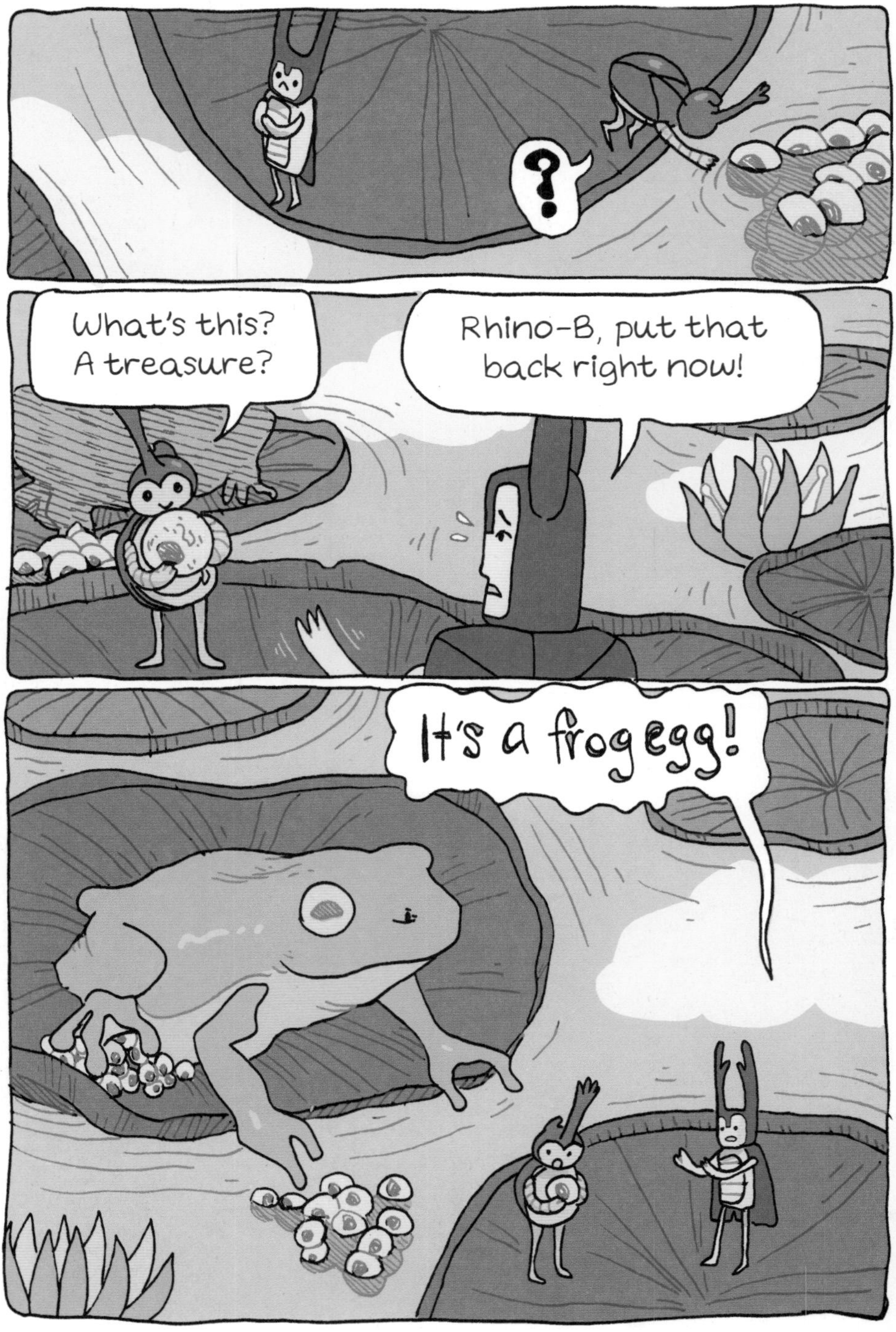
?
What's this? A treasure?
Rhino-B, put that back right now!
It's a frog egg!

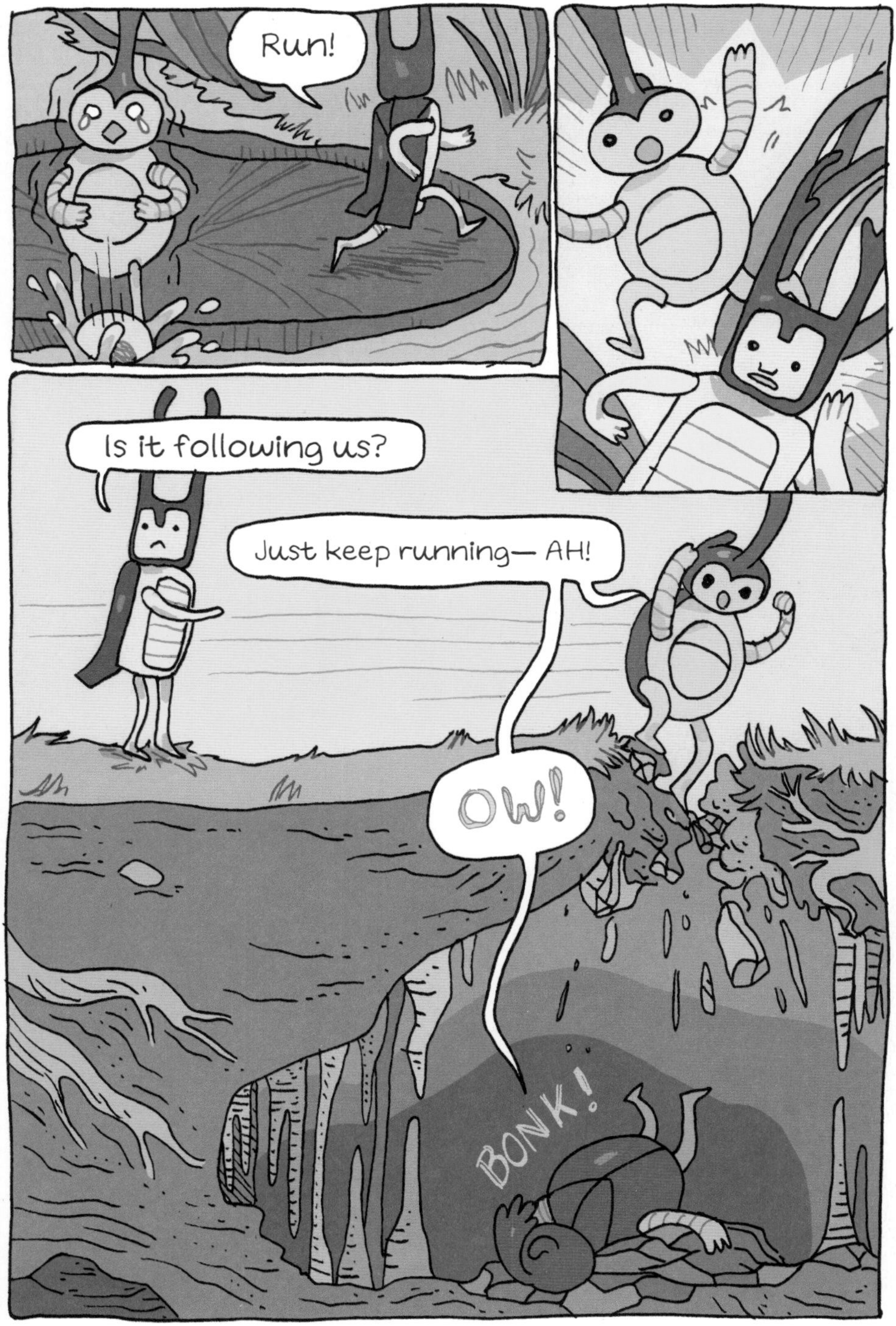
Run!
Is it following us?
Just keep running— AH!
OW!
BONK!

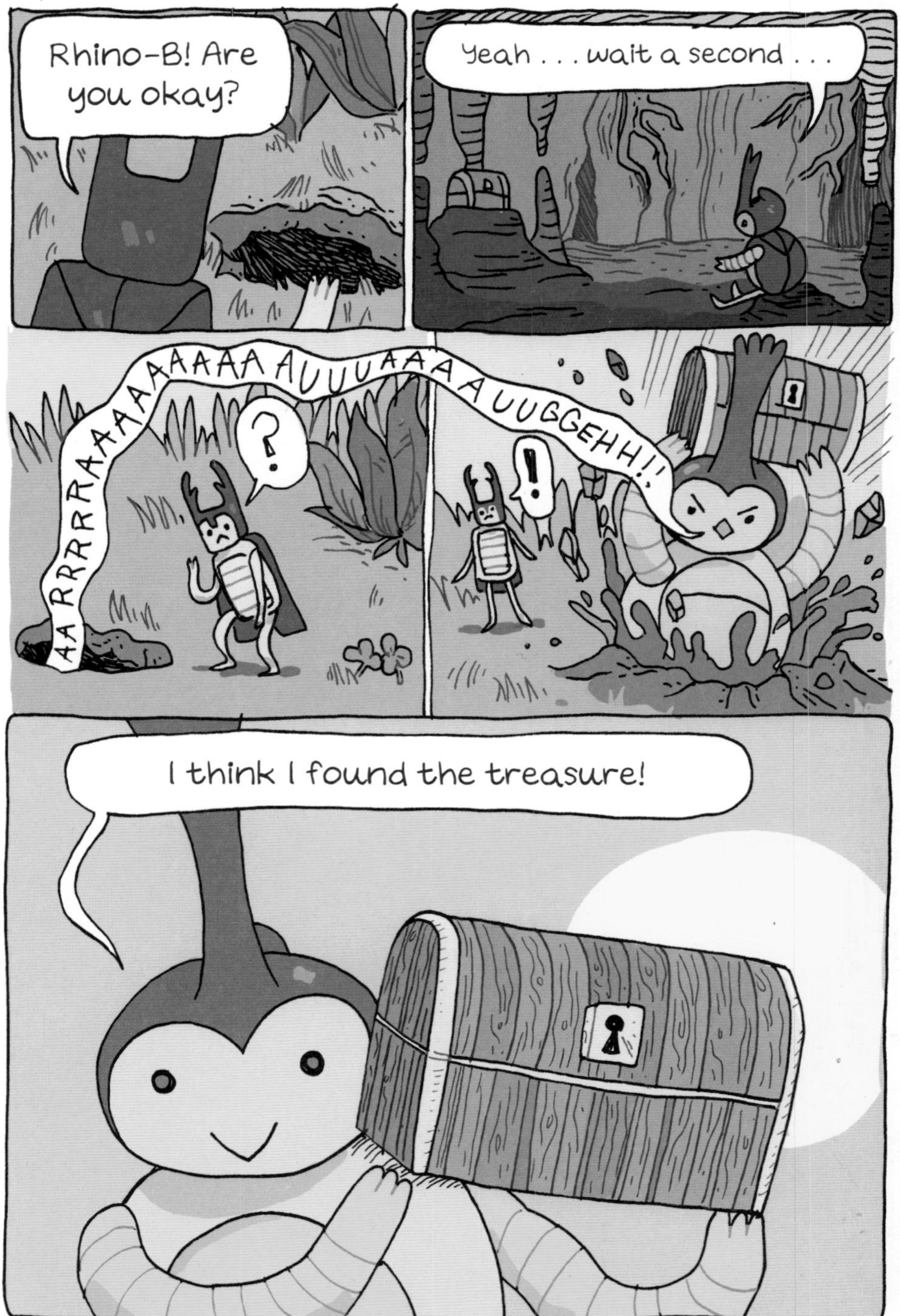
Rhino-B! Are you okay?
Yeah . . . wait a second . . .
AARRRRRAAAAAAAAAA AUUUAAAA UUGGEHH!!
?
!
I think I found the treasure!

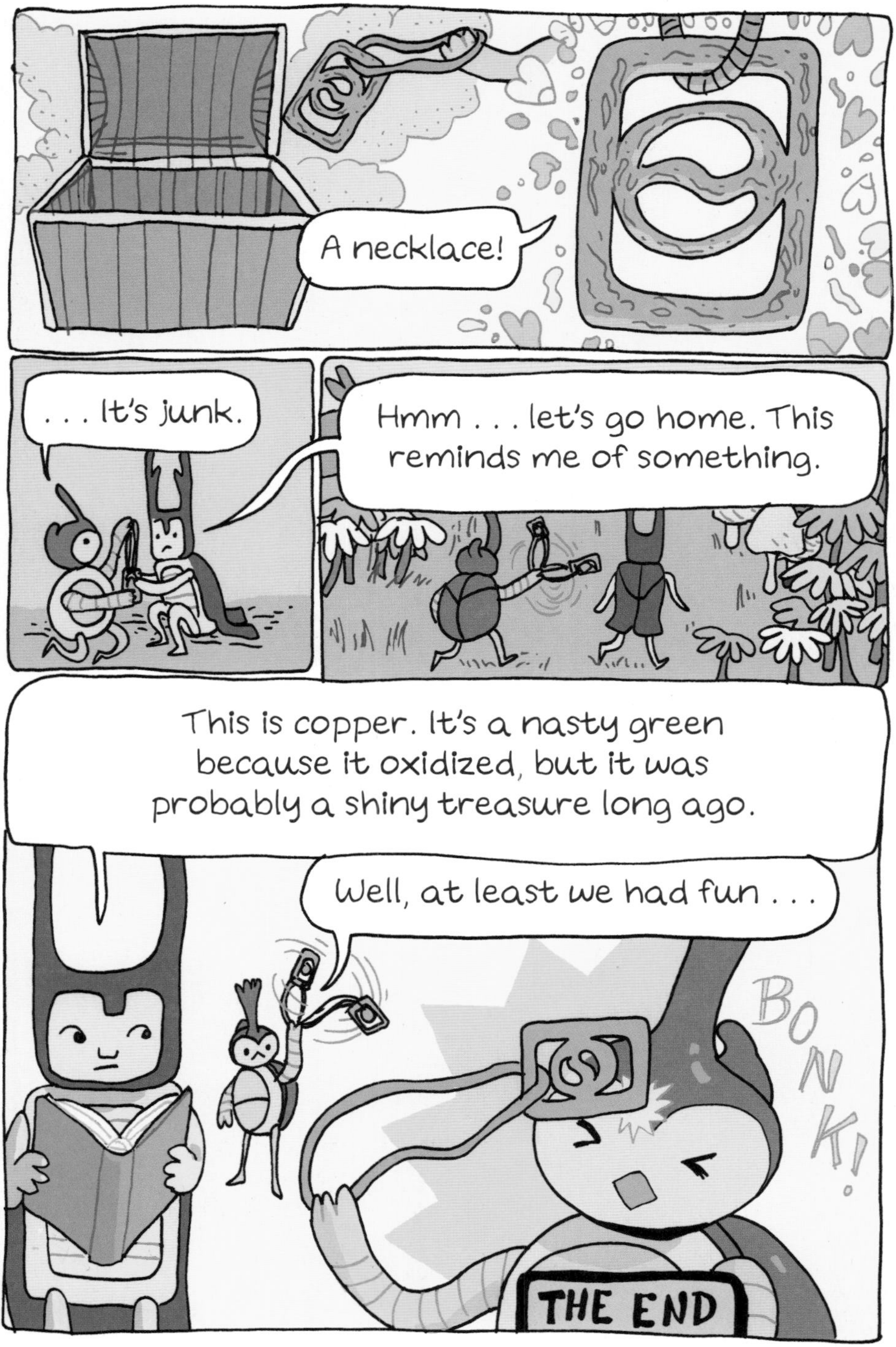
A necklace!
. . . It's junk.
Hmm . . . let's go home. This reminds me of something.
This is copper. It's a nasty green because it oxidized, but it was probably a shiny treasure long ago.
Well, at least we had fun . . .
BONK!
THE END

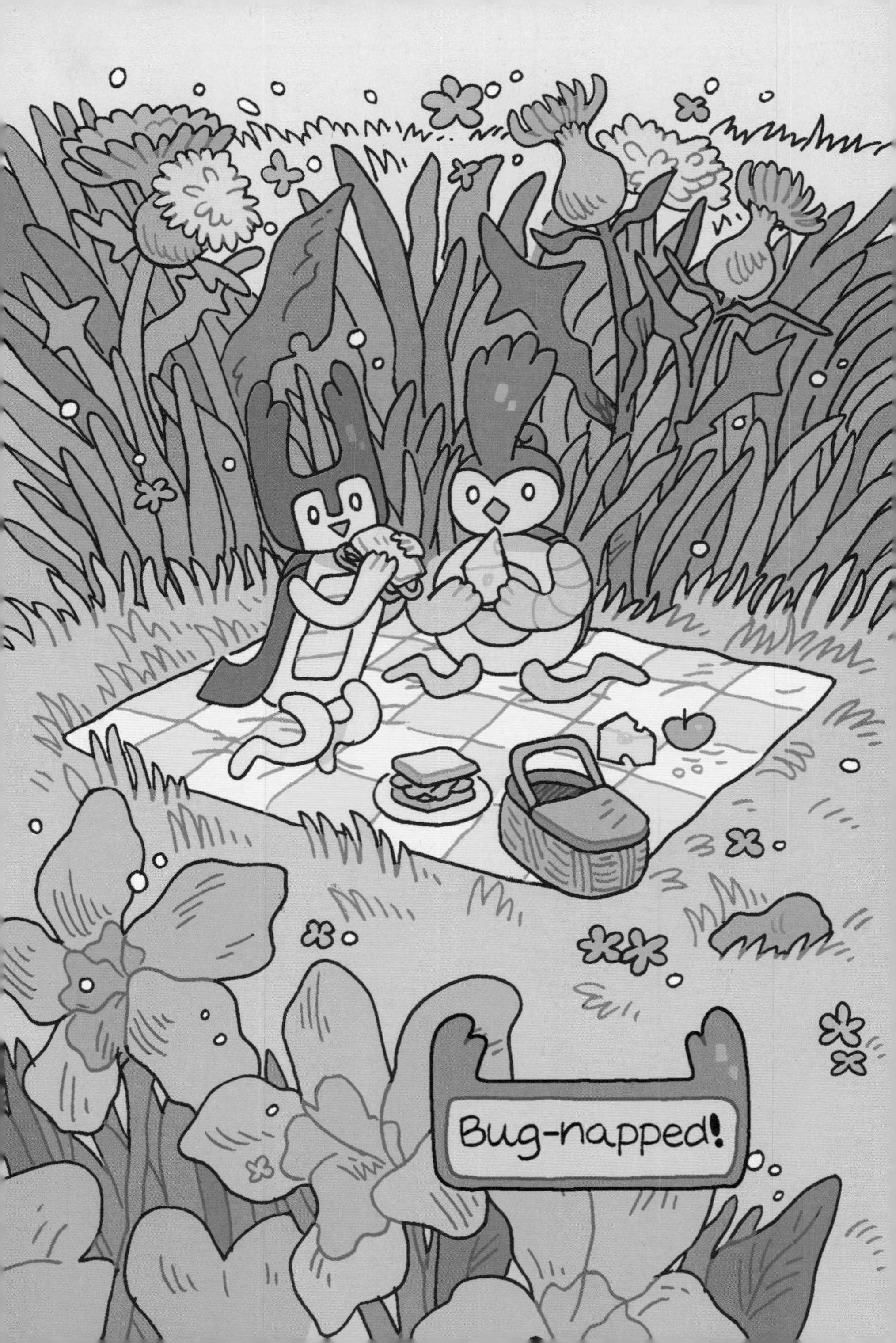
Bug-napped!

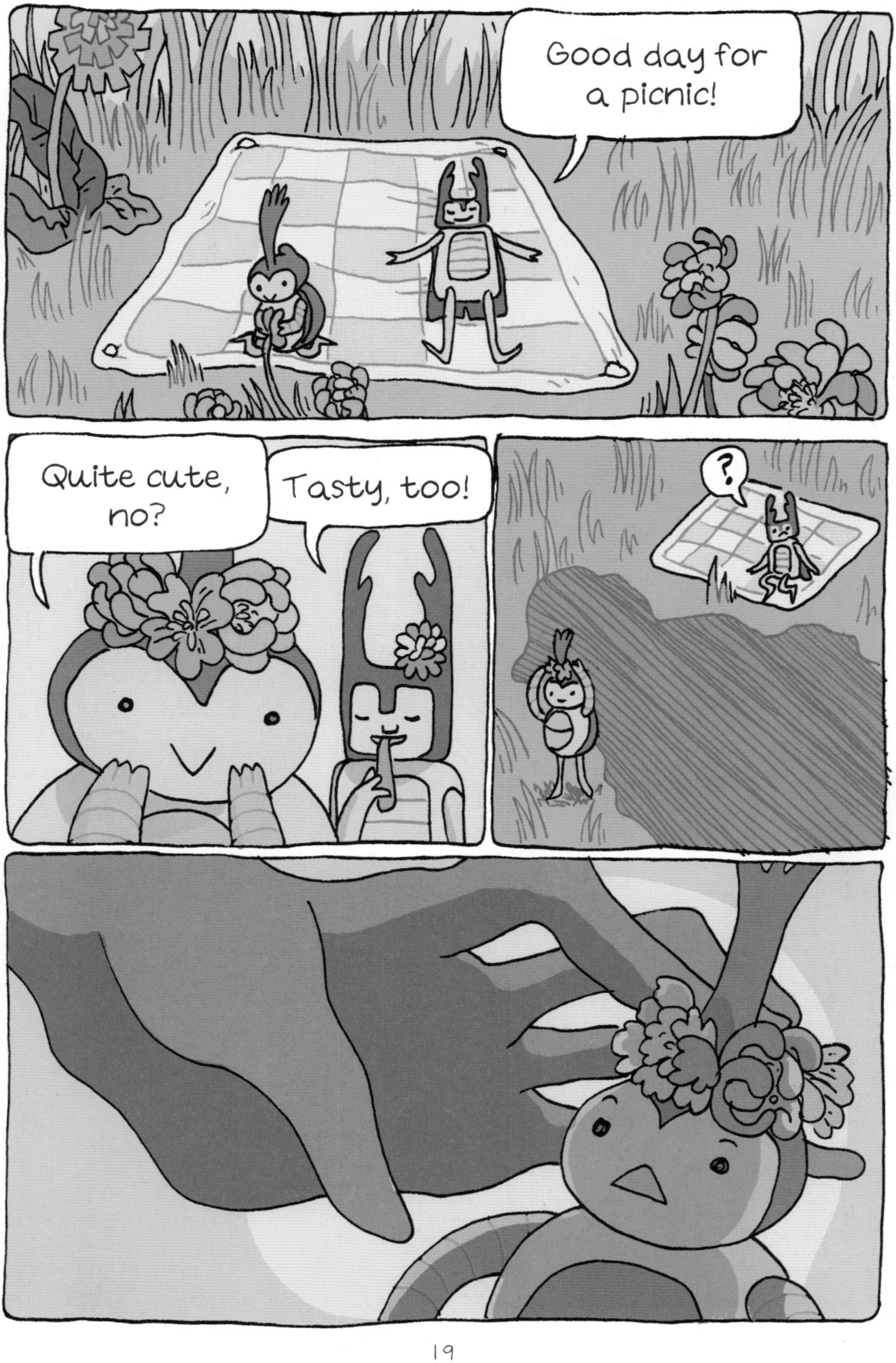
Good day for a picnic!
Quite cute, no?
Tasty, too!
?

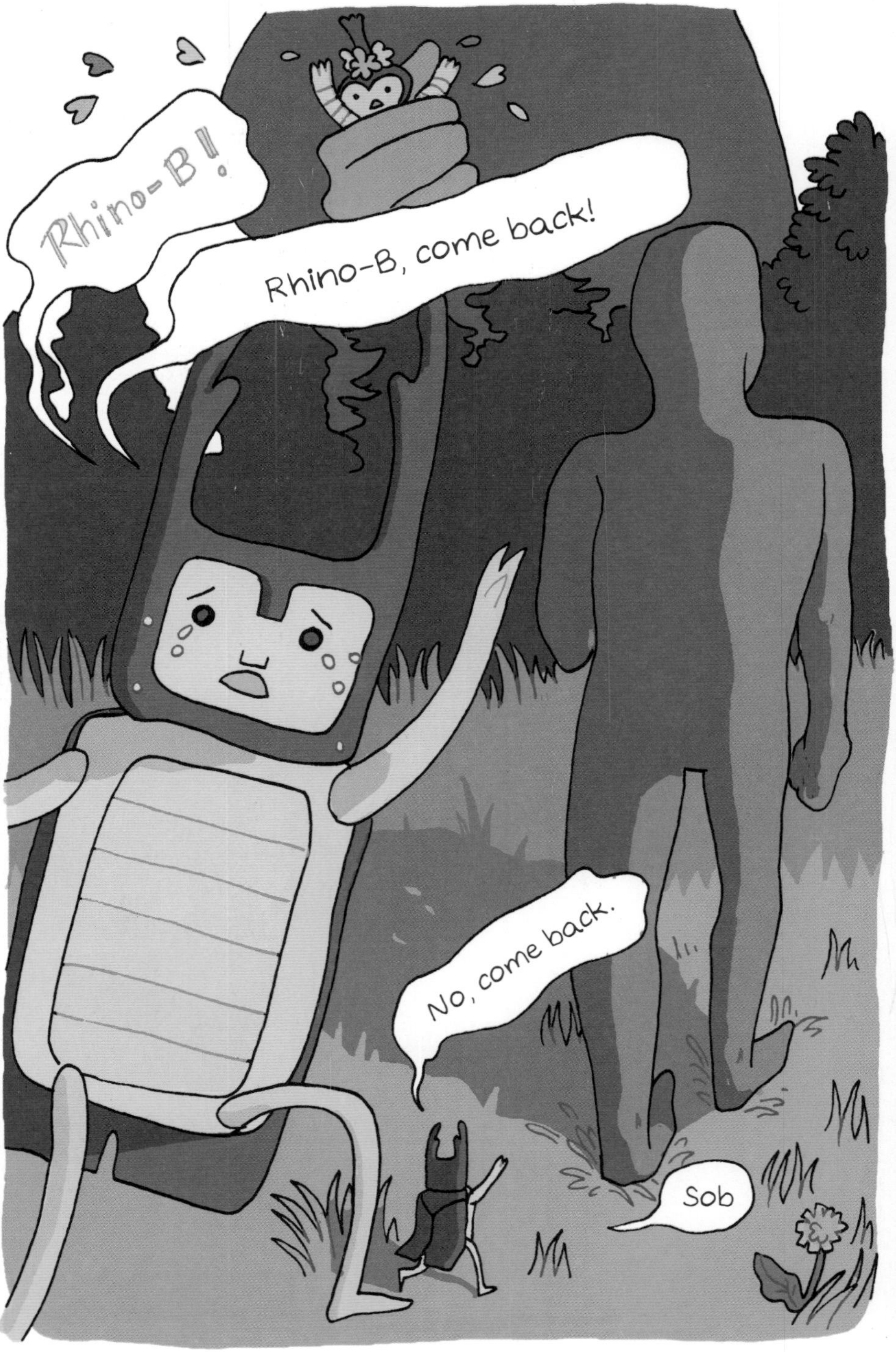
Rhino-B!
Rhino-B, come back!
No, come back.
Sob

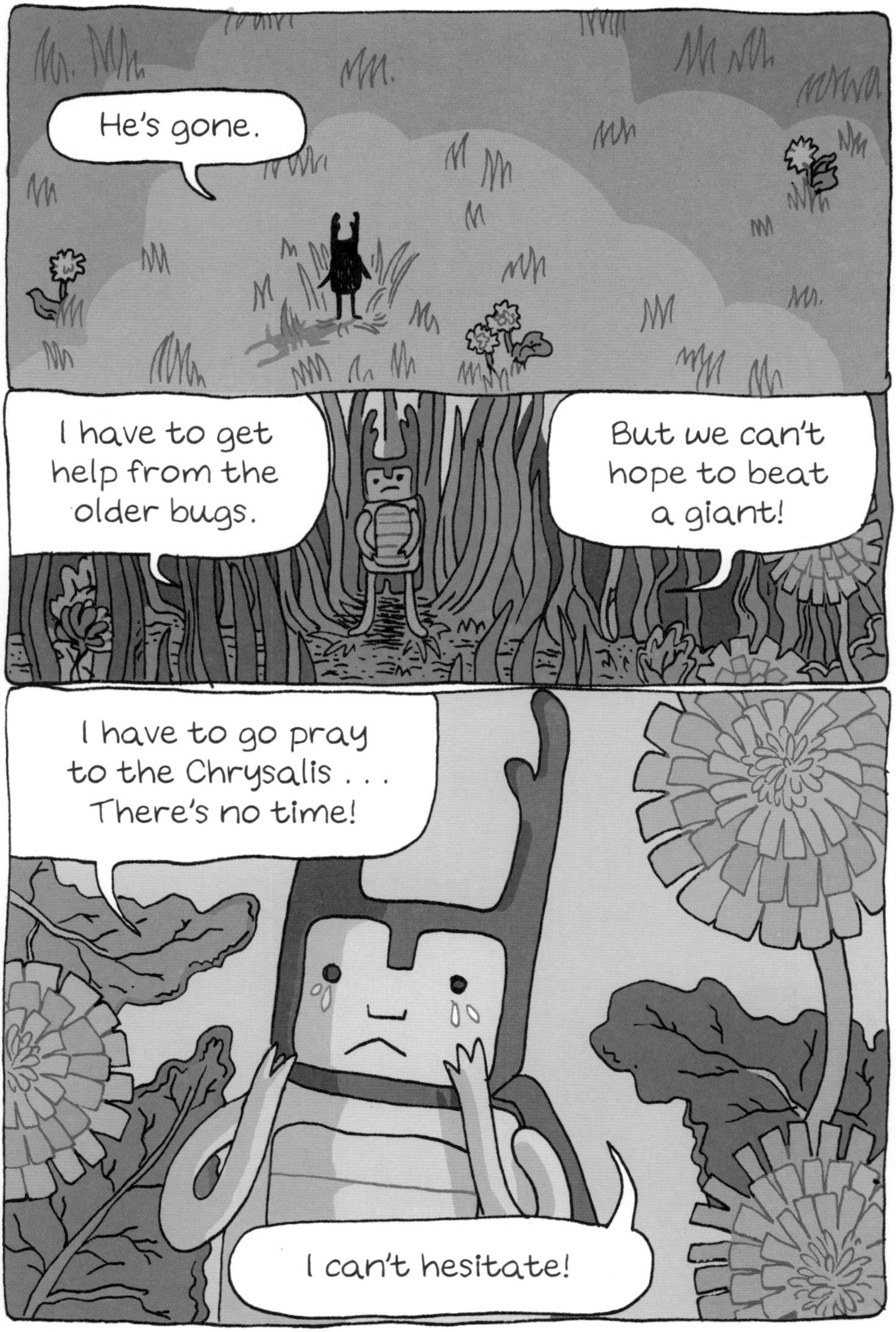
He's gone.
I have to get help from the older bugs.
But we can't hope to beat a giant!
I have to go pray to the Chrysalis . . . There's no time!
I can't hesitate!

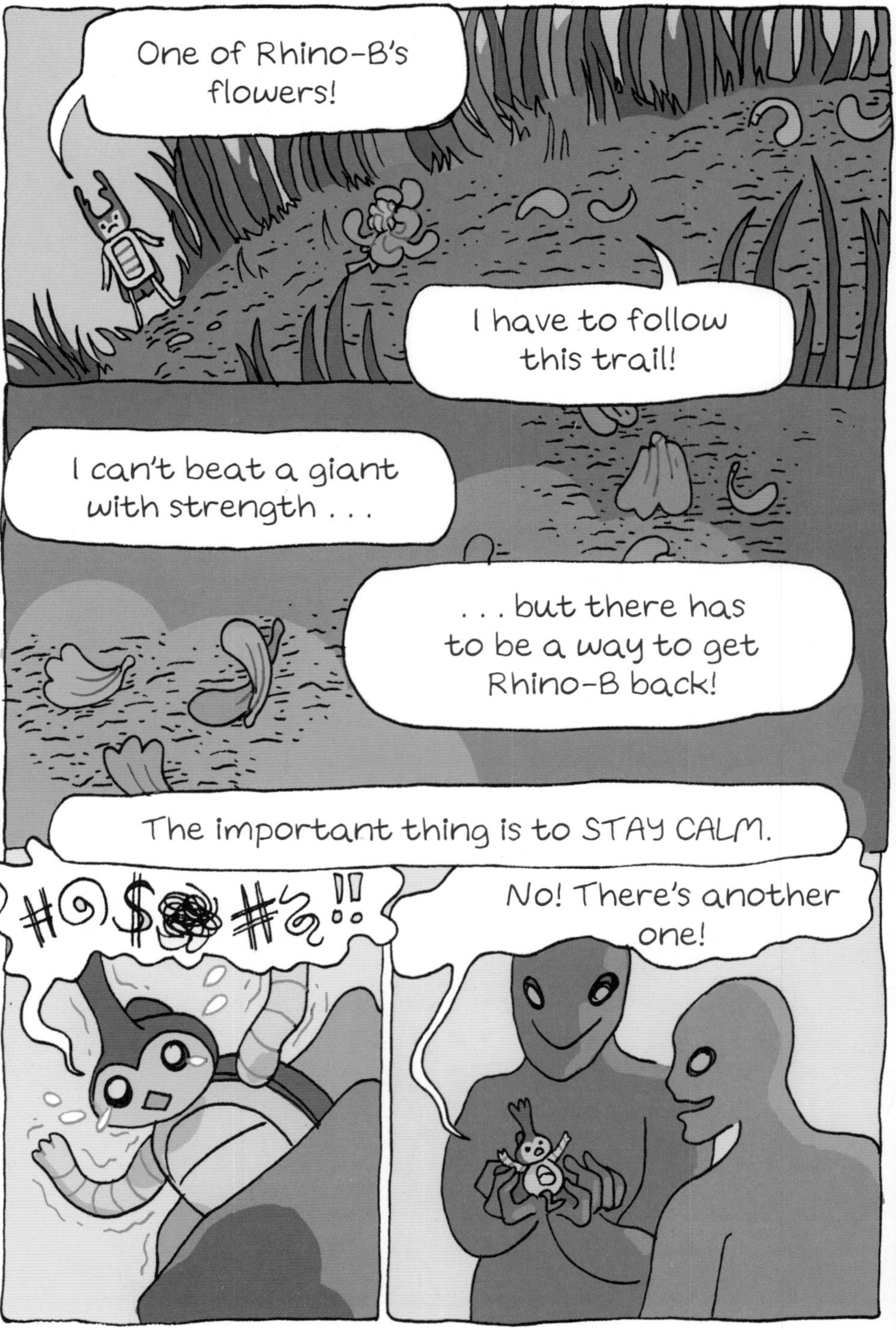

One of Rhino-B's flowers!
I have to follow this trail!
I can't beat a giant with strength . . .
. . . but there has to be a way to get Rhino-B back!
The important thing is to STAY CALM.
No! There's another one!

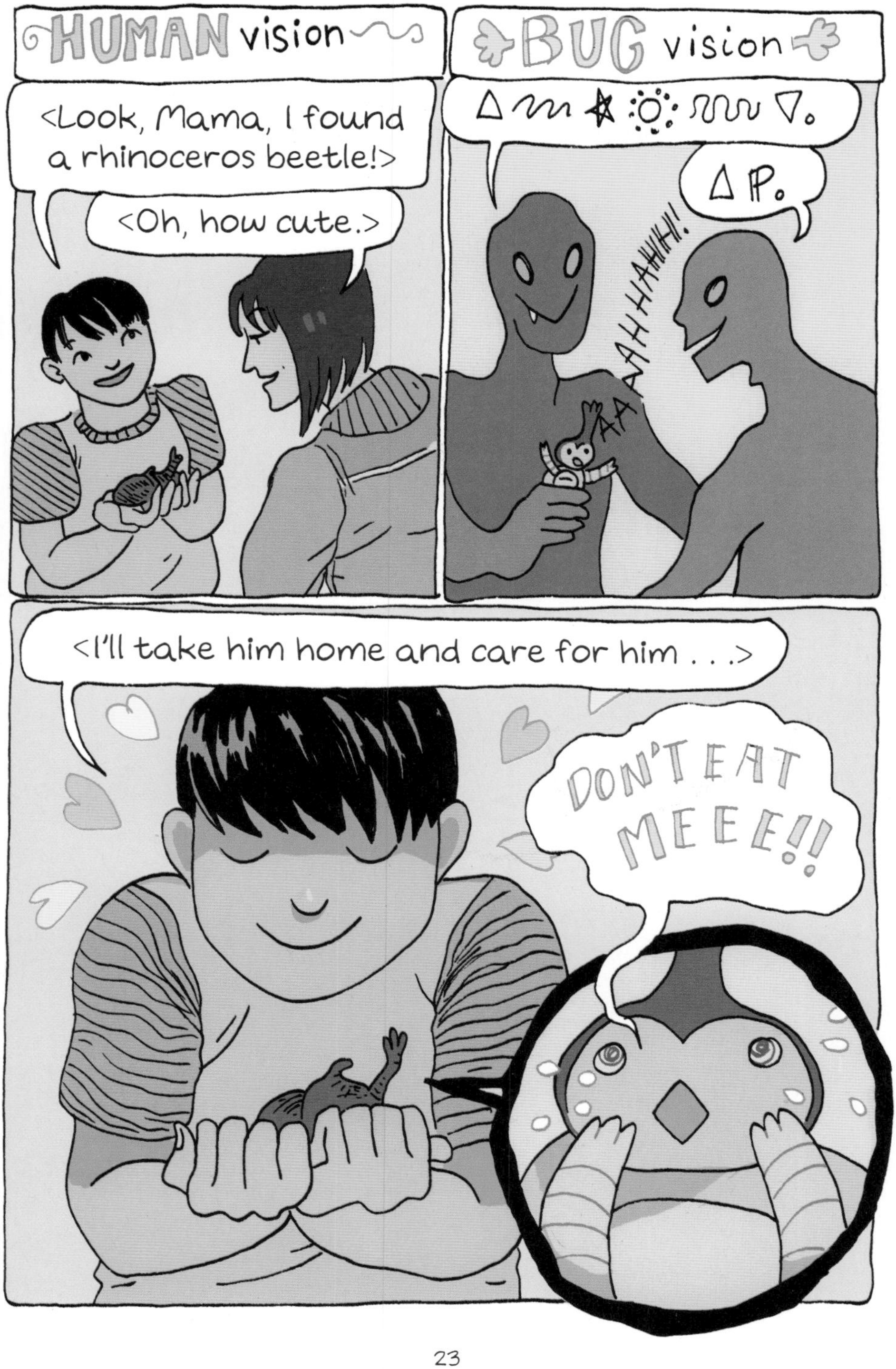
HUMAN vision
BUG vision
<Look, Mama, I found a rhinoceros beetle!>
<Oh, how cute.>
AAAAHHHAHHH!
<I'll take him home and care for him . . .>
DON'T EAT MEEE!!

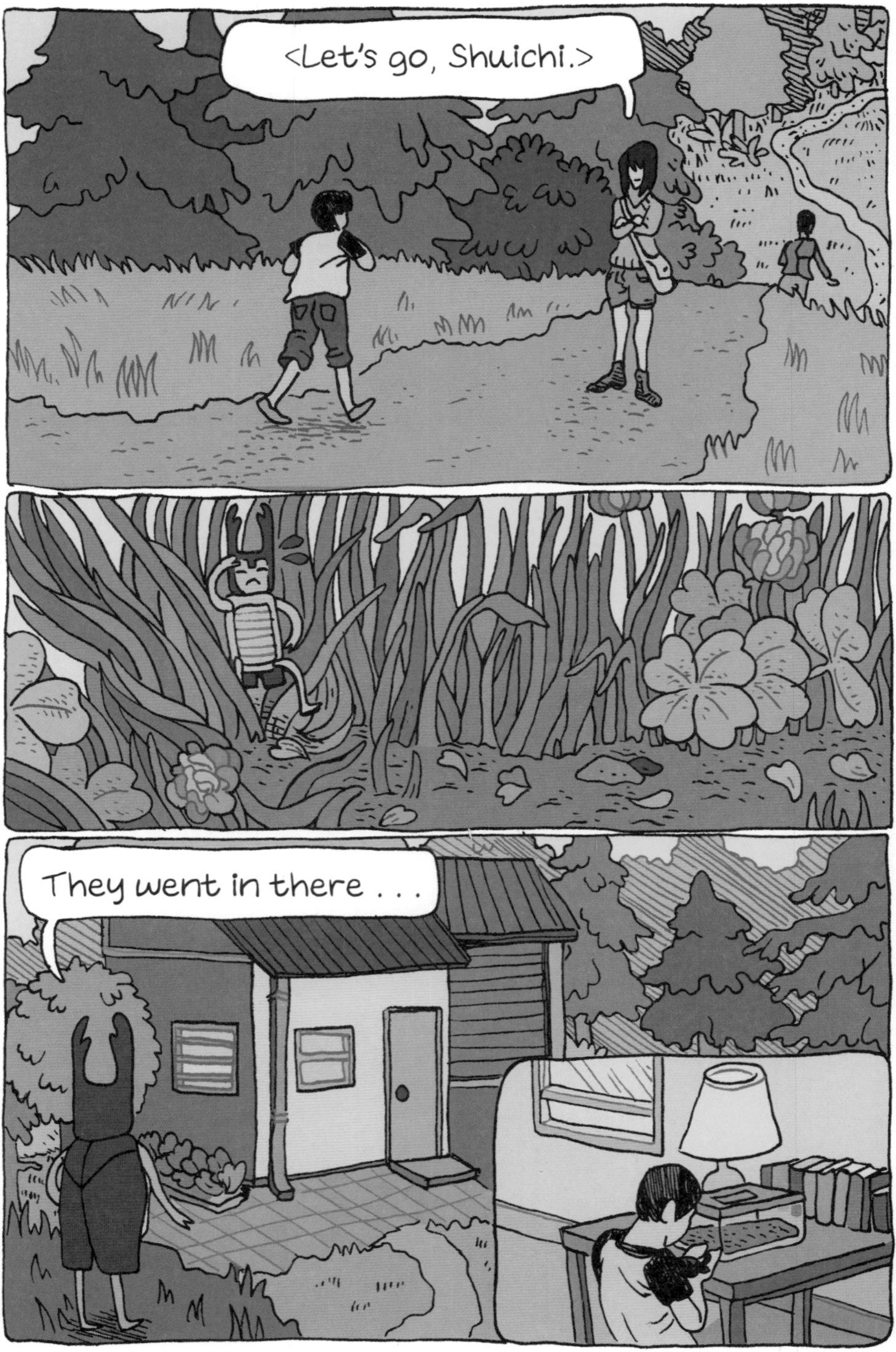
<Let’s go, Shuichi.>
They went in there . . .

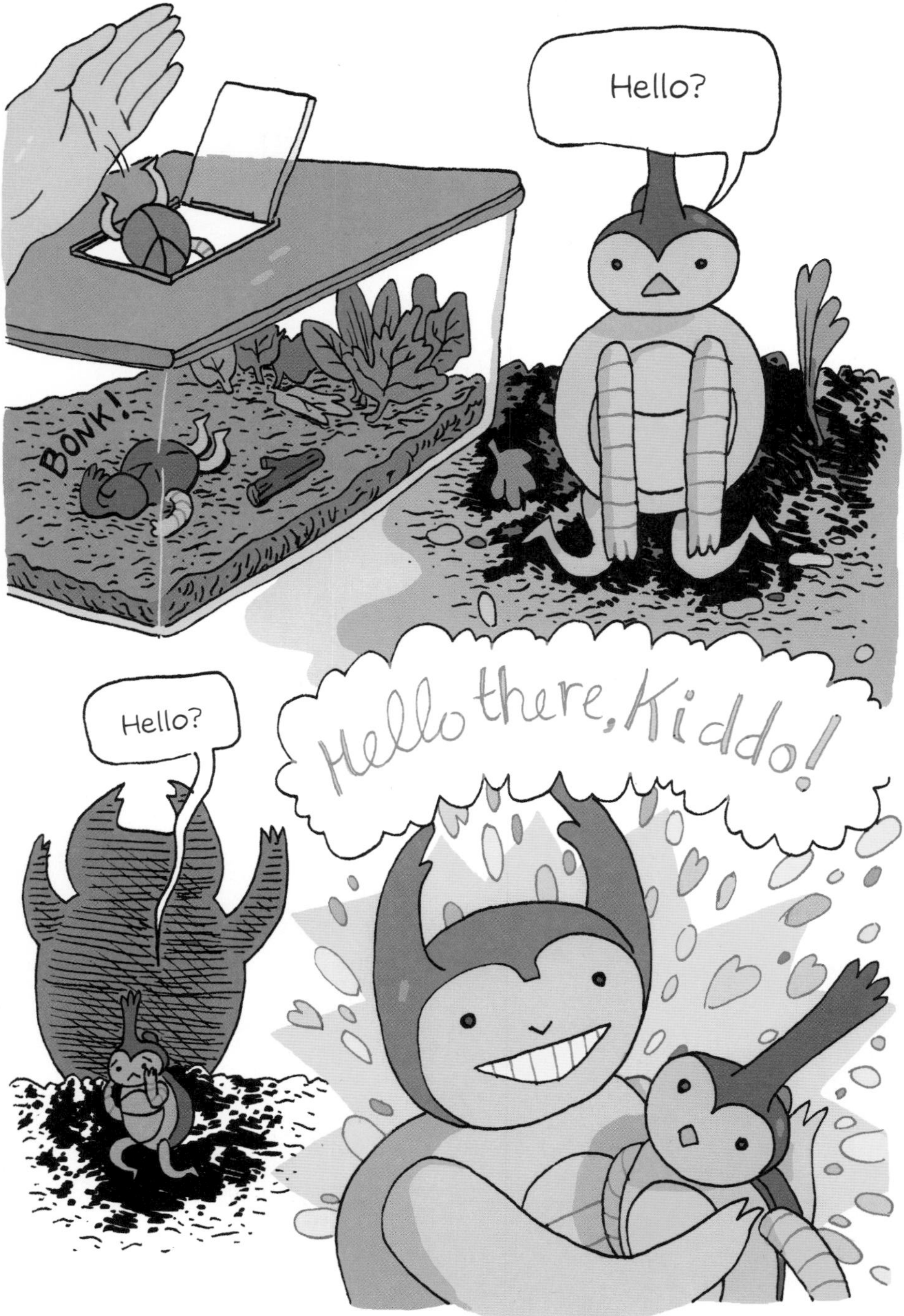
BONK!
Hello?
Hello?
Hello there, Kiddo!

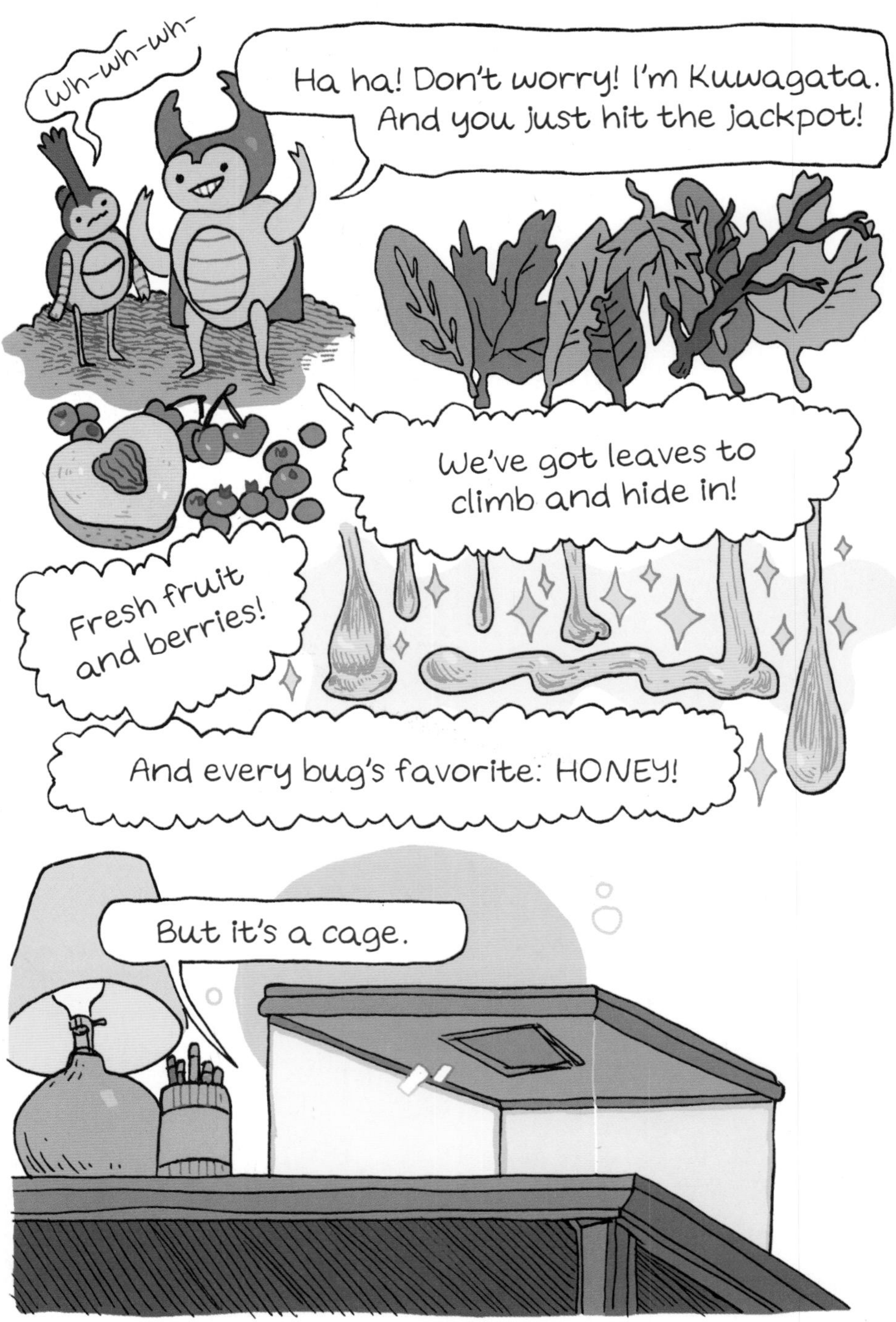
Wh-wh-wh-
Ha ha! Don't worry! I'm Kuwagata. And you just hit the jackpot!
We've got leaves to climb and hide in!
Fresh fruit and berries!
And every bug's favorite: HONEY!
But it's a cage.

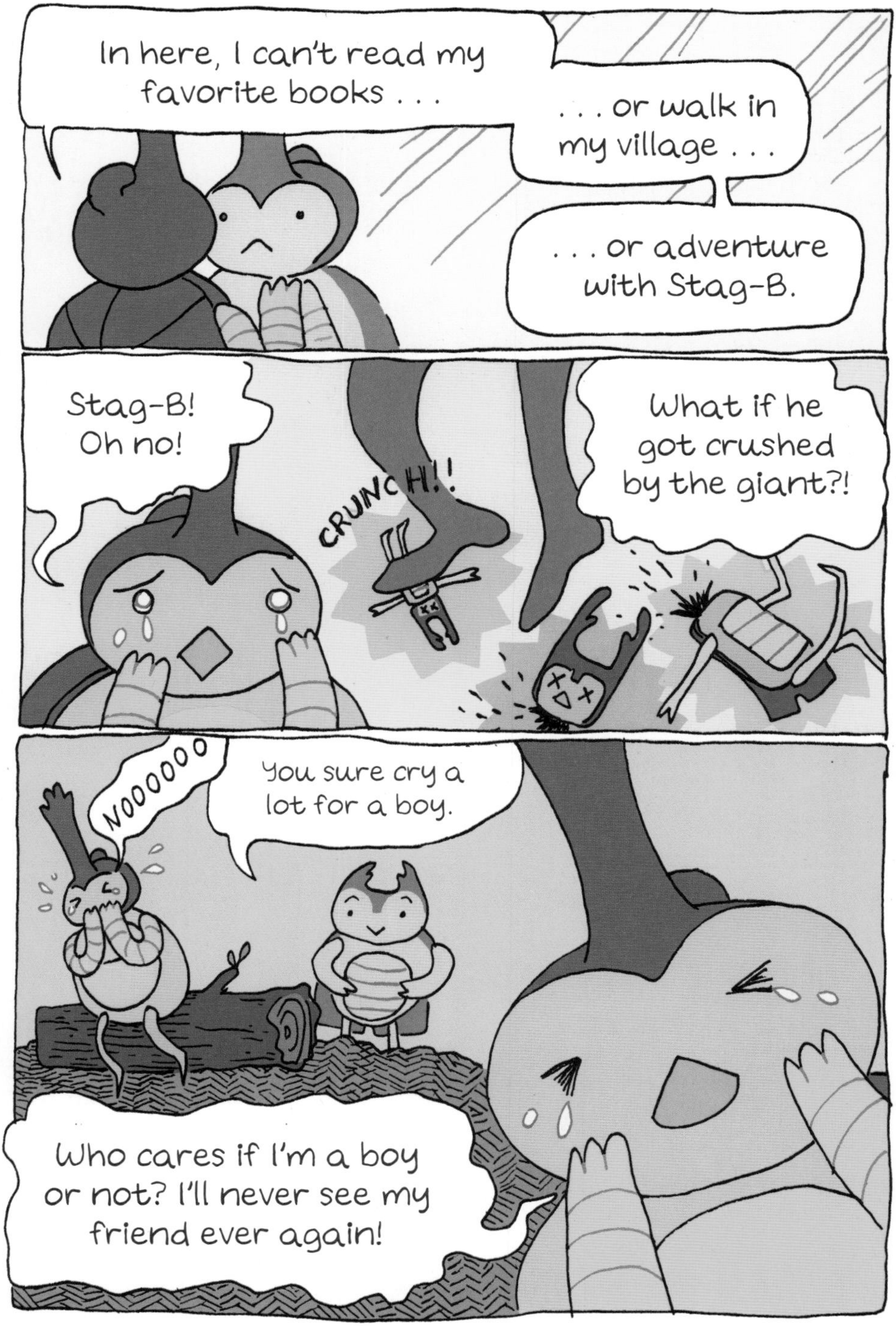
In here, I can't read my favorite books . . .
. . . or walk in my village . . .
. . . or adventure with Stag-B.
Stag-B! Oh no!
CRUNCH!!
What if he got crushed by the giant?!
NOOOOOO
You sure cry a lot for a boy.
Who cares if I'm a boy or not? I'll never see my friend ever again!

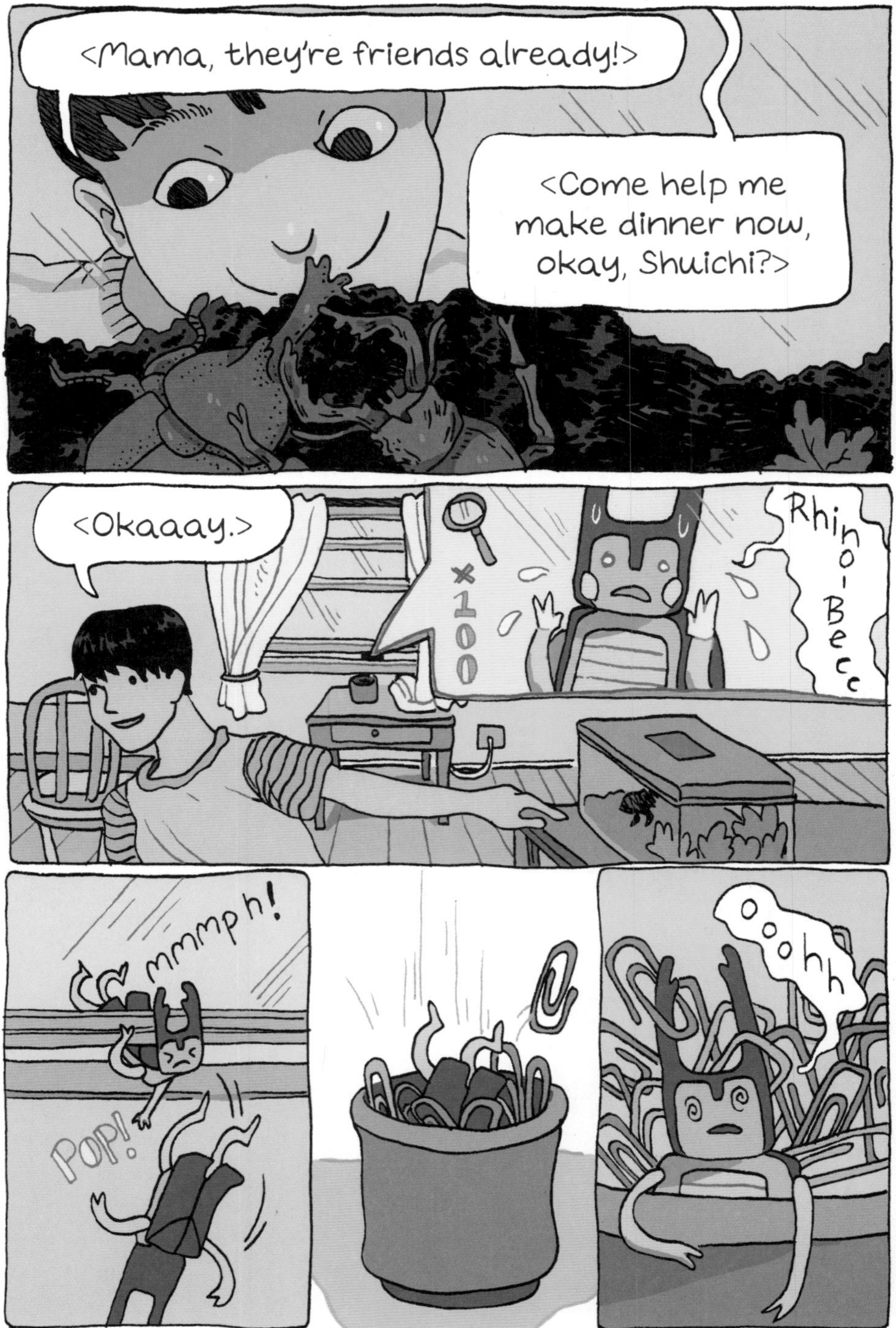
<Mama, they're friends already!>
<Come help me make dinner now, okay, Shuichi?>
<Okaaay.>
Rhino-Beeee
×100
mmmph!
POP!
Ooohh

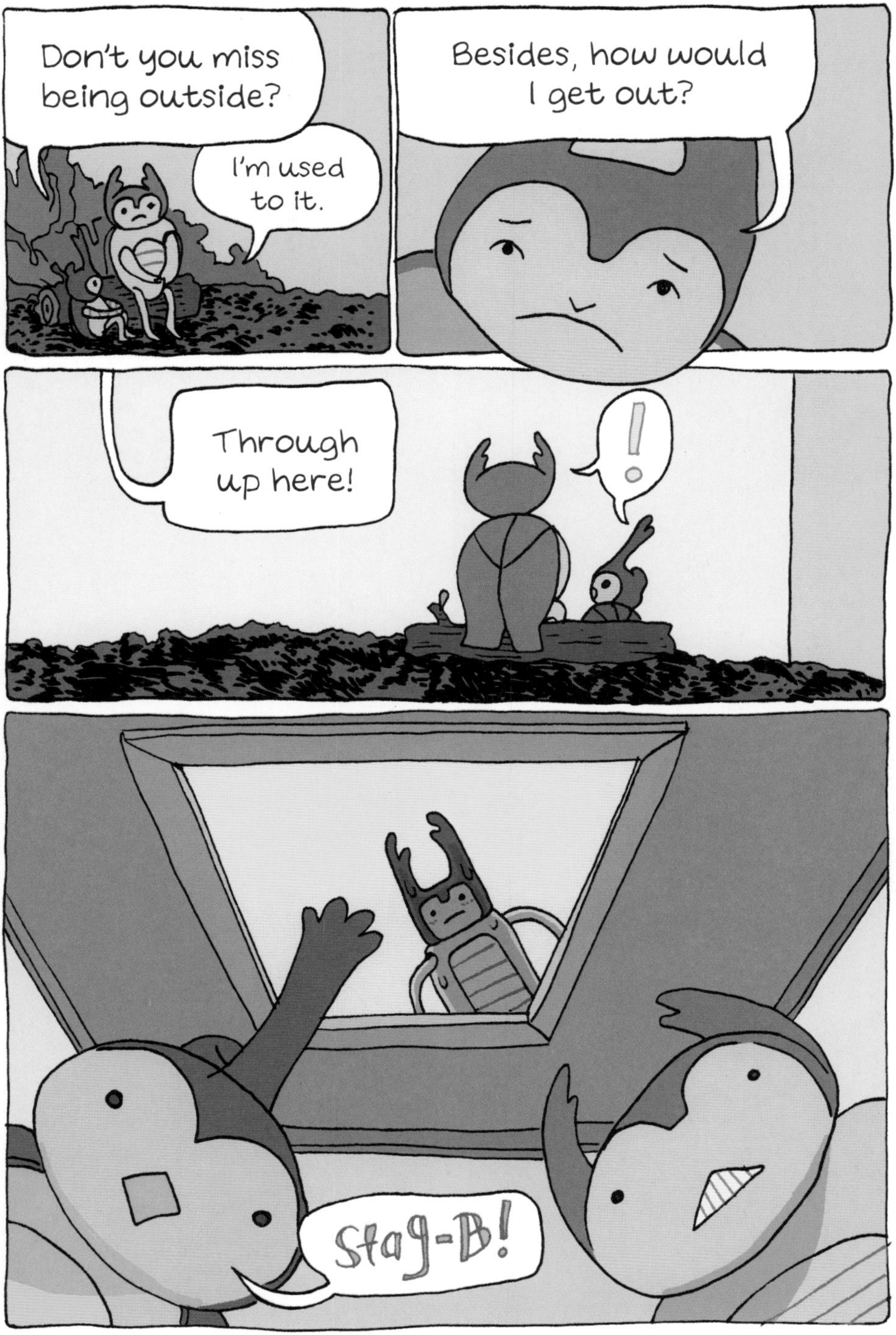
Don't you miss being outside?
I'm used to it.
Besides, how would I get out?
Through up here!
!
Stag-B!

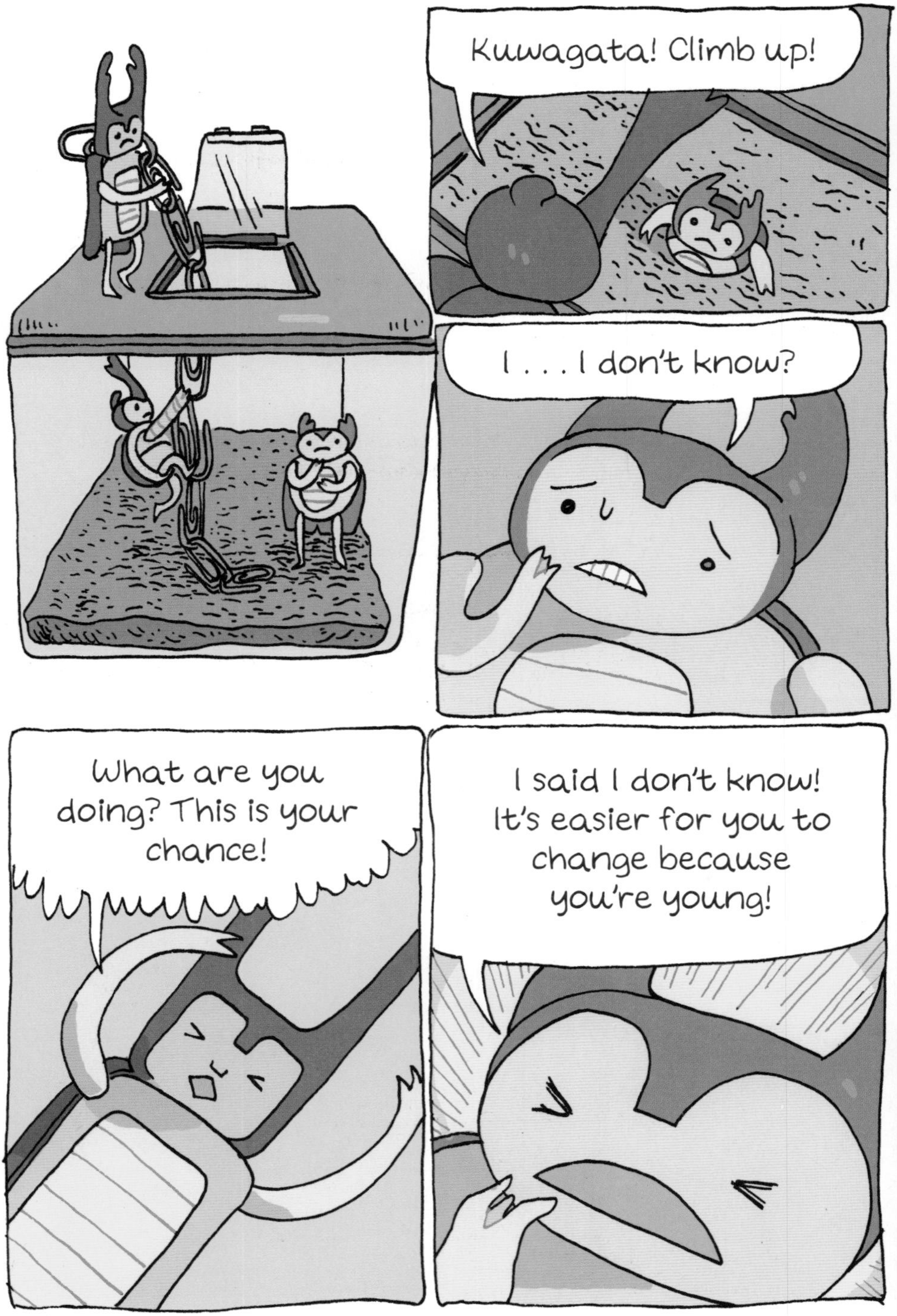
Kuwagata! Climb up!
I . . . I don't know?
What are you doing? This is your chance!
I said I don't know! It's easier for you to change because you're young!

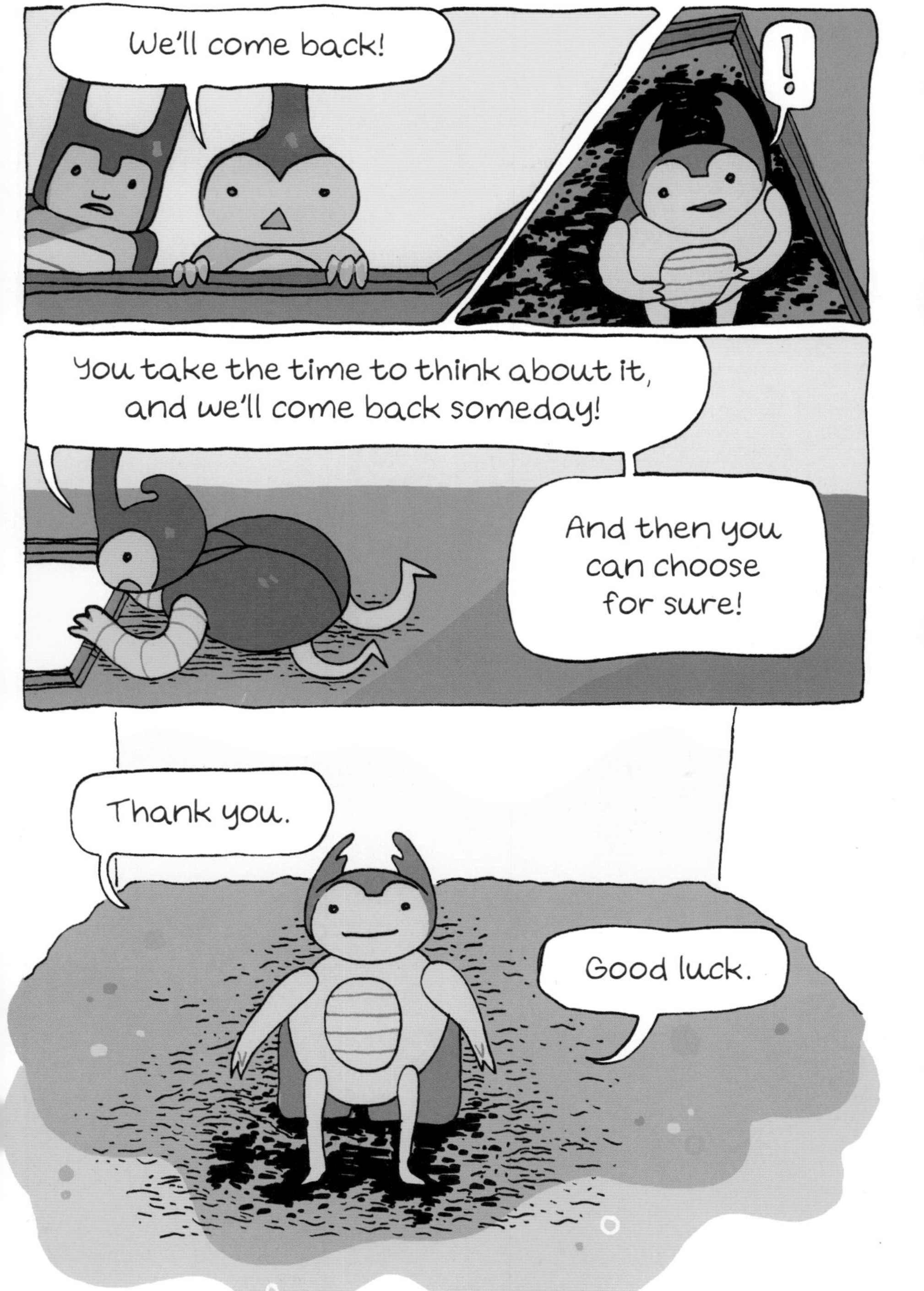
We'll come back!
!
You take the time to think about it, and we'll come back someday!
And then you can choose for sure!
Thank you.
Good luck.

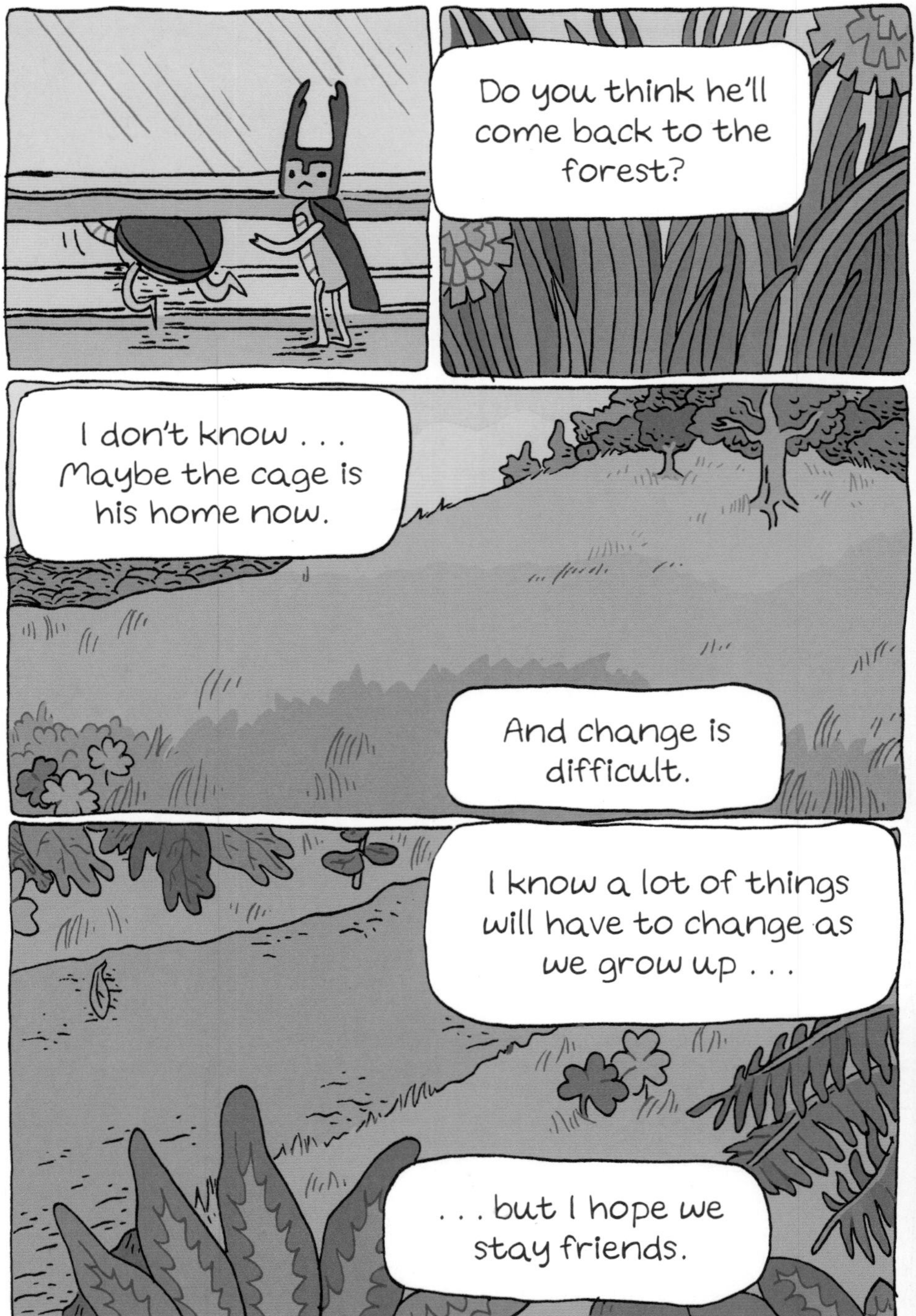
Do you think he'll come back to the forest?
I don't know . . . Maybe the cage is his home now.
And change is difficult.
I know a lot of things will have to change as we grow up . . .
. . . but I hope we stay friends.

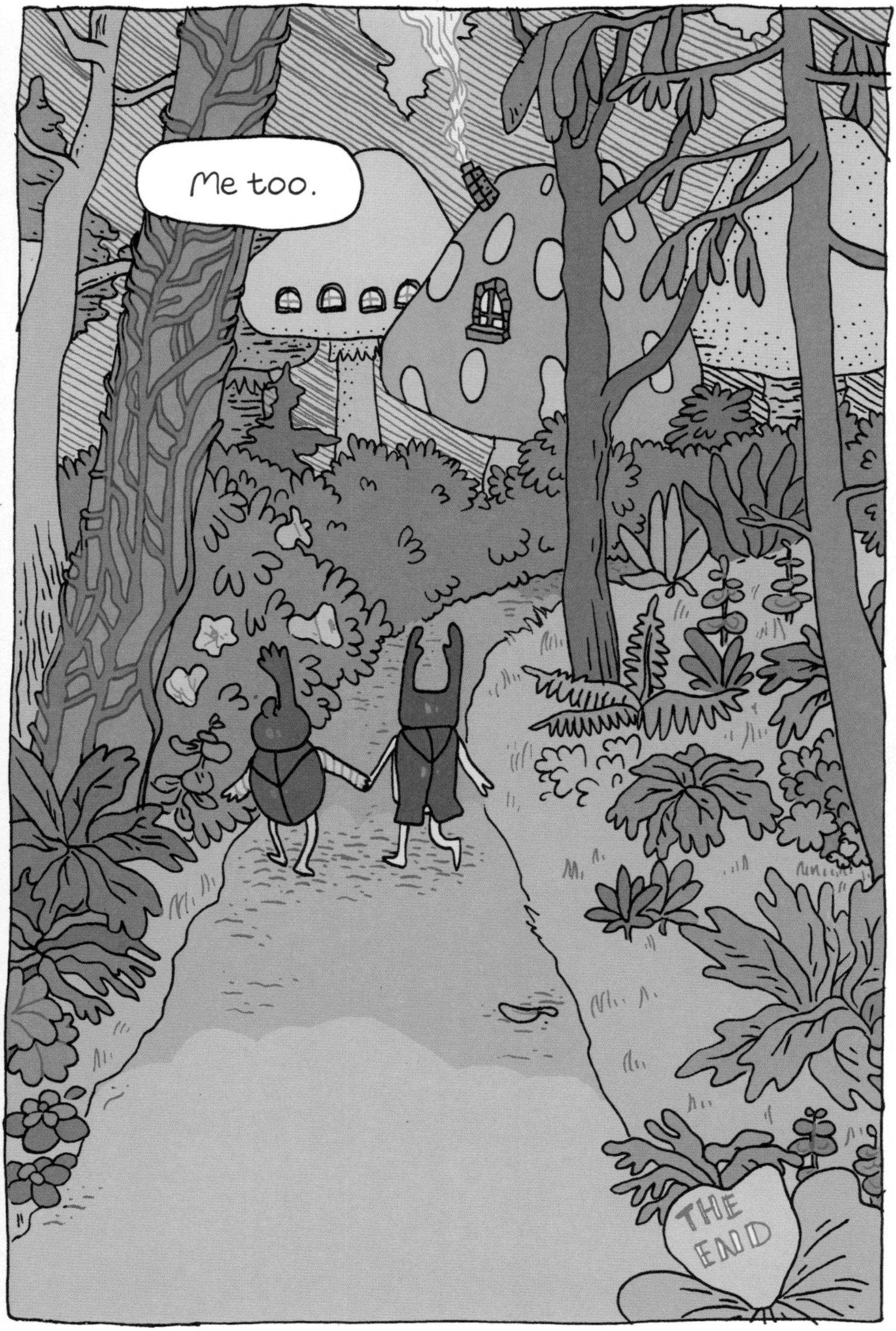
Me too.
THE END

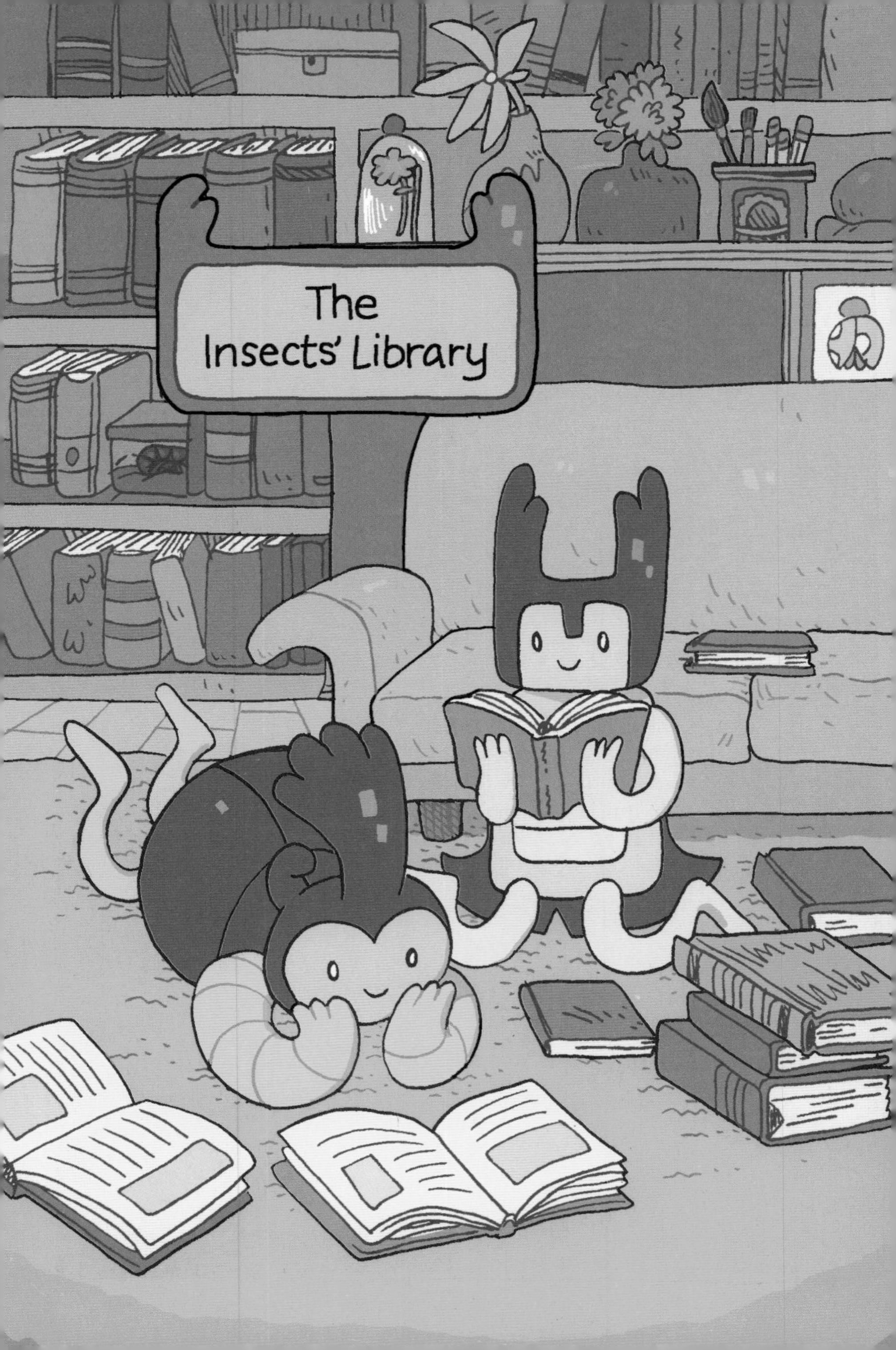
The
Insects' Library

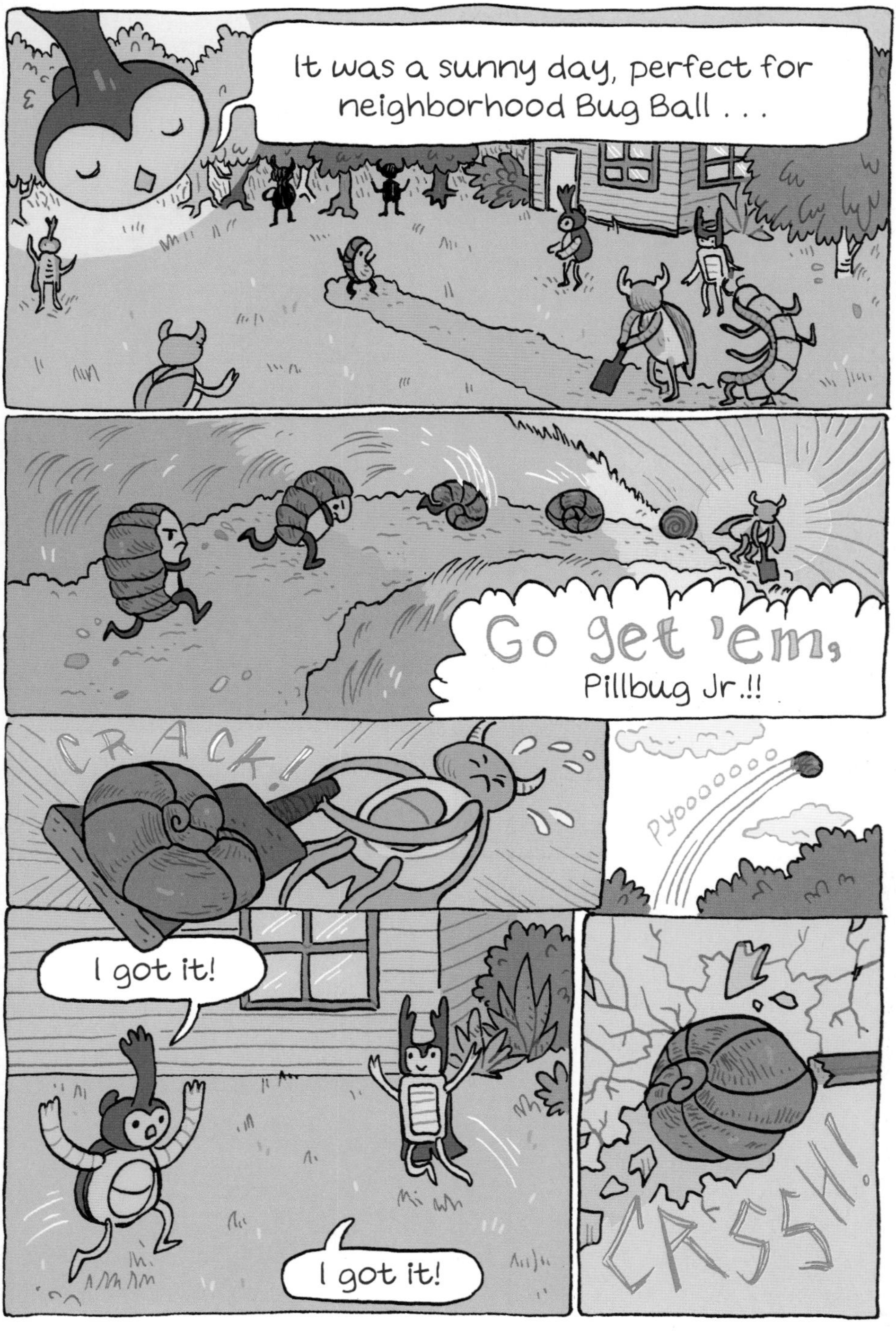
It was a sunny day, perfect for neighborhood Bug Ball . . .
Go get 'em, Pillbug Jr.!!
CRACK!
pyoooooooo
I got it!
I got it!
CRSSH!

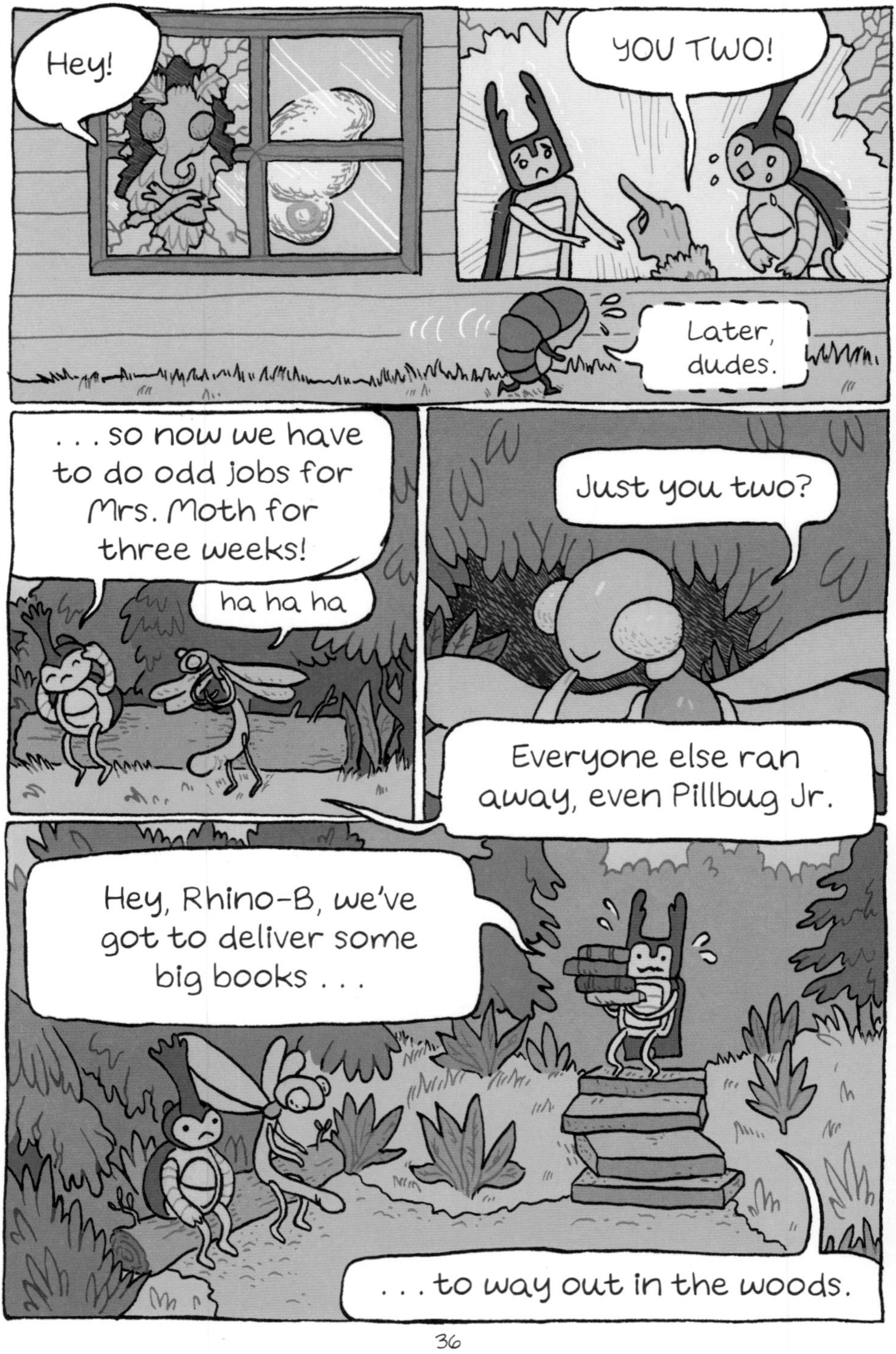
Hey!
YOU TWO!
Later, dudes.
. . . so now we have to do odd jobs for Mrs. Moth for three weeks!
ha ha ha
Just you two?
Everyone else ran away, even Pillbug Jr.
Hey, Rhino-B, we've got to deliver some big books . . .
. . . to way out in the woods.

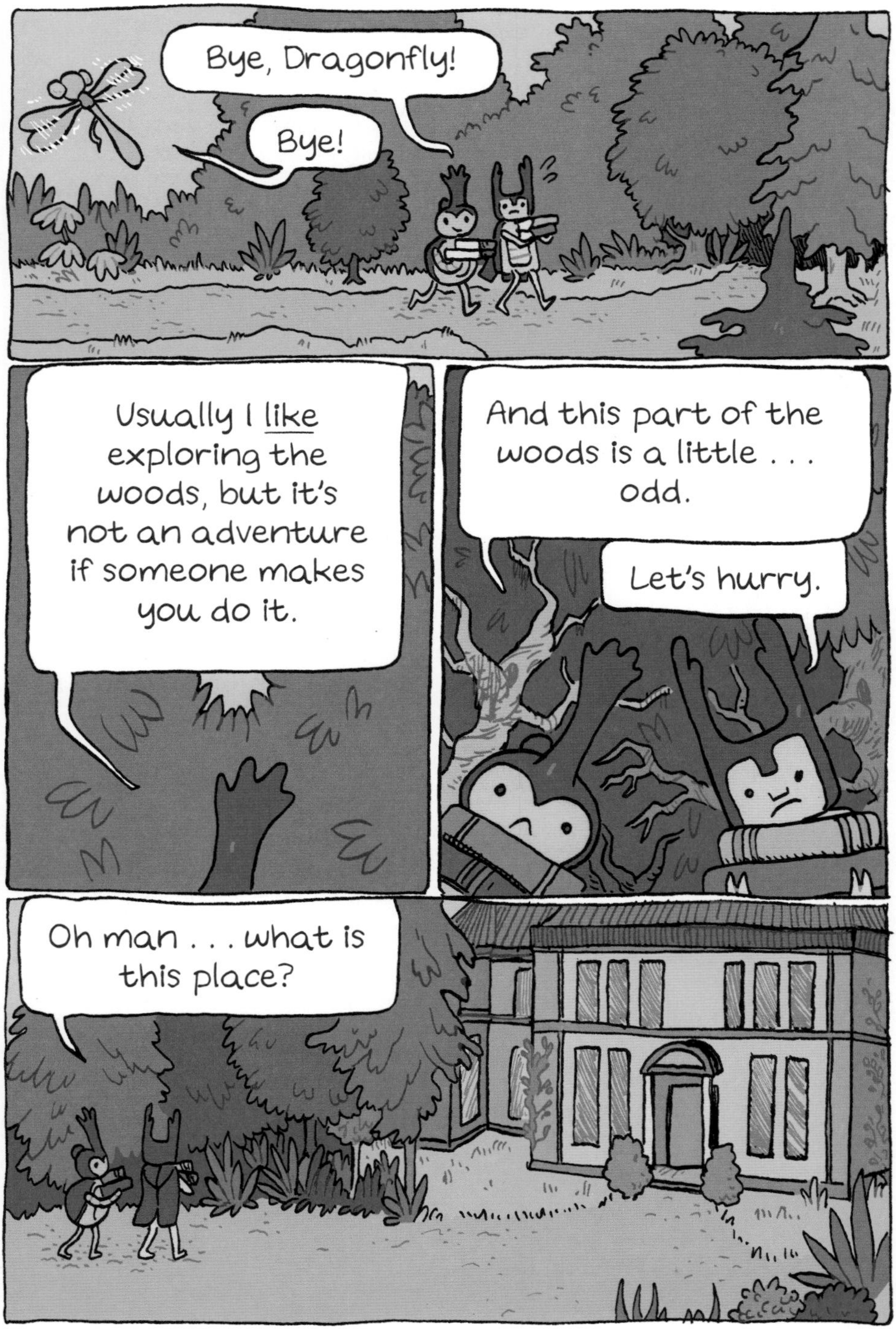
Bye, Dragonfly!
Bye!
Usually I like exploring the woods, but it's not an adventure if someone makes you do it.
And this part of the woods is a little . . . odd.
Let's hurry.
Oh man . . . what is this place?

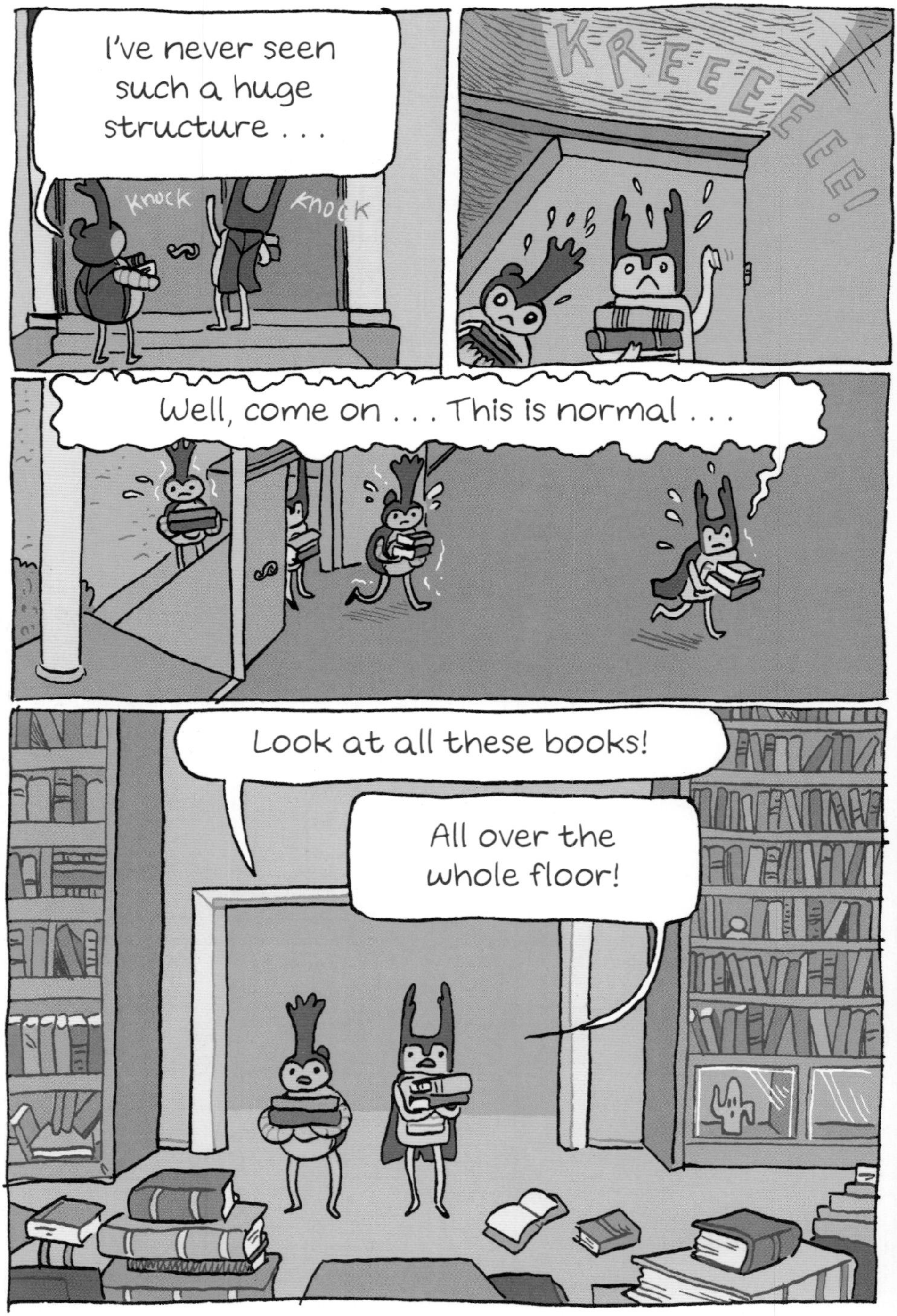
I've never seen such a huge structure . . .
KNOCK
KNOCK
KREEEEEE!
Well, come on . . . This is normal . . .
Look at all these books!
All over the whole floor!

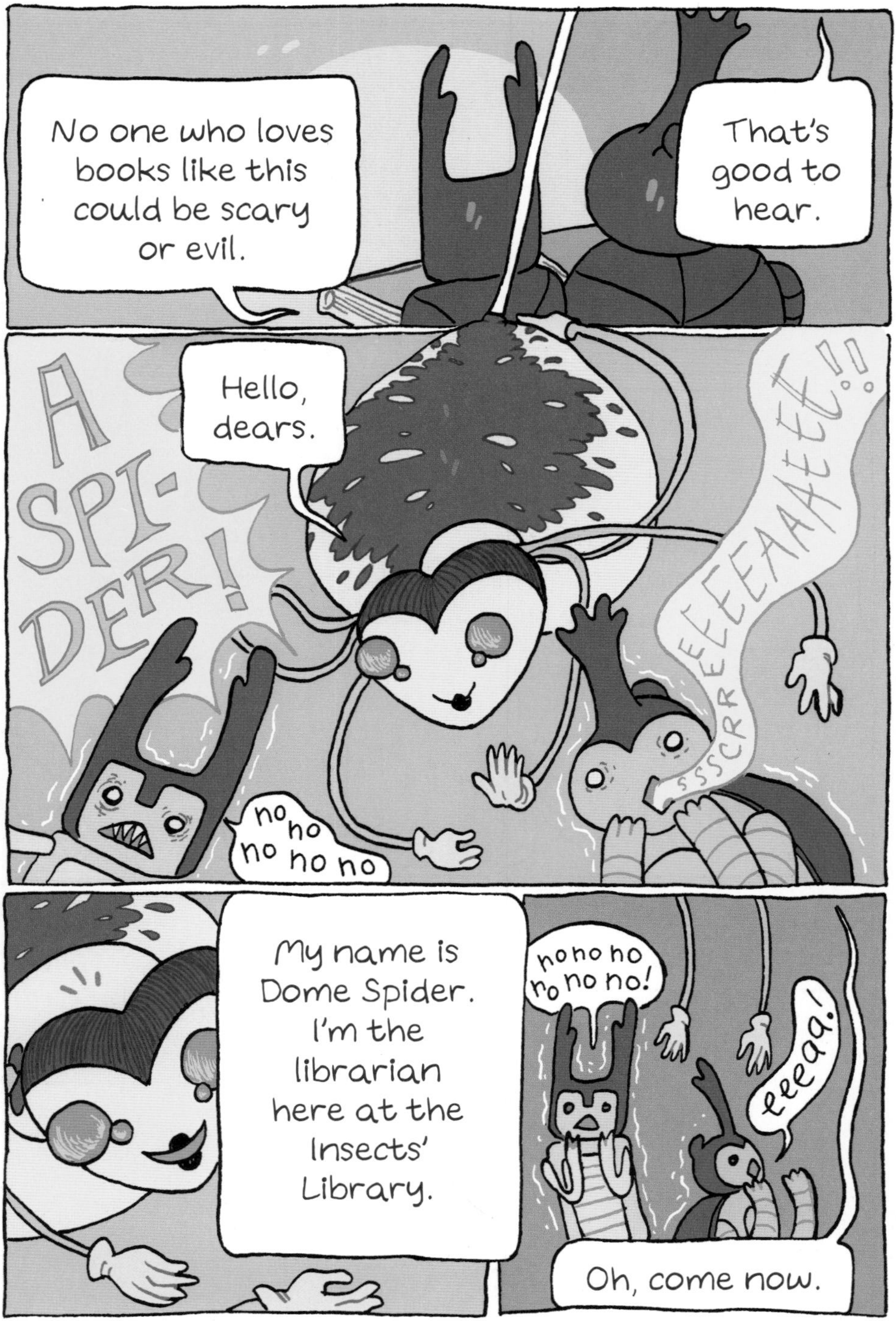

No one who loves books like this could be scary or evil.
That's good to hear.
A SPI-DER!
Hello, dears.
SSSCRREEEEEAAAEEE!!
no no no no no
My name is Dome Spider. I'm the librarian here at the Insects' Library.
no no no no no no no!
eeeaa!
Oh, come now.

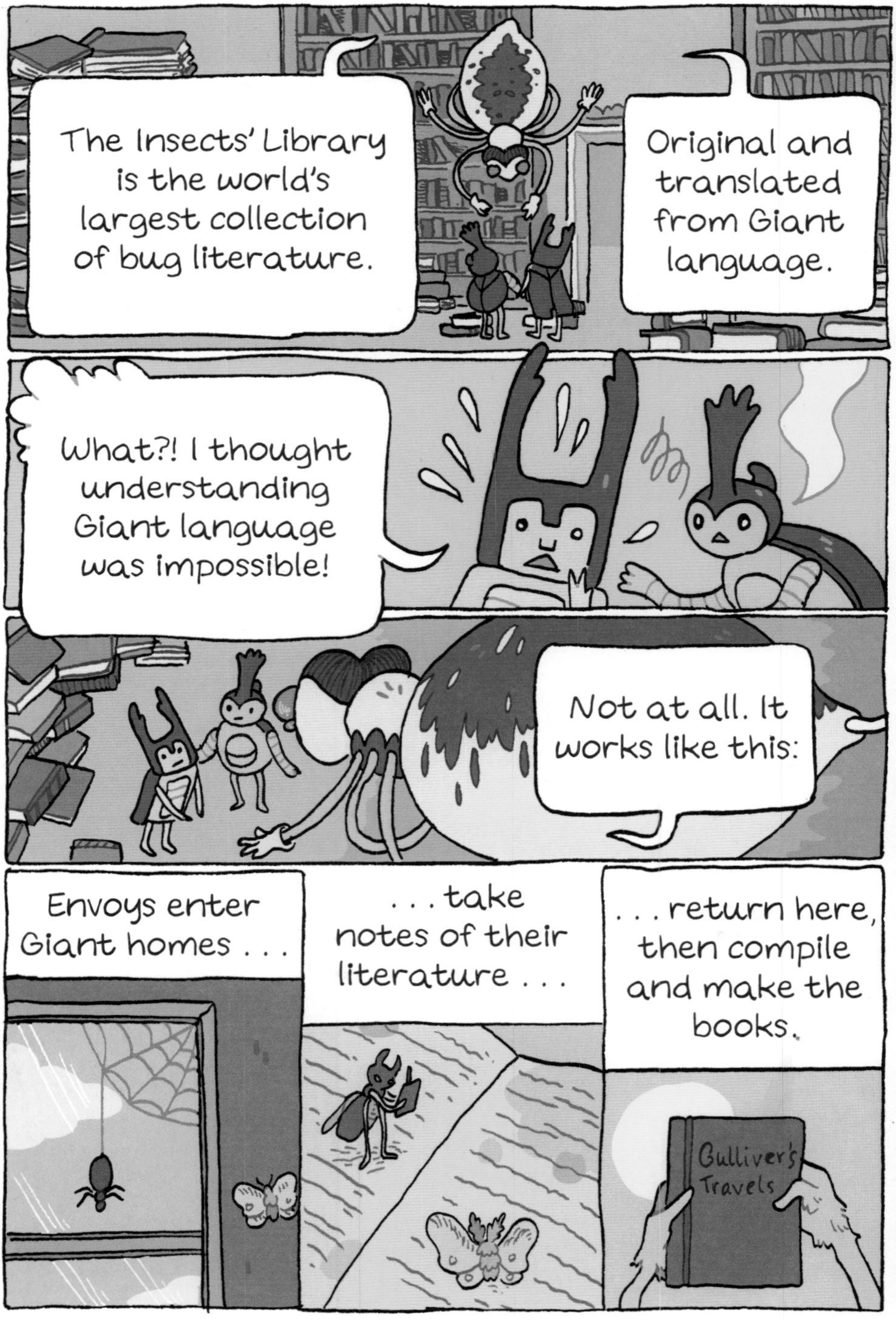
The Insects' Library is the world's largest collection of bug literature.
Original and translated from Giant language.
What?! I thought understanding Giant language was impossible!
Not at all. It works like this:
Envoys enter Giant homes . . .
. . . take notes of their literature . . .
. . . return here, then compile and make the books.
Gulliver's Travels

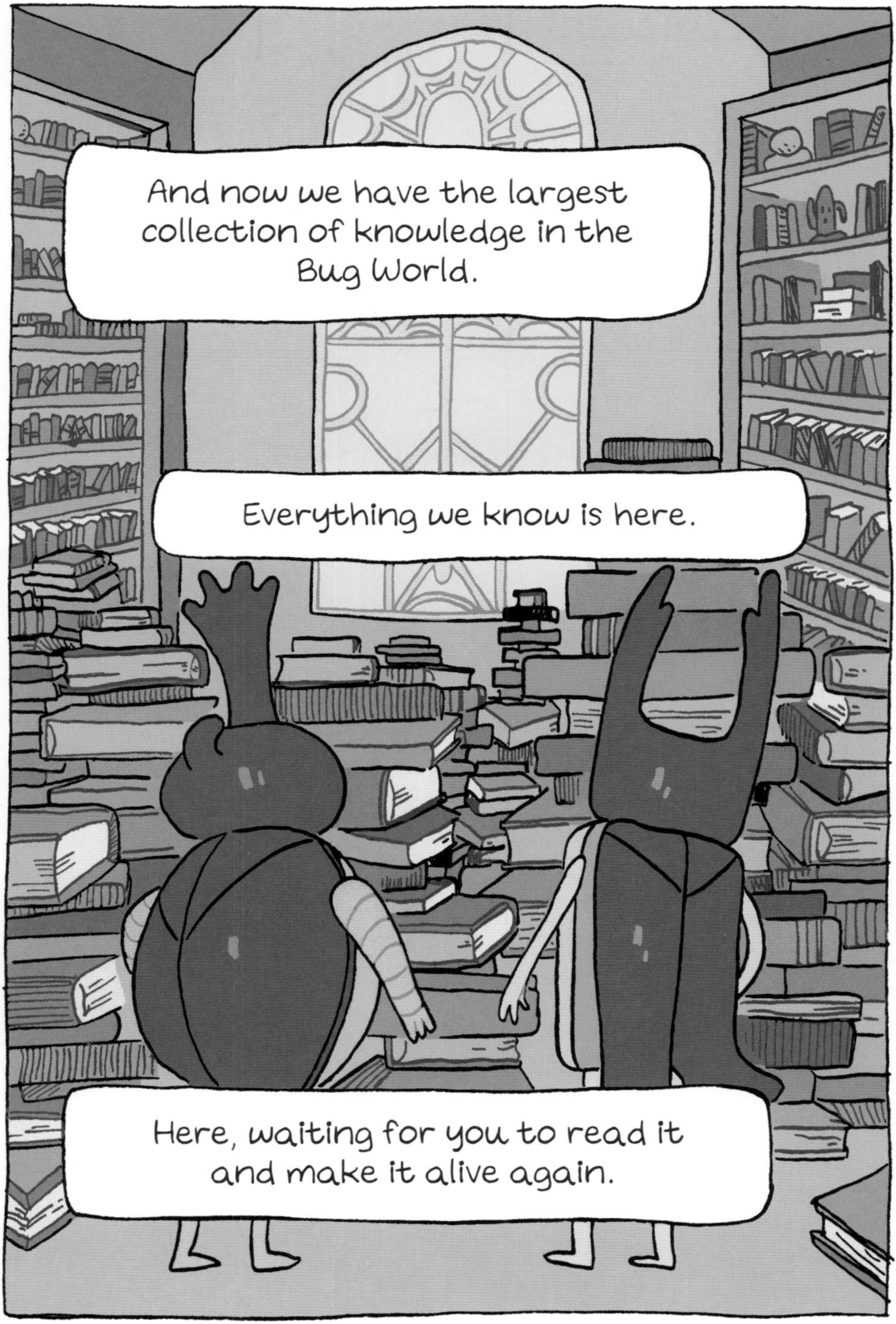
And now we have the largest collection of knowledge in the Bug World.
Everything we know is here.
Here, waiting for you to read it and make it alive again.

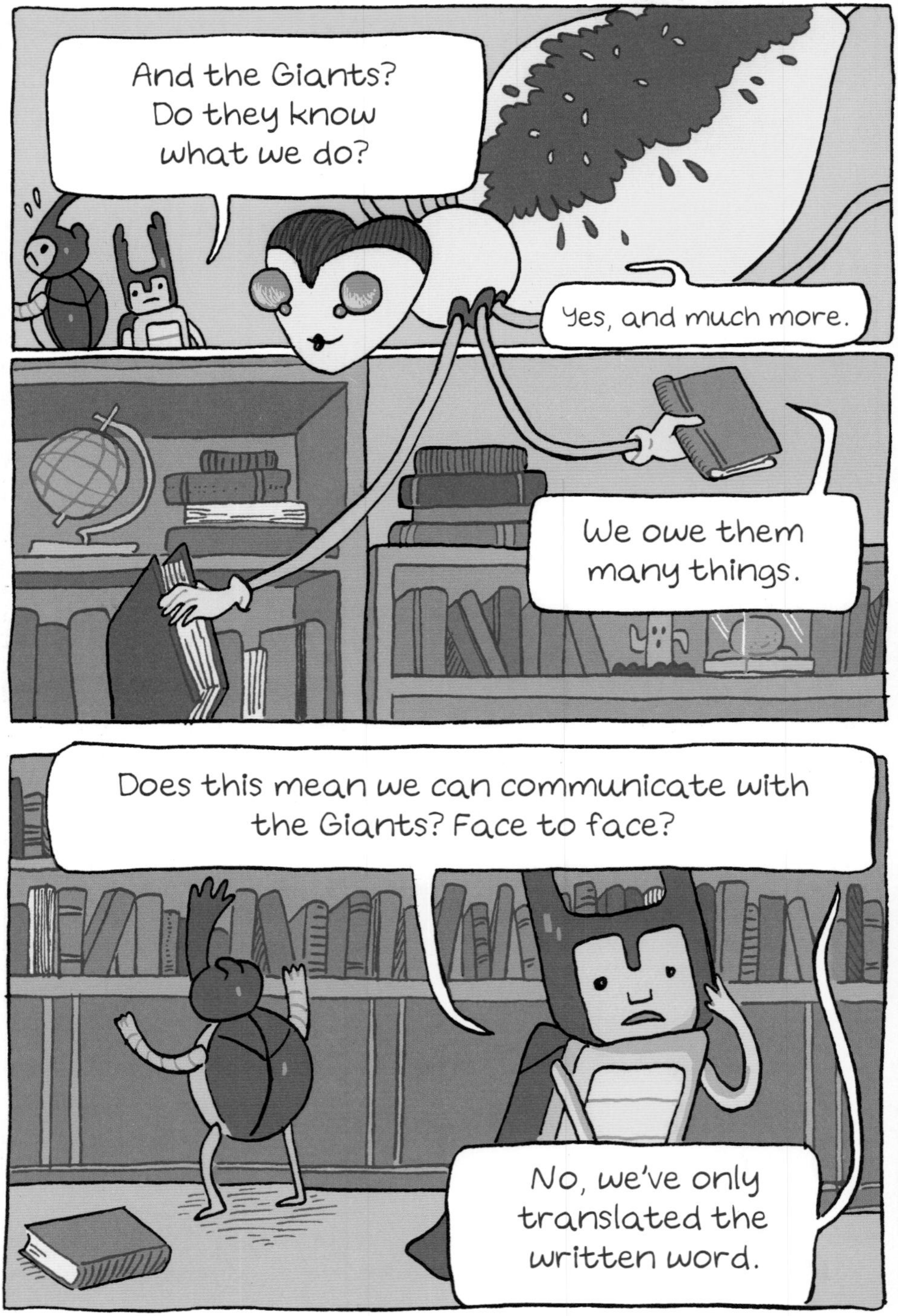
And the Giants? Do they know what we do?
Yes, and much more.
We owe them many things.
Does this mean we can communicate with the Giants? Face to face?
No, we've only translated the written word.

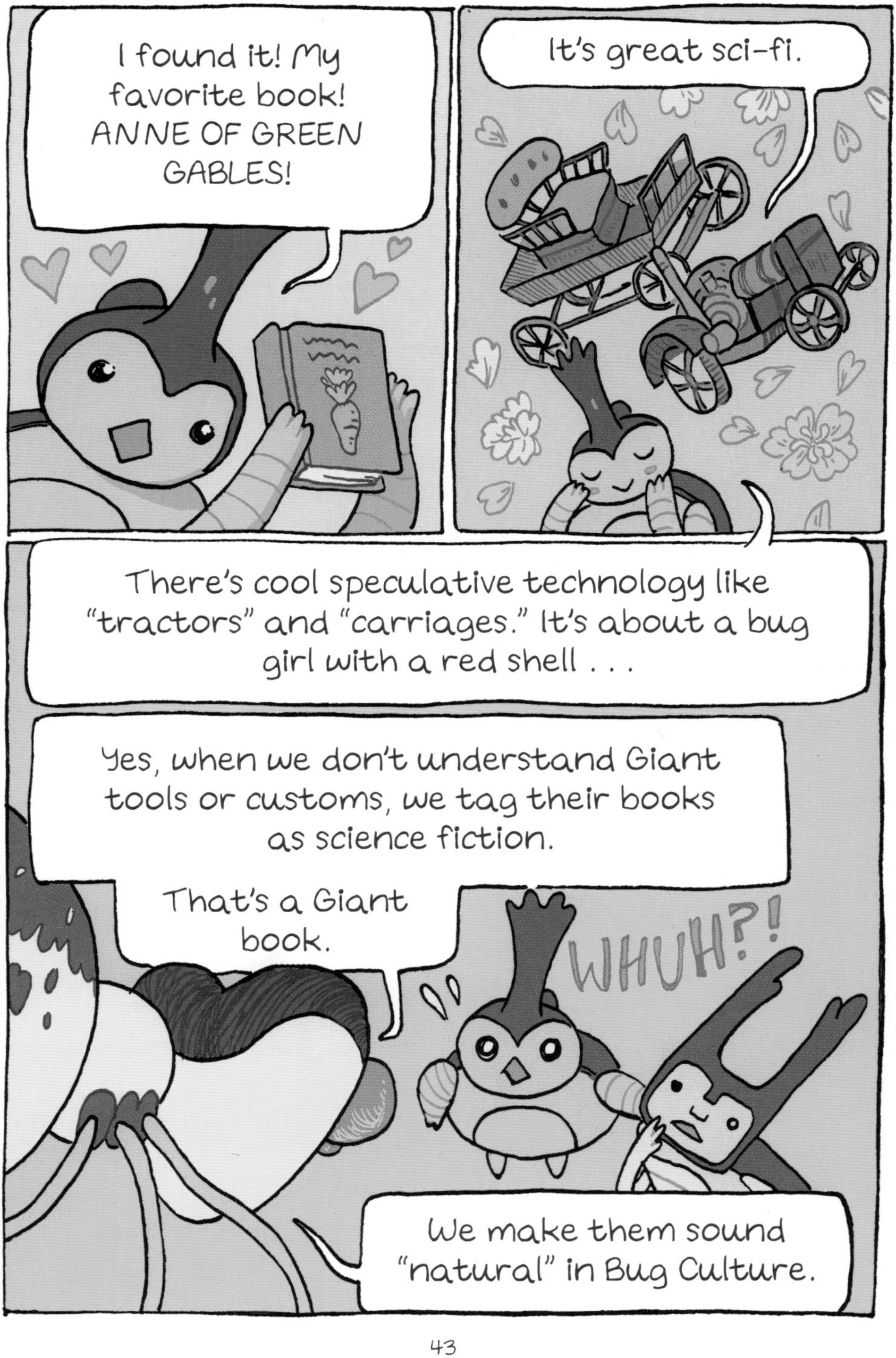
I found it! My favorite book! ANNE OF GREEN GABLES!
It's great sci-fi.
There's cool speculative technology like "tractors" and "carriages." It's about a bug girl with a red shell . . .
Yes, when we don't understand Giant tools or customs, we tag their books as science fiction.
That's a Giant book.
WHUH?!
We make them sound "natural" in Bug Culture.

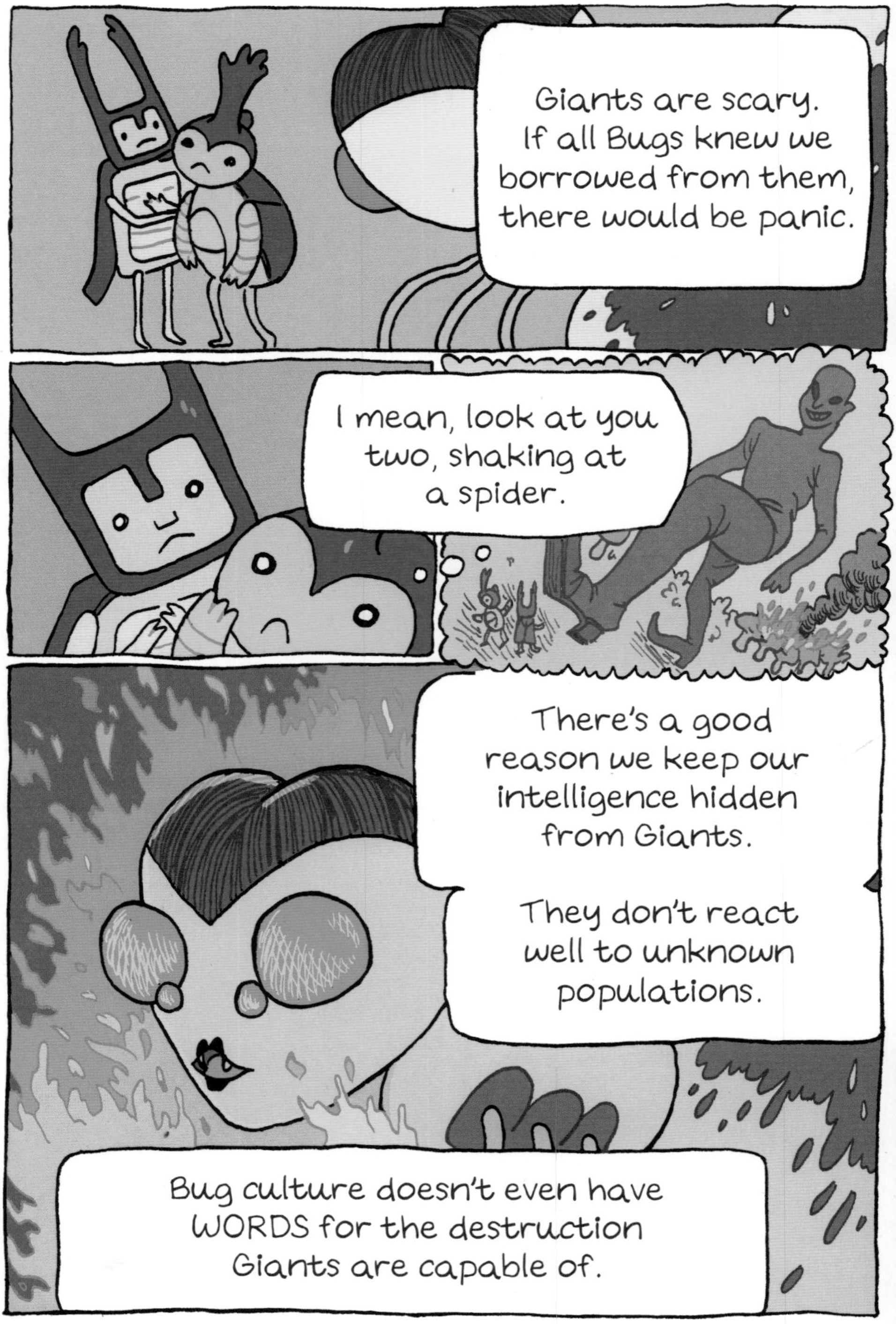
Giants are scary. If all Bugs knew we borrowed from them, there would be panic.
I mean, look at you two, shaking at a spider.
There's a good reason we keep our intelligence hidden from Giants.
They don't react well to unknown populations.
Bug culture doesn't even have WORDS for the destruction Giants are capable of.

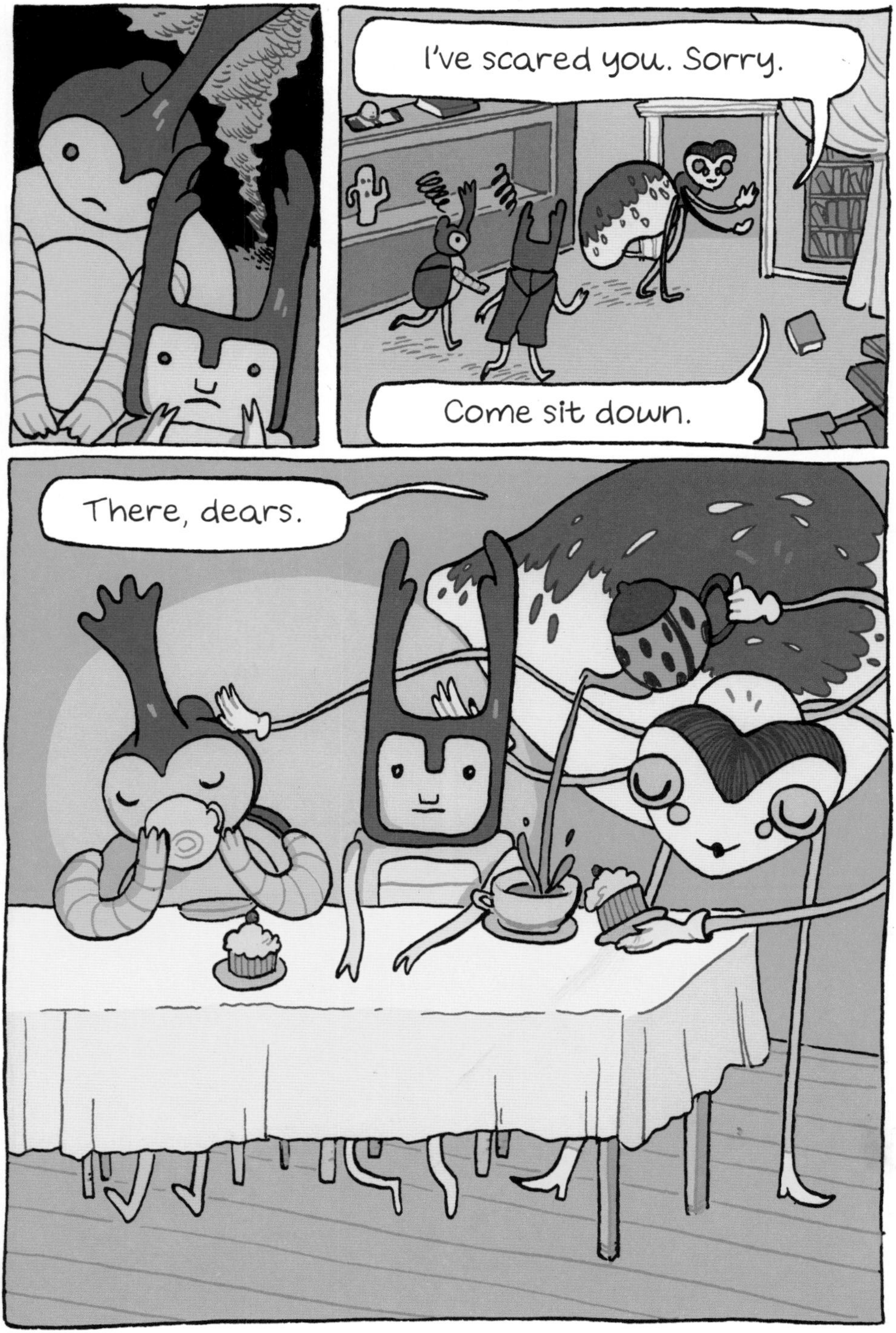
I've scared you. Sorry.
Come sit down.
There, dears.

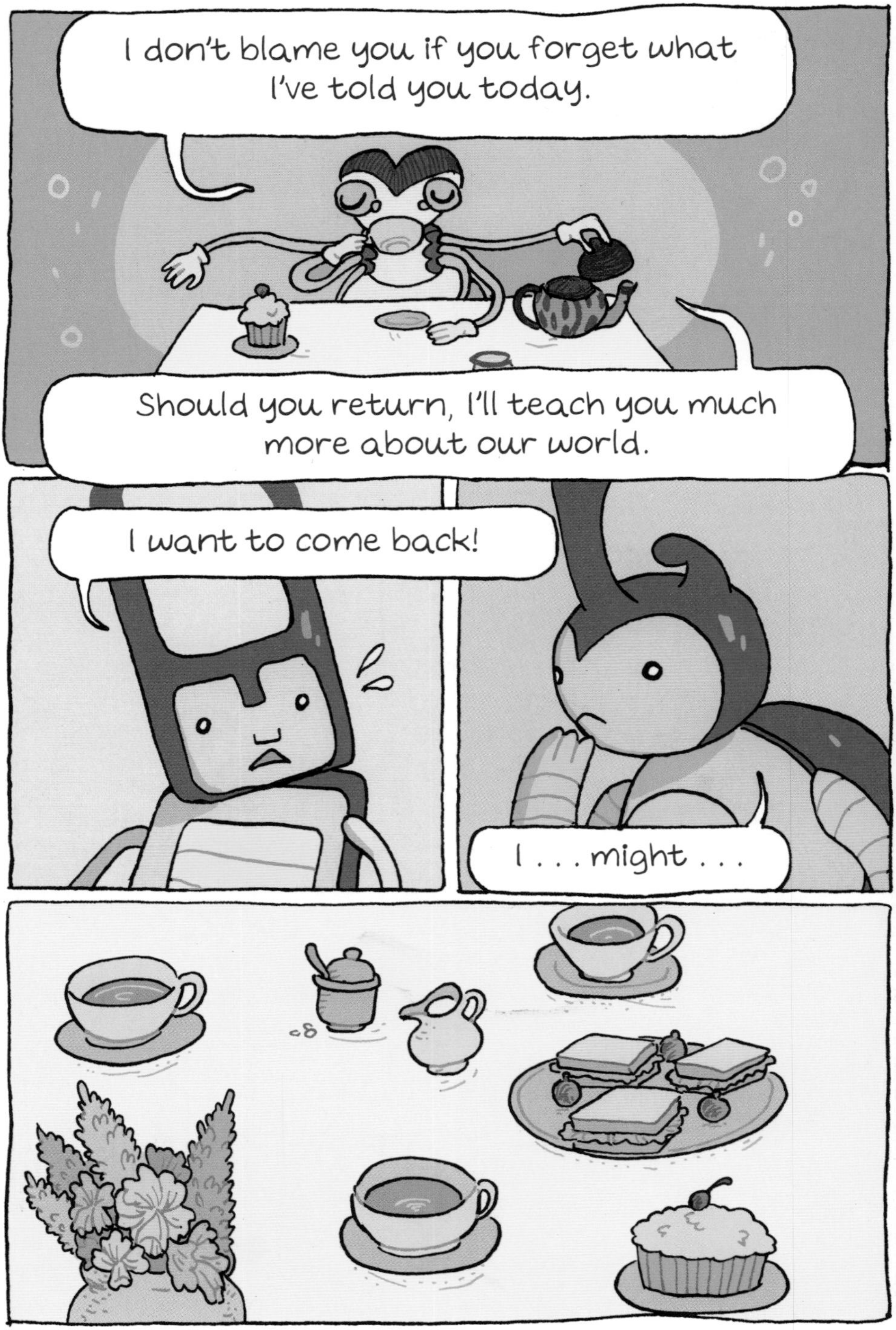

I don't blame you if you forget what I've told you today.
Should you return, I'll teach you much more about our world.
I want to come back!
I . . . might . . .

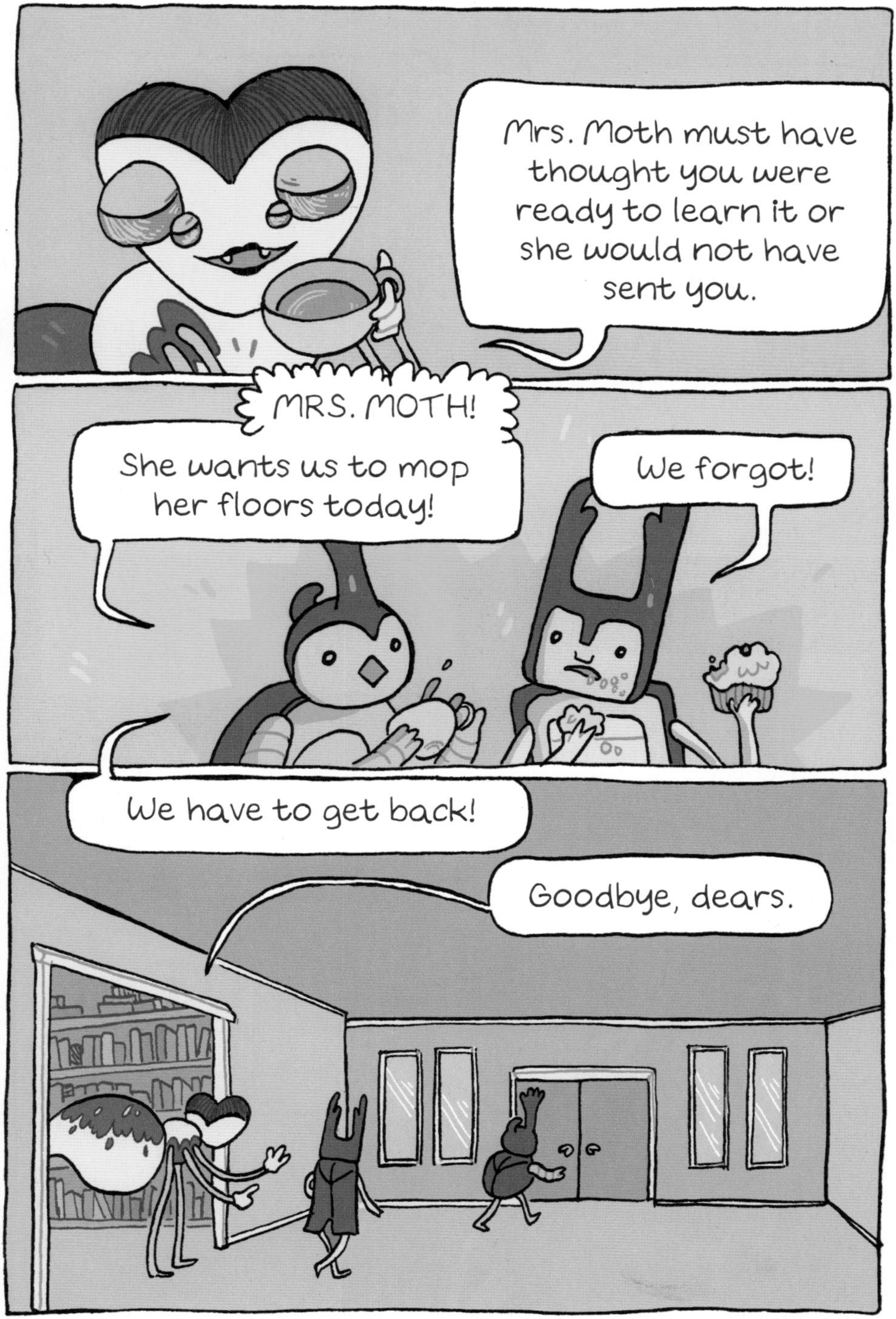
Mrs. Moth must have thought you were ready to learn it or she would not have sent you.
MRS. MOTH!
She wants us to mop her floors today!
We forgot!
We have to get back!
Goodbye, dears.

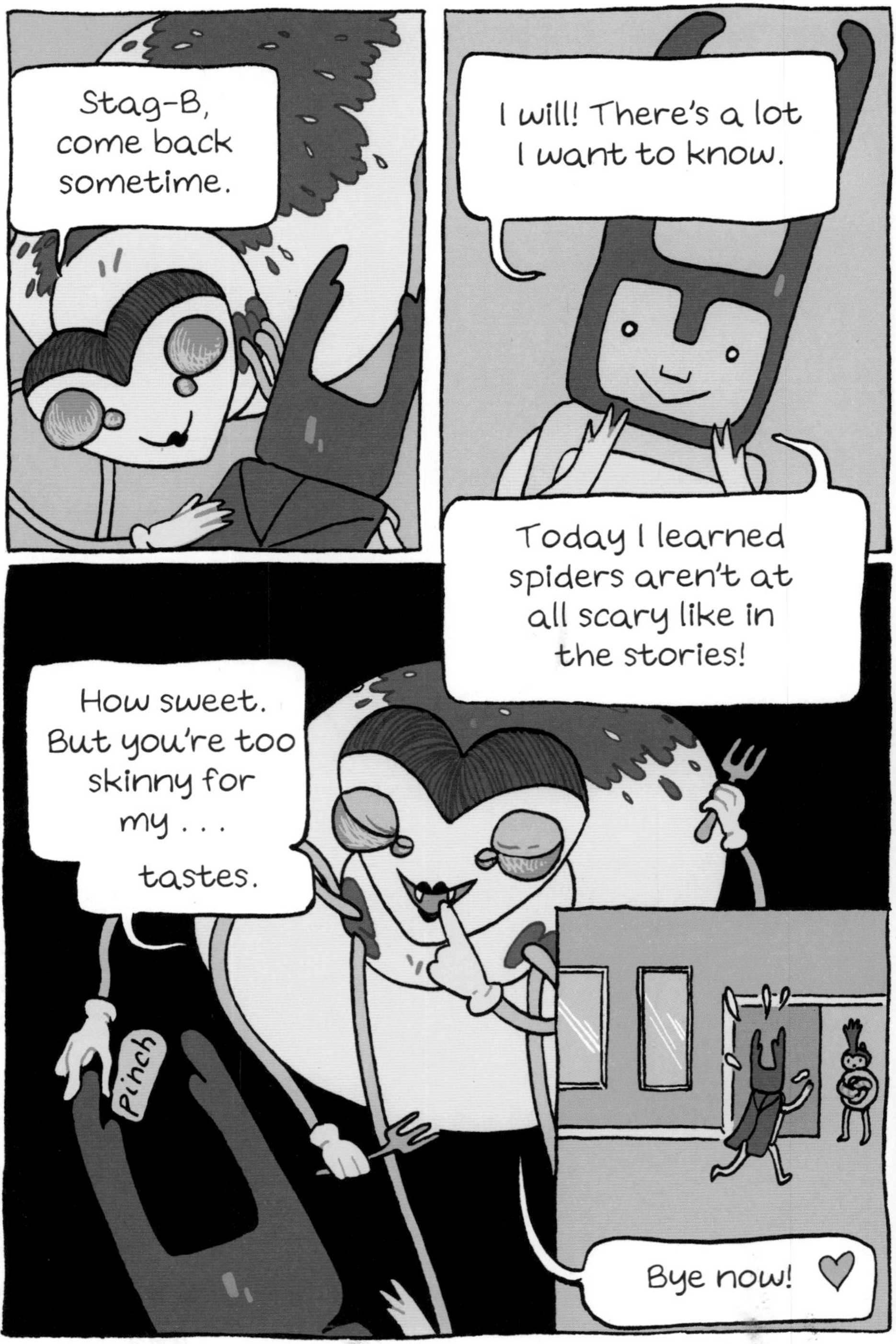
Stag-B, come back sometime.
I will! There's a lot I want to know.
Today I learned spiders aren't at all scary like in the stories!
How sweet. But you're too skinny for my . . . tastes.
Pinch
Bye now!

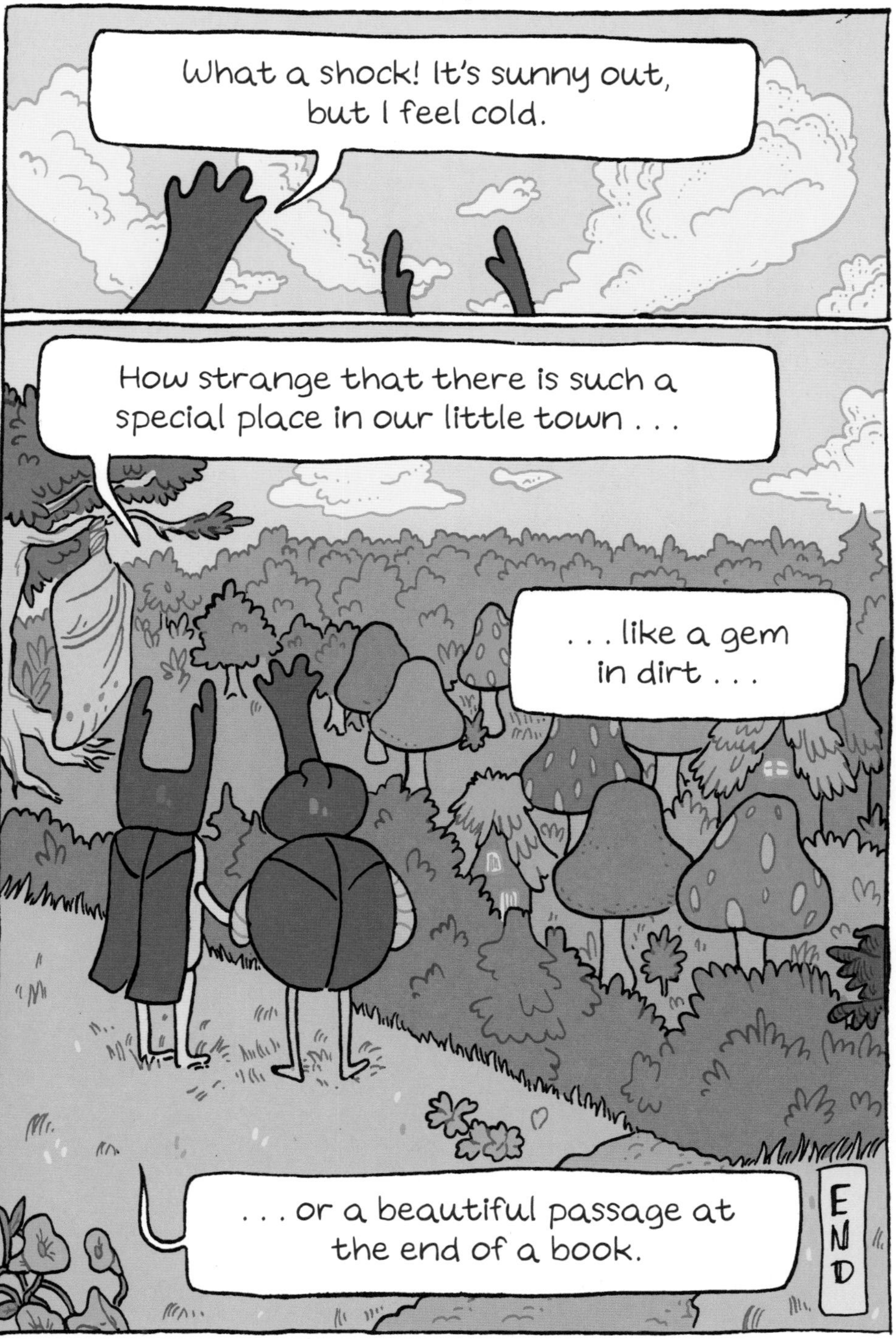
What a shock! It's sunny out, but I feel cold.
How strange that there is such a special place in our little town . . .
. . . like a gem in dirt . . .
. . . or a beautiful passage at the end of a book.
END

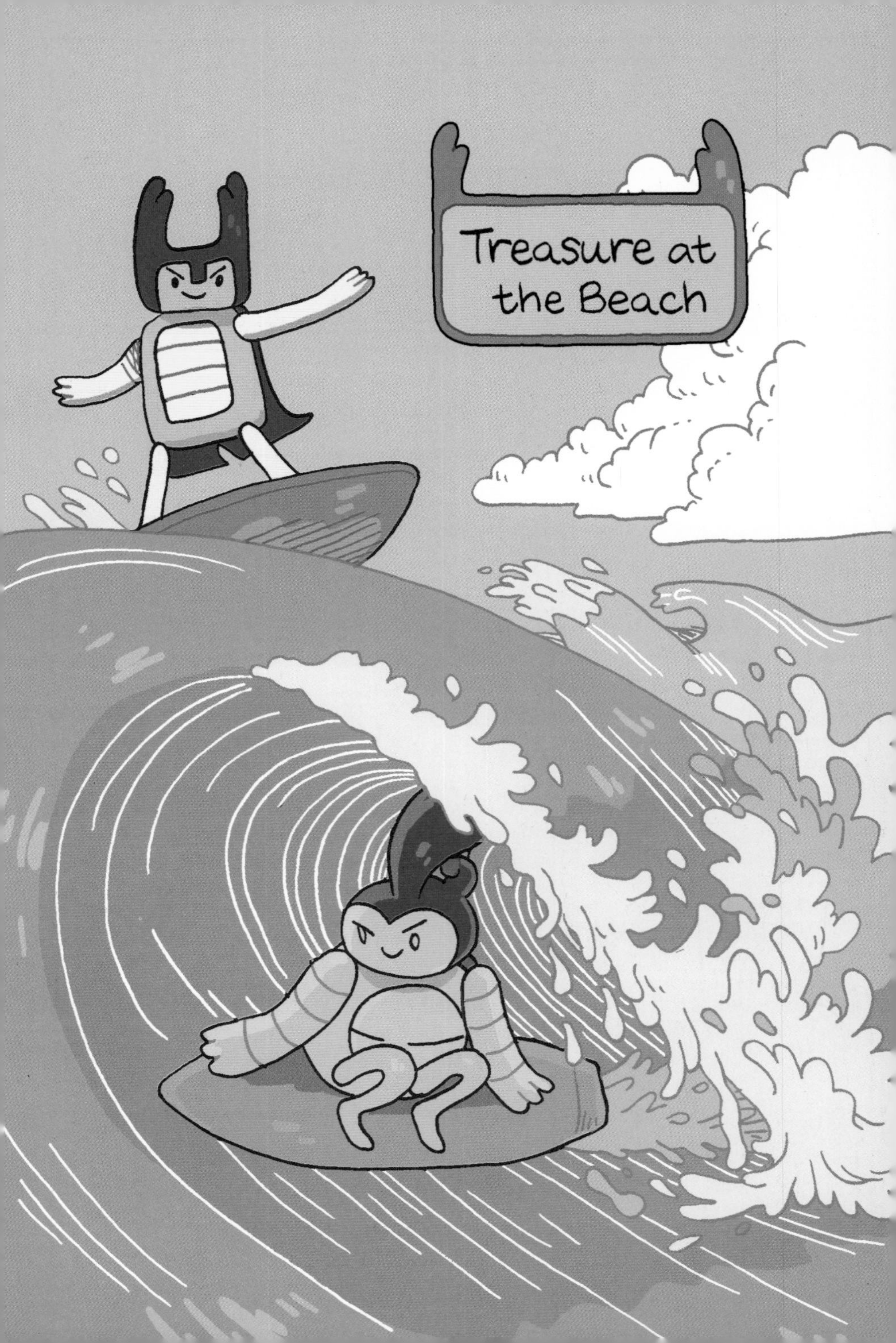
Treasure at the Beach

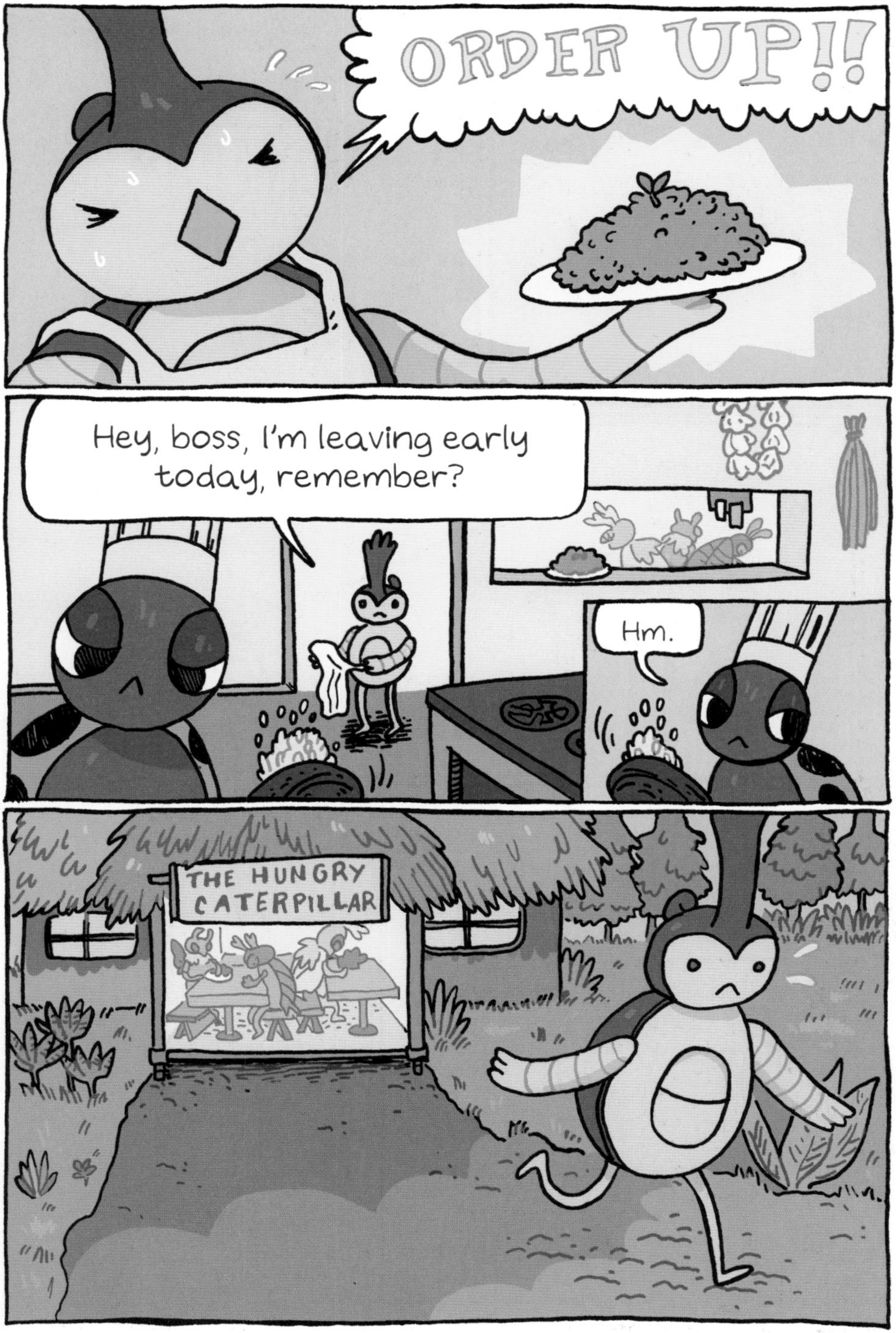

ORDER UP!!
Hey, boss, I'm leaving early today, remember?
Hm.
THE HUNGRY CATERPILLAR

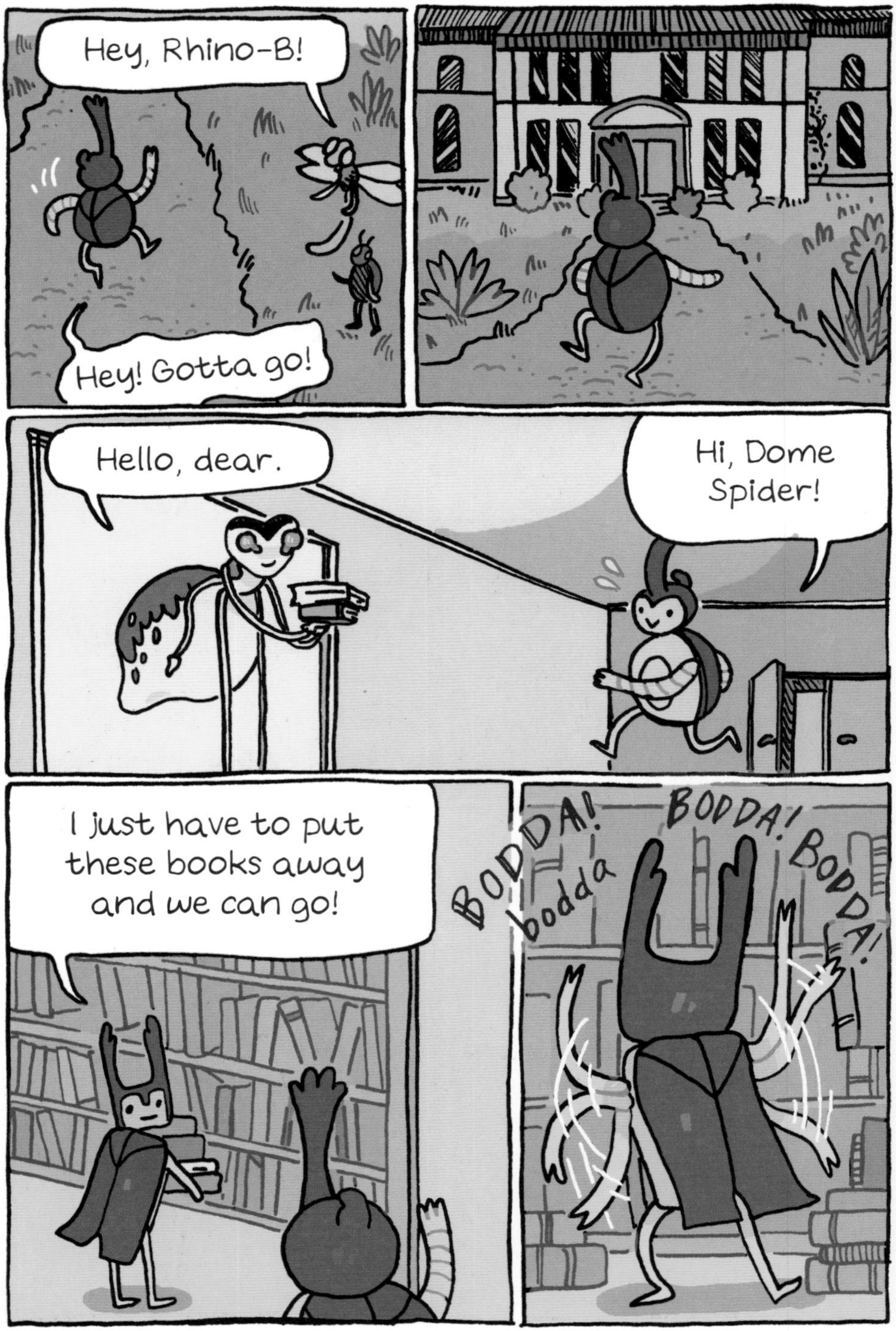
Hey, Rhino-B!
Hey! Gotta go!
Hello, dear.
Hi, Dome Spider!
I just have to put these books away and we can go!
BODDA! BODDA! BODDA! BODDA! bodda

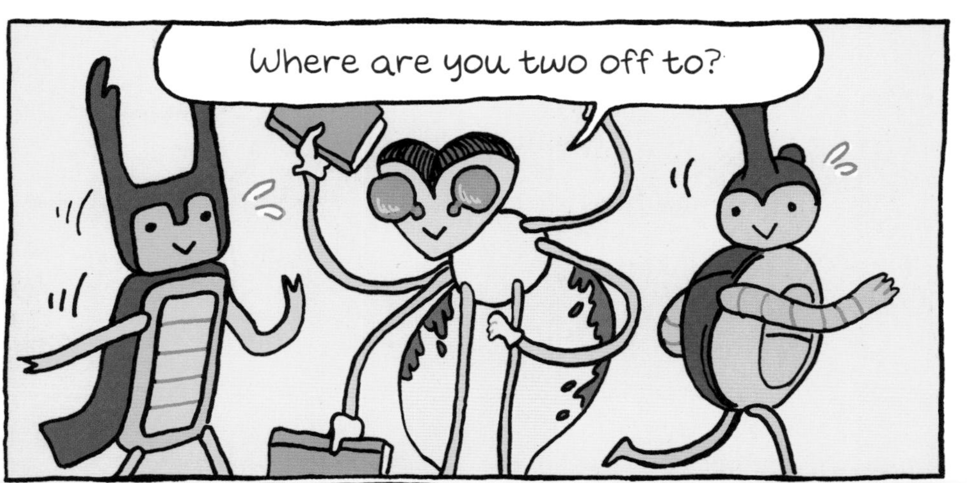
Where are you two off to?

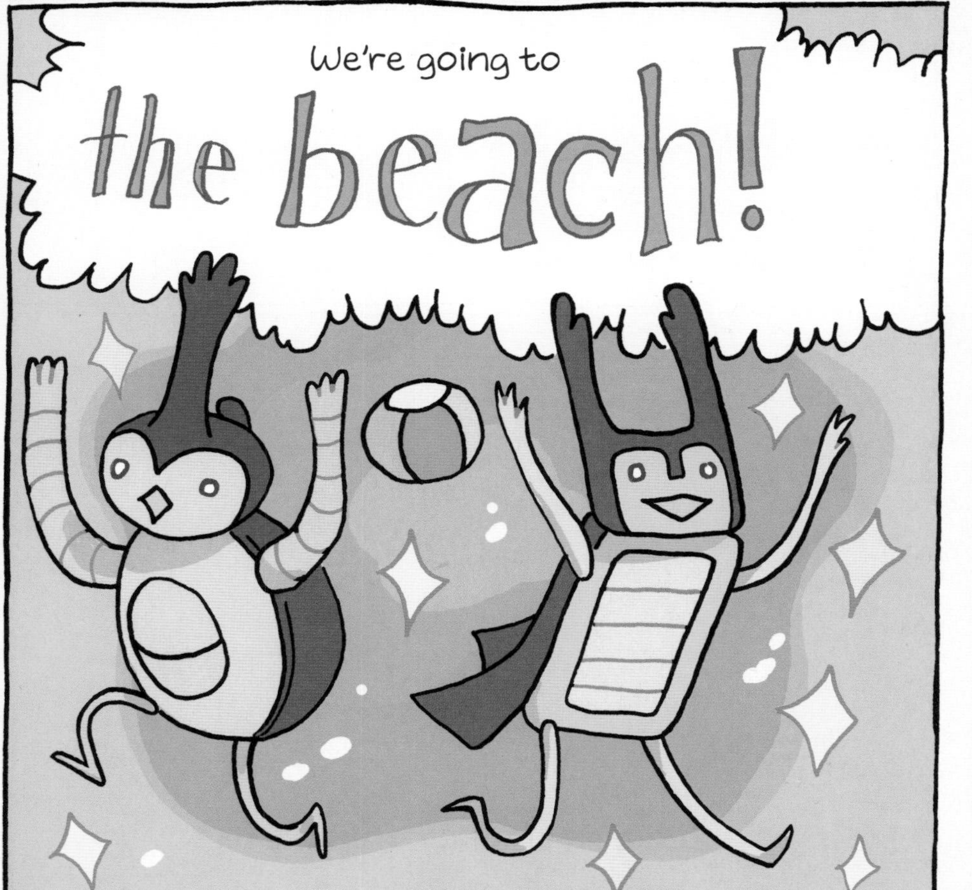
We're going to
the beach!

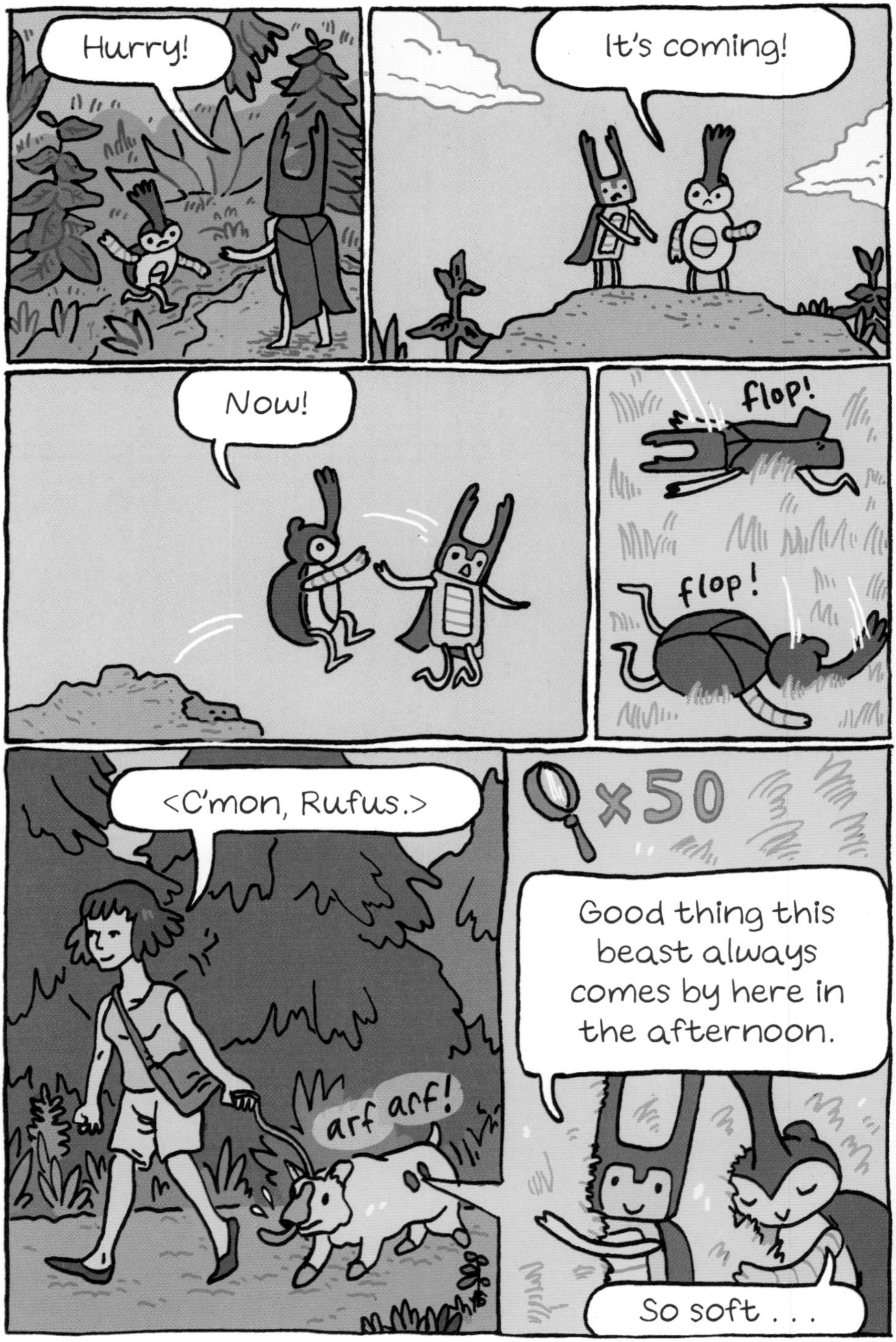
Hurry!
It's coming!
Now!
flop!
flop!
<C'mon, Rufus.>
arf arf!
x50
Good thing this beast always comes by here in the afternoon.
So soft . . .

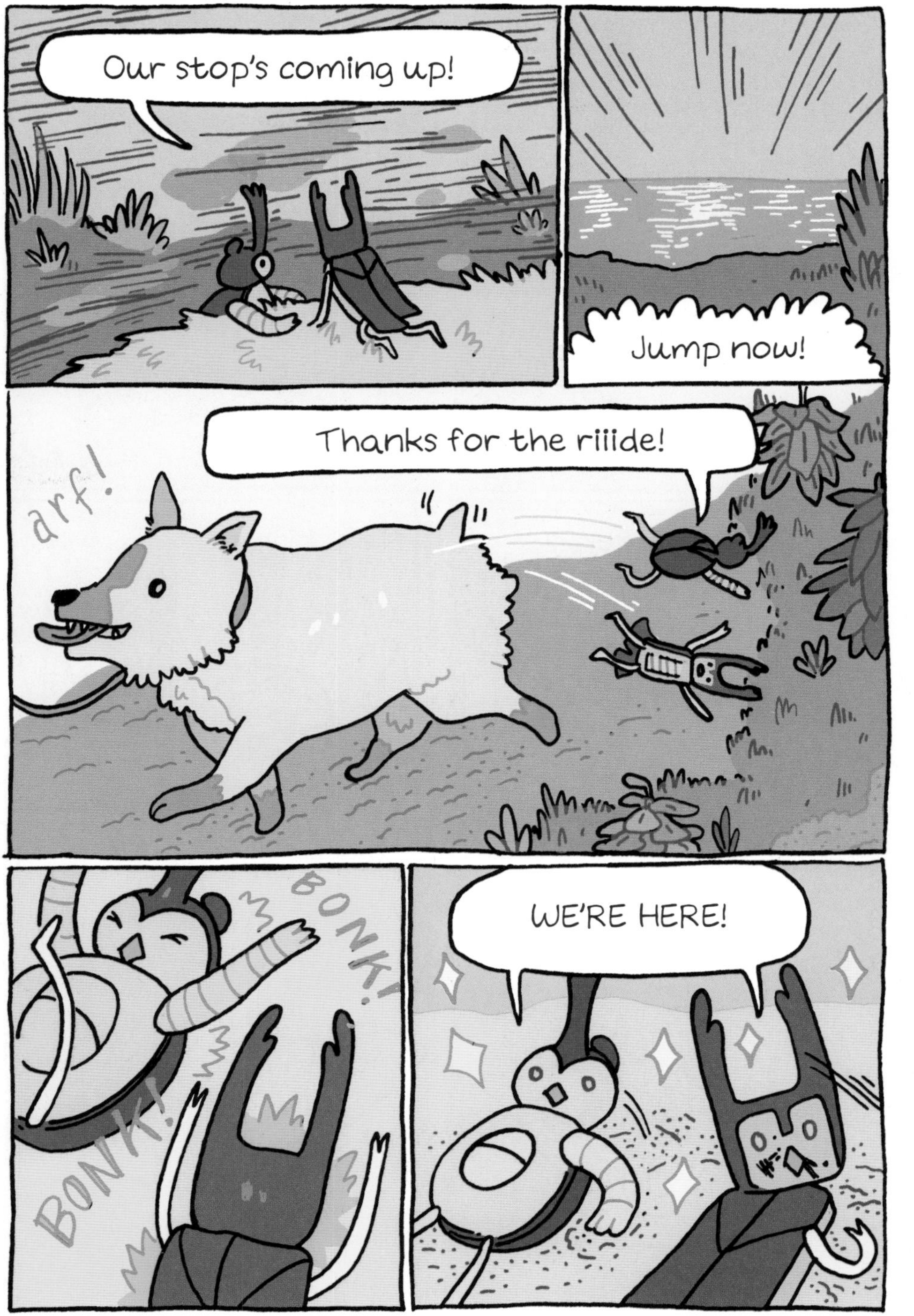
Our stop's coming up!
Jump now!
Thanks for the riiide!
arf!
BONK!
BONK!
WE'RE HERE!

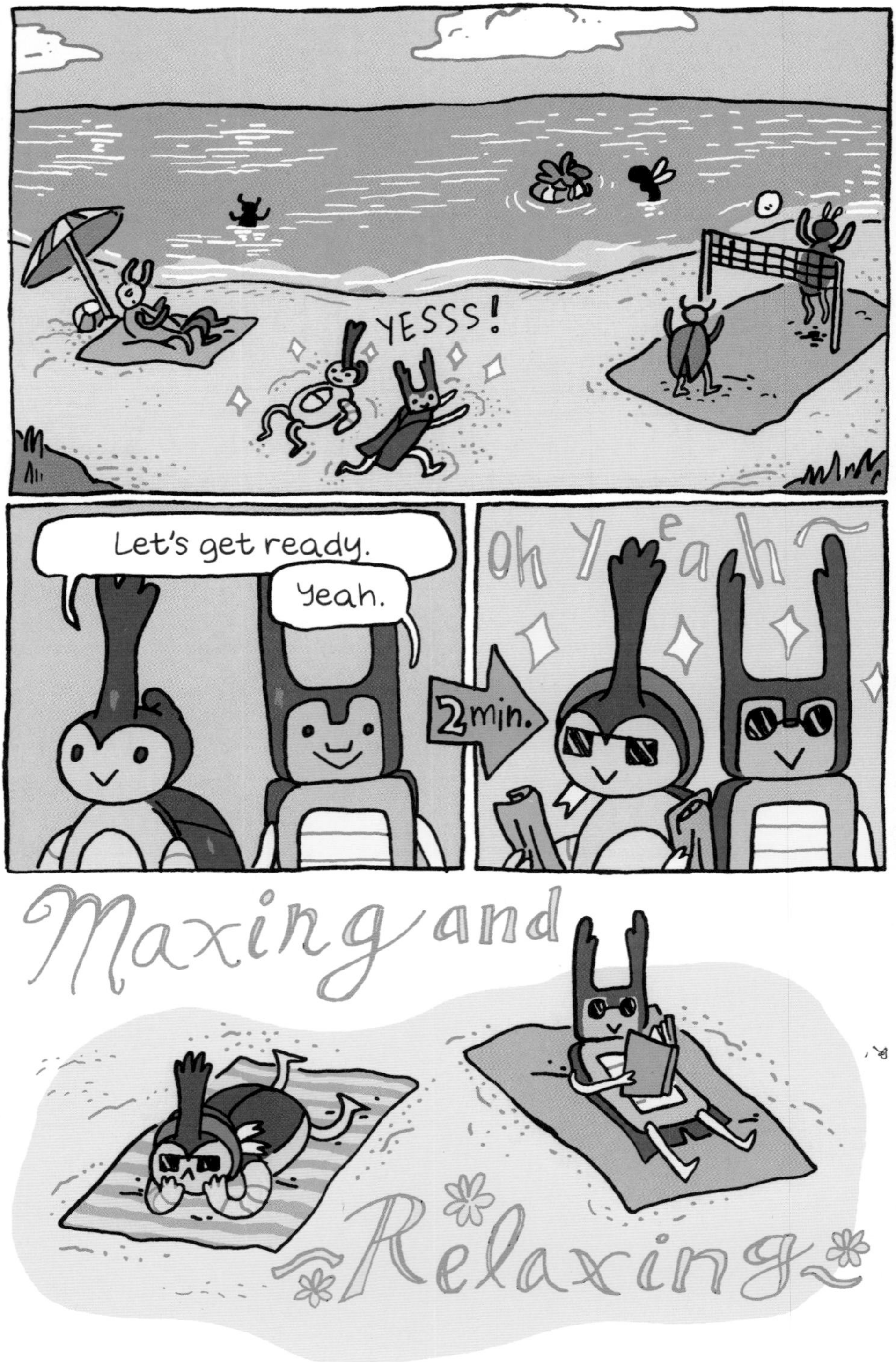
YESSS!
Let's get ready.
Yeah.
2 min.
Oh Yeah~
Maxing and
~Relaxing~

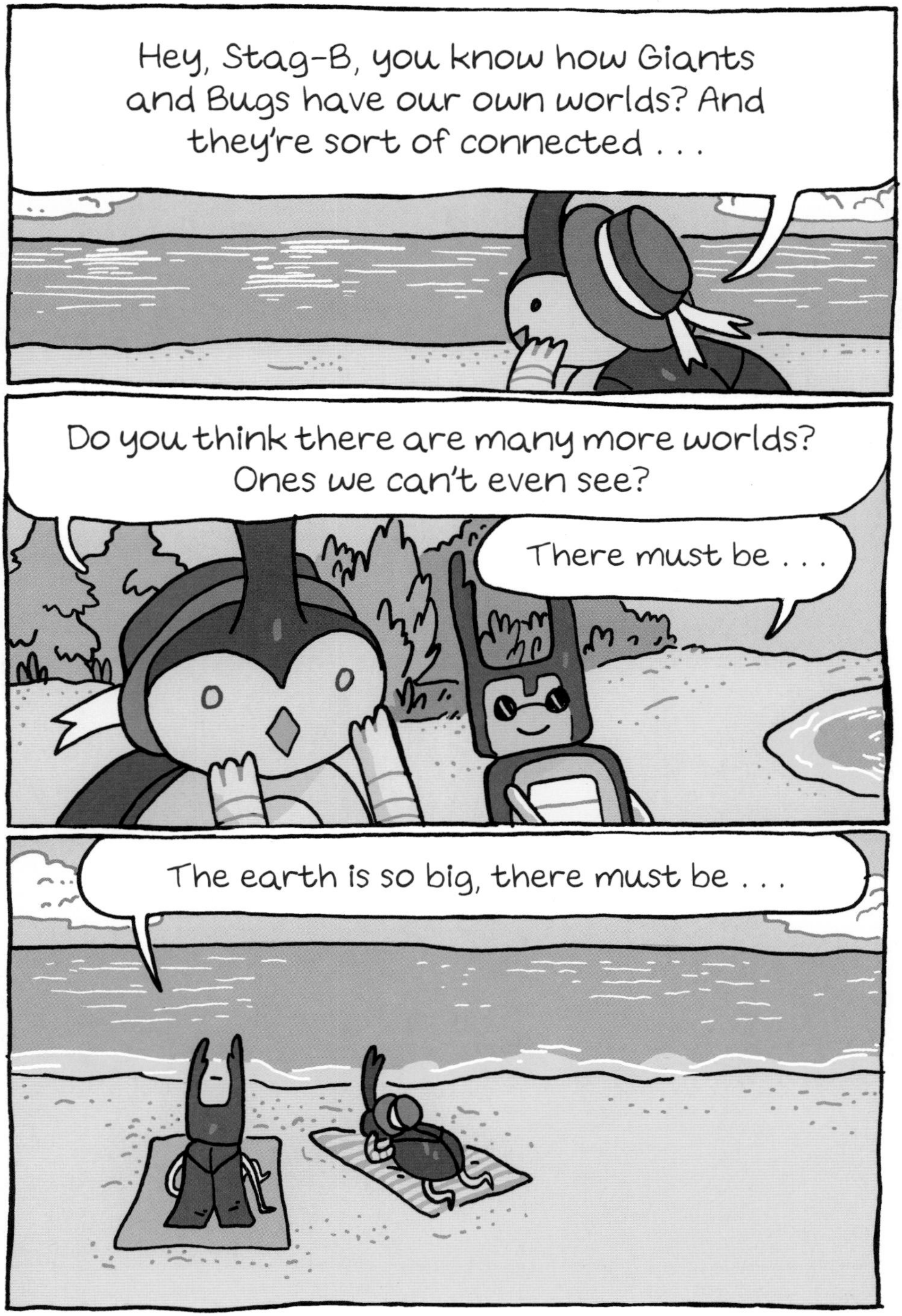
Hey, Stag-B, you know how Giants and Bugs have our own worlds? And they're sort of connected . . .
Do you think there are many more worlds? Ones we can't even see?
There must be . . .
The earth is so big, there must be . . .

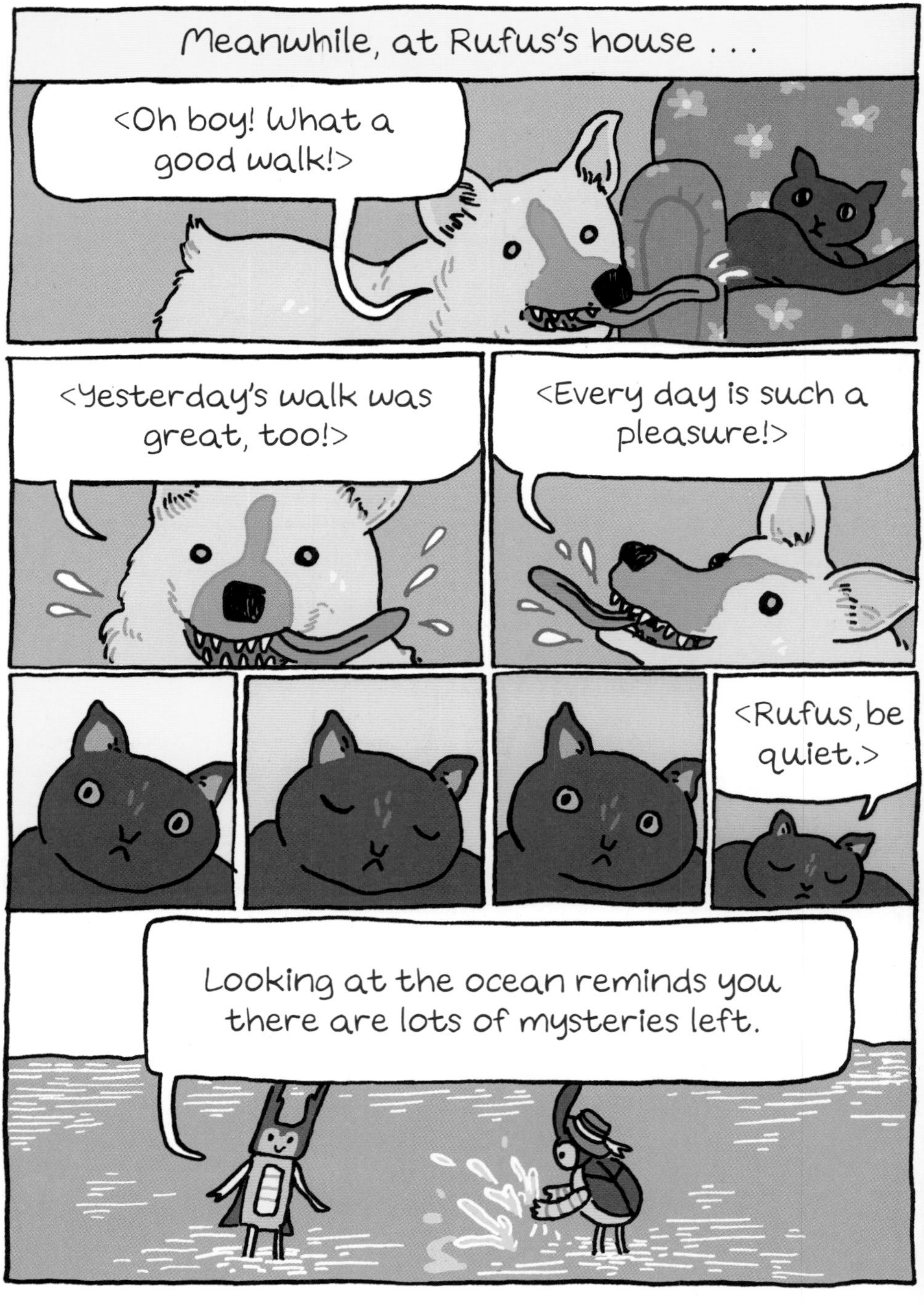
Meanwhile, at Rufus's house . . .
<Oh boy! What a good walk!>
<Yesterday's walk was great, too!>
<Every day is such a pleasure!>
<Rufus, be quiet.>
Looking at the ocean reminds you there are lots of mysteries left.

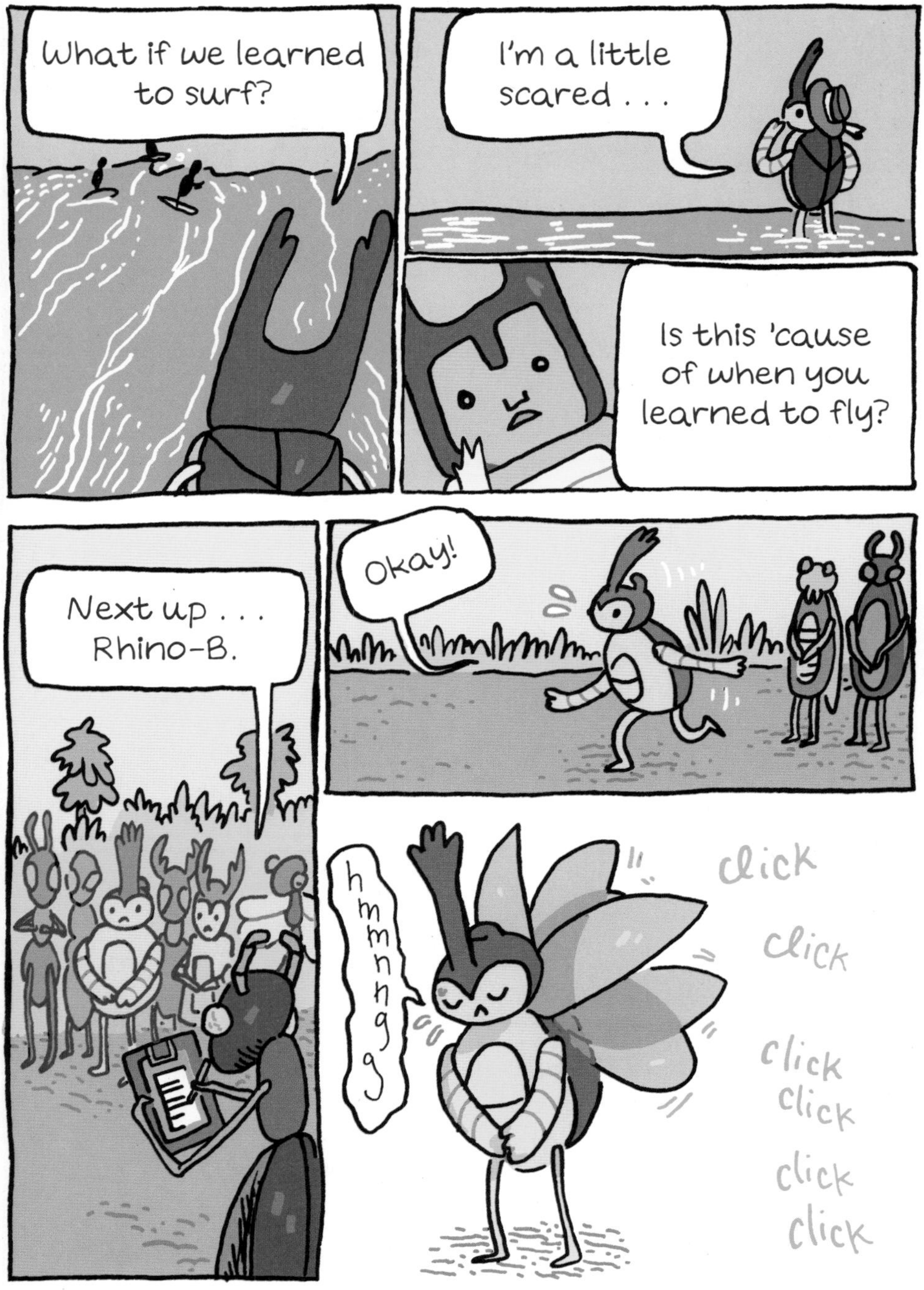
What if we learned to surf?
I'm a little scared . . .
Is this 'cause of when you learned to fly?
Next up . . . Rhino-B.
Okay!
hmmnngg
click
click
click
click
click
click

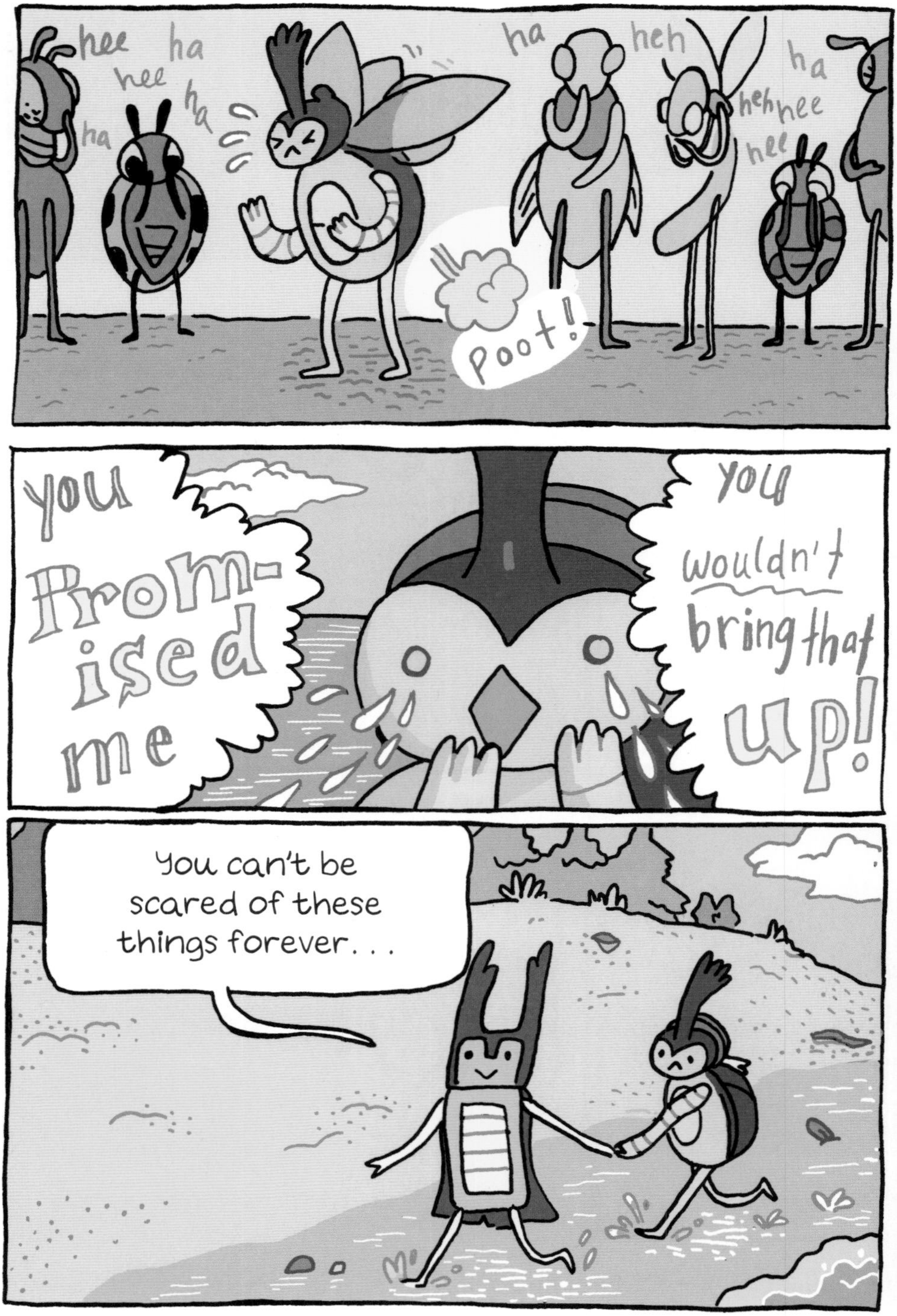
hee ha hee ha ha
ha heh ha heh hee hee
Poot!
you Prom-ised me
you wouldn't bring that up!
You can't be scared of these things forever. . .

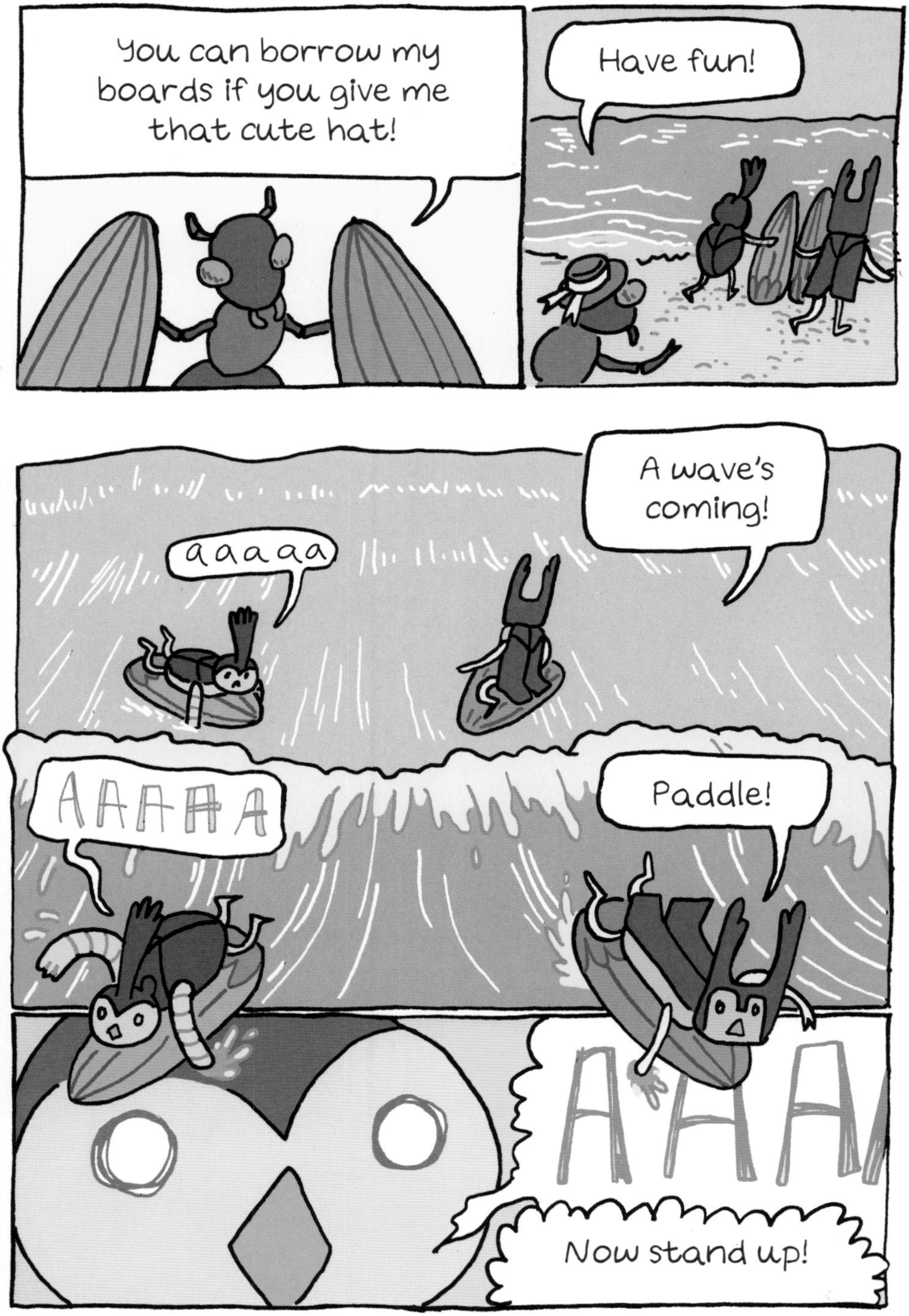
You can borrow my boards if you give me that cute hat!
Have fun!
A wave's coming!
aaaaa
AAAAA
Paddle!
AAAA
Now stand up!

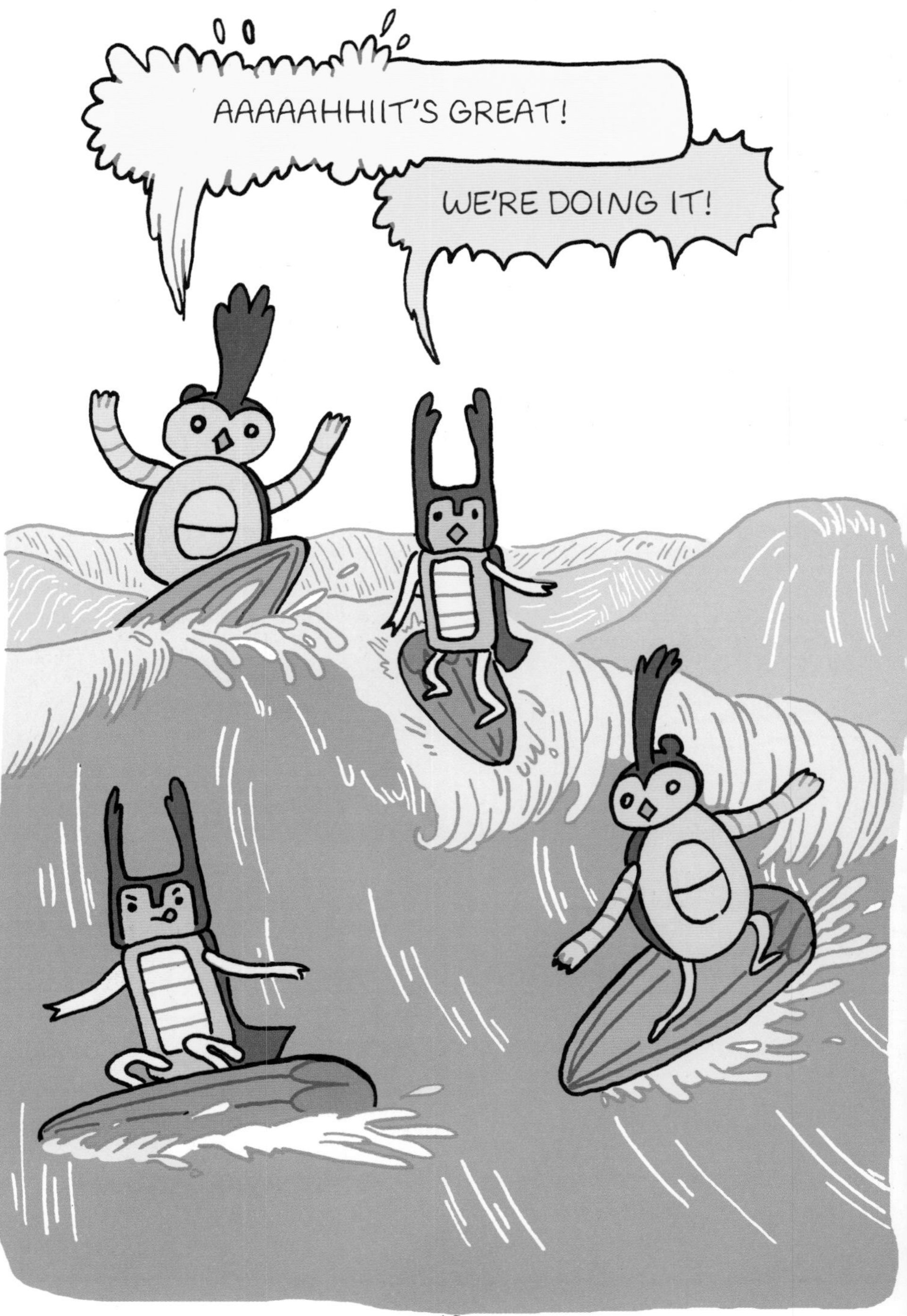
AAAAAHHIIT'S GREAT!
WE'RE DOING IT!

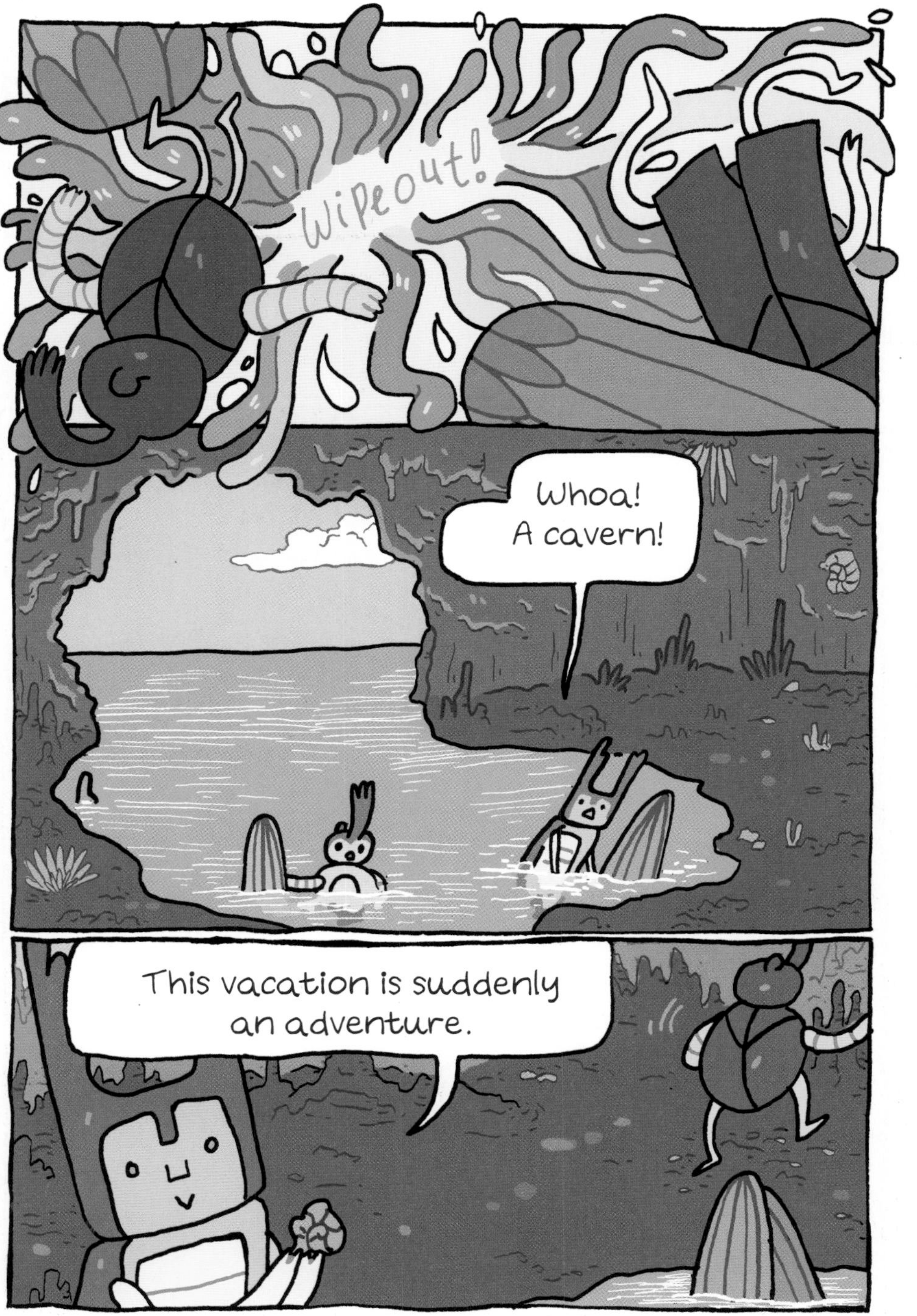
Wipeout!
Whoa!
A cavern!
This vacation is suddenly
an adventure.

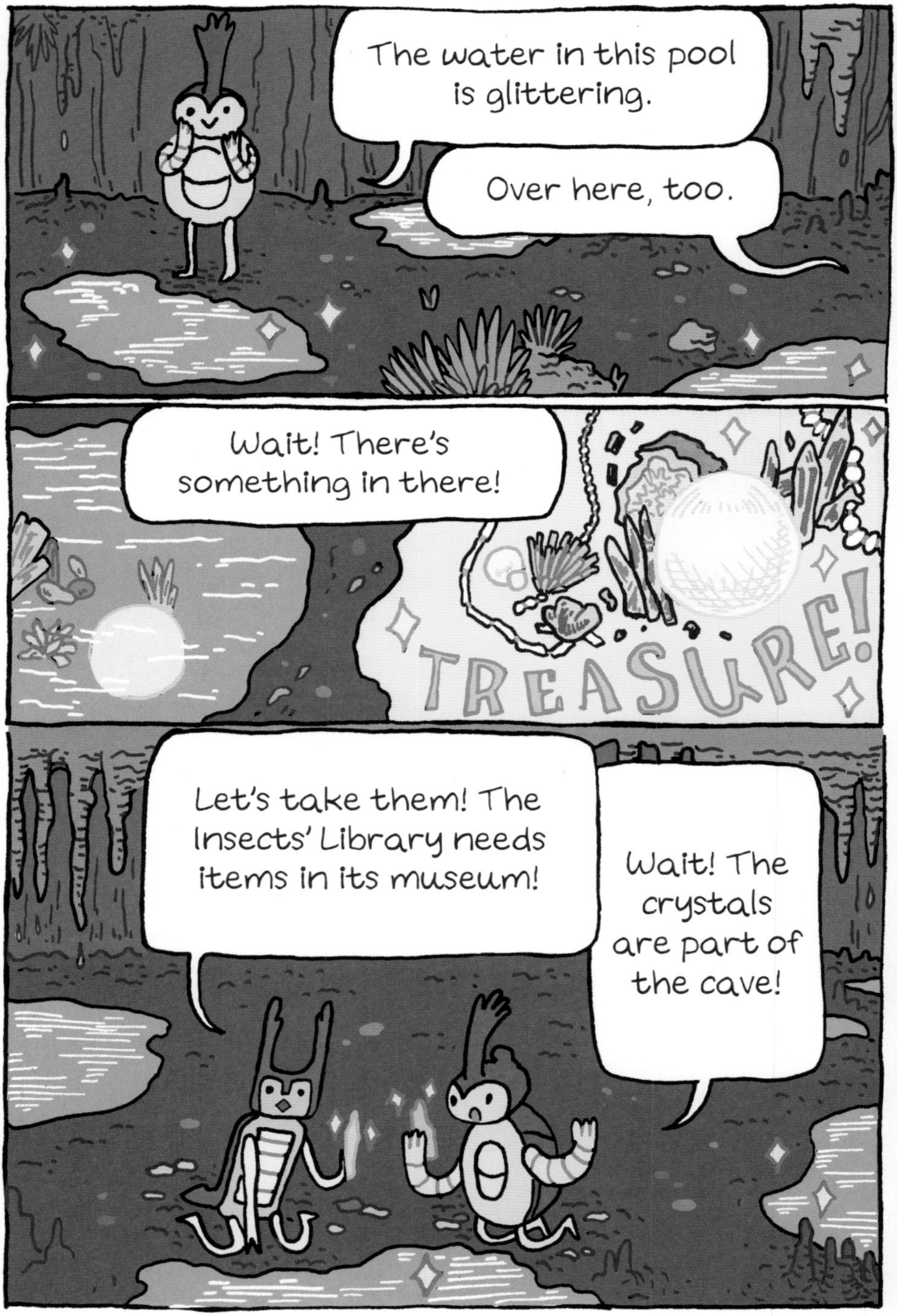

The water in this pool is glittering.
Over here, too.
Wait! There's something in there!
TREASURE!
Let's take them! The Insects' Library needs items in its museum!
Wait! The crystals are part of the cave!

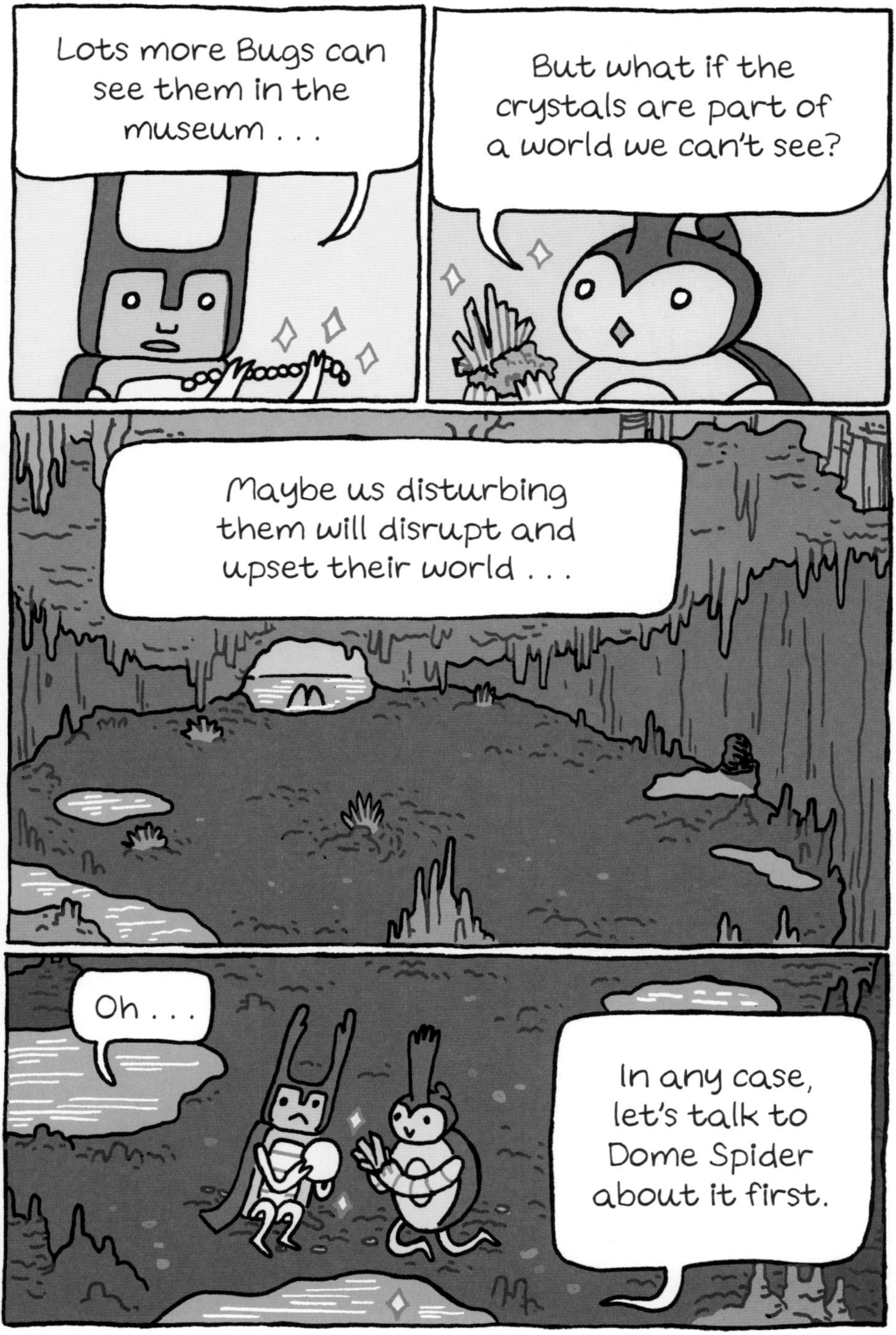
Lots more Bugs can see them in the museum . . .
But what if the crystals are part of a world we can't see?
Maybe us disturbing them will disrupt and upset their world . . .
Oh . . .
In any case, let's talk to Dome Spider about it first.

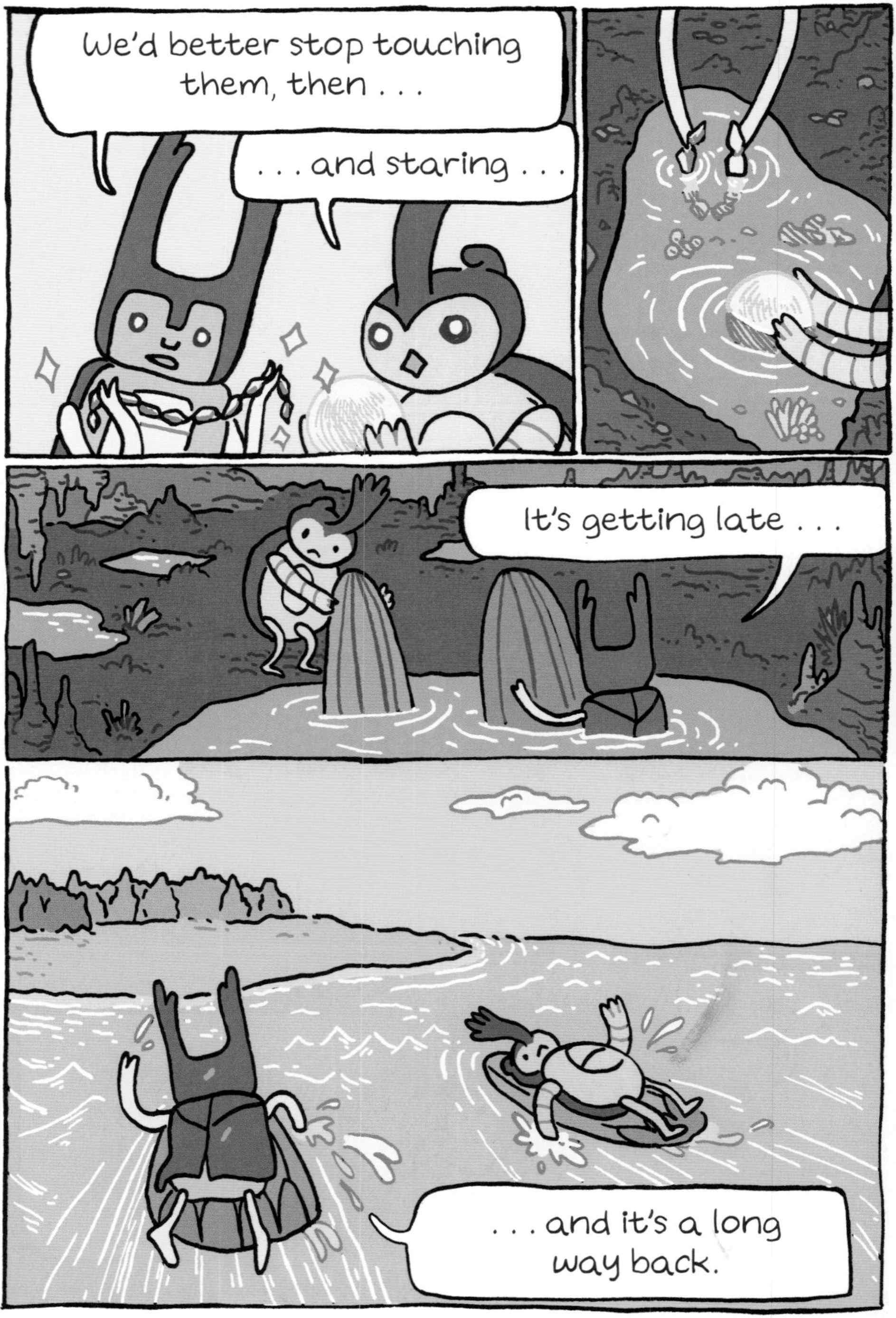
We'd better stop touching them, then . . .
. . . and staring . . .
It's getting late . . .
. . . and it's a long way back.

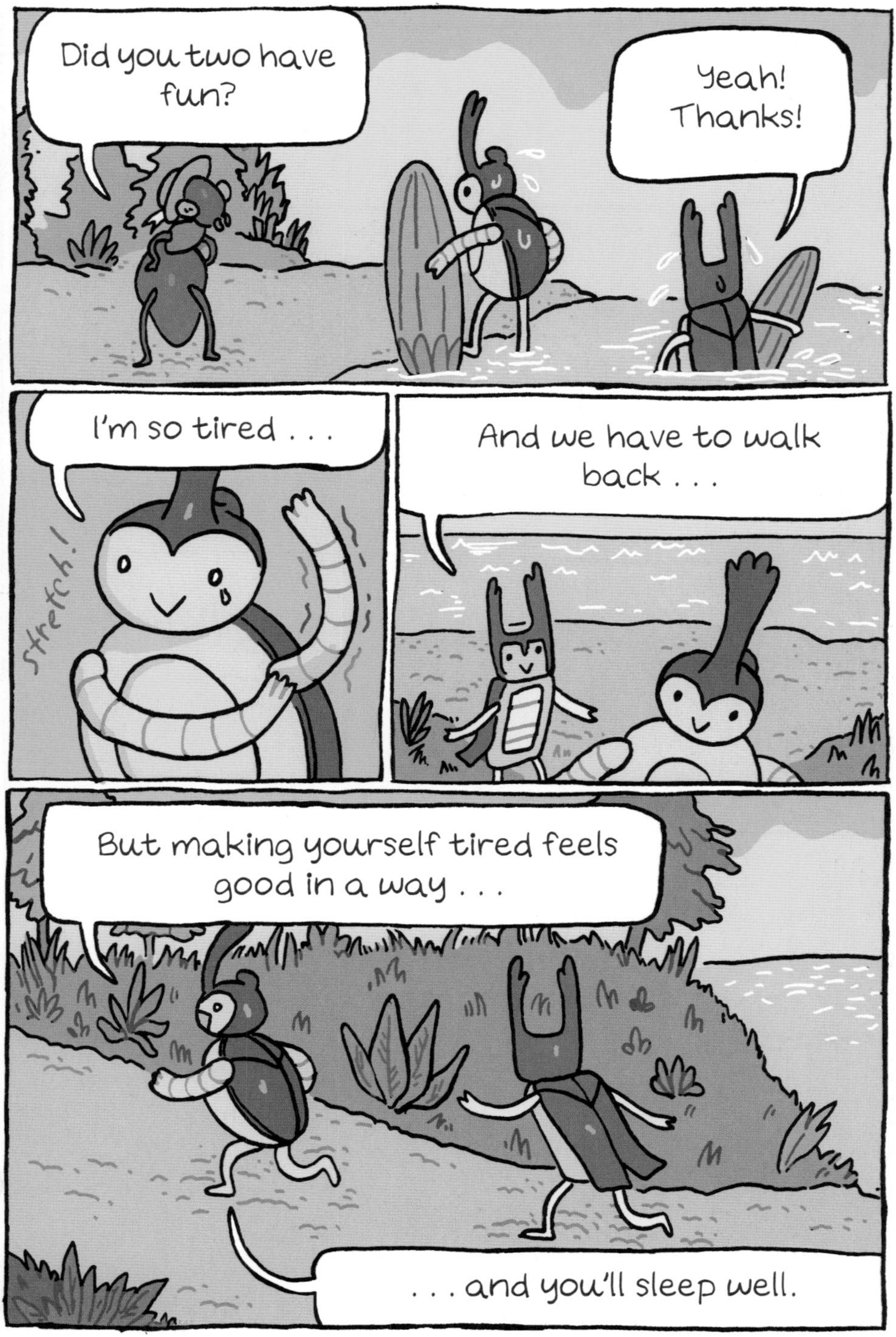

Did you two have fun?
Yeah! Thanks!
I'm so tired . . .
stretch!
And we have to walk back . . .
But making yourself tired feels good in a way . . .
. . . and you'll sleep well.

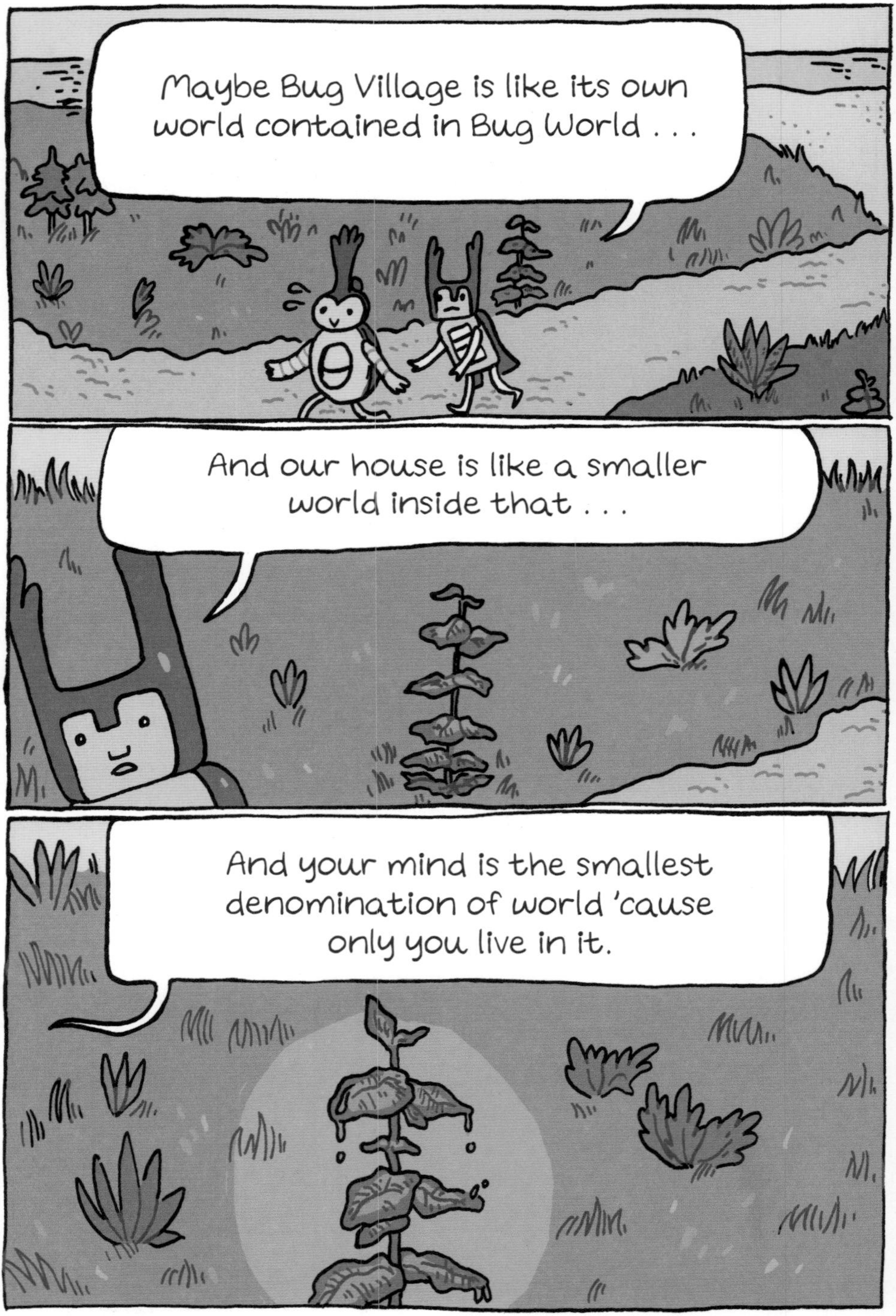
Maybe Bug Village is like its own world contained in Bug World . . .
And our house is like a smaller world inside that . . .
And your mind is the smallest denomination of world 'cause only you live in it.

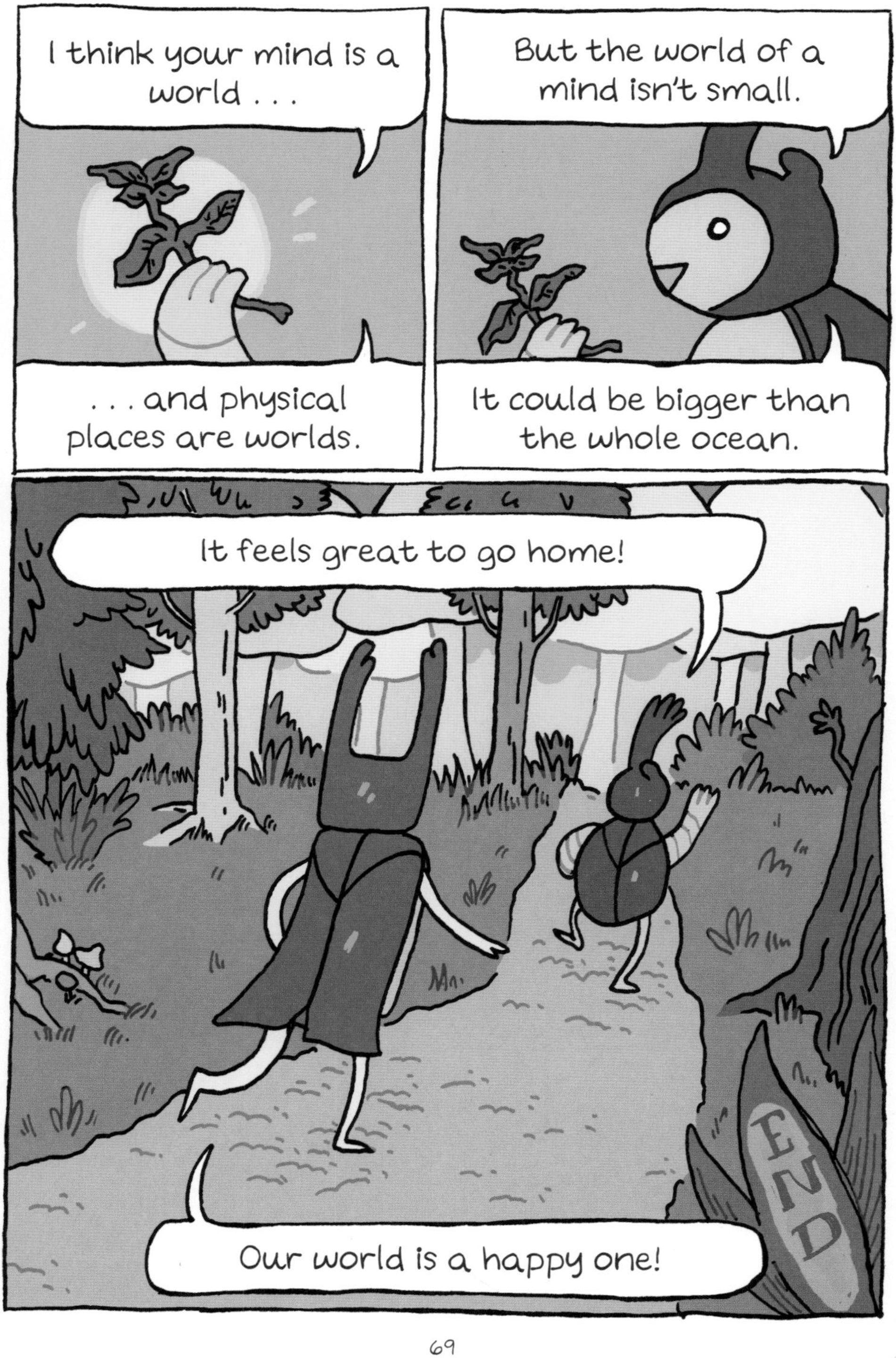
I think your mind is a world . . .
. . . and physical places are worlds.
But the world of a mind isn't small.
It could be bigger than the whole ocean.
It feels great to go home!
Our world is a happy one!
END

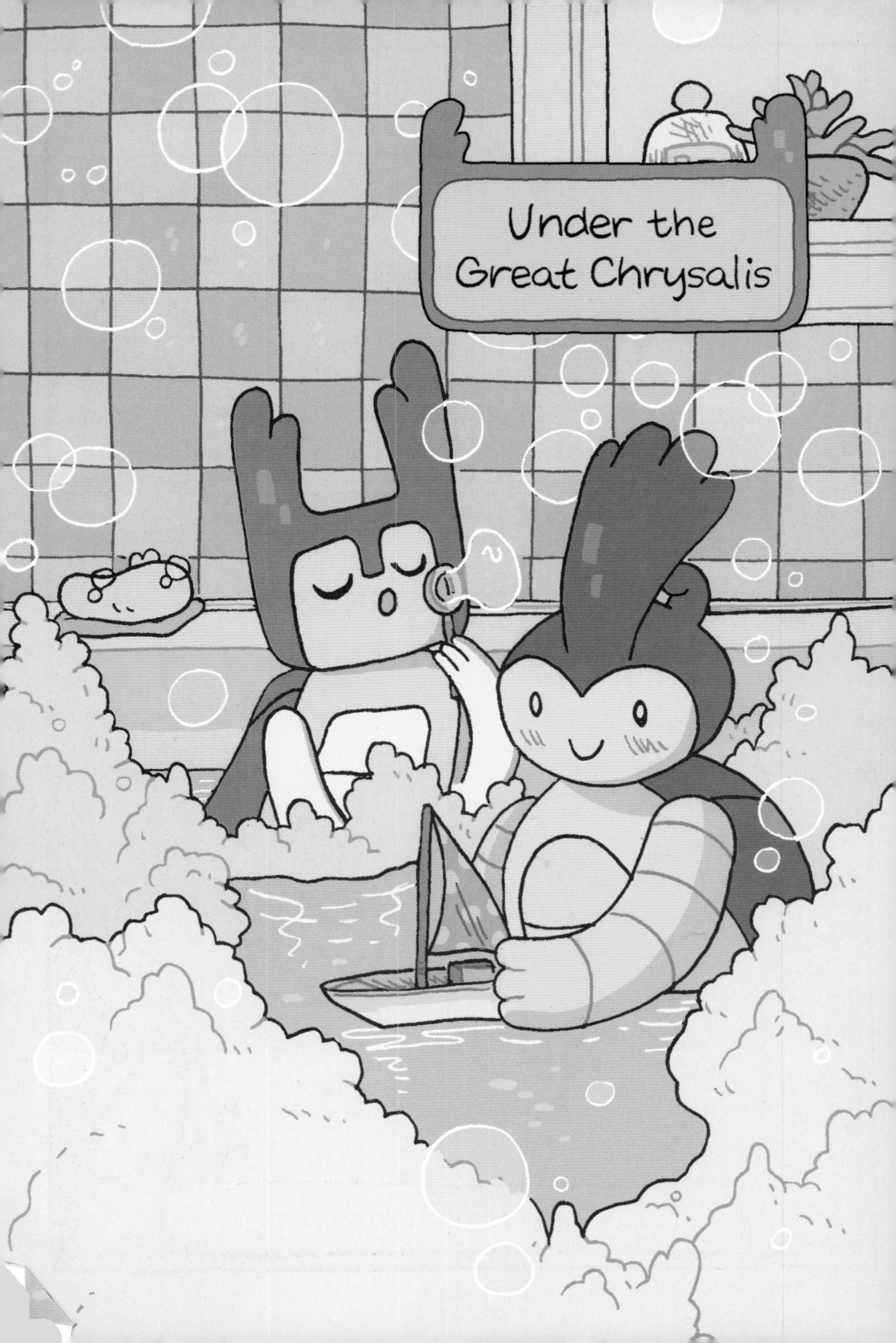
Under the
Great Chrysalis

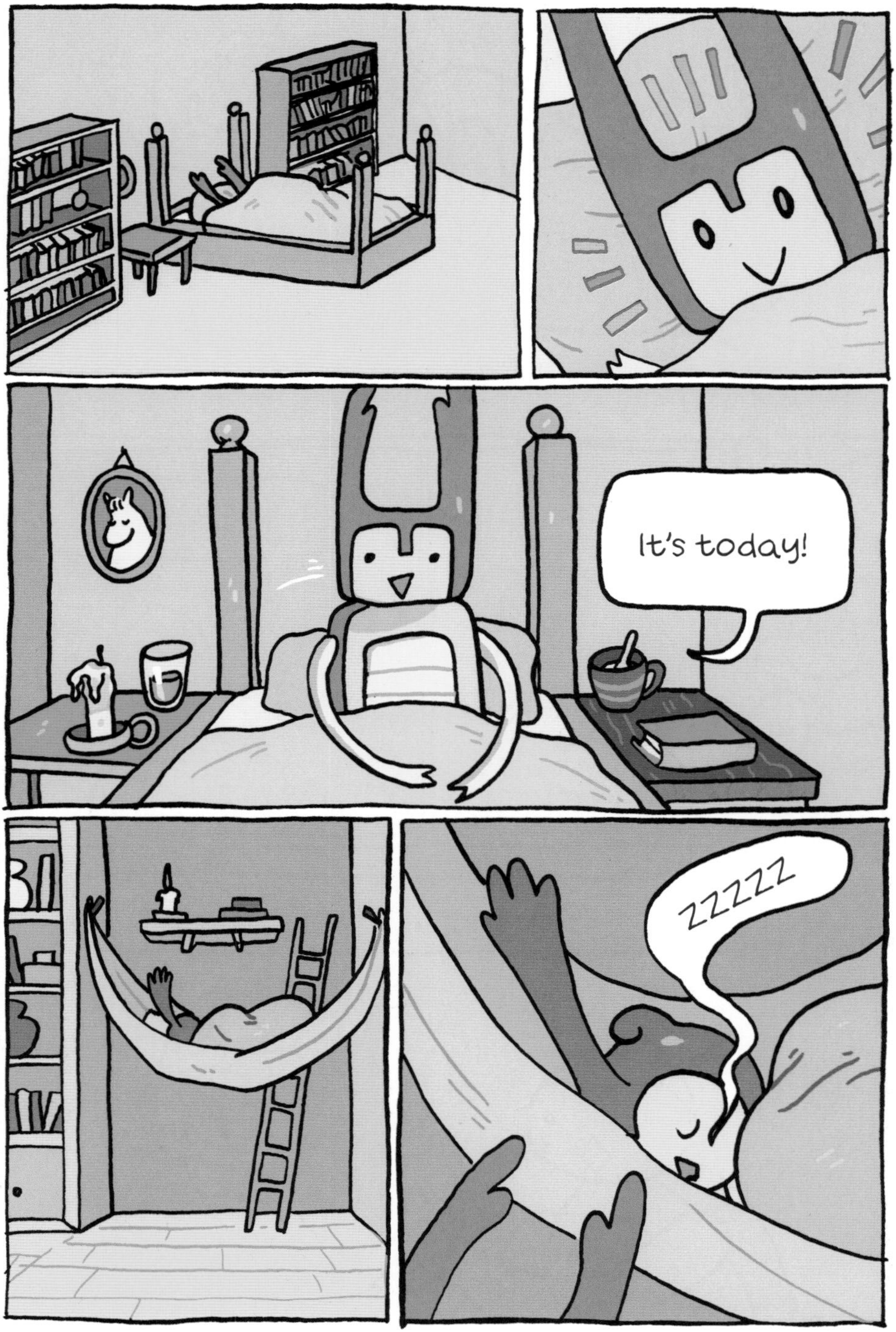
It's today!
ZZZZZ

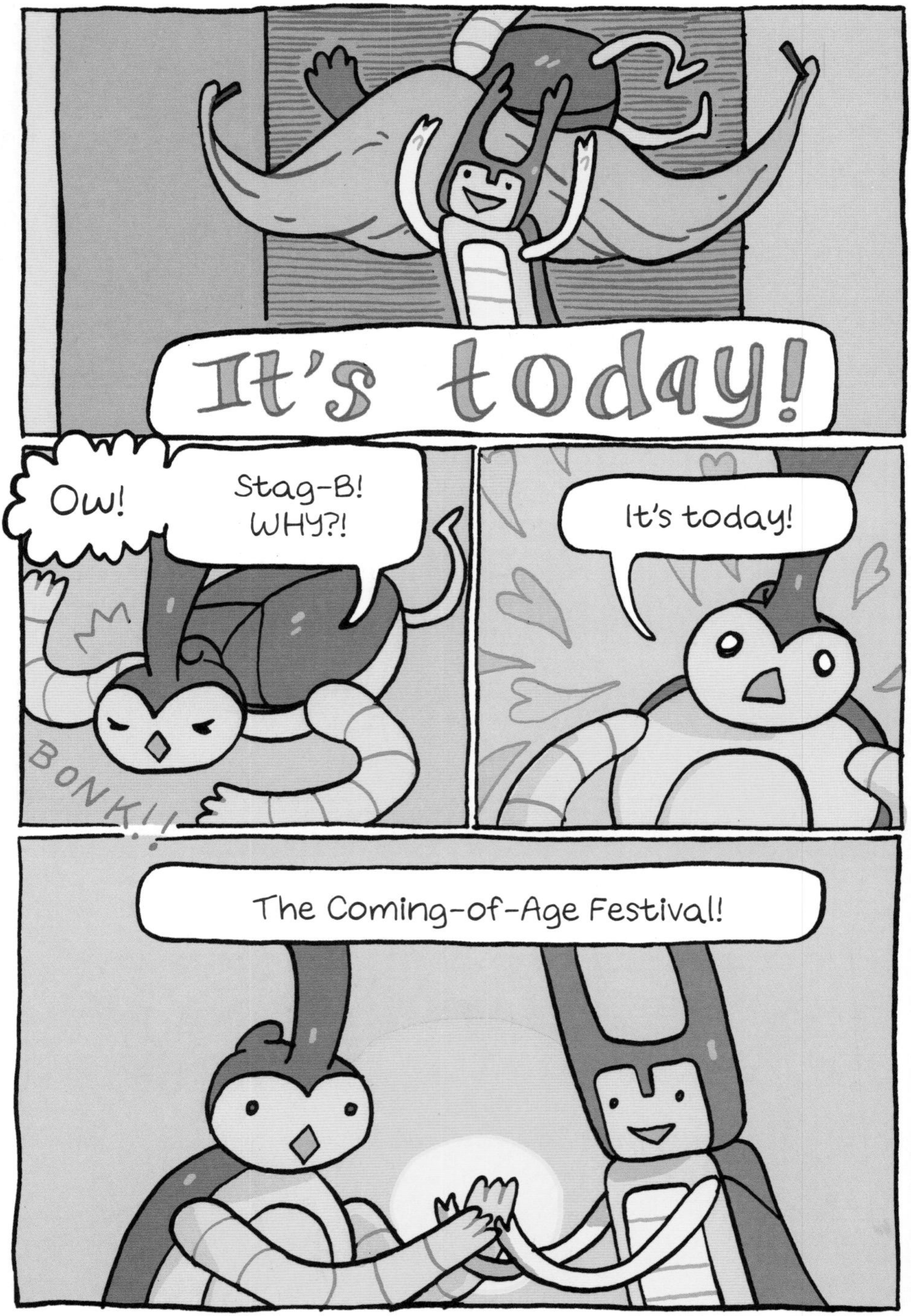
It's today!
Ow!
Stag-B! WHY?!
BONK!!
It's today!
The Coming-of-Age Festival!

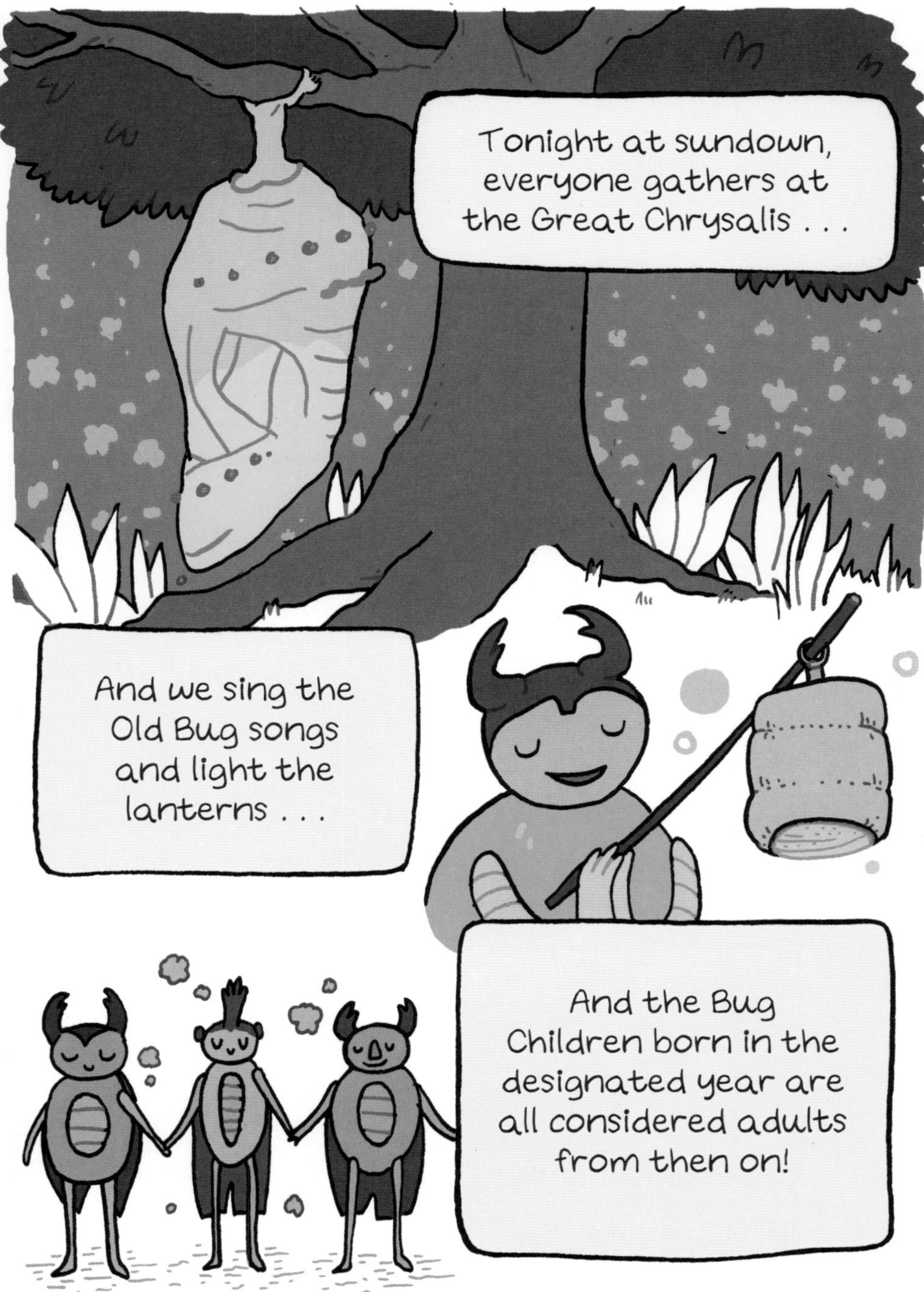
Tonight at sundown, everyone gathers at the Great Chrysalis . . .
And we sing the Old Bug songs and light the lanterns . . .
And the Bug Children born in the designated year are all considered adults from then on!

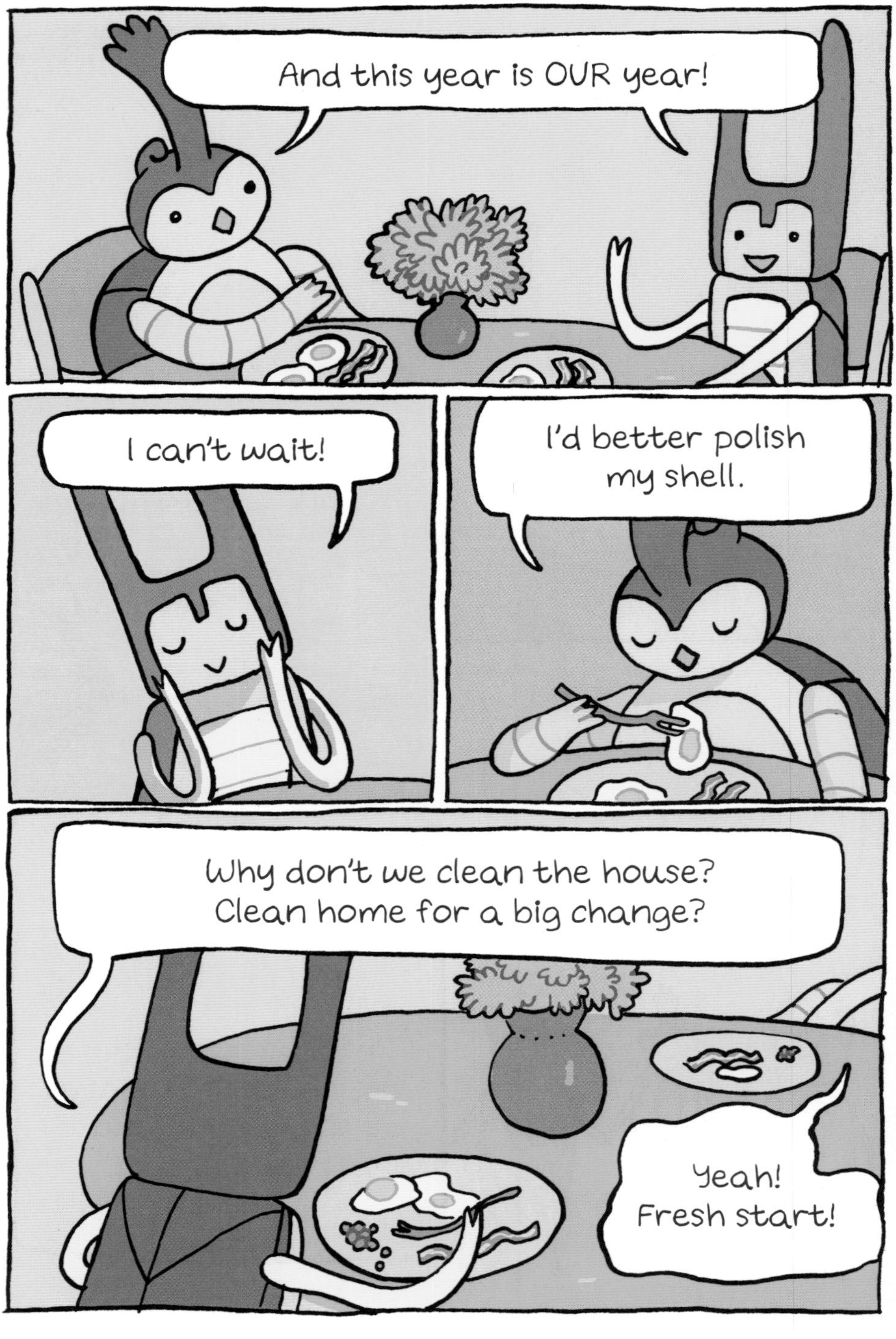
And this year is OUR year!
I can't wait!
I'd better polish my shell.
Why don't we clean the house? Clean home for a big change?
Yeah! Fresh start!

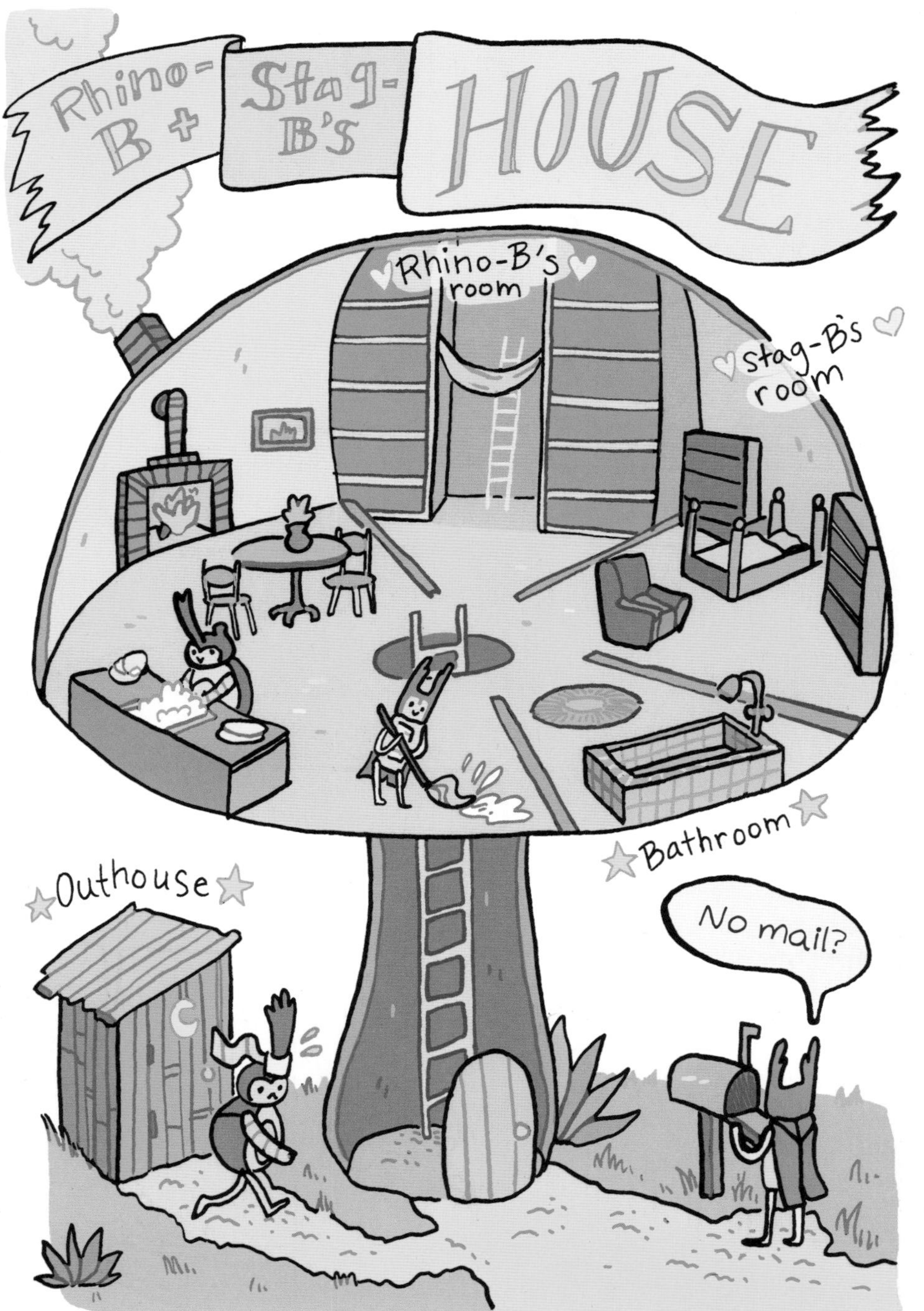
Rhino-B + Stag-B's HOUSE
Rhino-B's room
Stag-B's room
Bathroom
Outhouse
No mail?

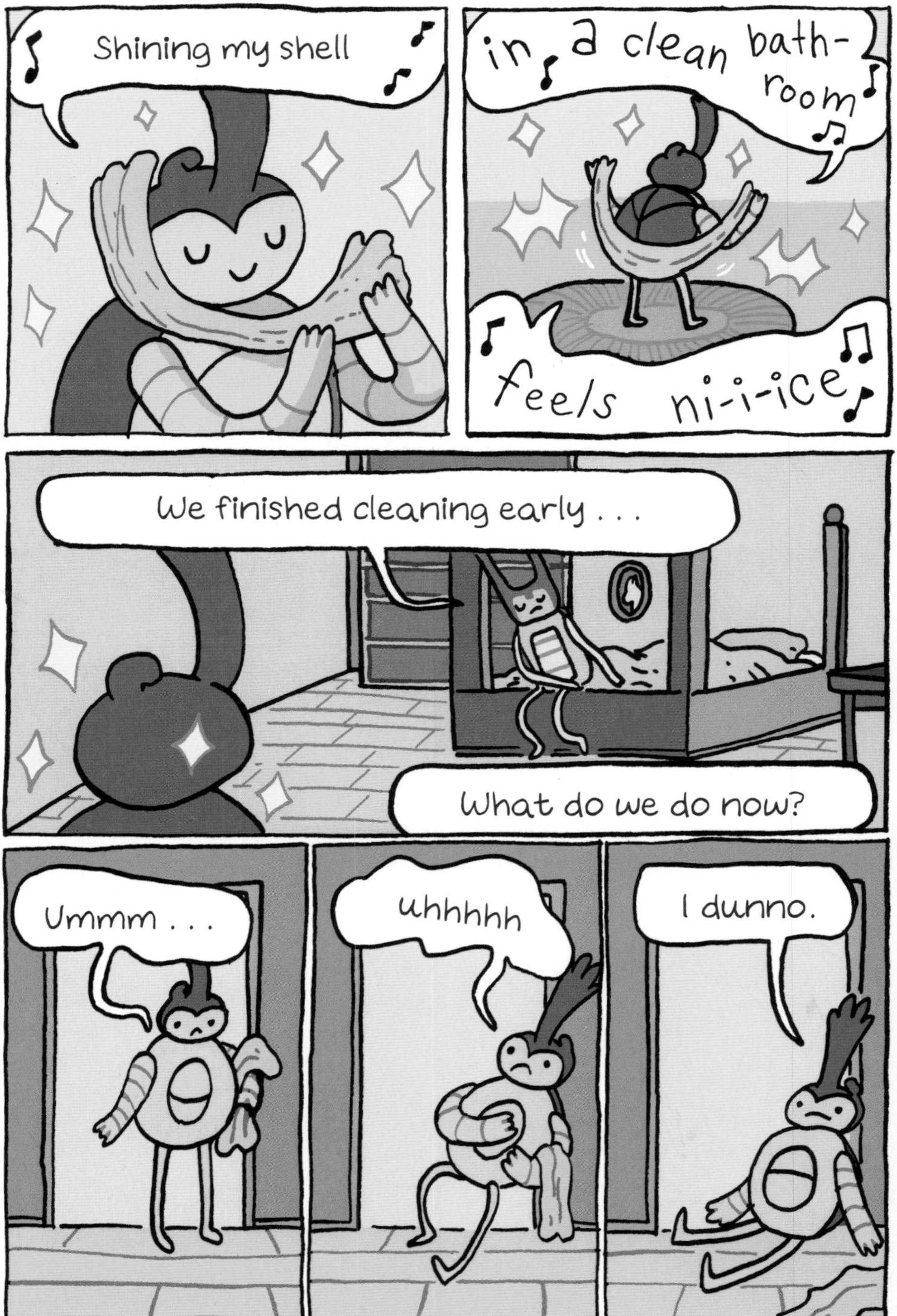
Shining my shell
in a clean bath-room
feels ni-i-ice
We finished cleaning early . . .
What do we do now?
Ummm . . .
uhhhhh
I dunno.

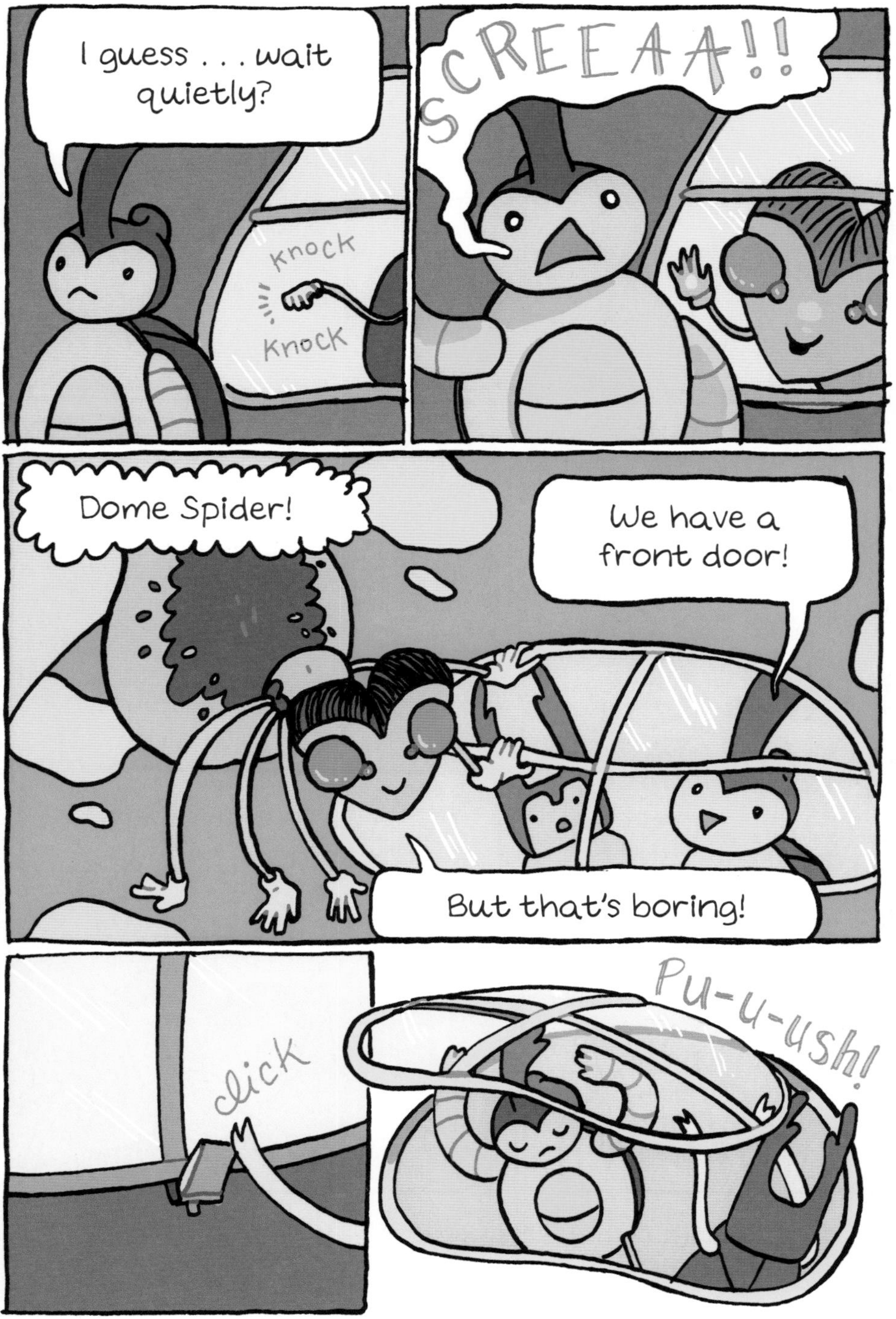
I guess . . . wait quietly?
KNOCK
KNOCK
SCREEAA!!
Dome Spider!
We have a front door!
But that's boring!
click
Pu-u-ush!

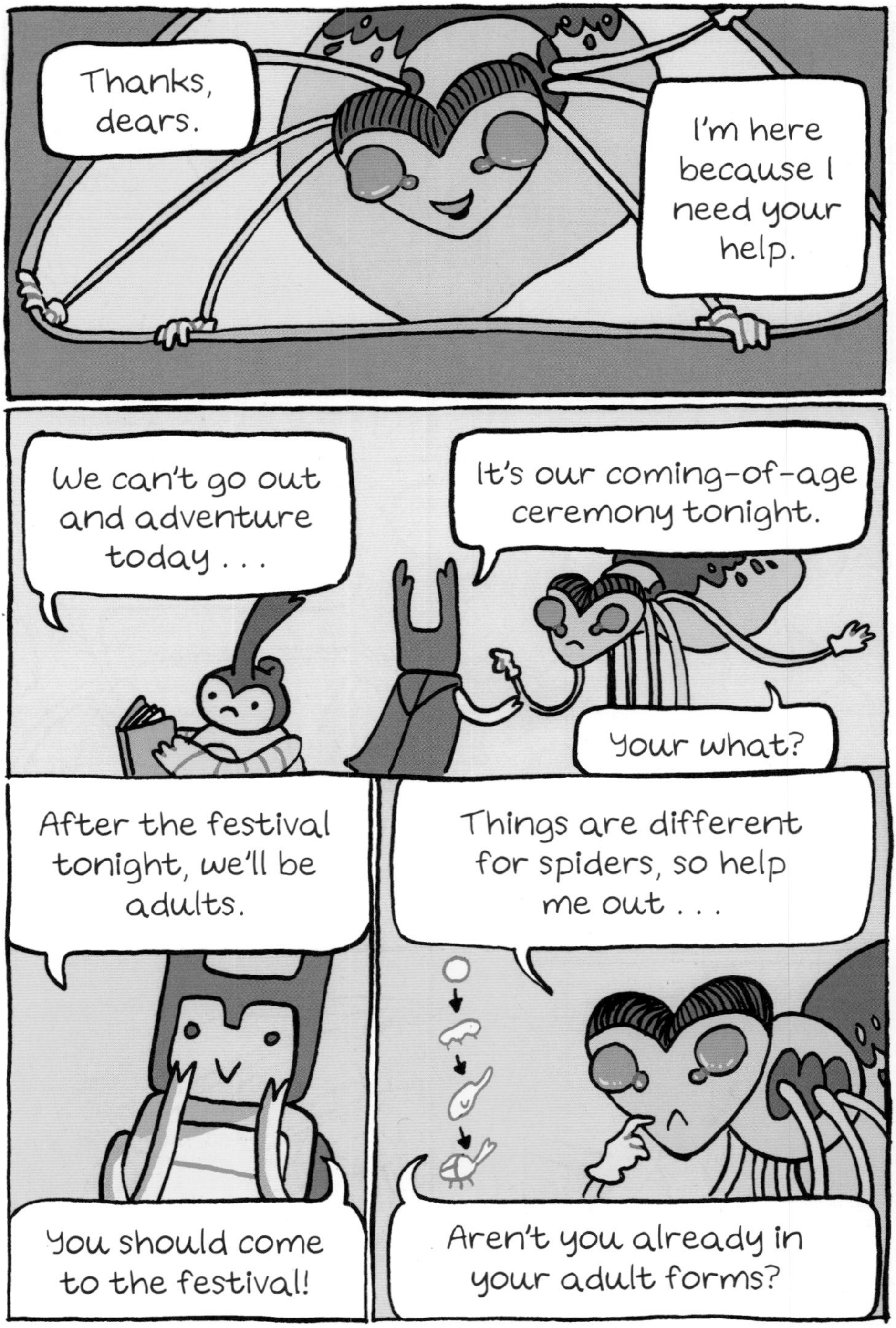
Thanks, dears.
I'm here because I need your help.
We can't go out and adventure today . . .
It's our coming-of-age ceremony tonight.
Your what?
After the festival tonight, we'll be adults.
You should come to the festival!
Things are different for spiders, so help me out . . .
Aren't you already in your adult forms?

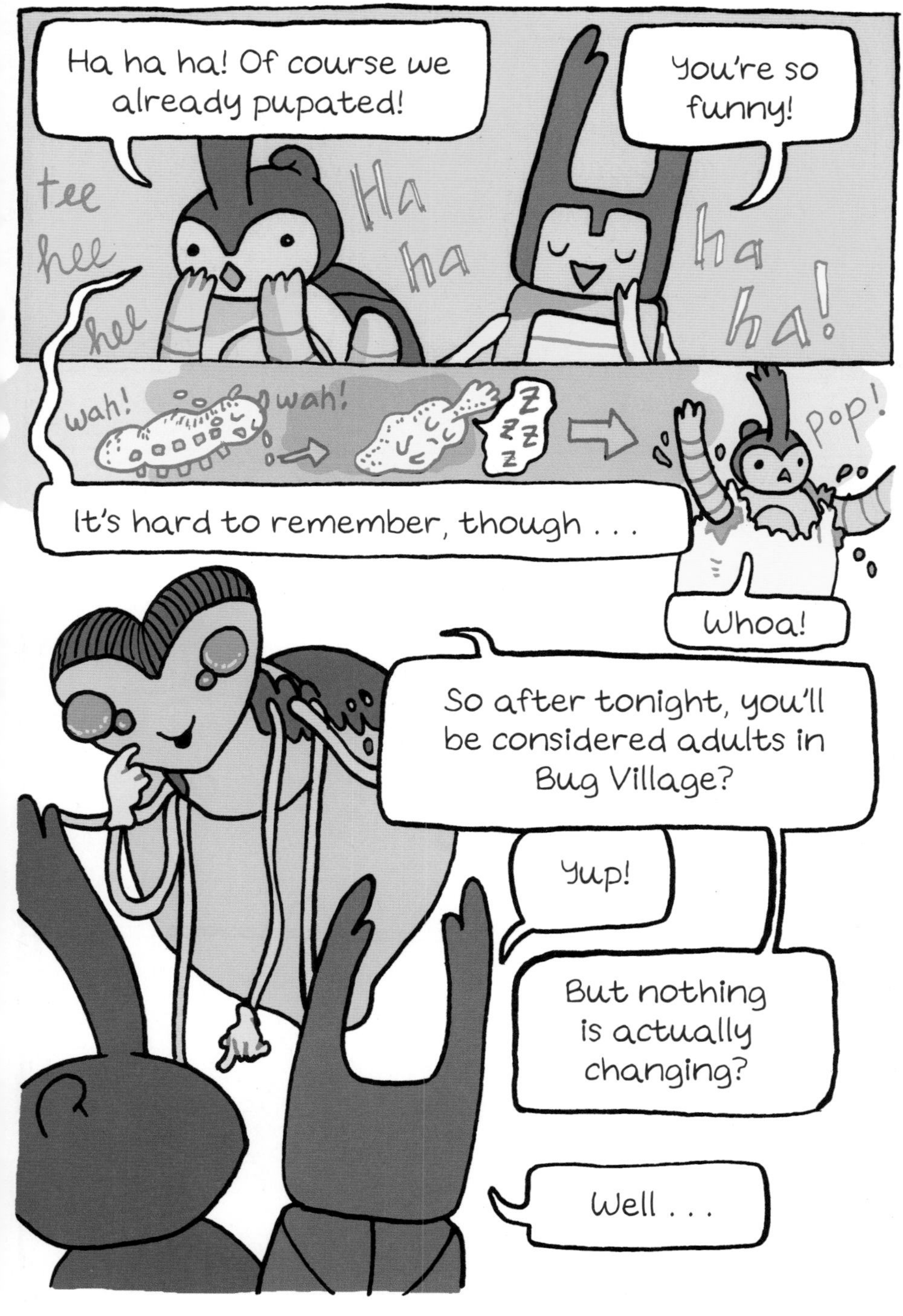

Ha ha ha! Of course we already pupated!
You're so funny!
tee hee hee
Ha ha
ha ha ha!
wah! wah!
Z Z Z Z
pop!
It's hard to remember, though . . .
Whoa!
So after tonight, you'll be considered adults in Bug Village?
Yup!
But nothing is actually changing?
Well . . .

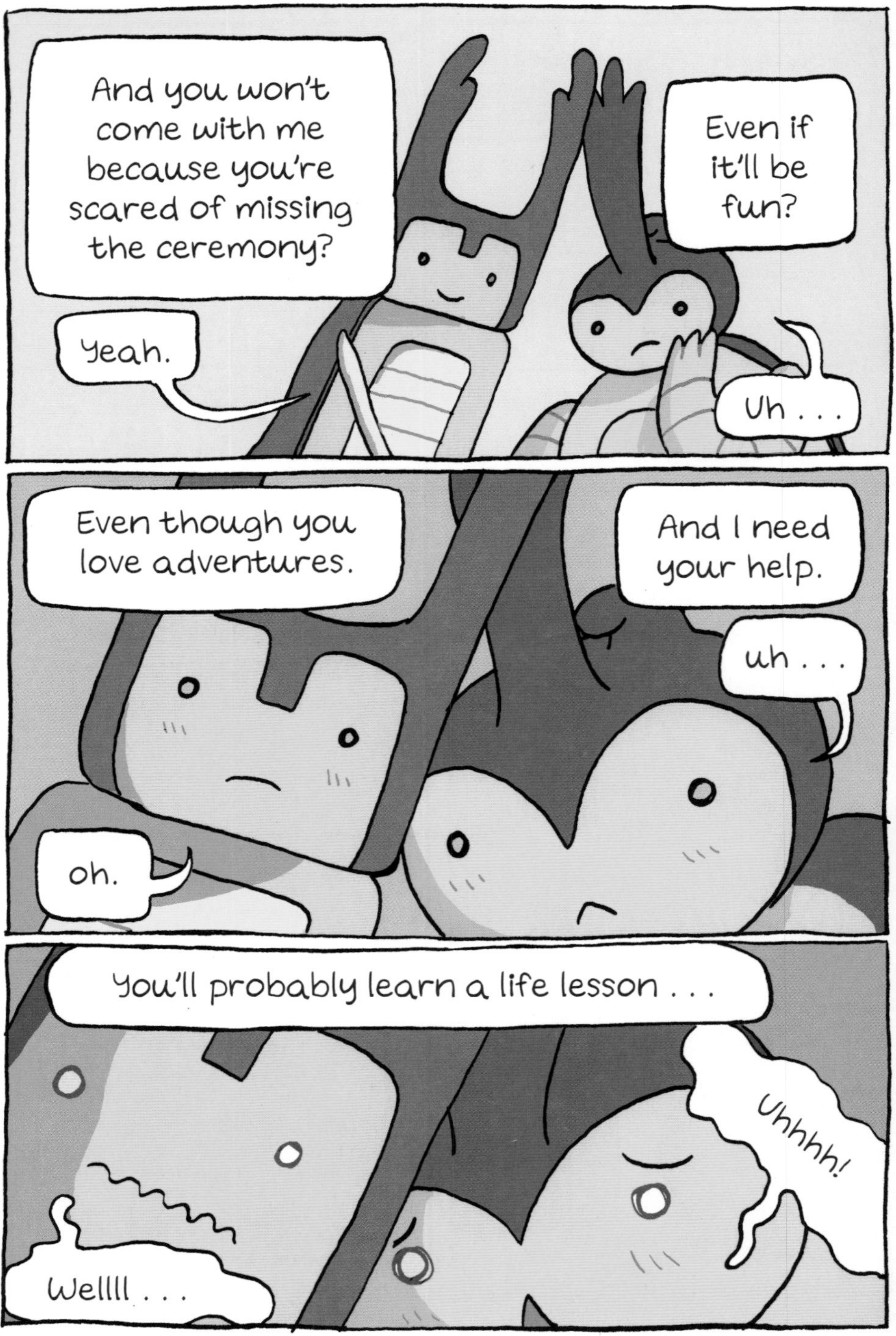
And you won't come with me because you're scared of missing the ceremony?
Yeah.
Even if it'll be fun?
Uh . . .
Even though you love adventures.
And I need your help.
uh . . .
oh.
You'll probably learn a life lesson . . .
Uhhhh!
Wellll . . .

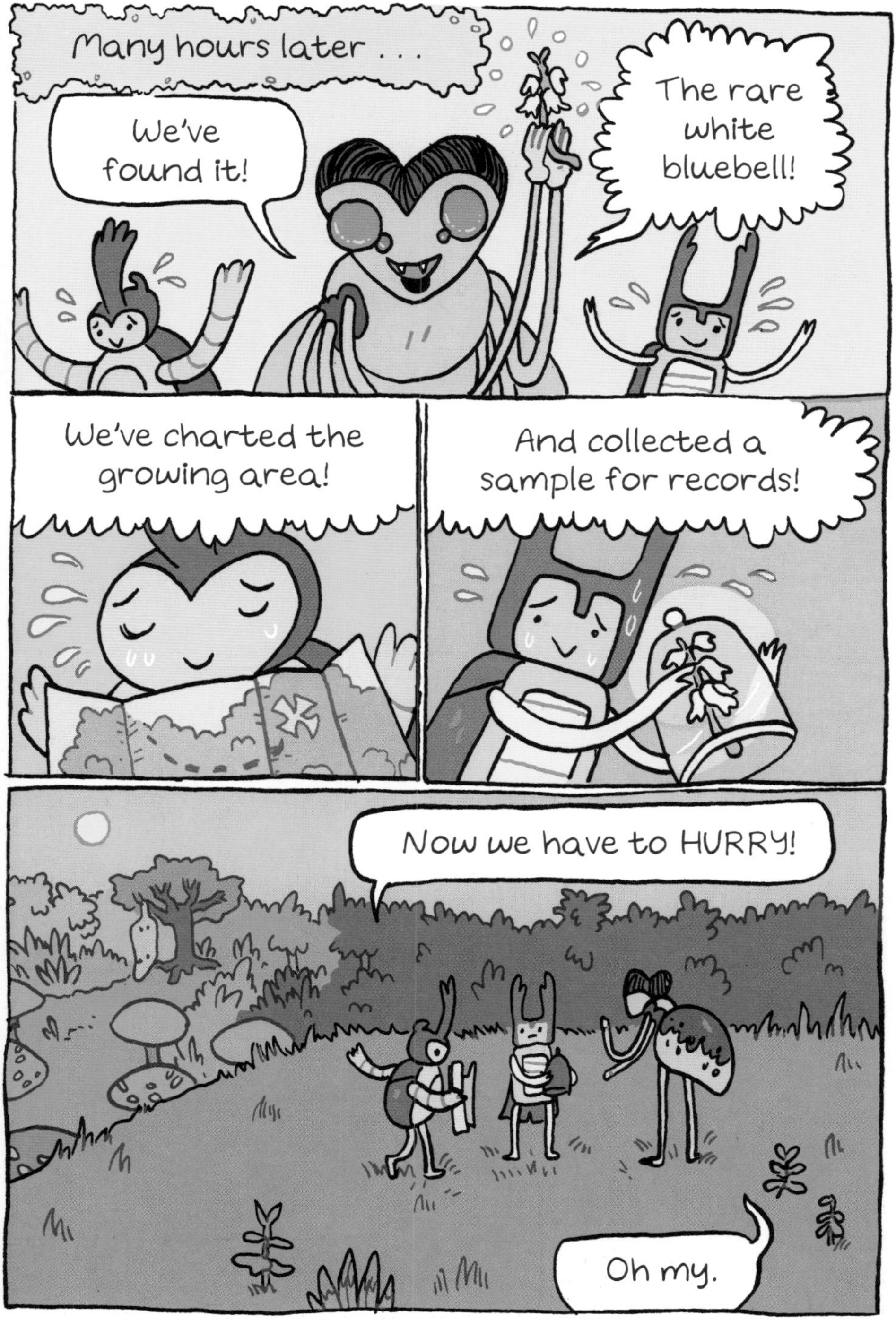
Many hours later . . .
We've found it!
The rare white bluebell!
We've charted the growing area!
And collected a sample for records!
Now we have to HURRY!
Oh my.

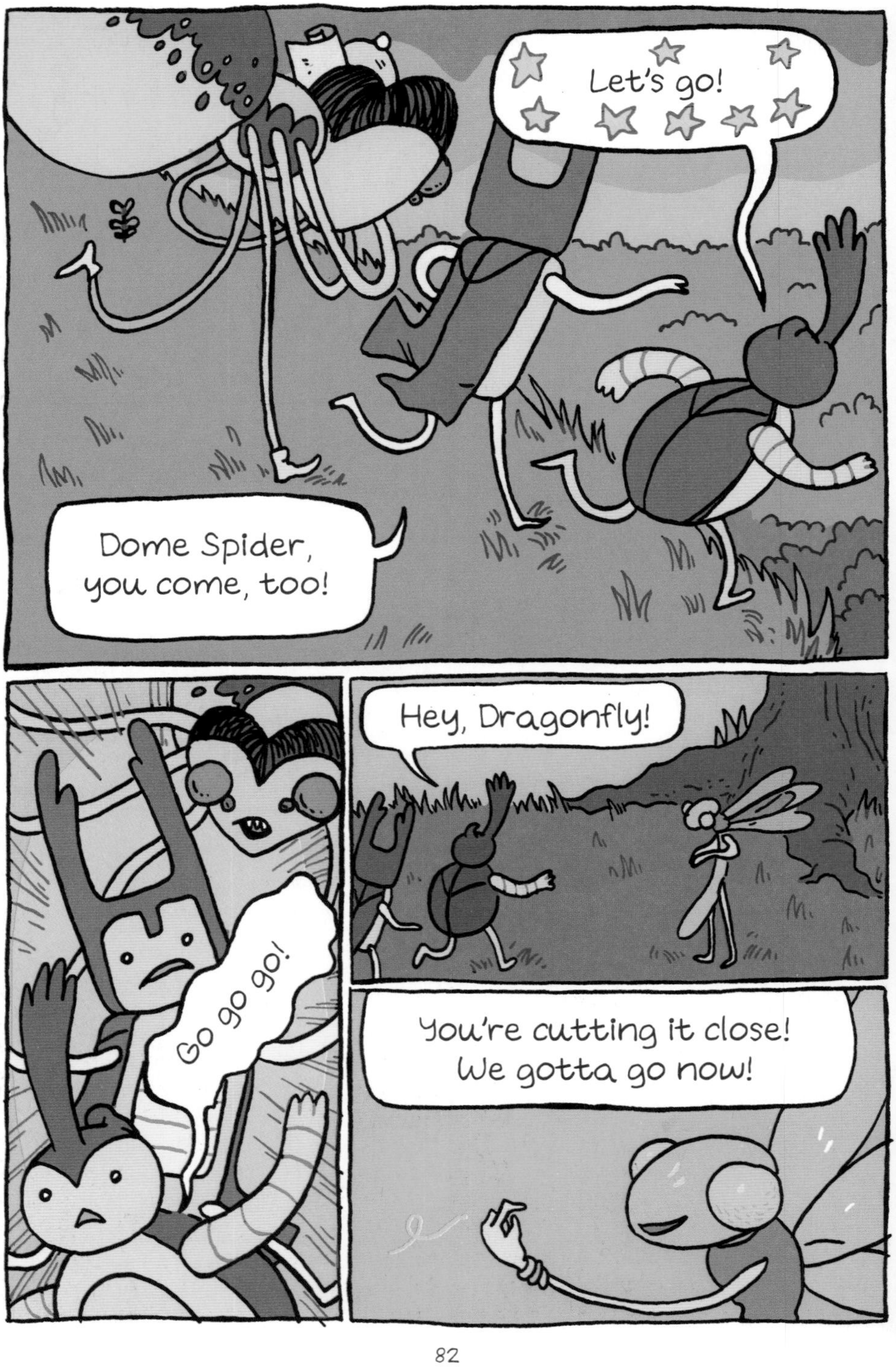
Let's go!
Dome Spider, you come, too!
Go go go!
Hey, Dragonfly!
You're cutting it close! We gotta go now!

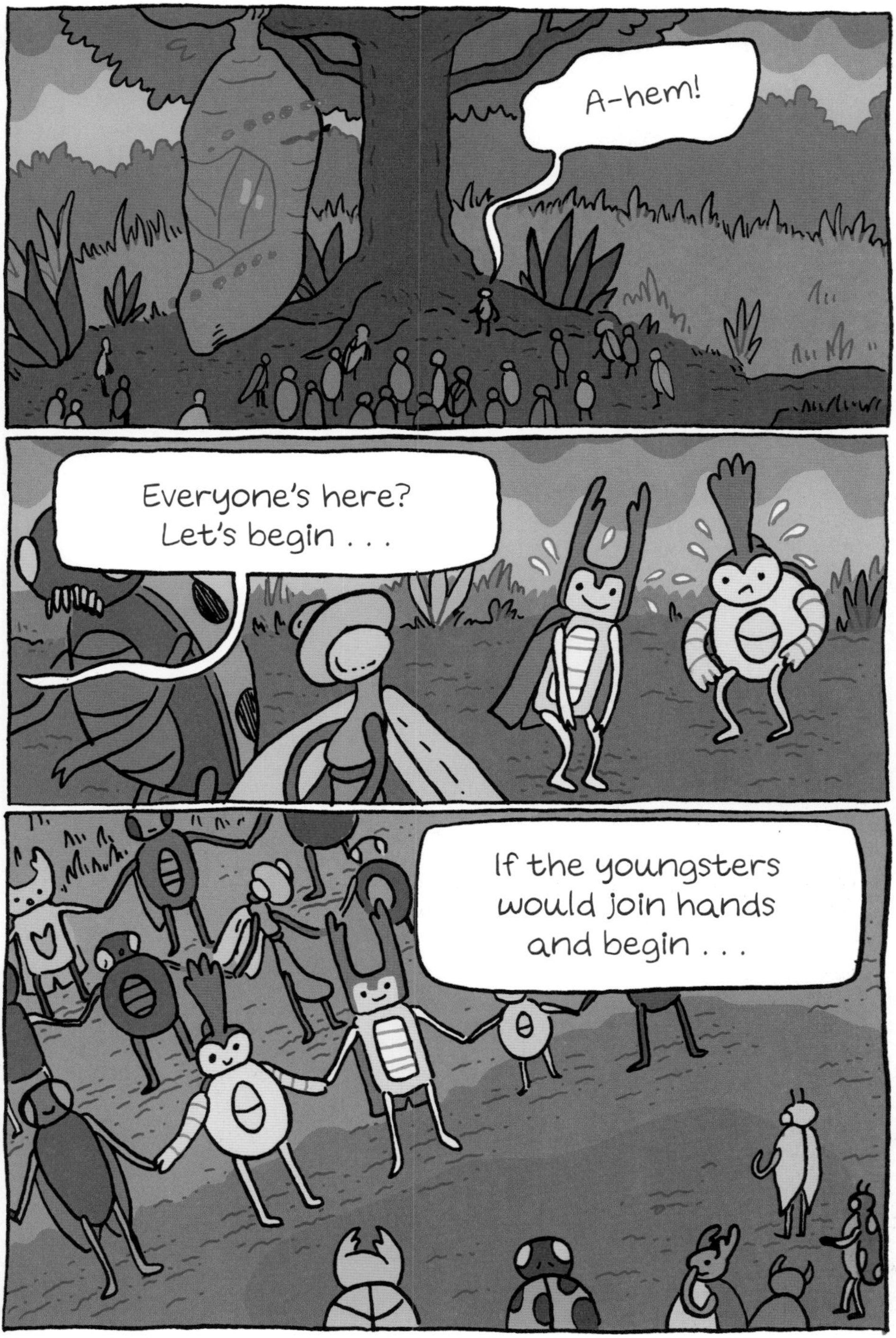
A-hem!
Everyone's here? Let's begin . . .
If the youngsters would join hands and begin . . .

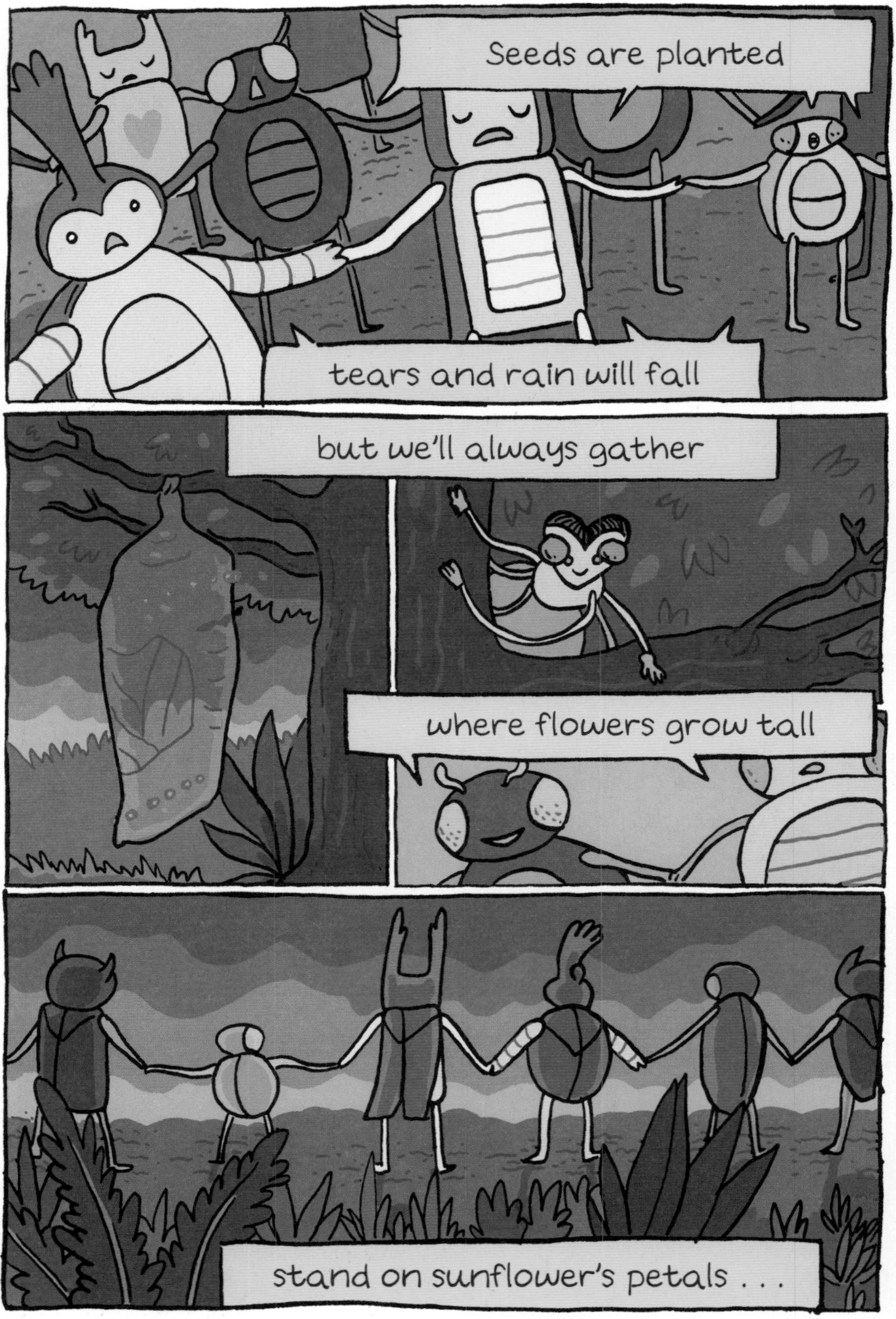
Seeds are planted
tears and rain will fall
but we'll always gather
where flowers grow tall
stand on sunflower's petals . . .

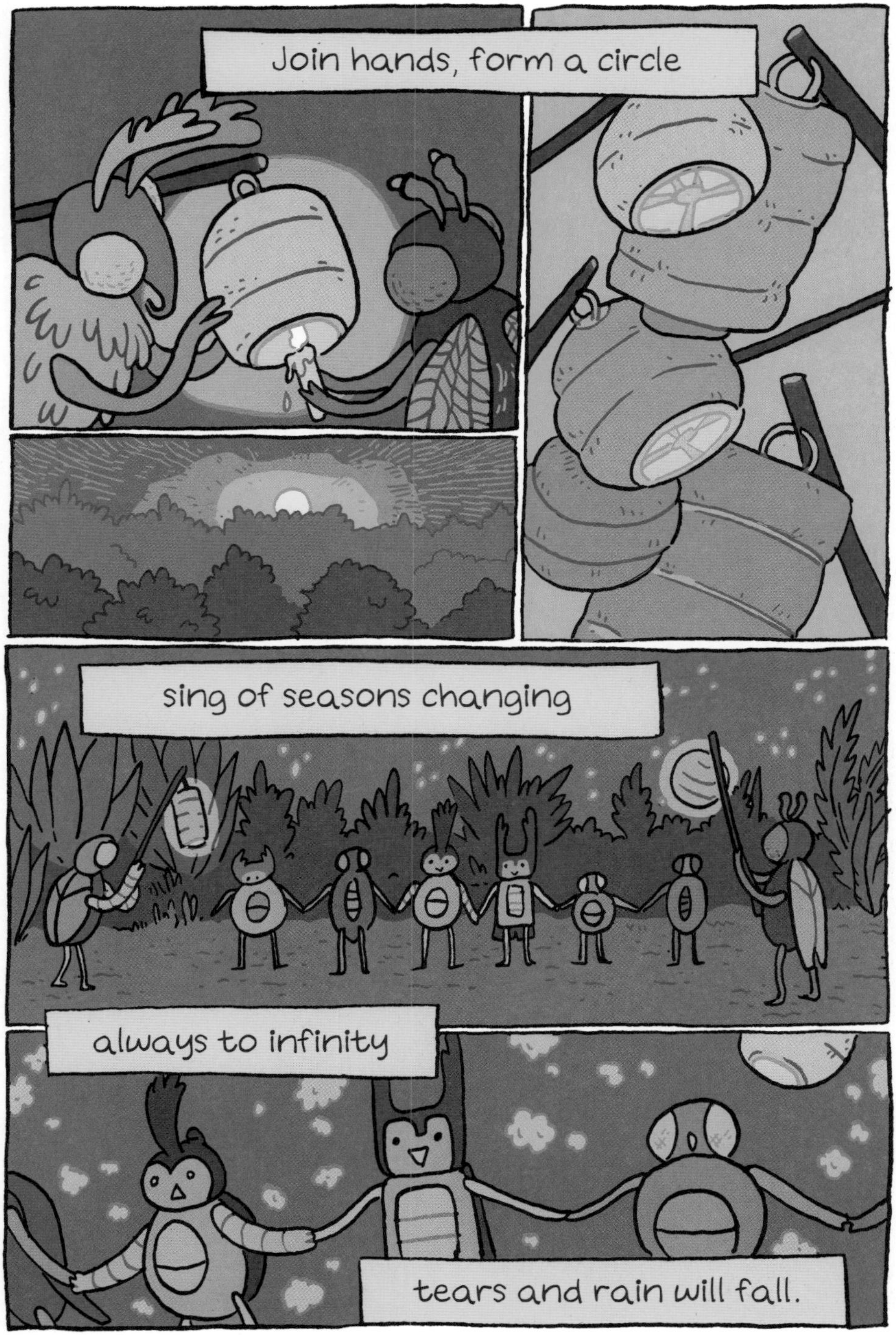
Join hands, form a circle
sing of seasons changing
always to infinity
tears and rain will fall.

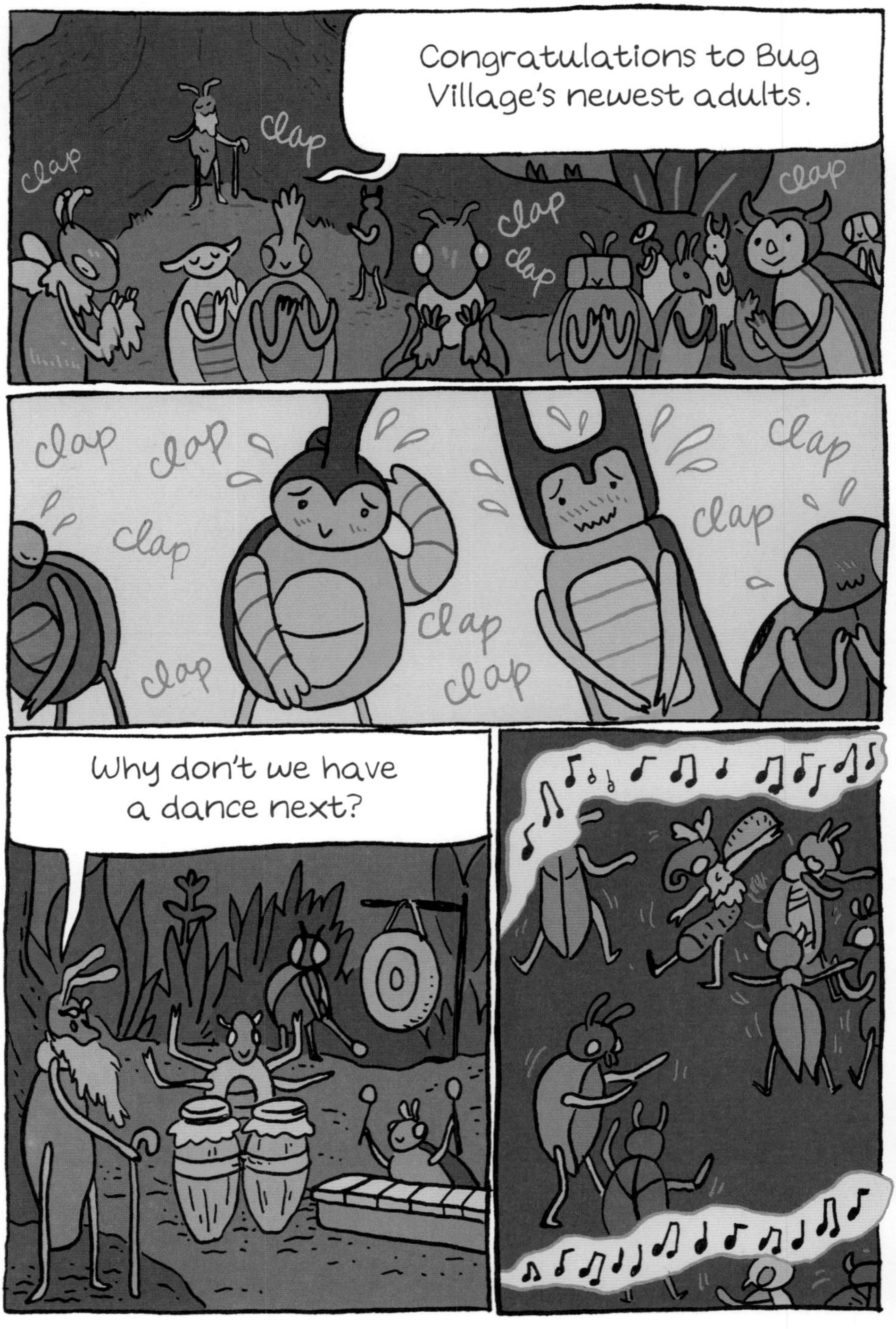
Congratulations to Bug Village's newest adults.
clap
clap
clap
clap
clap
clap
clap
clap
clap
clap
clap
clap
clap
Why don't we have a dance next?

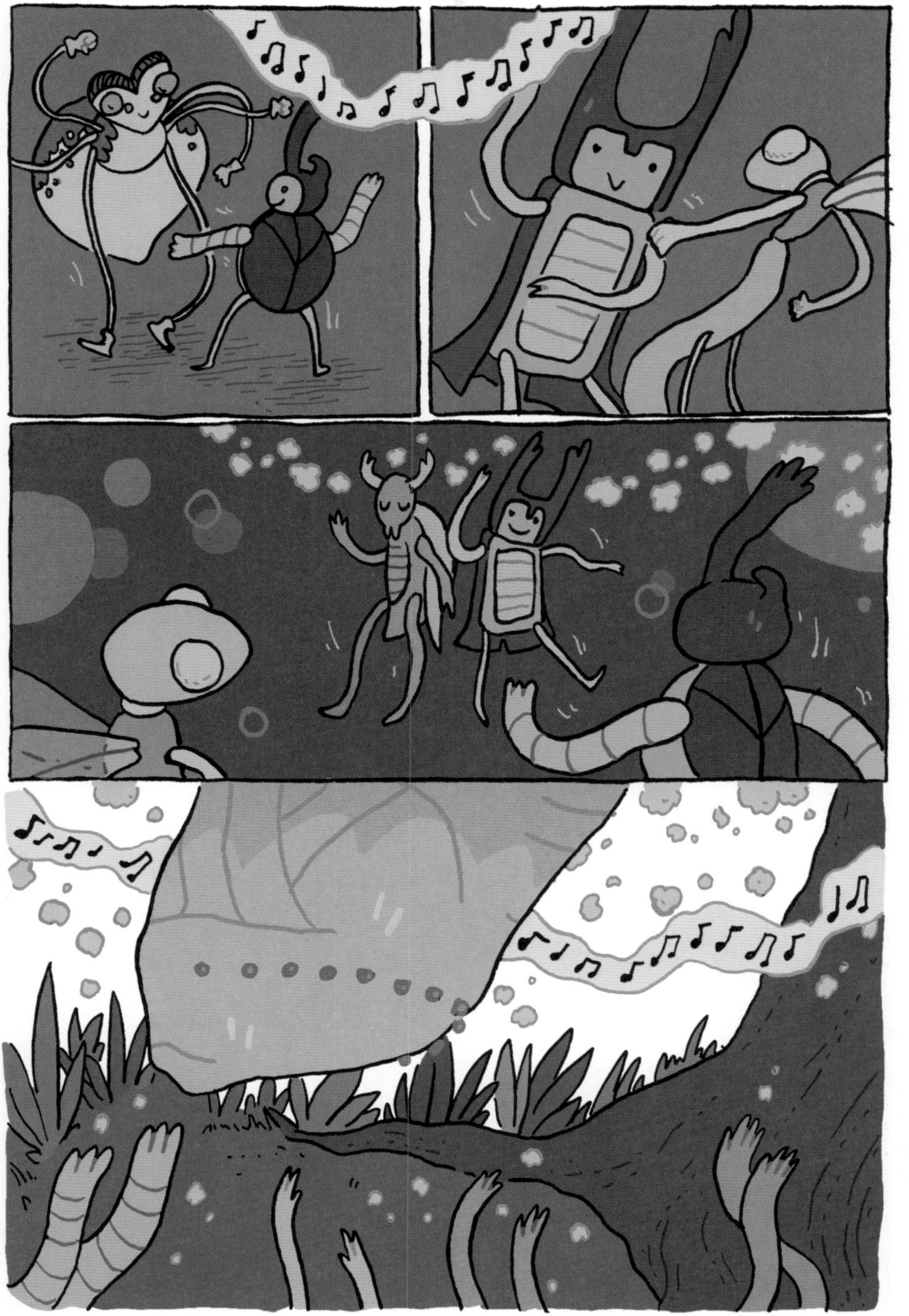

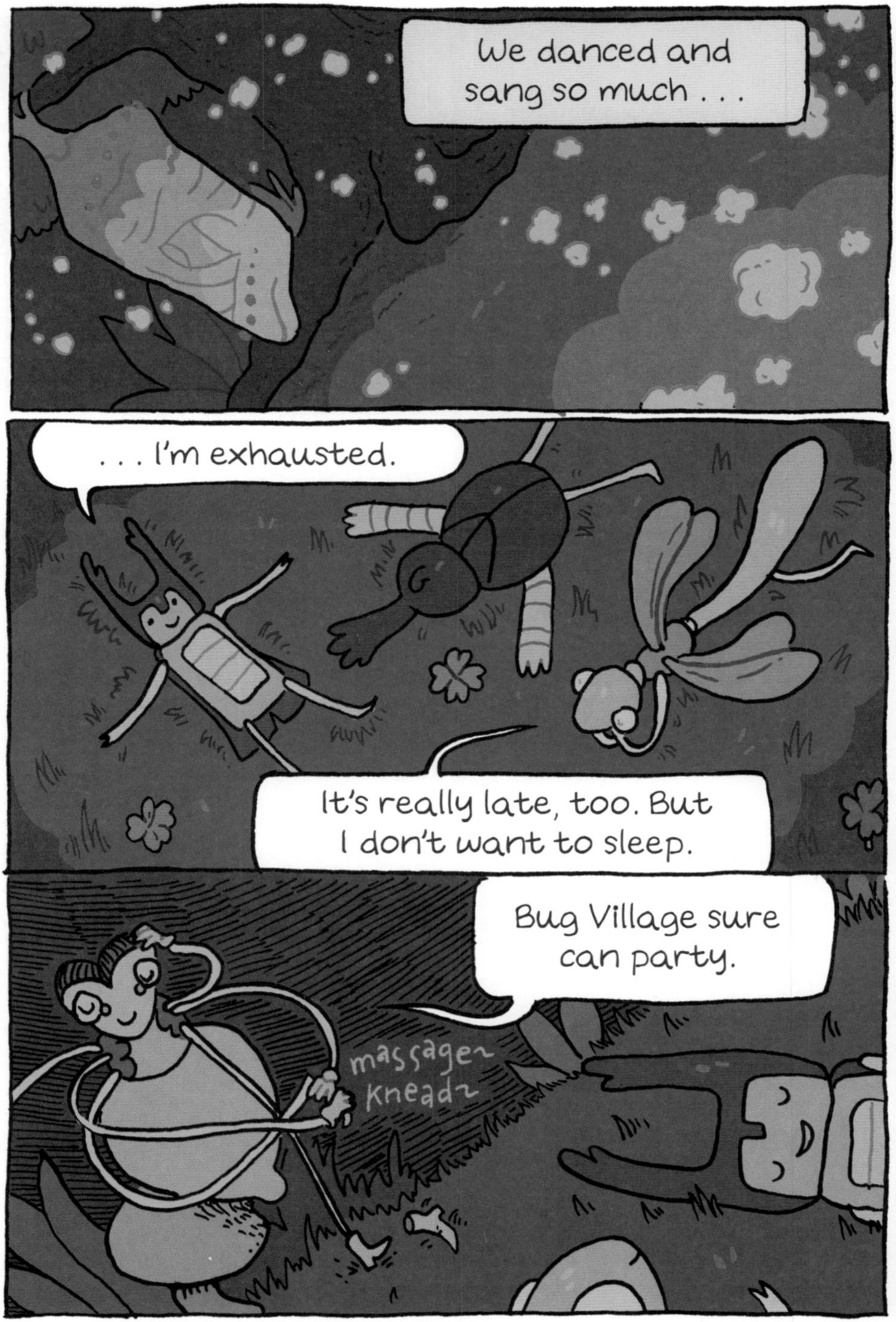
We danced and sang so much . . .
. . . I'm exhausted.
It's really late, too. But I don't want to sleep.
Bug Village sure can party.
massage~ knead~

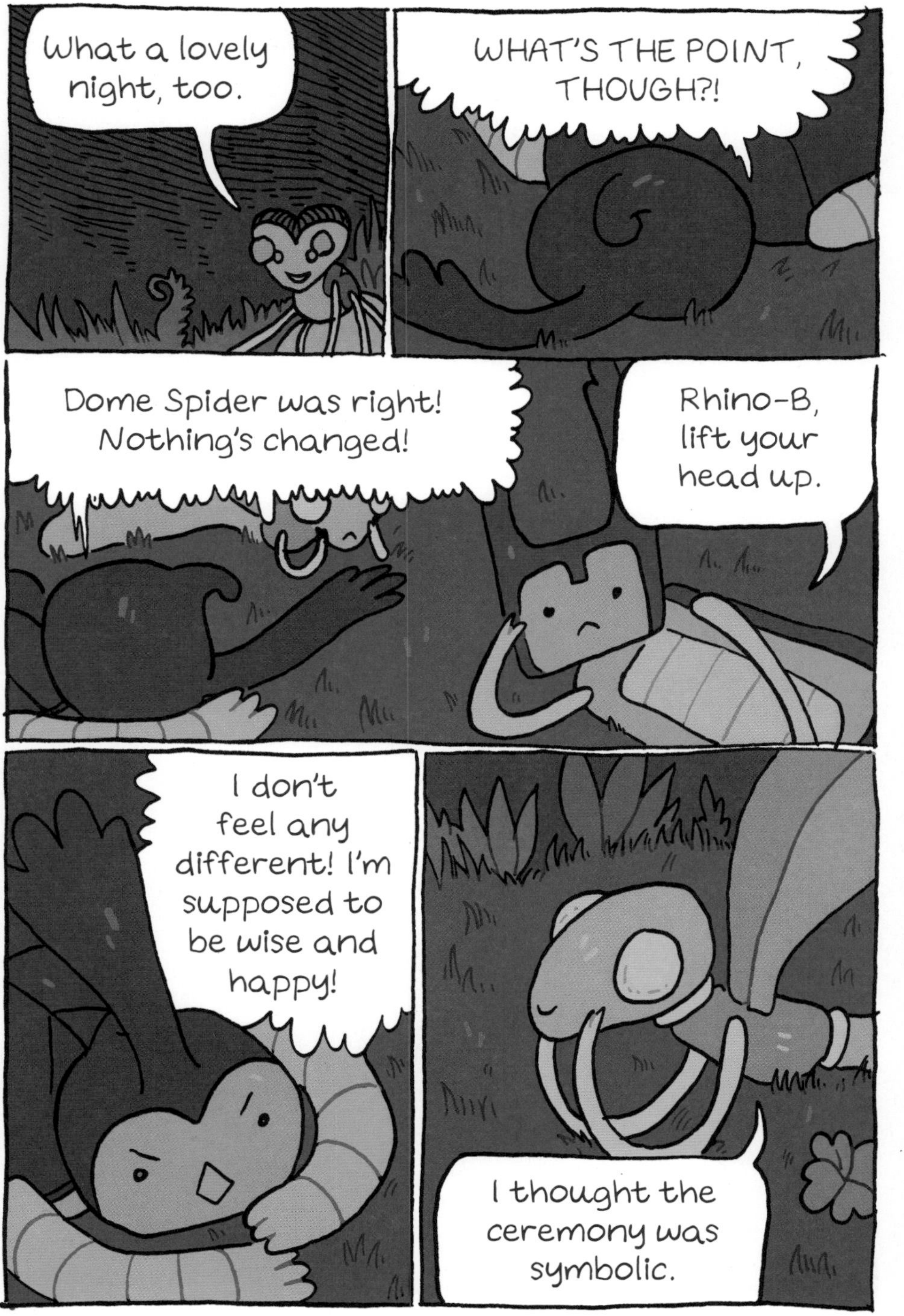
What a lovely night, too.
WHAT'S THE POINT, THOUGH?!
Dome Spider was right! Nothing's changed!
Rhino-B, lift your head up.
I don't feel any different! I'm supposed to be wise and happy!
I thought the ceremony was symbolic.

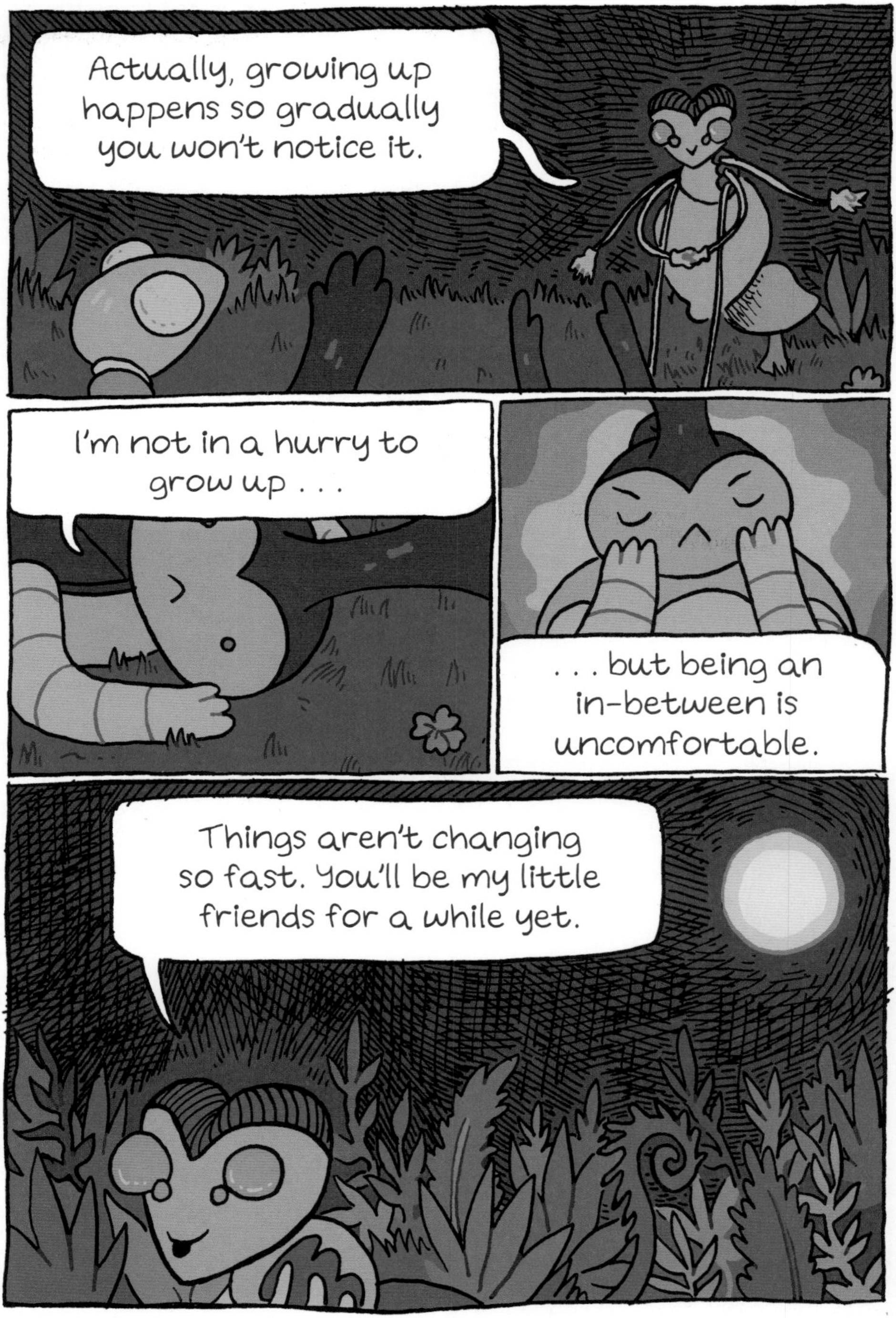
Actually, growing up happens so gradually you won't notice it.
I'm not in a hurry to grow up . . .
. . . but being an in-between is uncomfortable.
Things aren't changing so fast. You'll be my little friends for a while yet.

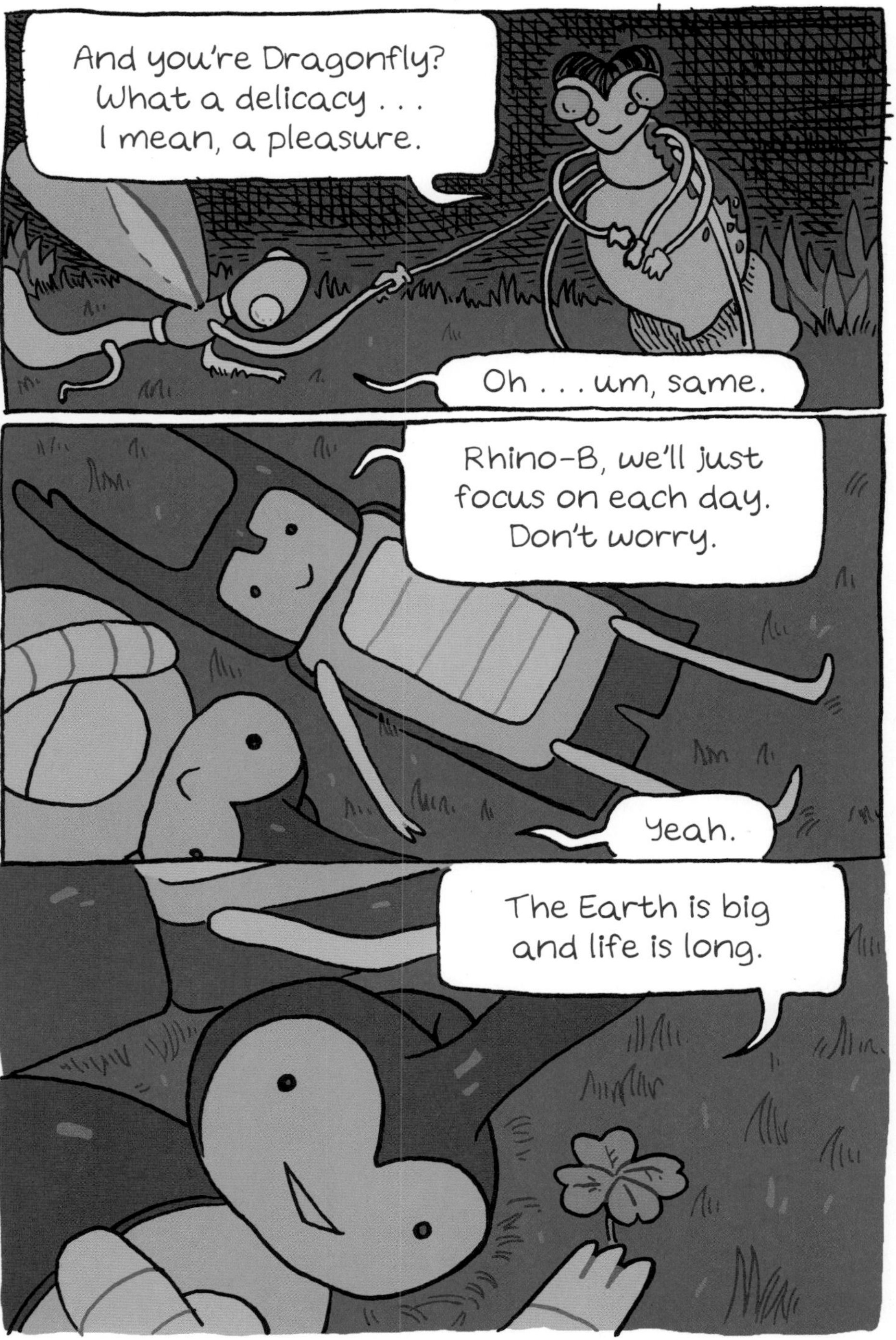
And you're Dragonfly? What a delicacy . . . I mean, a pleasure.
Oh . . . um, same.
Rhino-B, we'll just focus on each day. Don't worry.
Yeah.
The Earth is big and life is long.

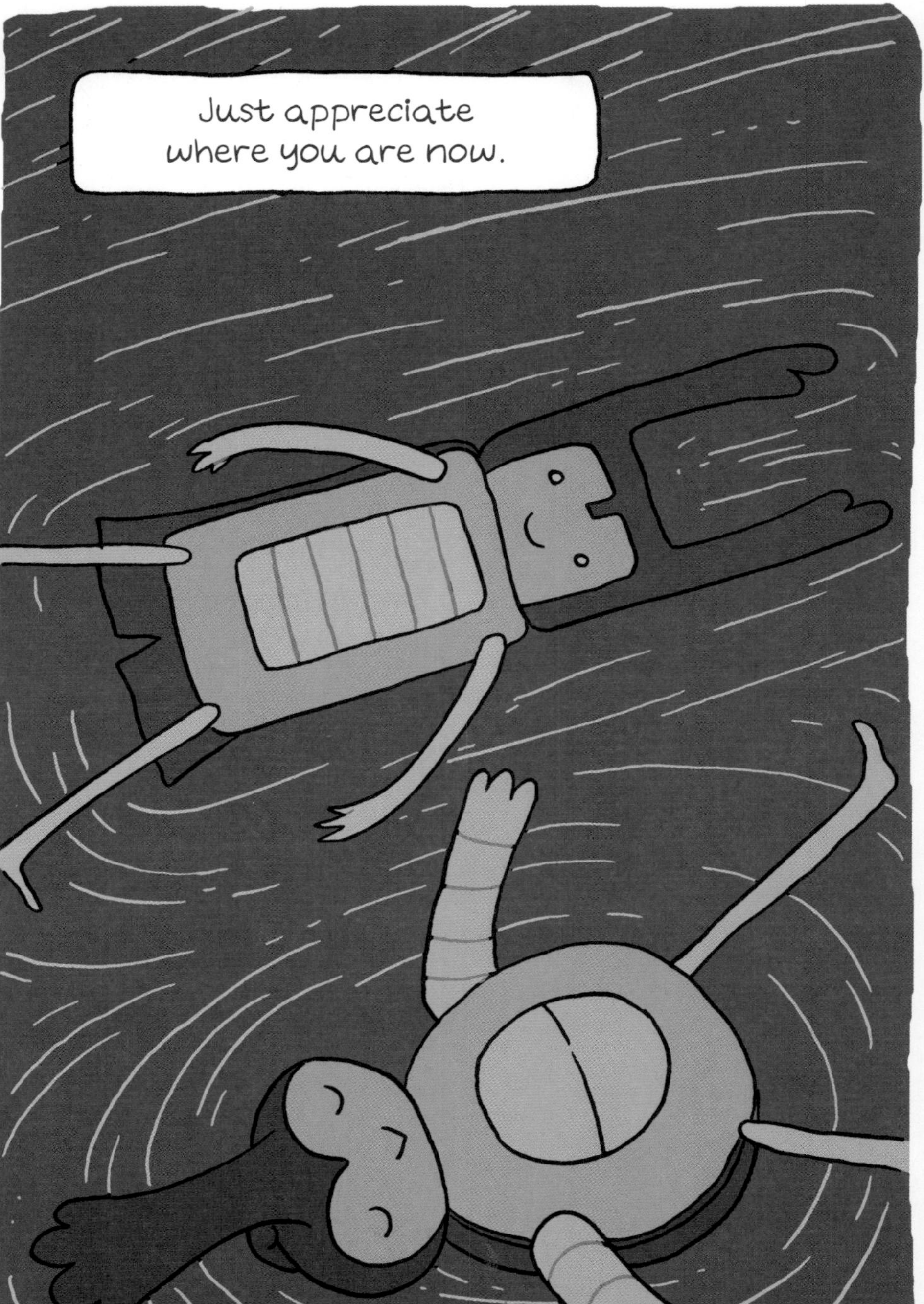
Just appreciate
where you are now.

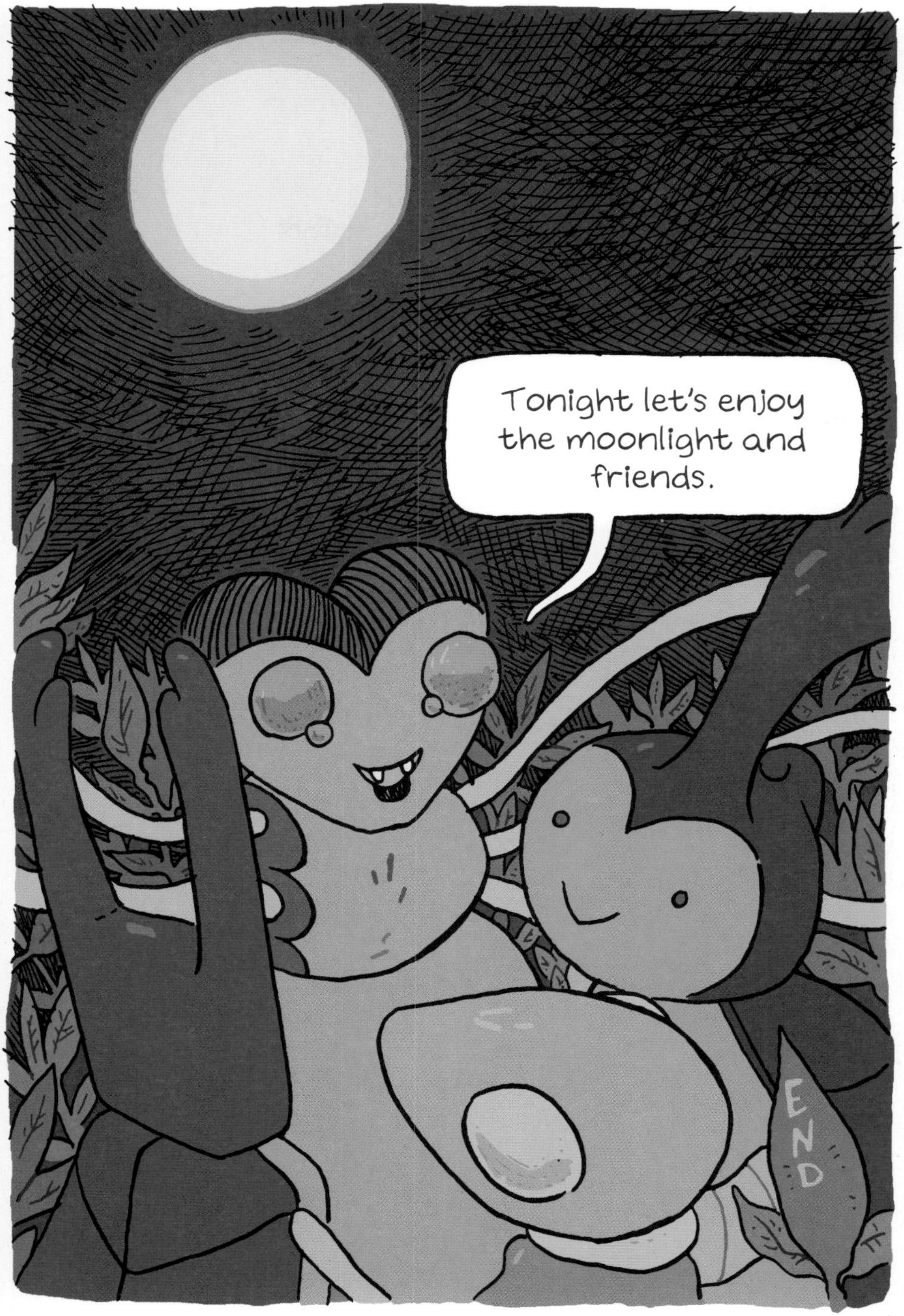
Tonight let's enjoy the moonlight and friends.
END

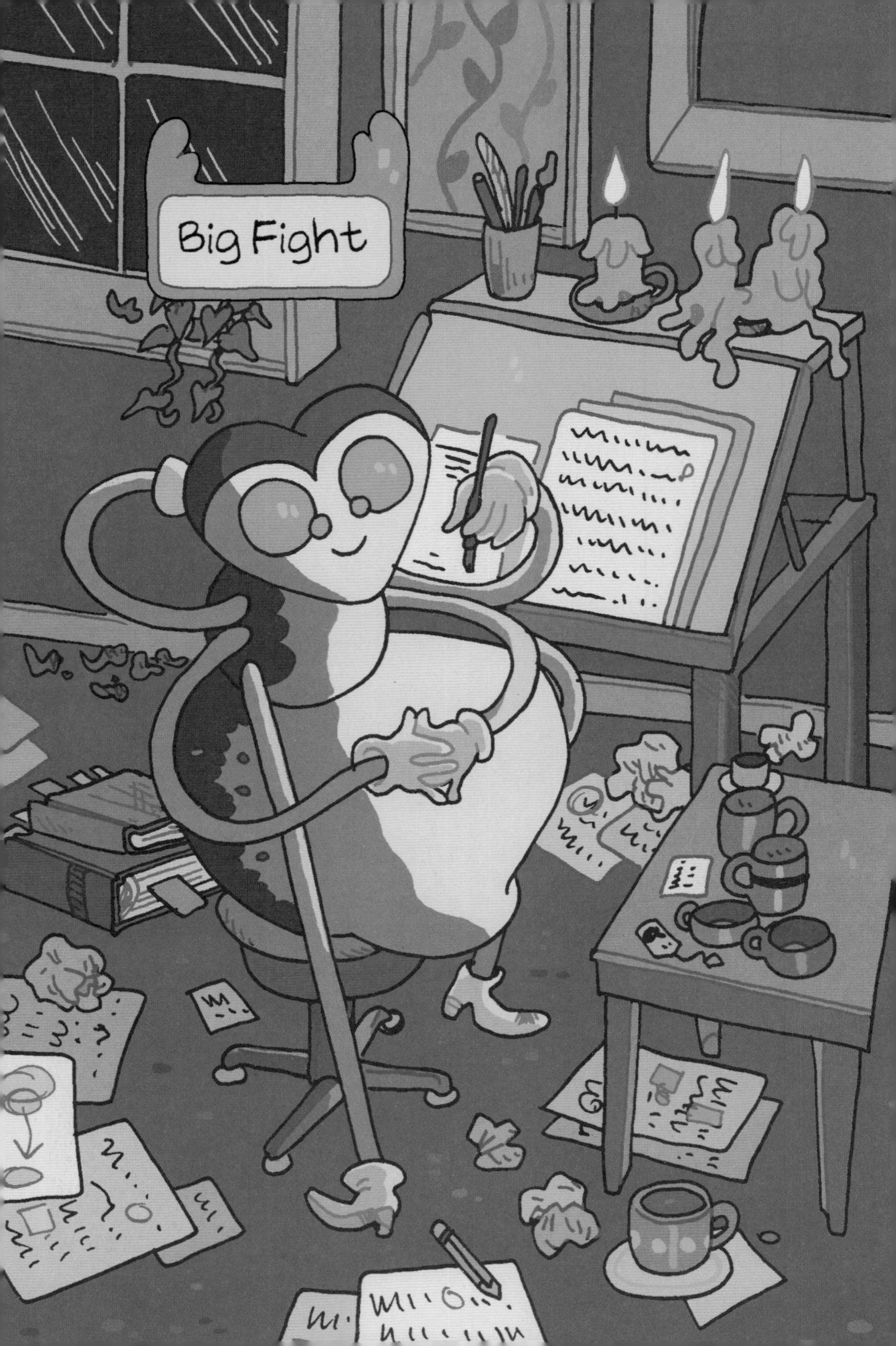
Big Fight

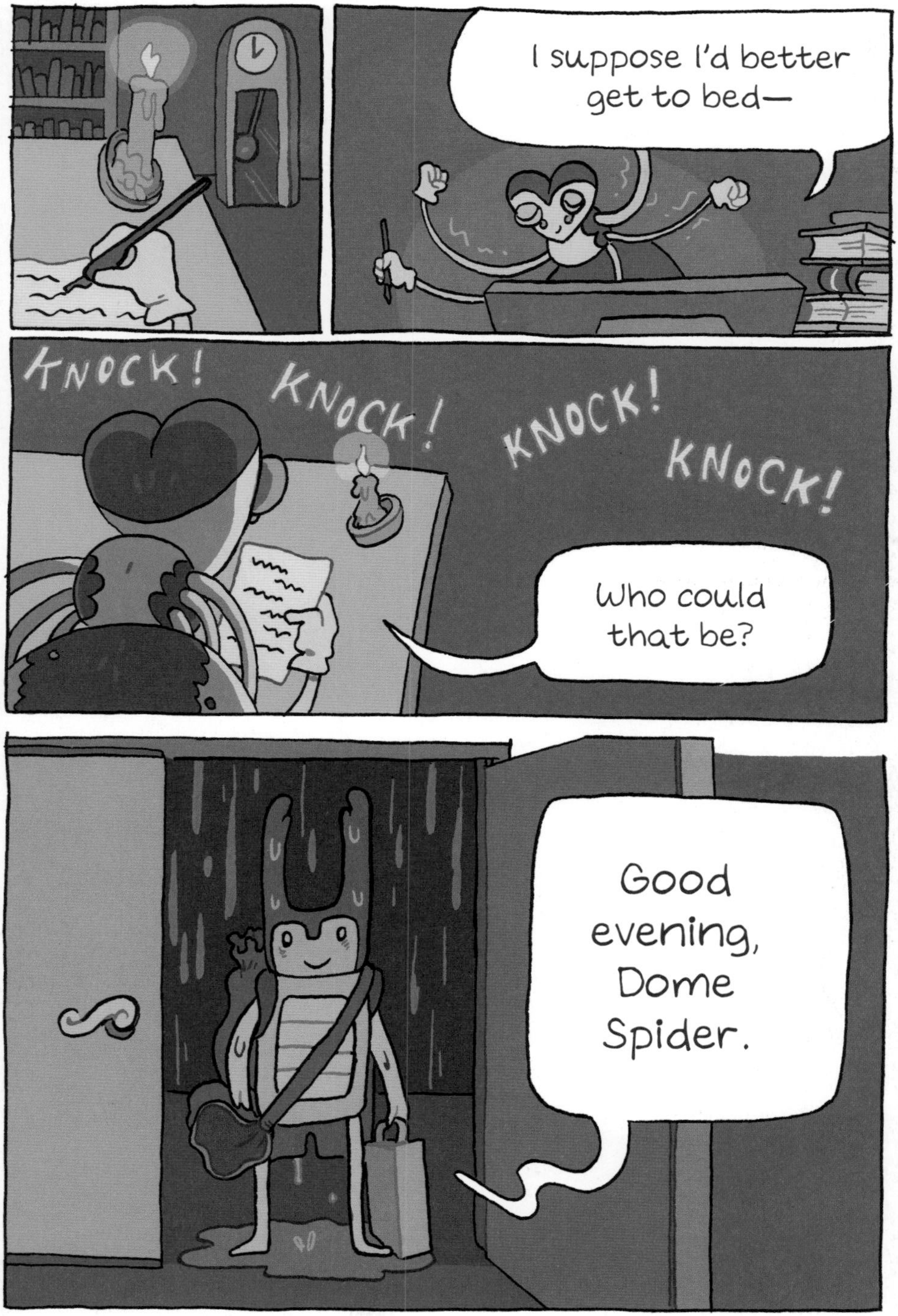

I suppose I'd better get to bed—
KNOCK!
KNOCK!
KNOCK!
KNOCK!
Who could that be?
Good evening, Dome Spider.

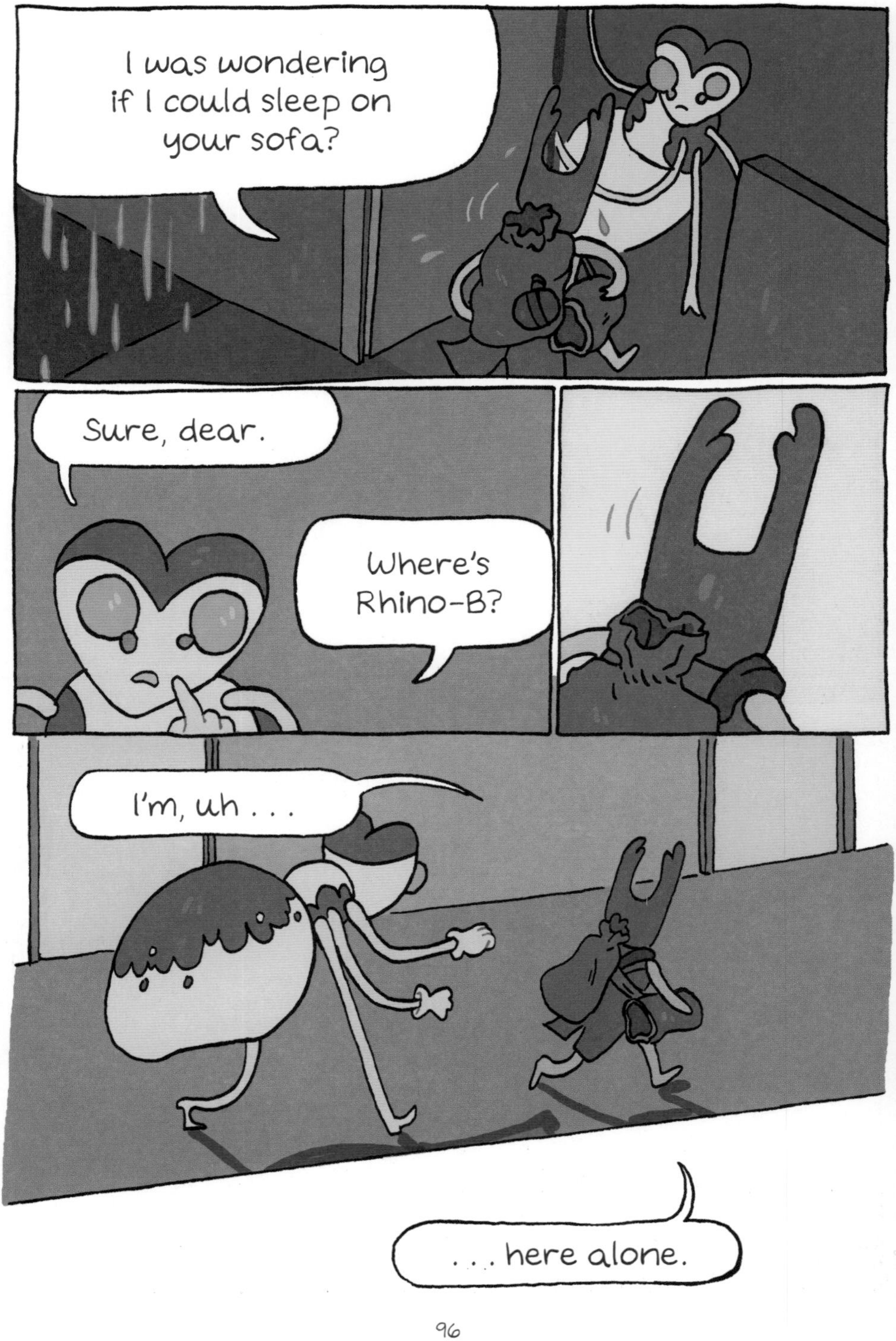
I was wondering if I could sleep on your sofa?
Sure, dear.
Where's Rhino-B?
I'm, uh . . .
. . . here alone.

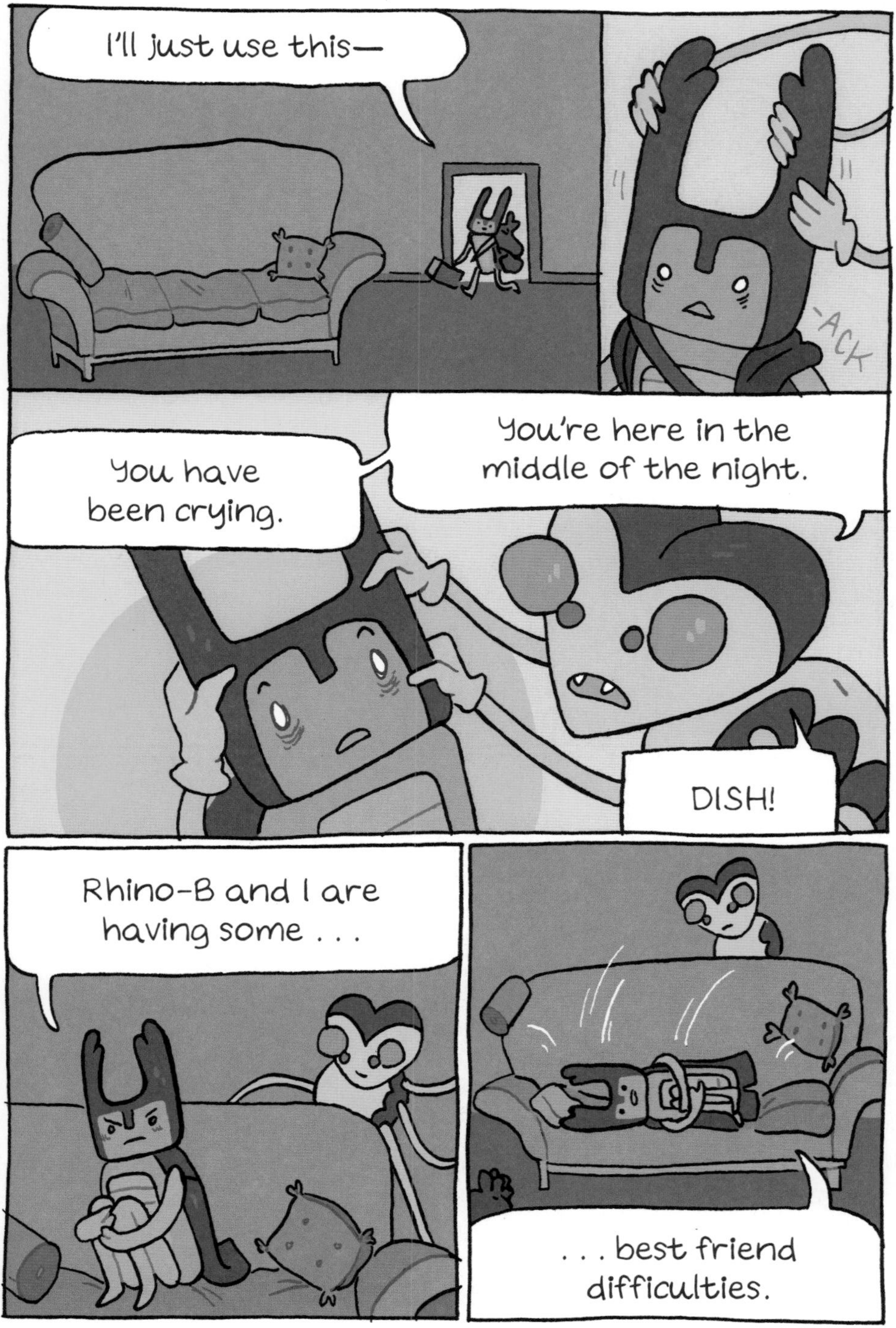
I'll just use this—
-ACK
You have been crying.
You're here in the middle of the night.
DISH!
Rhino-B and I are having some . . .
. . . best friend difficulties.

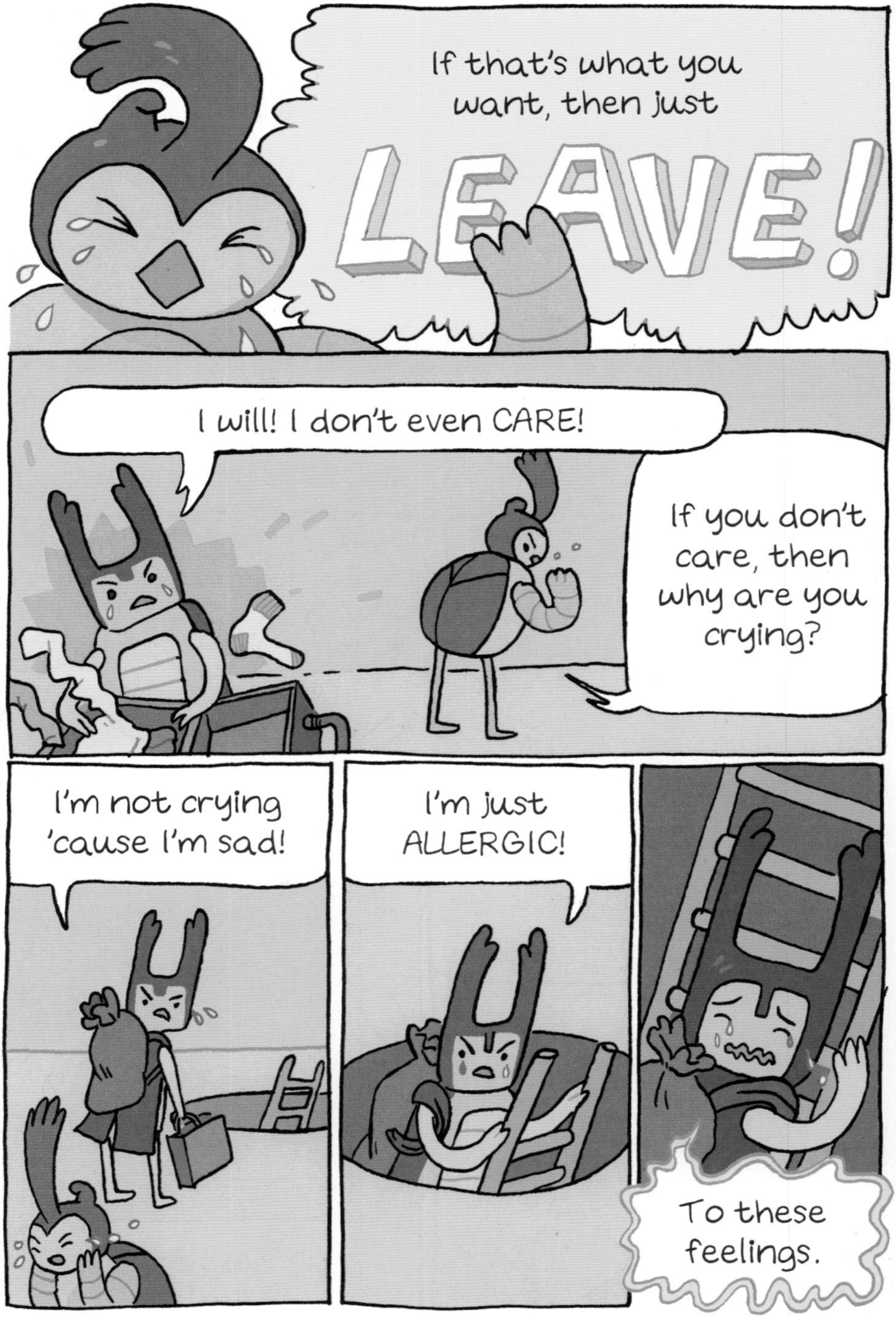
If that's what you want, then just
LEAVE!
I will! I don't even CARE!
If you don't care, then why are you crying?
I'm not crying 'cause I'm sad!
I'm just ALLERGIC!
To these feelings.

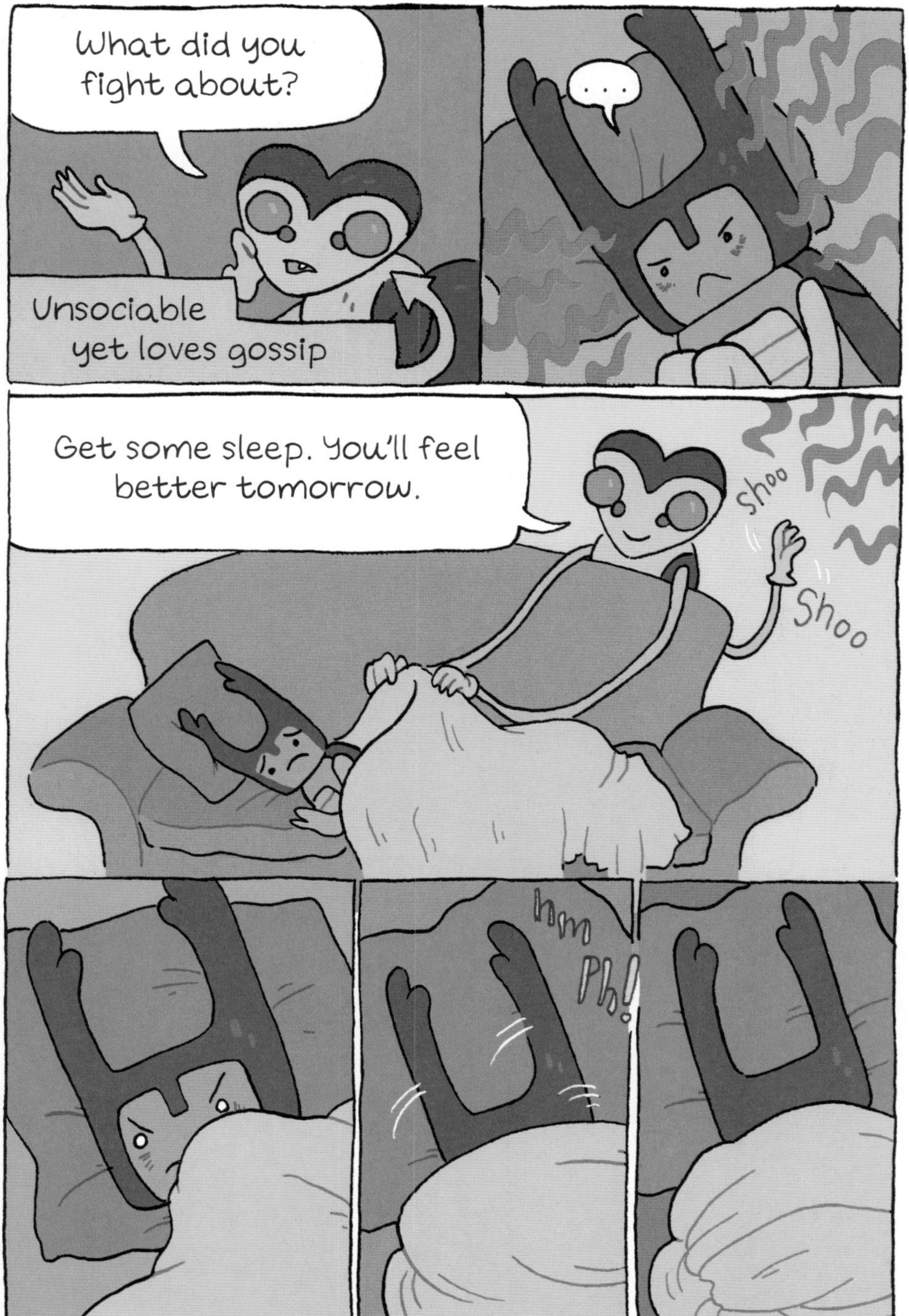
What did you fight about?
Unsociable yet loves gossip
. . .
Get some sleep. You'll feel better tomorrow.
Shoo
Shoo
hm
Ph!

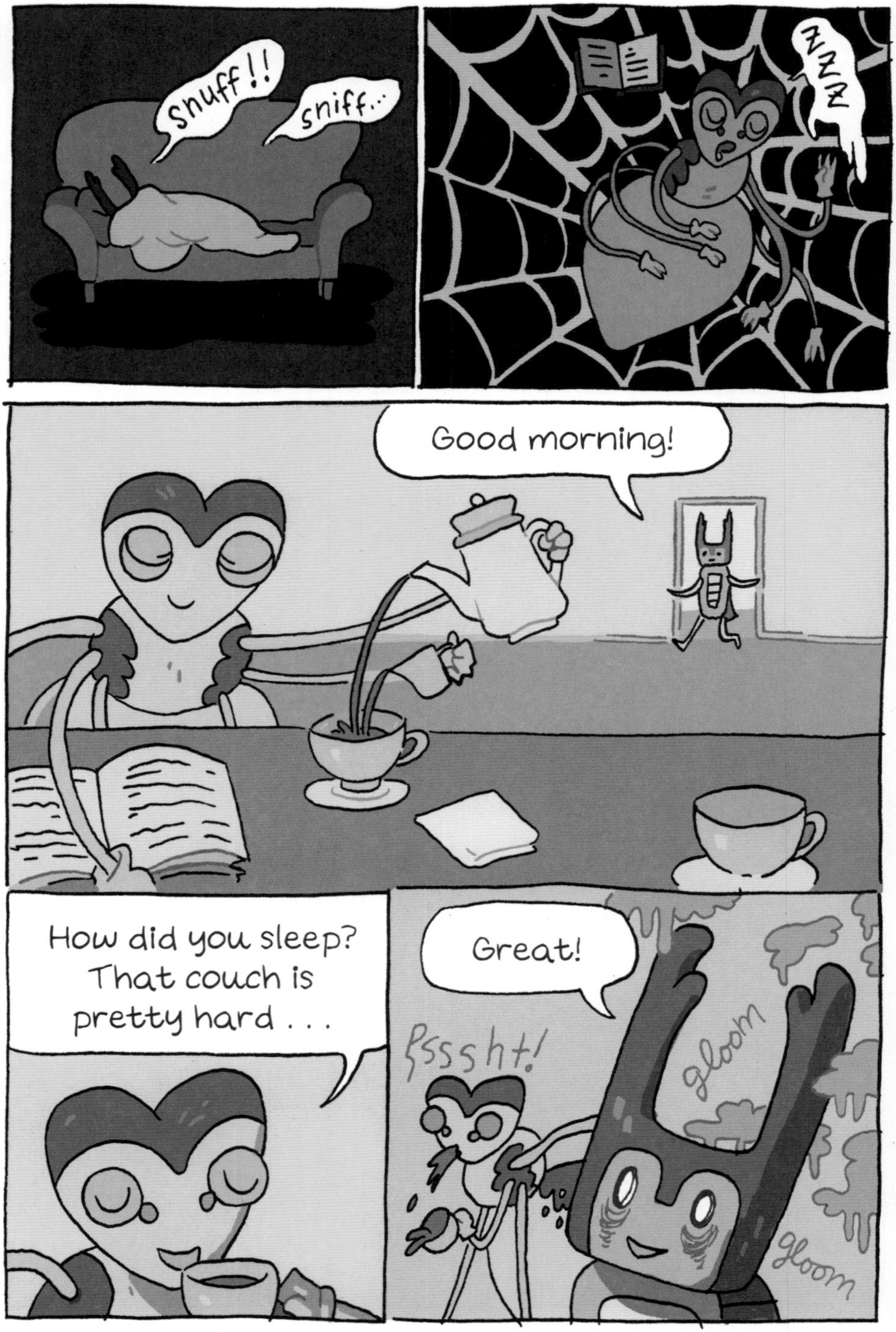
snuff!!
sniff...
ZZZ
Good morning!
How did you sleep? That couch is pretty hard . . .
Great!
Psssht!
gloom
gloom

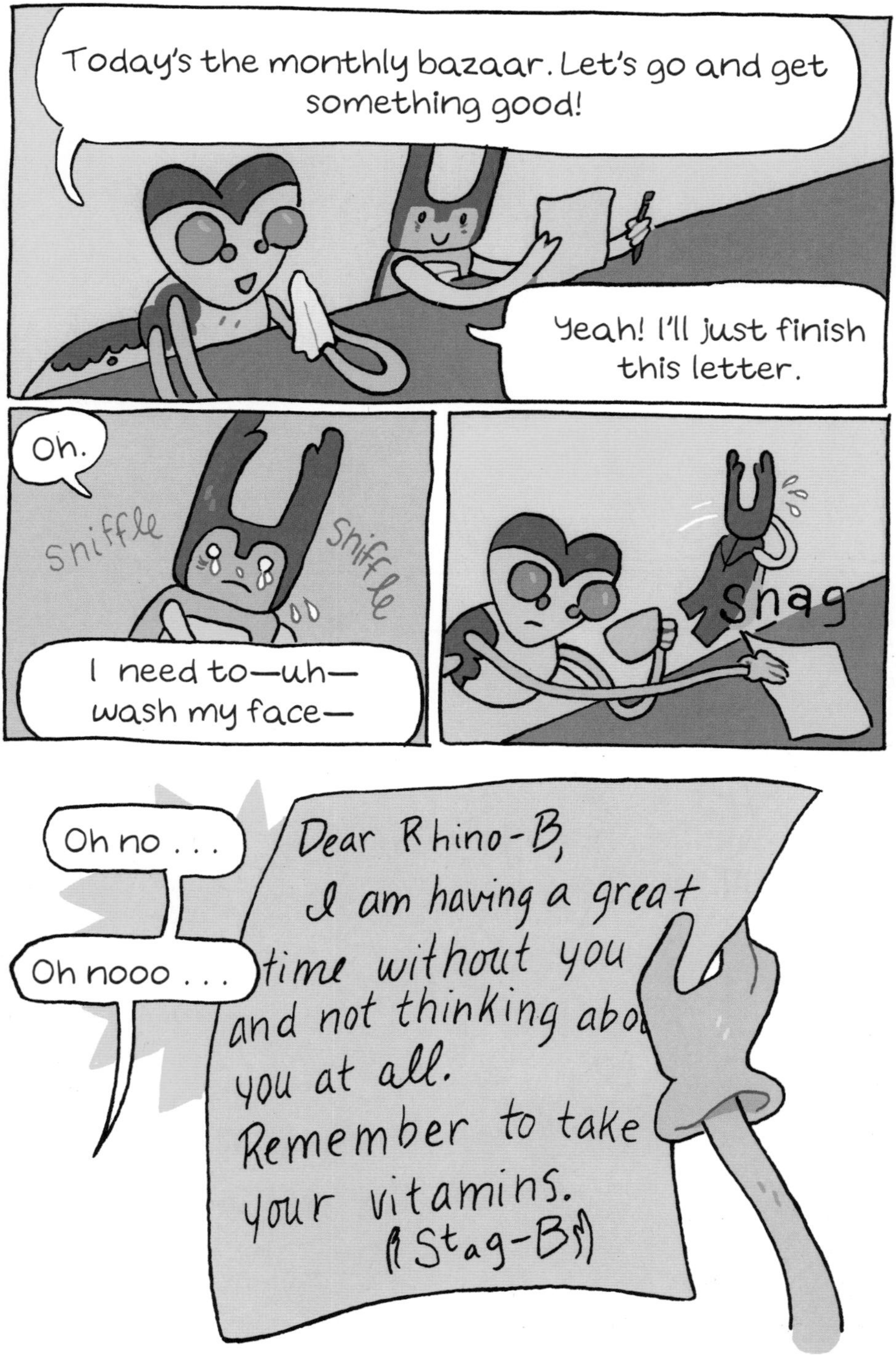
Today's the monthly bazaar. Let's go and get something good!
Yeah! I'll just finish this letter.
Oh.
sniffle
sniffle
I need to—uh—wash my face—
Snag
Oh no . . .
Oh nooo . . .
Dear Rhino-B,
I am having a great time without you and not thinking abo you at all.
Remember to take your vitamins.
(Stag-B)

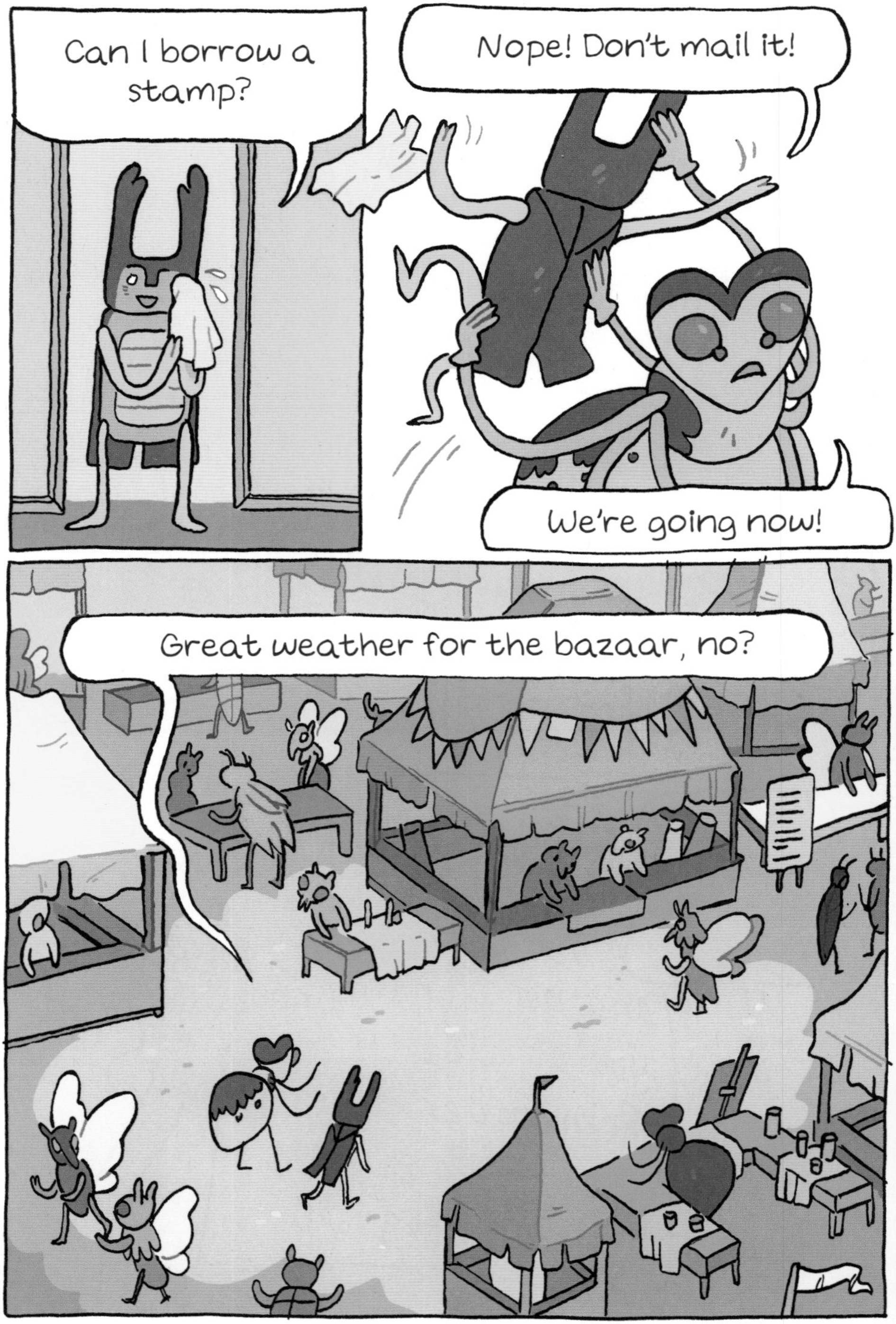
Can I borrow a stamp?
Nope! Don't mail it!
We're going now!
Great weather for the bazaar, no?

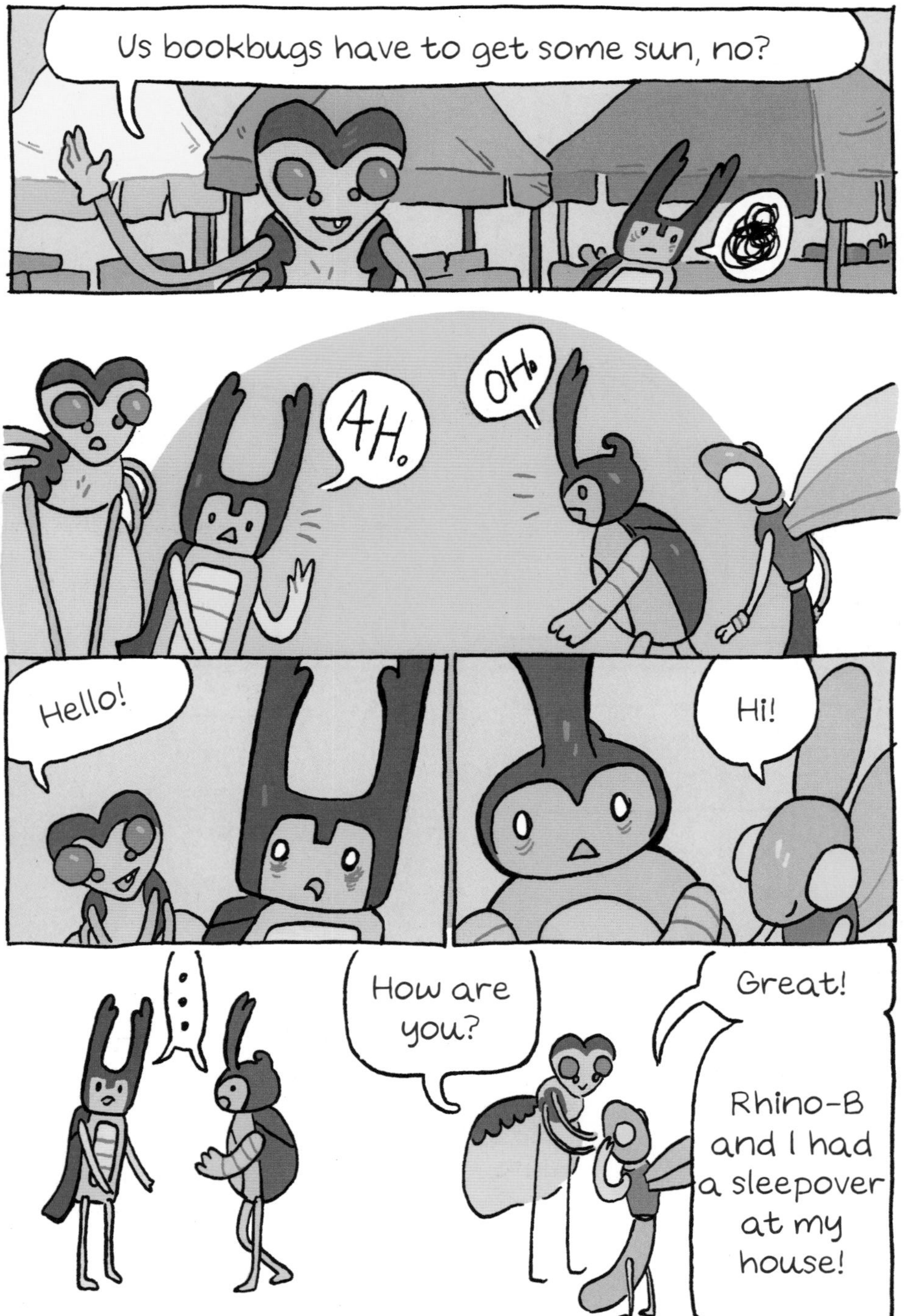
Us bookbugs have to get some sun, no?
AH.
OH.
Hello!
Hi!
...
How are you?
Great!
Rhino-B and I had a sleepover at my house!

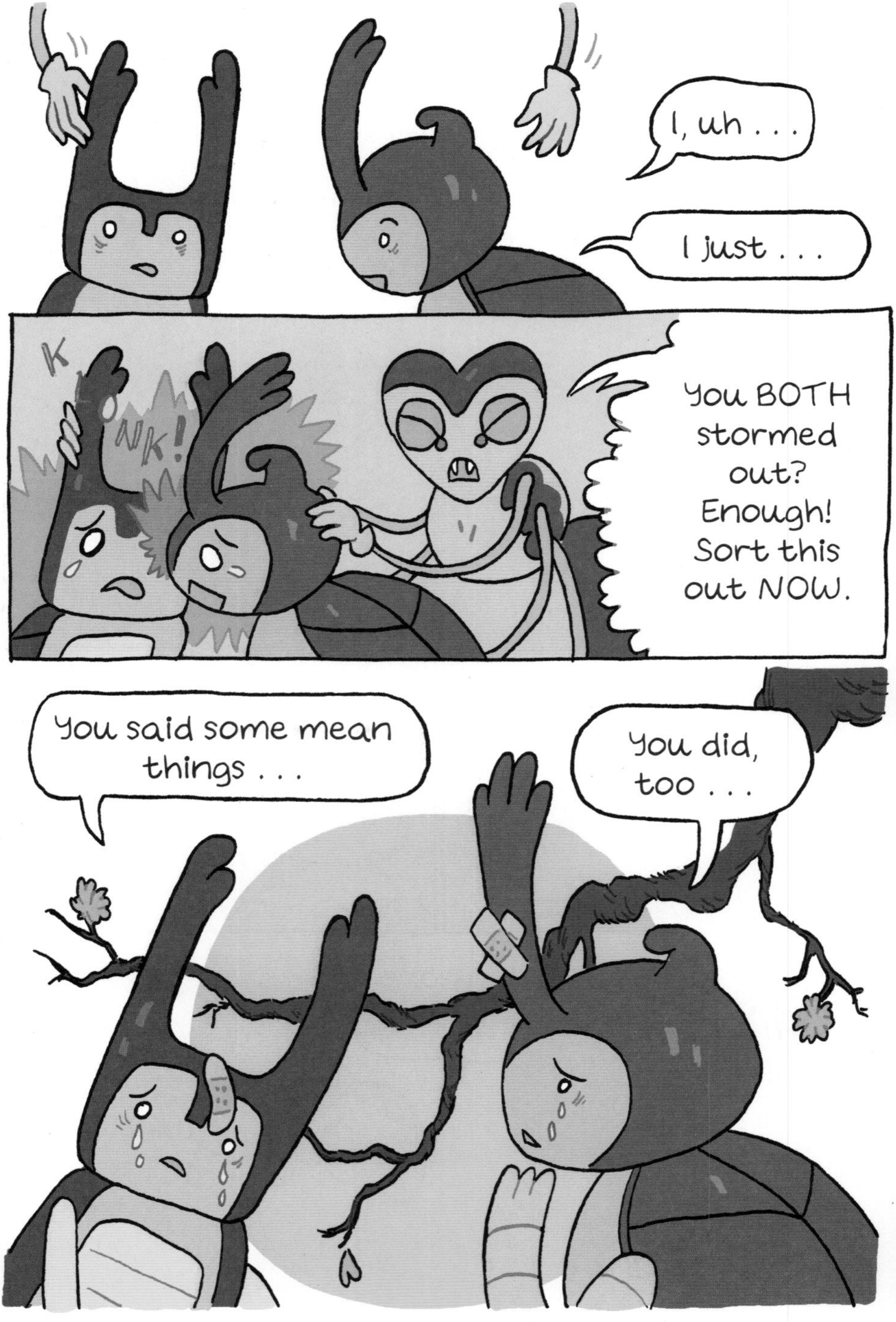
I, uh . . .
I just . . .
K
NK!
You BOTH stormed out? Enough! Sort this out NOW.
You said some mean things . . .
You did, too . . .

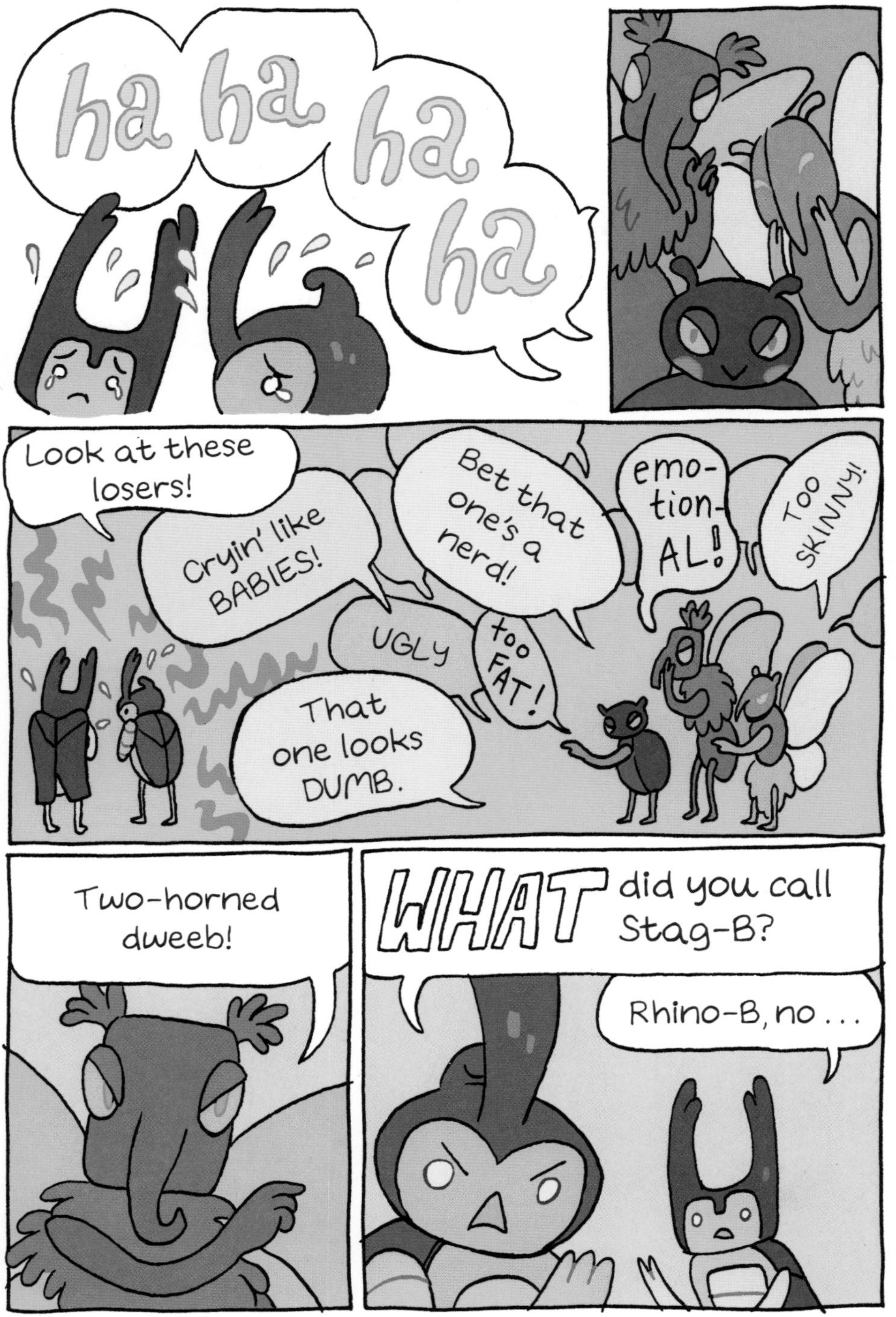
ha ha ha ha
Look at these losers!
Cryin' like BABIES!
Bet that one's a nerd!
emo-tion-AL!
Too SKINNY!
UGLY
too FAT!
That one looks DUMB.
Two-horned dweeb!
WHAT did you call Stag-B?
Rhino-B, no . . .

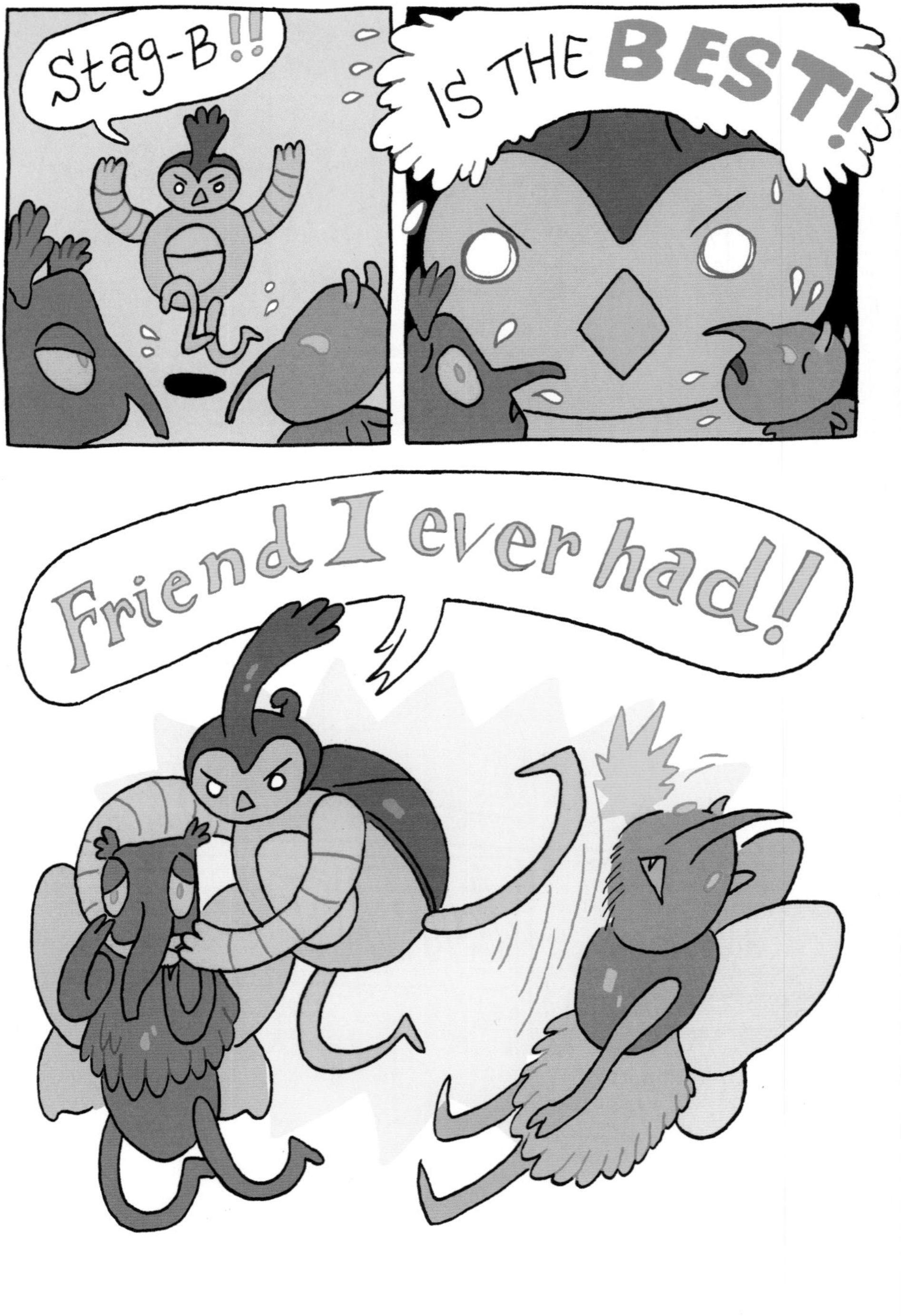
Stag-B!!
IS THE BEST!
Friend I ever had!

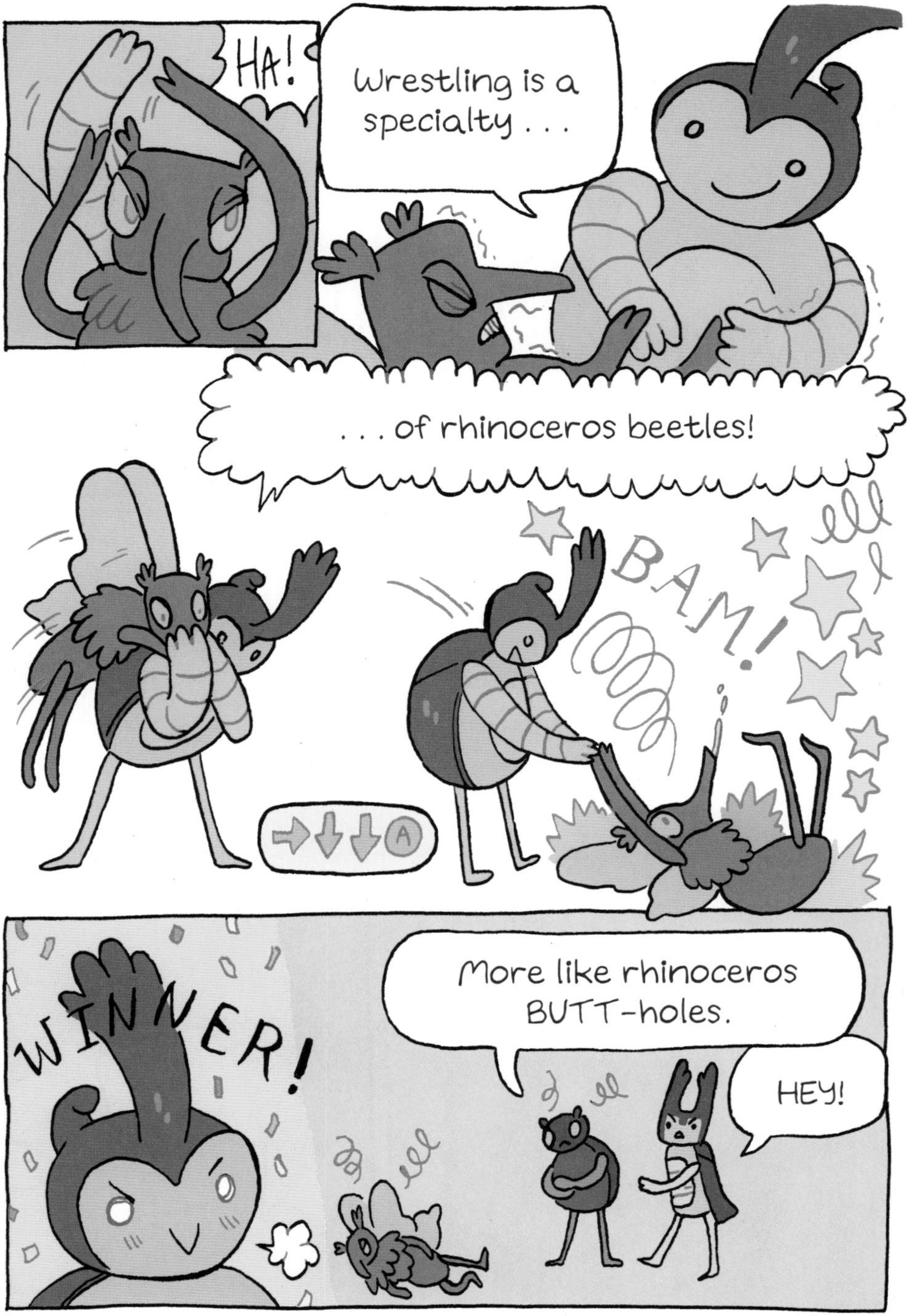
HA!
Wrestling is a specialty . . .
. . . of rhinoceros beetles!
BAM!
A
WINNER!
More like rhinoceros BUTT-holes.
HEY!

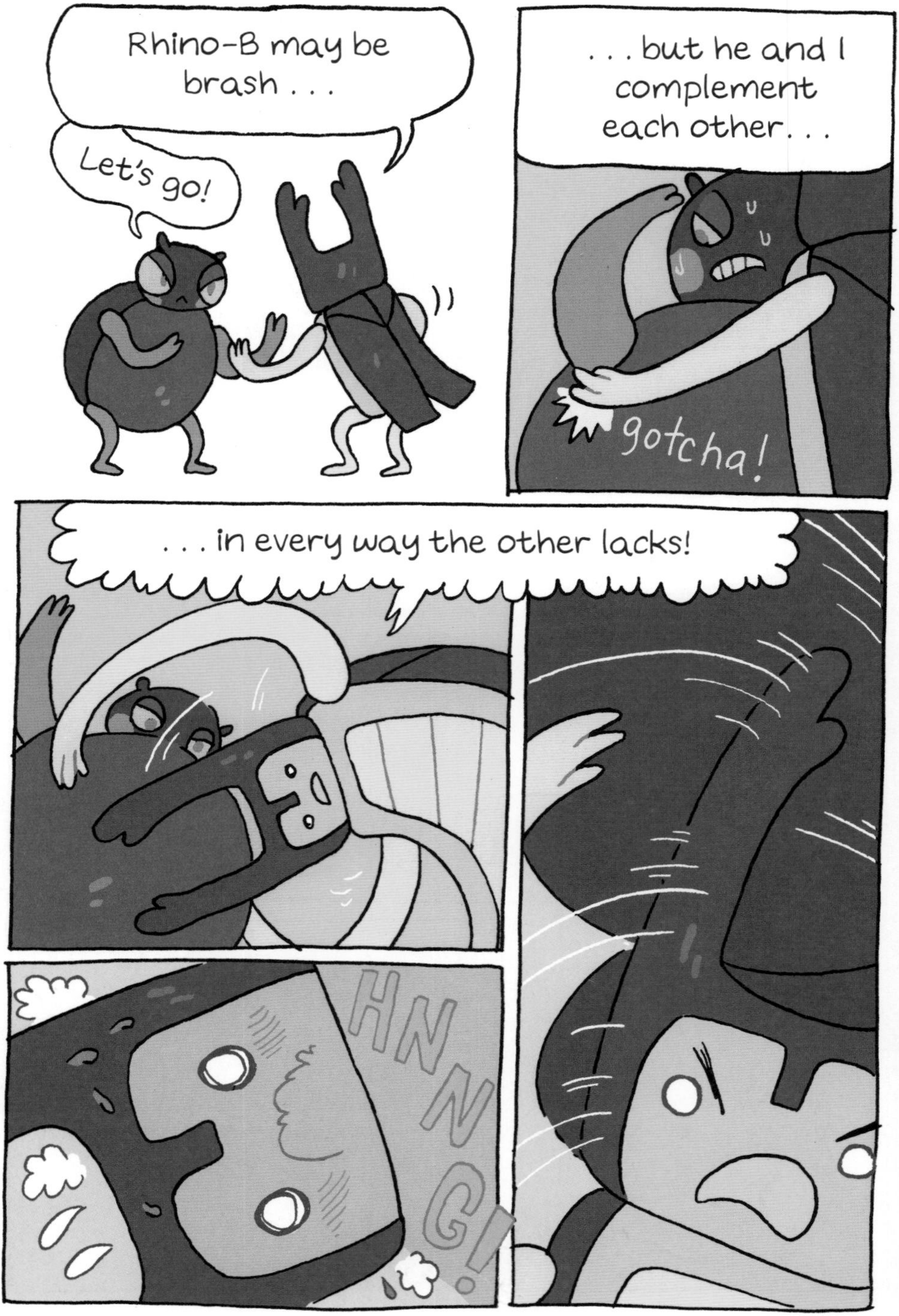
Rhino-B may be brash . . .
Let's go!
. . . but he and I complement each other . . .
gotcha!
. . . in every way the other lacks!
HNNG!

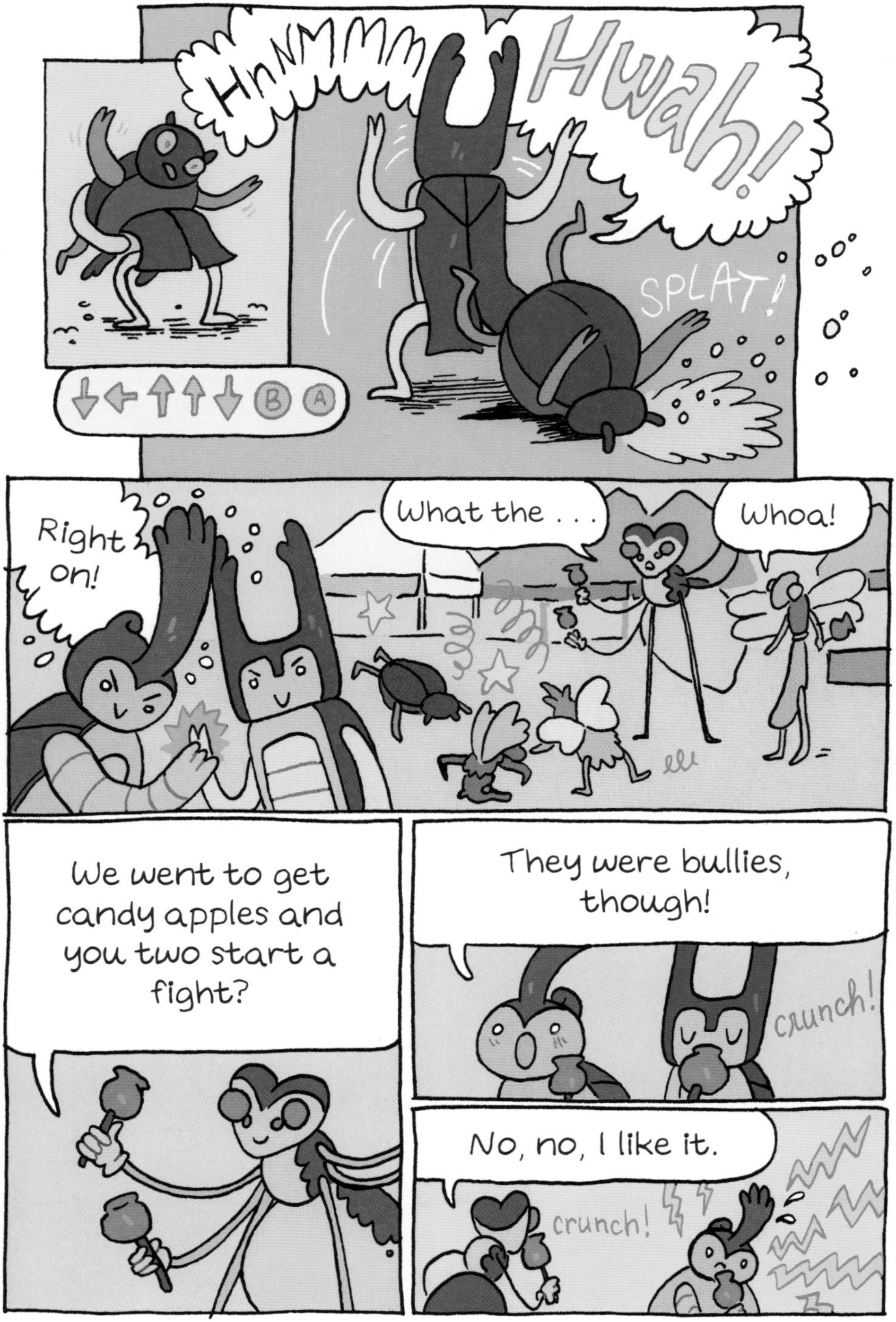
HnNMMM
Hwah!
SPLAT!
B A
Right on!
What the . . .
Whoa!
We went to get candy apples and you two start a fight?
They were bullies, though!
crunch!
No, no, I like it.
crunch!

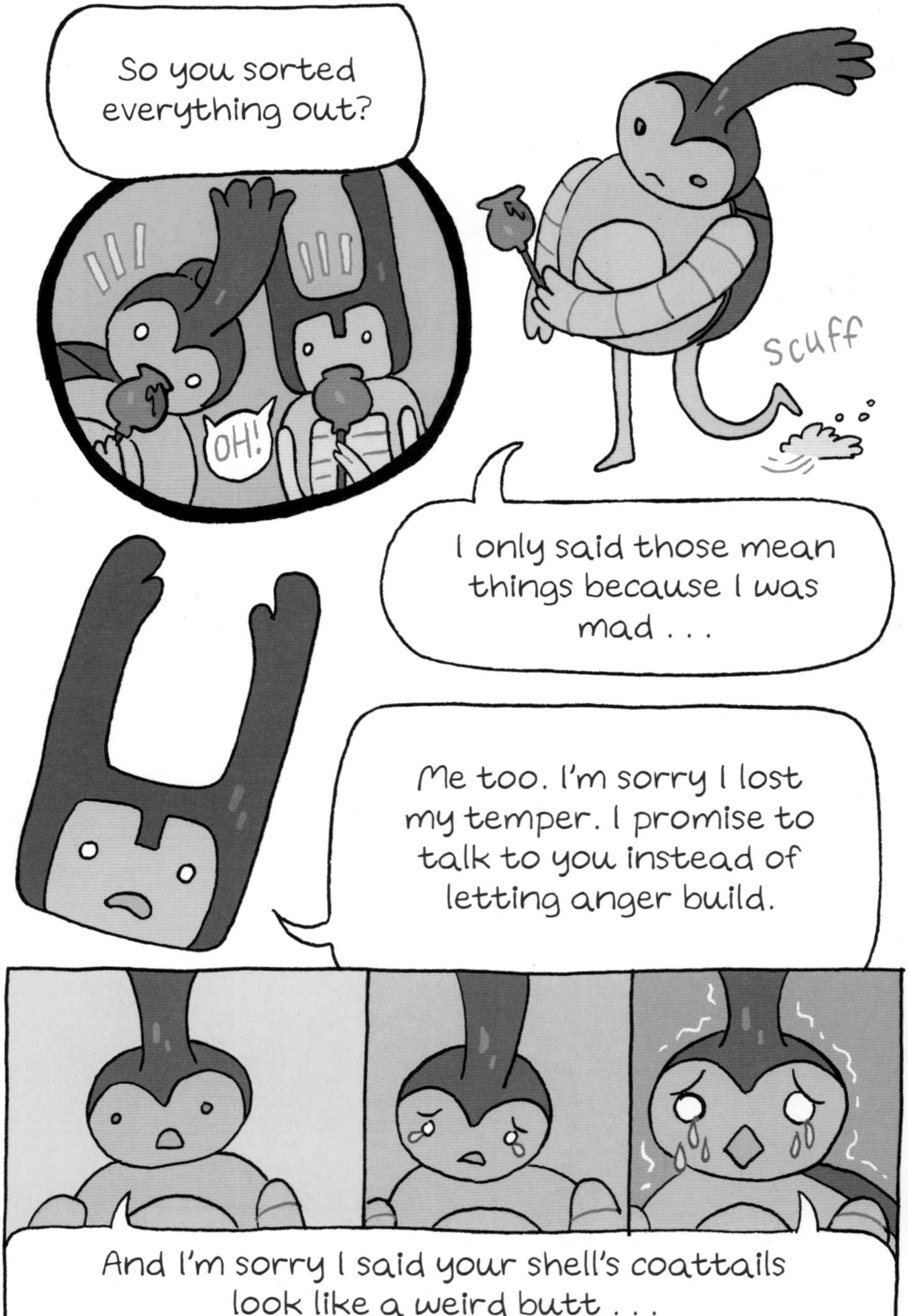
So you sorted everything out?
OH!
SCUFF
I only said those mean things because I was mad . . .
Me too. I'm sorry I lost my temper. I promise to talk to you instead of letting anger build.
And I'm sorry I said your shell's coattails look like a weird butt . . .

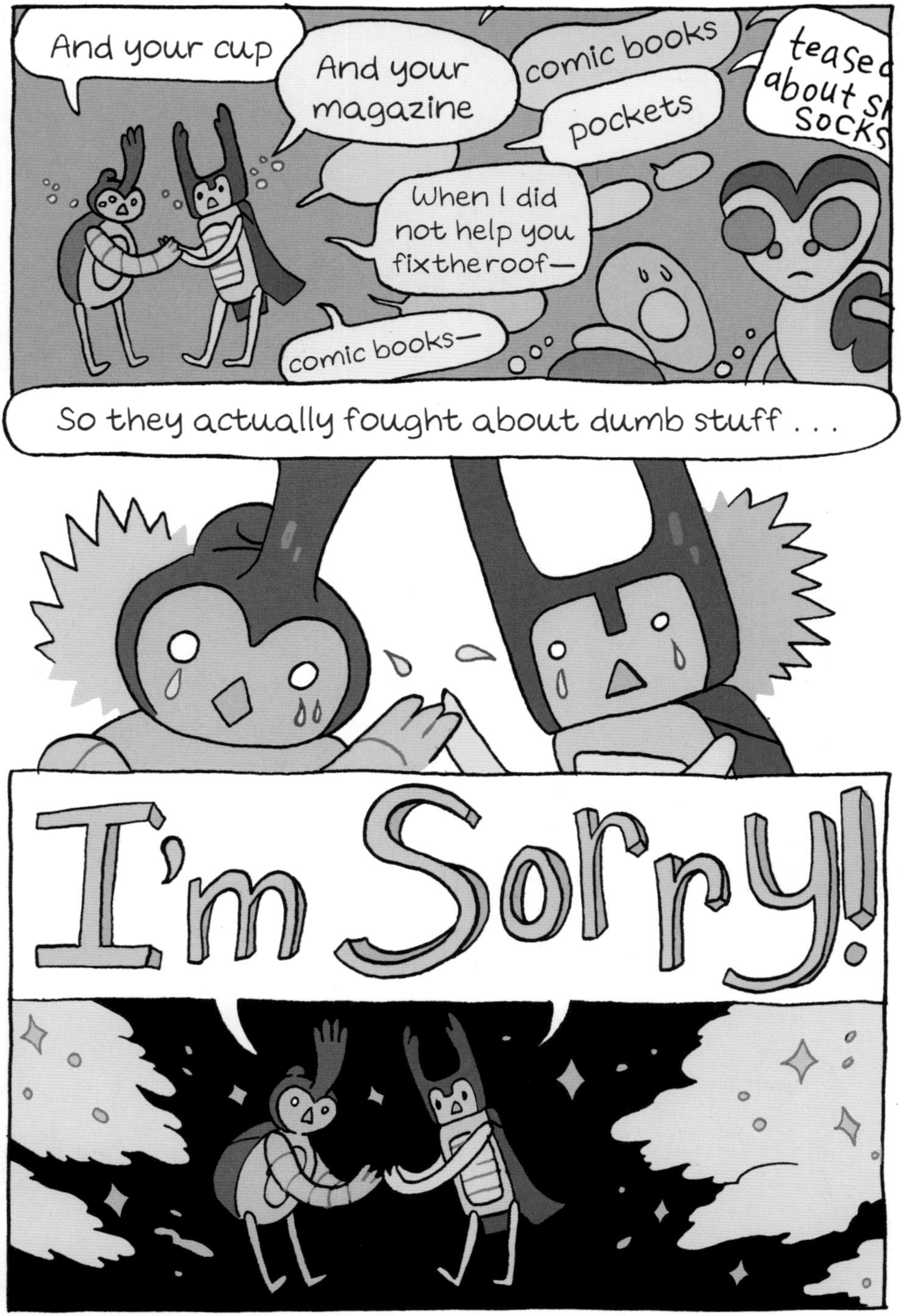
And your cup
And your magazine
comic books
pockets
tease about socks
When I did not help you fixtheroof—
comic books—
So they actually fought about dumb stuff . . .
I'm Sorry!

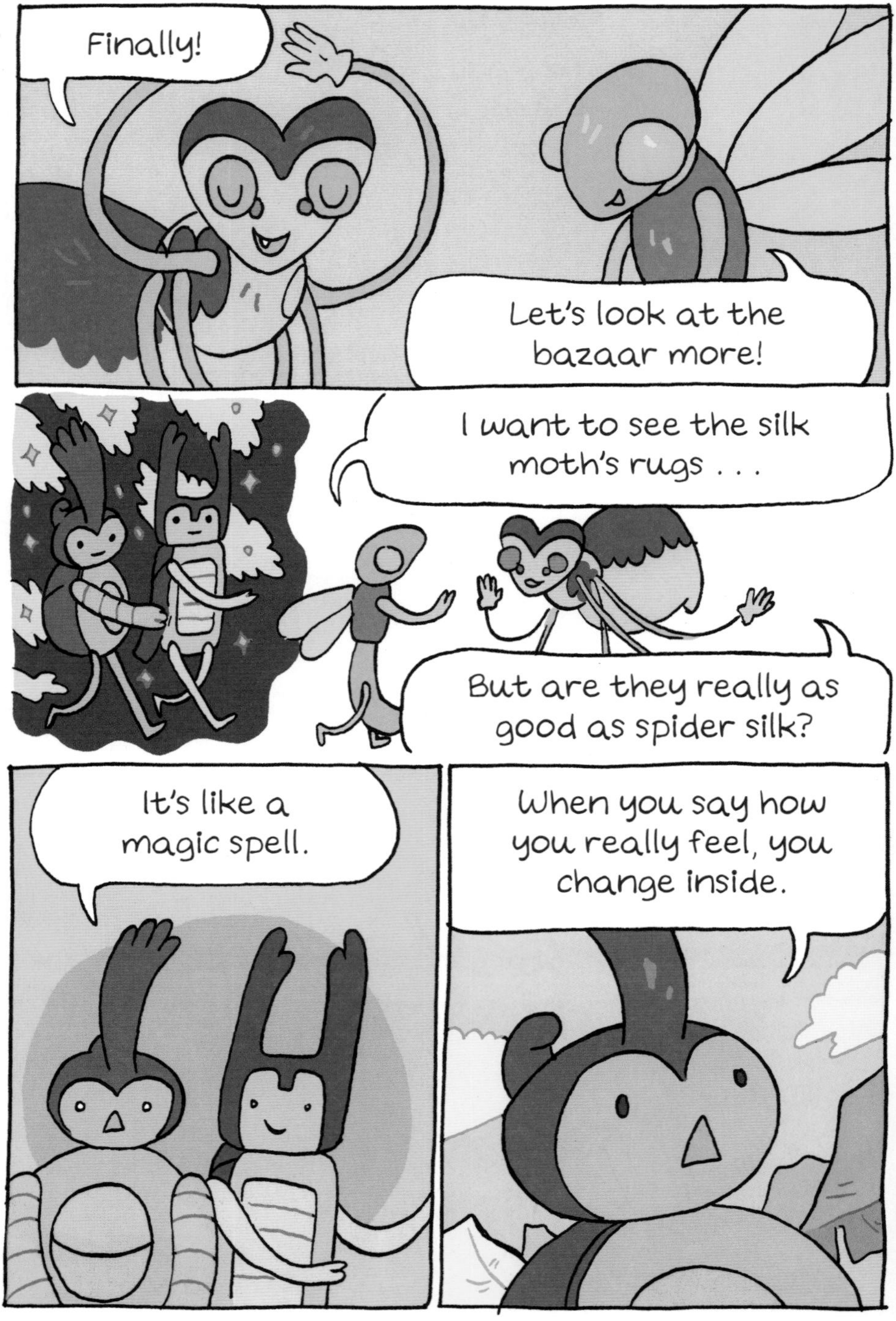
Finally!
Let's look at the bazaar more!
I want to see the silk moth's rugs . . .
But are they really as good as spider silk?
It's like a magic spell.
When you say how you really feel, you change inside.

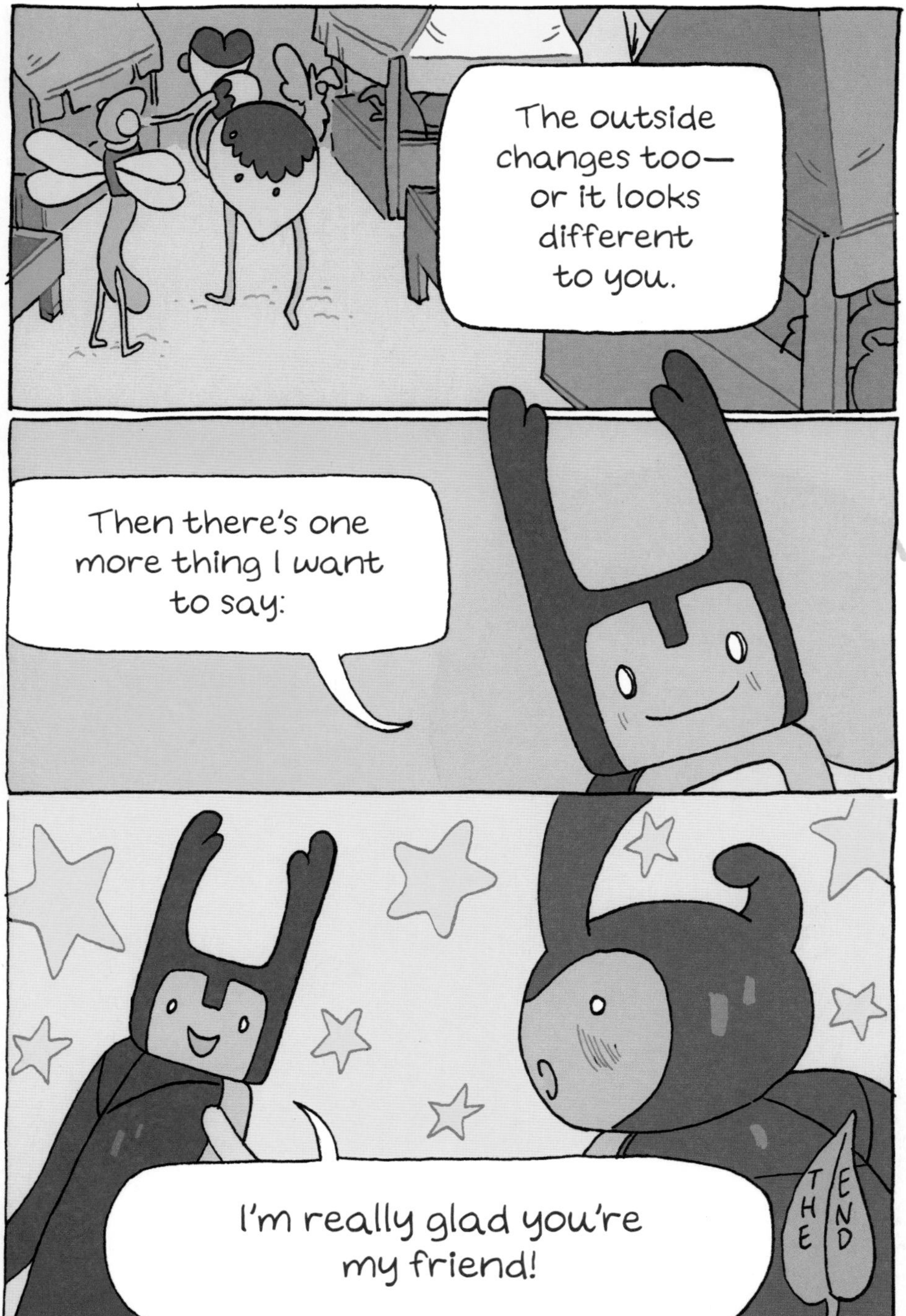
The outside changes too—or it looks different to you.
Then there's one more thing I want to say:
I'm really glad you're my friend!
THE END

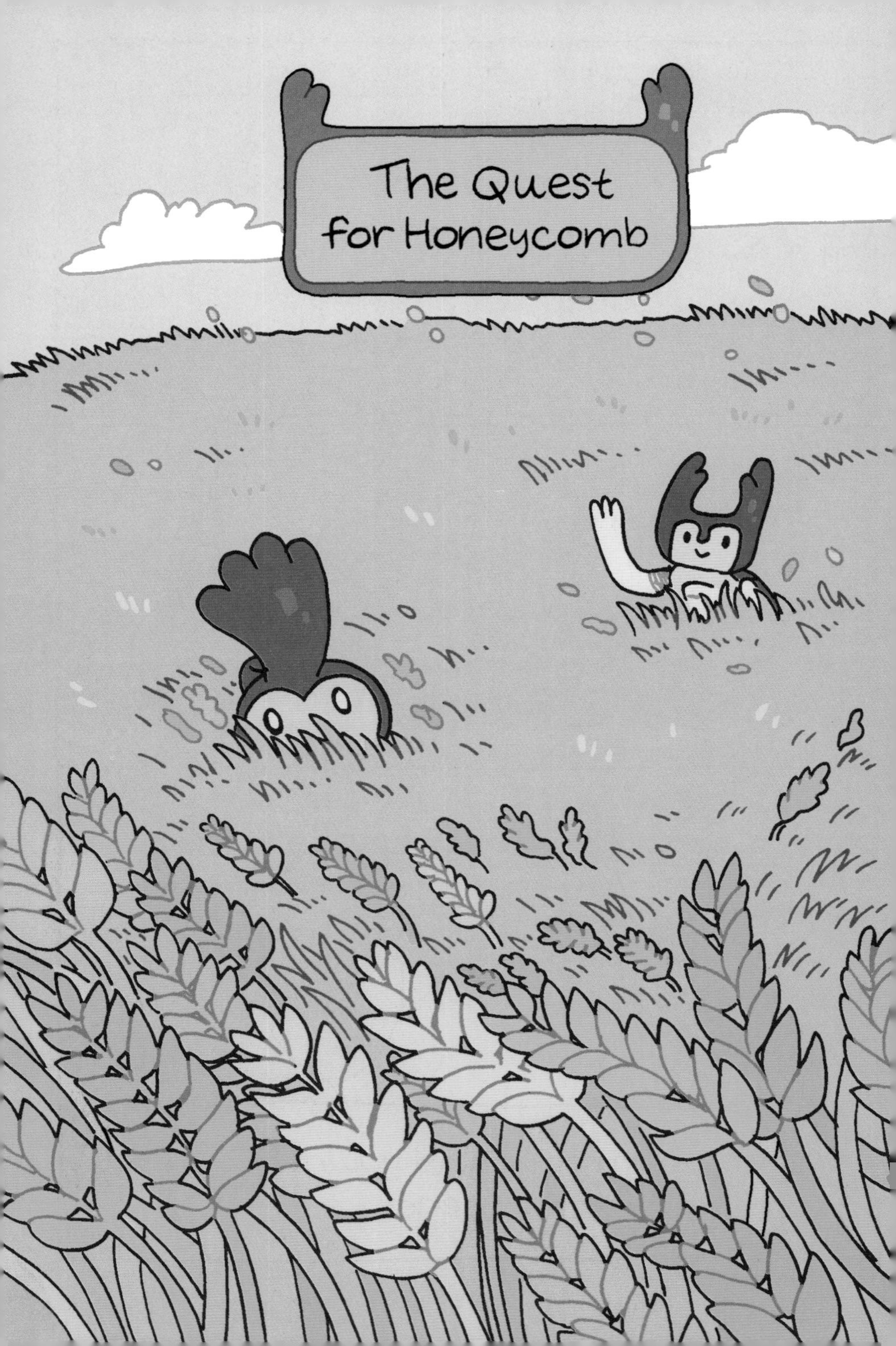
The Quest
for Honeycomb

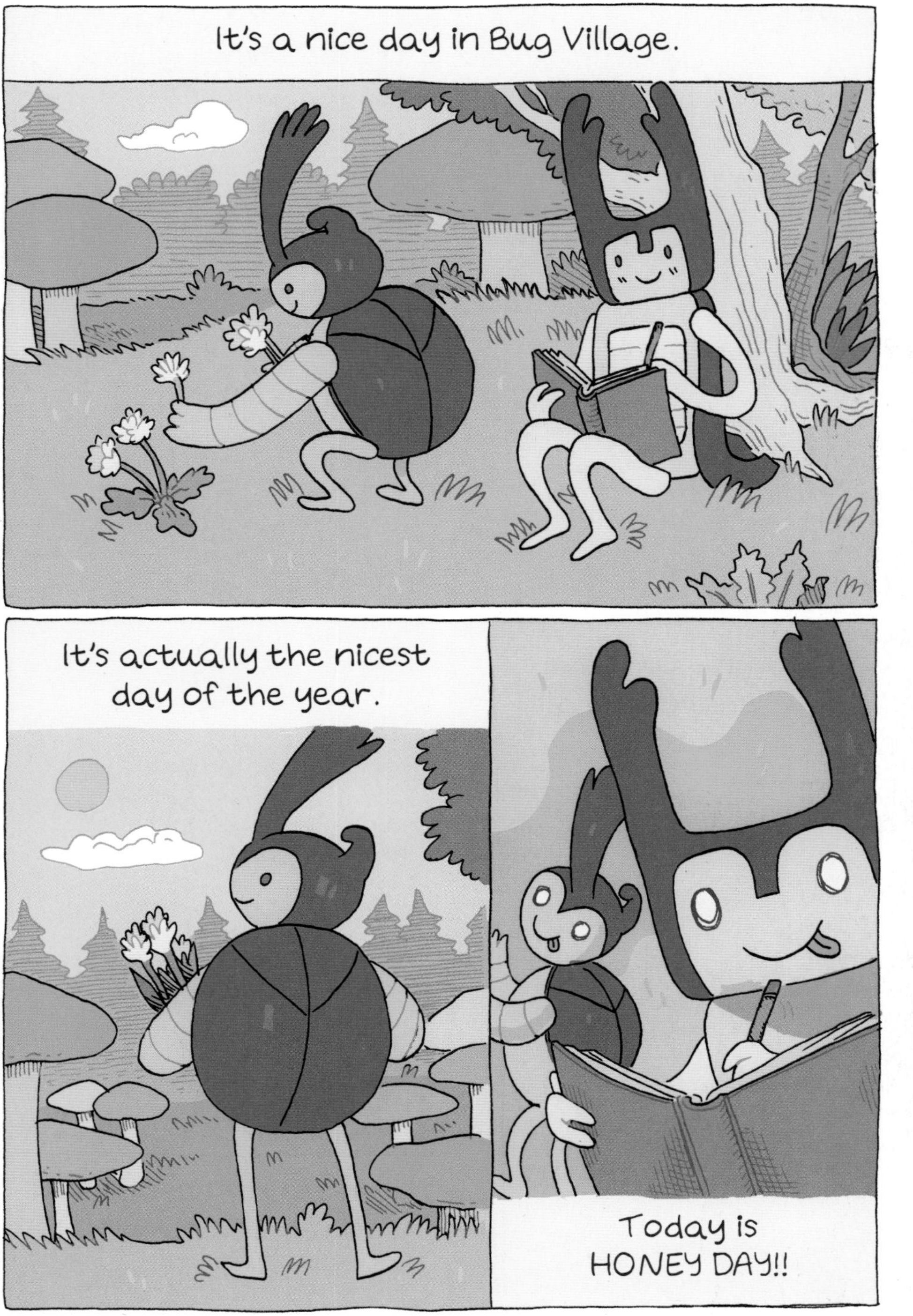
It's a nice day in Bug Village.
It's actually the nicest day of the year.
Today is HONEY DAY!!

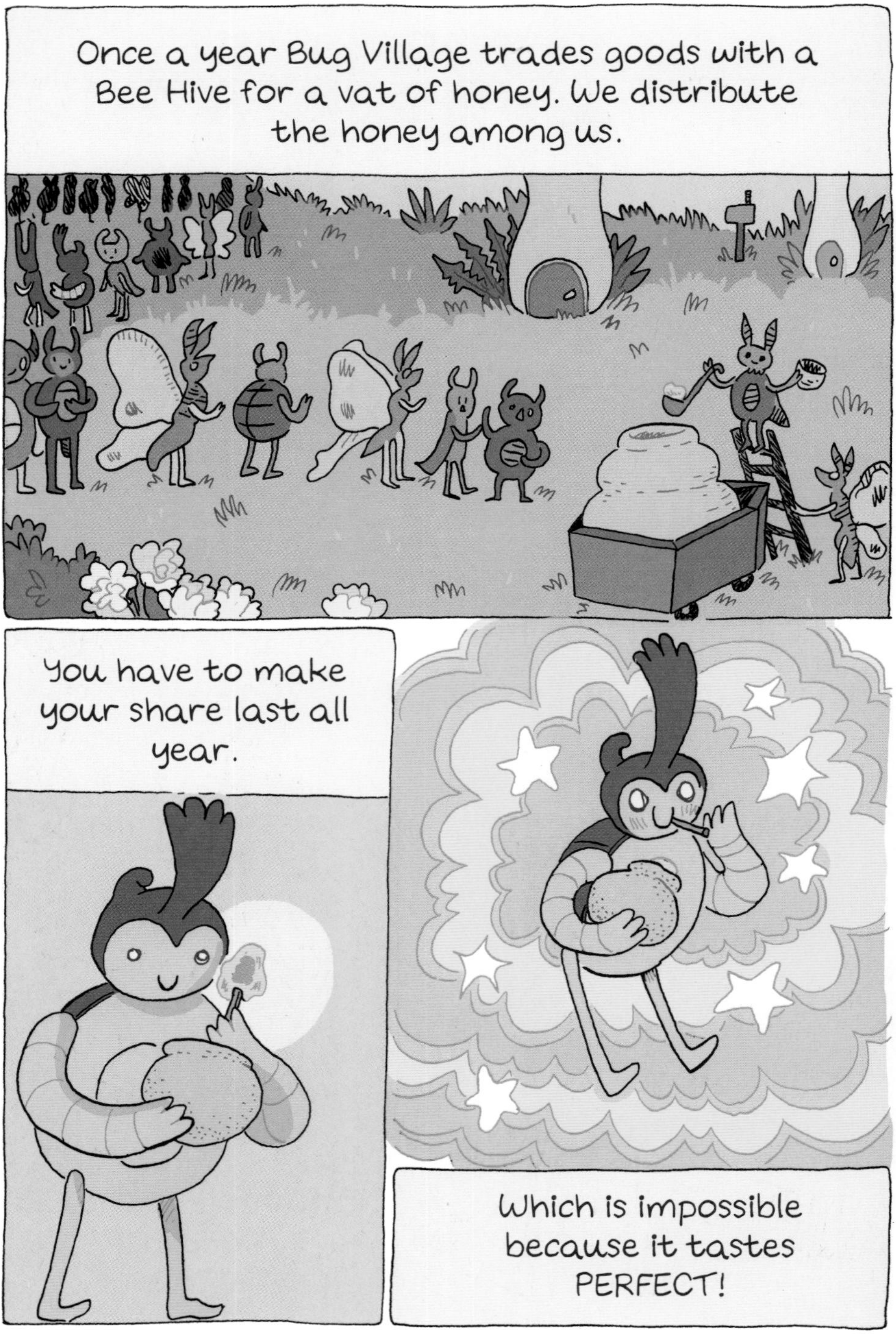
Once a year Bug Village trades goods with a Bee Hive for a vat of honey. We distribute the honey among us.
You have to make your share last all year.
Which is impossible because it tastes PERFECT!

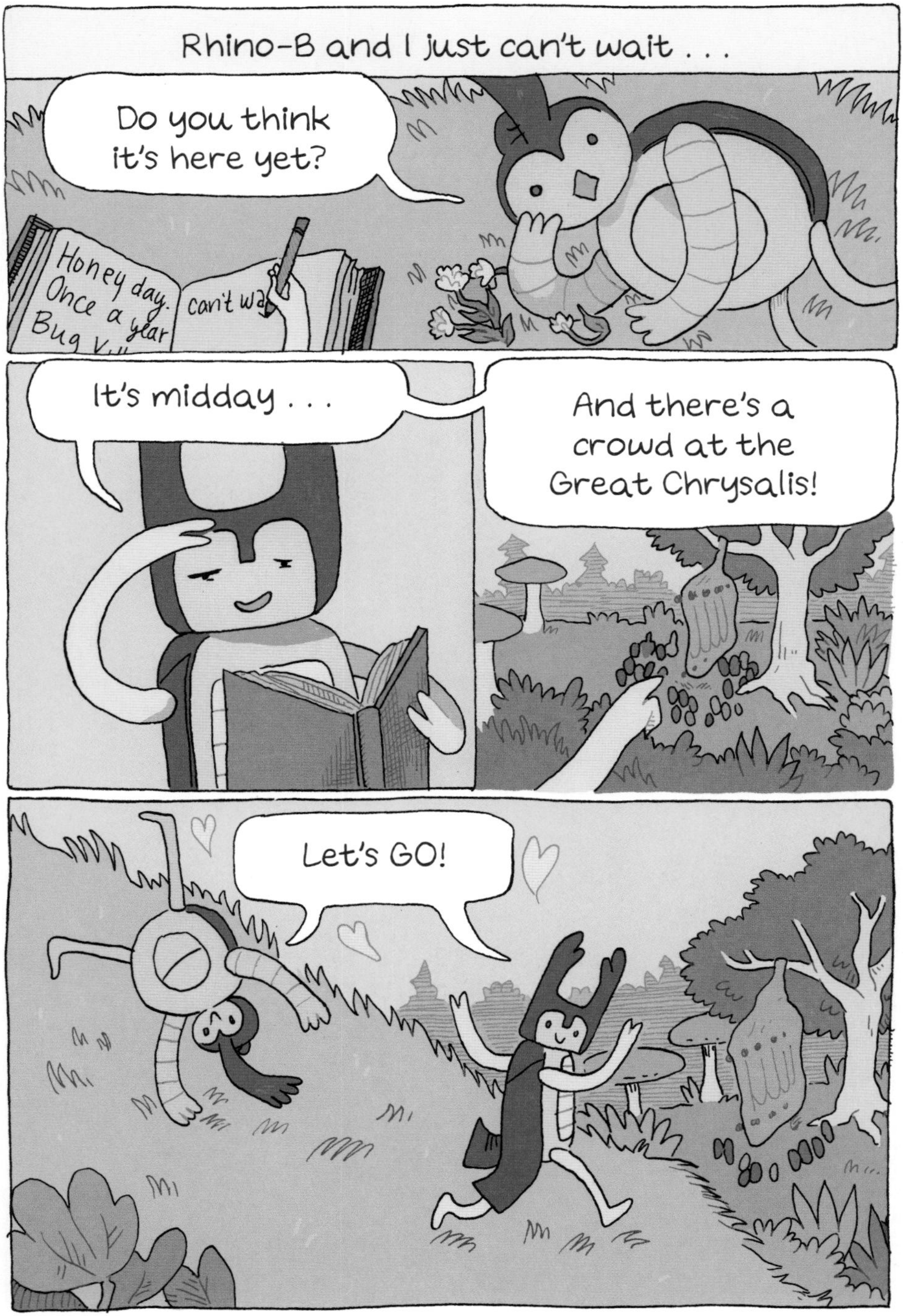
Rhino-B and I just can't wait . . .
Do you think it's here yet?
Honey day. Once a year
It's midday . . .
And there's a crowd at the Great Chrysalis!
Let's GO!

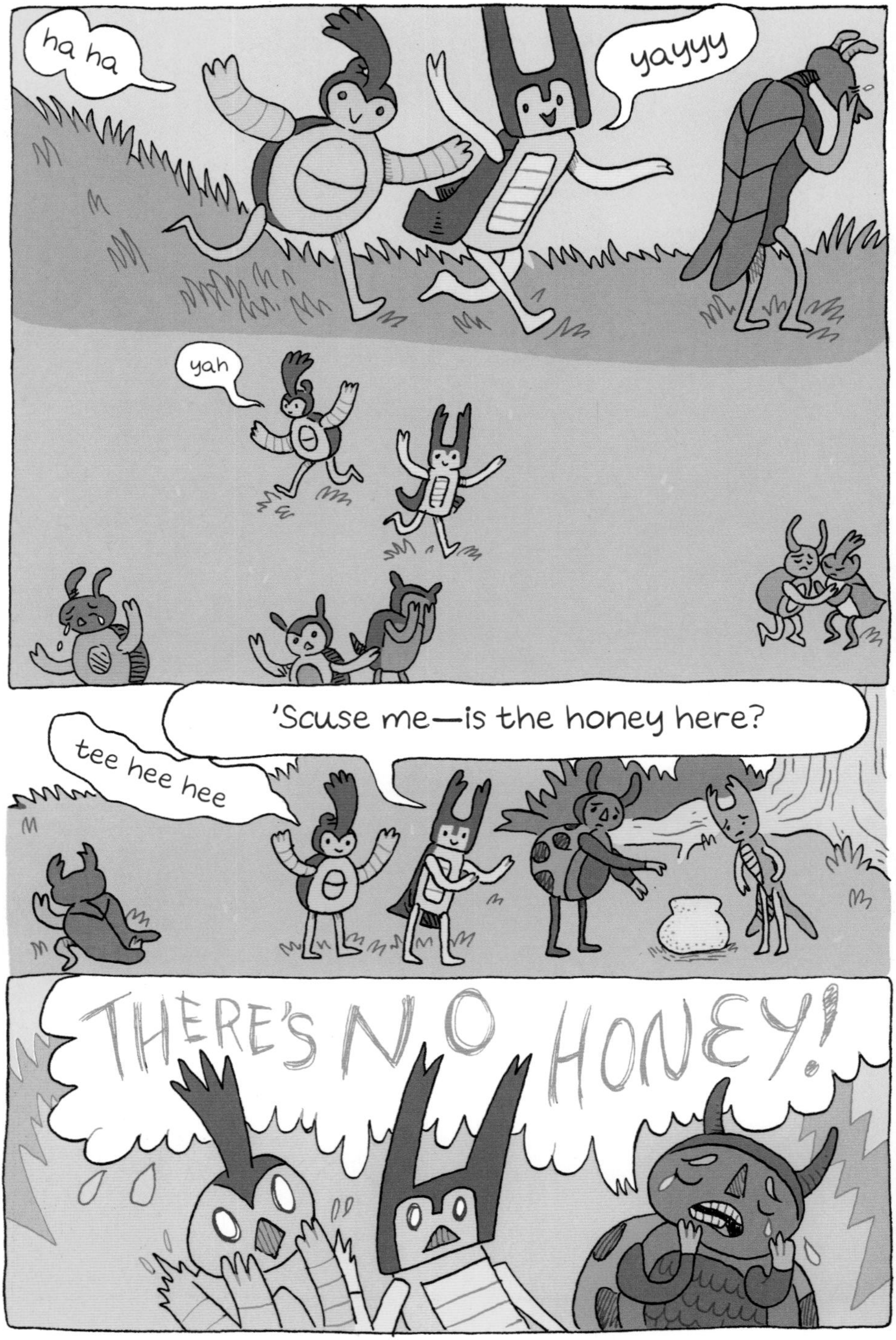
ha ha
yayyy
yah
'Scuse me—is the honey here?
tee hee hee
THERE'S NO HONEY!

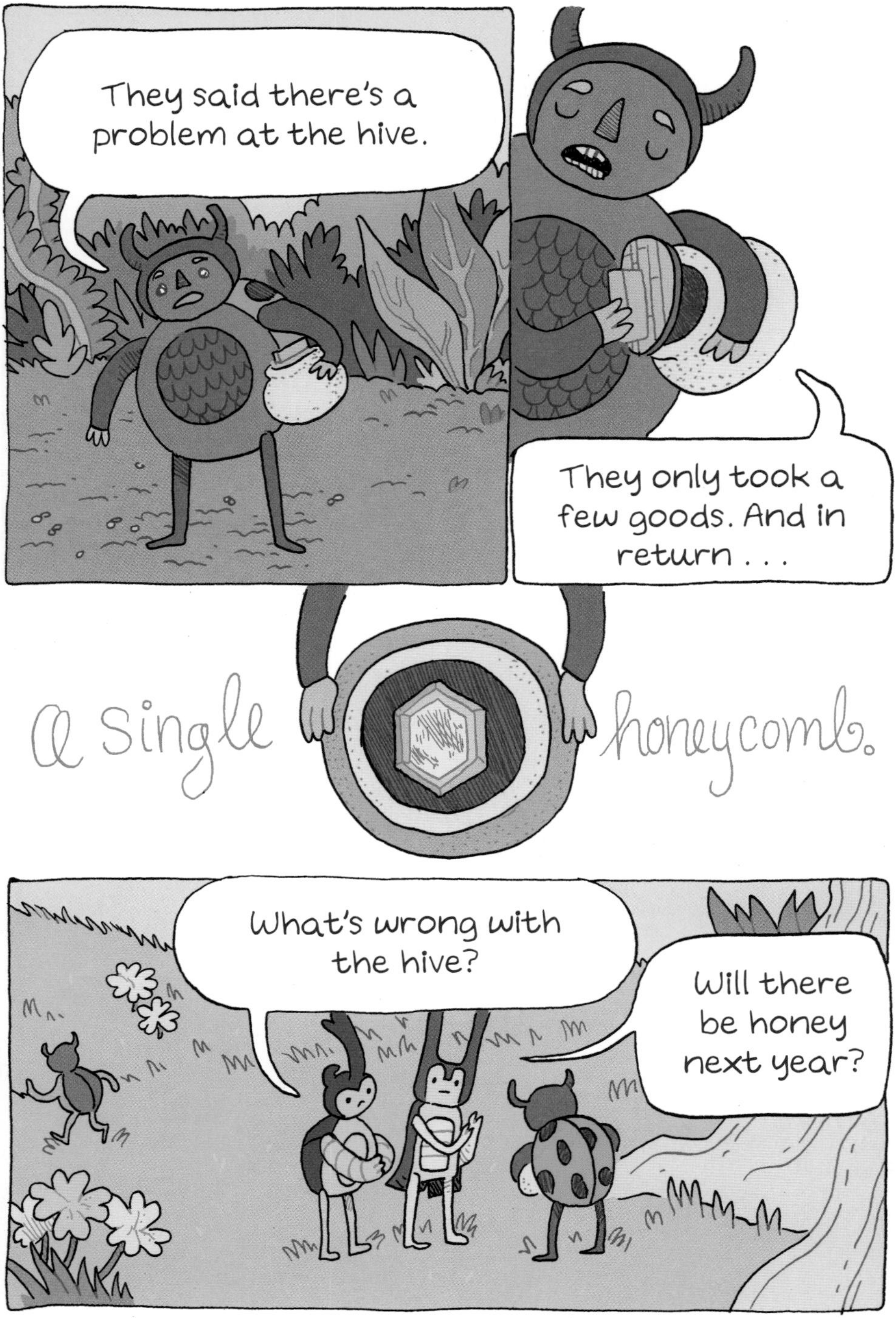
They said there's a problem at the hive.
They only took a few goods. And in return . . .
a single honeycomb.
What's wrong with the hive?
Will there be honey next year?

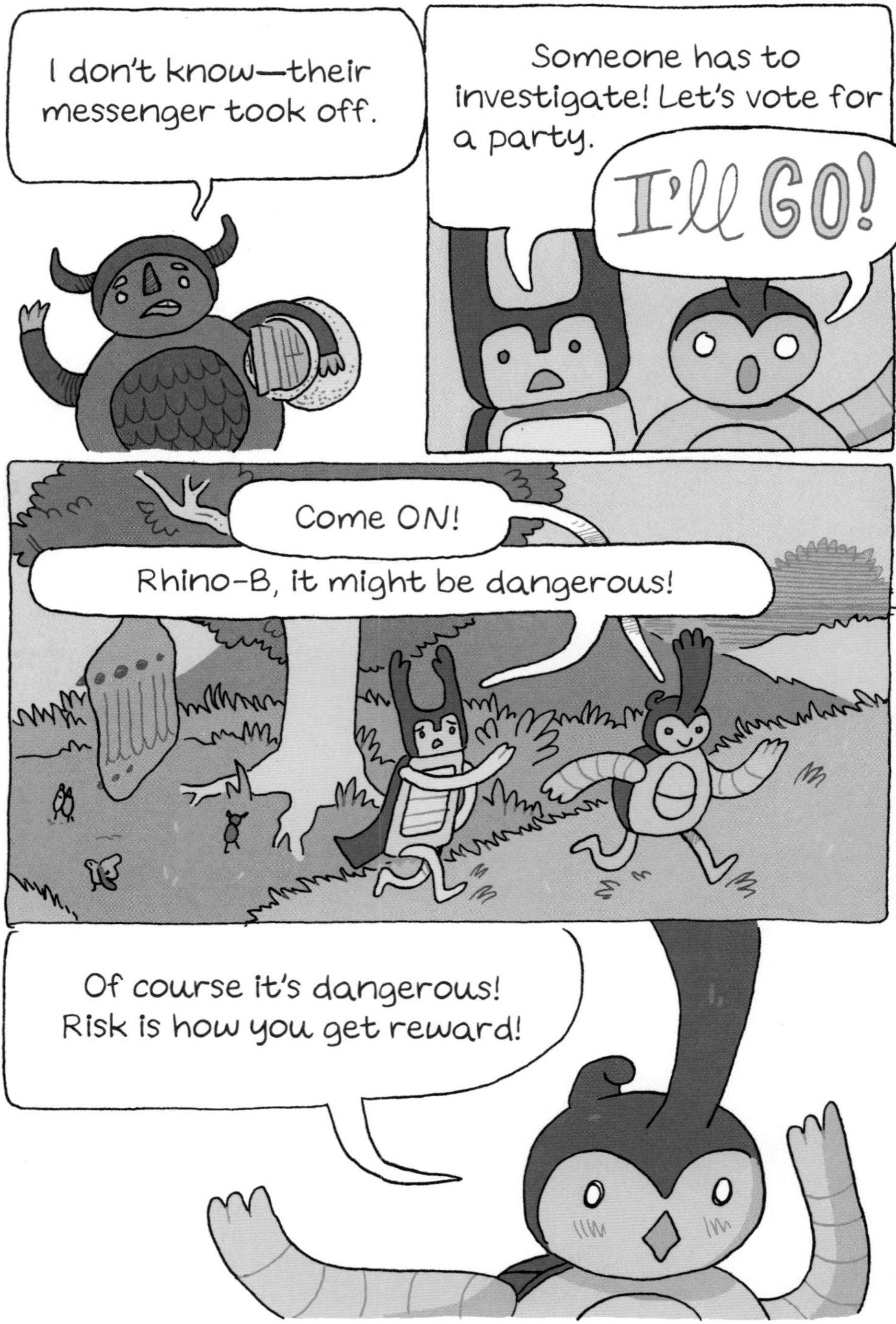
I don't know—their messenger took off.
Someone has to investigate! Let's vote for a party.
I'LL GO!
Come ON!
Rhino-B, it might be dangerous!
Of course it's dangerous! Risk is how you get reward!

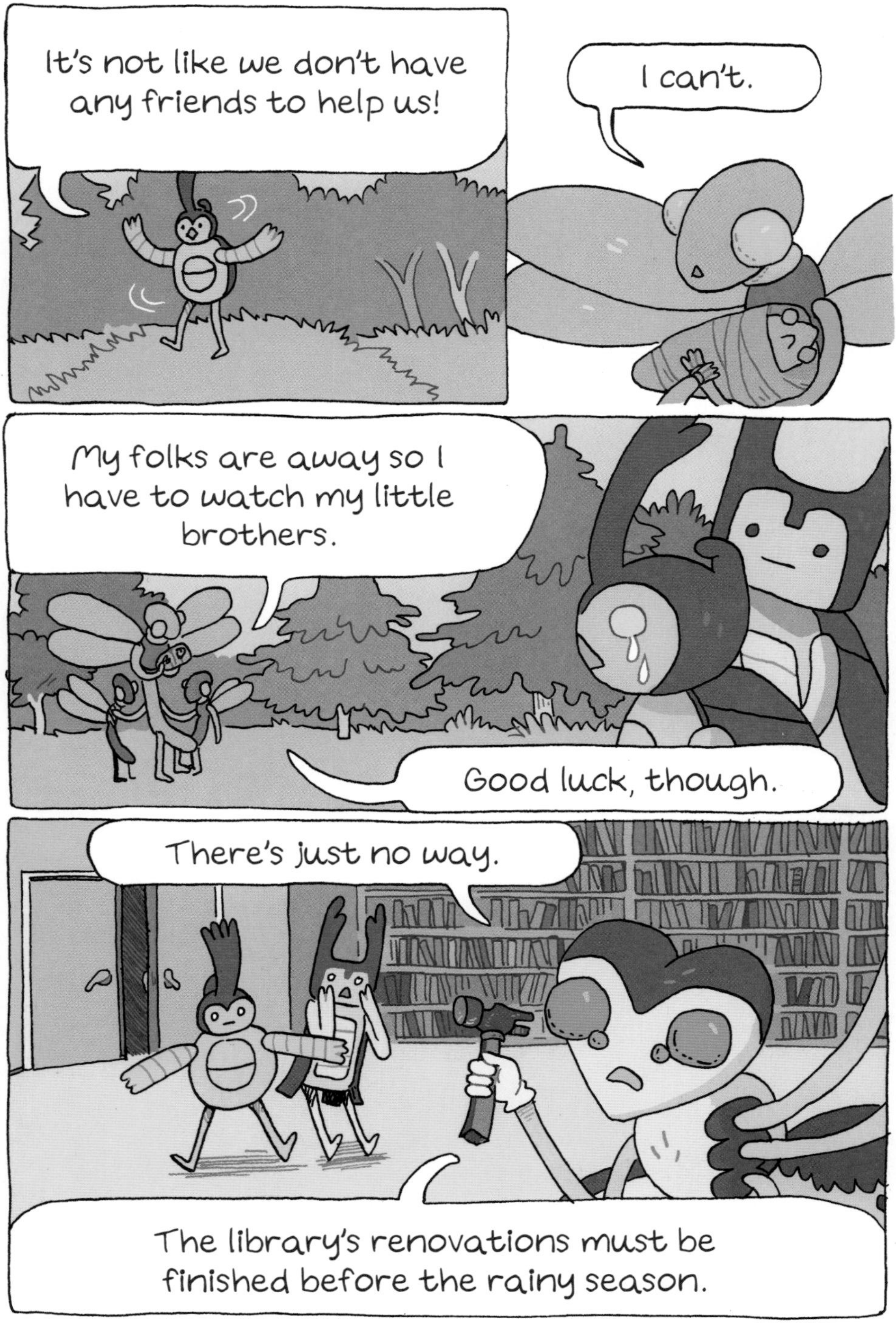
It's not like we don't have any friends to help us!
I can't.
My folks are away so I have to watch my little brothers.
Good luck, though.
There's just no way.
The library's renovations must be finished before the rainy season.

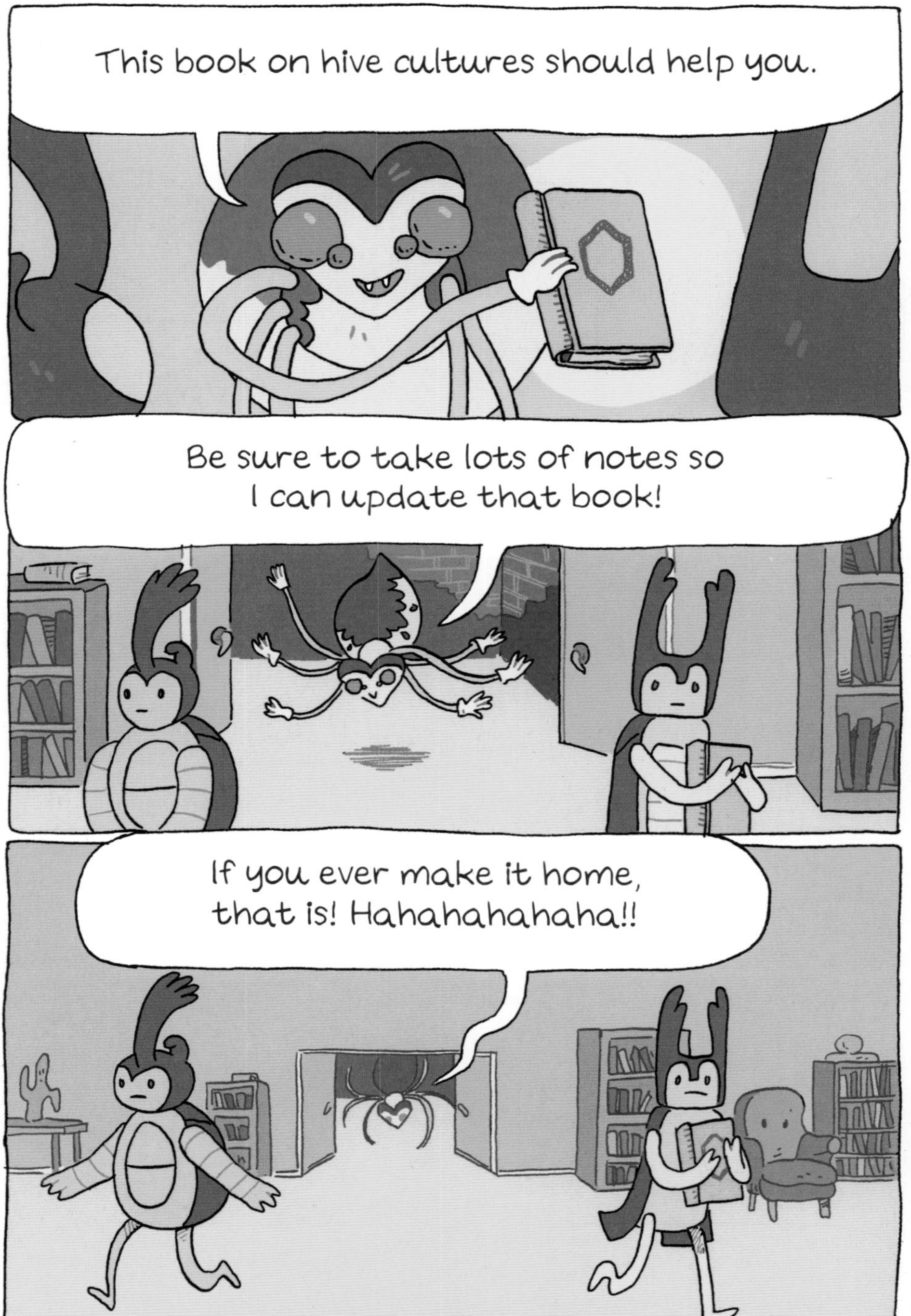
This book on hive cultures should help you.
Be sure to take lots of notes so I can update that book!
If you ever make it home, that is! Hahahahahaha!!

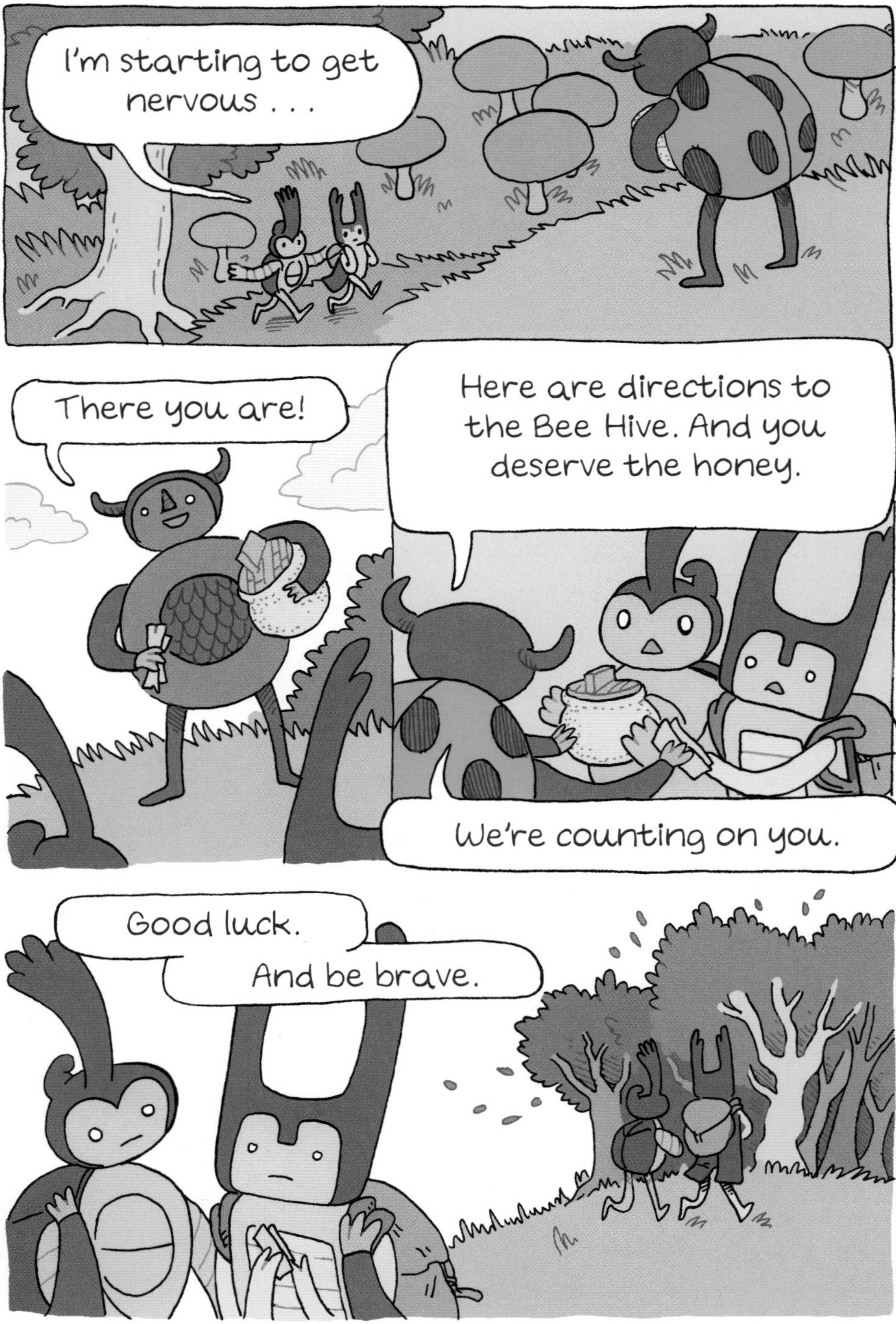
I'm starting to get nervous . . .
There you are!
Here are directions to the Bee Hive. And you deserve the honey.
We're counting on you.
Good luck.
And be brave.

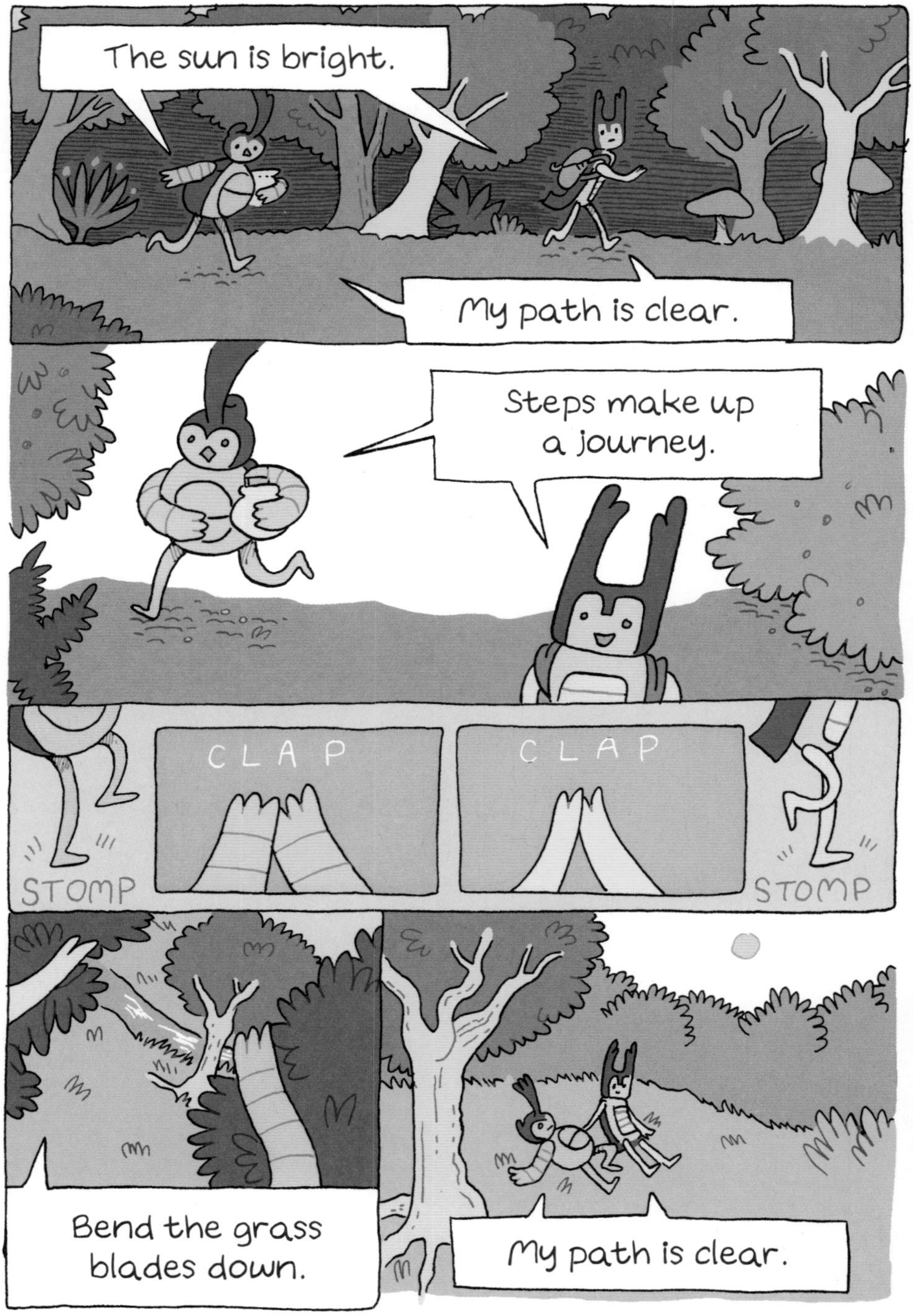
The sun is bright.
My path is clear.
Steps make up a journey.
STOMP
CLAP
CLAP
STOMP
Bend the grass blades down.
My path is clear.

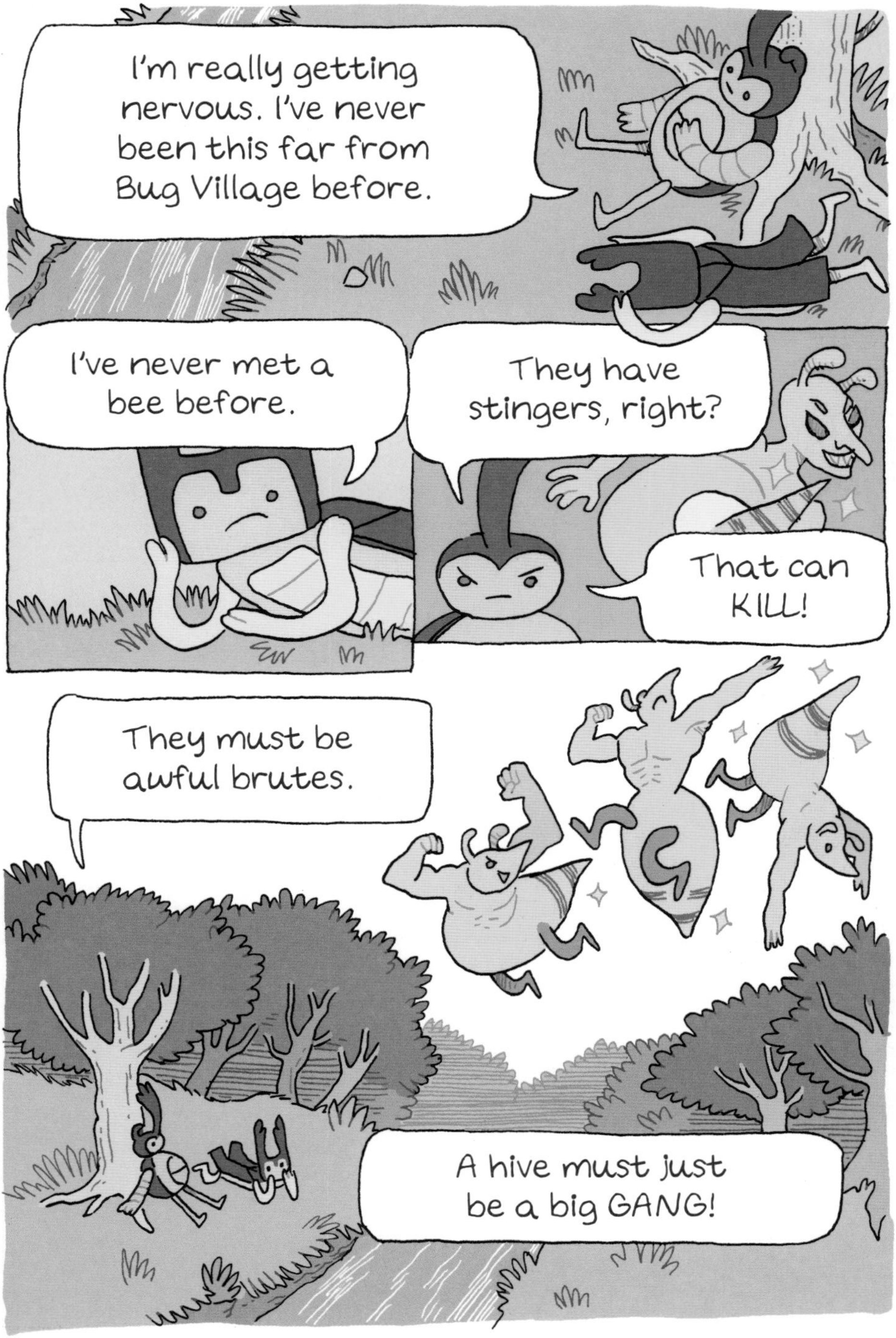

I'm really getting nervous. I've never been this far from Bug Village before.
I've never met a bee before.
They have stingers, right?
That can KILL!
They must be awful brutes.
A hive must just be a big GANG!

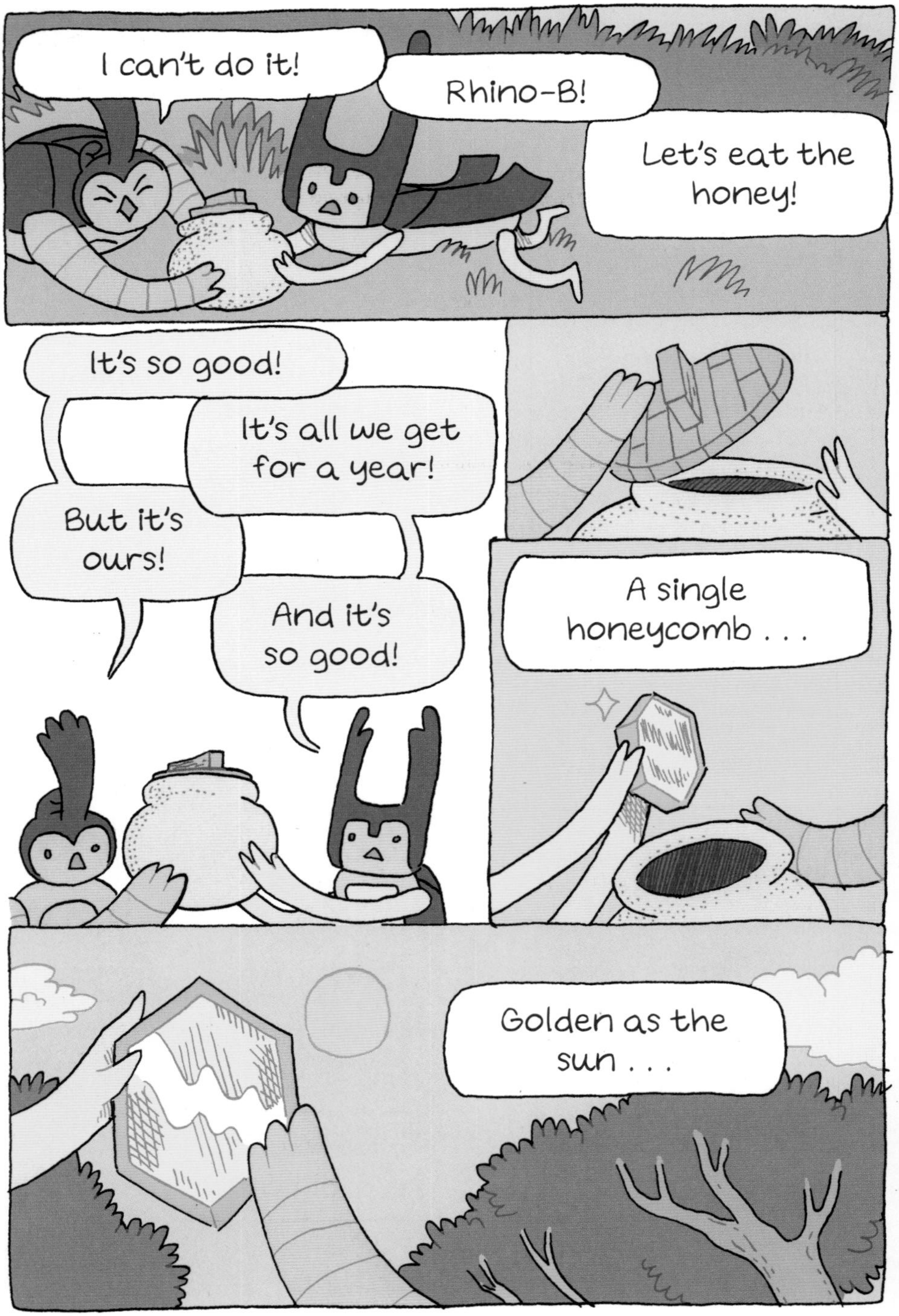
I can't do it!
Rhino-B!
Let's eat the honey!
It's so good!
It's all we get for a year!
But it's ours!
And it's so good!
A single honeycomb . . .
Golden as the sun . . .

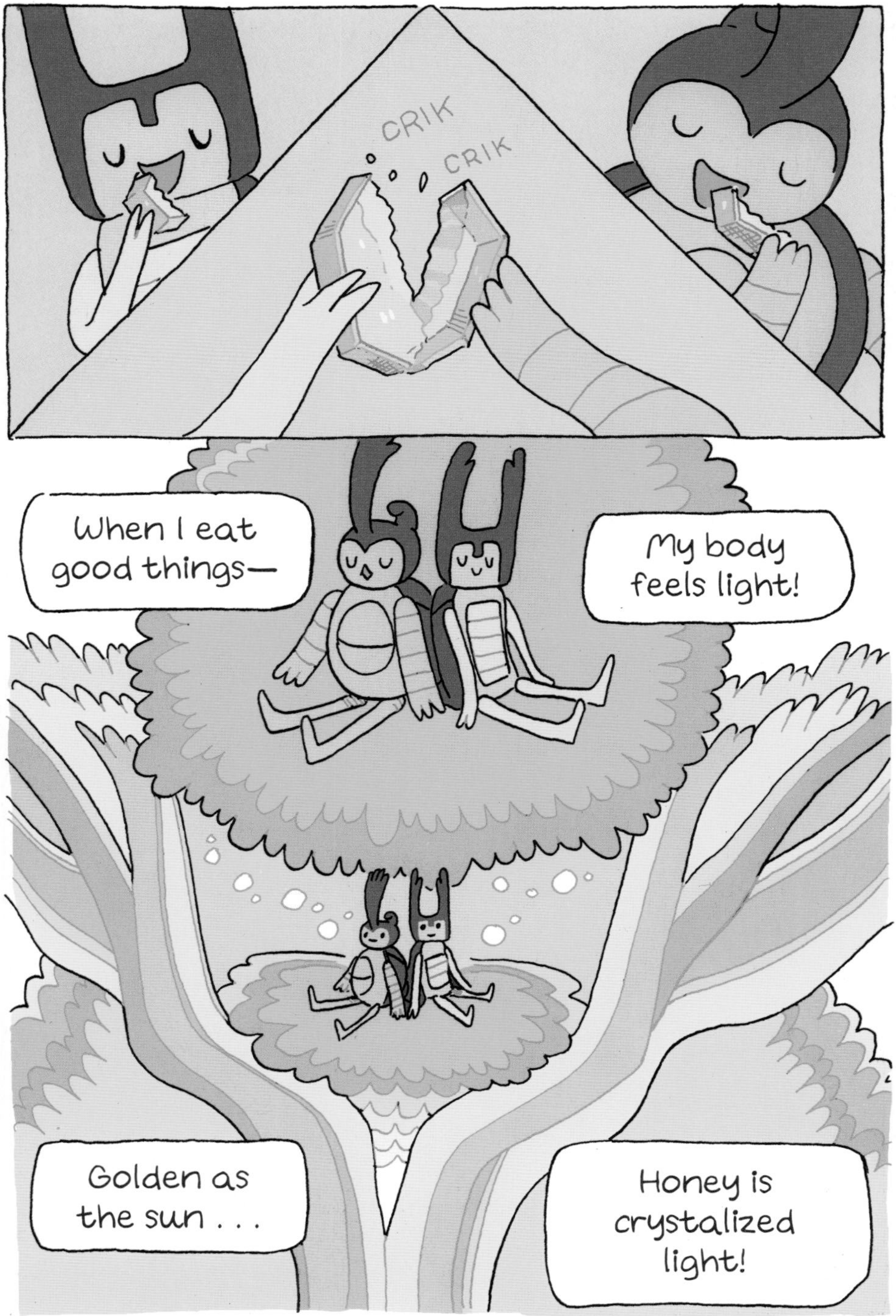
CRIK
CRIK
When I eat good things—
My body feels light!
Golden as the sun . . .
Honey is crystalized light!

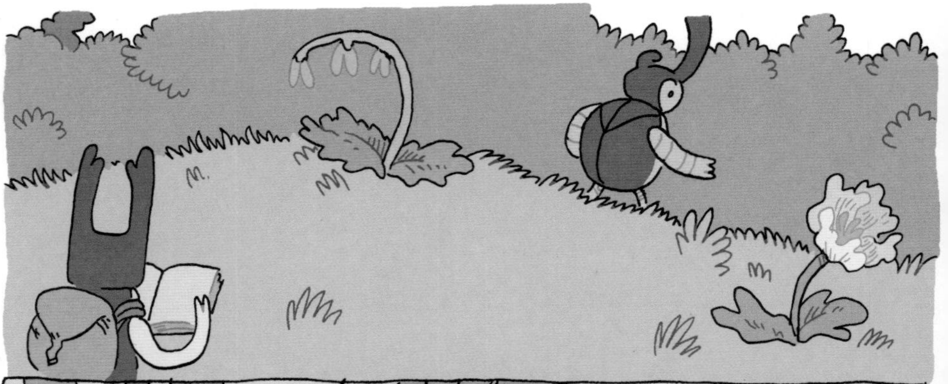

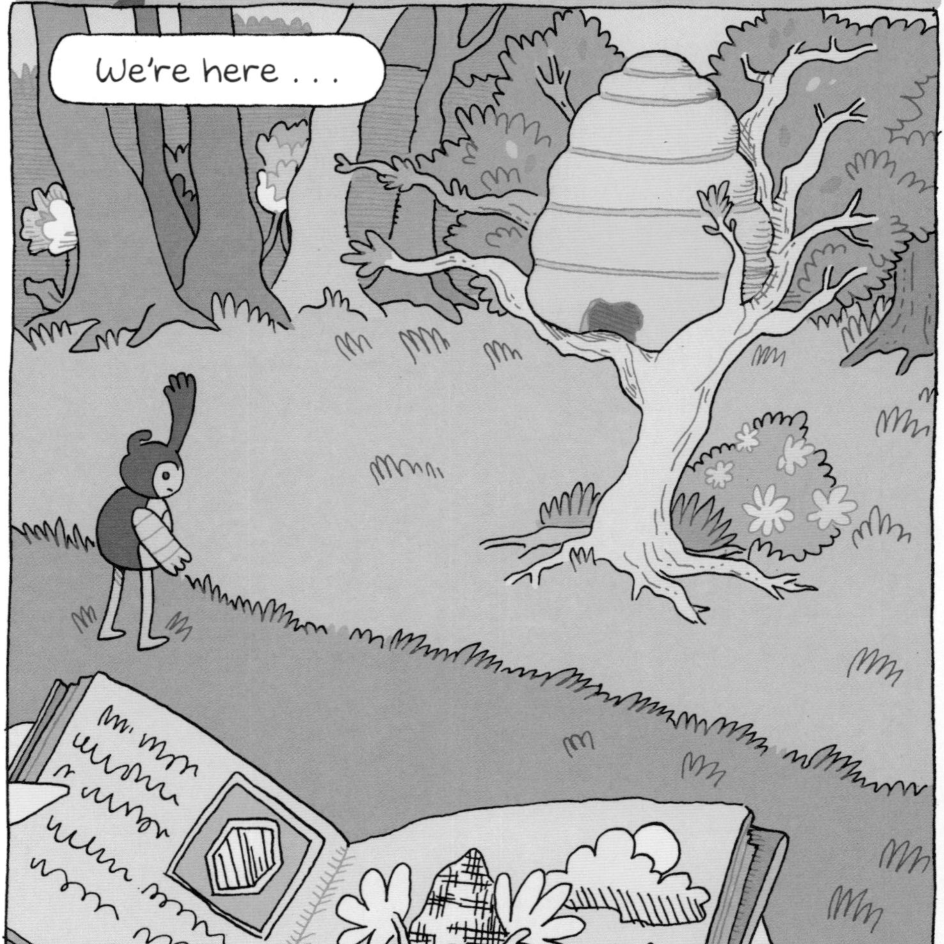
We're here . . .

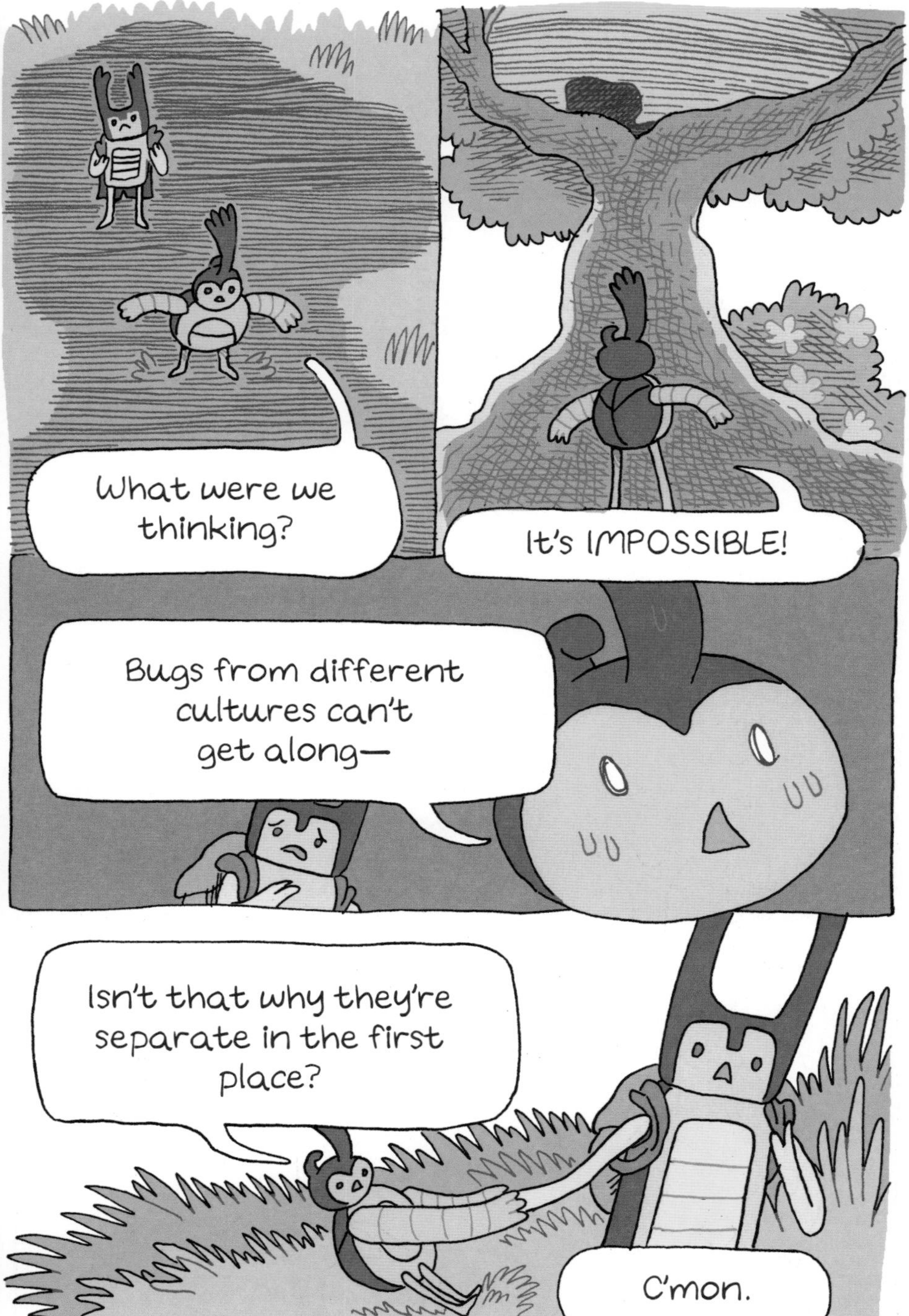
What were we thinking?
It's IMPOSSIBLE!
Bugs from different cultures can't get along—
Isn't that why they're separate in the first place?
C'mon.

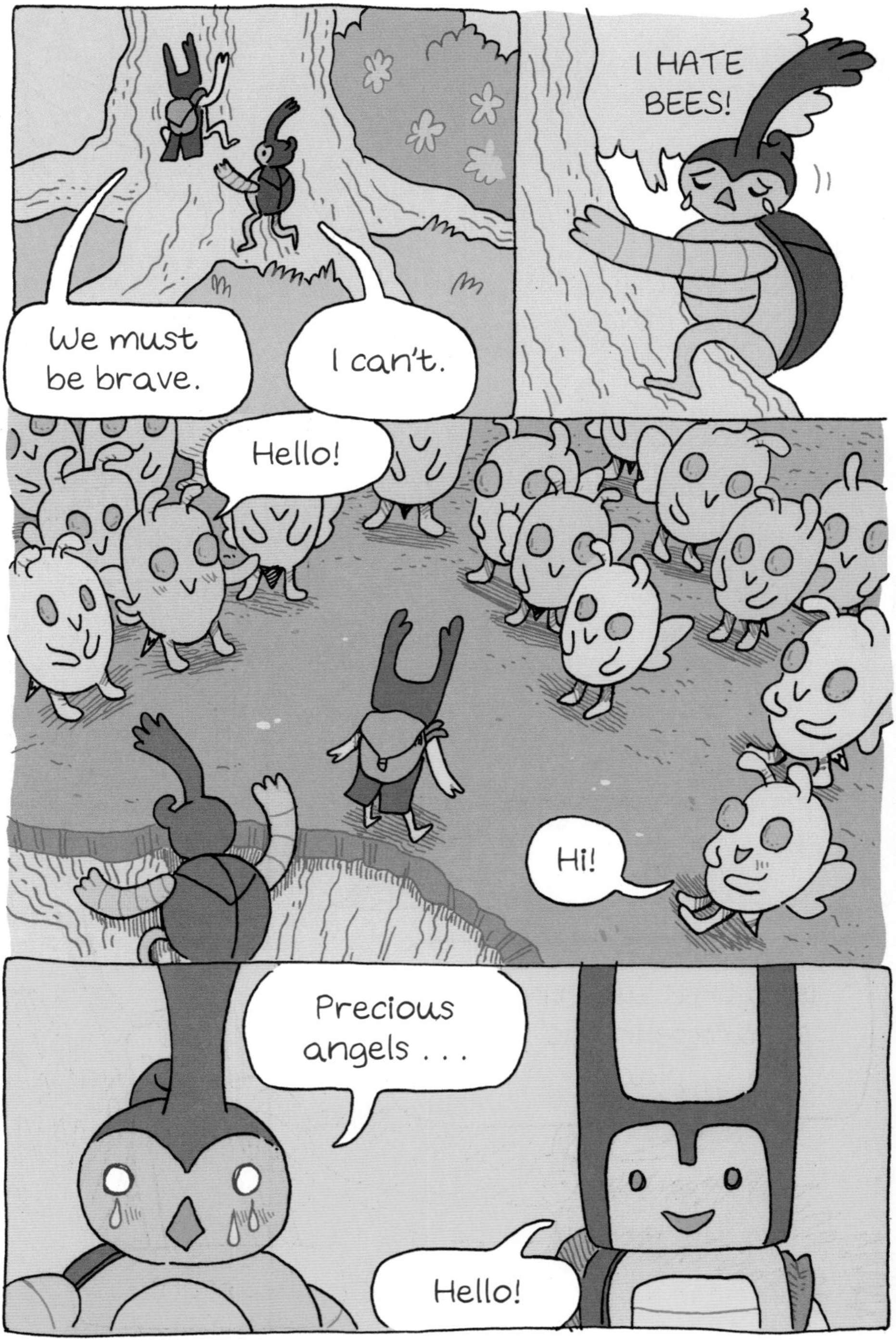
We must be brave.
I can't.
I HATE BEES!
Hello!
Hi!
Precious angels . . .
Hello!

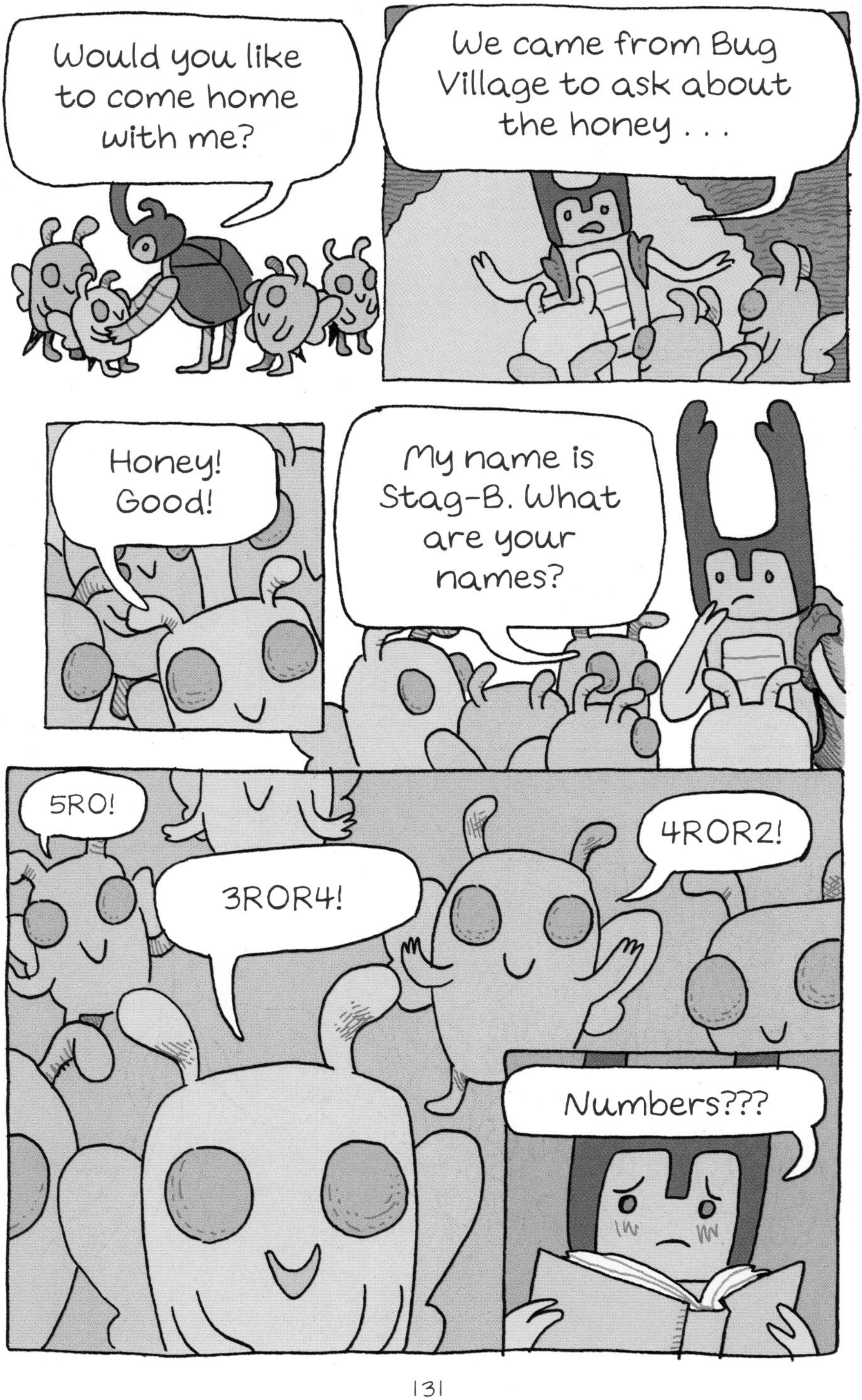
Would you like to come home with me?
We came from Bug Village to ask about the honey . . .
Honey! Good!
My name is Stag-B. What are your names?
5RO!
3ROR4!
4ROR2!
Numbers???

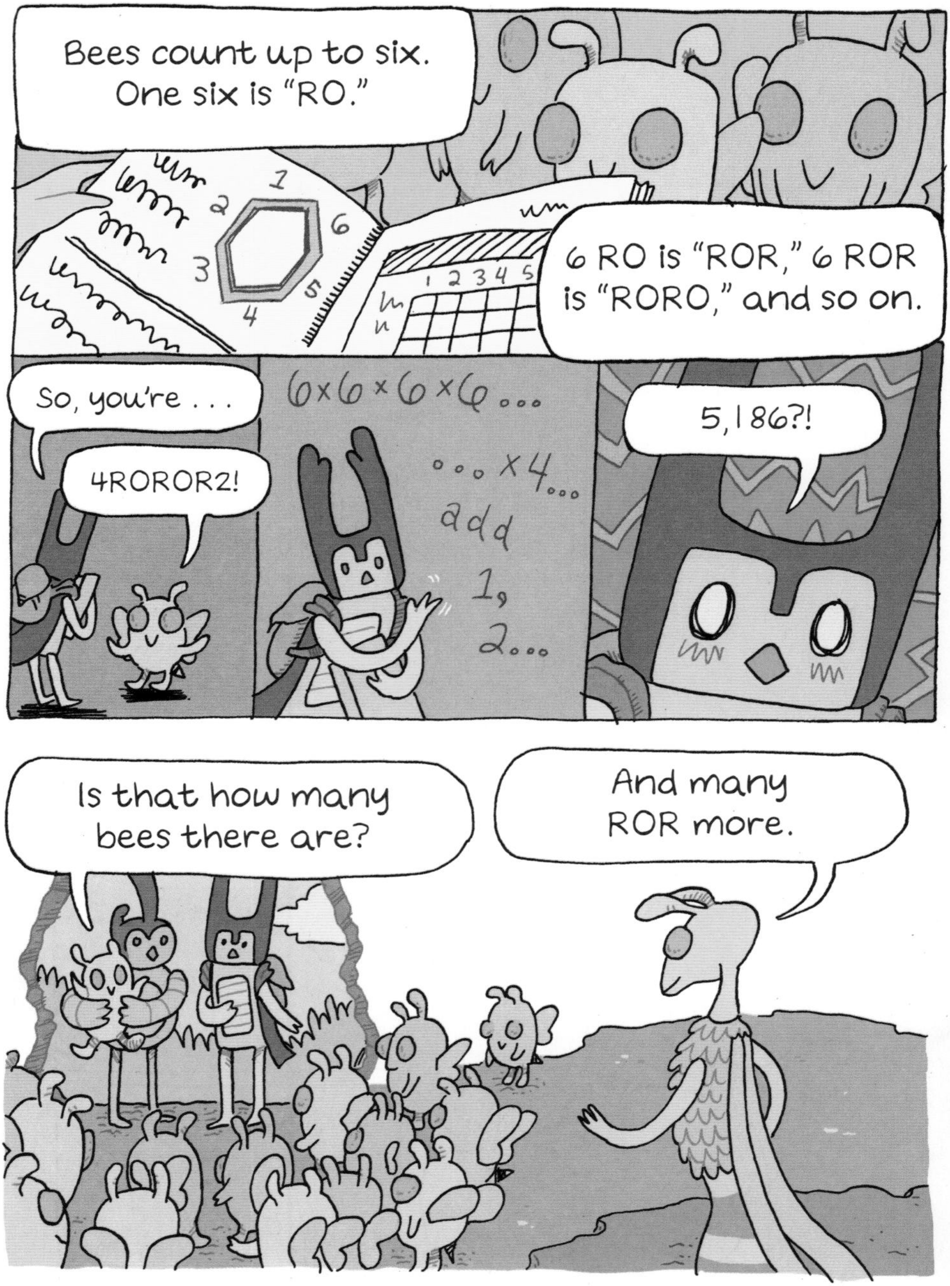
Bees count up to six. One six is "RO."
1
2
3
4
5
6
1 2 3 4 5
6 RO is "ROR," 6 ROR is "RORO," and so on.
So, you're . . .
4ROROR2!
6×6×6×6...
...×4...
add
1,
2...
5,186?!
Is that how many bees there are?
And many ROR more.

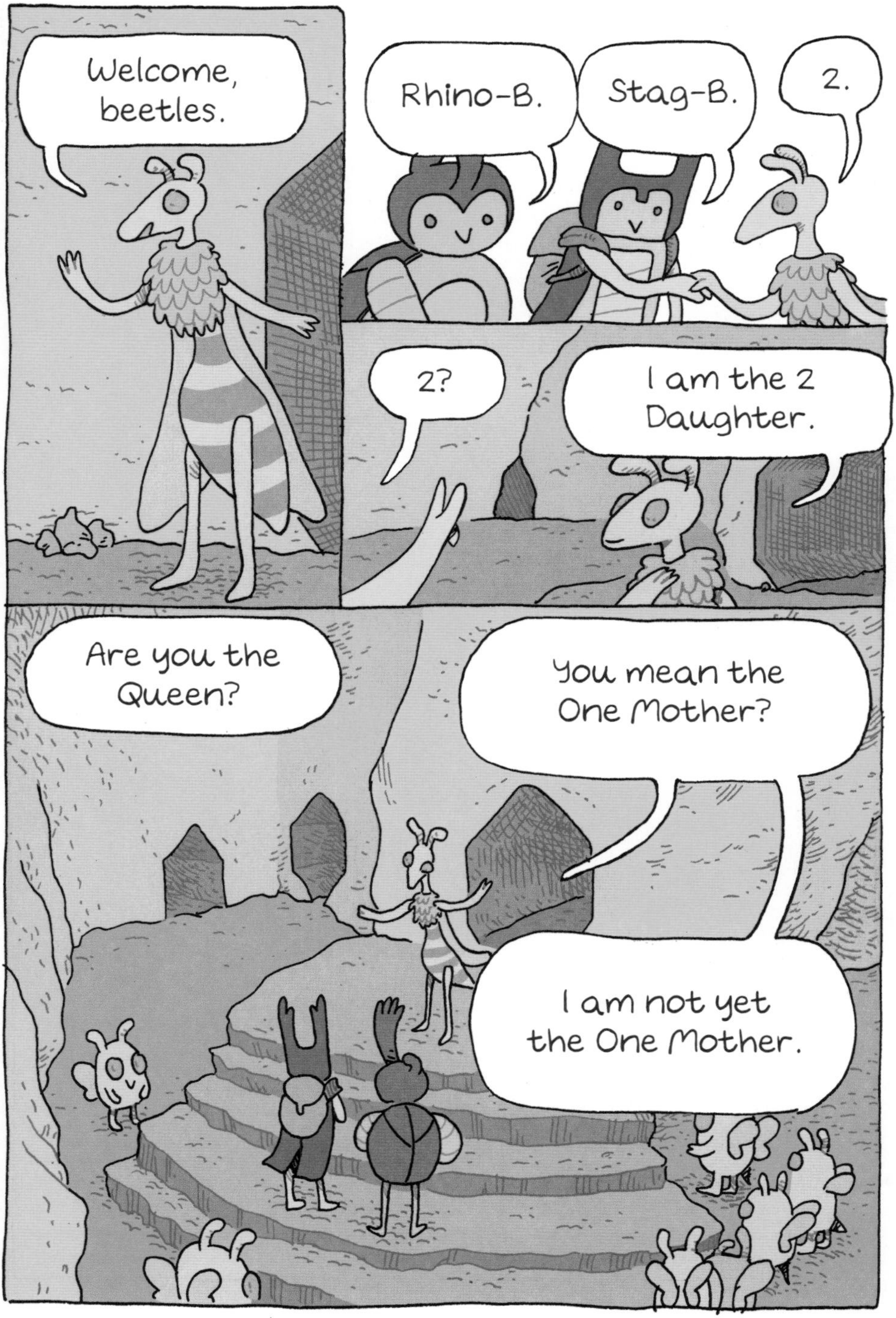
Welcome, beetles.
Rhino-B.
Stag-B.
2.
2?
I am the 2 Daughter.
Are you the Queen?
You mean the One Mother?
I am not yet the One Mother.

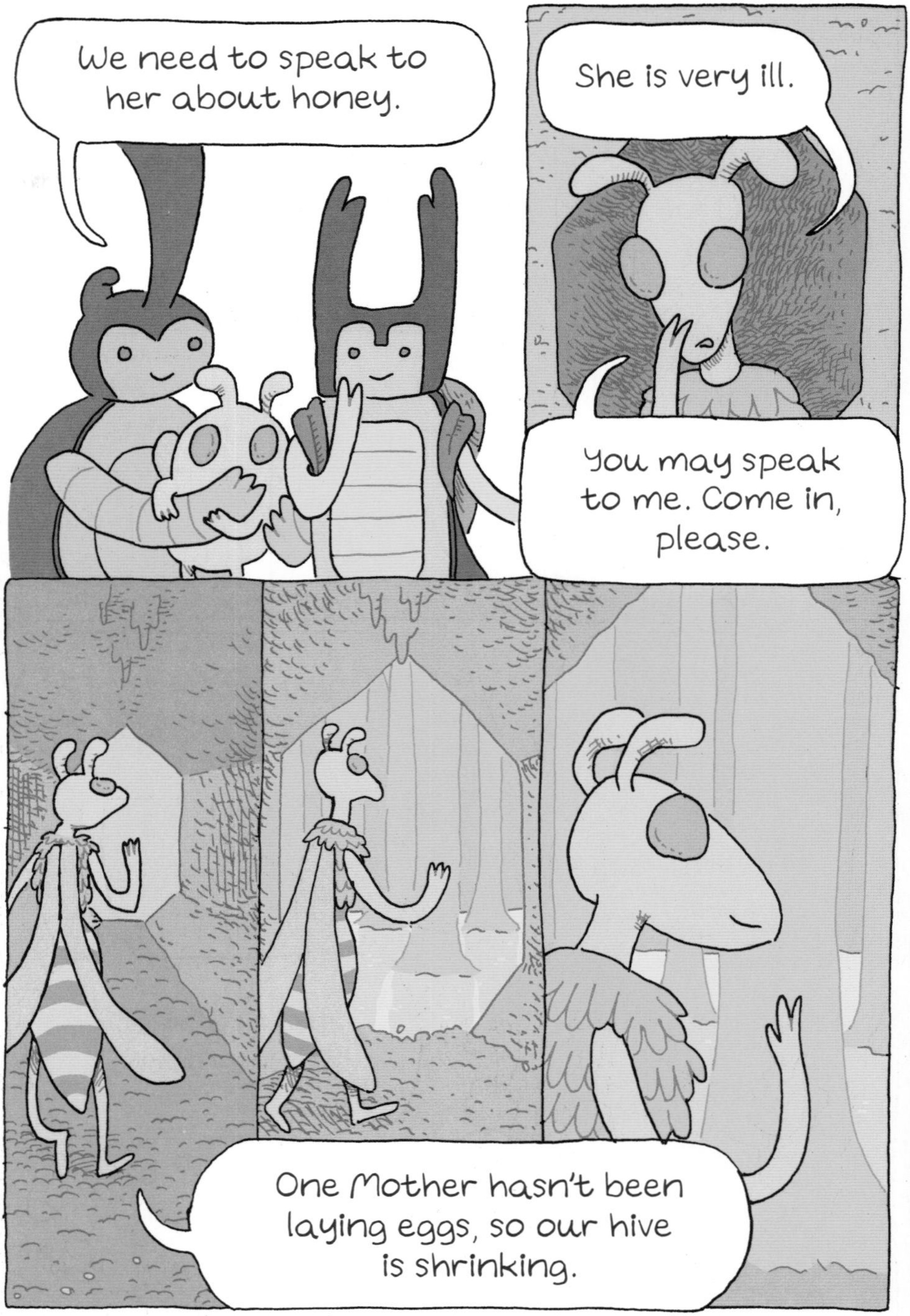
We need to speak to her about honey.
She is very ill.
You may speak to me. Come in, please.
One Mother hasn't been laying eggs, so our hive is shrinking.

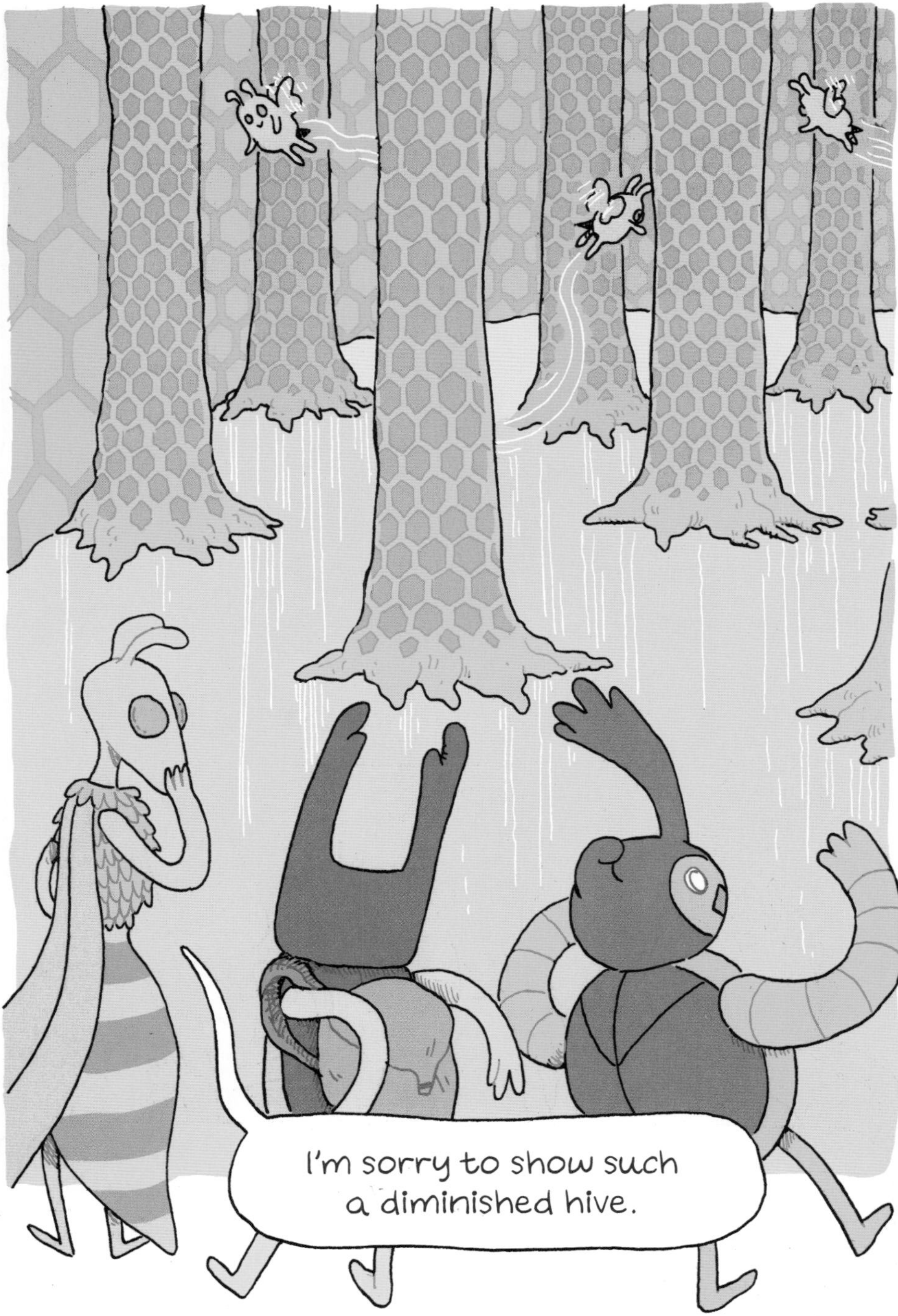
I'm sorry to show such a diminished hive.

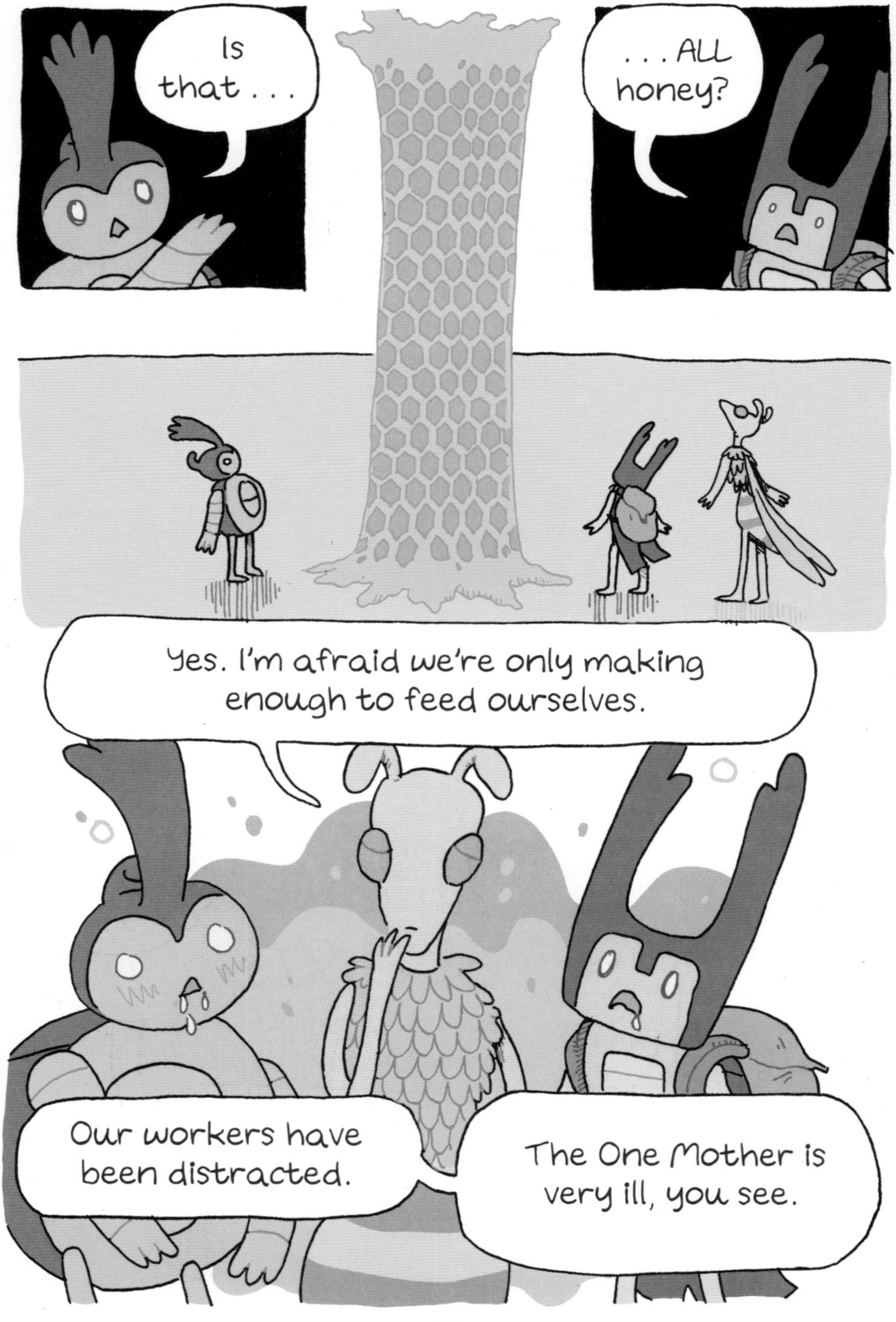
Is that . . .
. . . ALL honey?
Yes. I'm afraid we're only making enough to feed ourselves.
Our workers have been distracted.
The One Mother is very ill, you see.

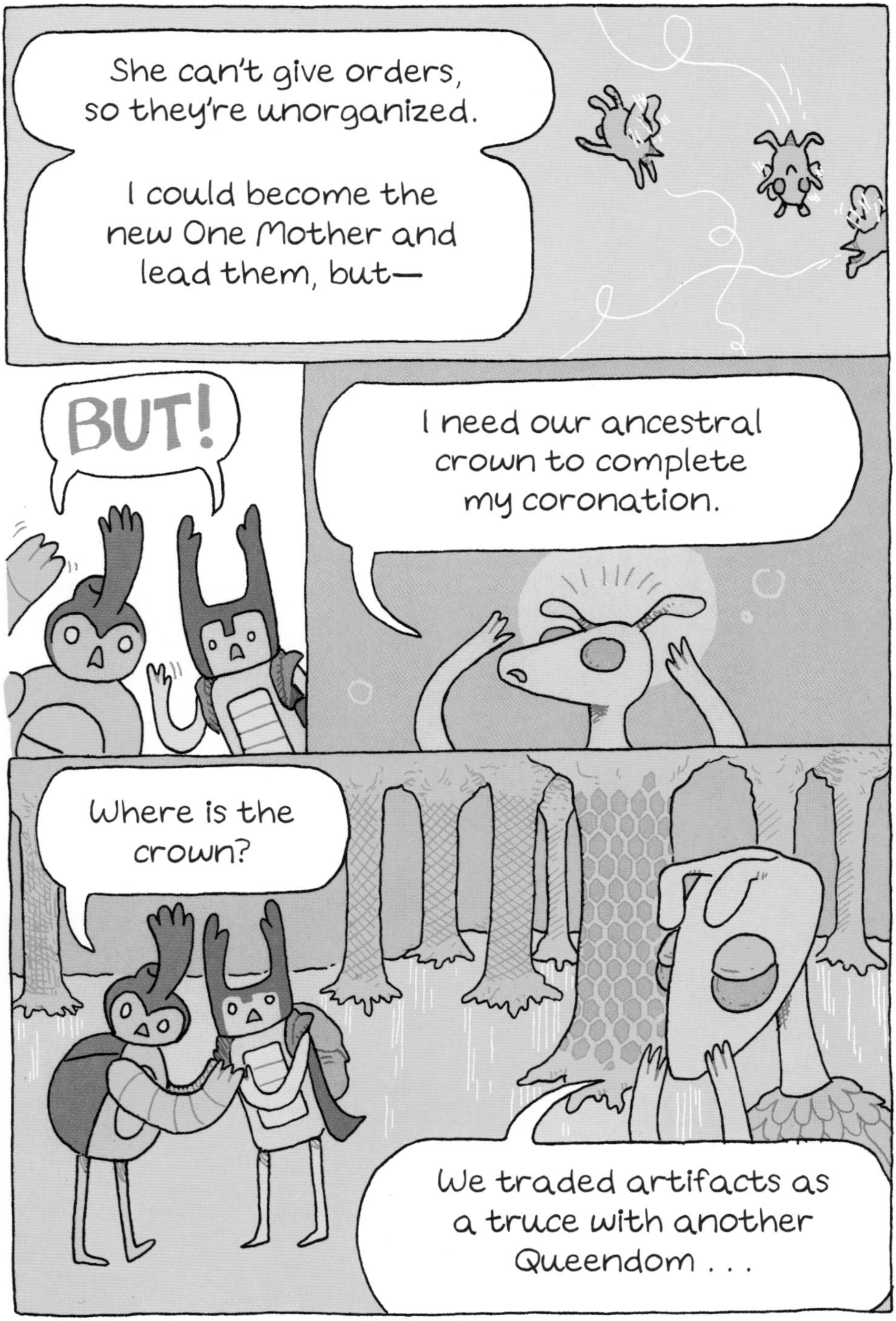
She can't give orders, so they're unorganized.
I could become the new One Mother and lead them, but—
BUT!
I need our ancestral crown to complete my coronation.
Where is the crown?
We traded artifacts as a truce with another Queendom . . .

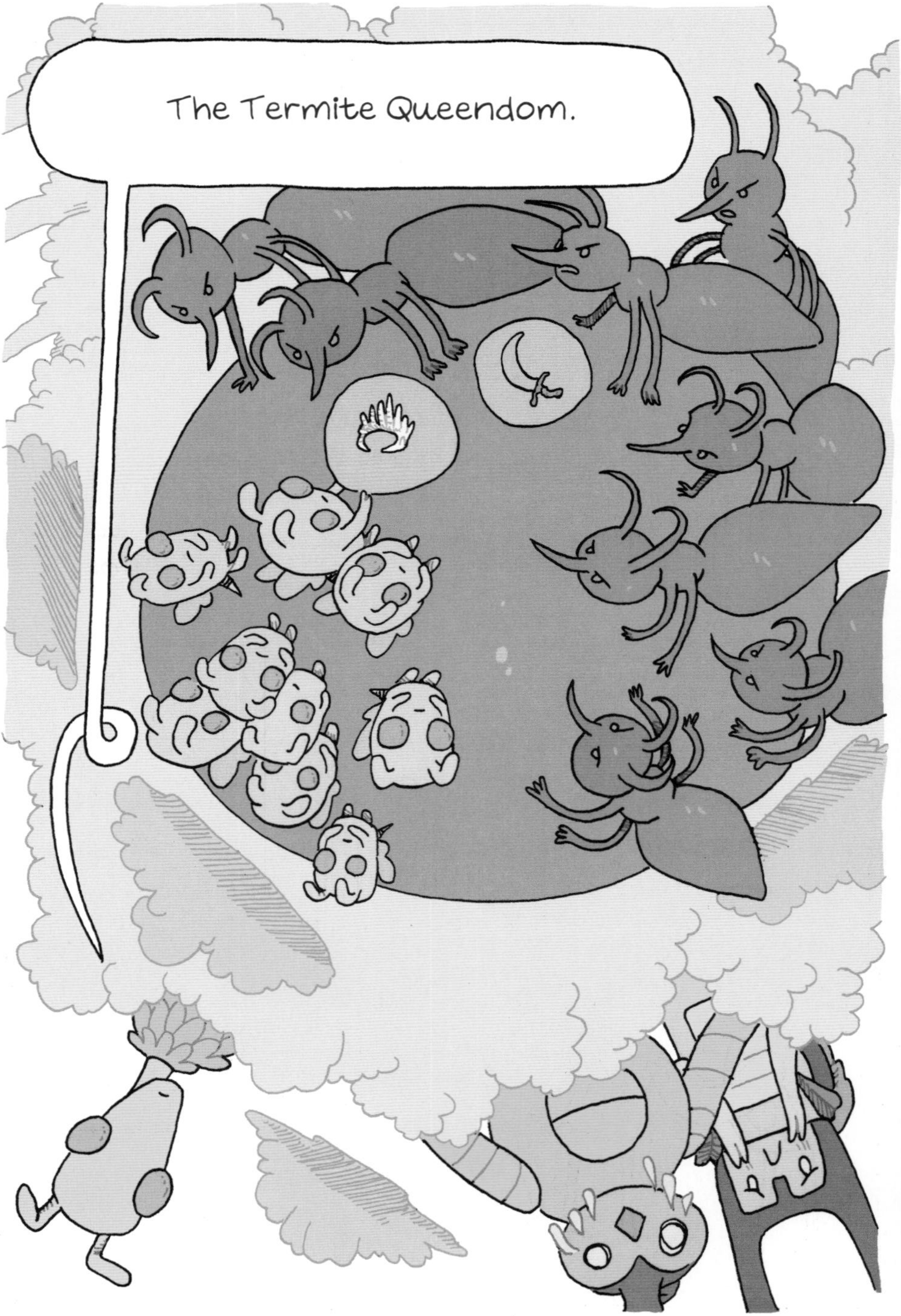
The Termite Queendom.

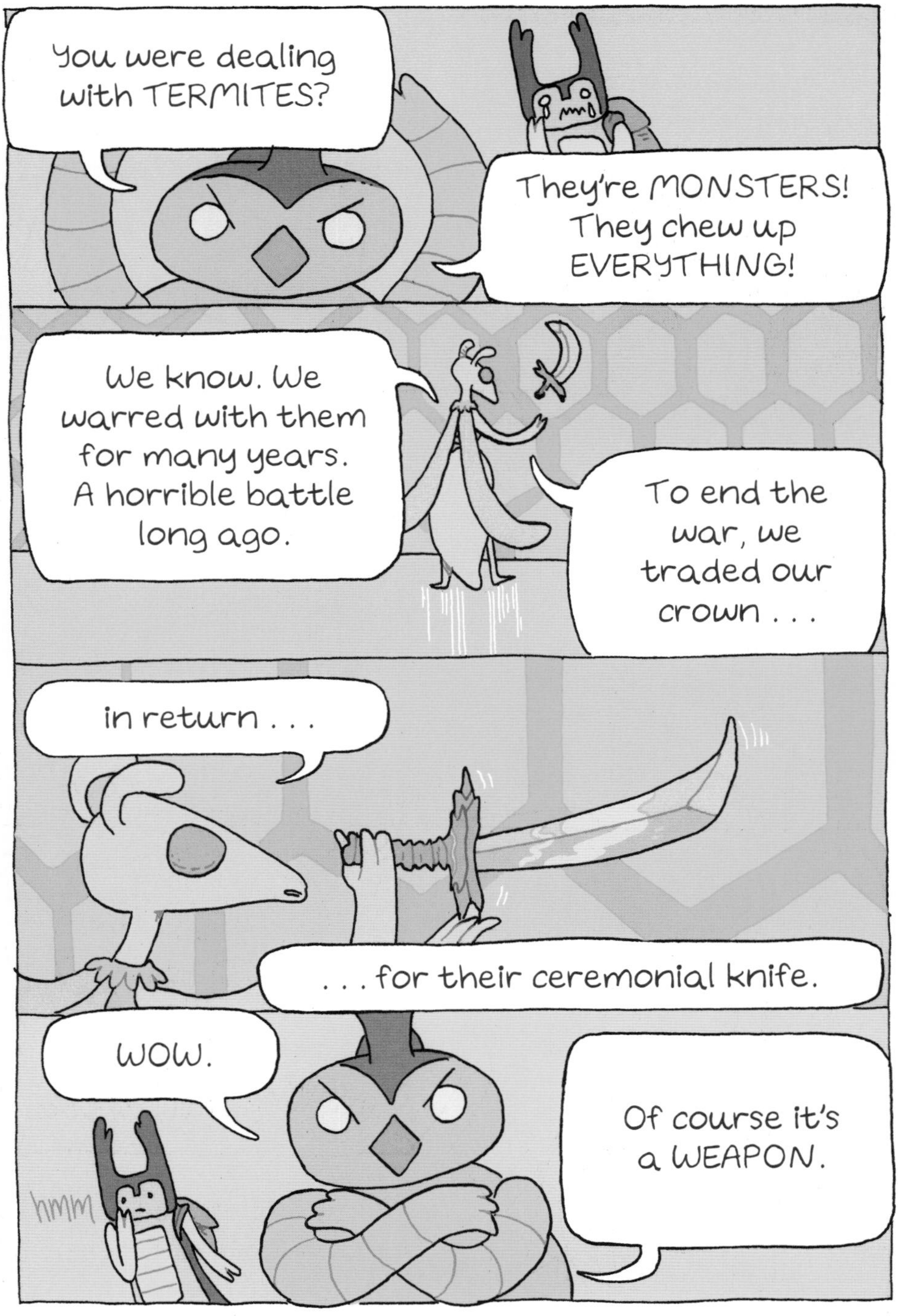
You were dealing with TERMITES?
They're MONSTERS! They chew up EVERYTHING!
We know. We warred with them for many years. A horrible battle long ago.
To end the war, we traded our crown . . .
in return . . .
. . . for their ceremonial knife.
WOW.
Of course it's a WEAPON.
hmm

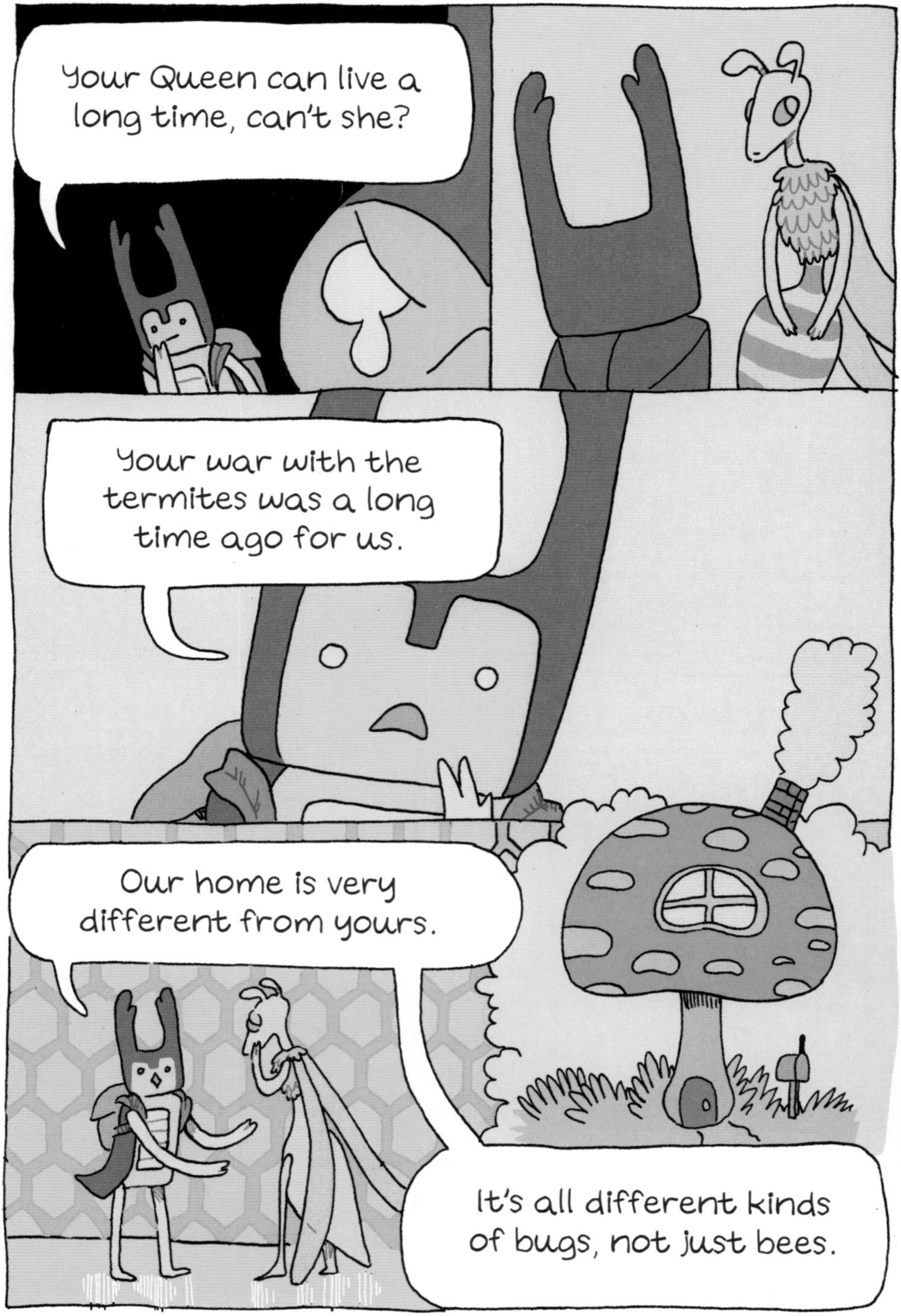
Your Queen can live a long time, can't she?
Your war with the termites was a long time ago for us.
Our home is very different from yours.
It's all different kinds of bugs, not just bees.

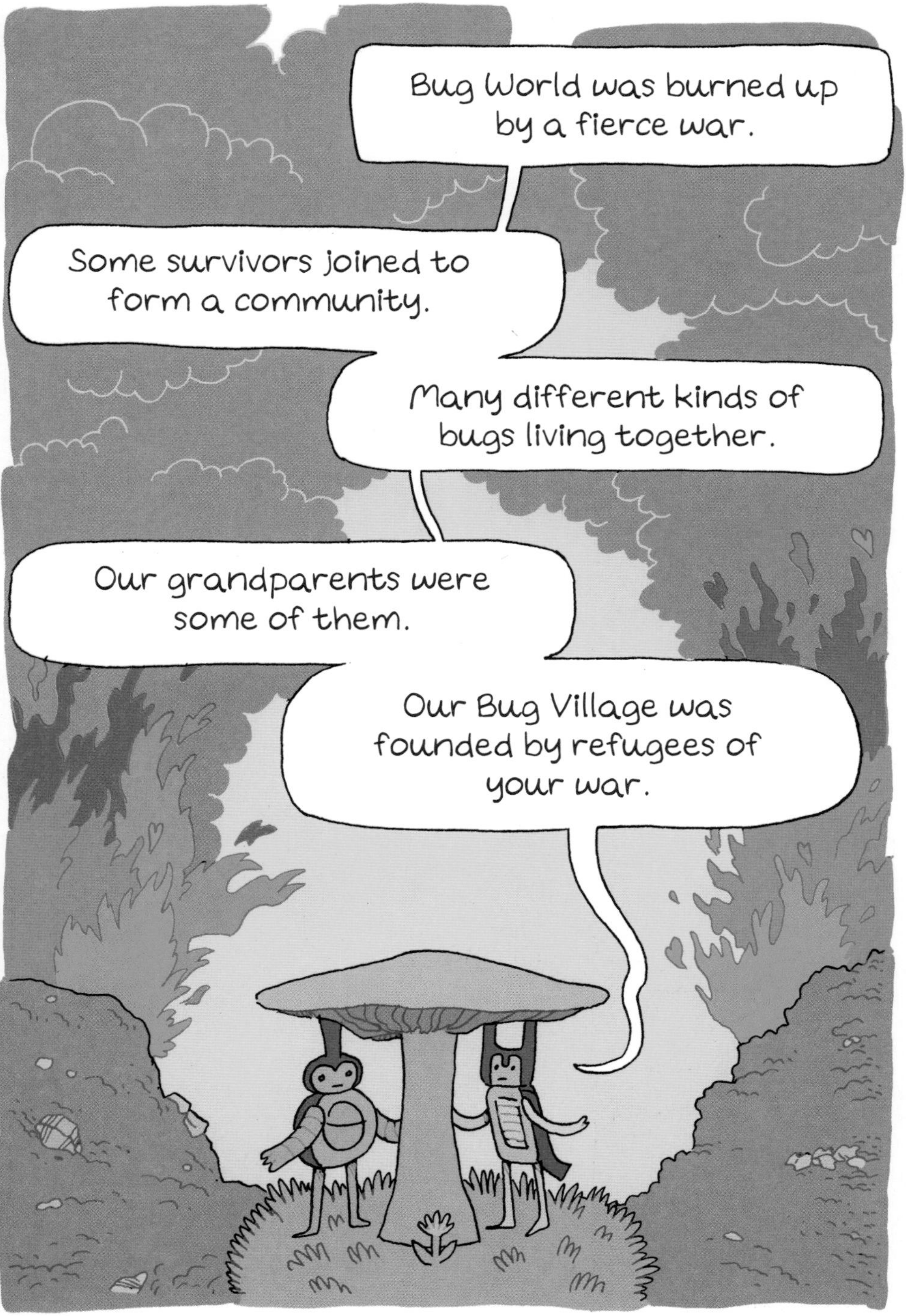
Bug World was burned up by a fierce war.
Some survivors joined to form a community.
Many different kinds of bugs living together.
Our grandparents were some of them.
Our Bug Village was founded by refugees of your war.

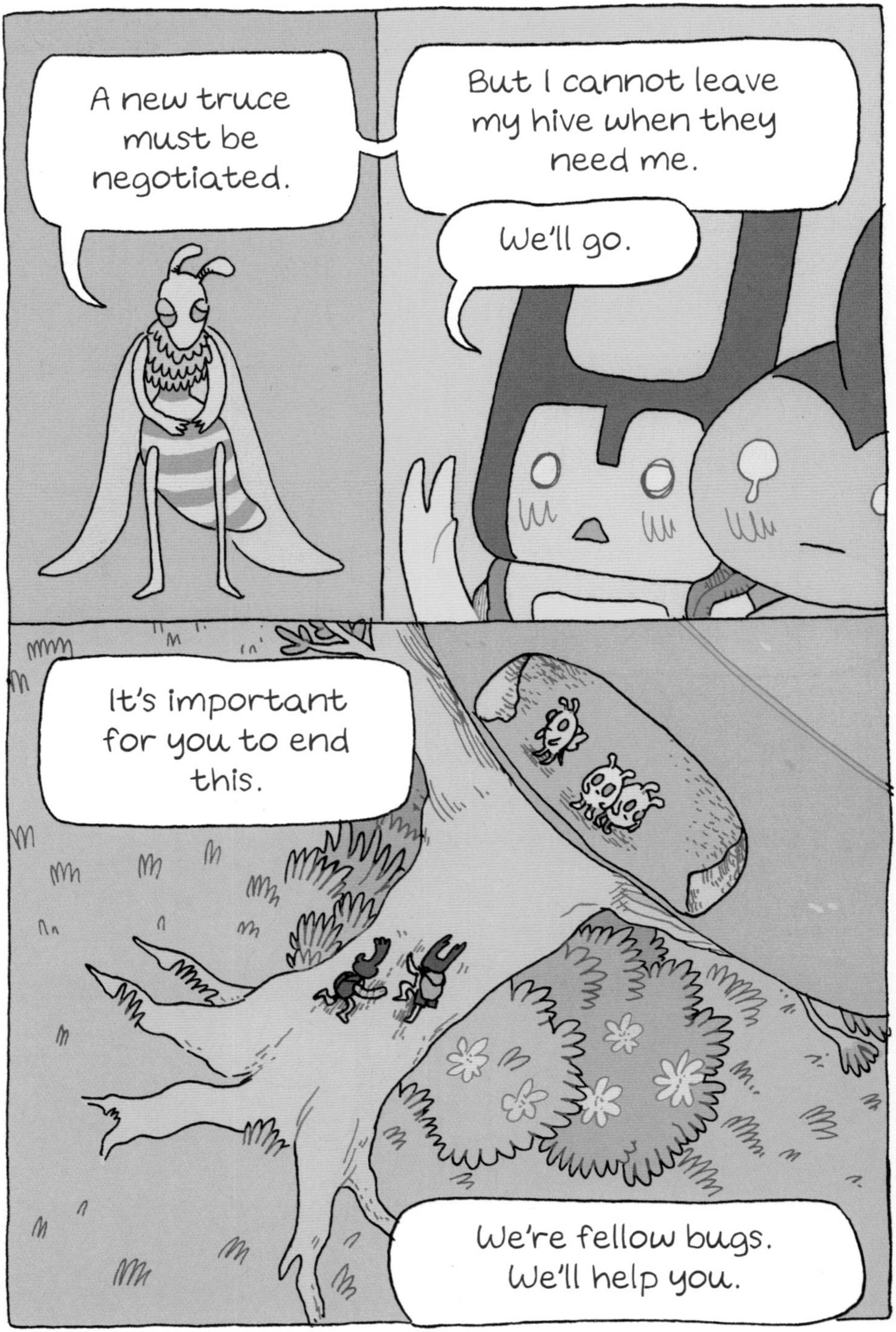
A new truce must be negotiated.
But I cannot leave my hive when they need me.
We'll go.
It's important for you to end this.
We're fellow bugs. We'll help you.

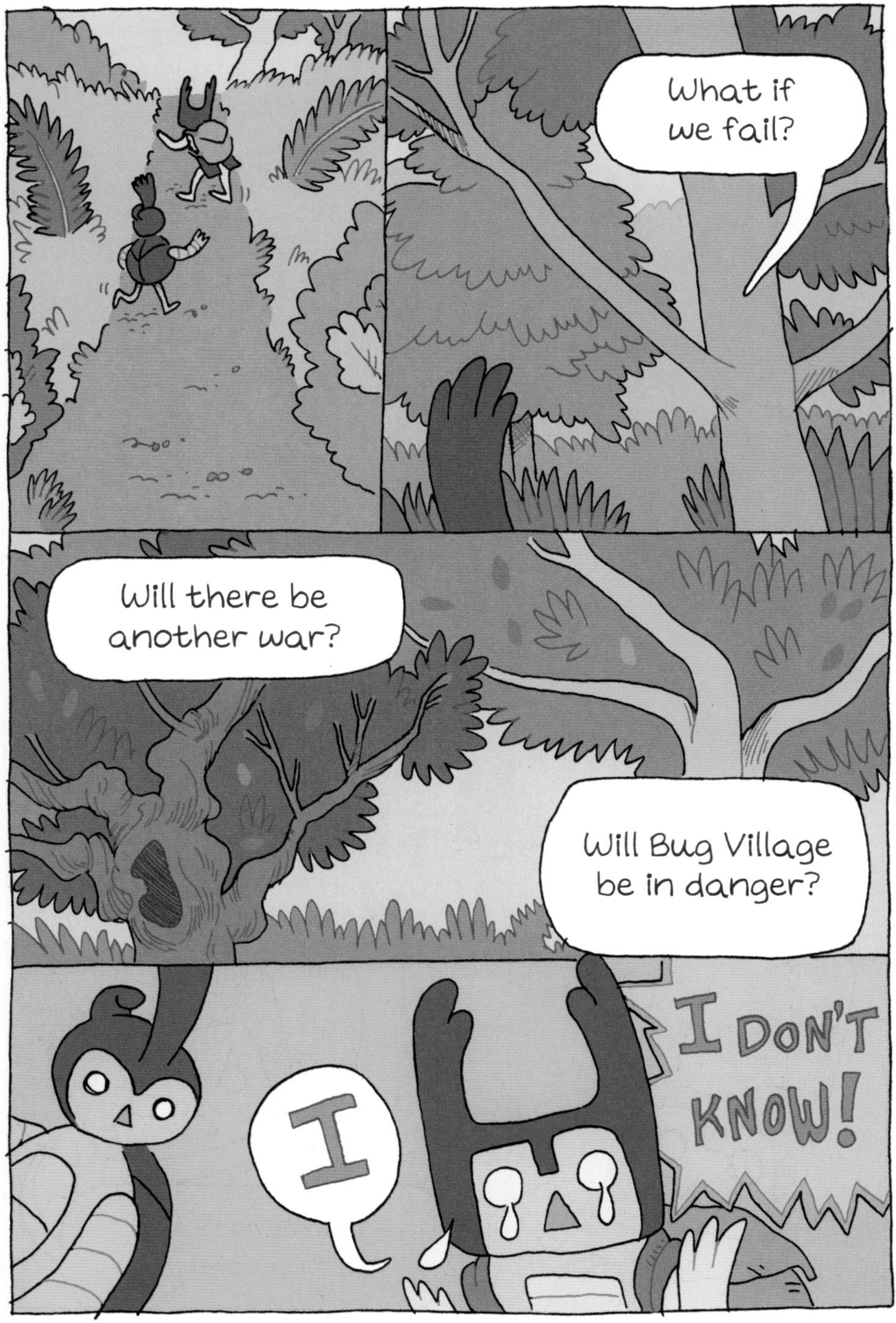
What if we fail?
Will there be another war?
Will Bug Village be in danger?
I
I DON'T KNOW!

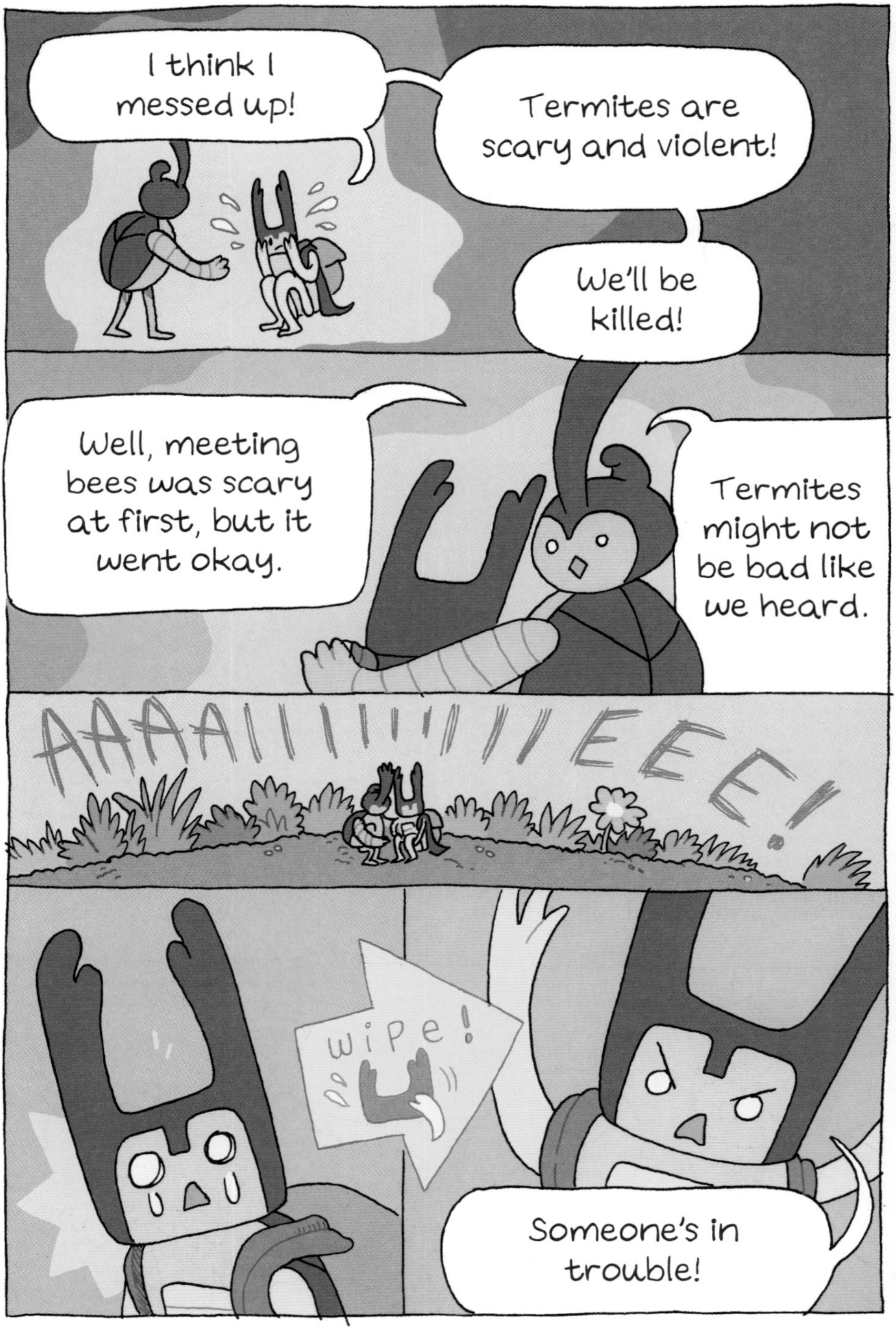
I think I messed up!
Termites are scary and violent!
We'll be killed!
Well, meeting bees was scary at first, but it went okay.
Termites might not be bad like we heard.
AAAAIIIIIIIIIEEEE!
wipe!
Someone's in trouble!

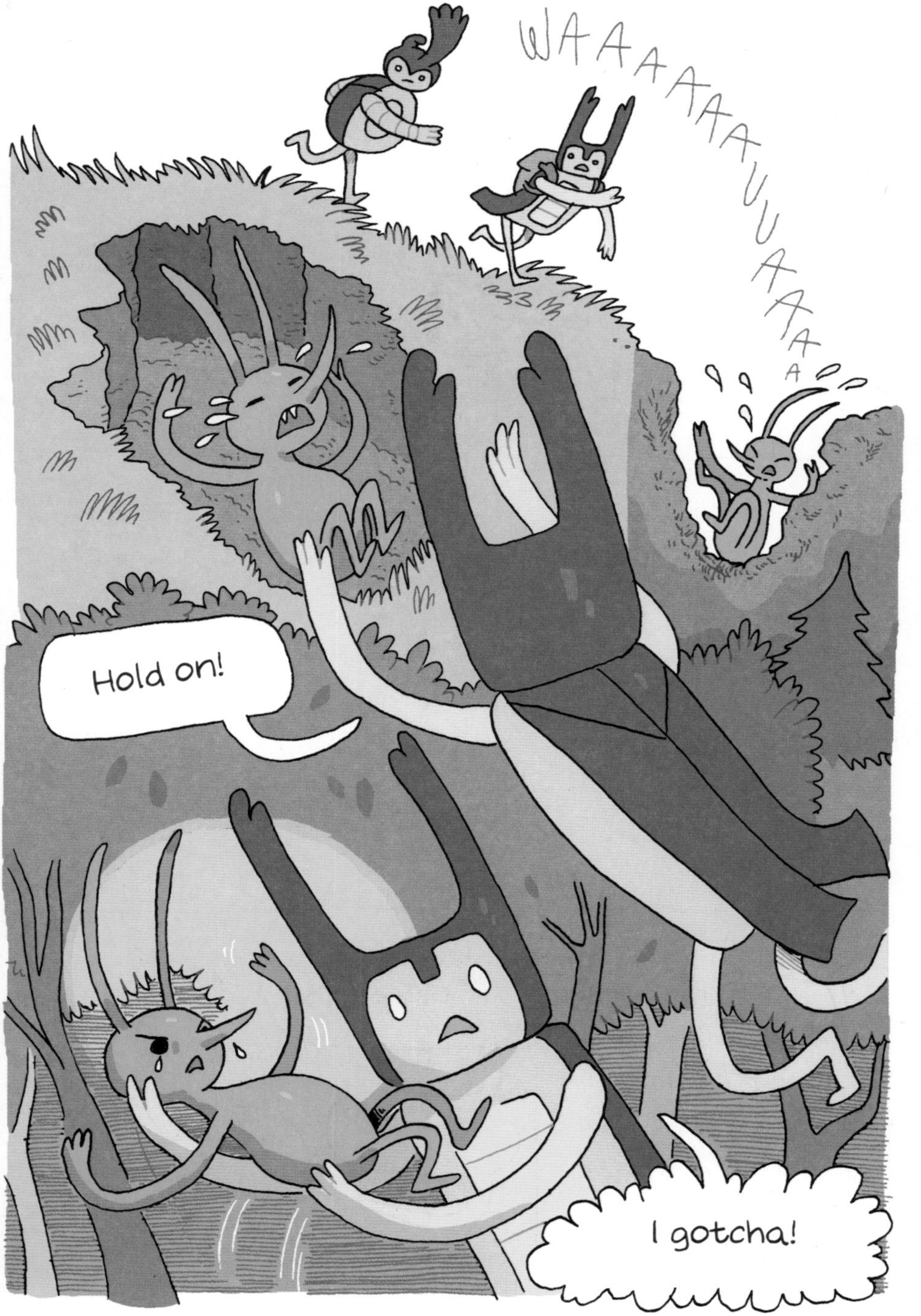
WAAAAAAUUAAAA
Hold on!
I gotcha!

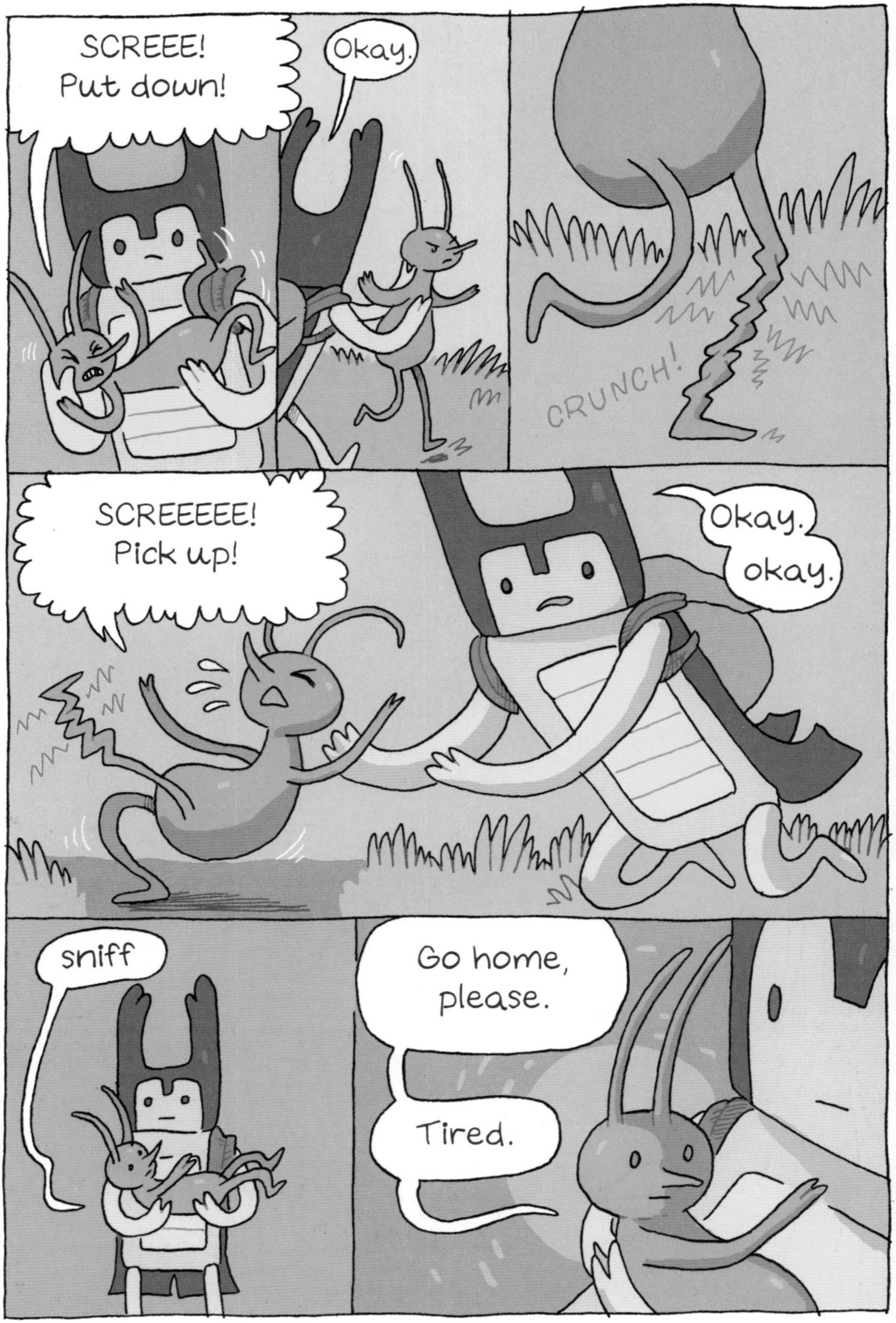
SCREEE! Put down!
Okay.
CRUNCH!
SCREEEEEE! Pick up!
Okay.
okay.
sniff
Go home, please.
Tired.

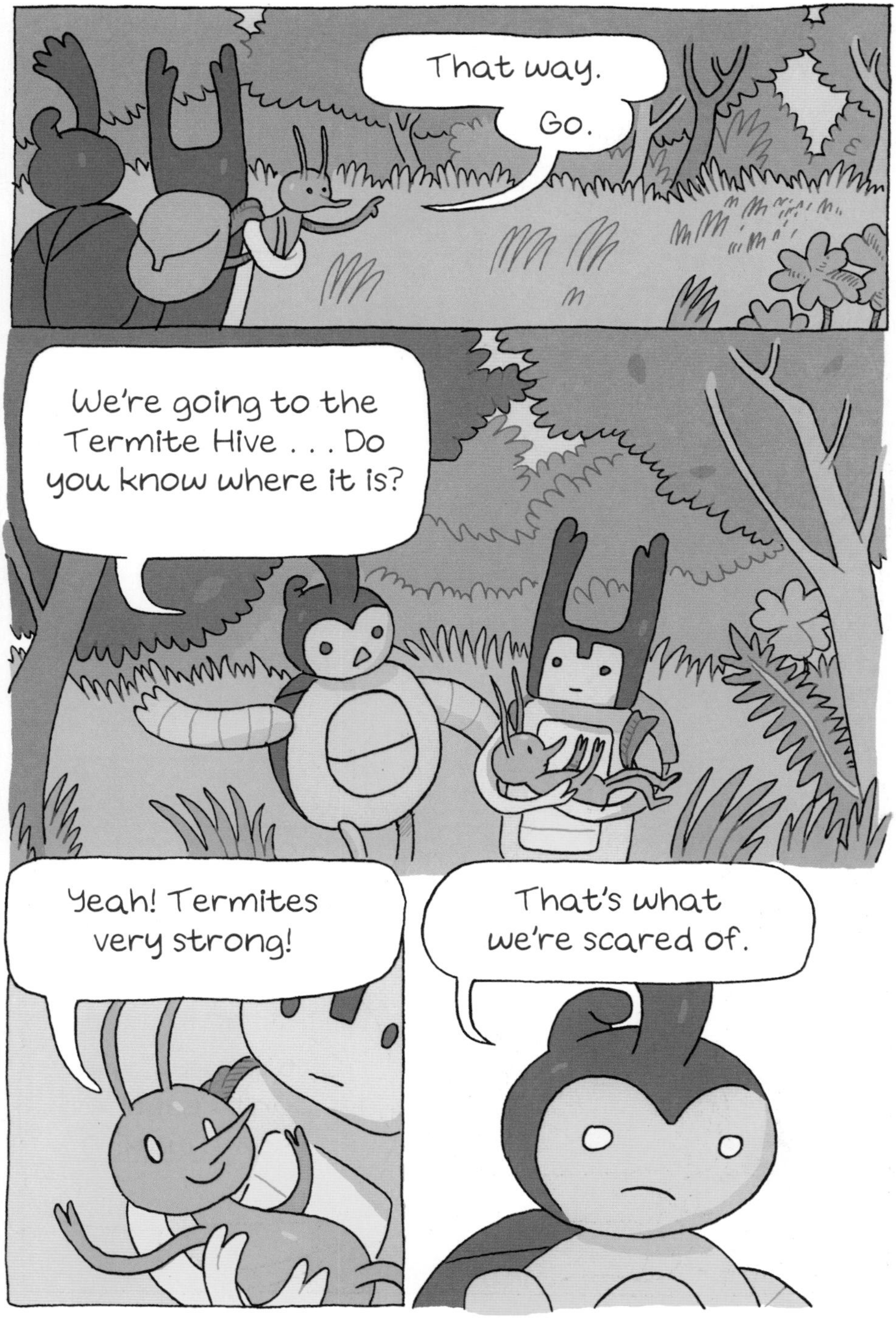
That way.
Go.
We're going to the Termite Hive . . . Do you know where it is?
Yeah! Termites very strong!
That's what we're scared of.

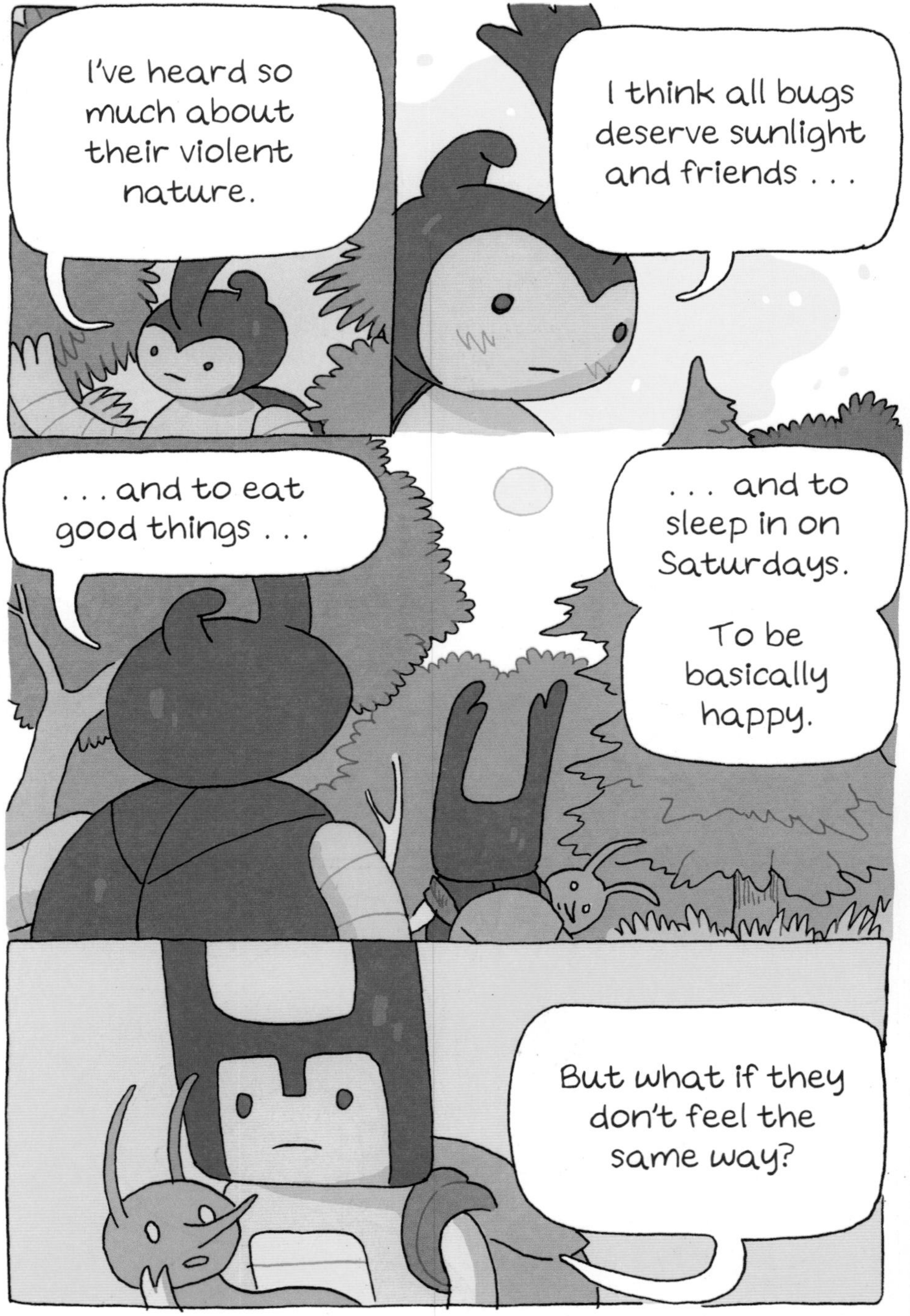
I've heard so much about their violent nature.
I think all bugs deserve sunlight and friends . . .
. . . and to eat good things . . .
. . . and to sleep in on Saturdays.
To be basically happy.
But what if they don't feel the same way?

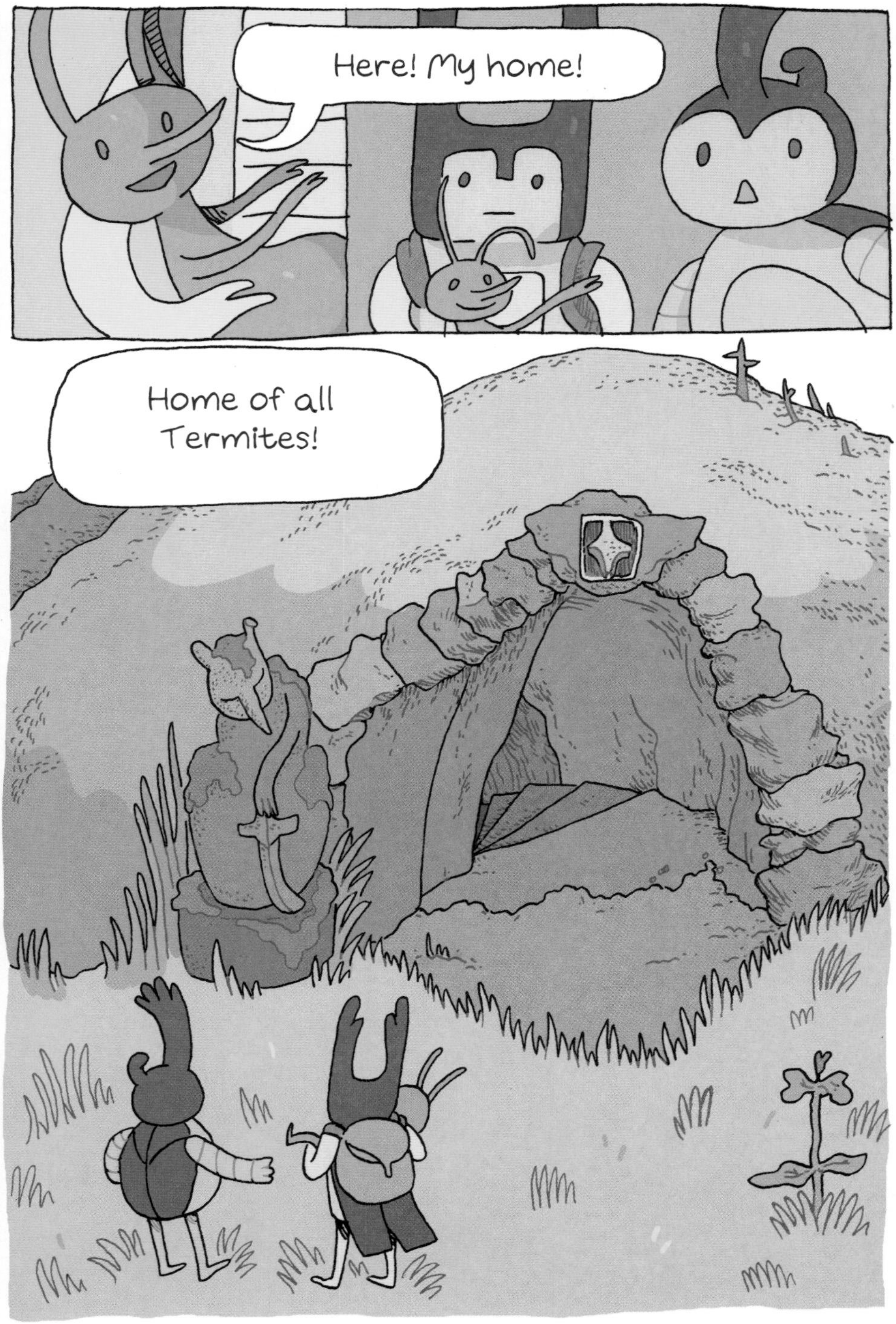
Here! My home!
Home of all Termites!

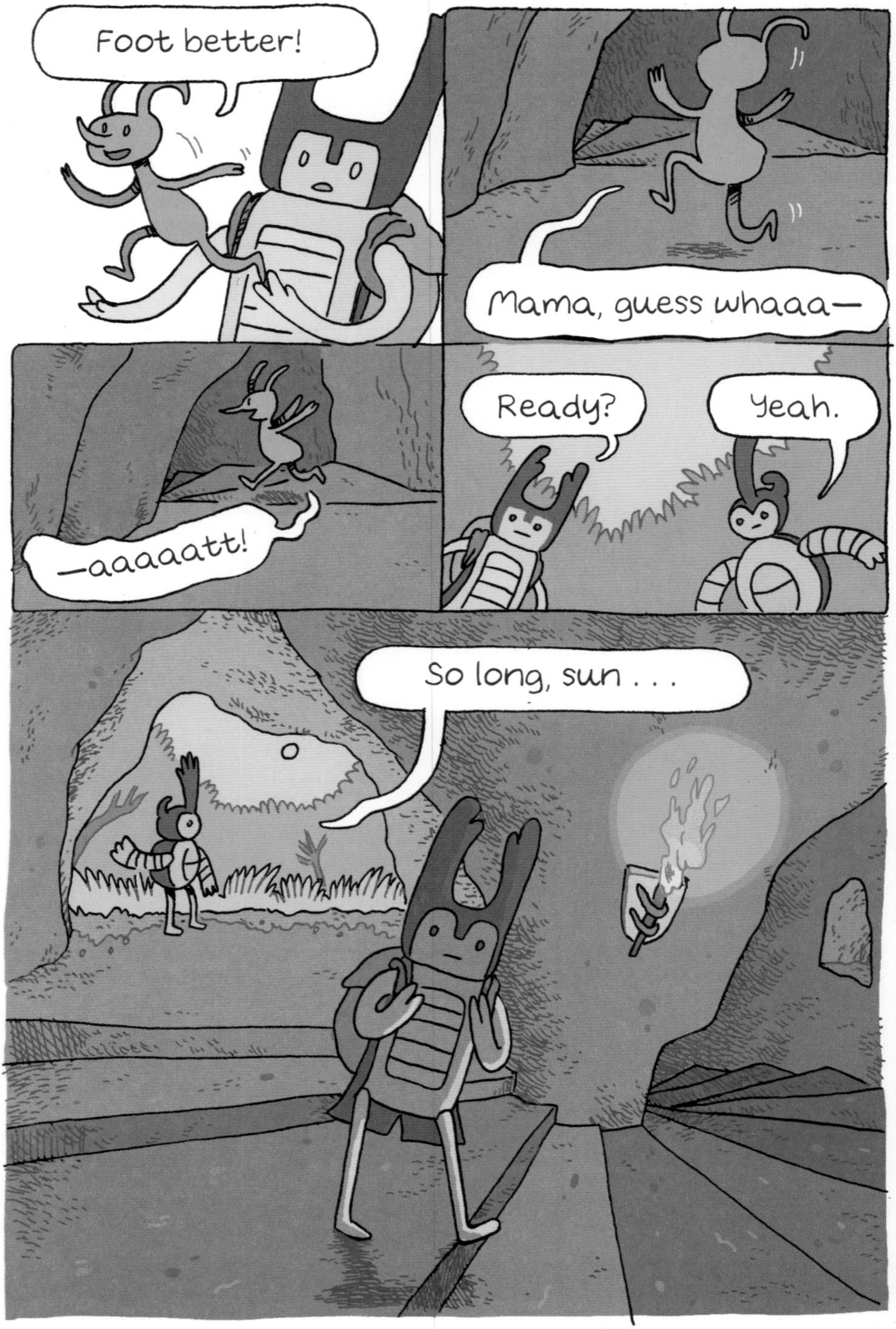
Foot better!
Mama, guess whaaa—
—aaaaatt!
Ready?
Yeah.
So long, sun . . .

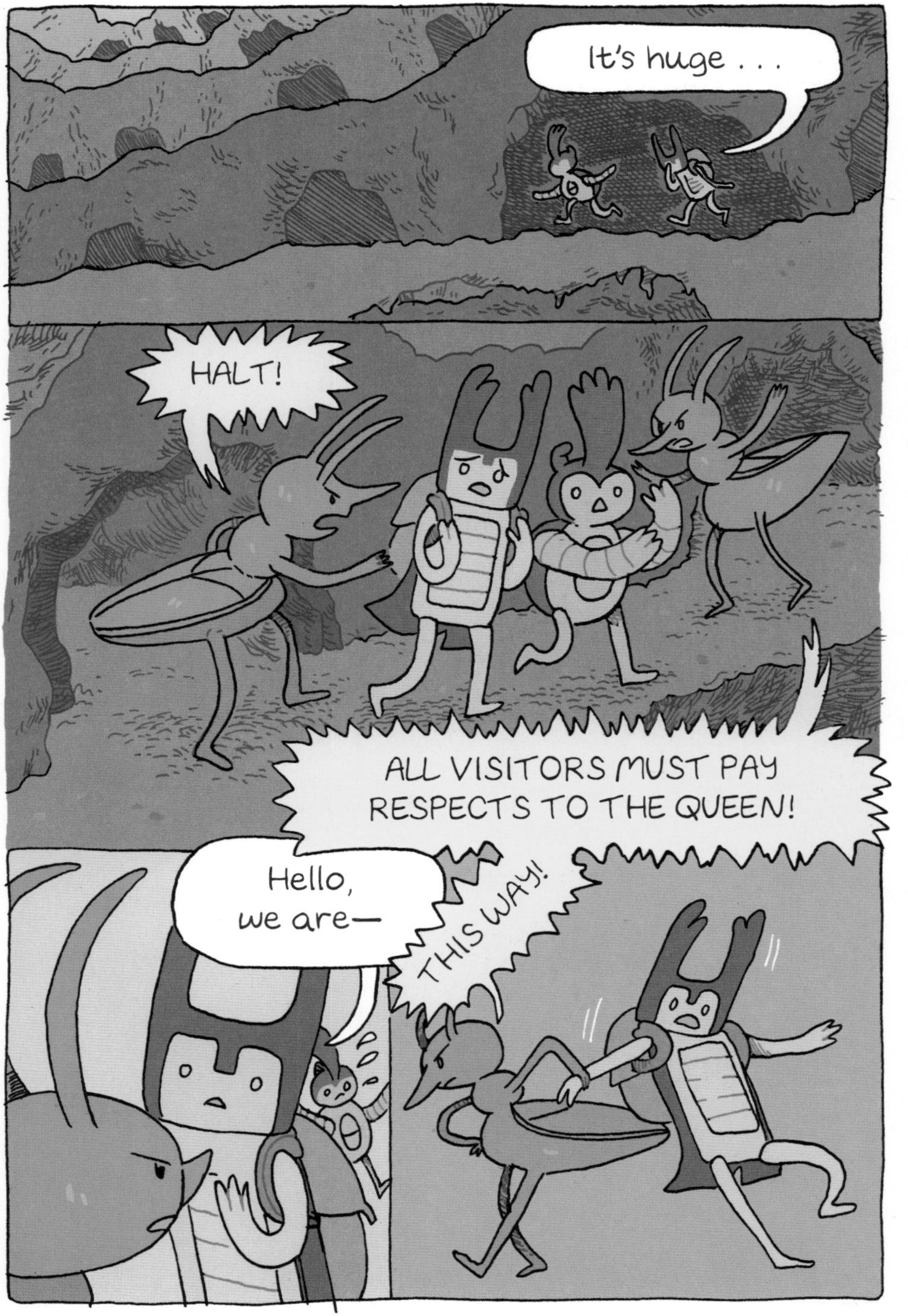
It's huge . . .
HALT!
ALL VISITORS MUST PAY RESPECTS TO THE QUEEN!
Hello, we are—
THIS WAY!

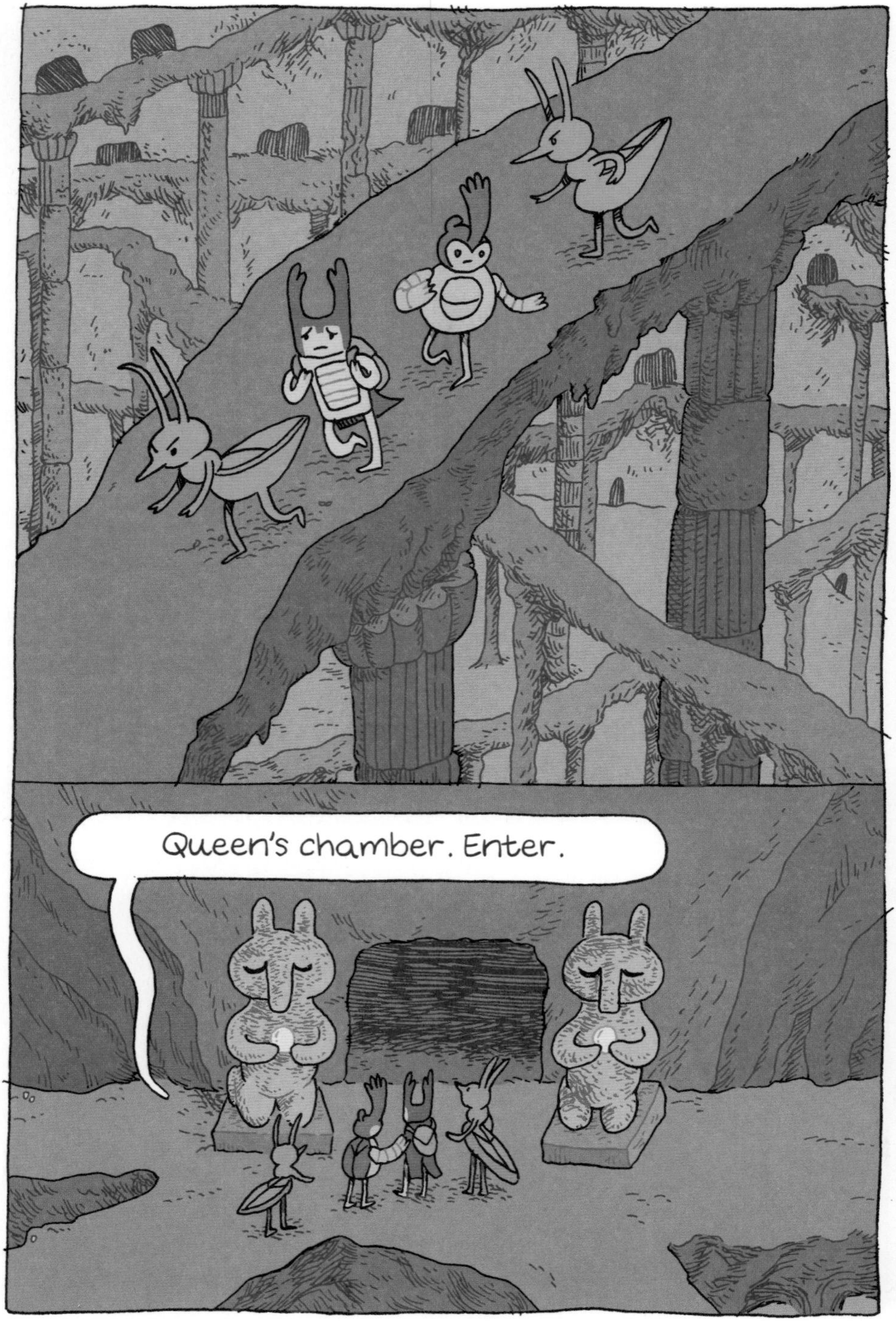
Queen's chamber. Enter.

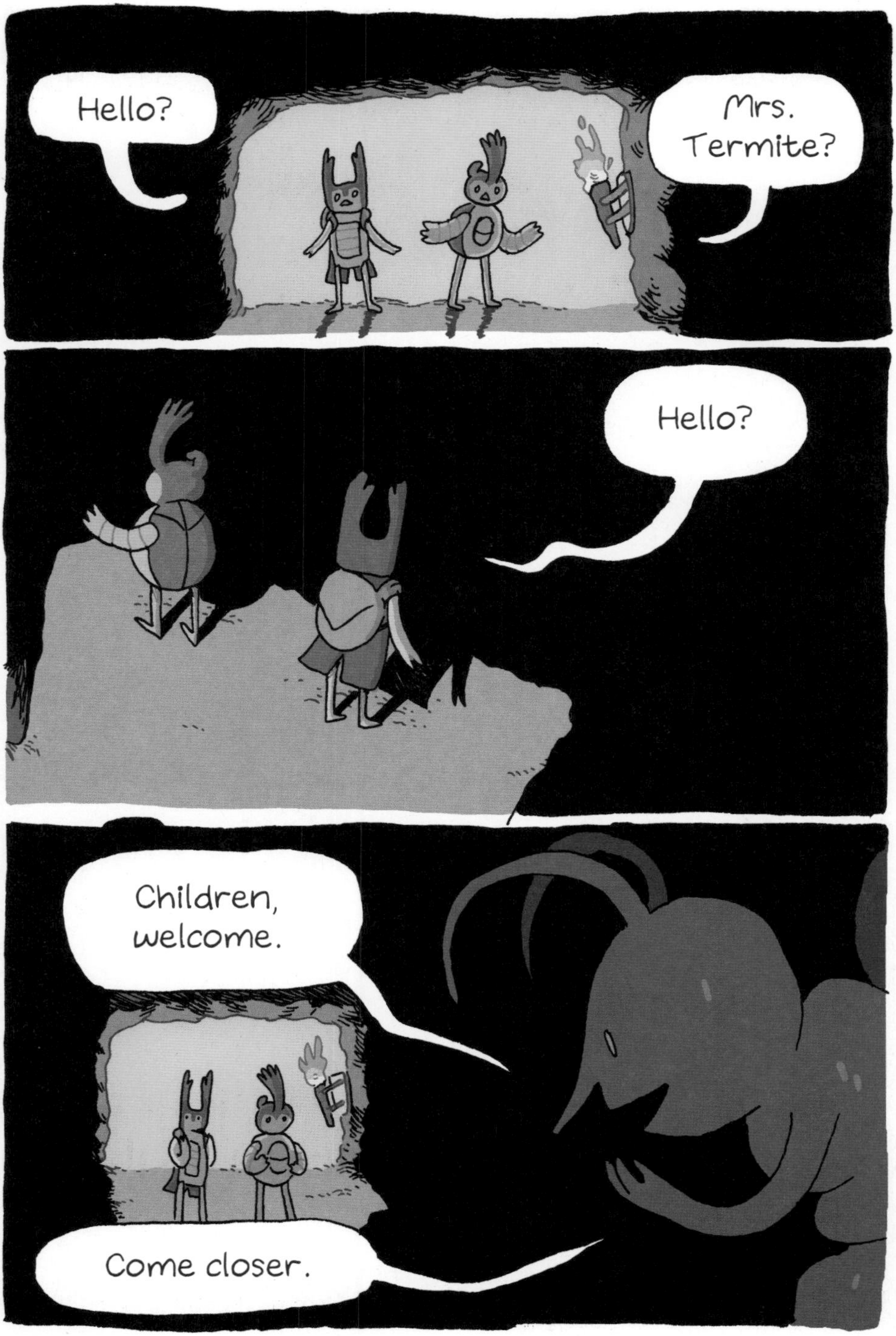
Hello?
Mrs. Termite?
Hello?
Children, welcome.
Come closer.

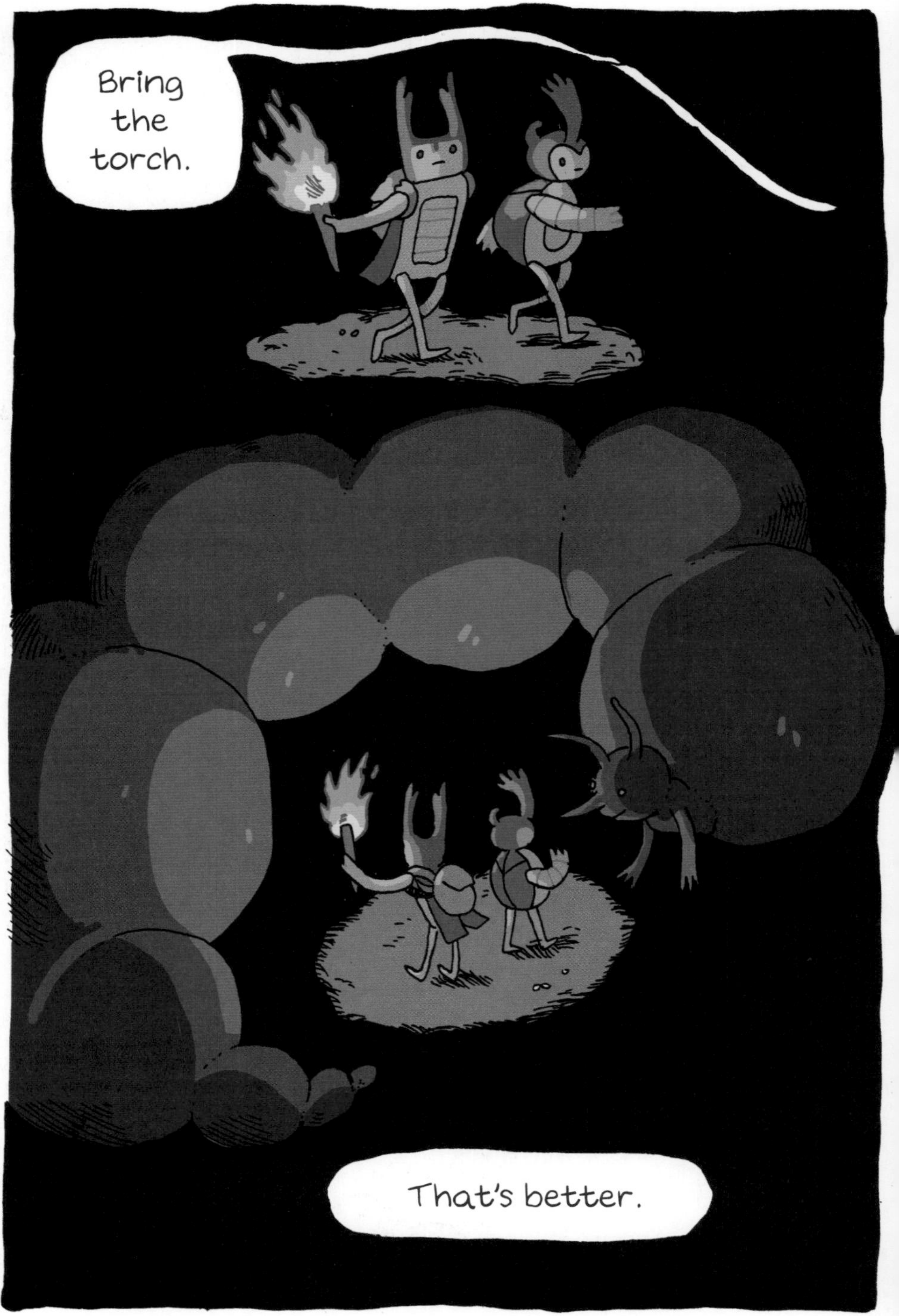
Bring the torch.
That's better.

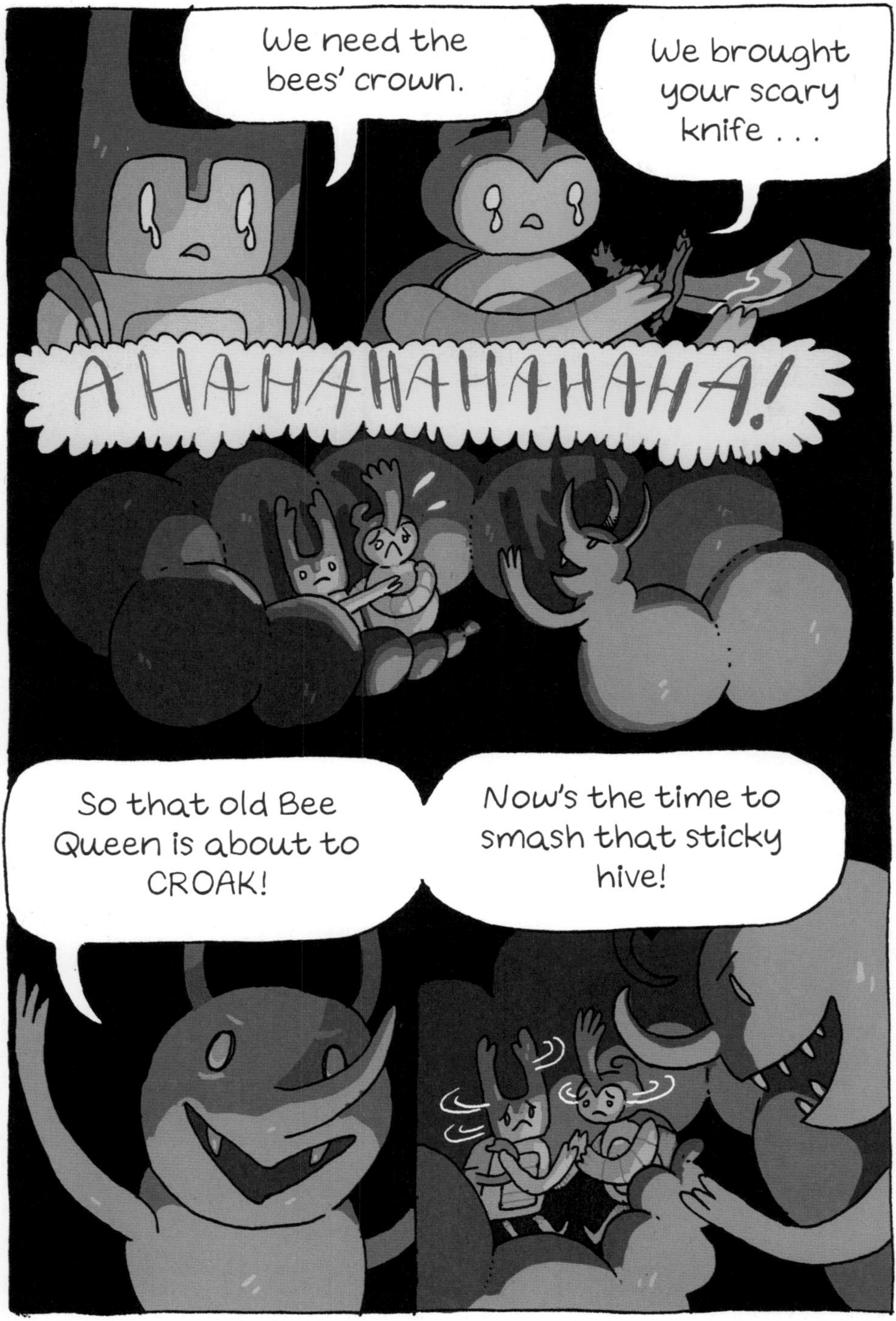
We need the bees' crown.
We brought your scary knife . . .
AHAHAHAHAHAHAHA!
So that old Bee Queen is about to CROAK!
Now's the time to smash that sticky hive!

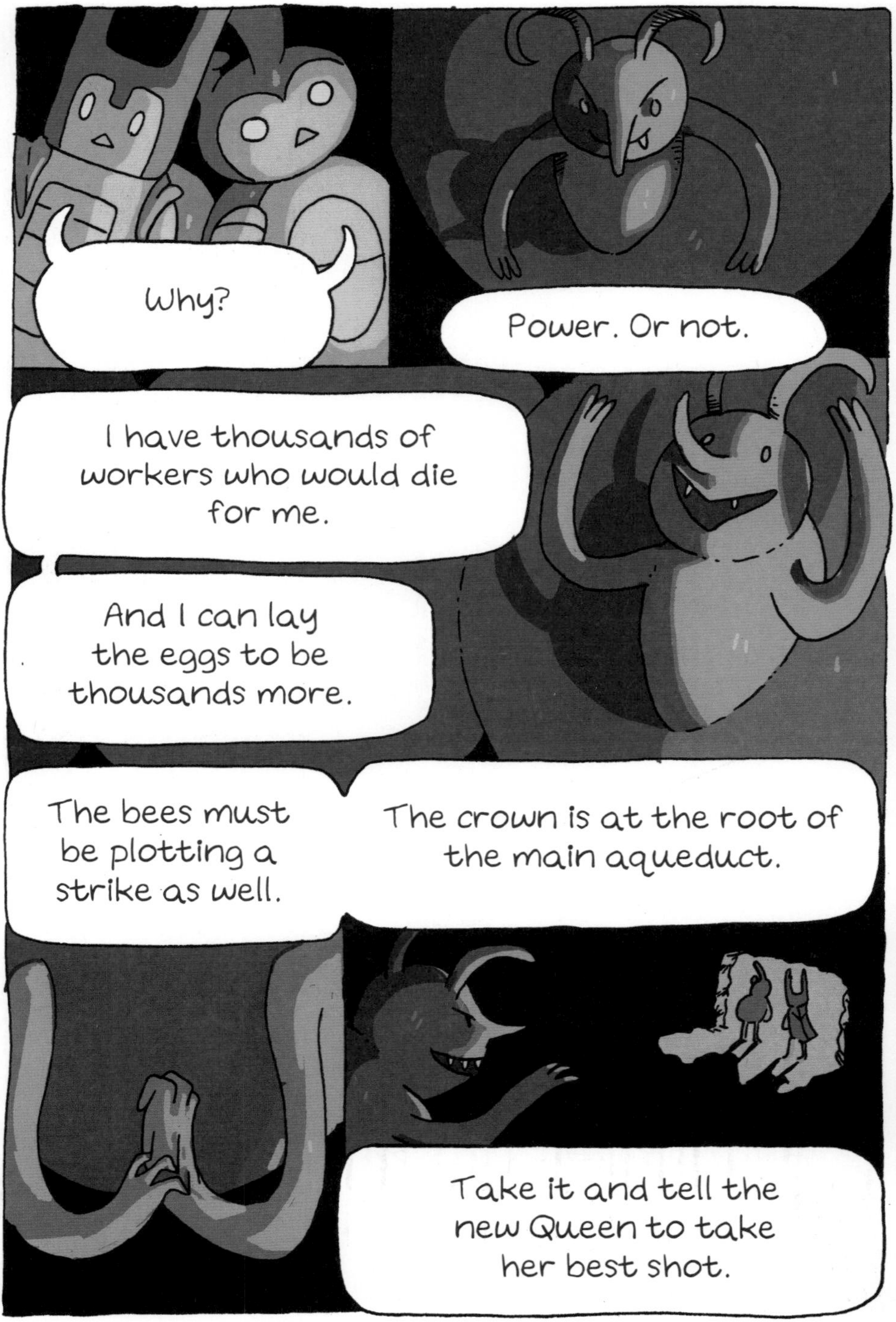

Why?

Power. Or not.

I have thousands of workers who would die for me.

And I can lay the eggs to be thousands more.

The bees must be plotting a strike as well.

The crown is at the root of the main aqueduct.

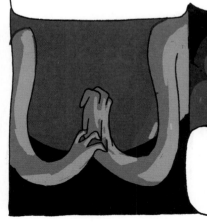

Take it and tell the new Queen to take her best shot.

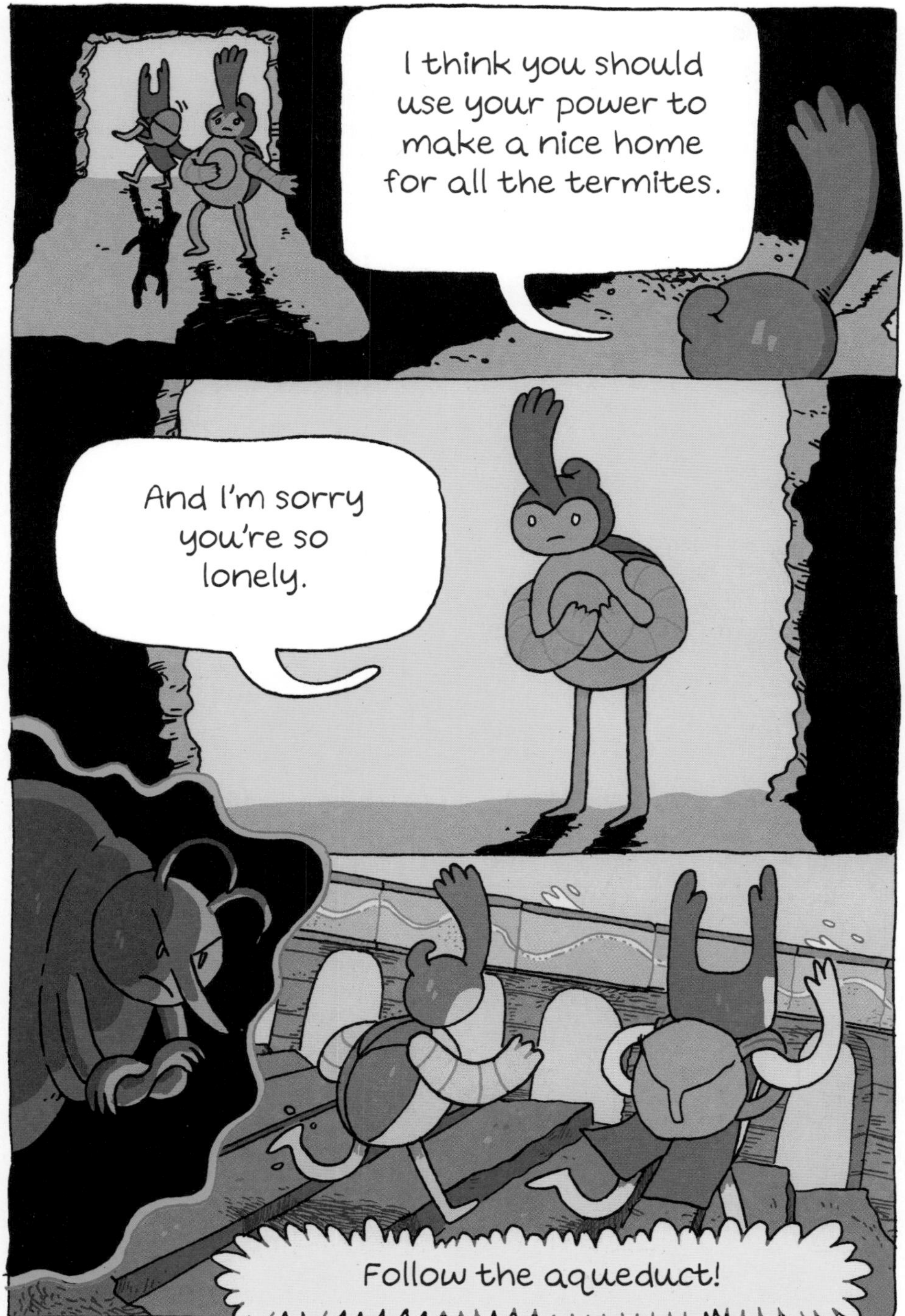
I think you should use your power to make a nice home for all the termites.
And I'm sorry you're so lonely.
Follow the aqueduct!

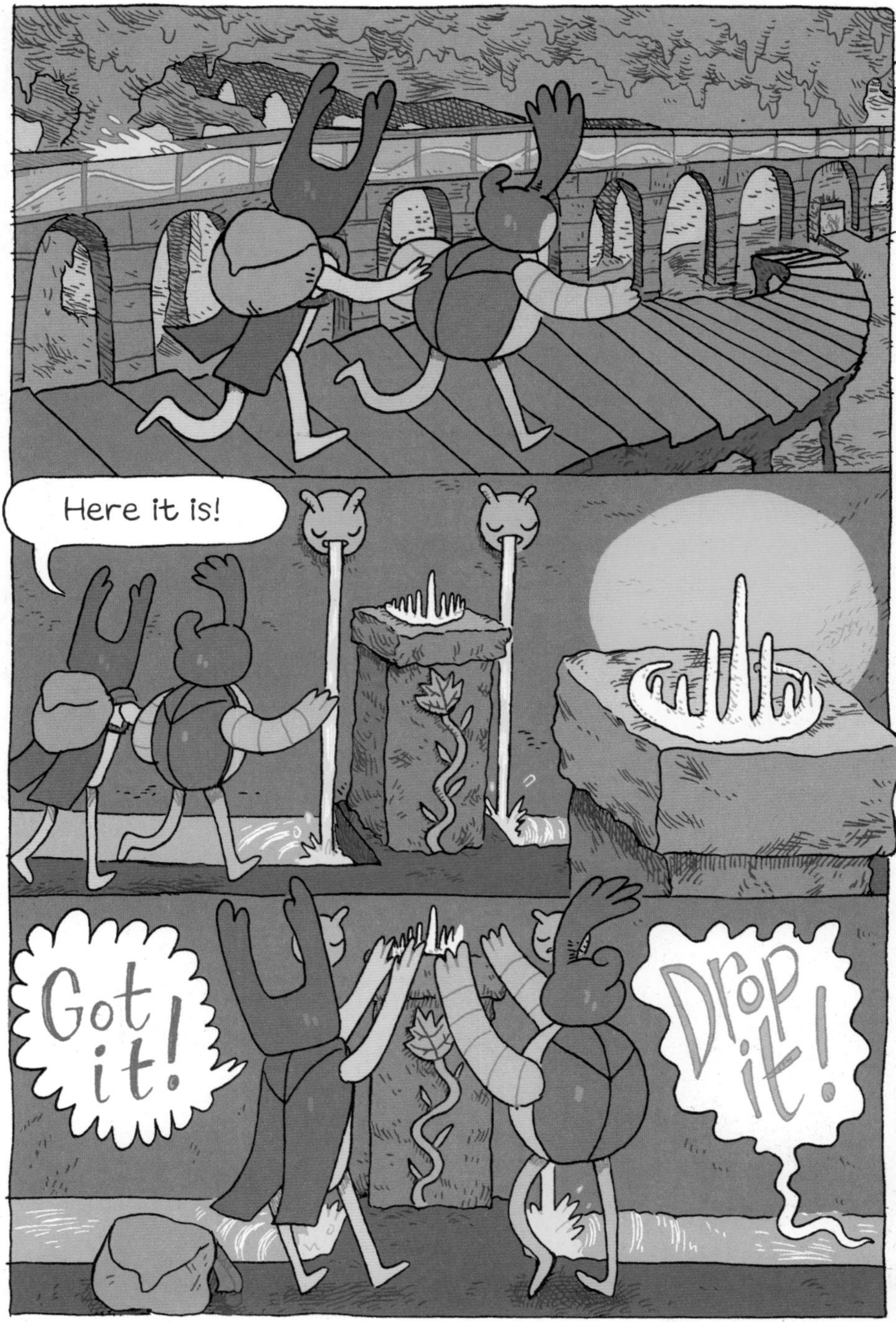
Here it is!
Got it!
Drop it!

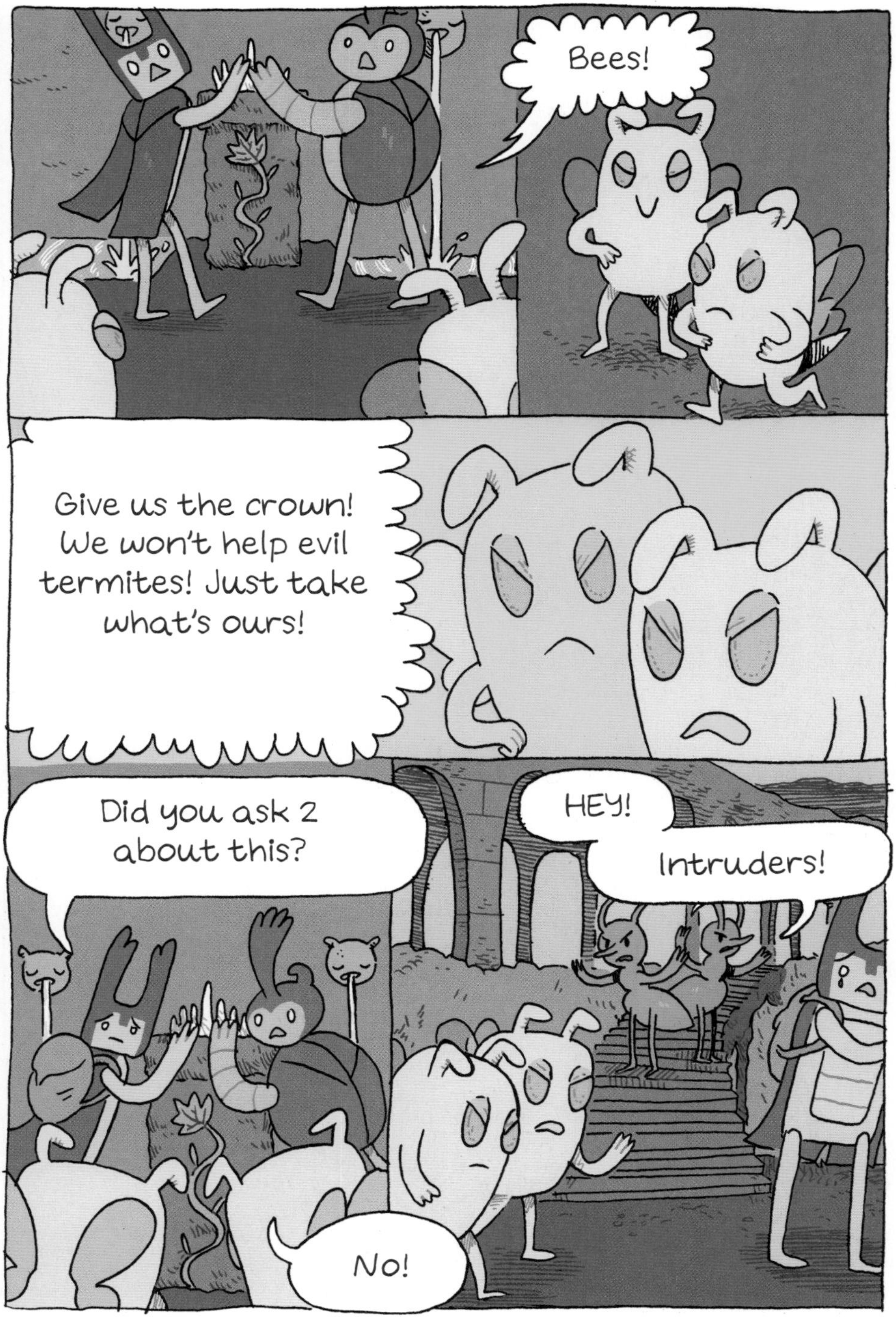
Bees!
Give us the crown! We won't help evil termites! Just take what's ours!
Did you ask 2 about this?
No!
HEY!
Intruders!

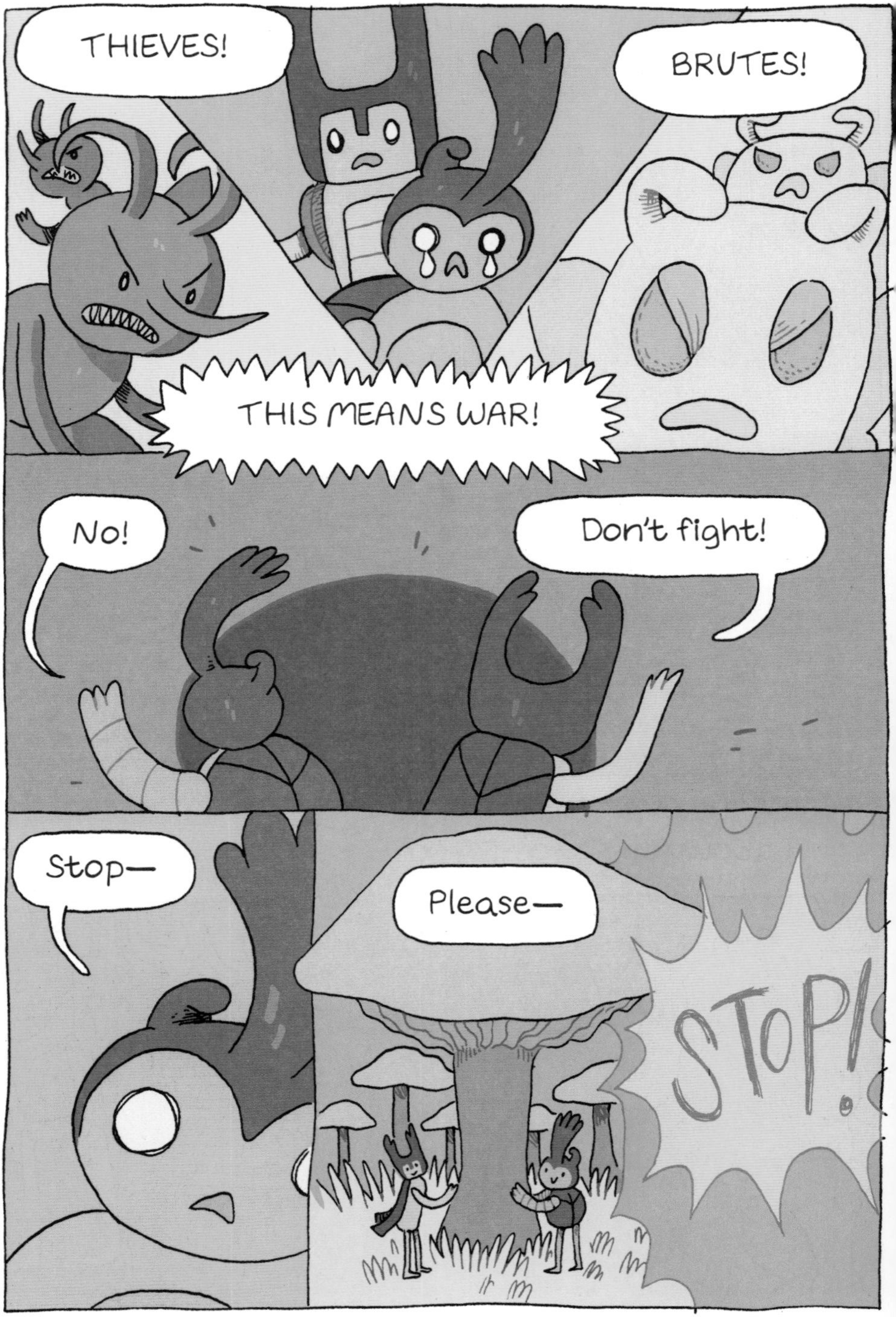
THIEVES!
BRUTES!
THIS MEANS WAR!
No!
Don't fight!
Stop—
Please—
STOP!

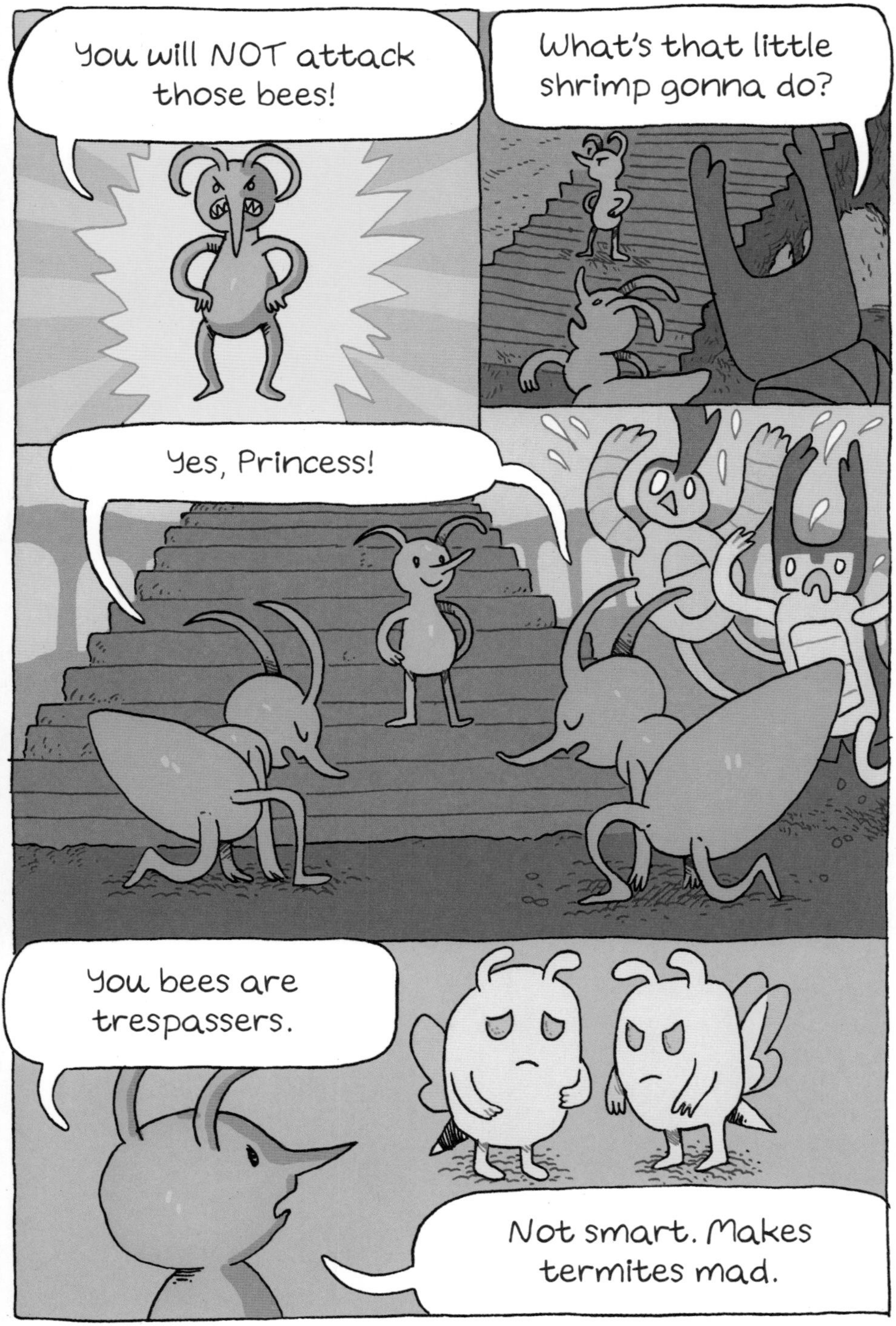
You will NOT attack those bees!
What's that little shrimp gonna do?
Yes, Princess!
You bees are trespassers.
Not smart. Makes termites mad.

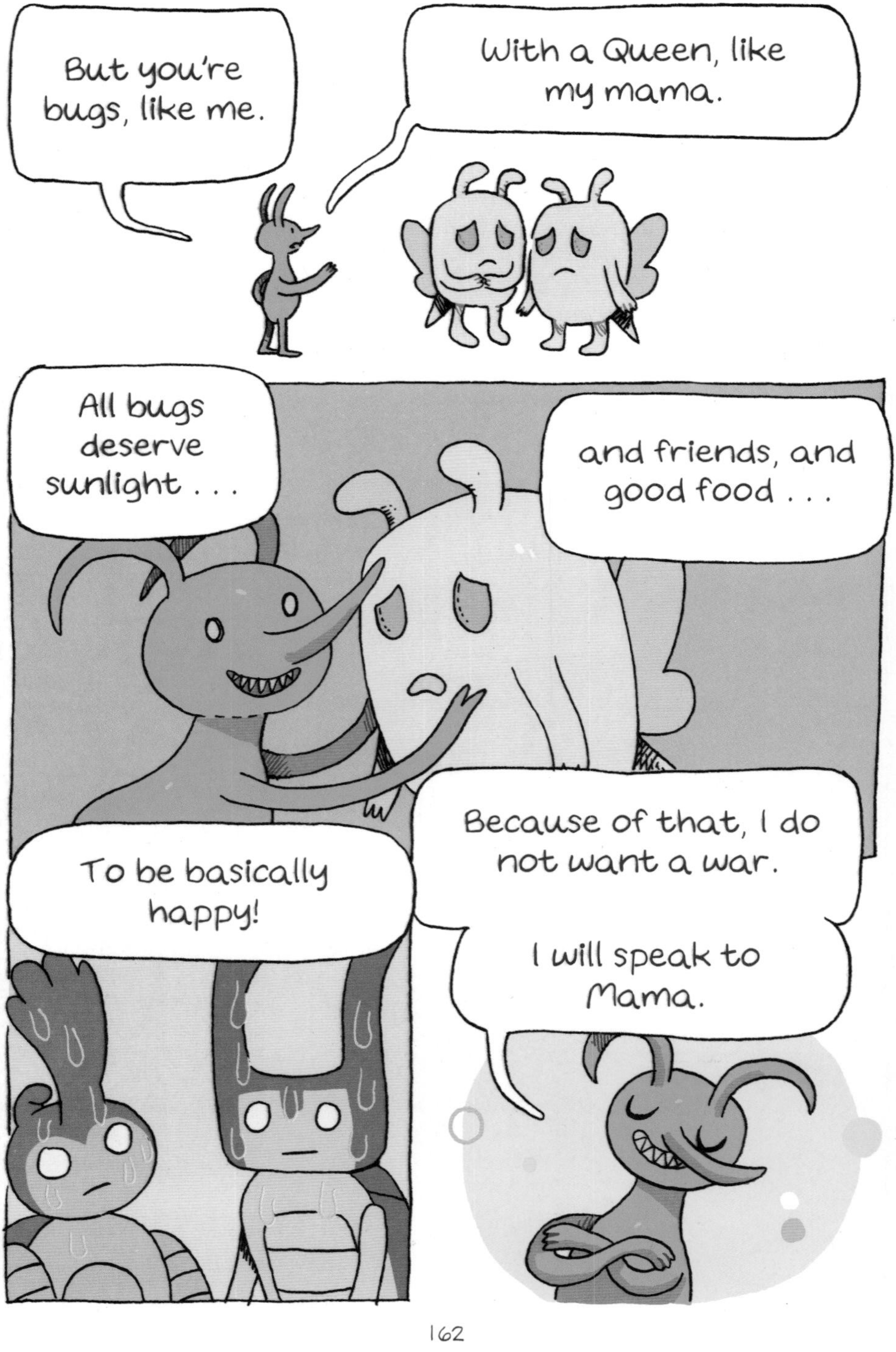
But you're bugs, like me.
With a Queen, like my mama.
All bugs deserve sunlight . . .
and friends, and good food . . .
To be basically happy!
Because of that, I do not want a war.
I will speak to Mama.

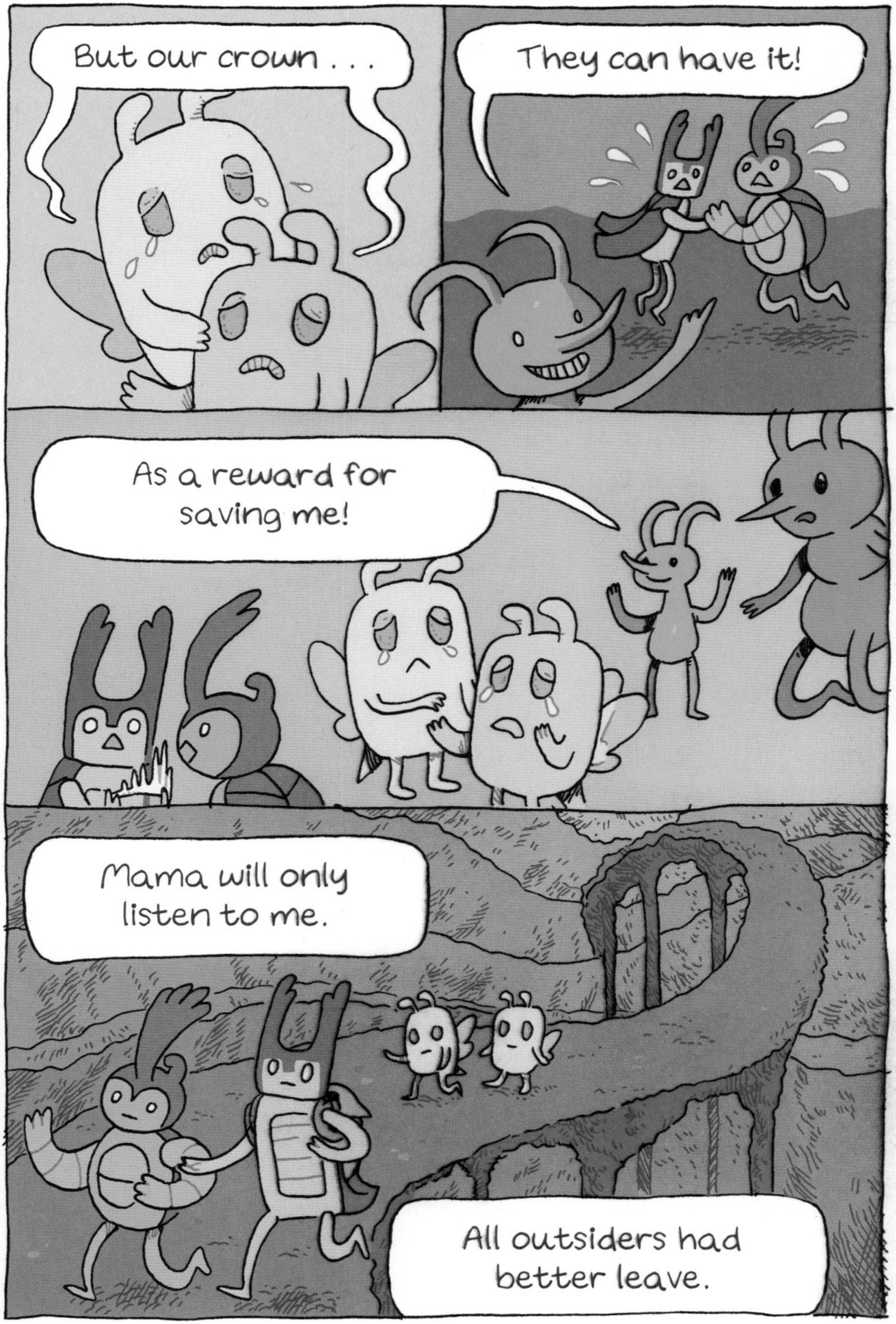
But our crown . . .
They can have it!
As a reward for saving me!
Mama will only listen to me.
All outsiders had better leave.

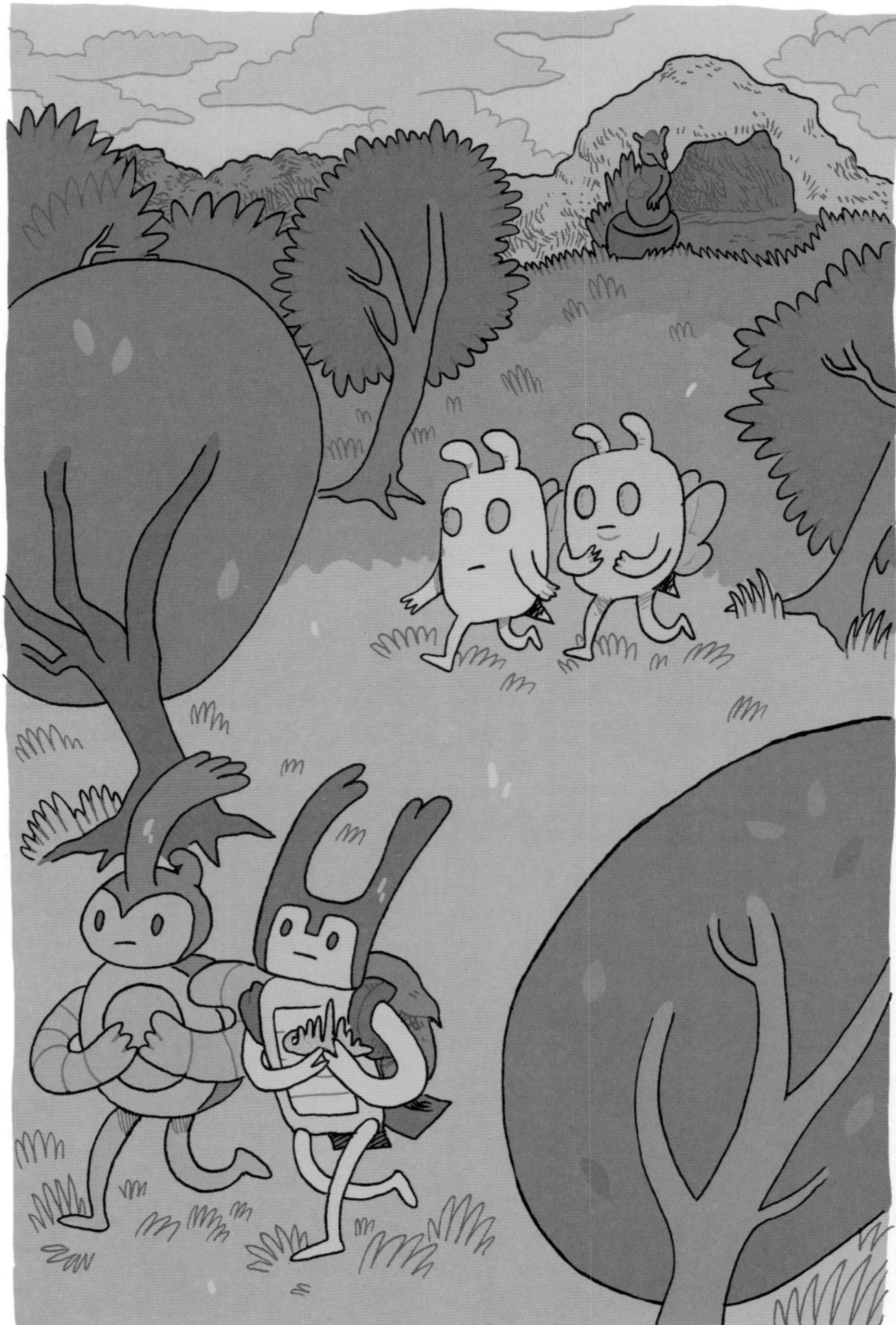

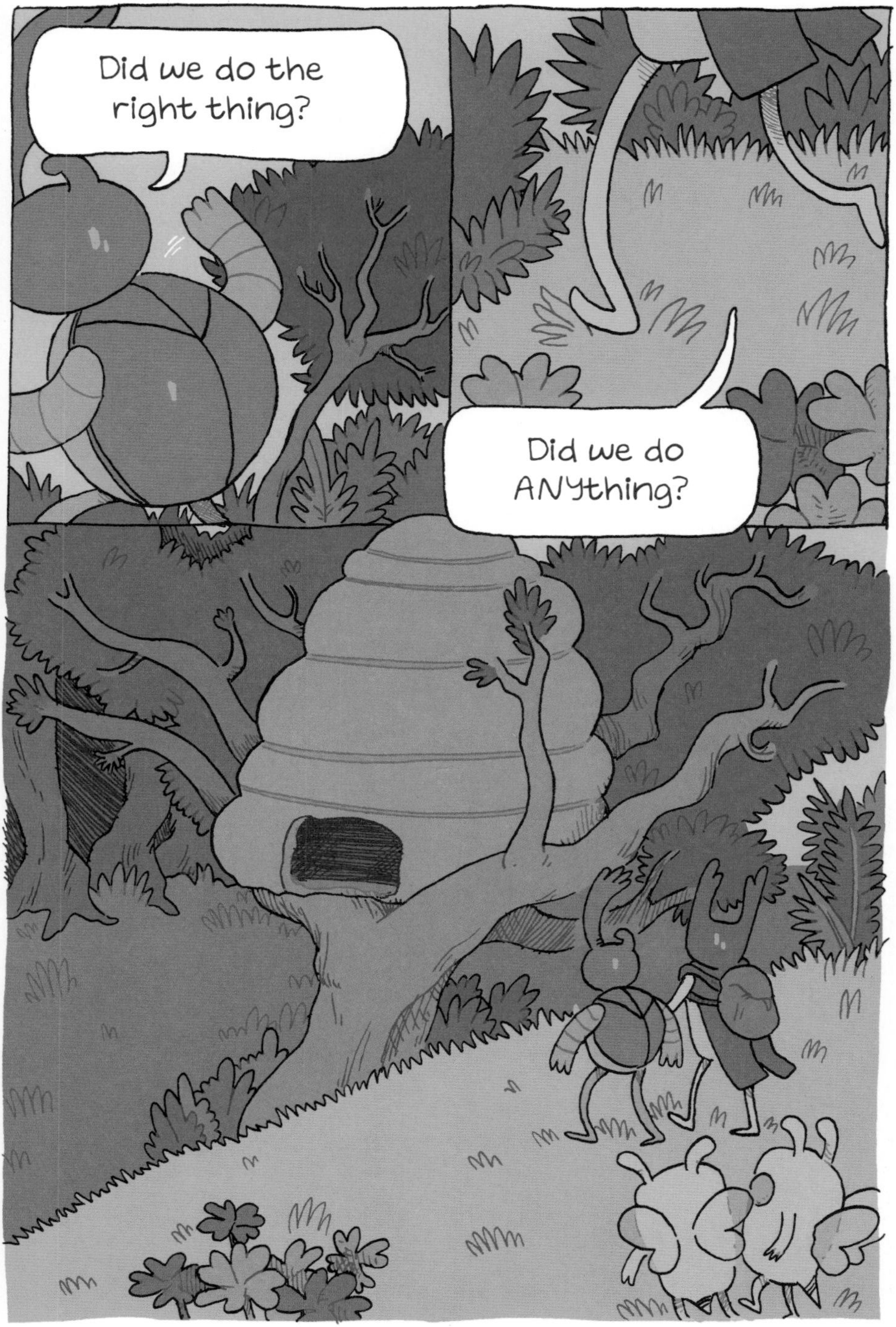
Did we do the right thing?
Did we do ANYthing?

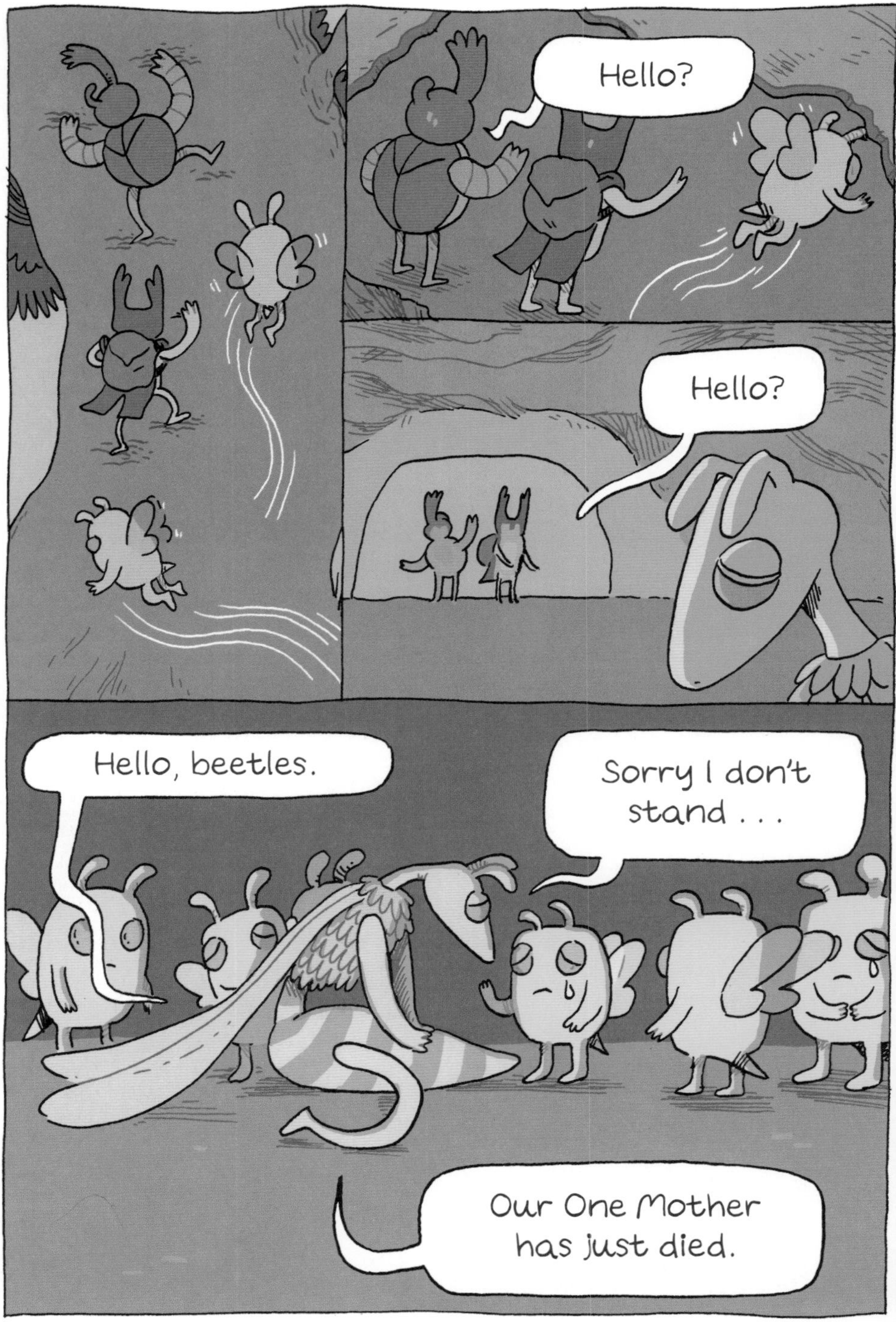
Hello?
Hello?
Hello, beetles.
Sorry I don't stand . . .
Our One Mother has just died.

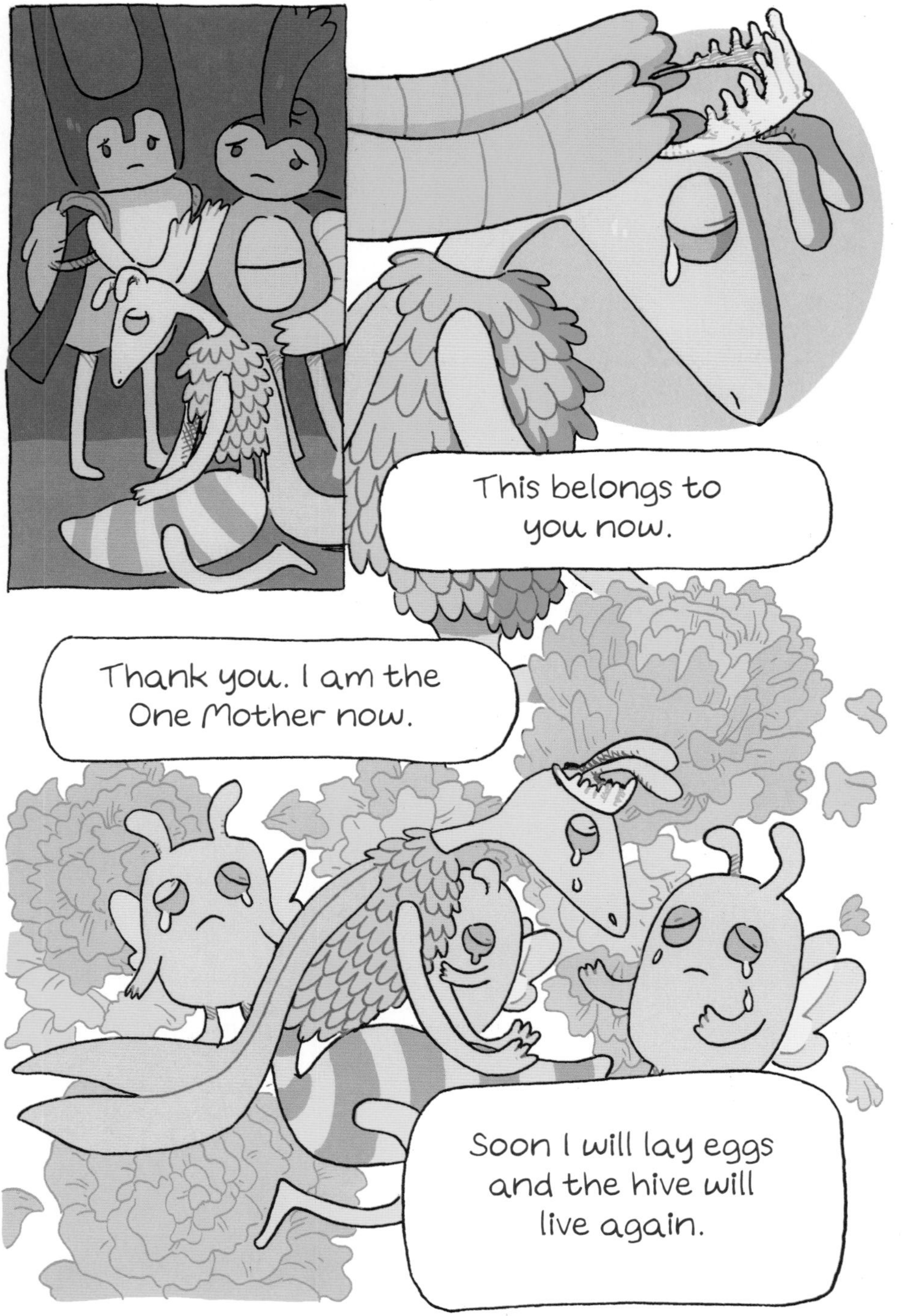
This belongs to you now.
Thank you. I am the One Mother now.
Soon I will lay eggs and the hive will live again.

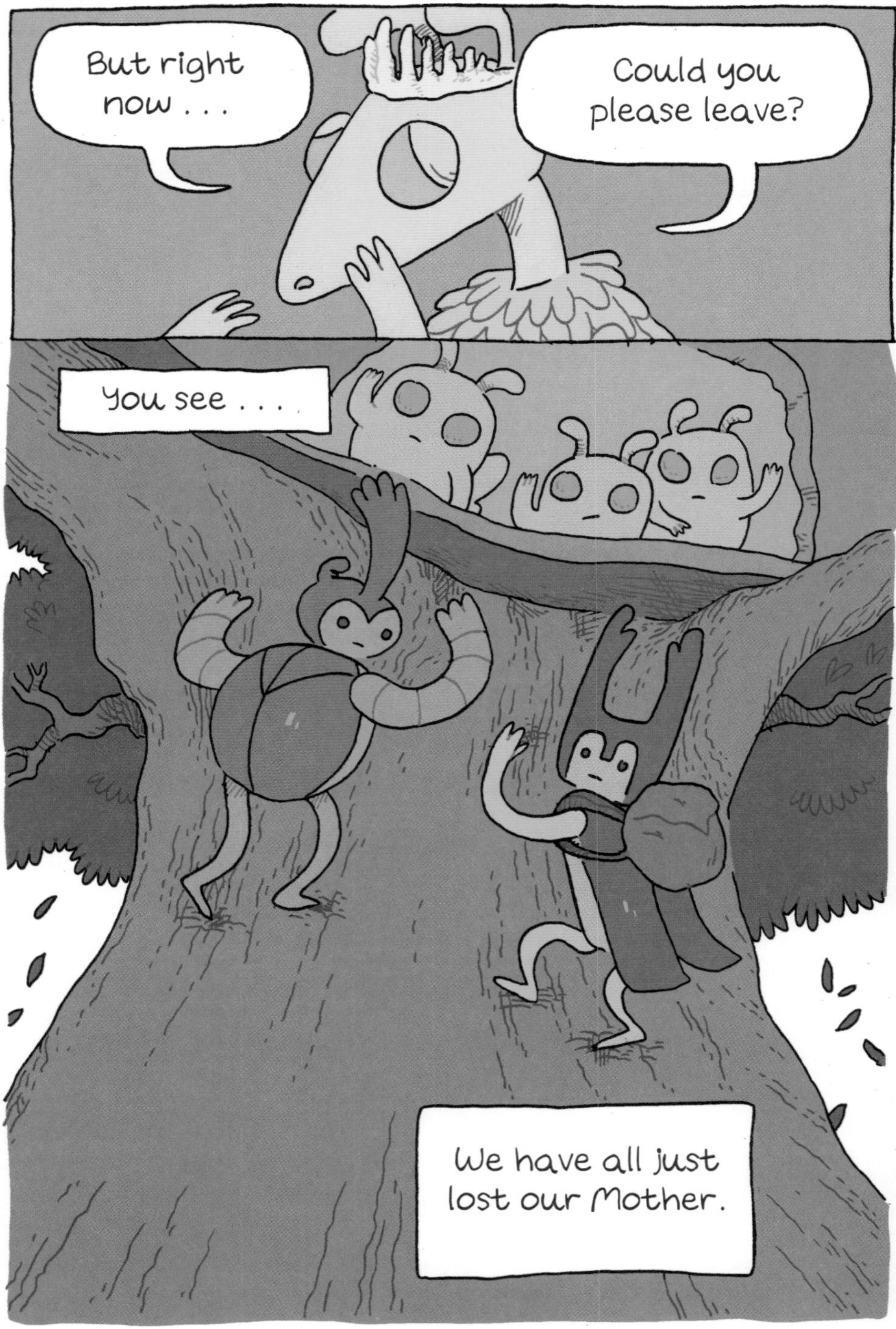
But right now . . .
Could you please leave?
You see . . .
We have all just lost our Mother.

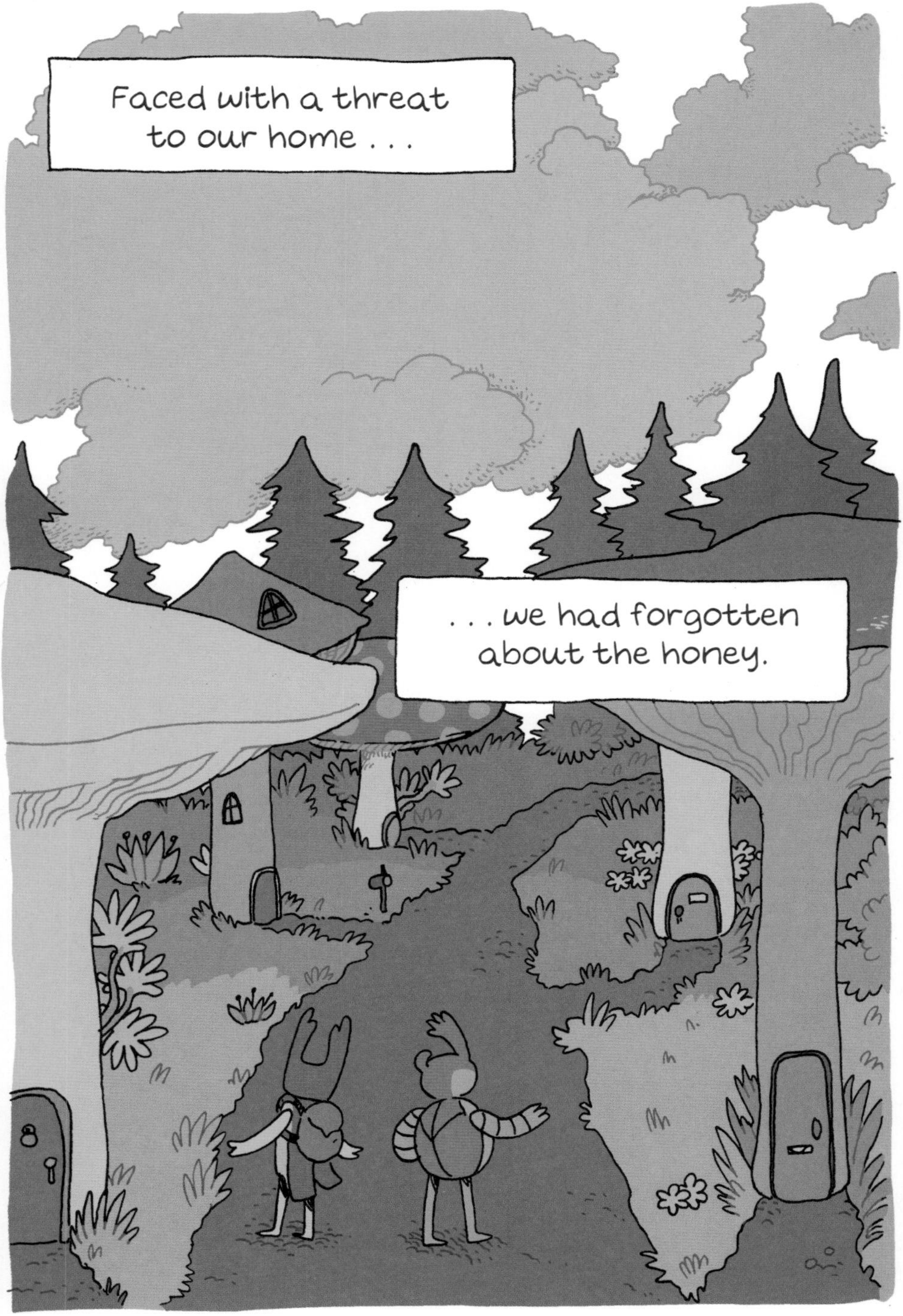
Faced with a threat to our home . . .
. . . we had forgotten about the honey.

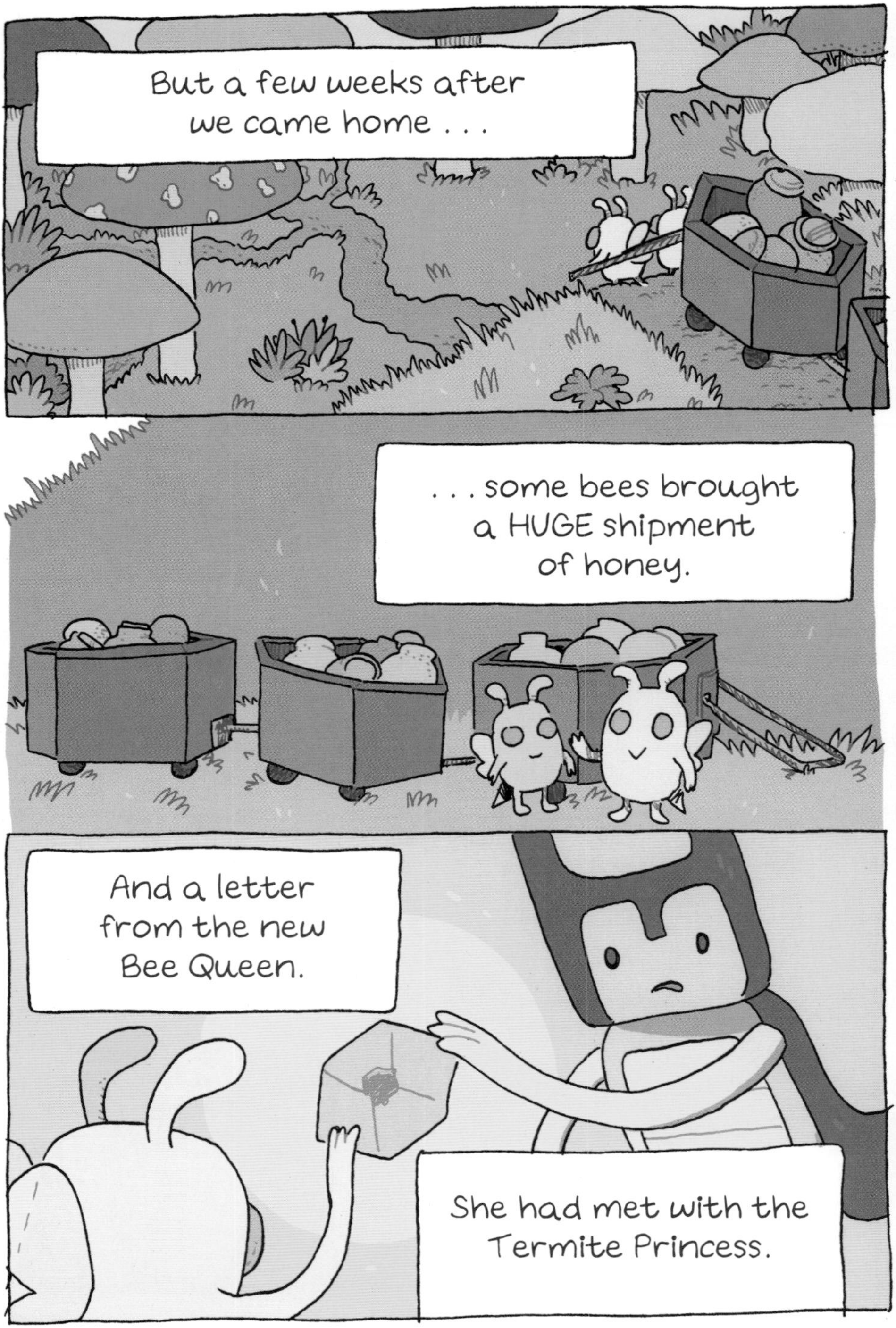
But a few weeks after we came home . . .
. . . some bees brought a HUGE shipment of honey.
And a letter from the new Bee Queen.
She had met with the Termite Princess.

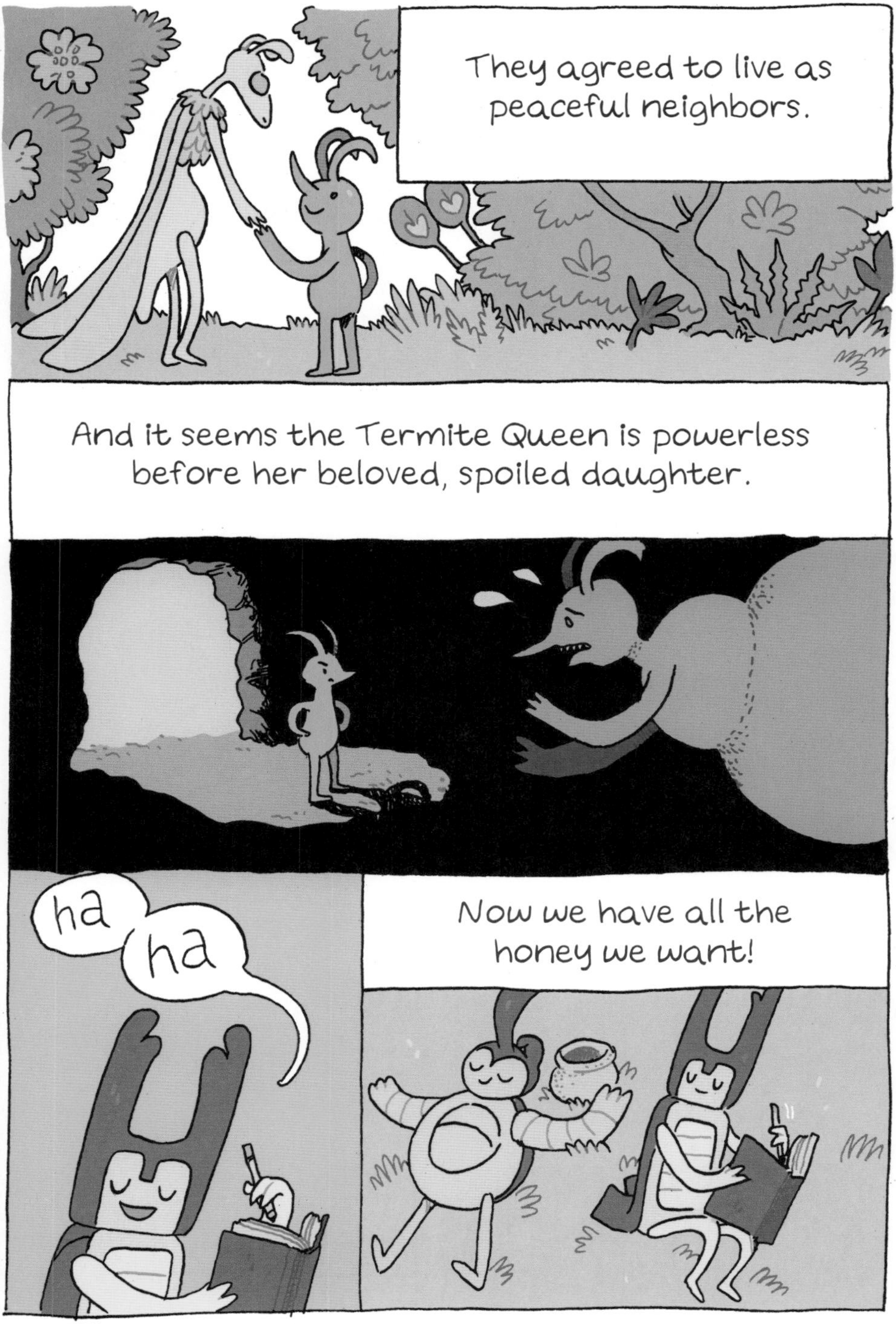

They agreed to live as peaceful neighbors.
And it seems the Termite Queen is powerless before her beloved, spoiled daughter.
ha
ha
Now we have all the honey we want!

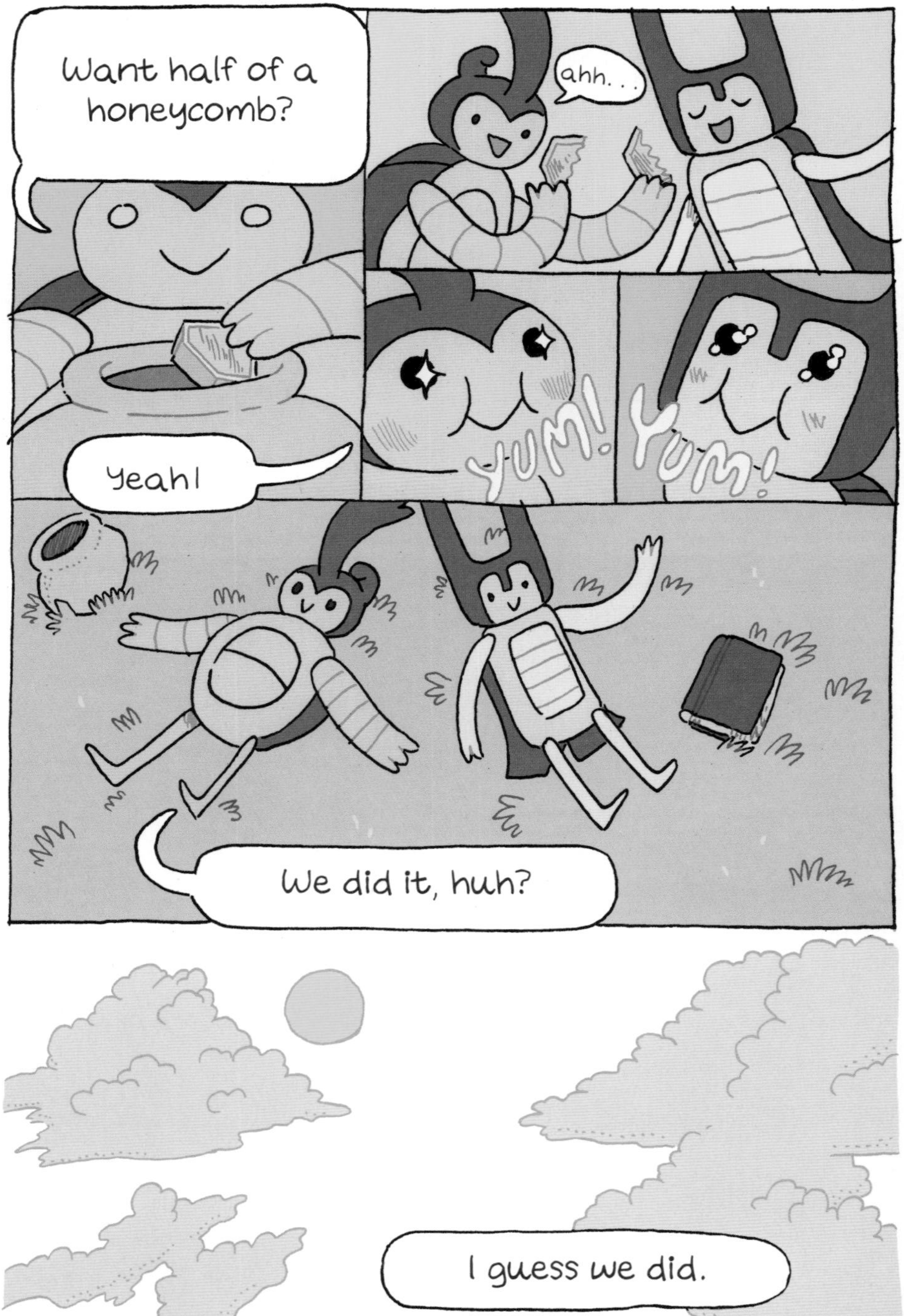
Want half of a honeycomb?
Yeah!
ahh. . .
YUM!
YUM!
We did it, huh?
I guess we did.

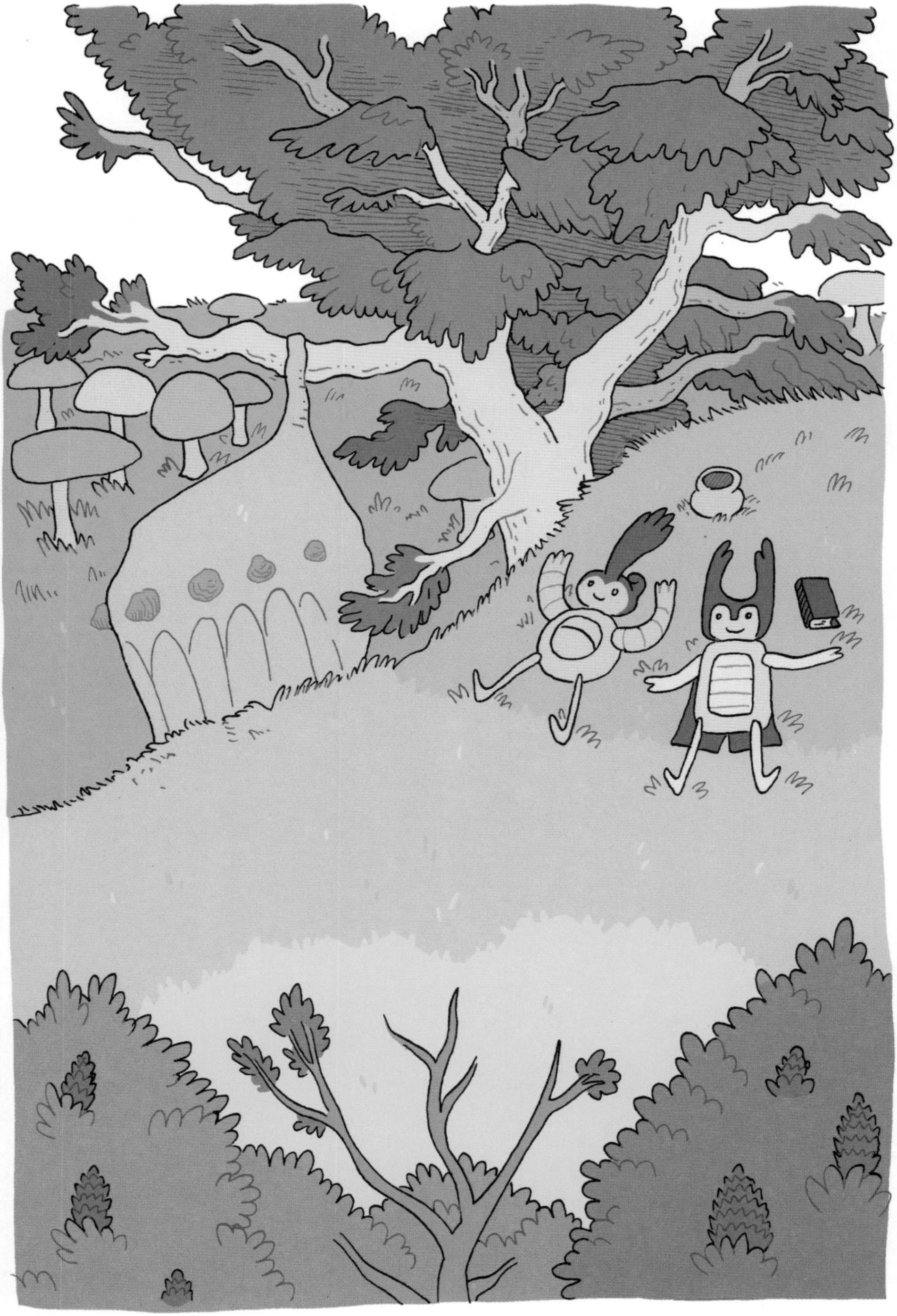

In the Dark

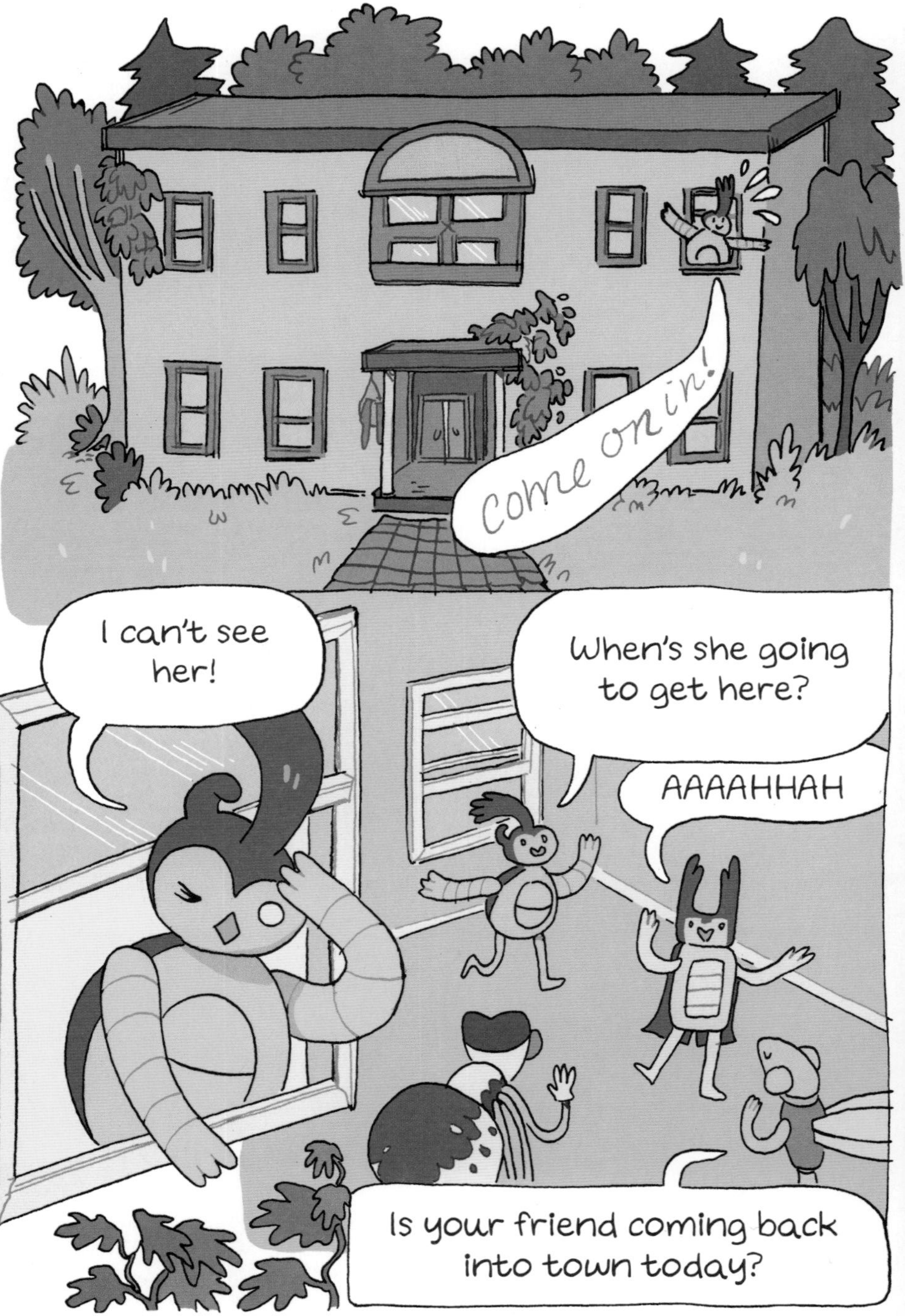
Come on in!
I can't see her!
When's she going to get here?
AAAAHHAH
Is your friend coming back into town today?

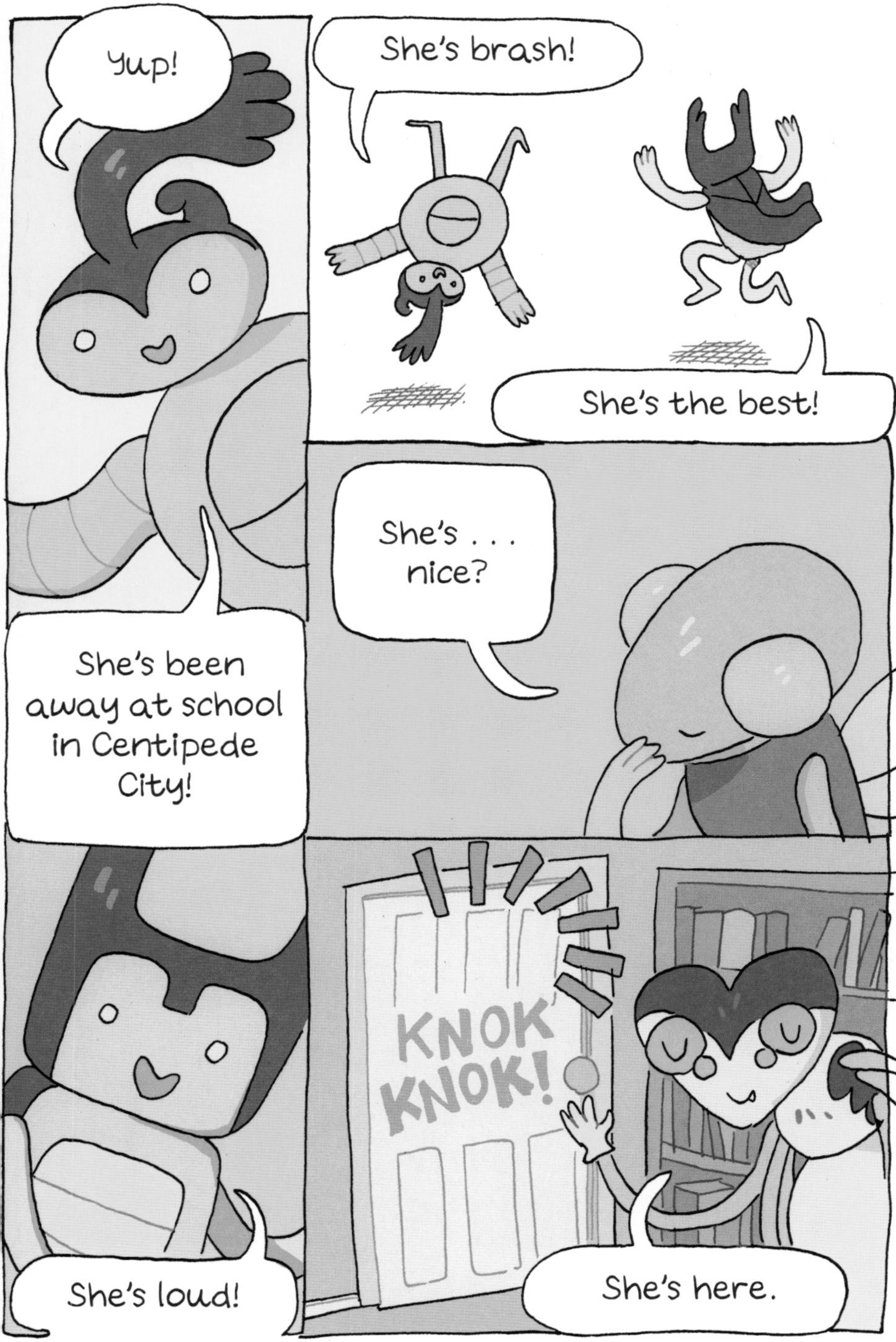
Yup!
She's brash!
She's the best!
She's been away at school in Centipede City!
She's . . . nice?
She's loud!
KNOK KNOK!
She's here.

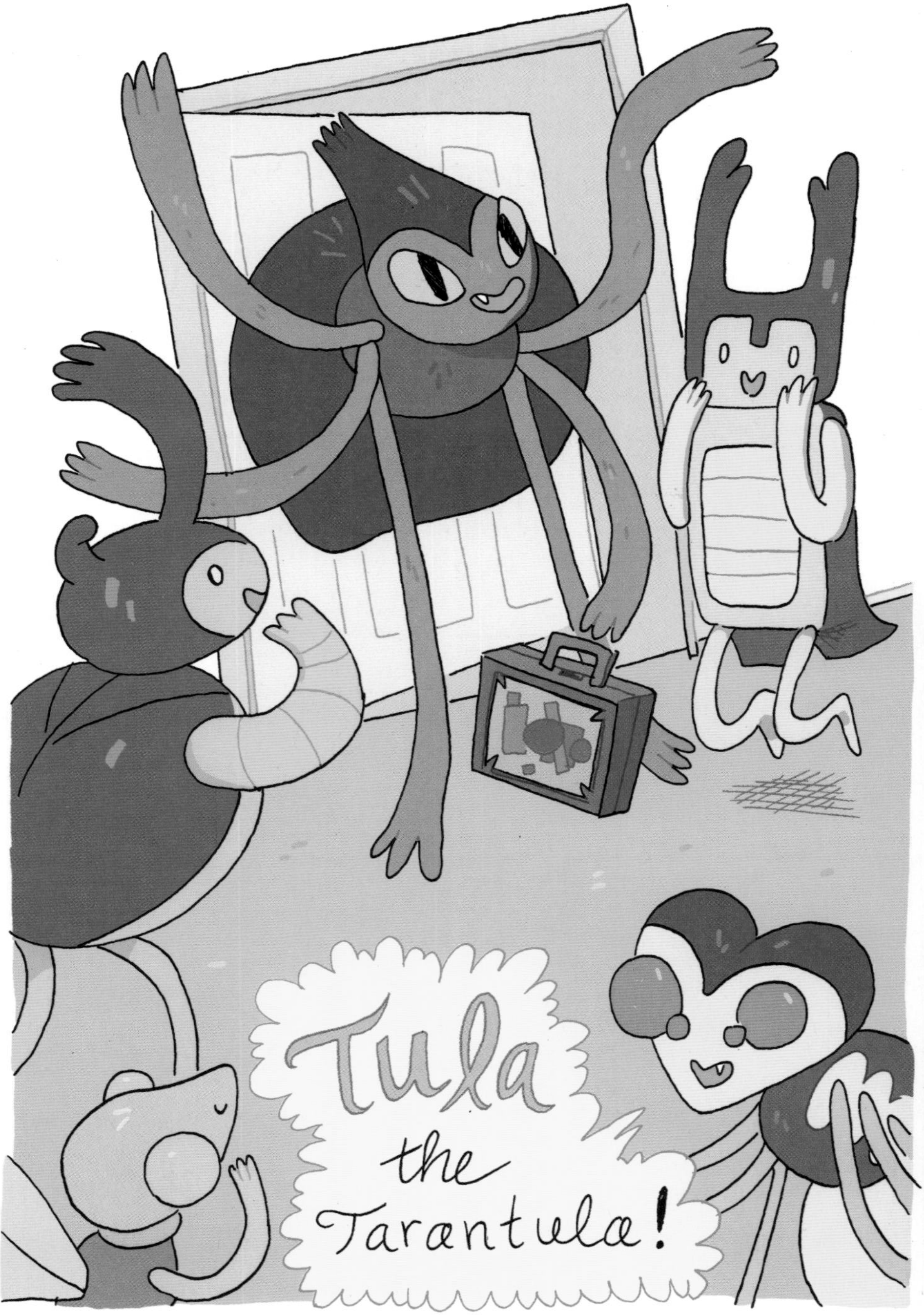
Tula the Tarantula!

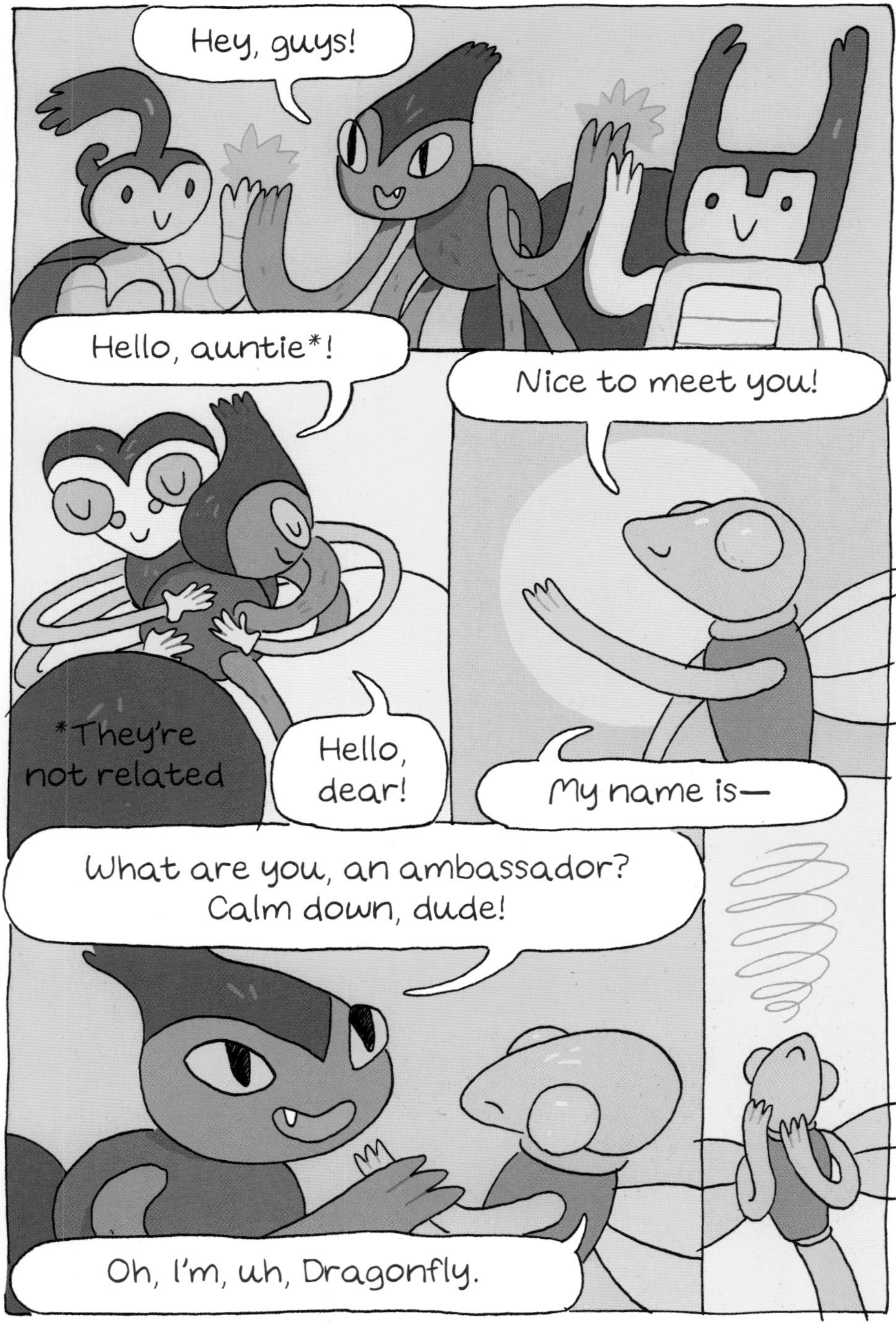
Hey, guys!
Hello, auntie*!
*They're not related
Hello, dear!
Nice to meet you!
My name is—
What are you, an ambassador? Calm down, dude!
Oh, I'm, uh, Dragonfly.

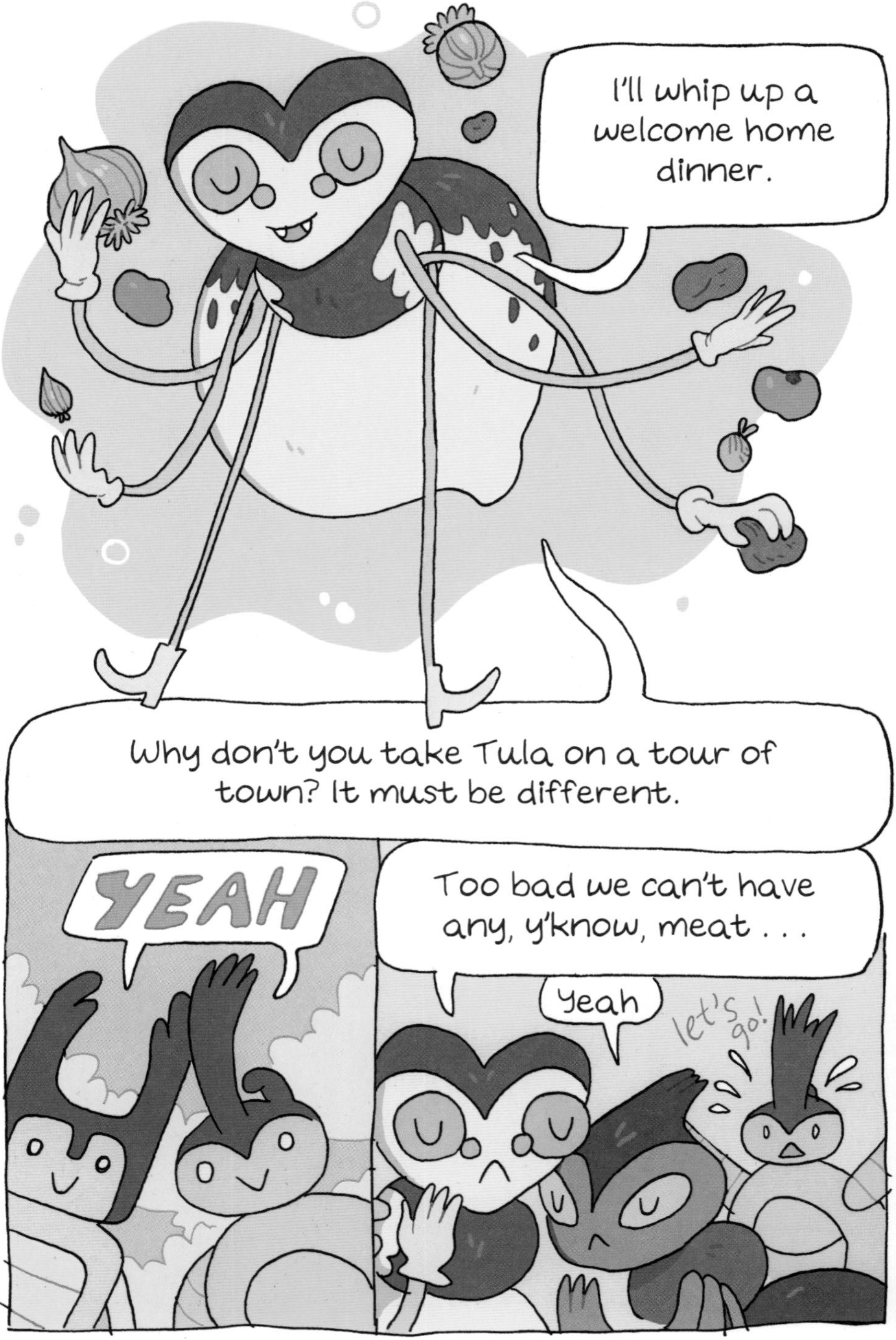
I'll whip up a welcome home dinner.
Why don't you take Tula on a tour of town? It must be different.
YEAH
Too bad we can't have any, y'know, meat . . .
Yeah
let's go!

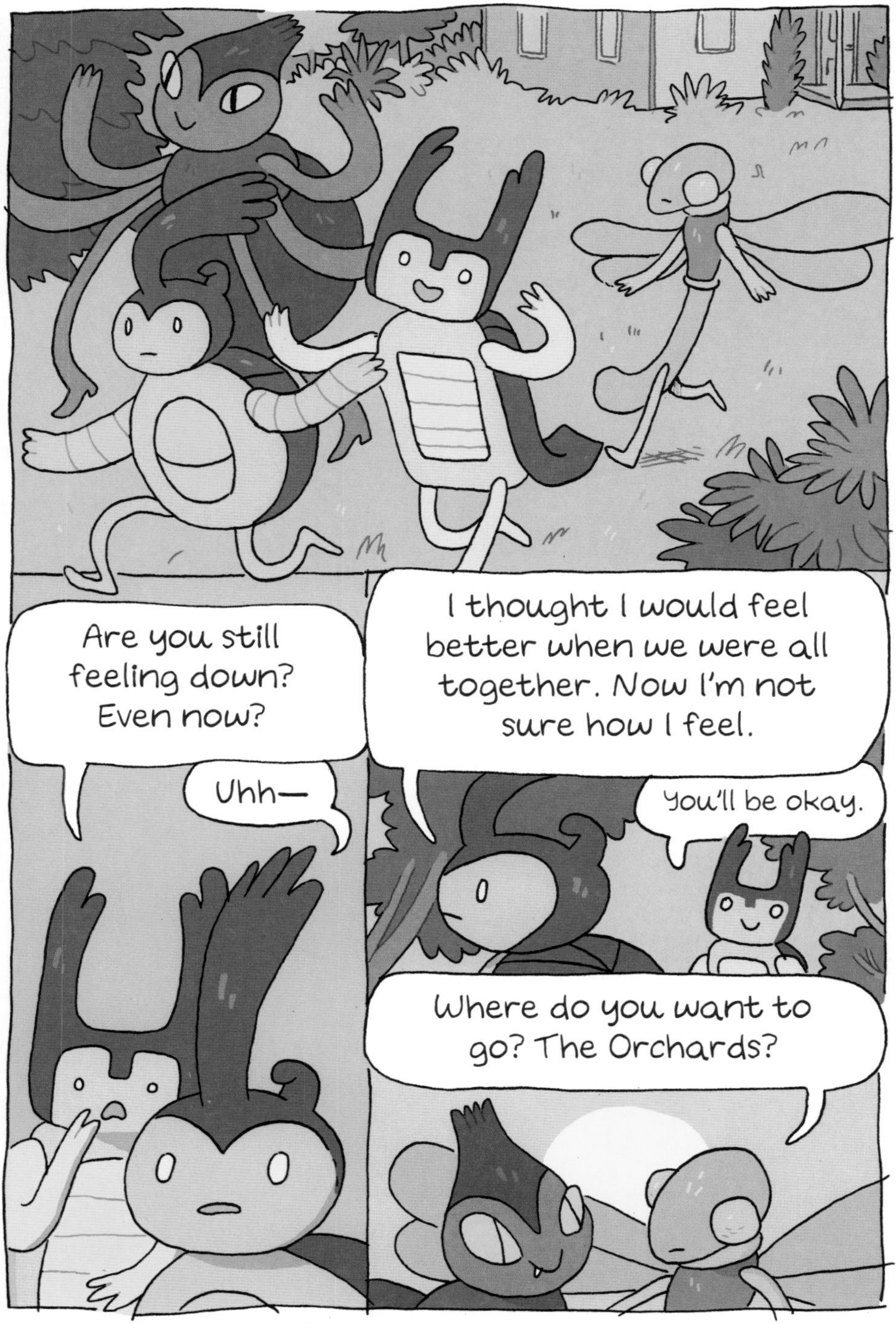
Are you still feeling down? Even now?
I thought I would feel better when we were all together. Now I'm not sure how I feel.
Uhh—
You'll be okay.
Where do you want to go? The Orchards?

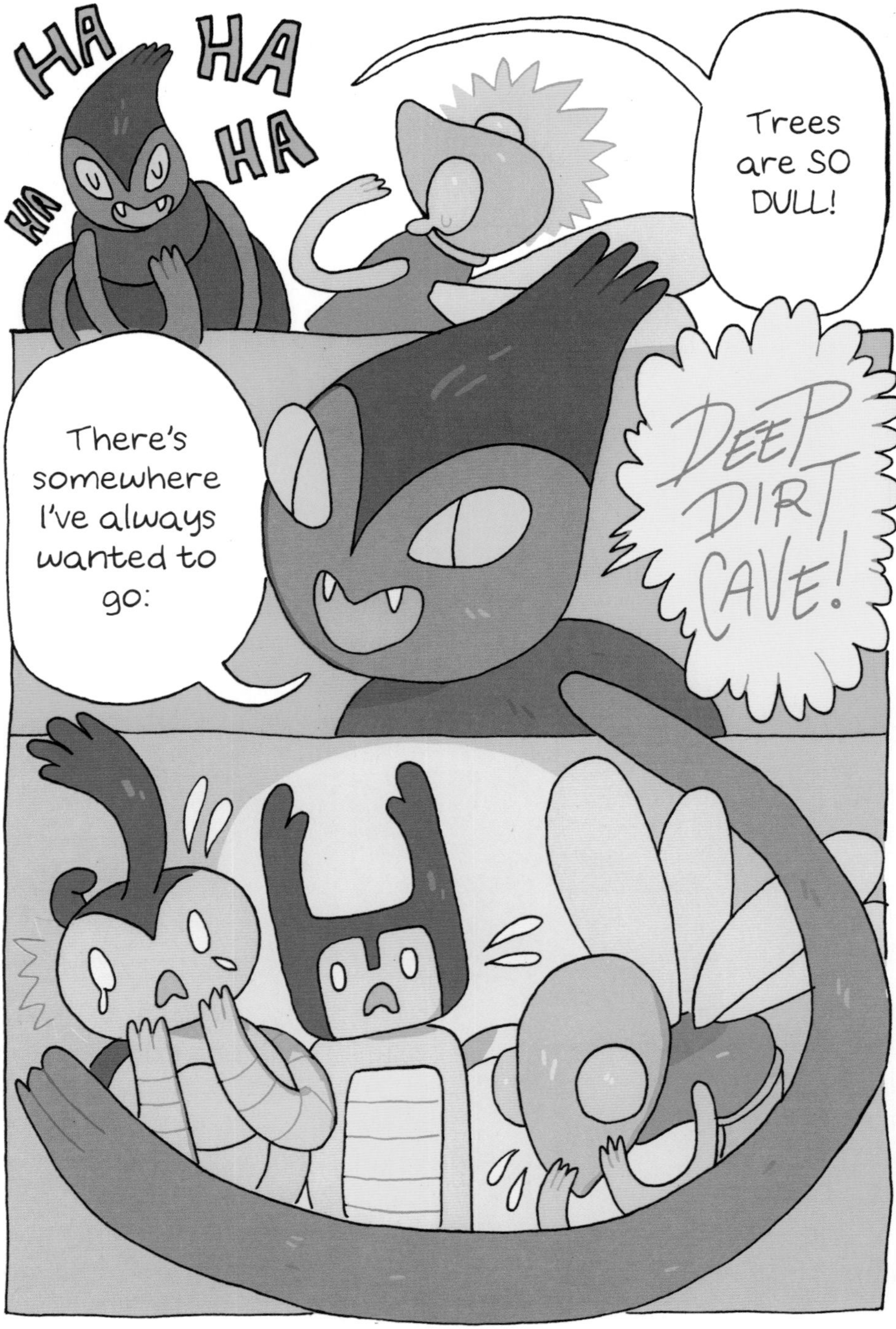
HA
HA
HA
HA
Trees are SO DULL!
There's somewhere I've always wanted to go:
DEEP DIRT CAVE!

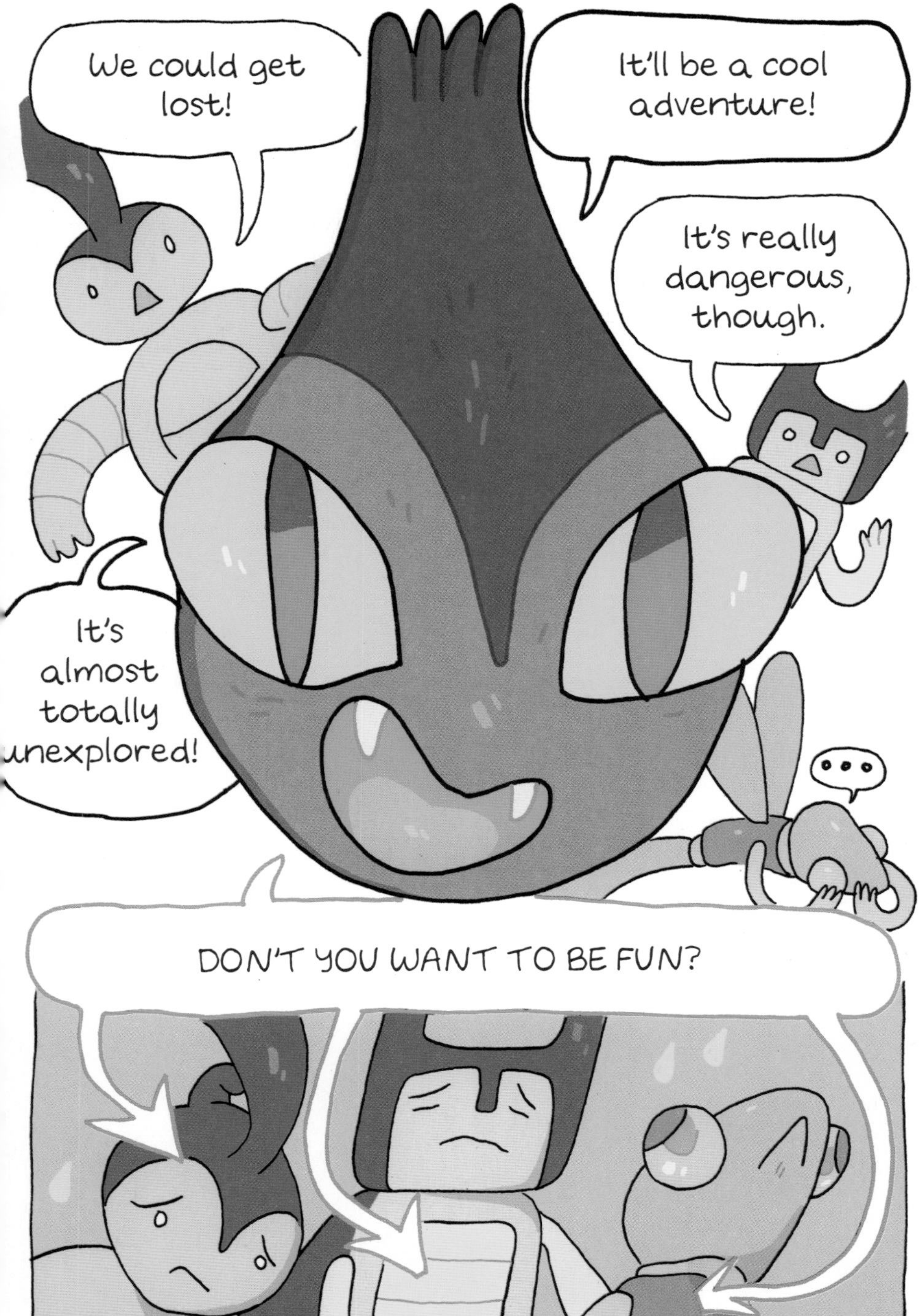
We could get lost!
It'll be a cool adventure!
It's really dangerous, though.
It's almost totally unexplored!
• • •
DON'T YOU WANT TO BE FUN?

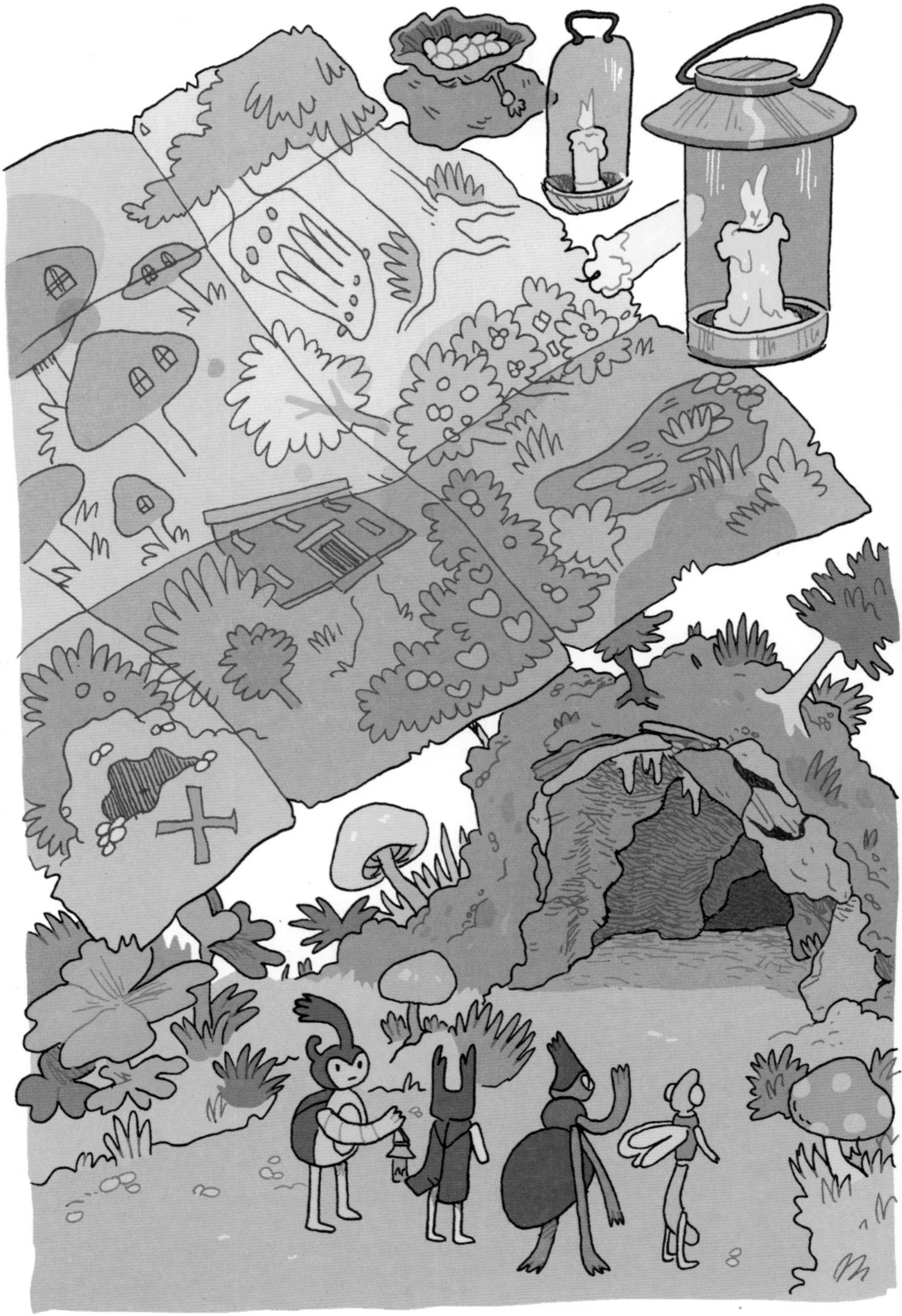

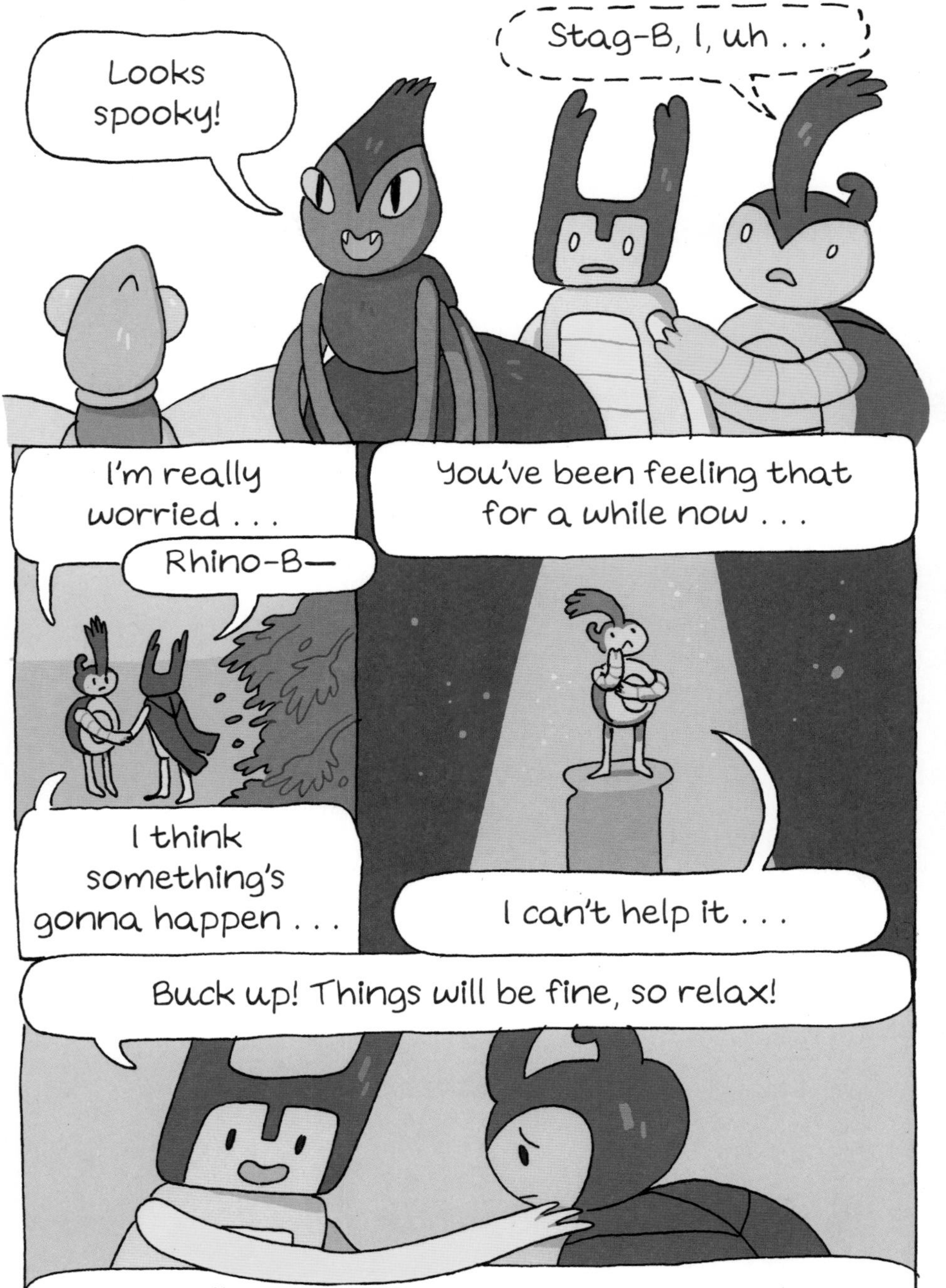

Looks spooky!
Stag-B, I, uh . . .
I'm really worried . . .
Rhino-B—
You've been feeling that for a while now . . .
I think something's gonna happen . . .
I can't help it . . .
Buck up! Things will be fine, so relax!
Usually you're the one cheering me up!

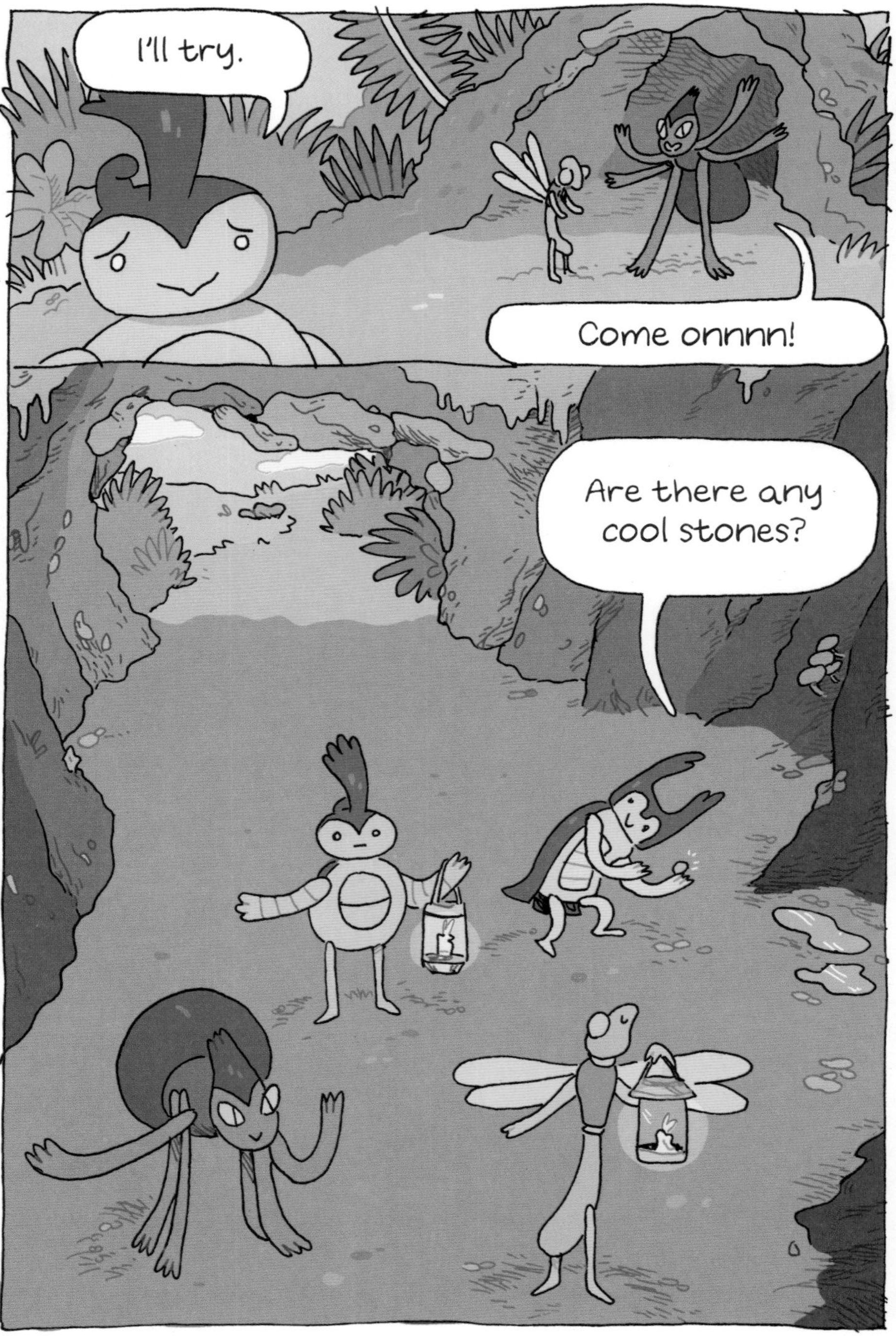
I'll try.
Come onnnn!
Are there any cool stones?

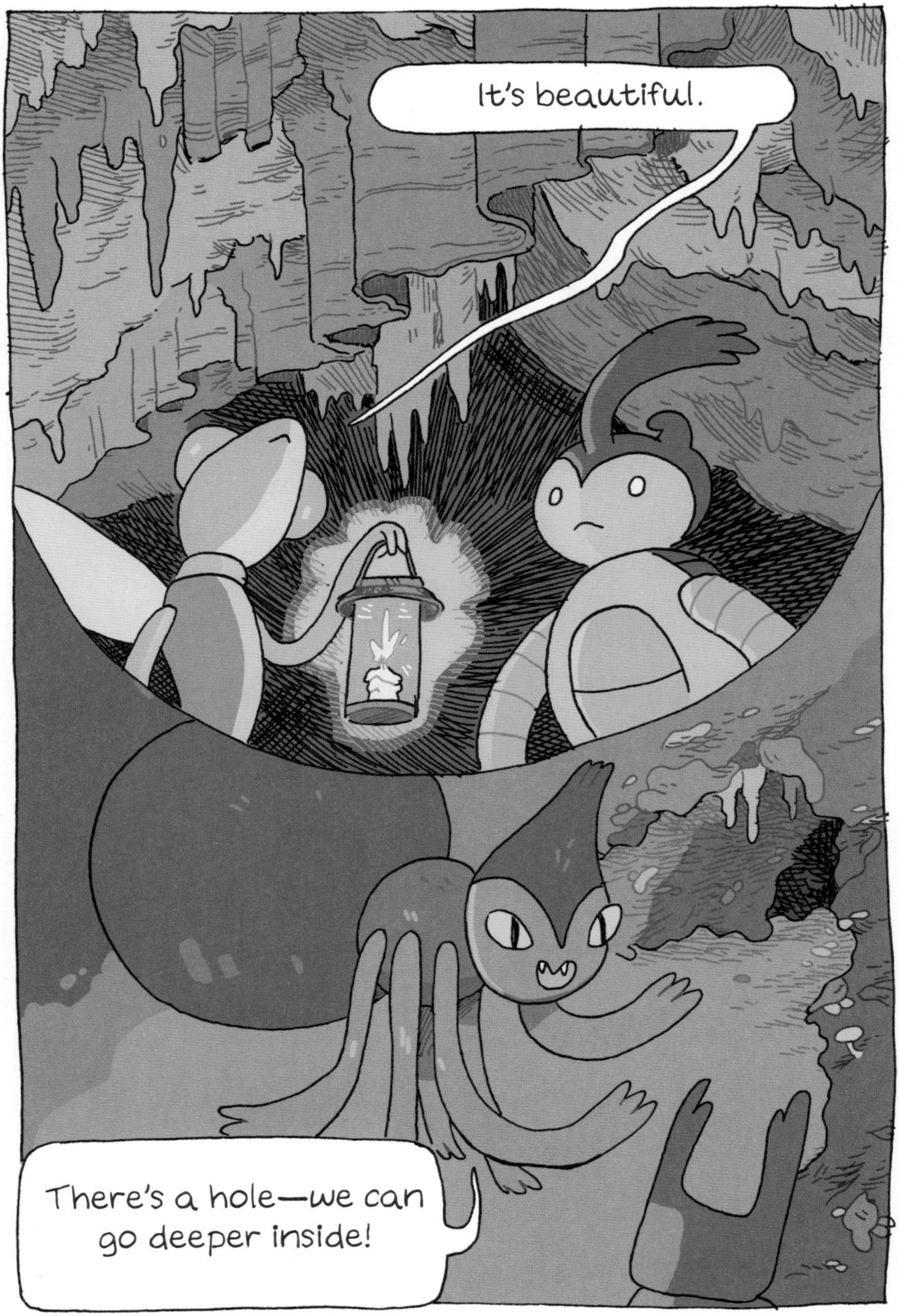
It's beautiful.
There's a hole—we can go deeper inside!

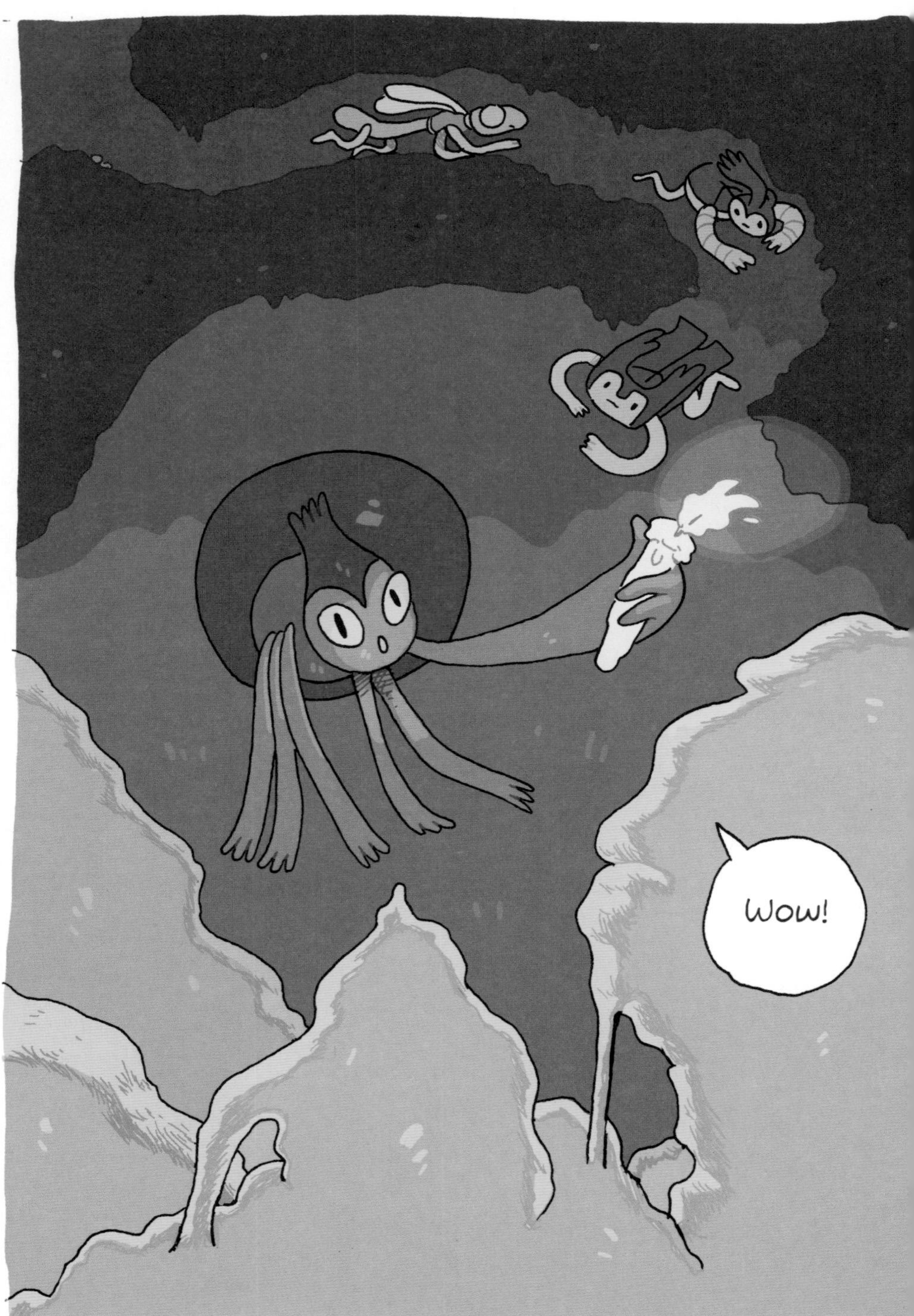
WOW!

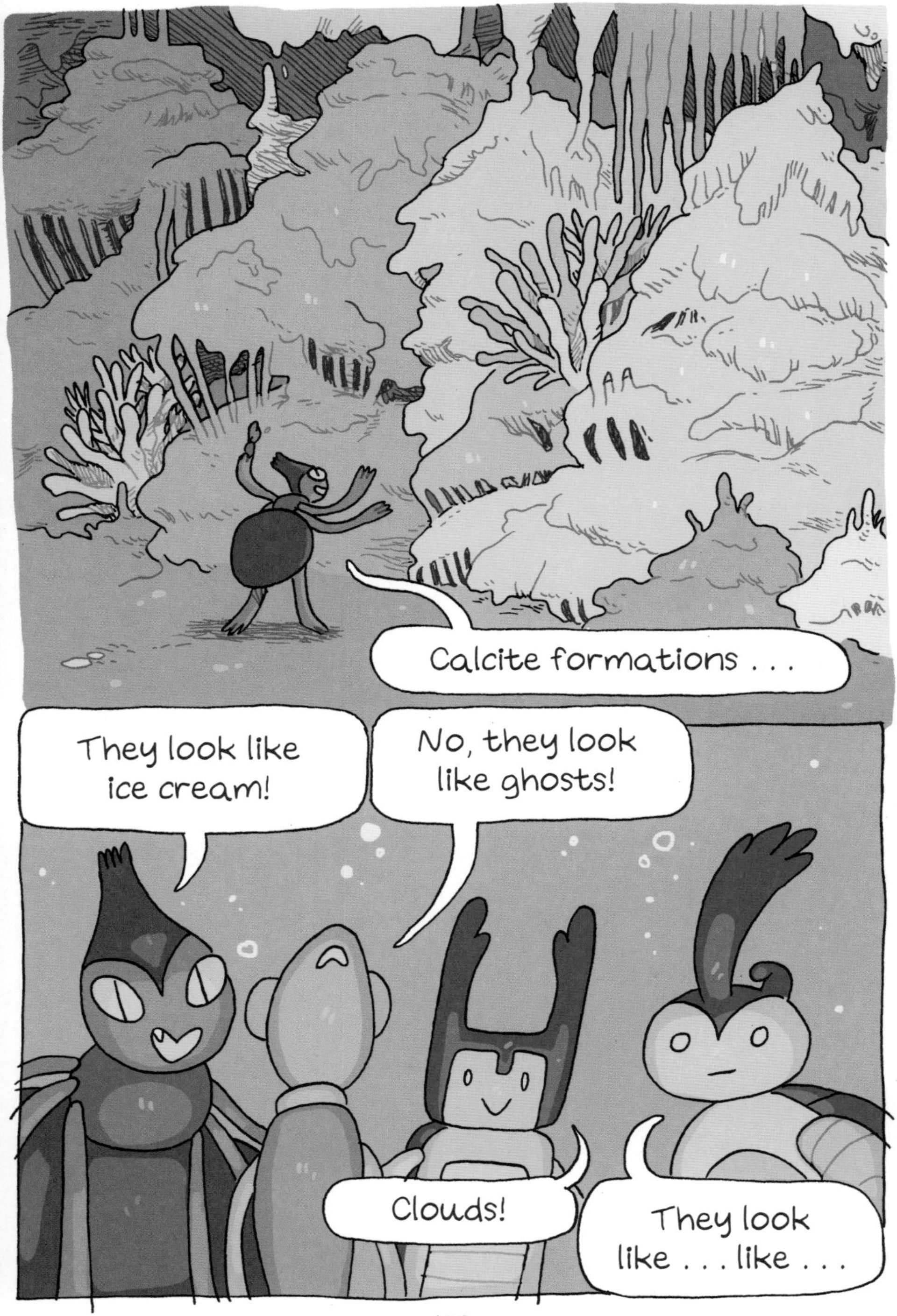
Calcite formations . . .
They look like ice cream!
No, they look like ghosts!
Clouds!
They look like . . . like . . .

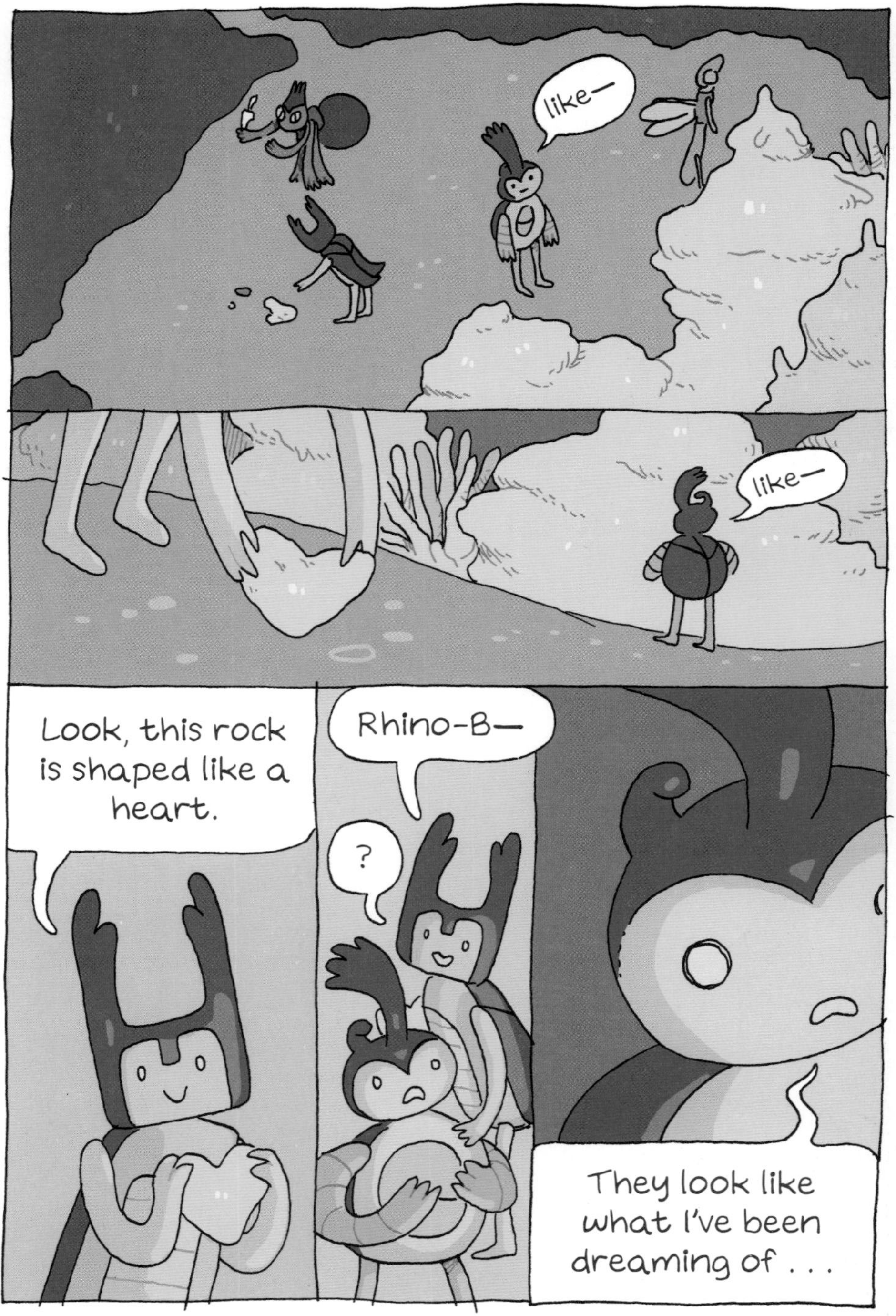
like—
like—
Look, this rock is shaped like a heart.
Rhino-B—
?
They look like what I've been dreaming of . . .

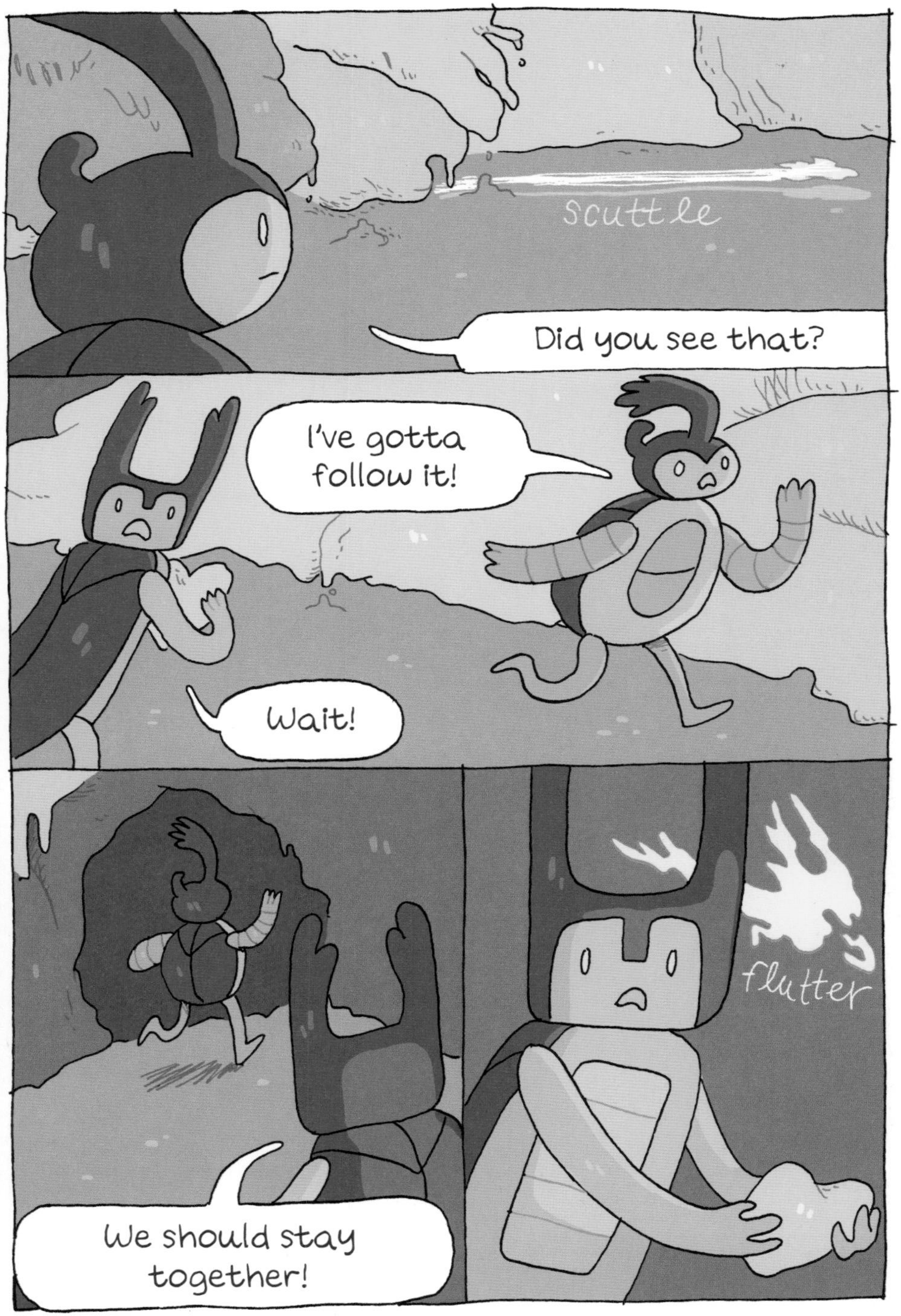
scuttle
Did you see that?
I've gotta follow it!
Wait!
We should stay together!
flutter

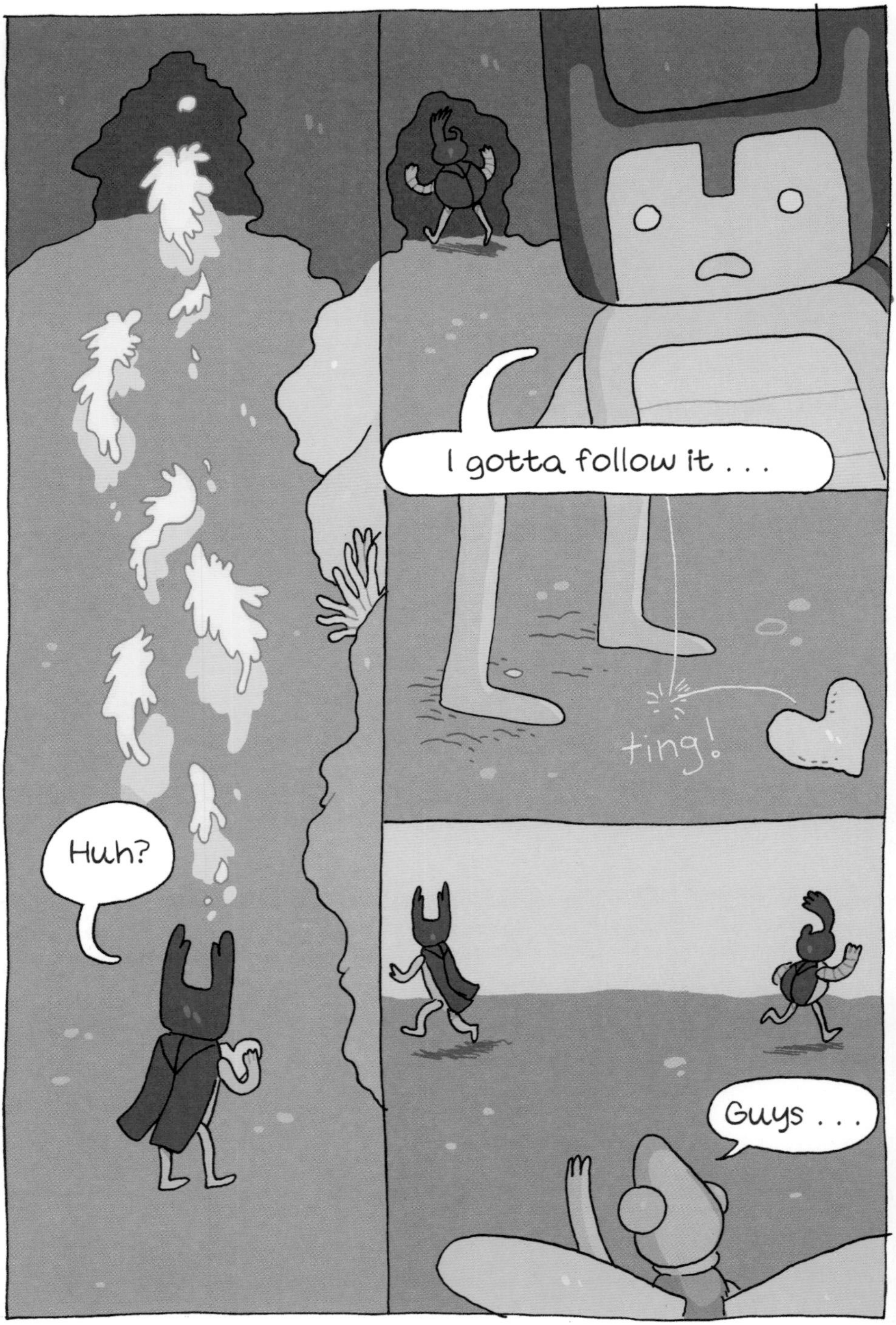
Huh?
I gotta follow it . . .
ting!
Guys . . .

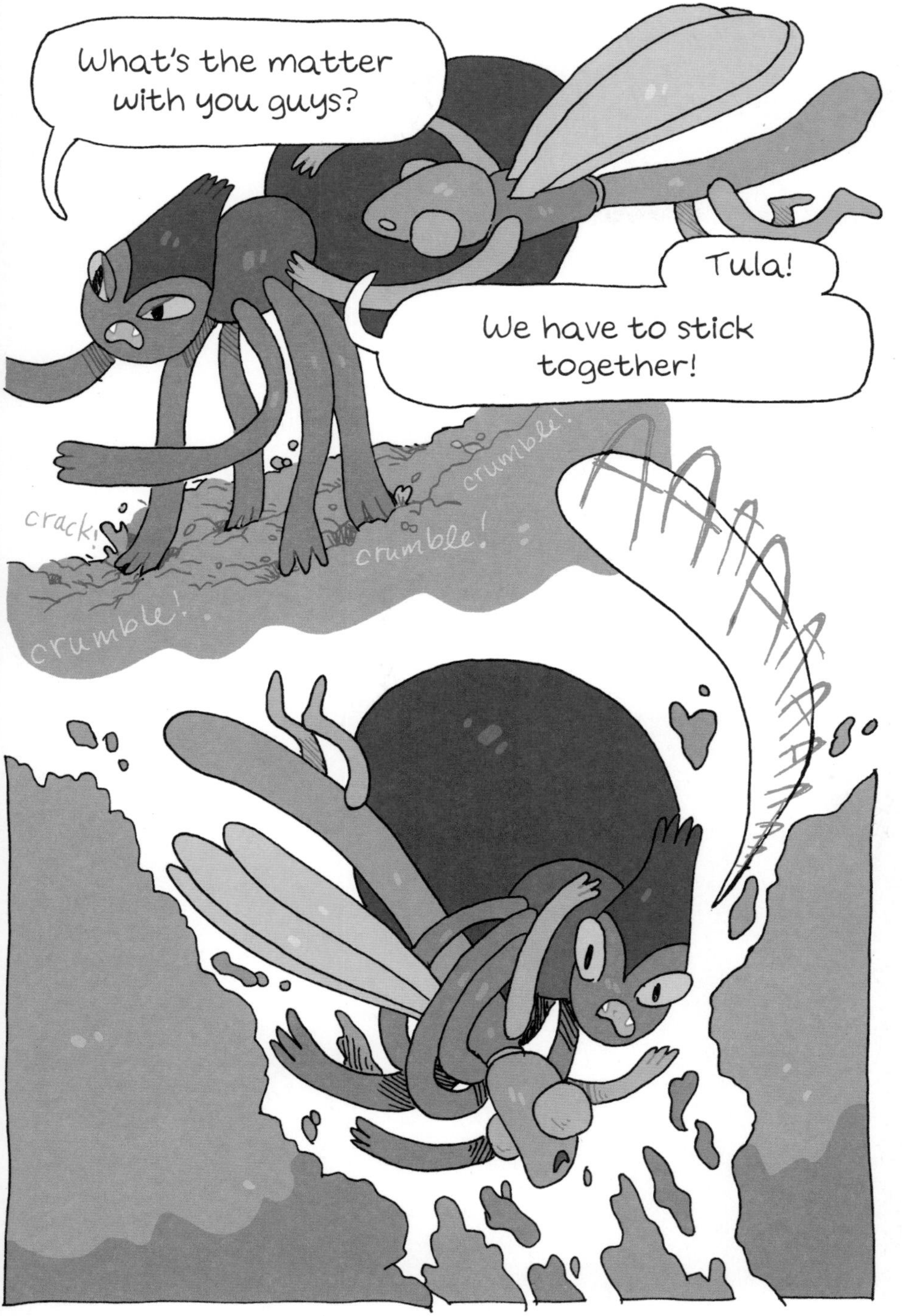
What's the matter with you guys?
Tula!
We have to stick together!
crack!
crumble!
crumble!
crumble!
crumble!
AAAAAAAAAAAAA

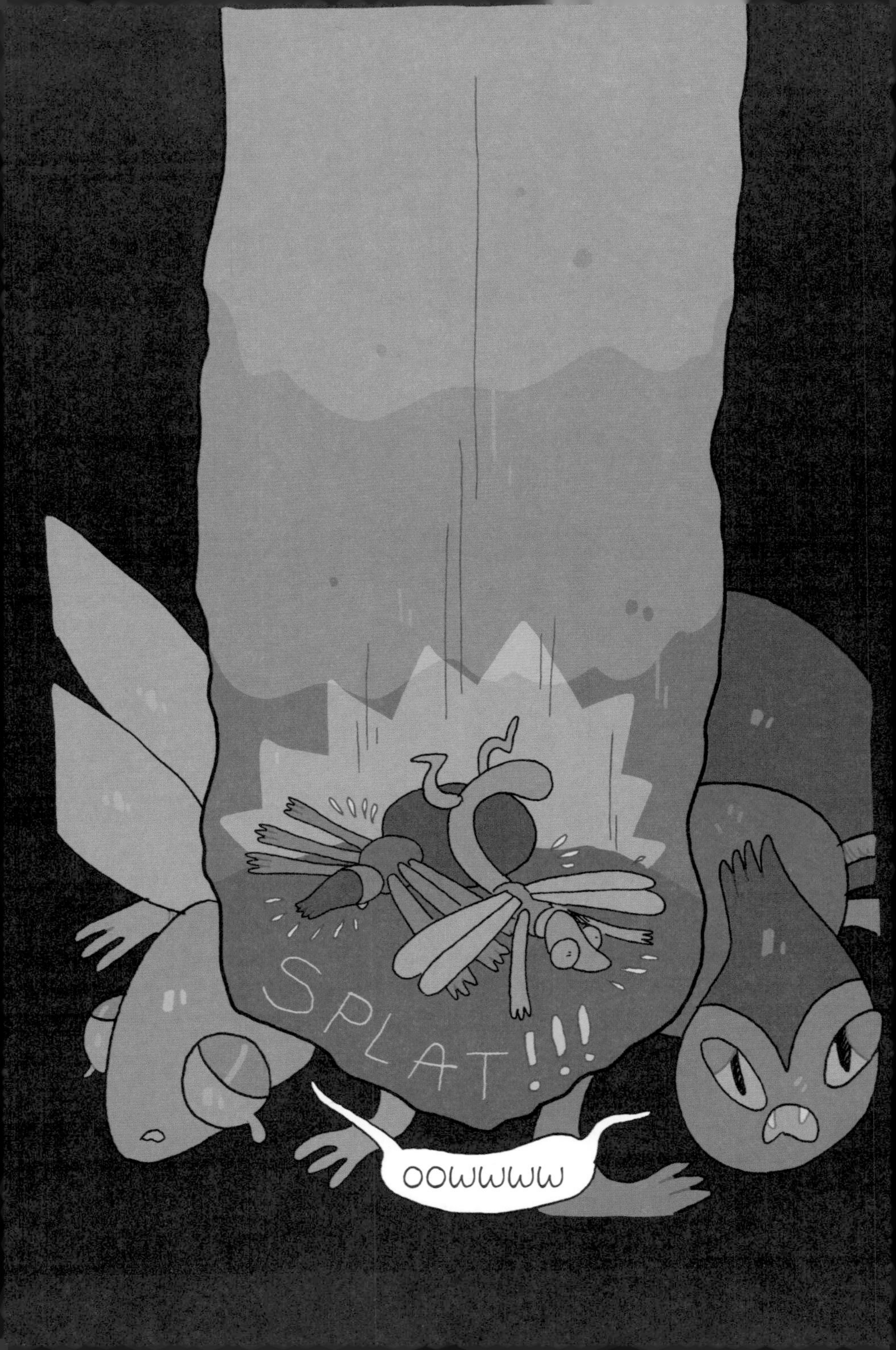
SPLAT!!!
OOWWWW

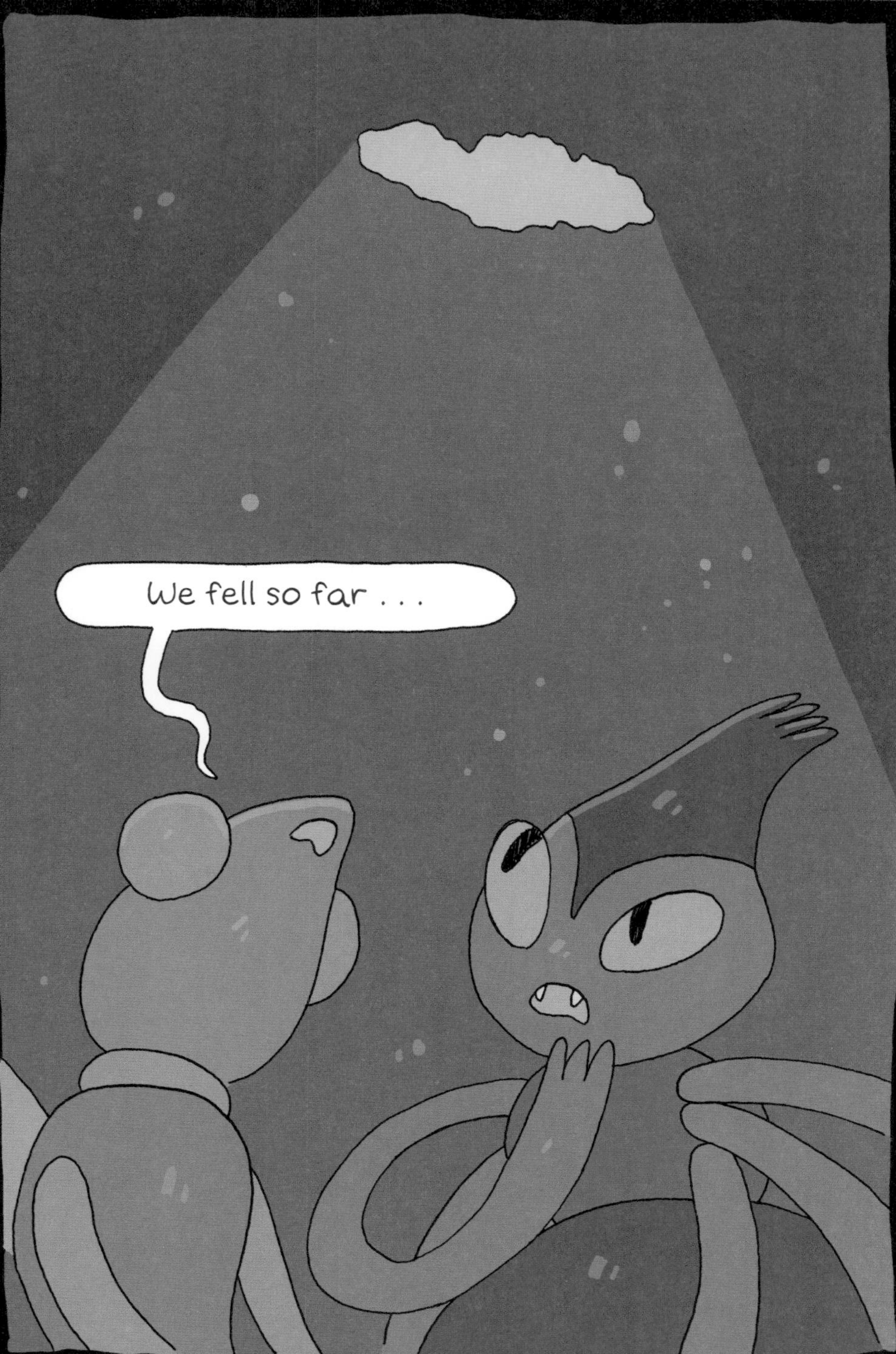
We fell so far . . .

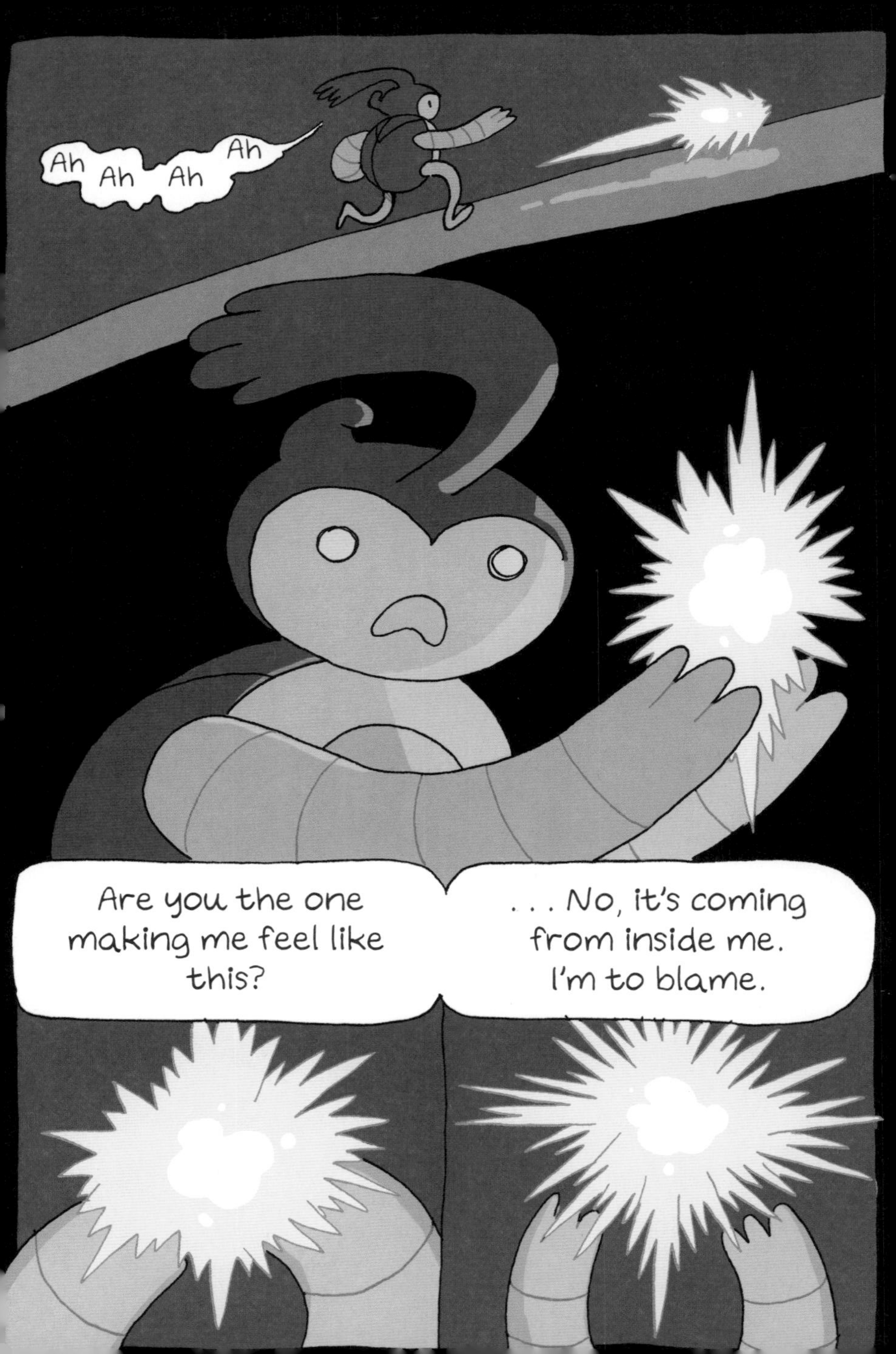
Ah Ah Ah Ah
Are you the one making me feel like this?
. . . No, it's coming from inside me. I'm to blame.

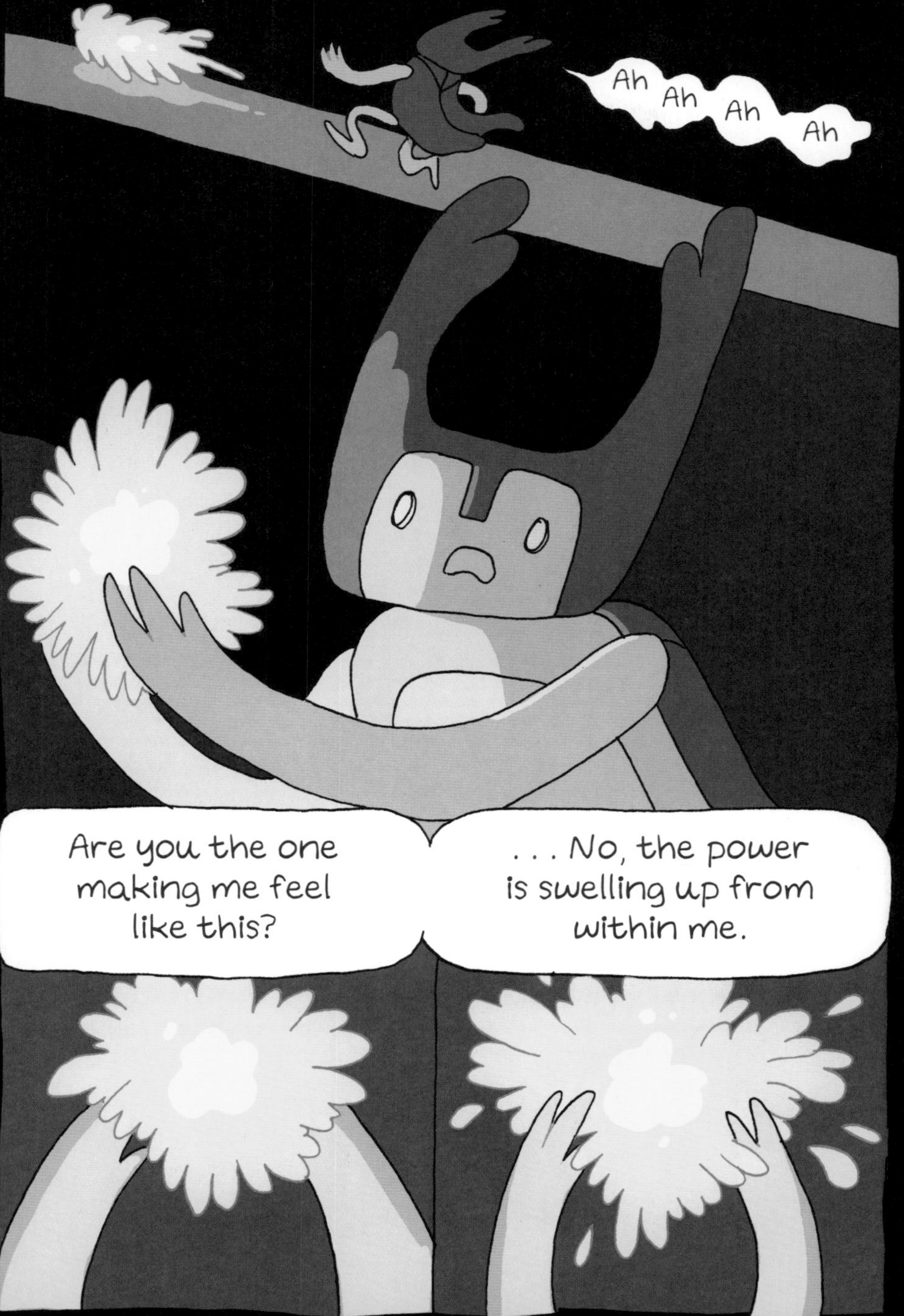
Ah Ah Ah Ah
Are you the one making me feel like this?
. . . No, the power is swelling up from within me.

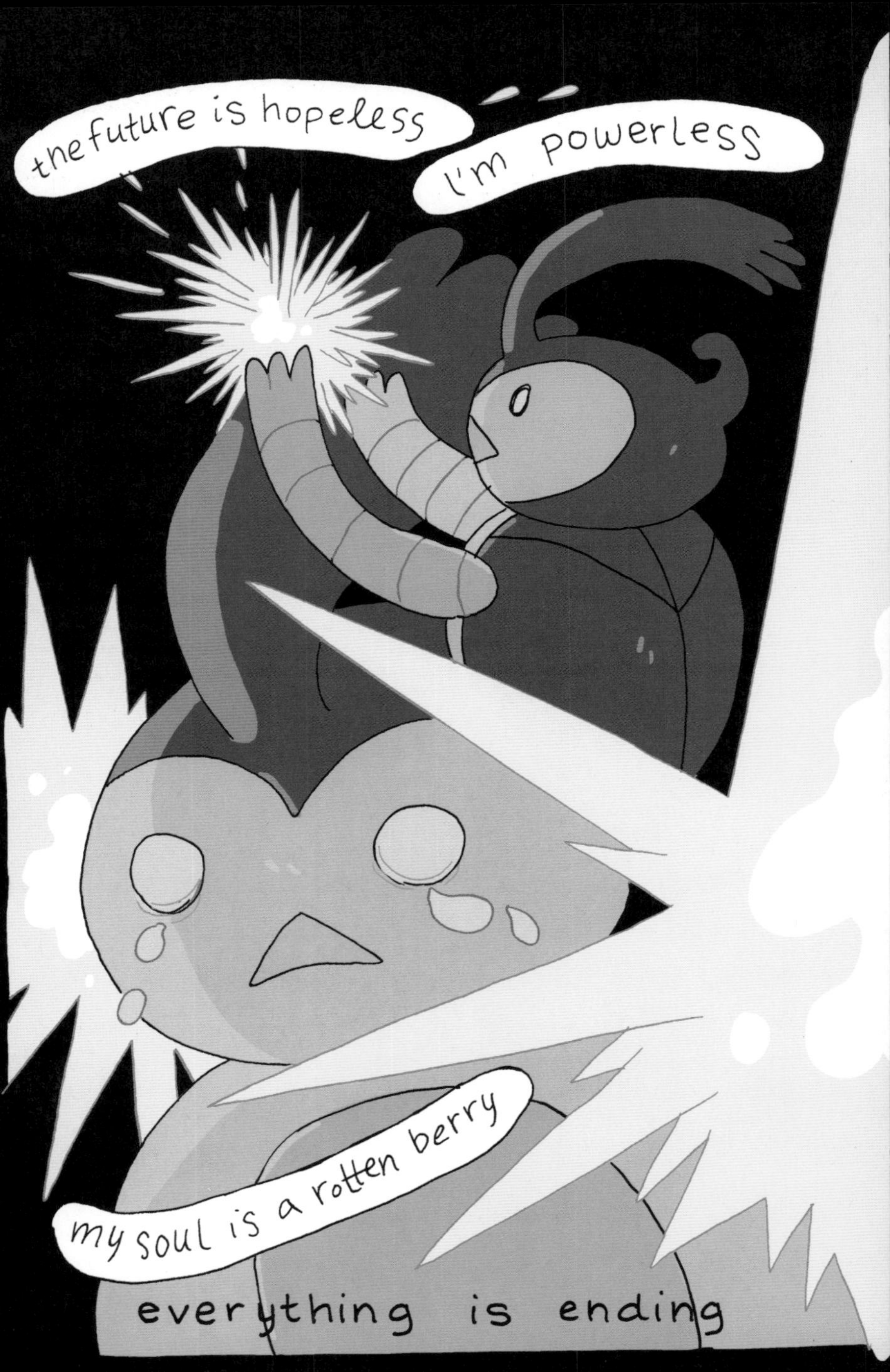
the future is hopeless
i'm powerless
my soul is a rotten berry
everything is ending

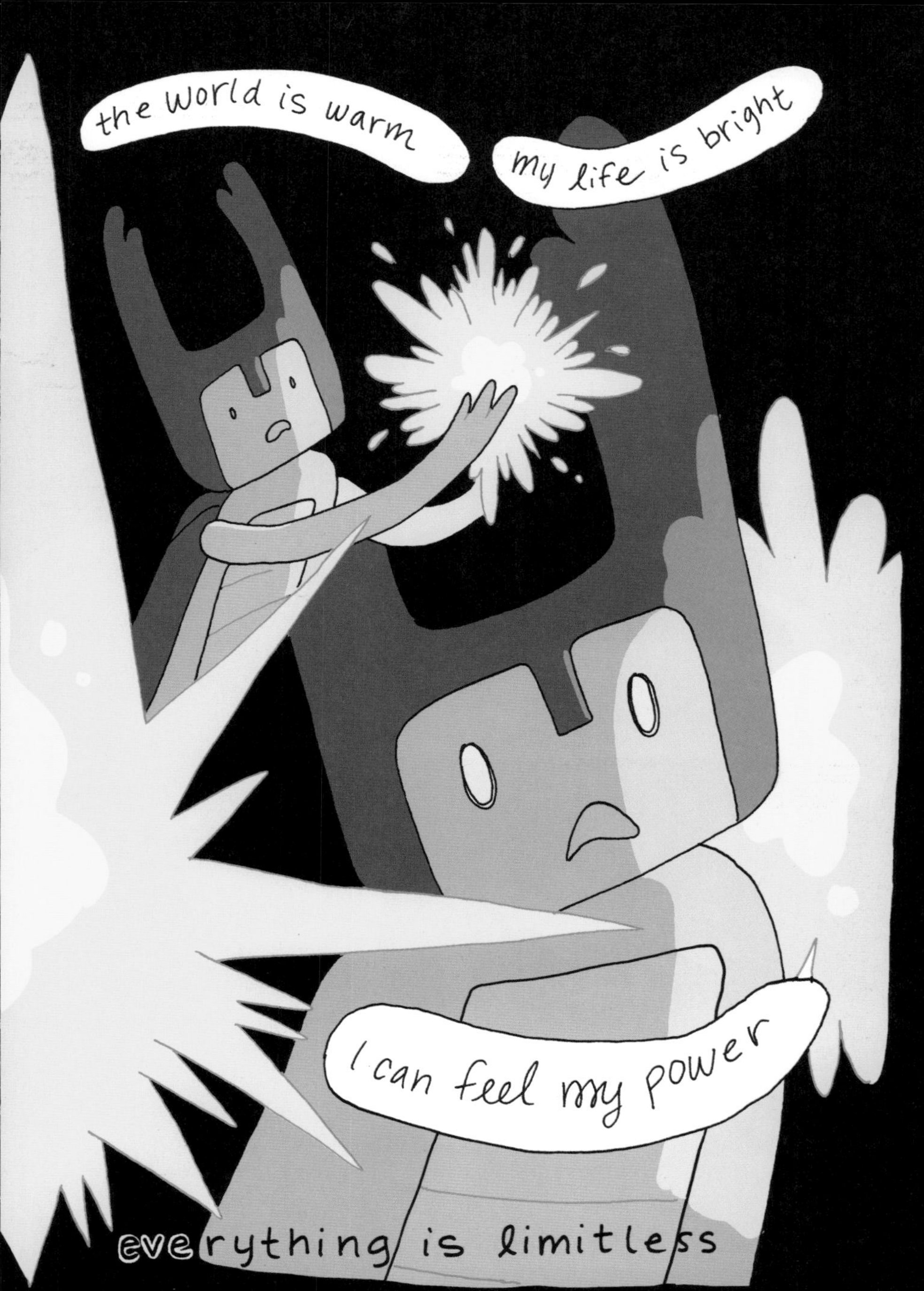
the world is warm
my life is bright
I can feel my power
everything is limitless

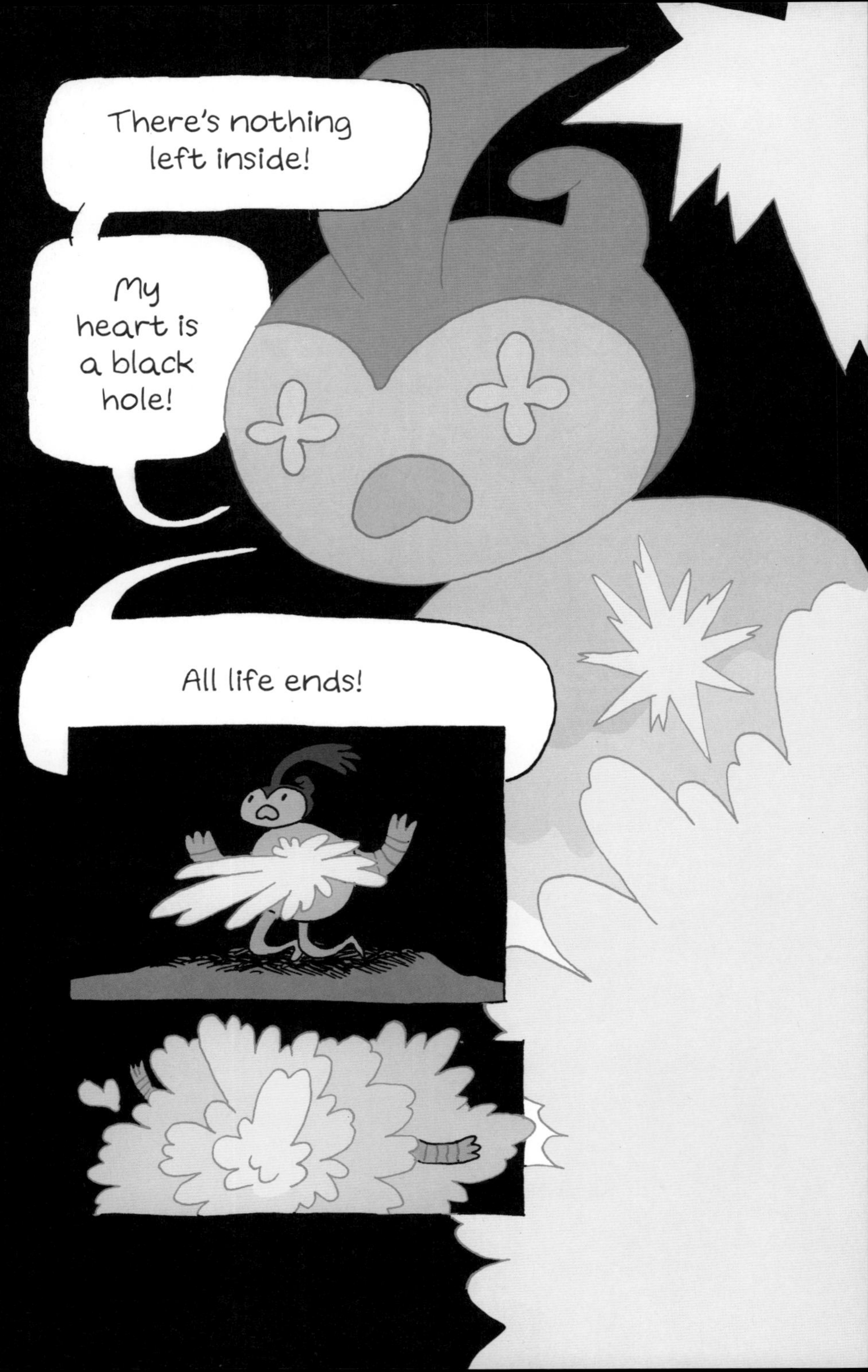
There's nothing left inside!
My heart is a black hole!
All life ends!

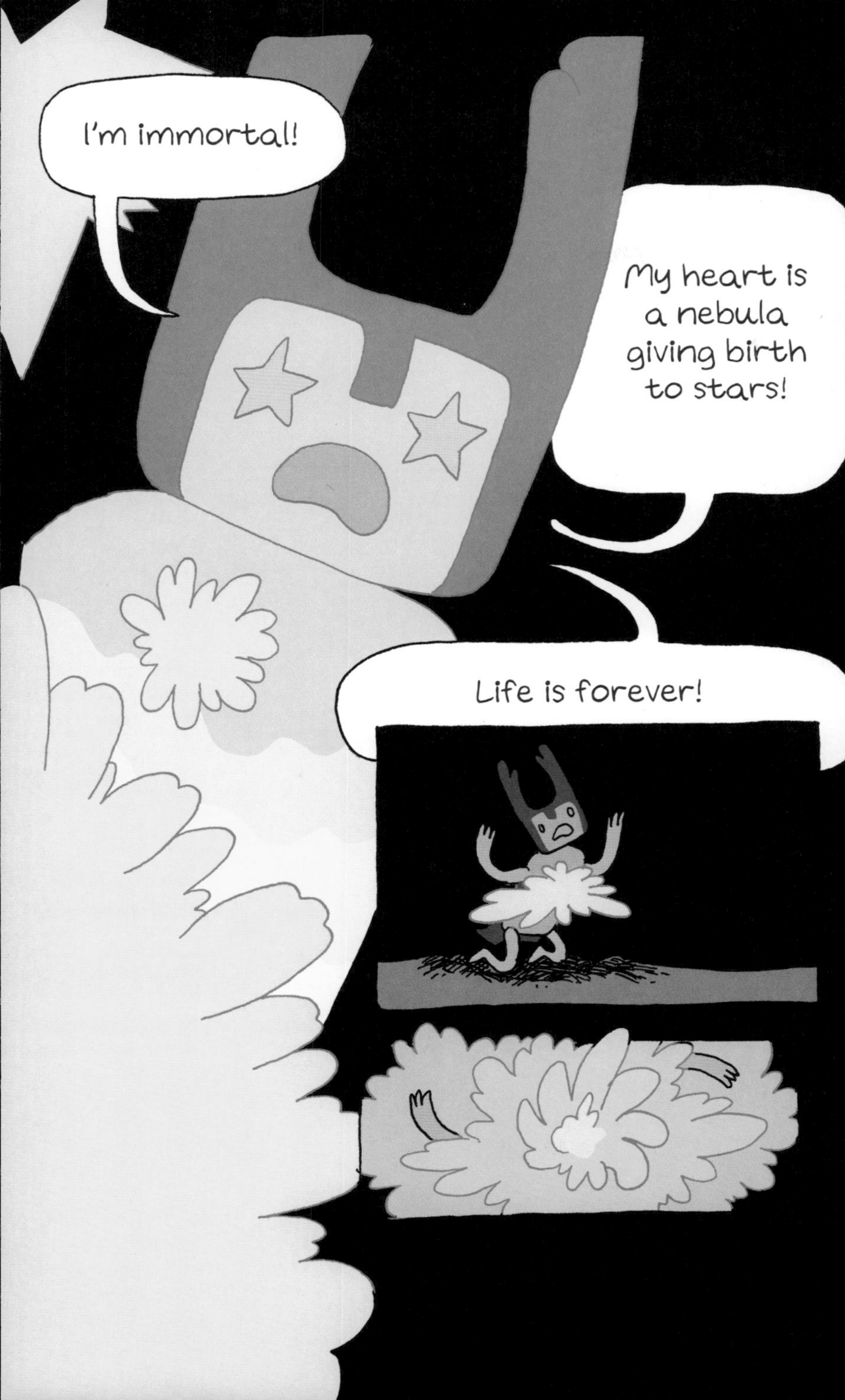
I'm immortal!
My heart is a nebula giving birth to stars!
Life is forever!

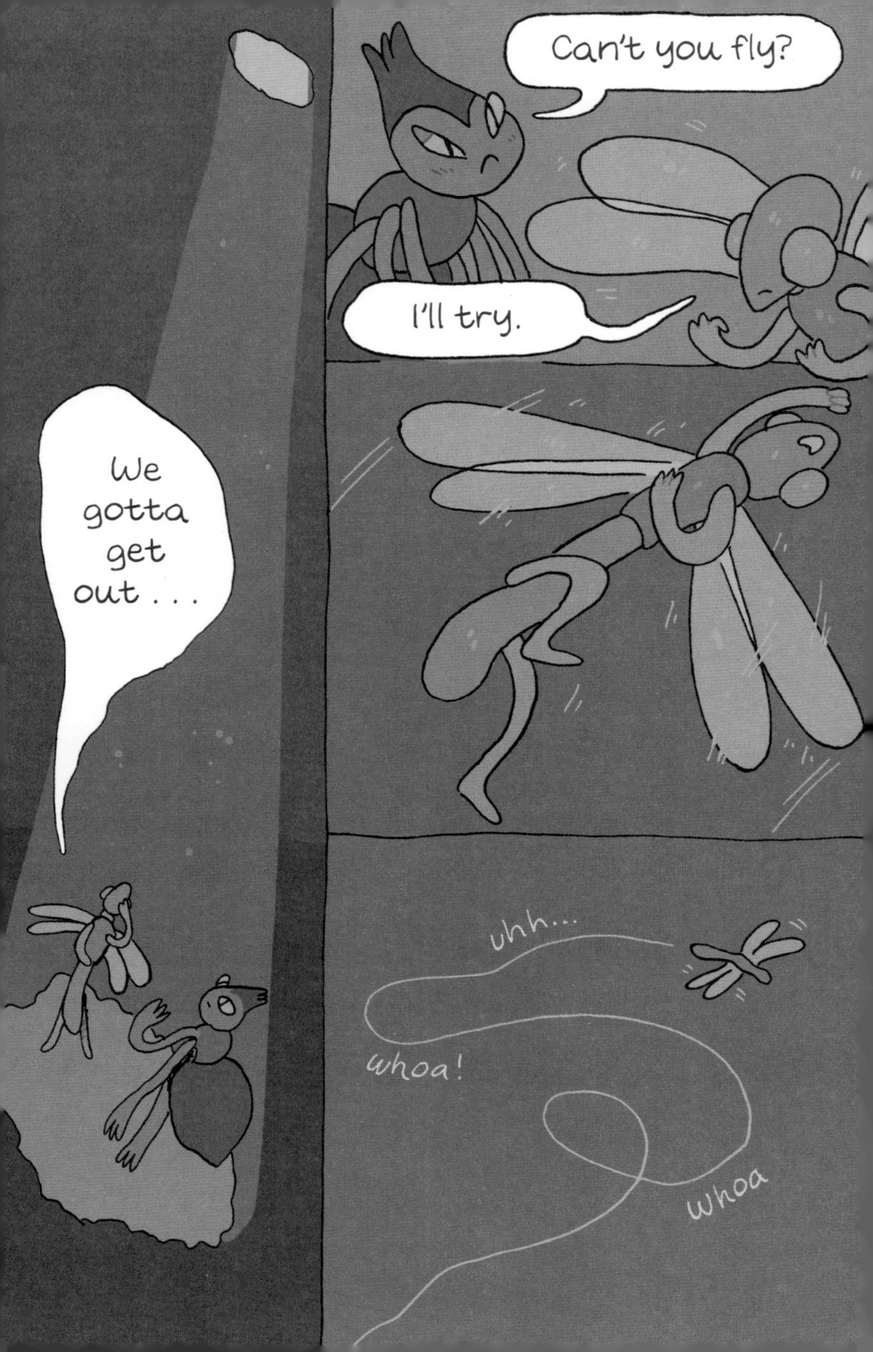
We gotta get out . . .
Can't you fly?
I'll try.
uhh...
whoa!
whoa

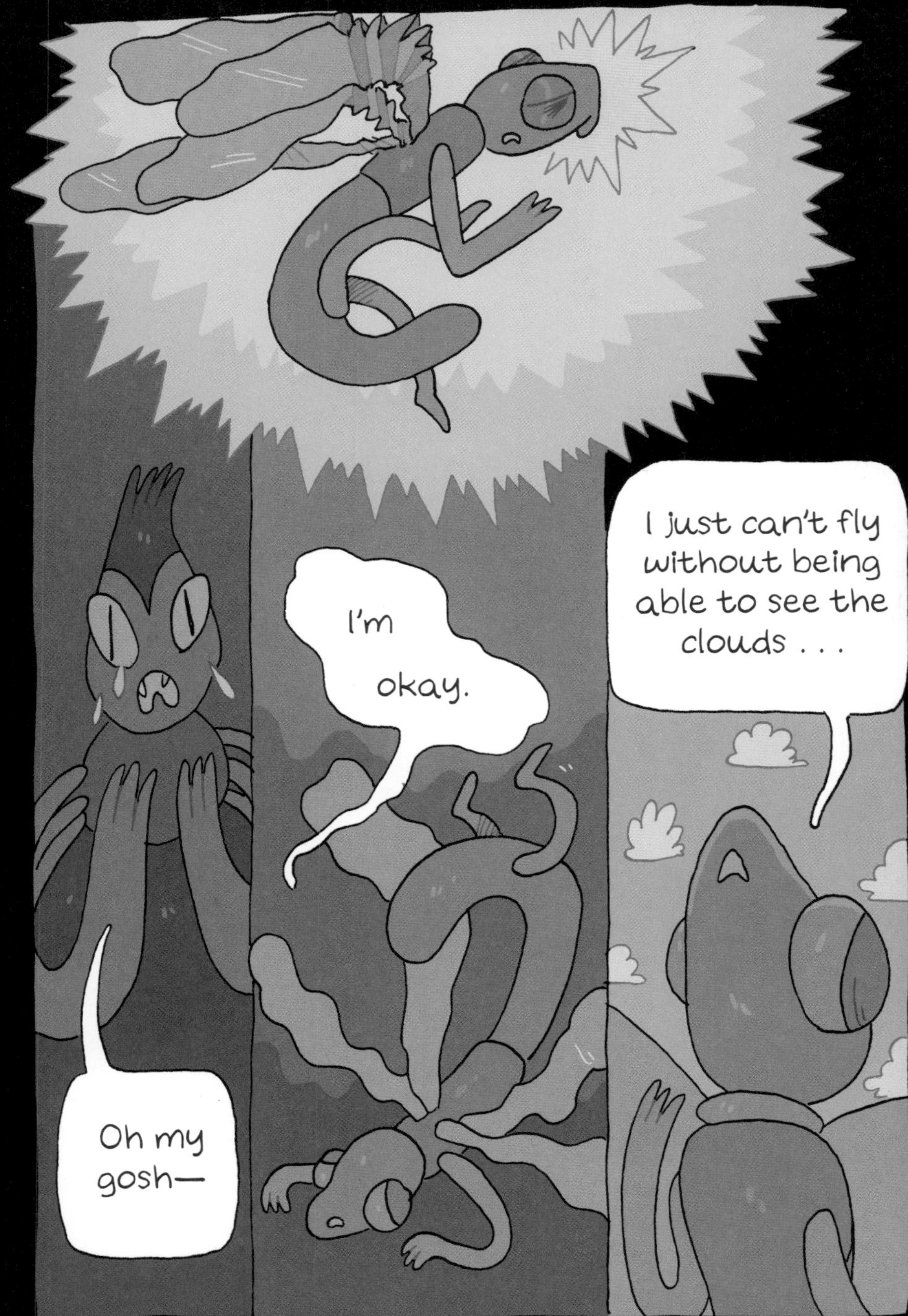
Oh my gosh—
I'm okay.
I just can't fly without being able to see the clouds . . .

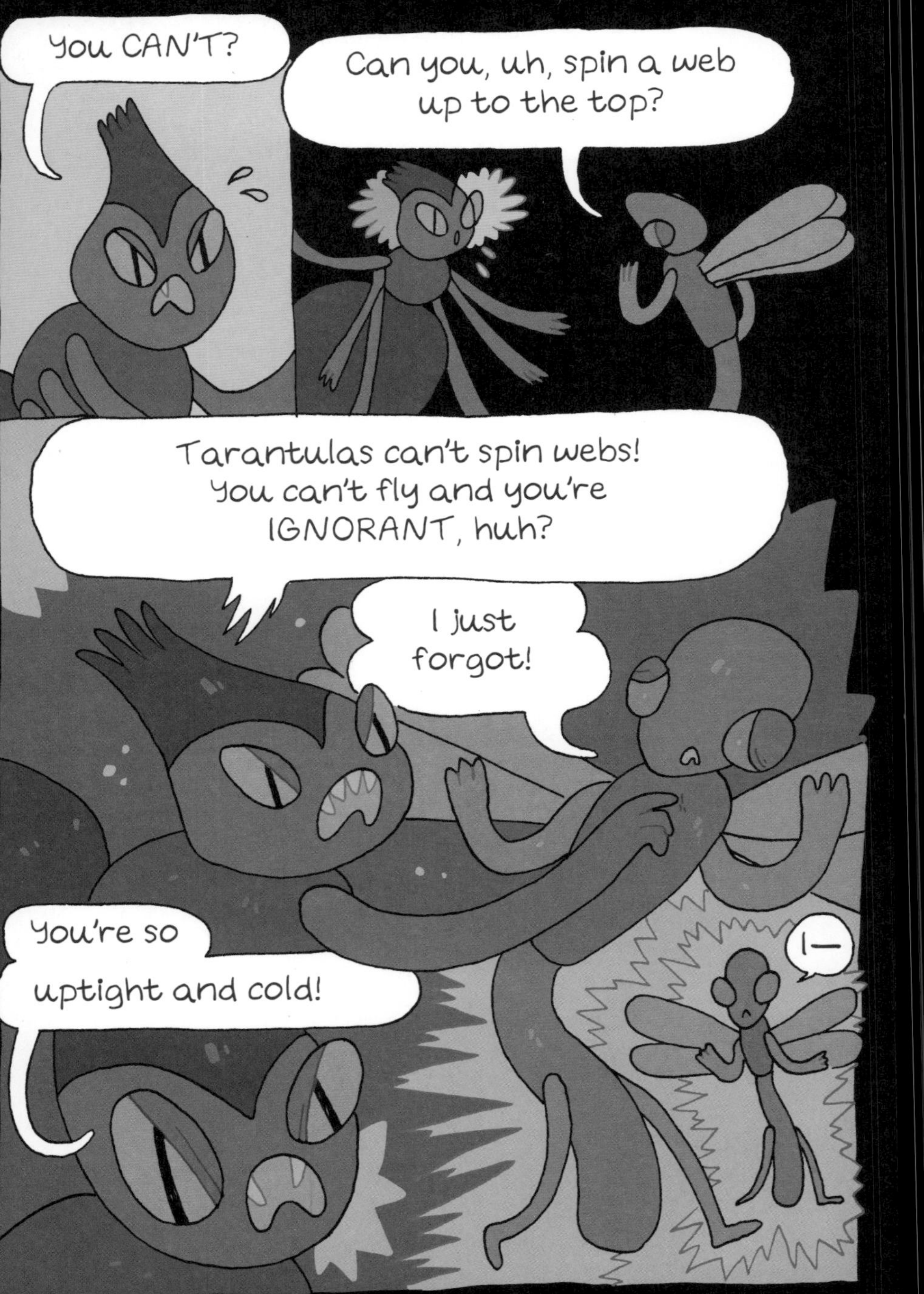
You CAN'T?
Can you, uh, spin a web up to the top?
Tarantulas can't spin webs! You can't fly and you're IGNORANT, huh?
I just forgot!
You're so
uptight and cold!
I—

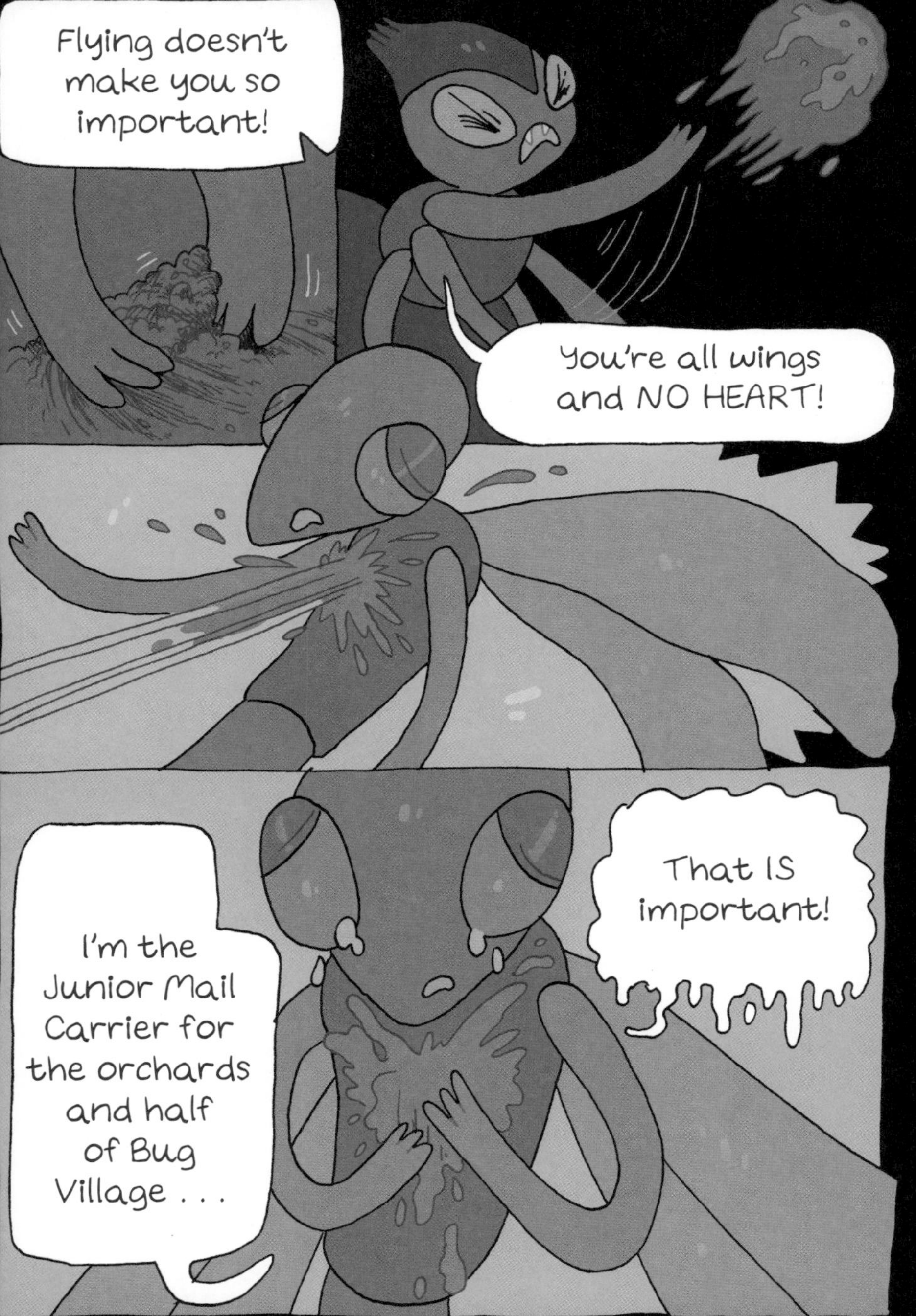
Flying doesn't make you so important!
You're all wings and NO HEART!
That IS important!
I'm the Junior Mail Carrier for the orchards and half of Bug Village . . .

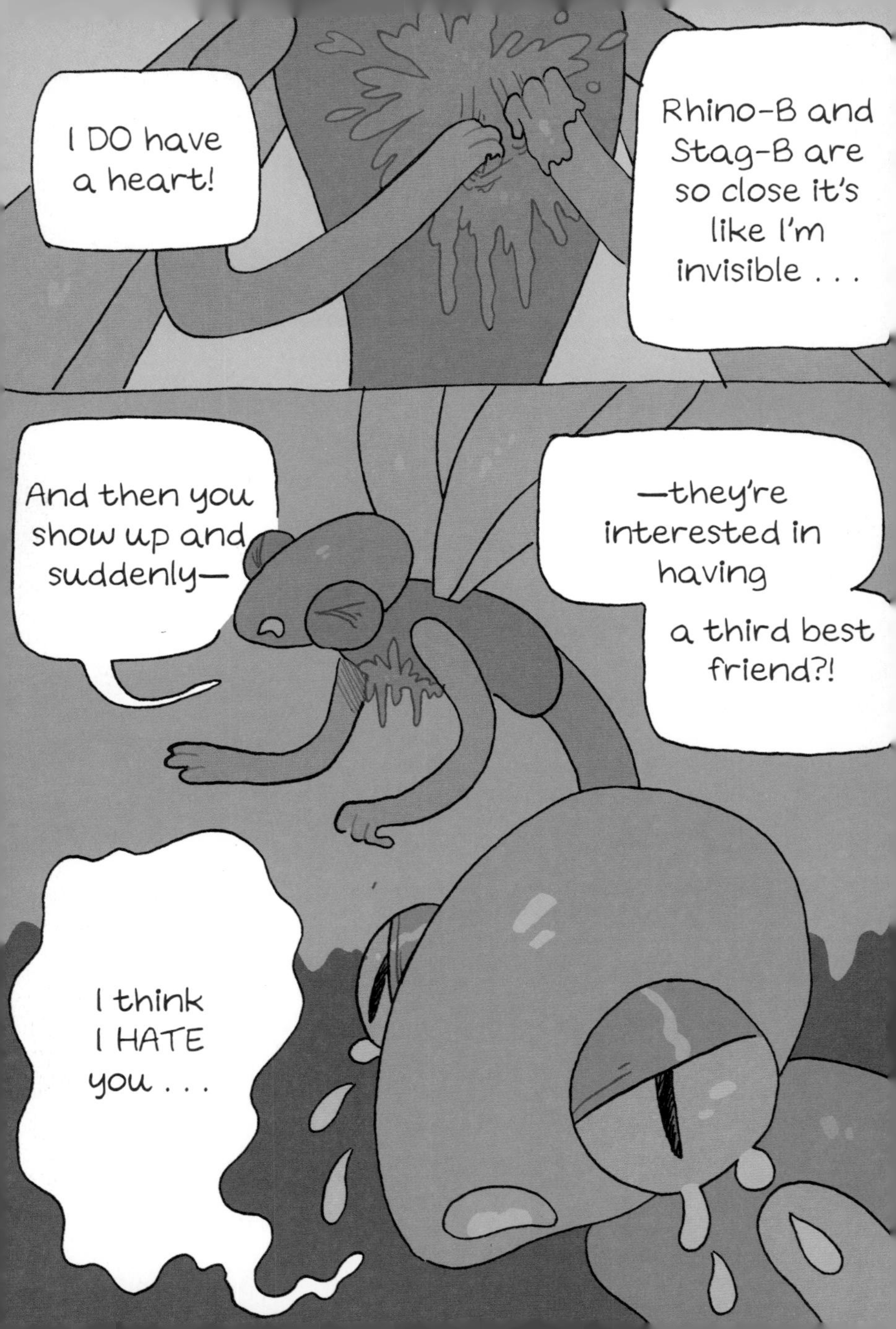
I DO have a heart!
Rhino-B and Stag-B are so close it's like I'm invisible . . .
And then you show up and suddenly—
—they're interested in having
a third best friend?!
I think I HATE you . . .

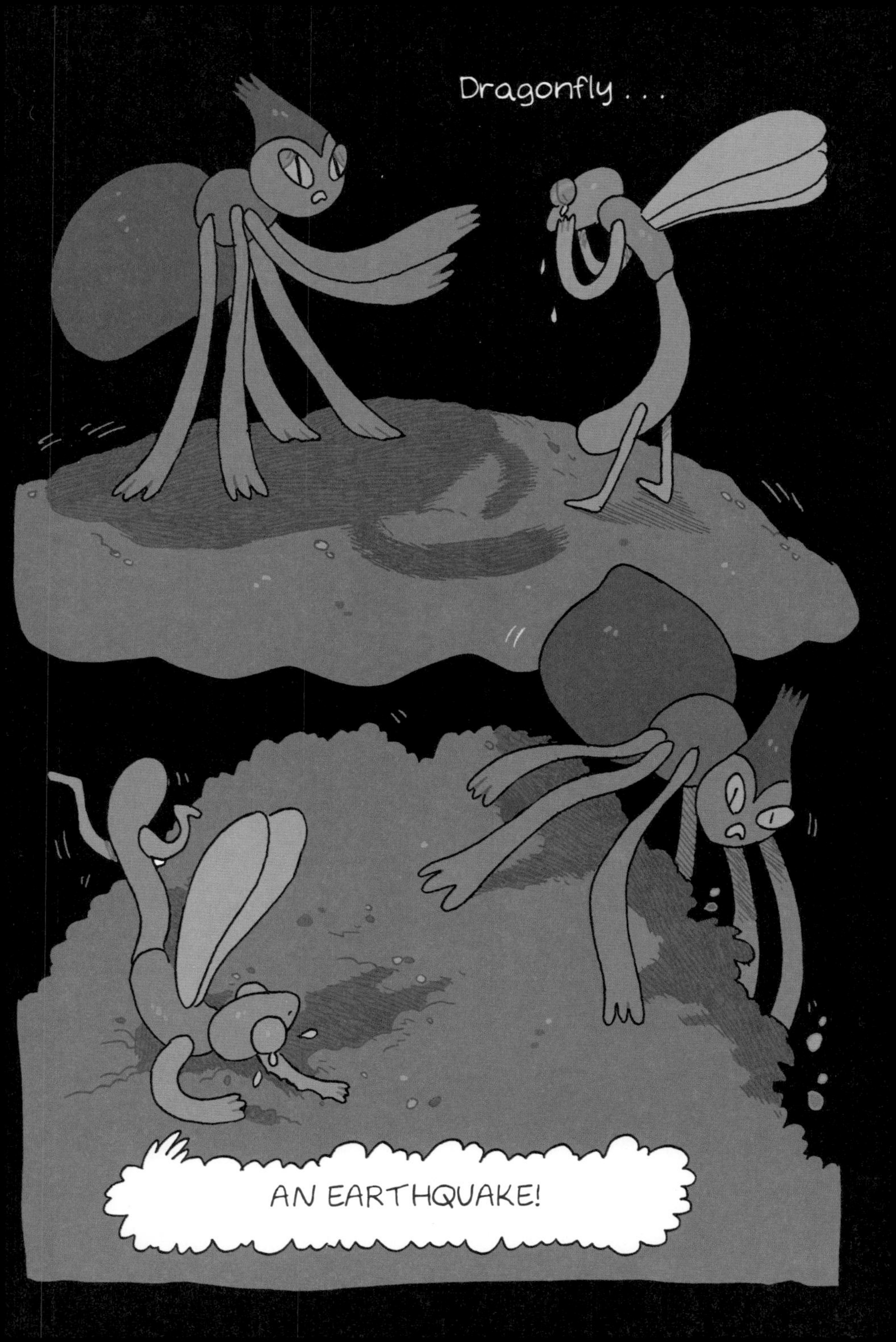
Dragonfly . . .
AN EARTHQUAKE!

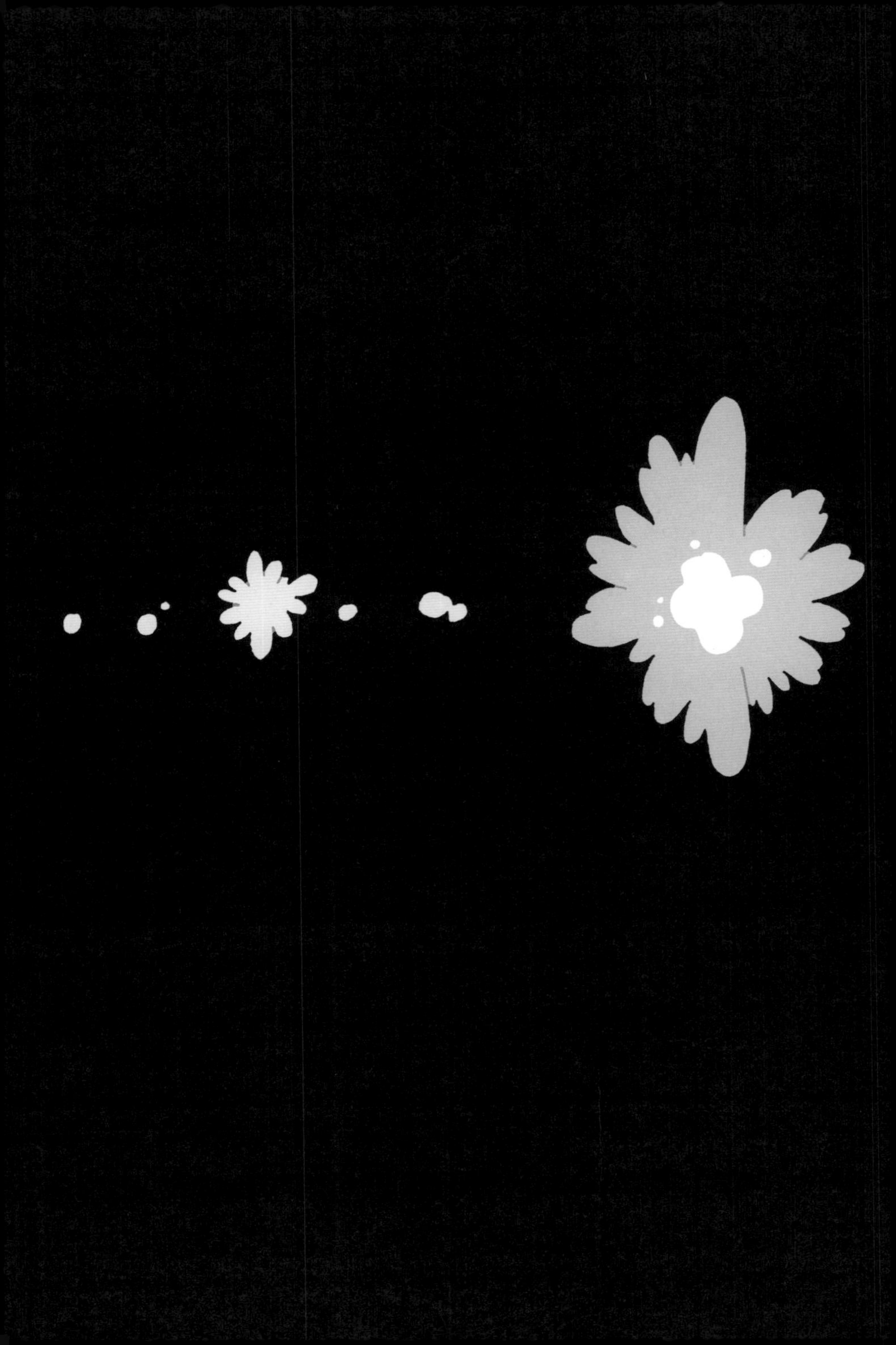

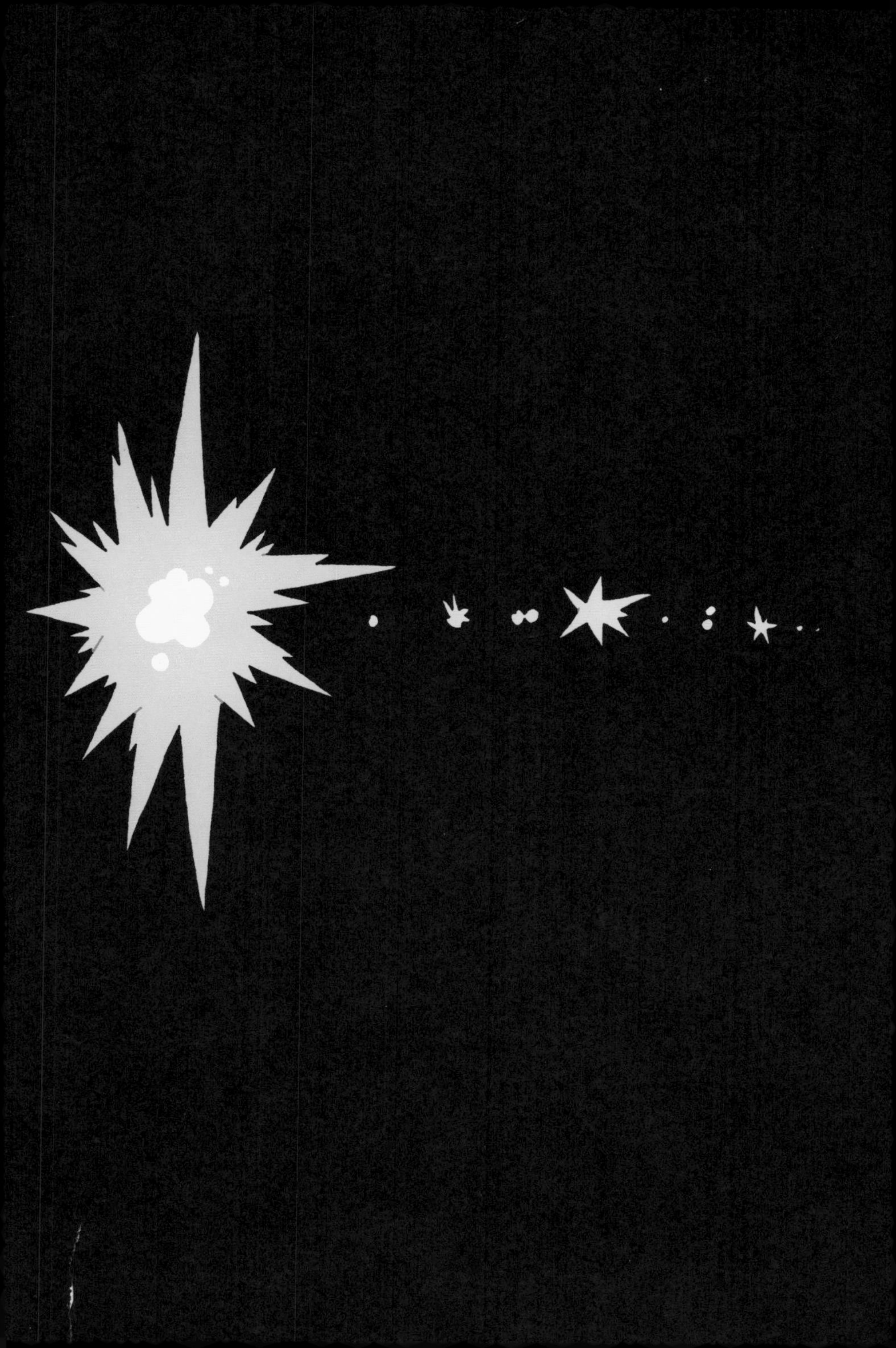

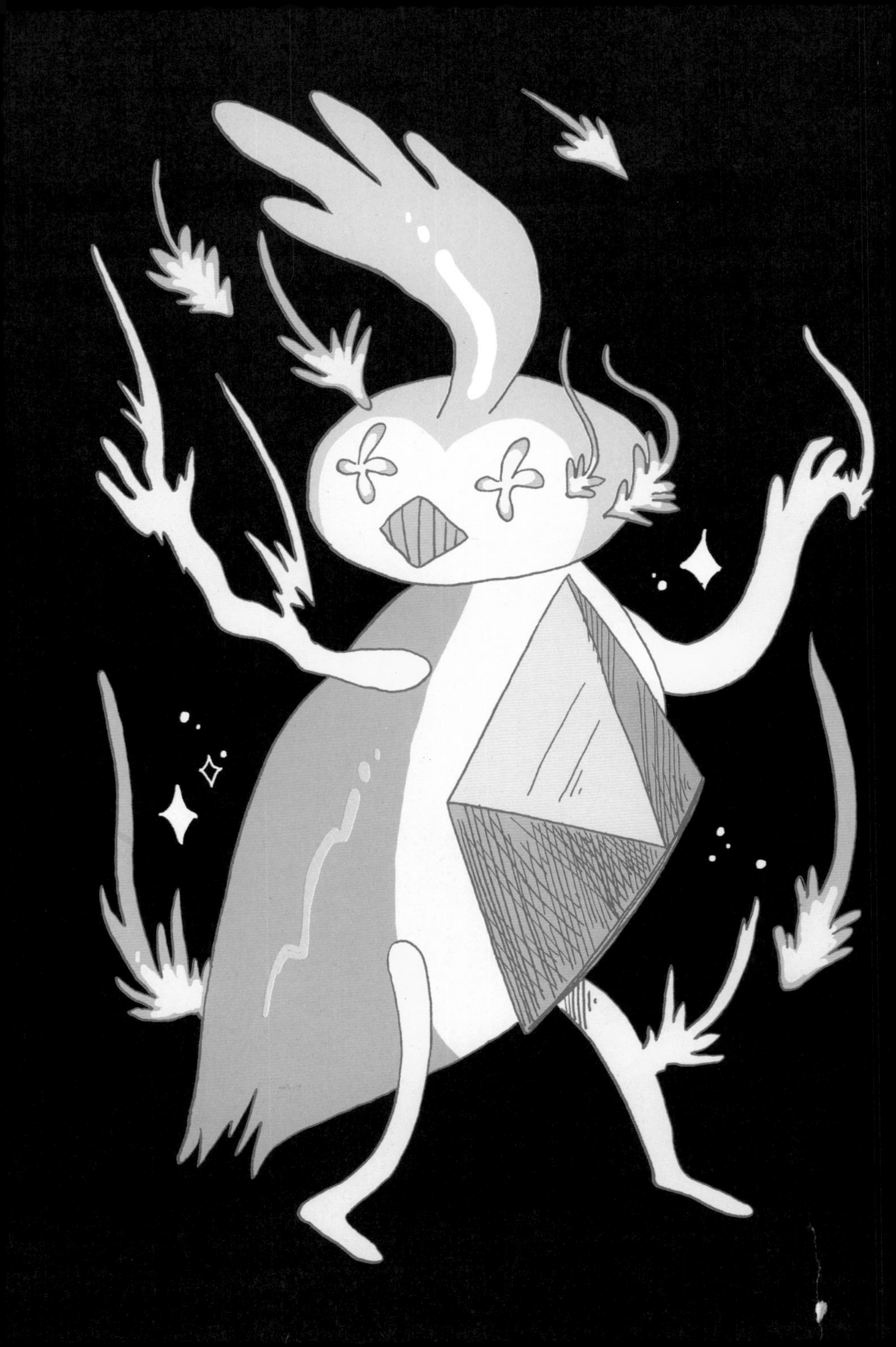

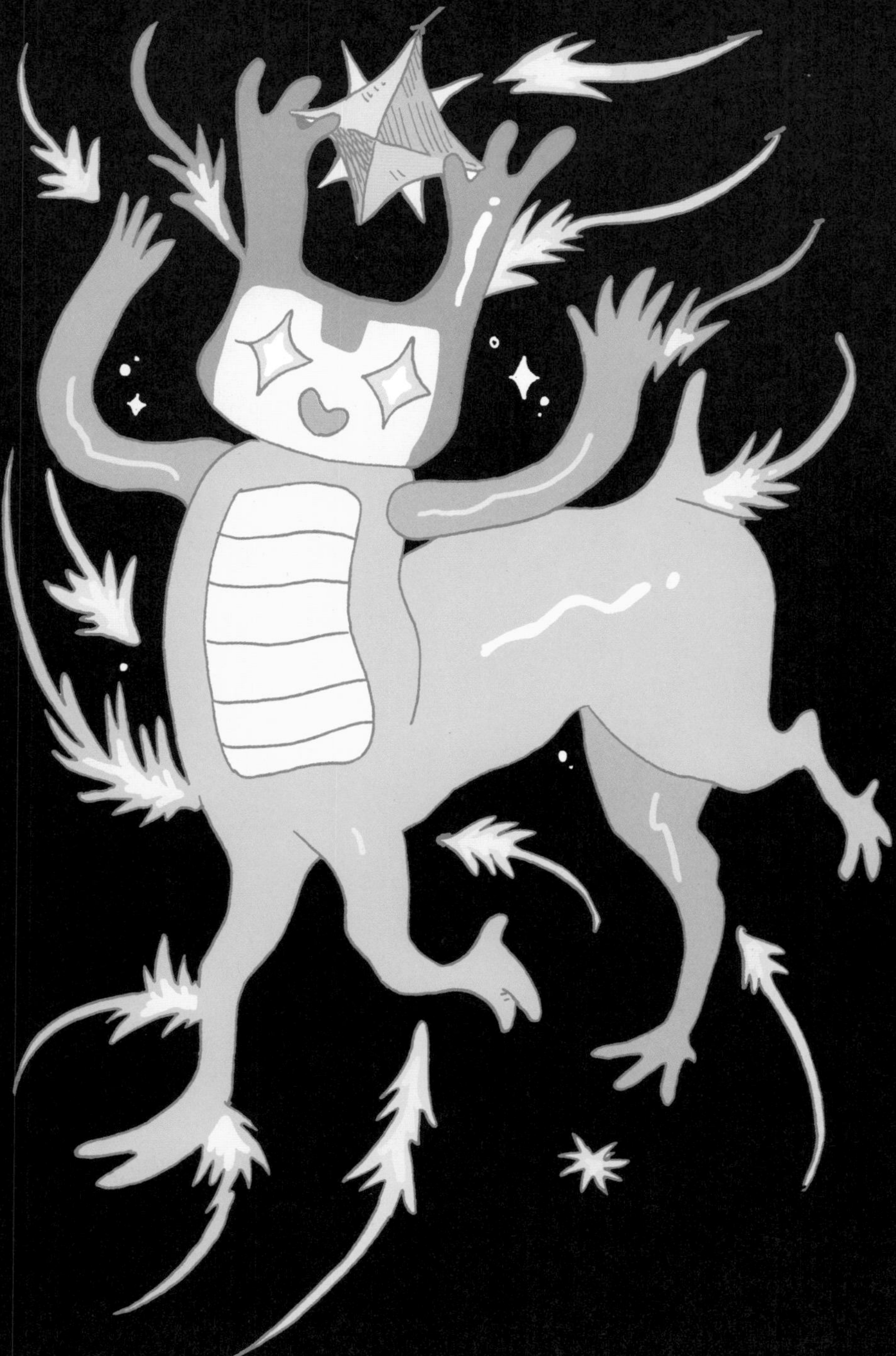

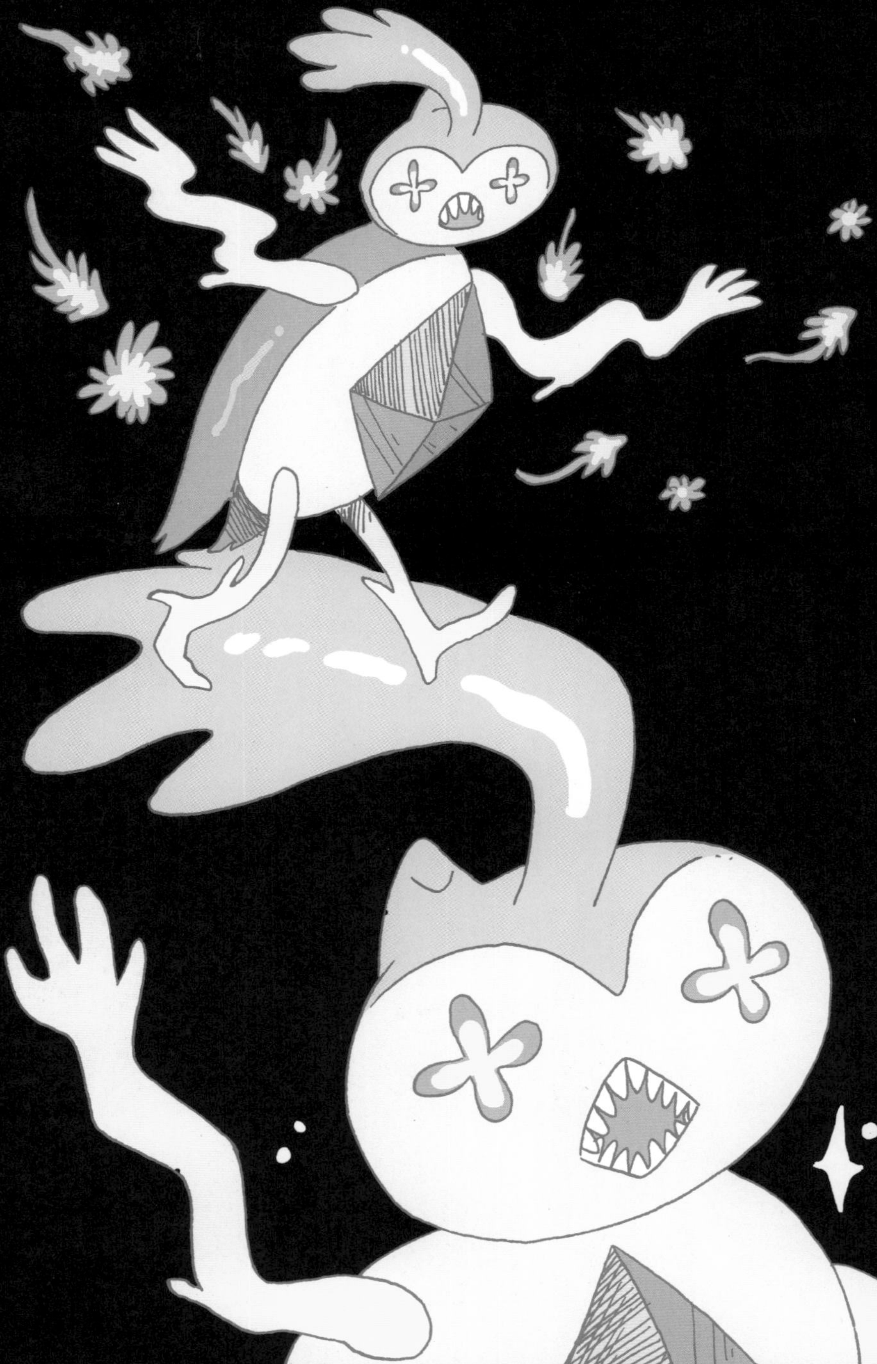

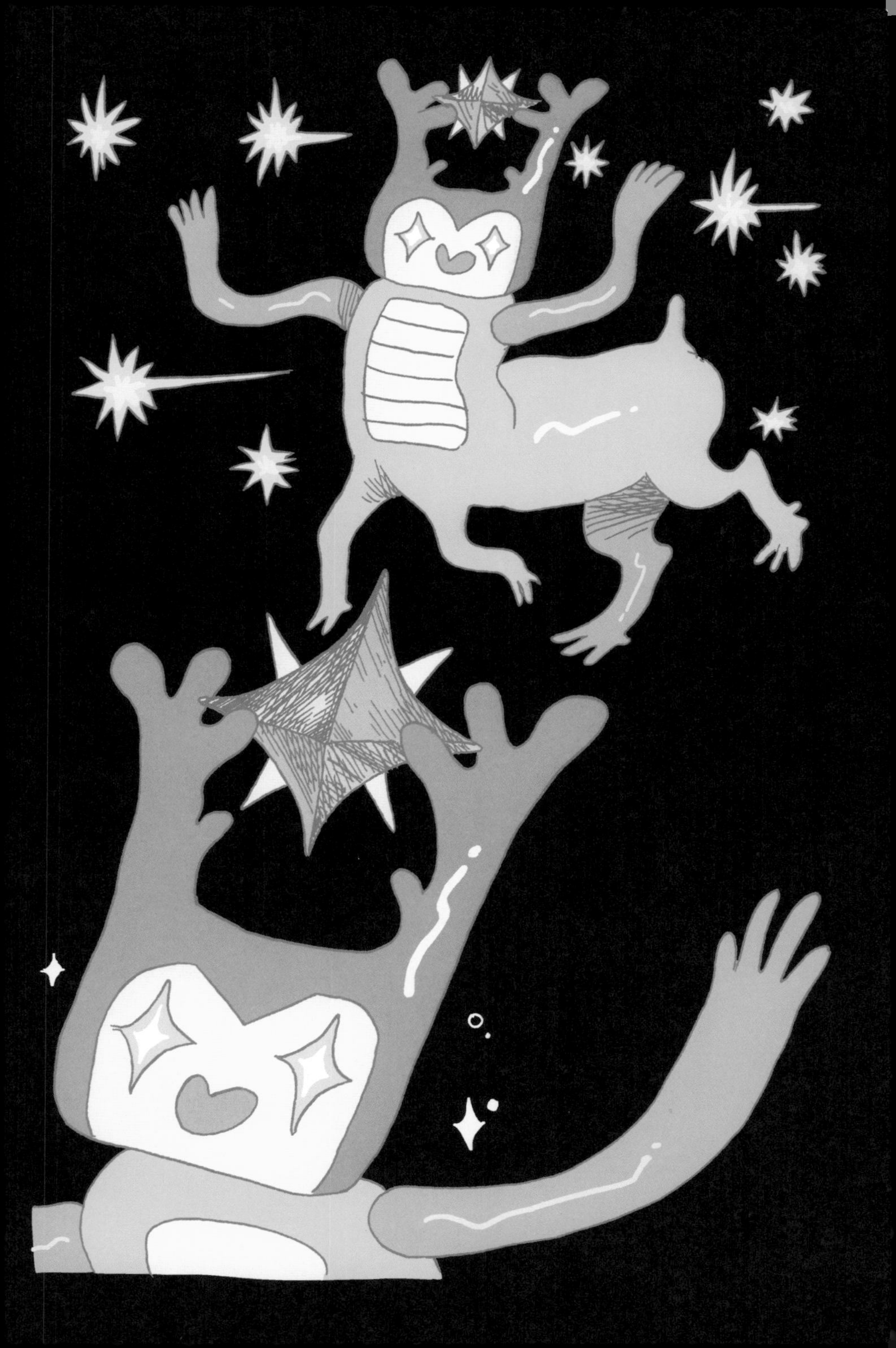

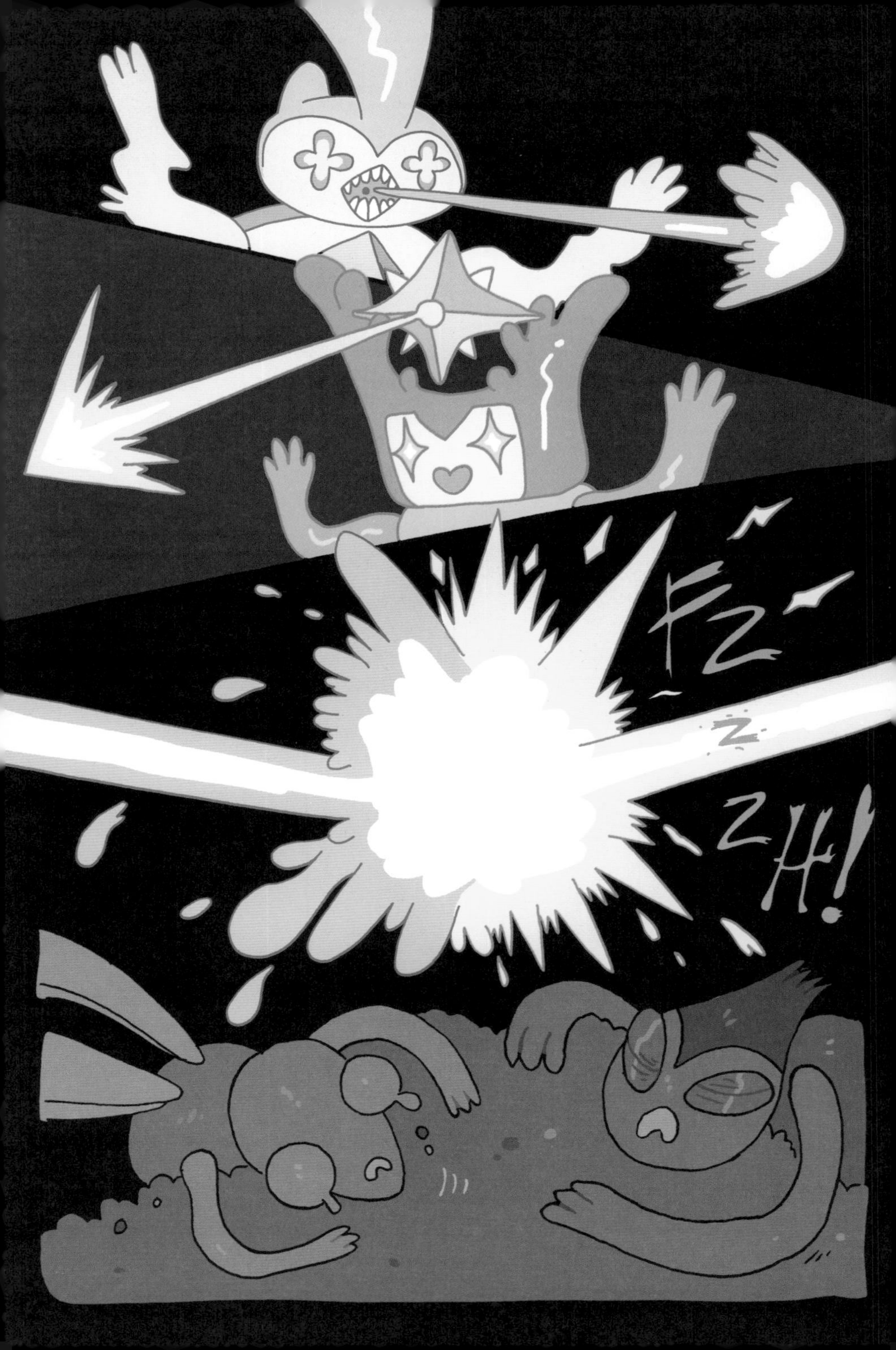
FZZZH!

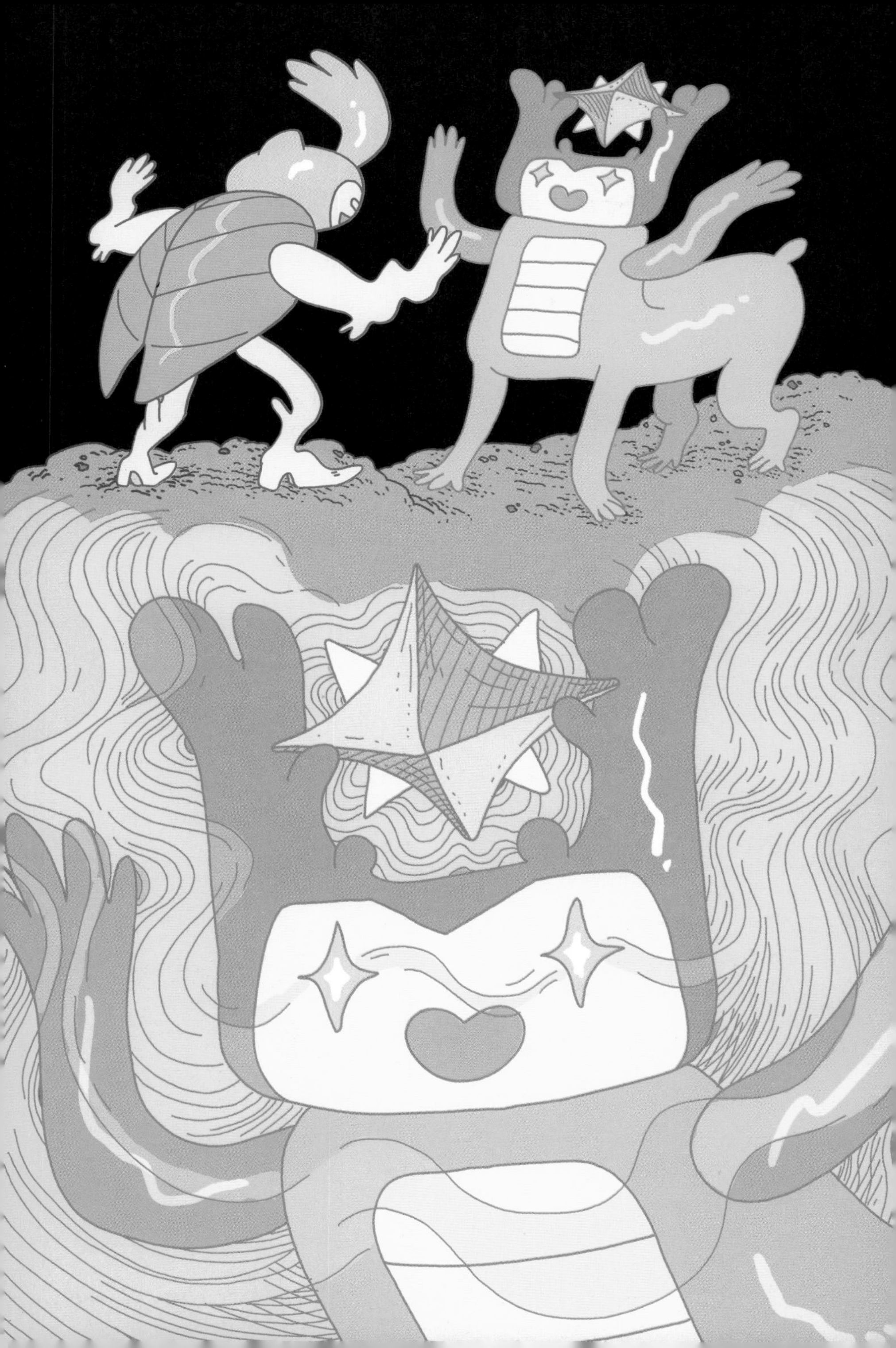

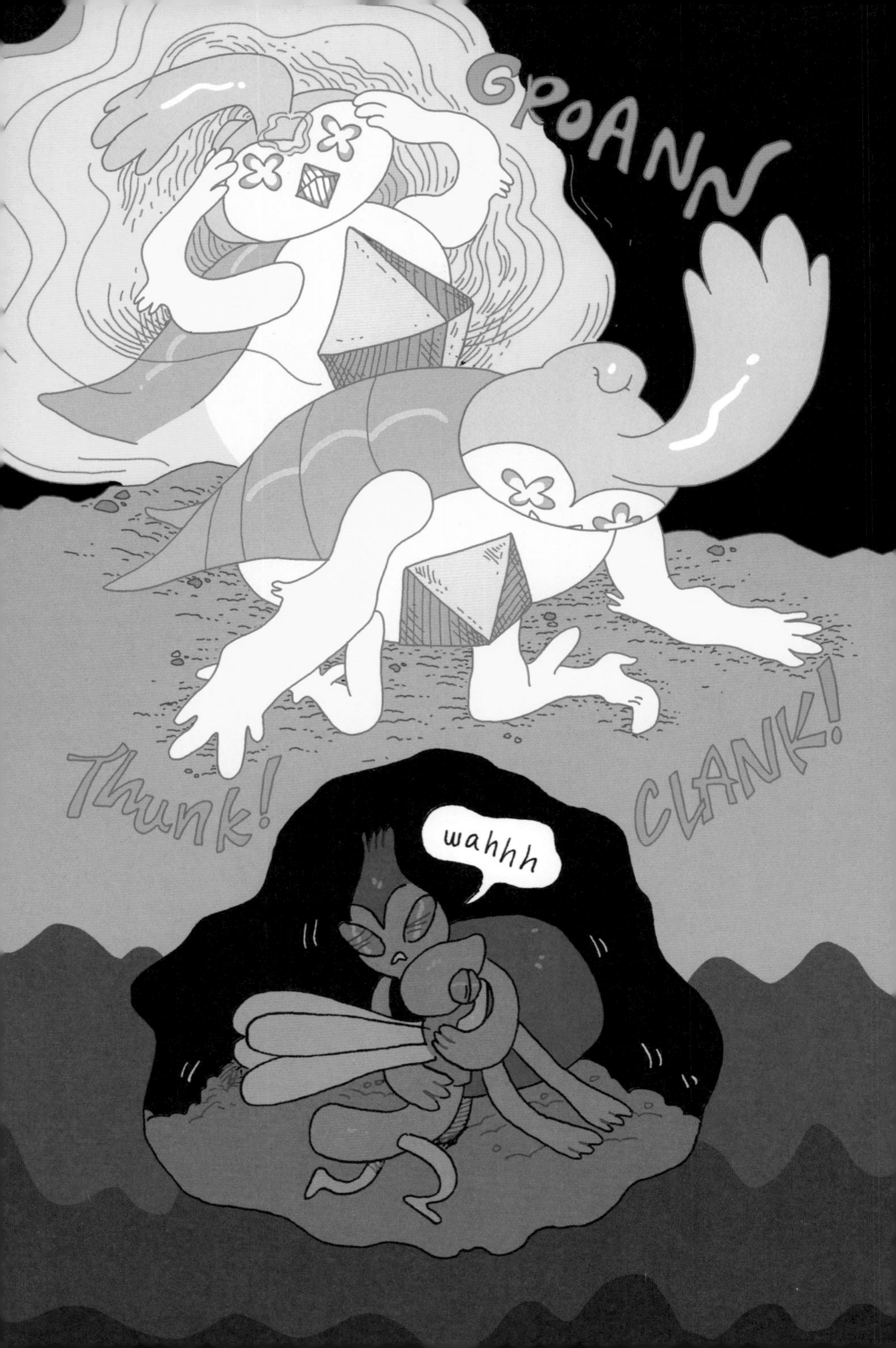
GROANN
Thunk!
CLANK!
wahhh

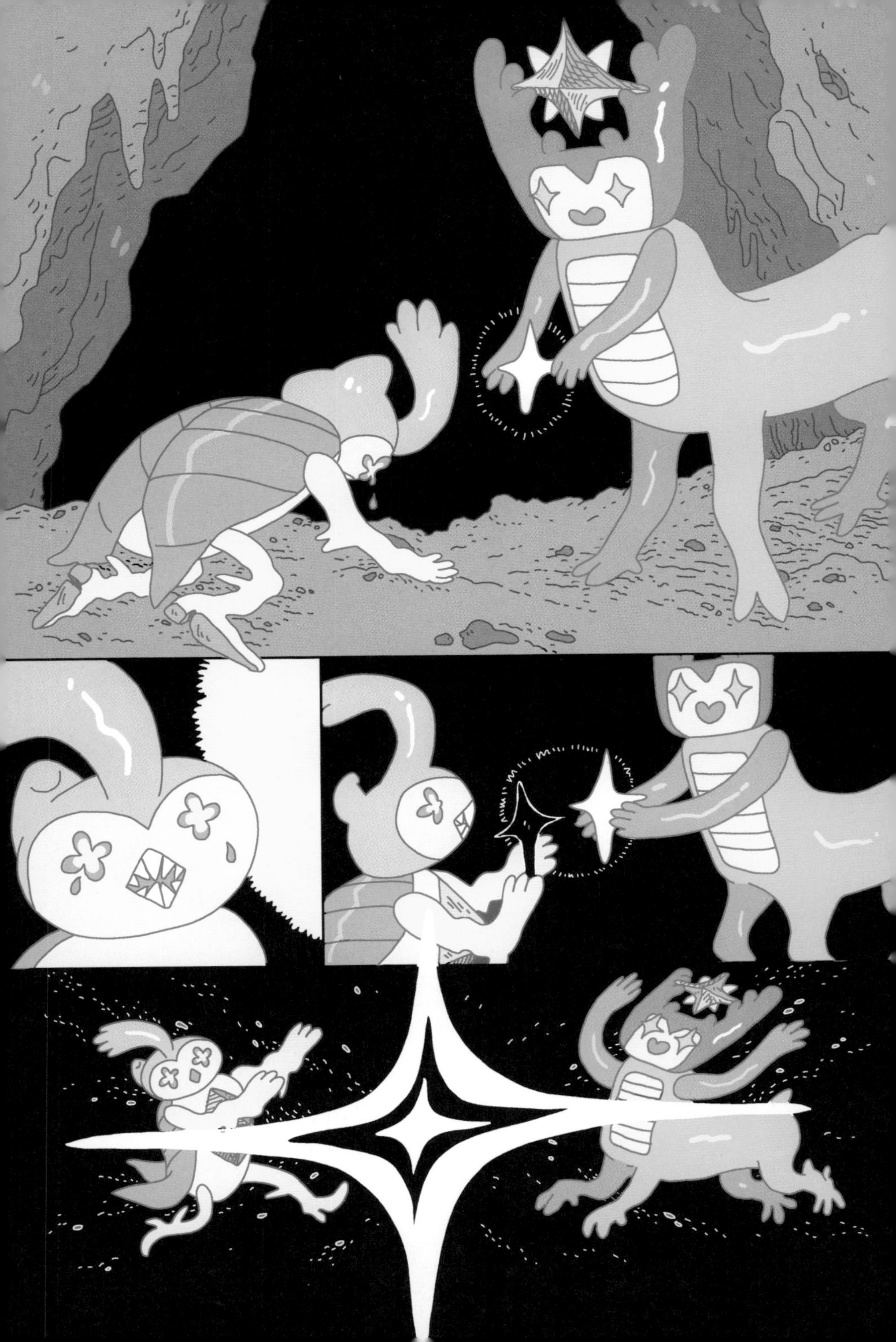

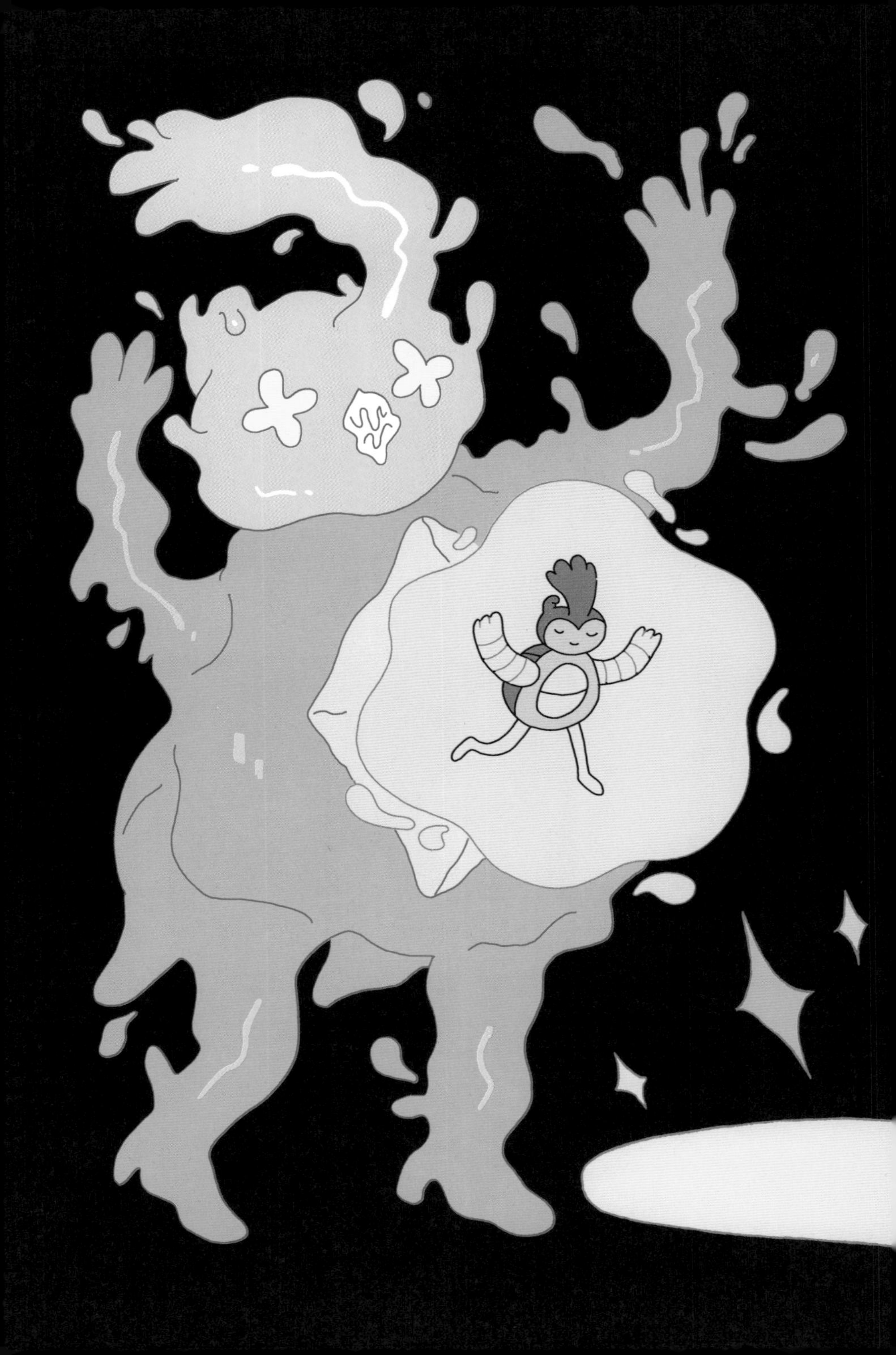

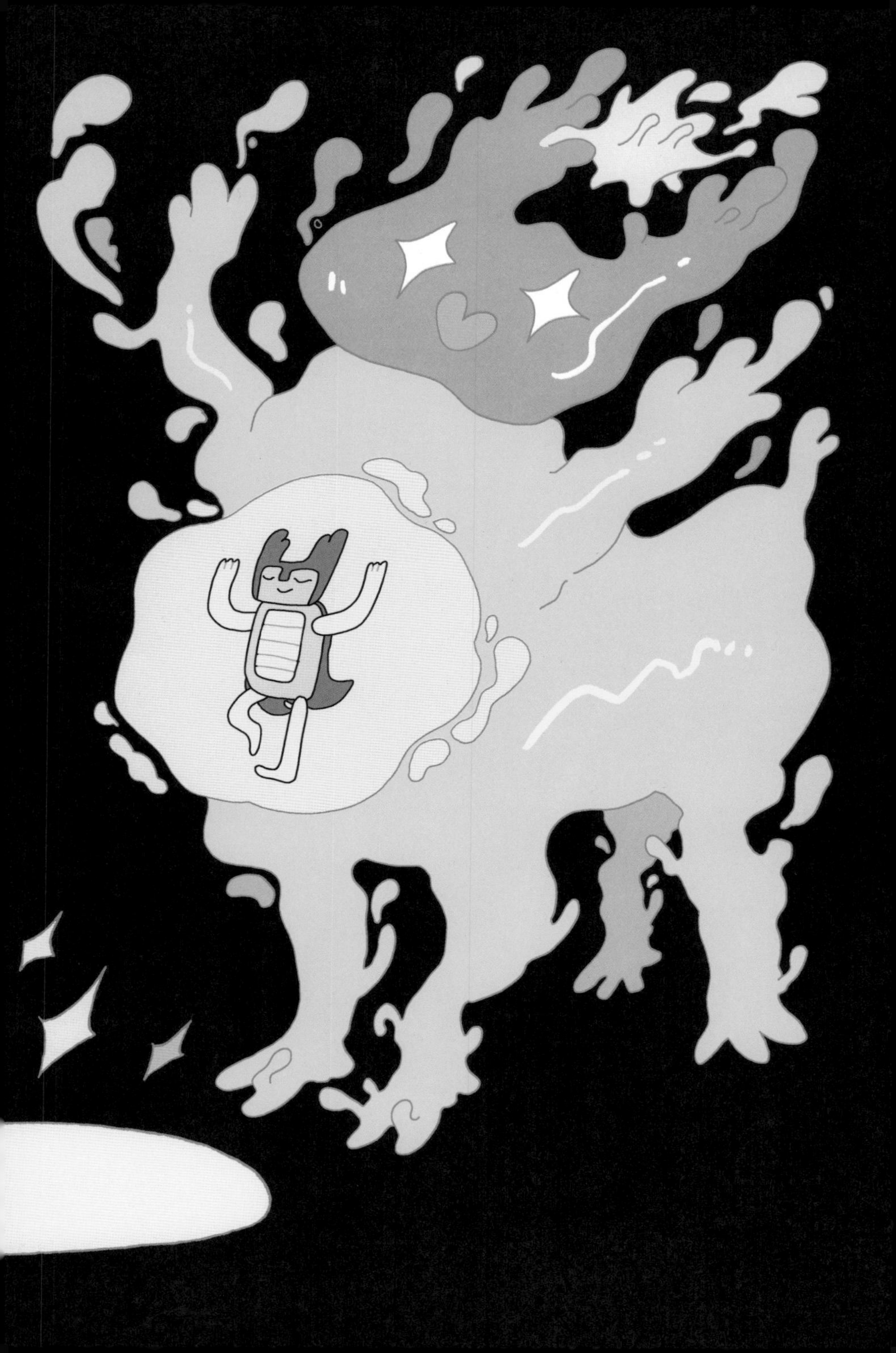

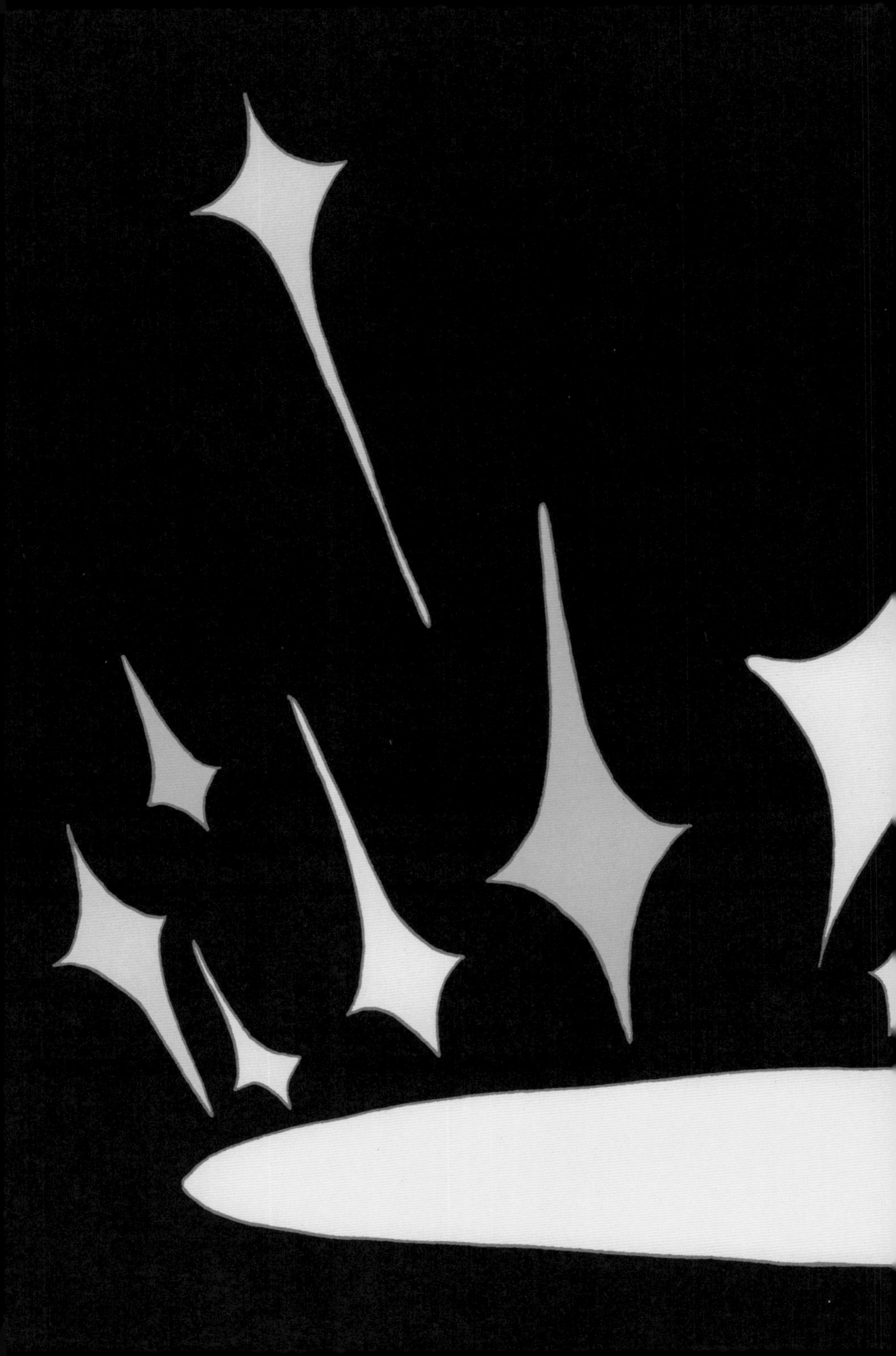

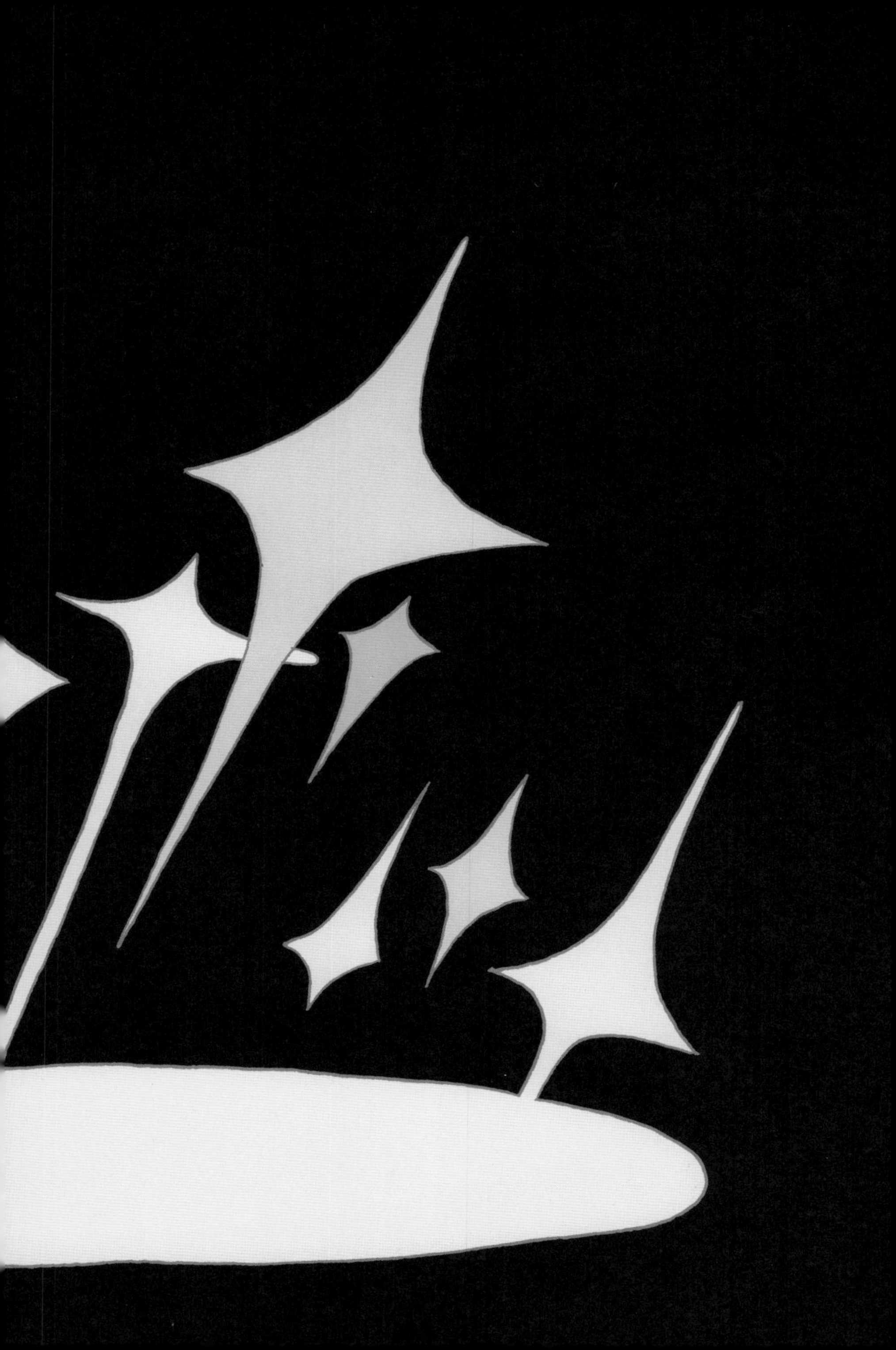

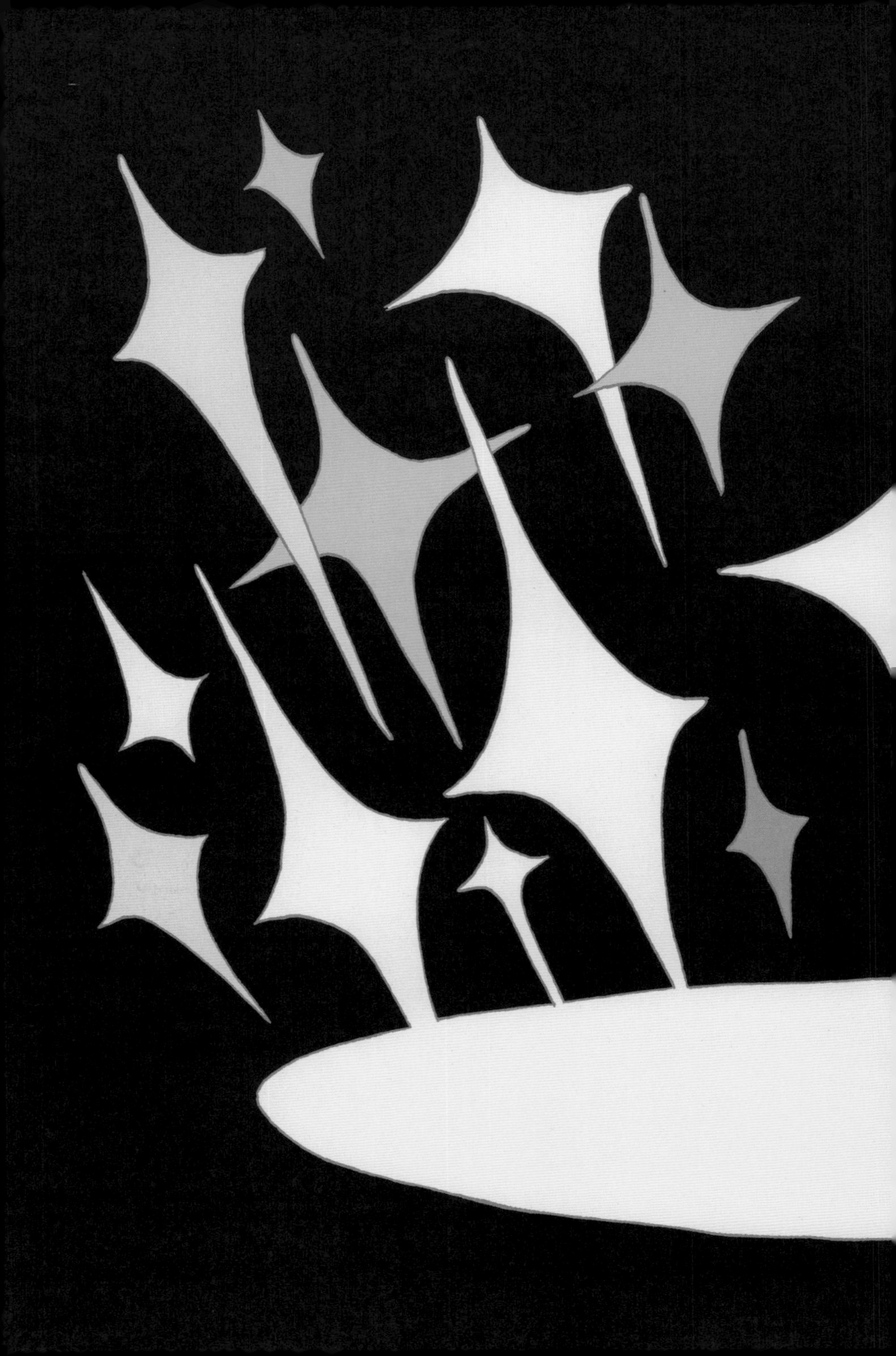

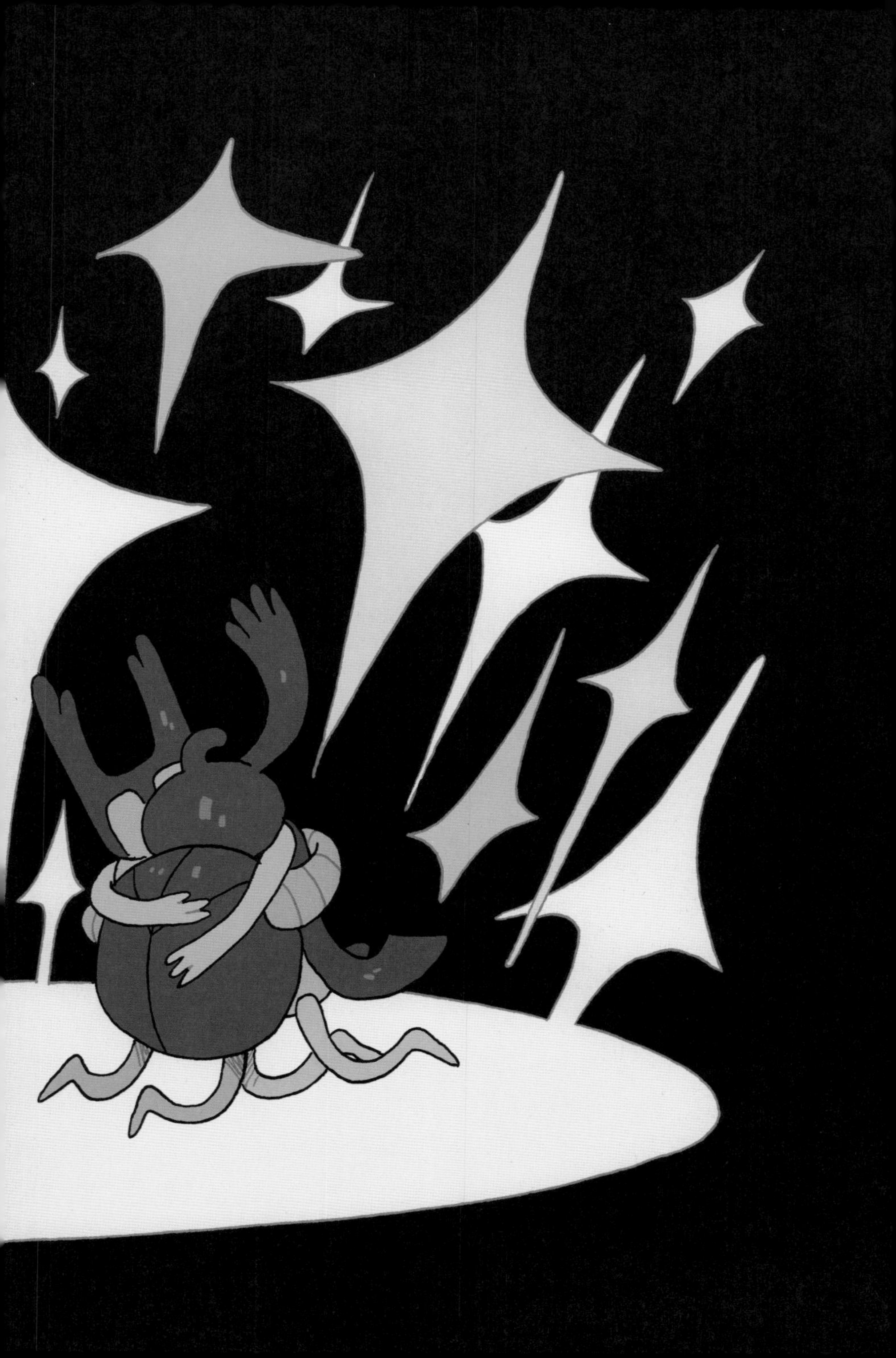

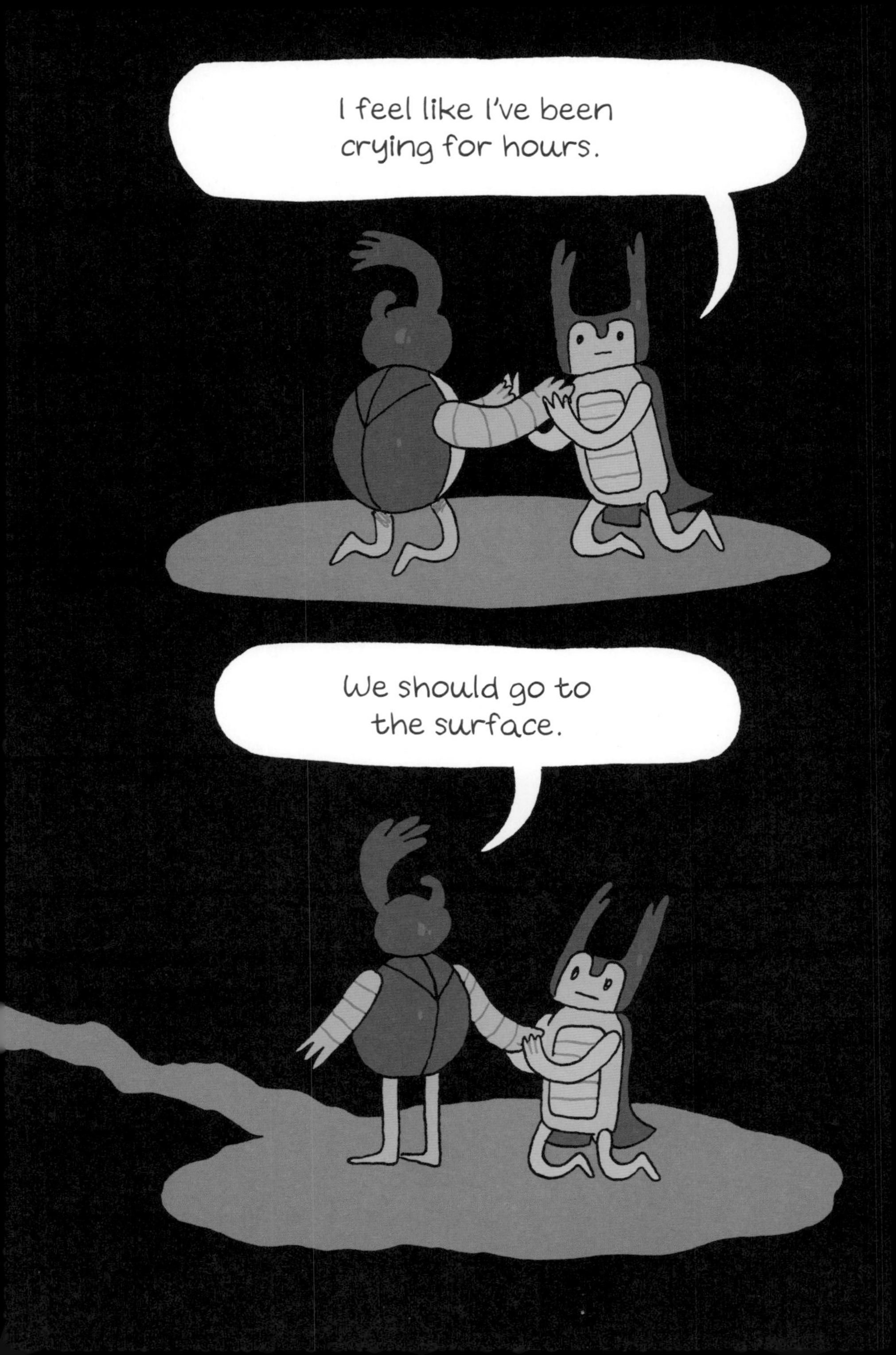
I feel like I've been crying for hours.
We should go to the surface.

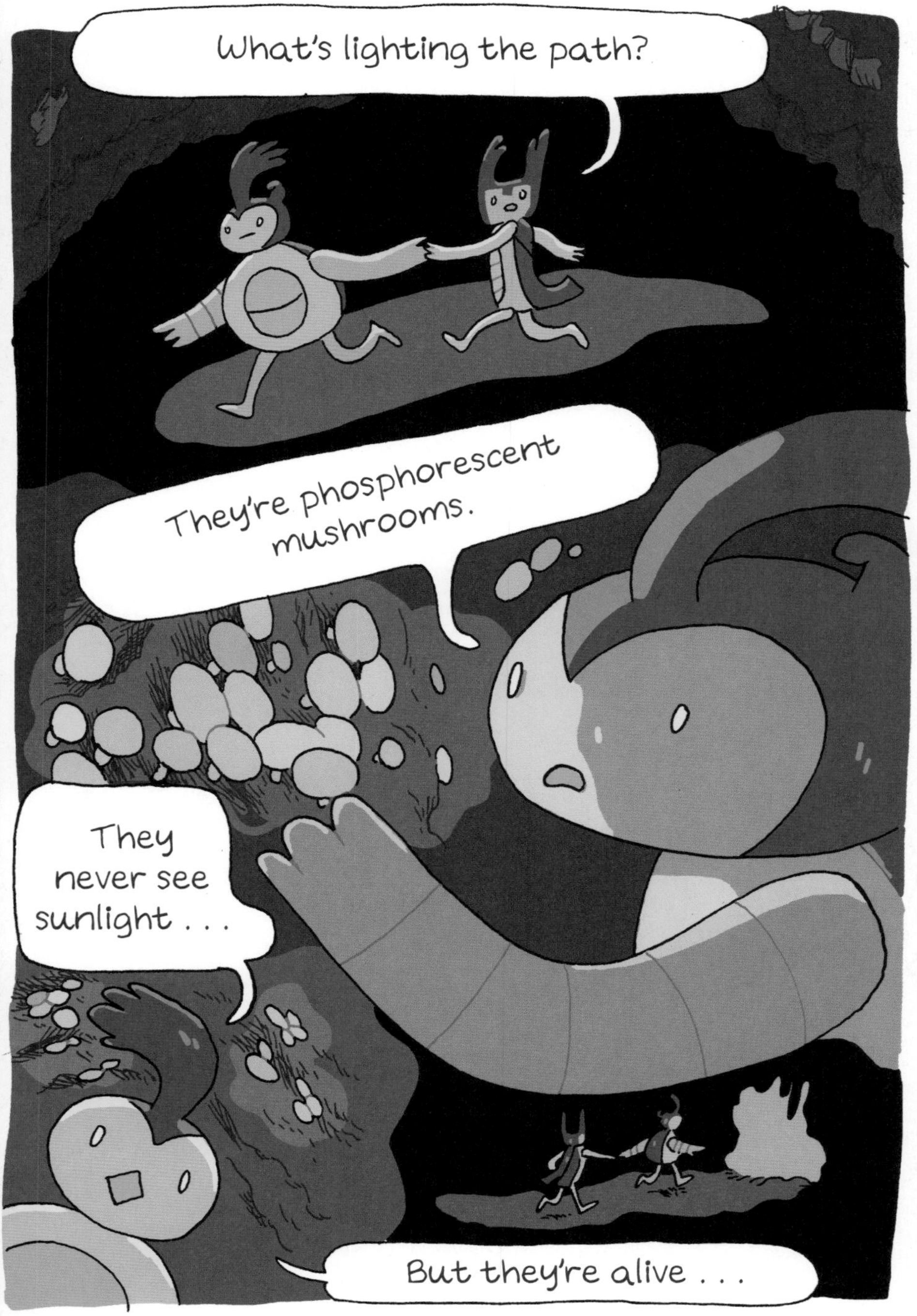
What's lighting the path?
They're phosphorescent mushrooms.
They never see sunlight . . .
But they're alive . . .

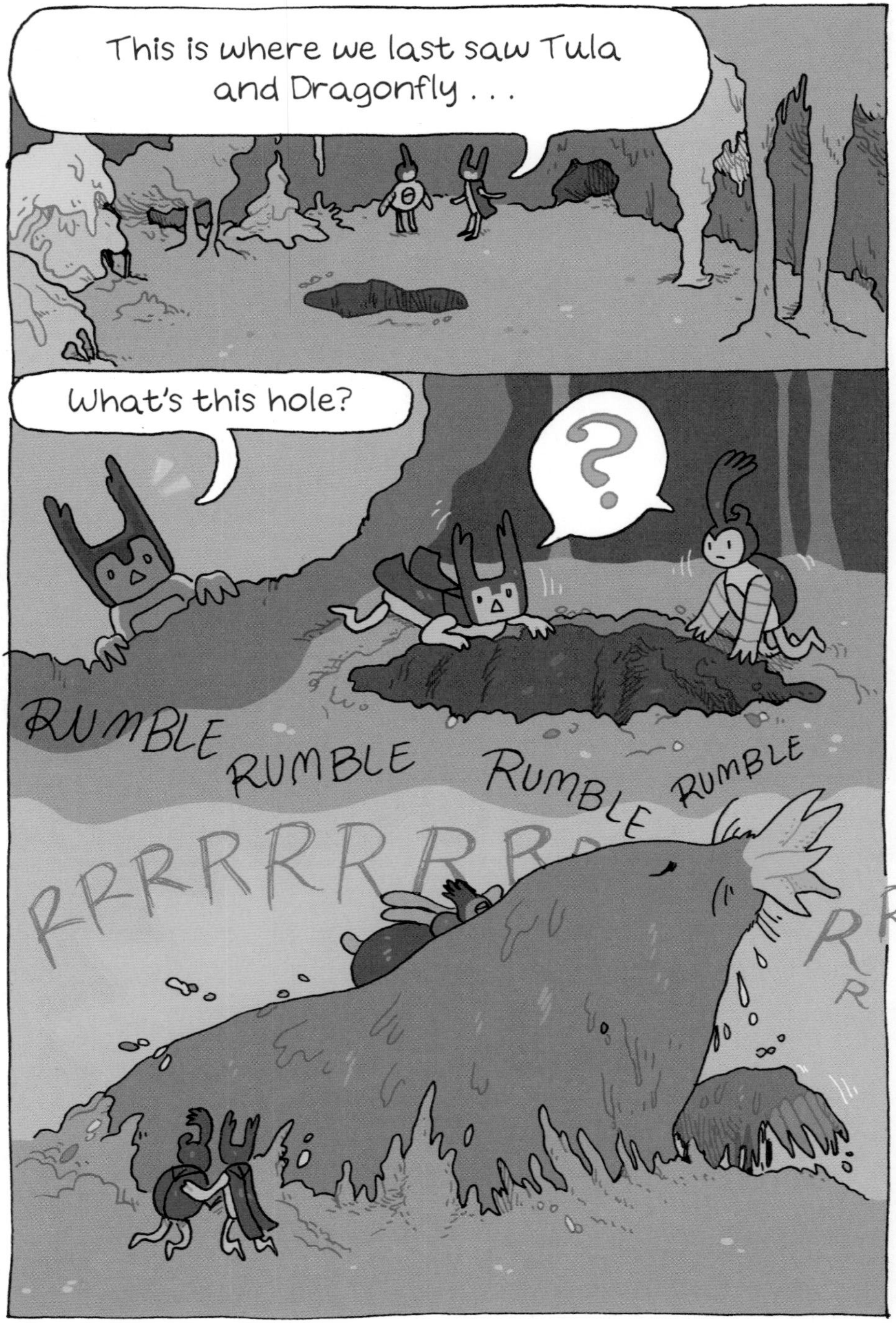
This is where we last saw Tula and Dragonfly . . .
What's this hole?
?
RUMBLE
RUMBLE
RUMBLE
RUMBLE
RRRRRRRRR
RR
R

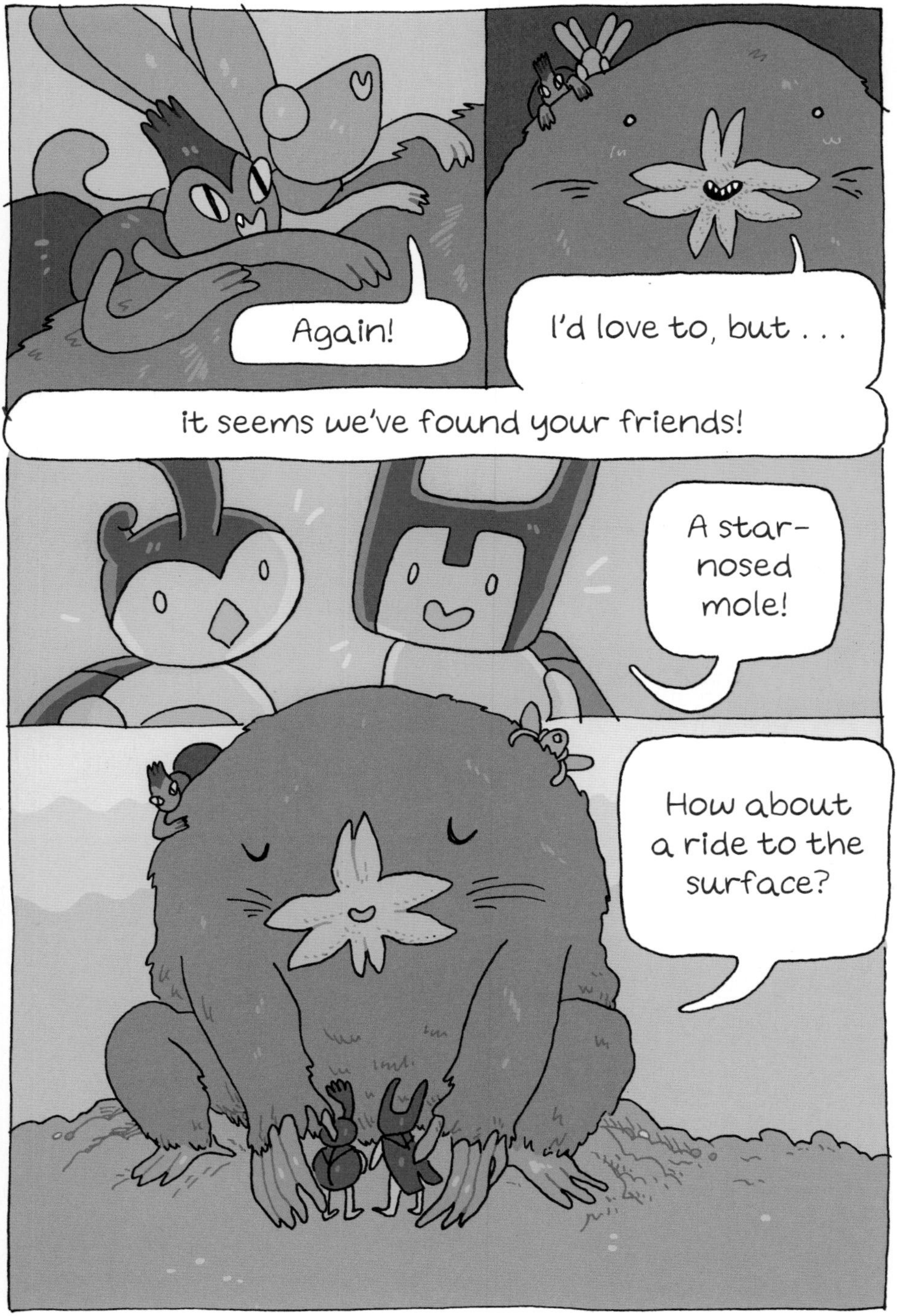
Again!
I'd love to, but . . .
it seems we've found your friends!
A star-nosed mole!
How about a ride to the surface?

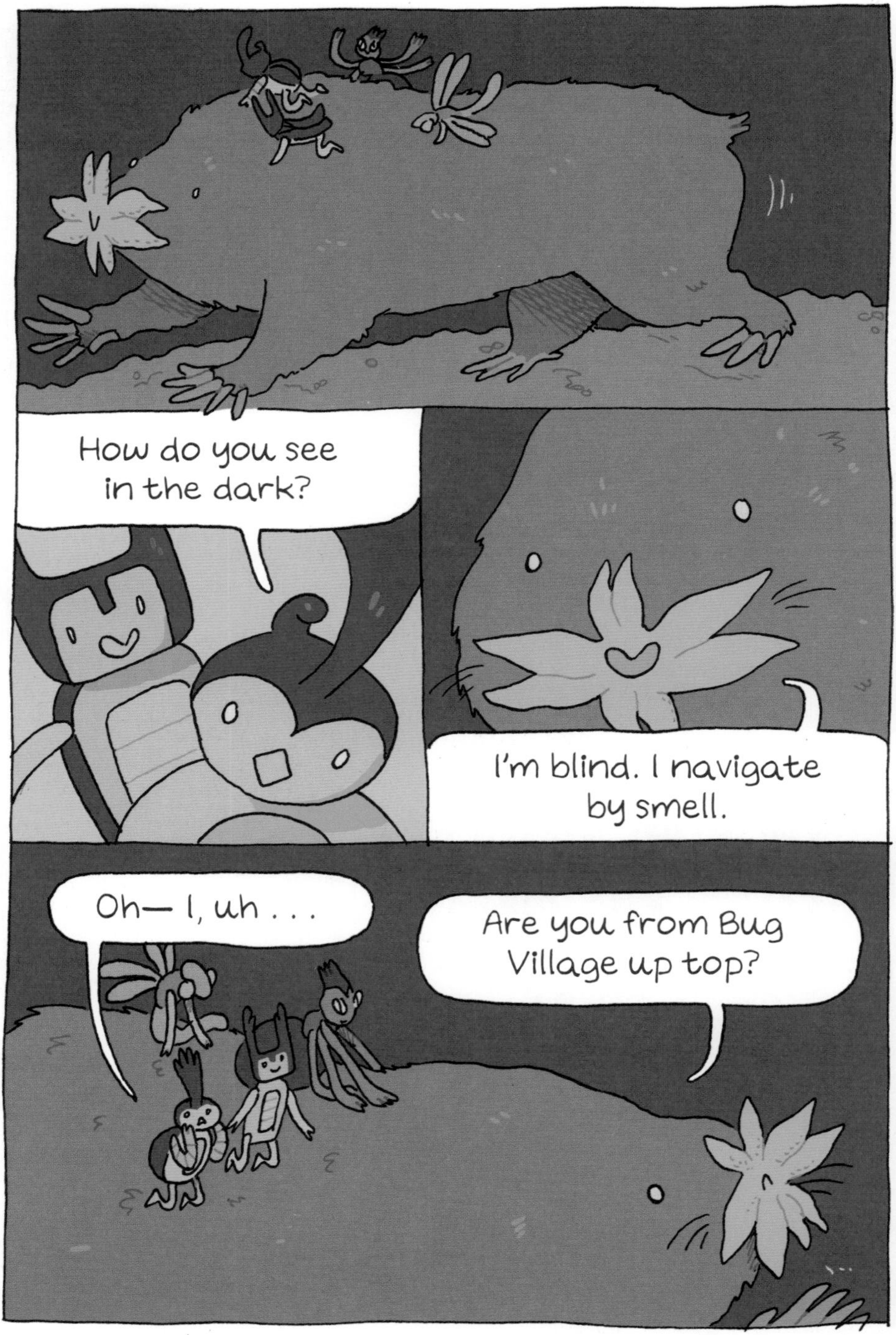
How do you see in the dark?
I'm blind. I navigate by smell.
Oh— I, uh . . .
Are you from Bug Village up top?

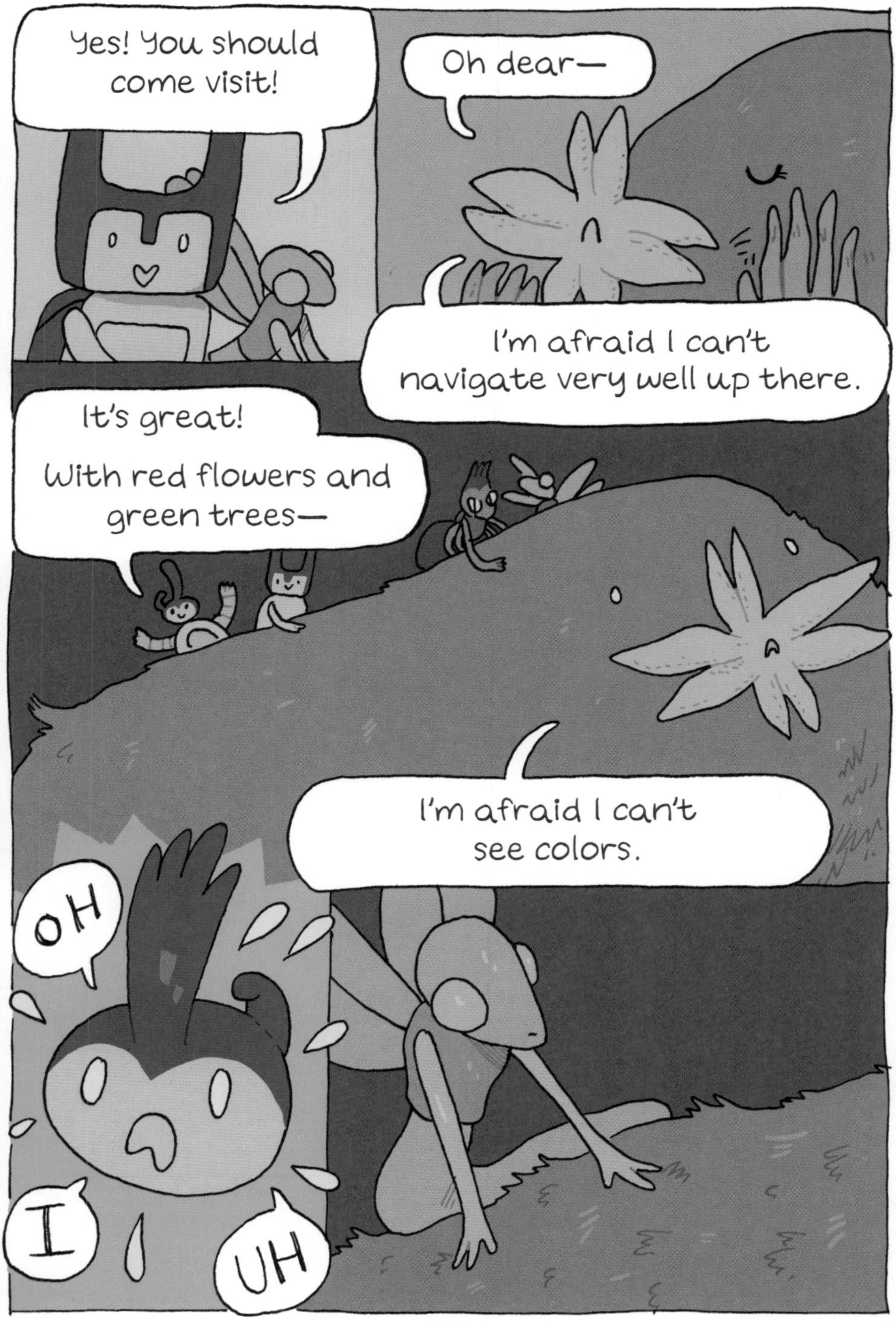
Yes! You should come visit!
Oh dear—
I'm afraid I can't navigate very well up there.
It's great!
With red flowers and green trees—
I'm afraid I can't see colors.
OH
I
UH

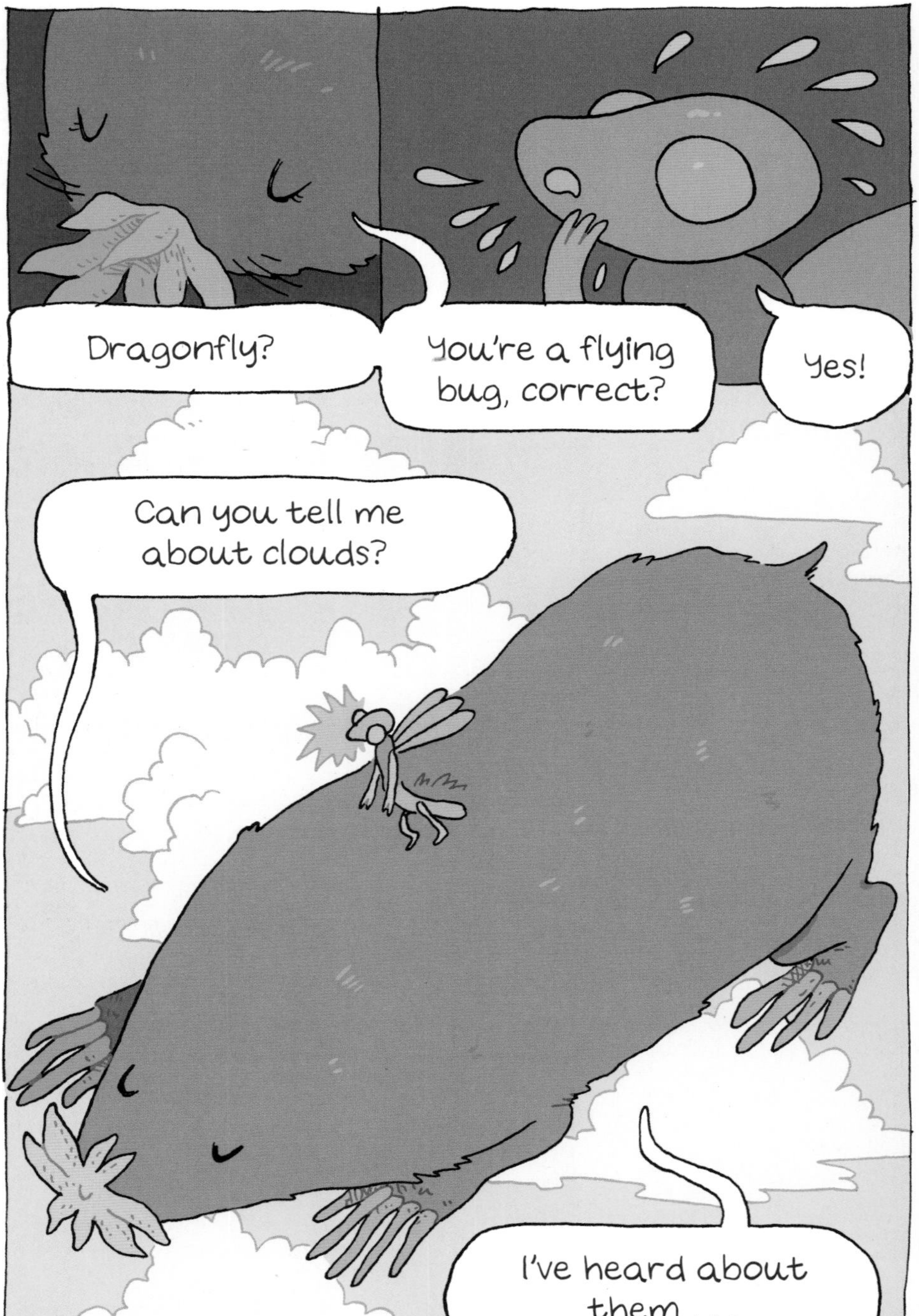
Dragonfly?
You're a flying bug, correct?
Yes!
Can you tell me about clouds?
I've heard about them . . .

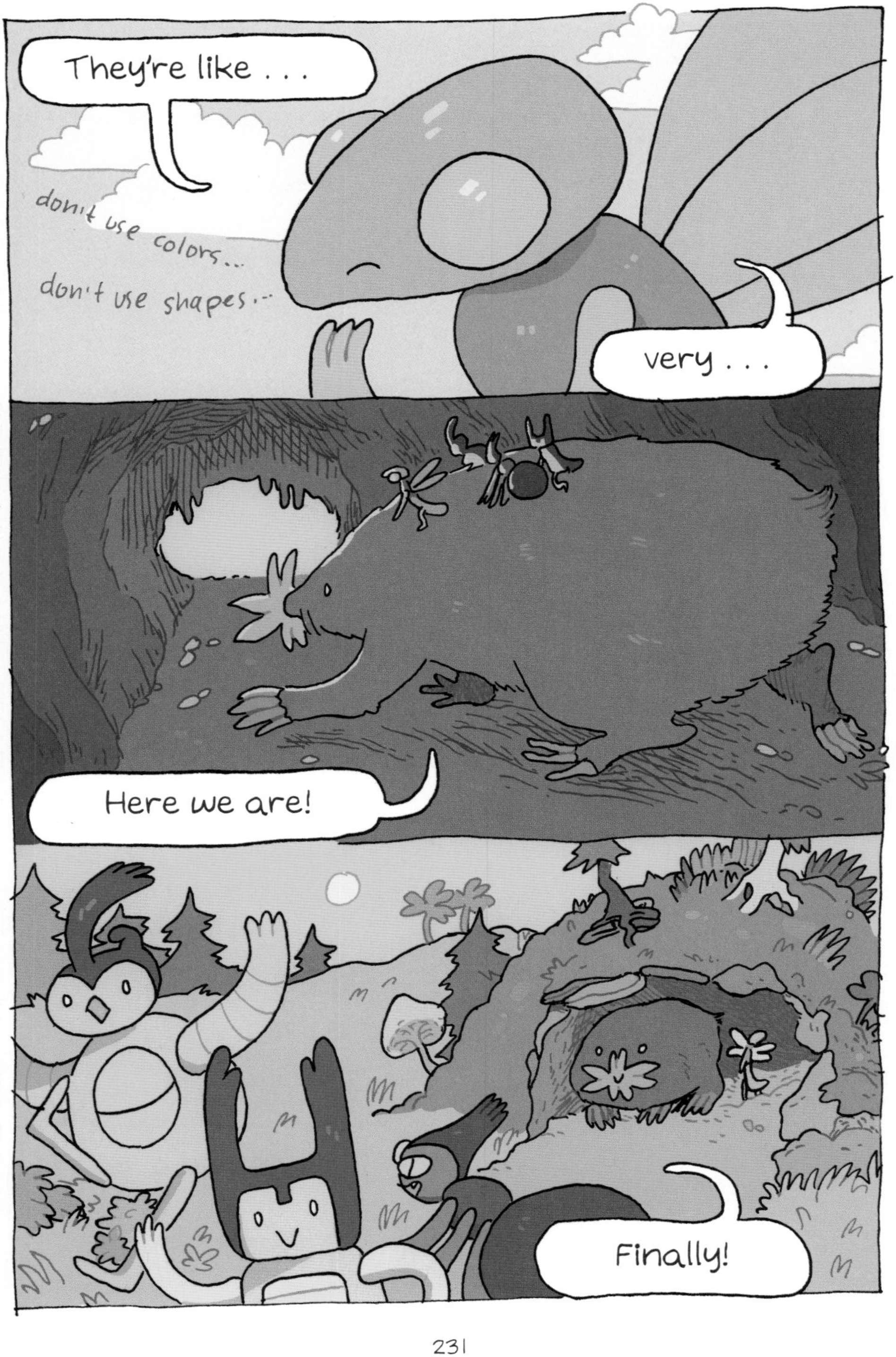
They're like . . .
don't use colors...
don't use shapes...
very . . .
Here we are!
Finally!

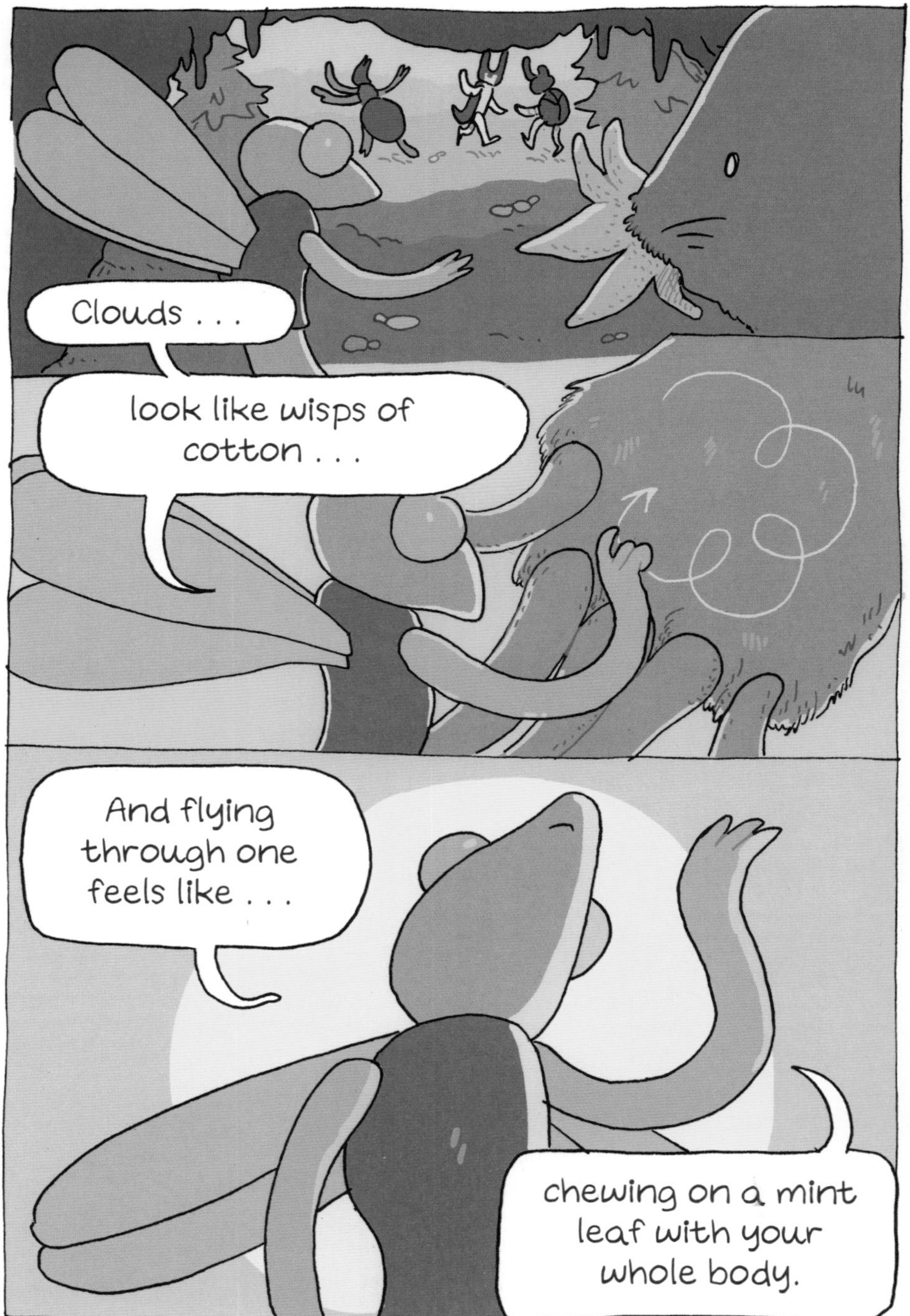
Clouds . . .
look like wisps of cotton . . .
And flying through one feels like . . .
chewing on a mint leaf with your whole body.

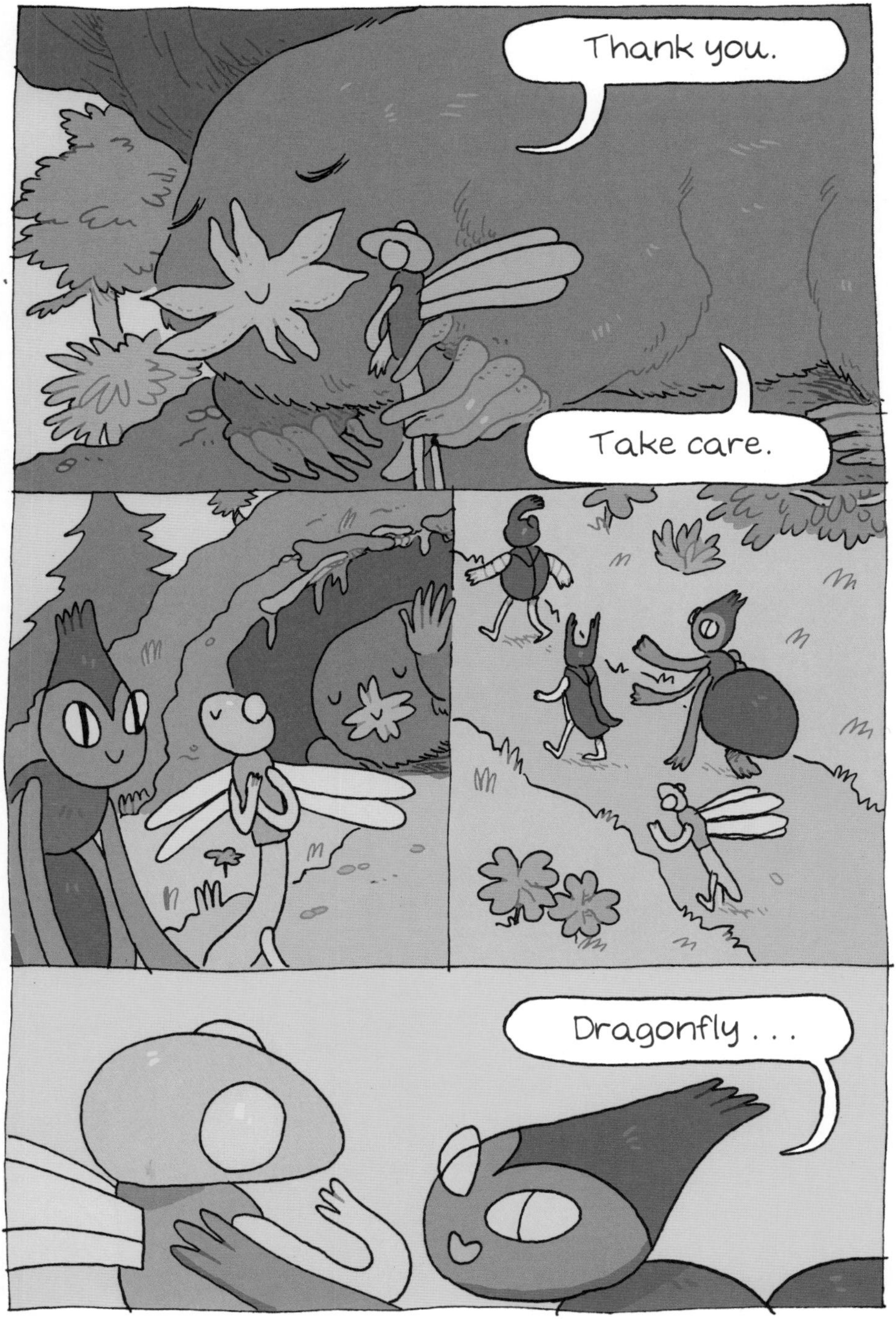
Thank you.
Take care.
Dragonfly . . .

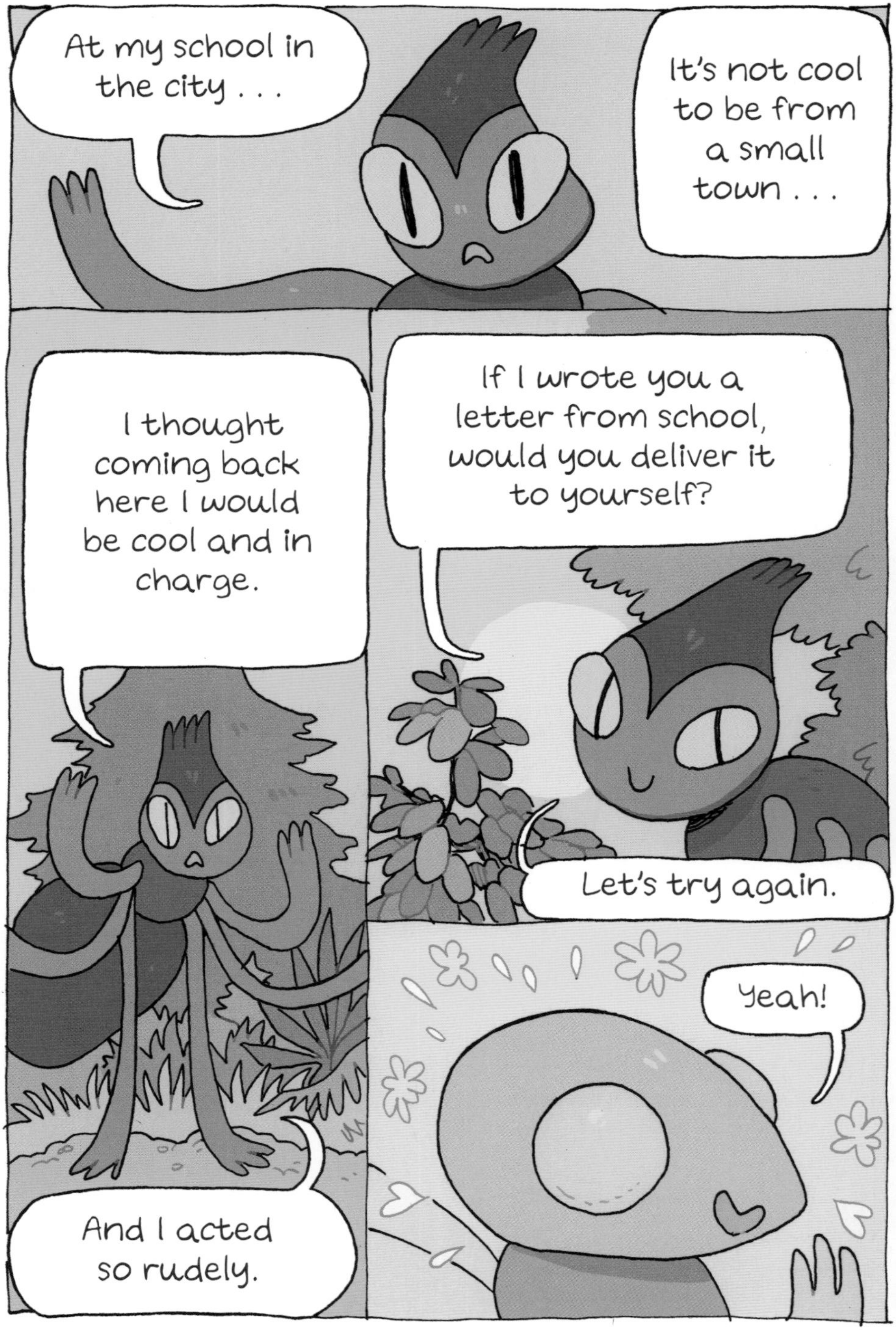
At my school in the city . . .
It's not cool to be from a small town . . .
I thought coming back here I would be cool and in charge.
And I acted so rudely.
If I wrote you a letter from school, would you deliver it to yourself?
Let's try again.
Yeah!

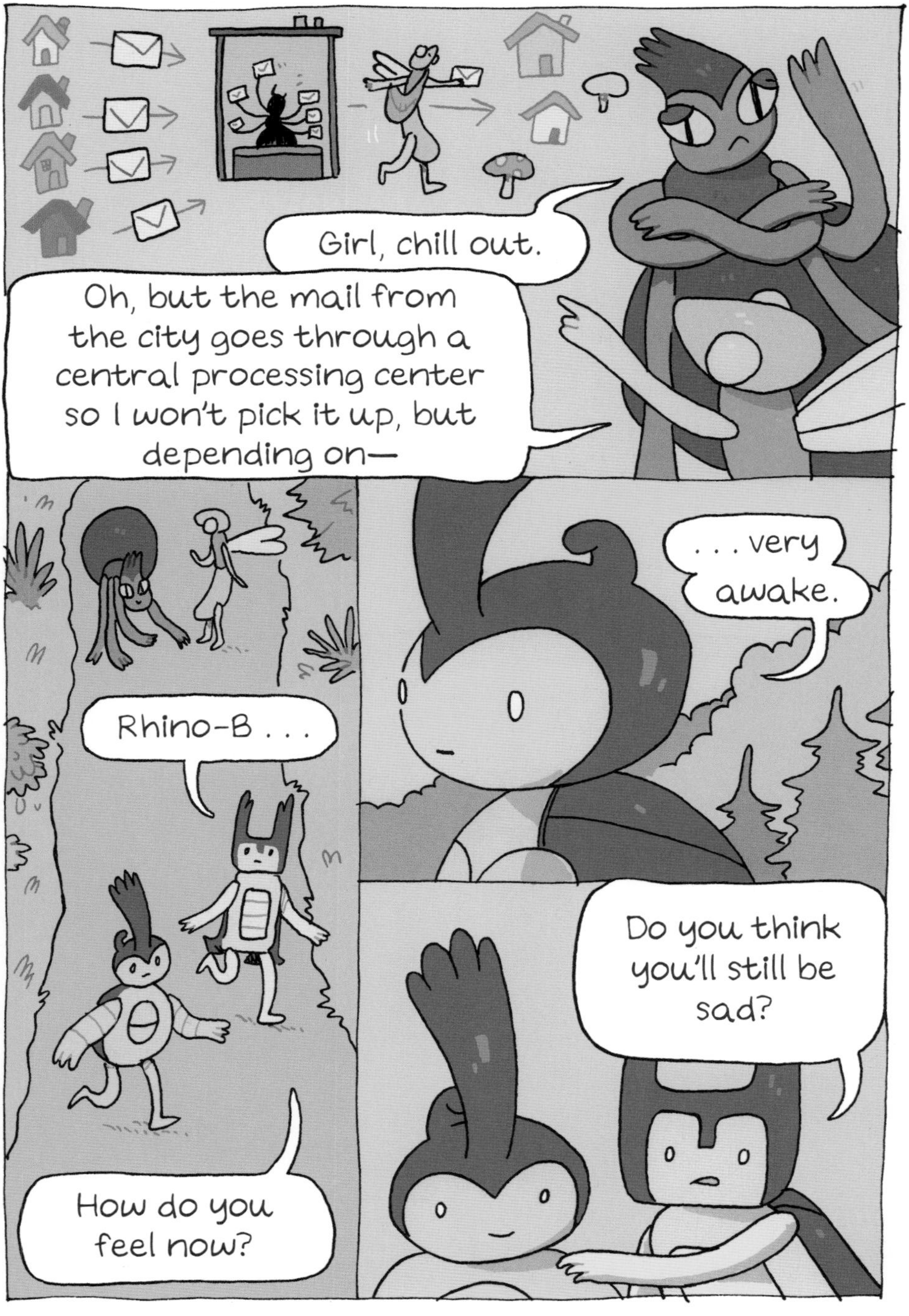
Girl, chill out.
Oh, but the mail from the city goes through a central processing center so I won't pick it up, but depending on—
Rhino-B . . .
How do you feel now?
. . . very awake.
Do you think you'll still be sad?

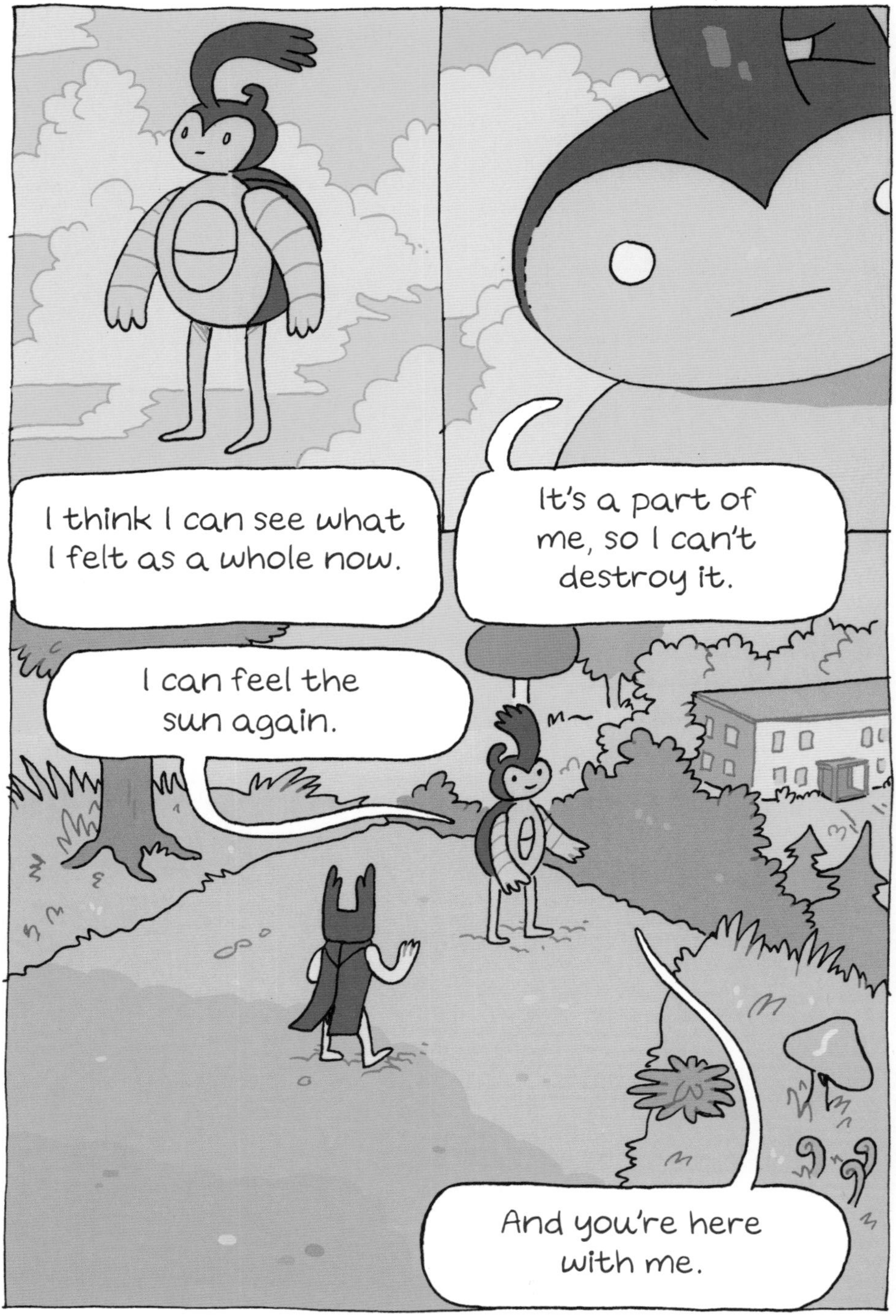
I think I can see what I felt as a whole now.
It's a part of me, so I can't destroy it.
I can feel the sun again.
m~
And you're here with me.

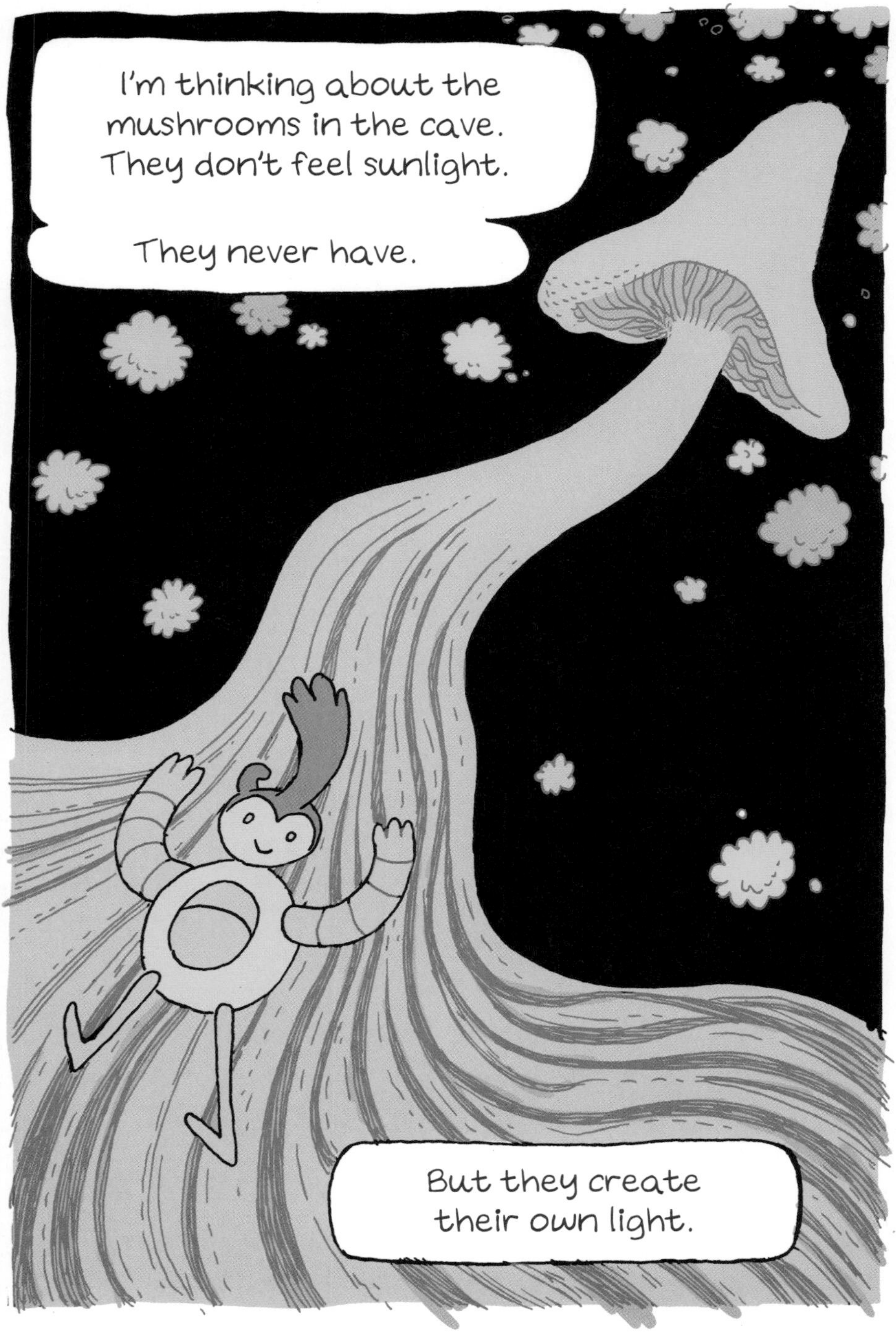
I'm thinking about the mushrooms in the cave. They don't feel sunlight.
They never have.
But they create their own light.

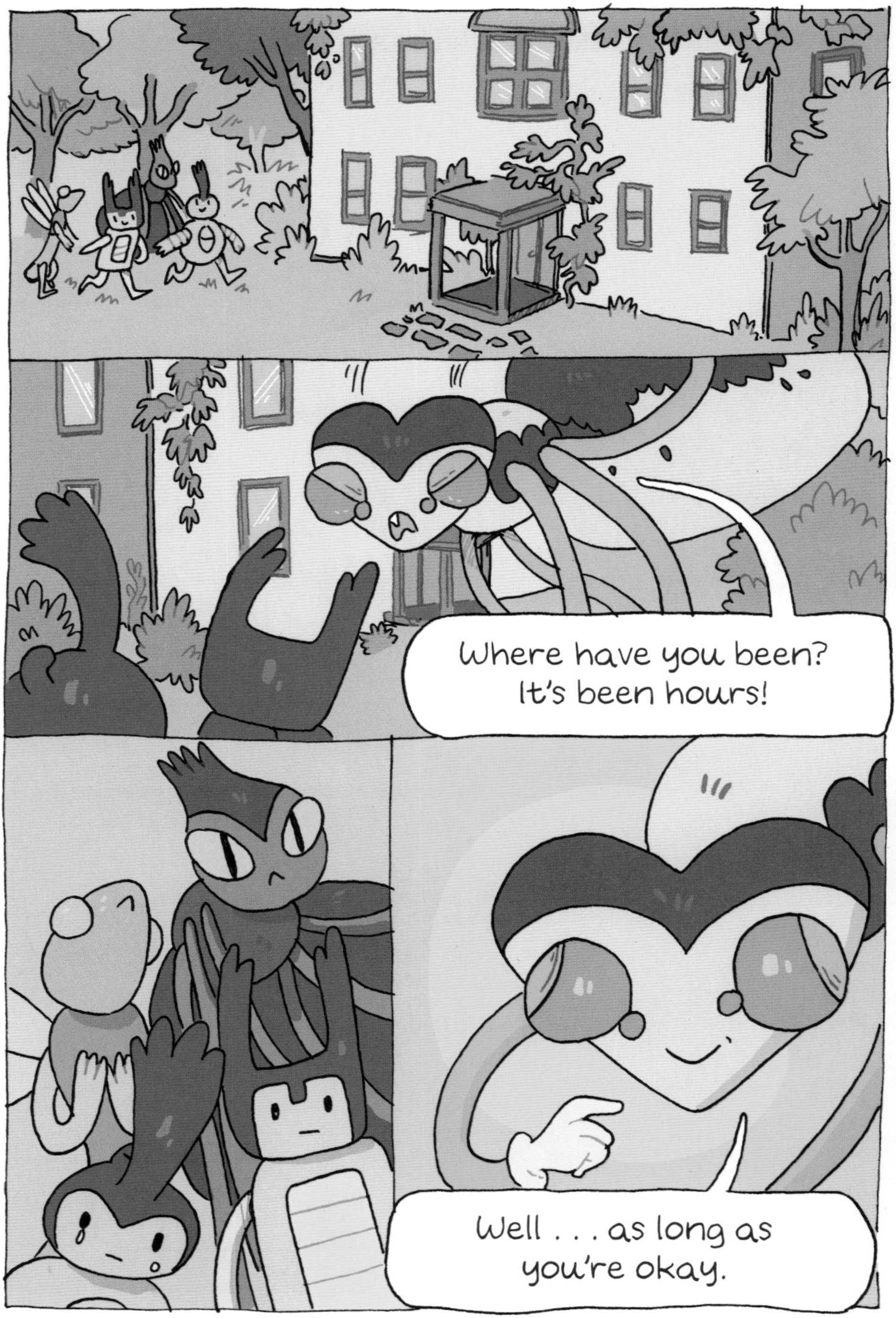
Where have you been? It's been hours!
Well . . . as long as you're okay.

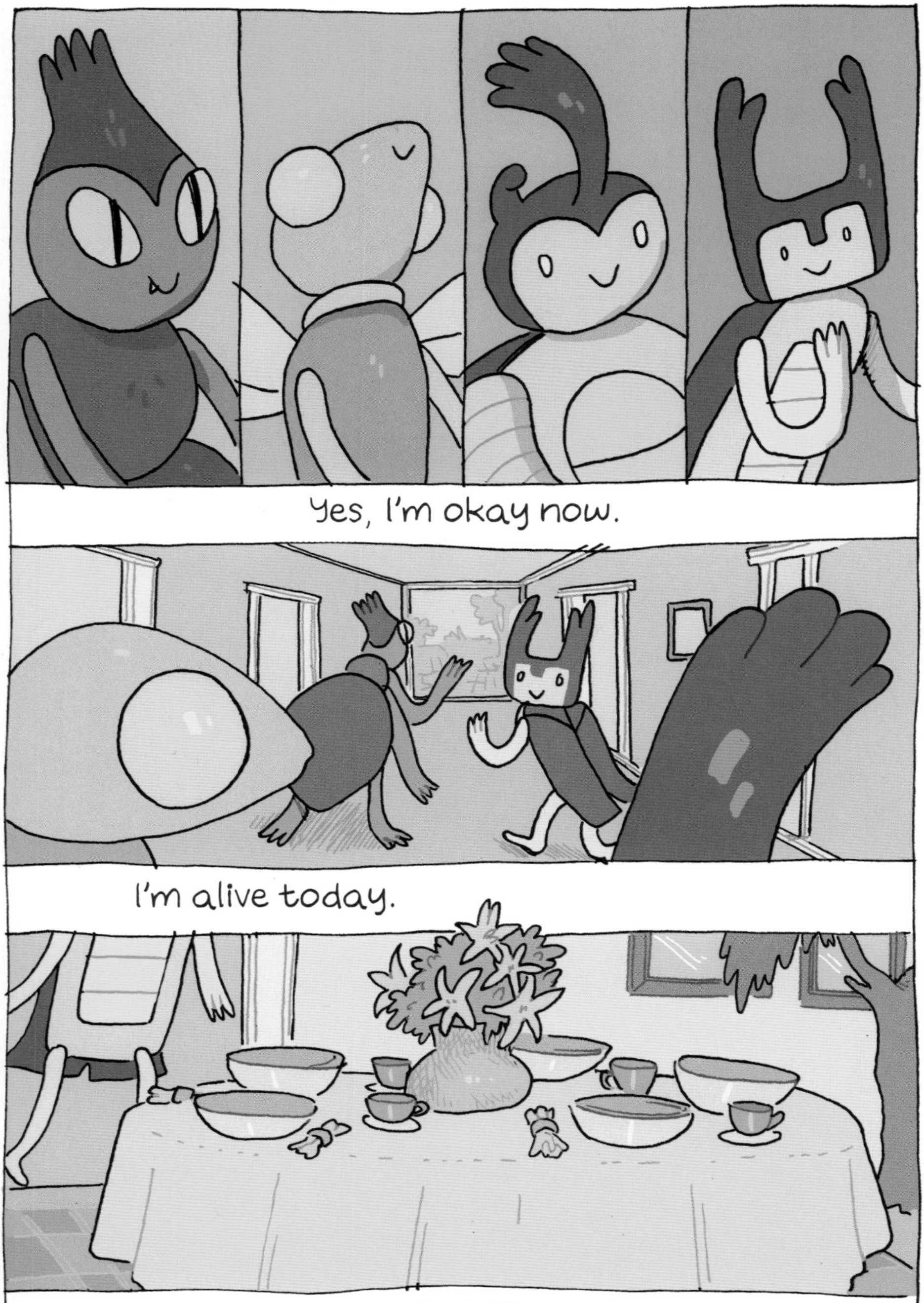
Yes, I'm okay now.
I'm alive today.
And I'll be alive tomorrow.

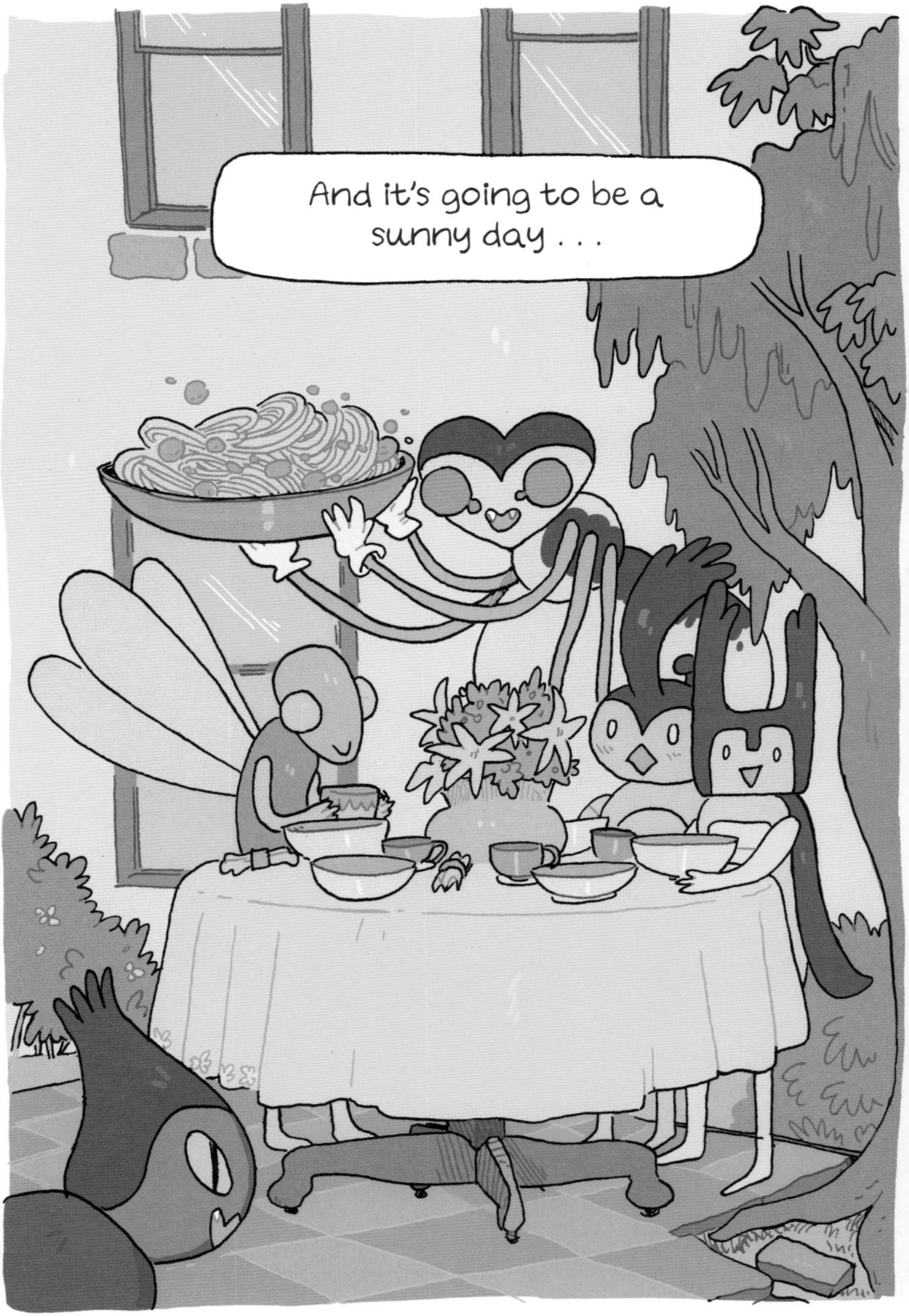
And it's going to be a sunny day . . .

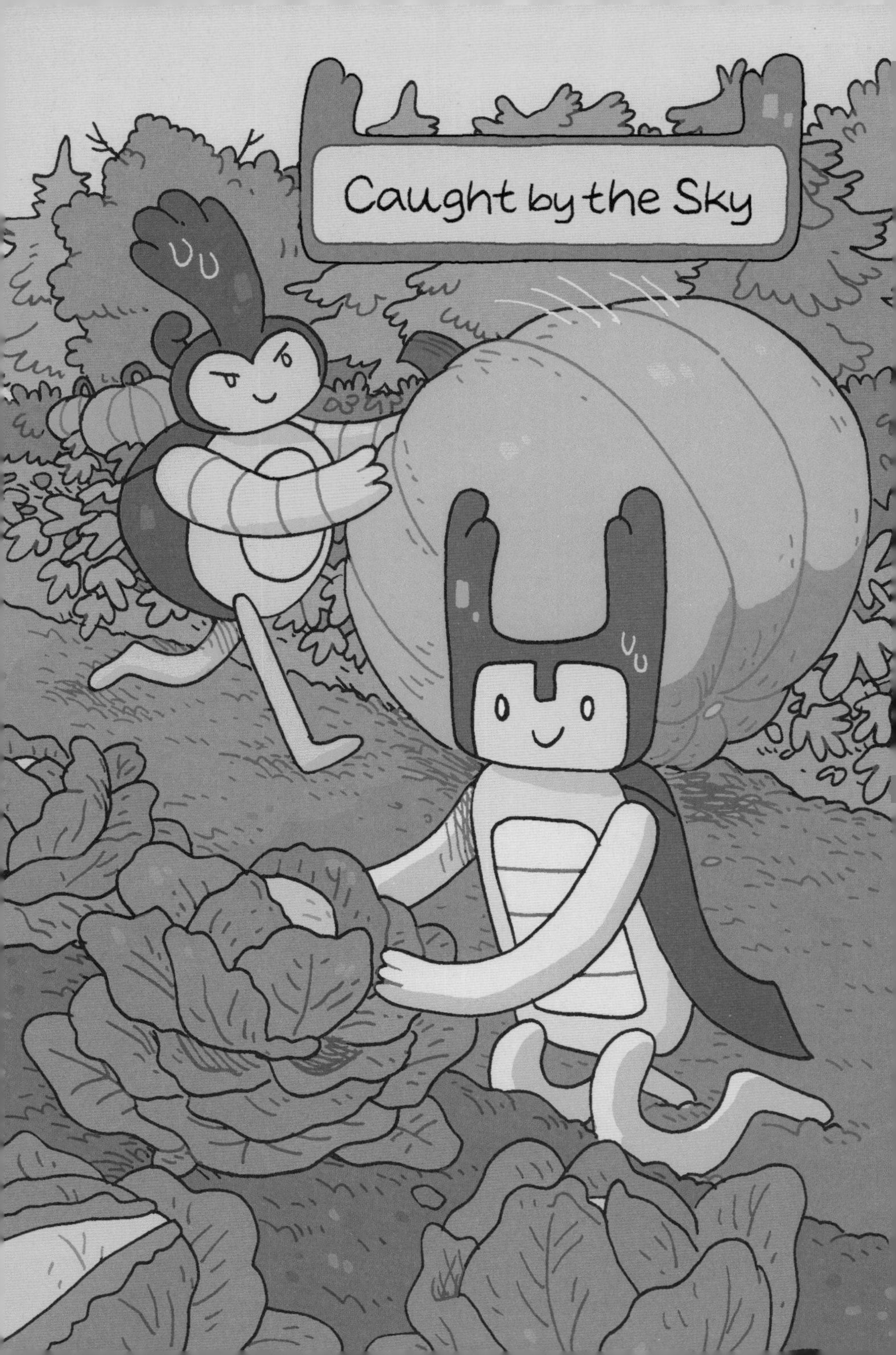
Caught by the Sky

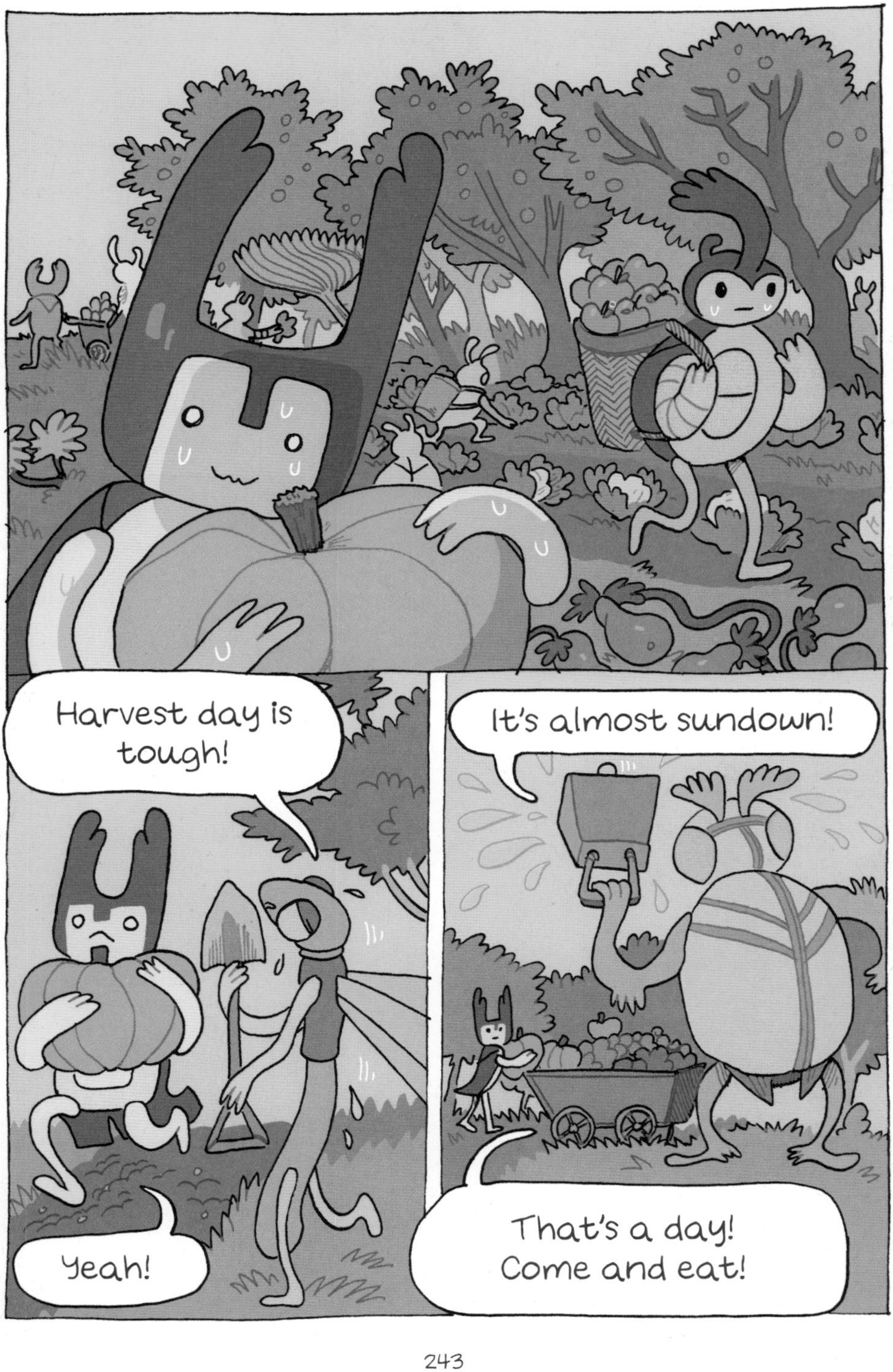

Harvest day is tough!
Yeah!
It's almost sundown!
That's a day! Come and eat!

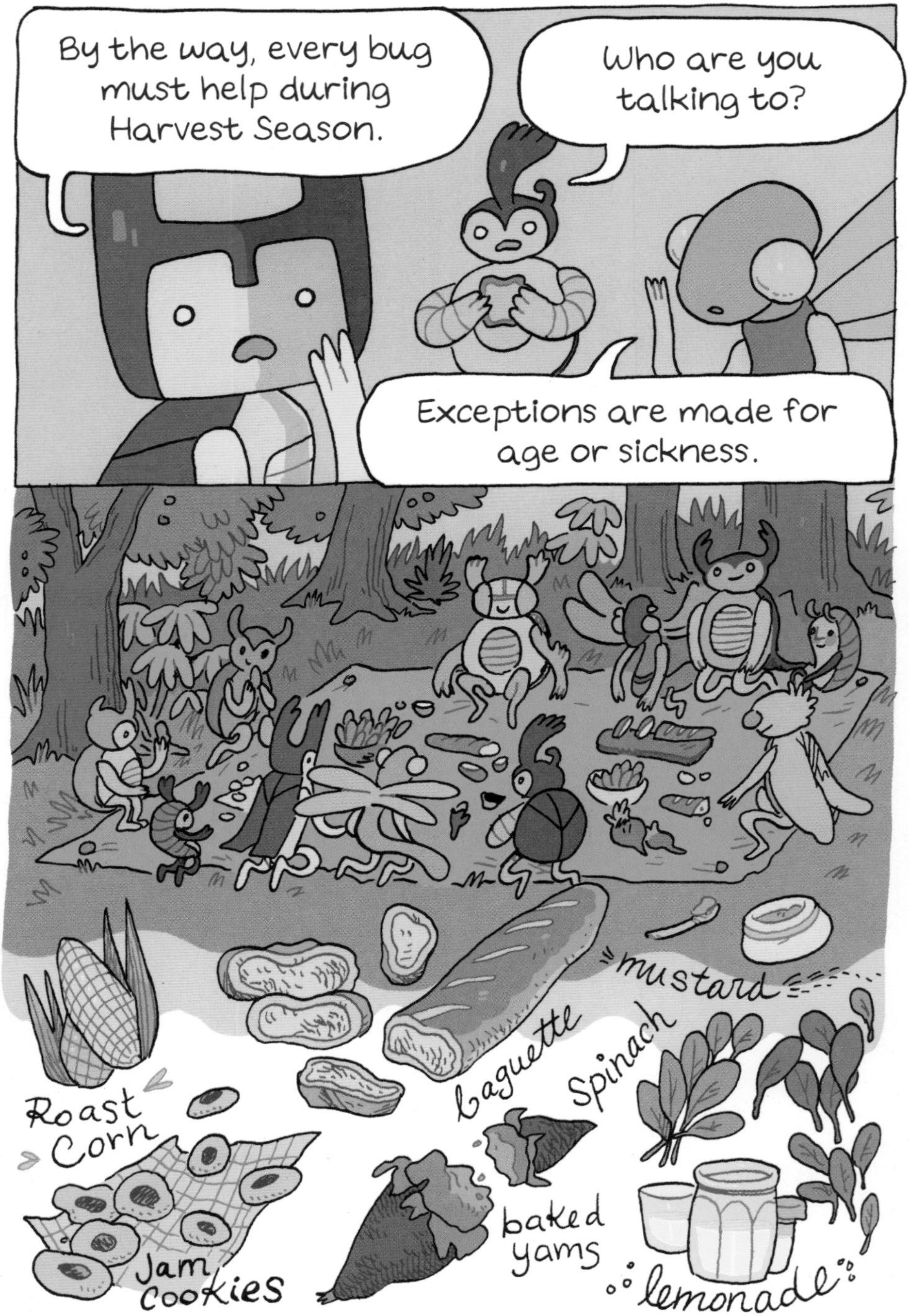
By the way, every bug must help during Harvest Season.
Who are you talking to?
Exceptions are made for age or sickness.
mustard
Baguette
Spinach
Roast Corn
Jam cookies
baked yams
lemonade

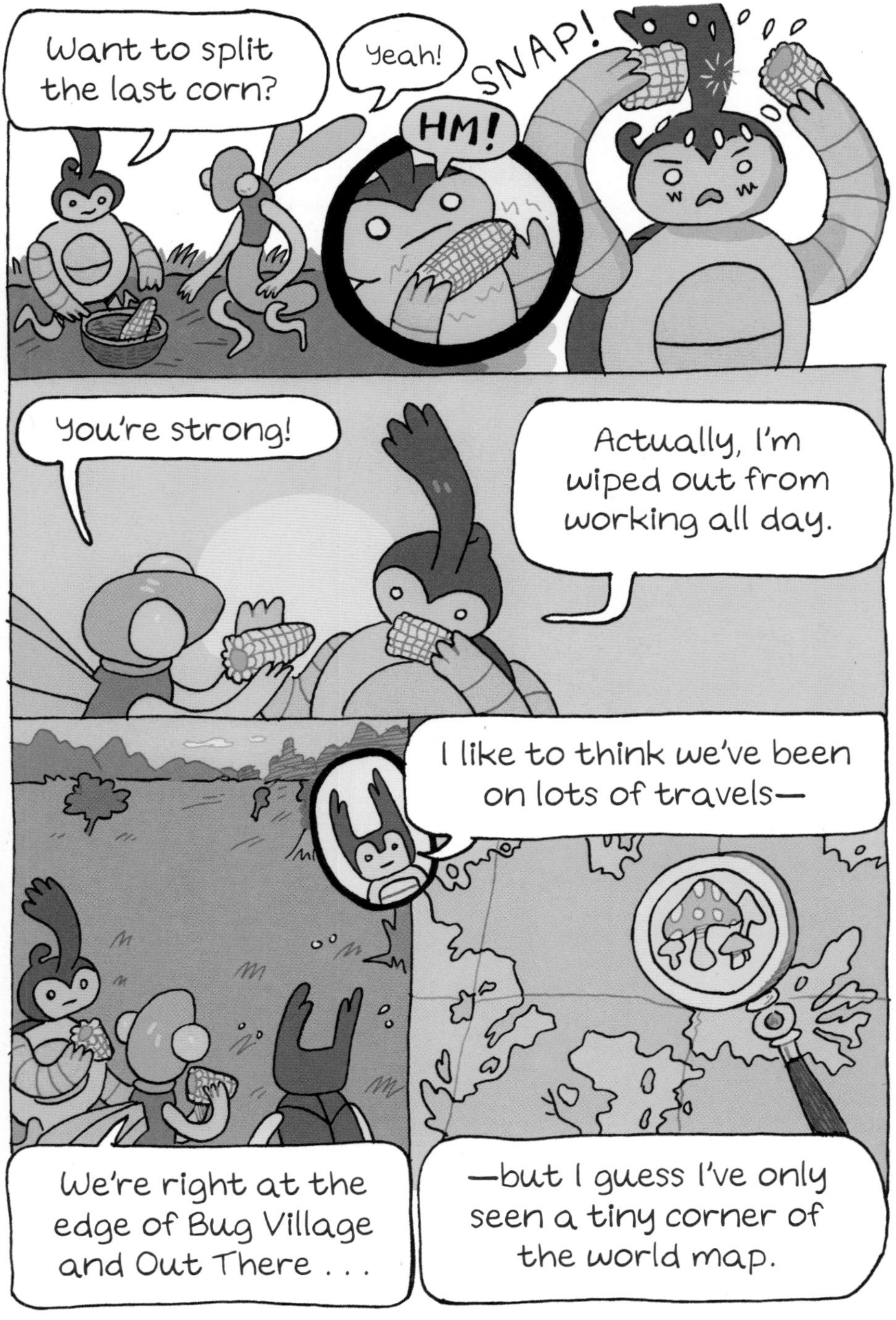
Want to split the last corn?
Yeah!
HM!
SNAP!
You're strong!
Actually, I'm wiped out from working all day.
I like to think we've been on lots of travels—
We're right at the edge of Bug Village and Out There . . .
—but I guess I've only seen a tiny corner of the world map.

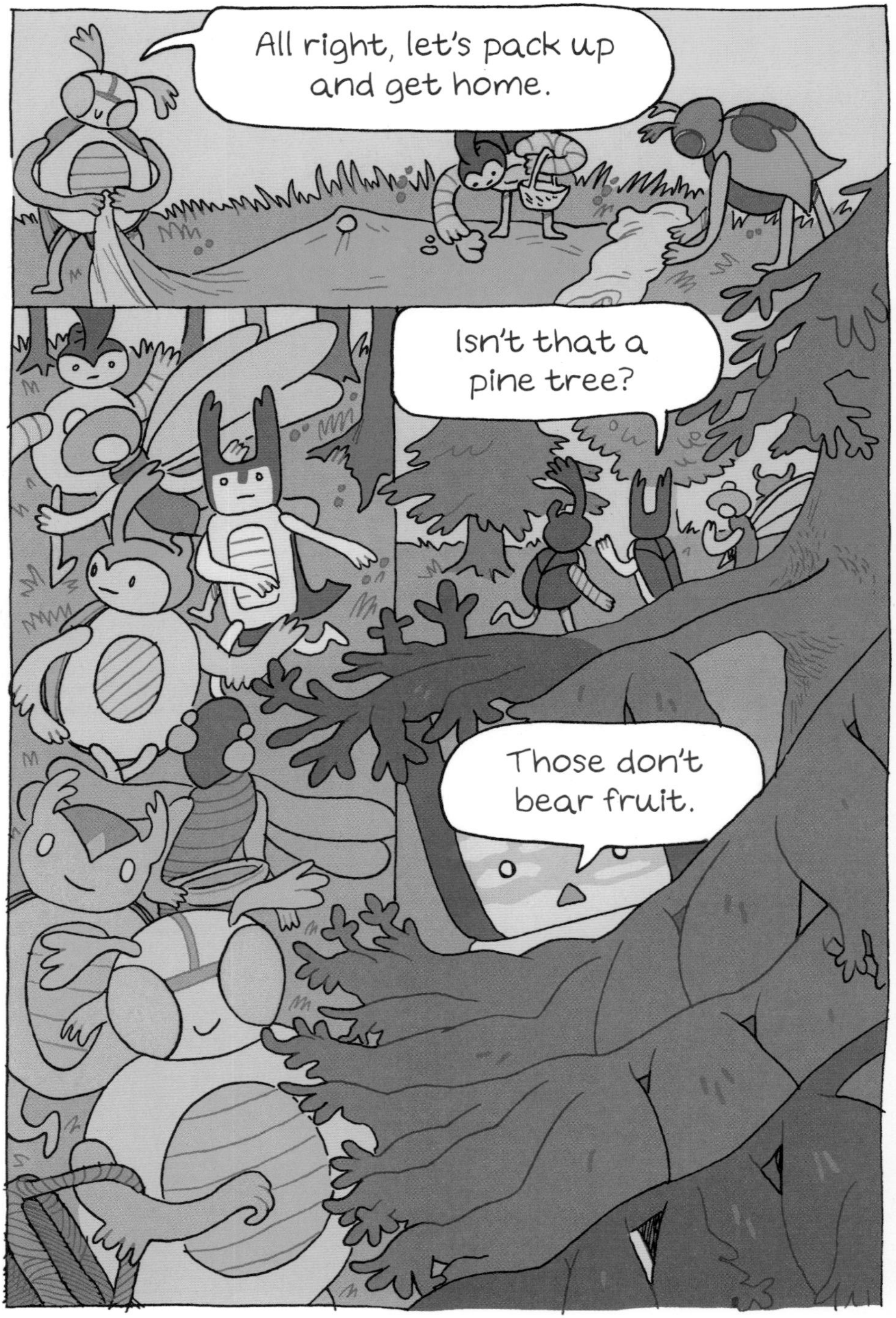
All right, let's pack up and get home.
Isn't that a pine tree?
Those don't bear fruit.

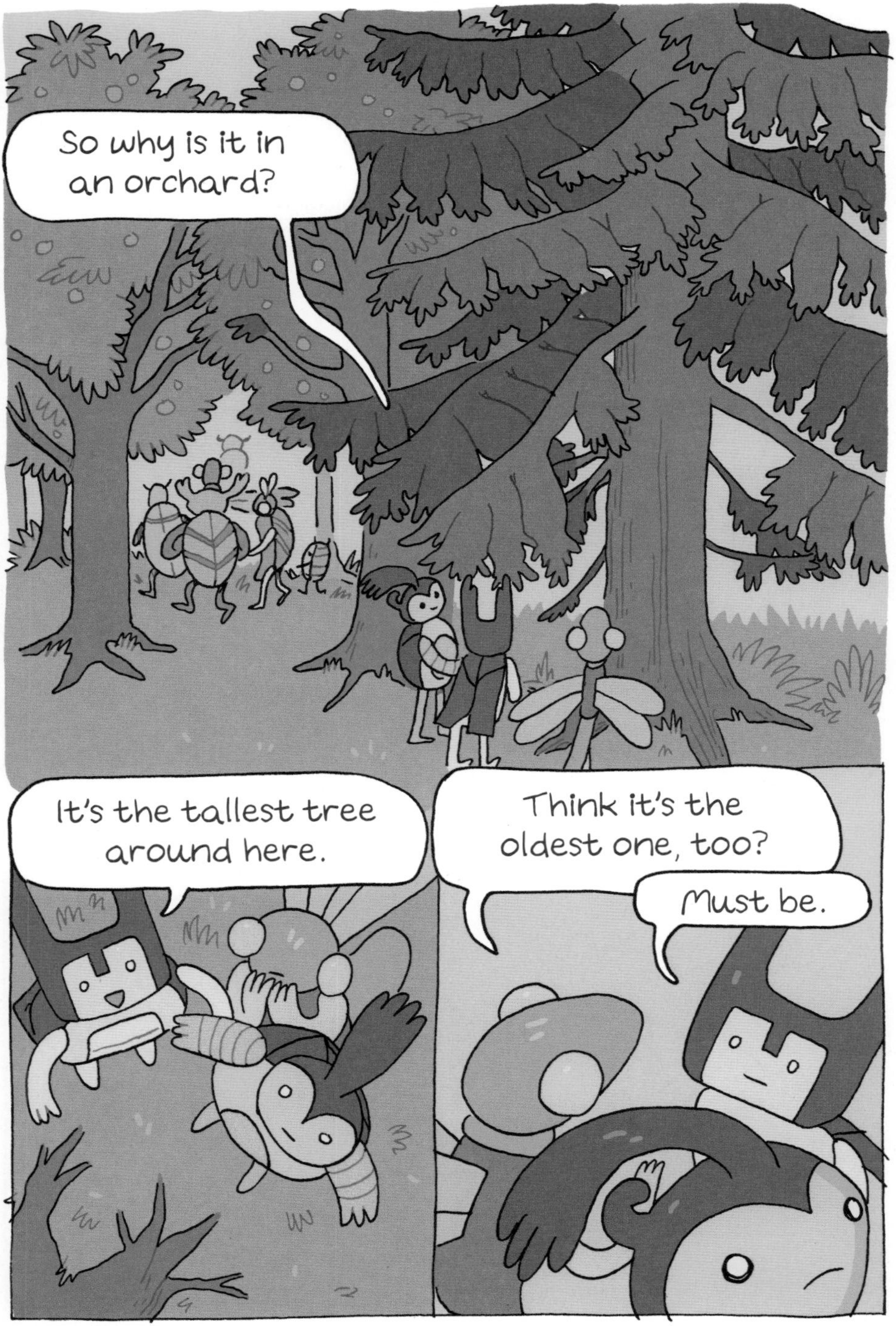
So why is it in an orchard?
It's the tallest tree around here.
Think it's the oldest one, too?
Must be.

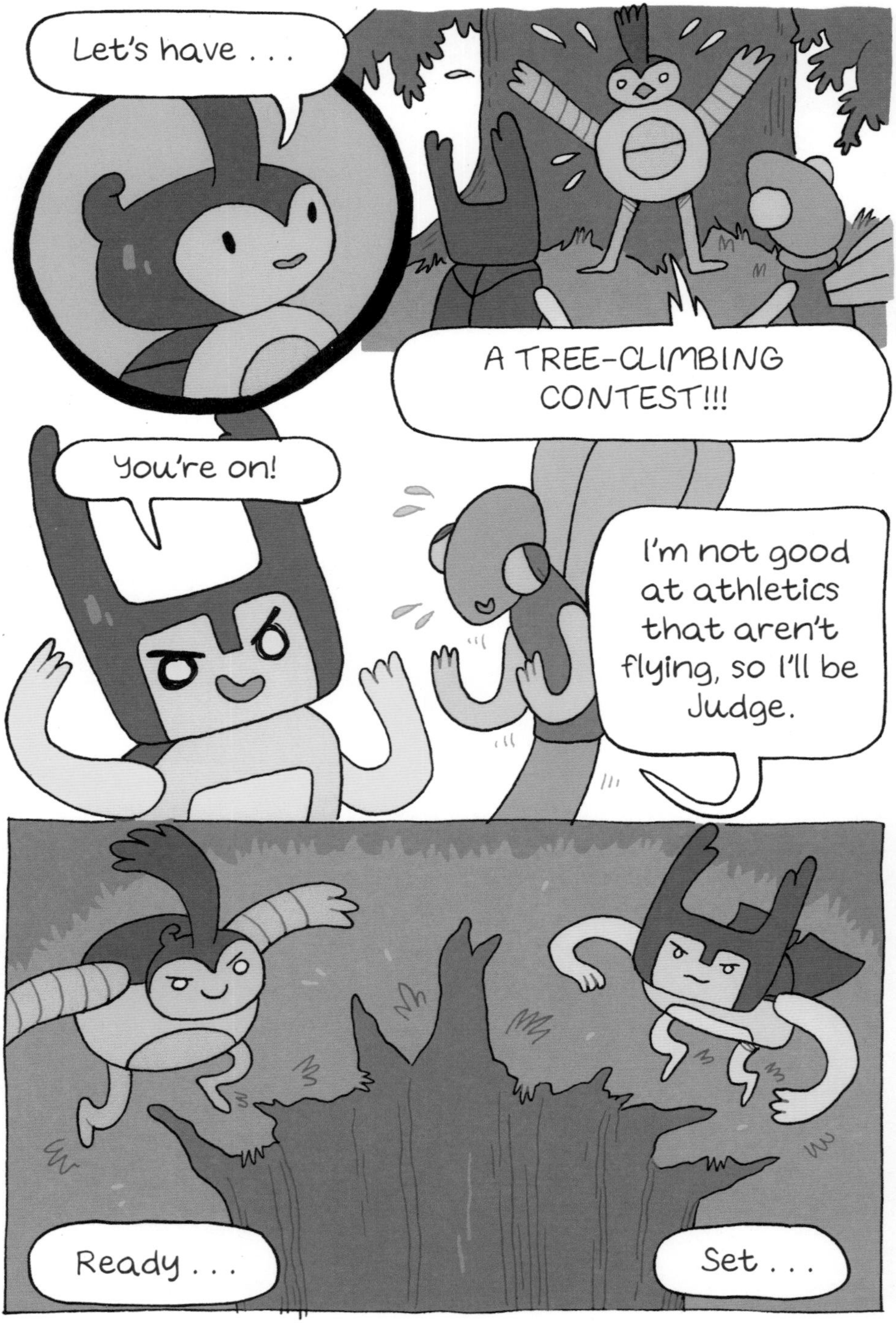
Let's have . . .
A TREE-CLIMBING CONTEST!!!
You're on!
I'm not good at athletics that aren't flying, so I'll be Judge.
Ready . . .
Set . . .

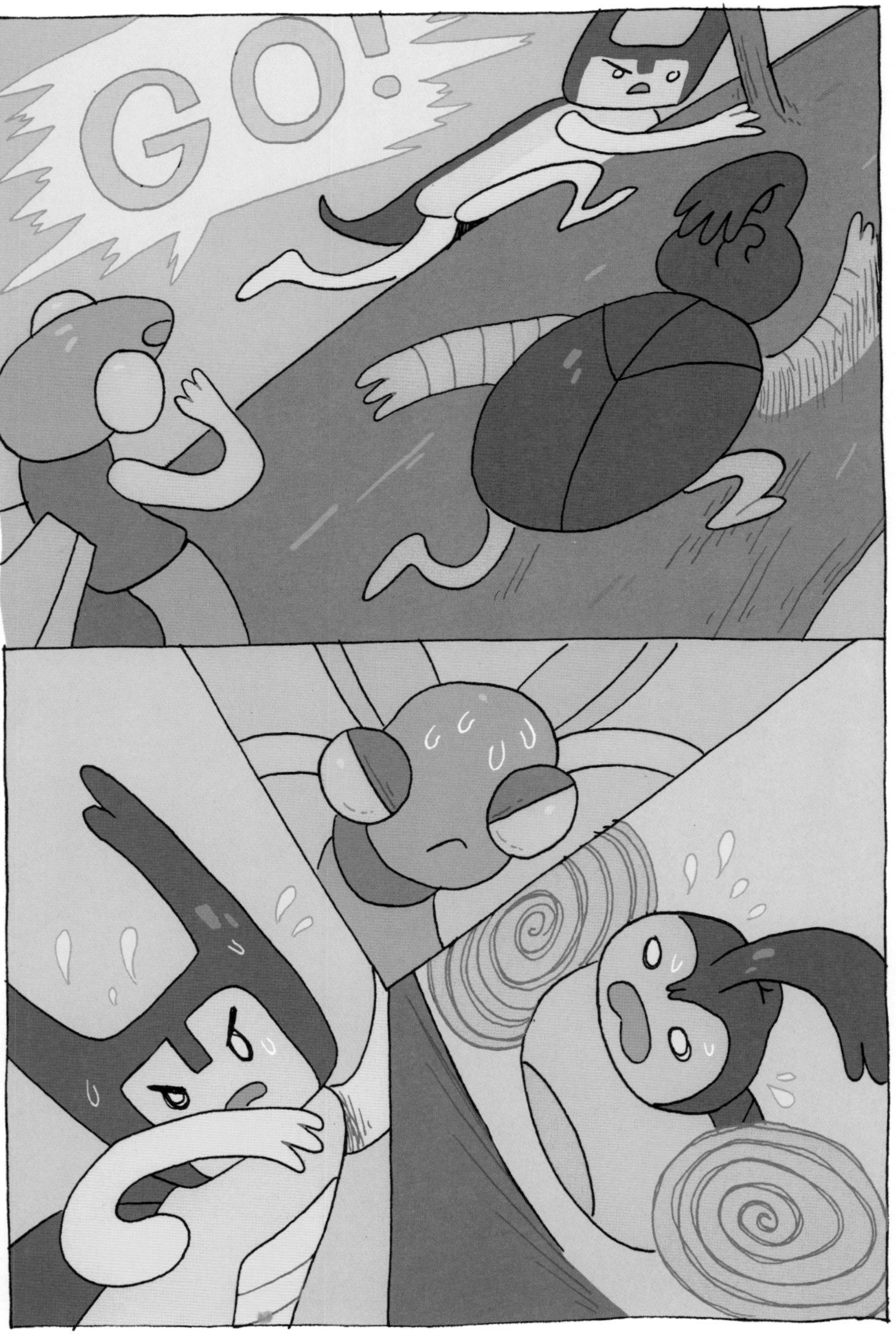
GO!

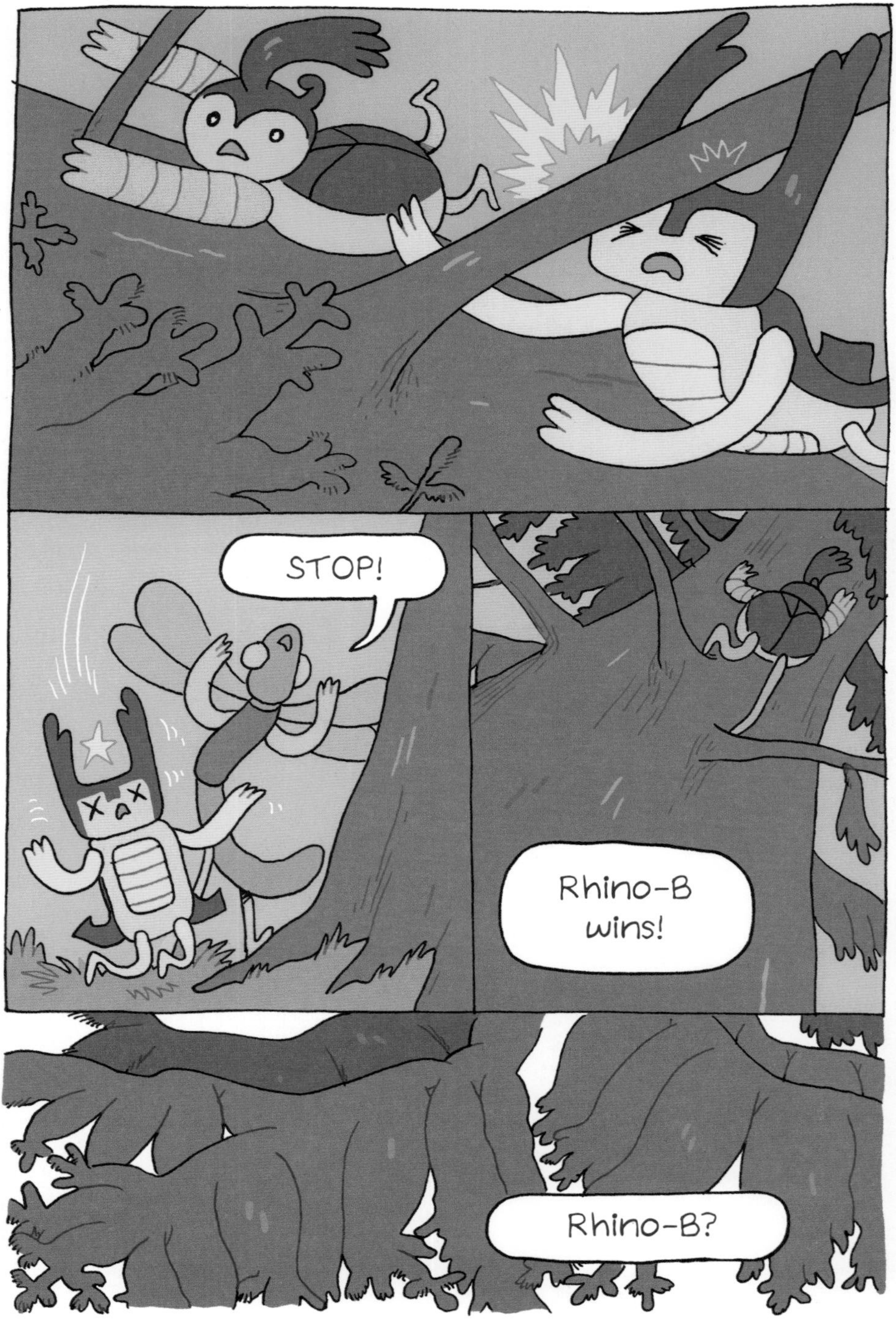
STOP!
Rhino-B wins!
Rhino-B?

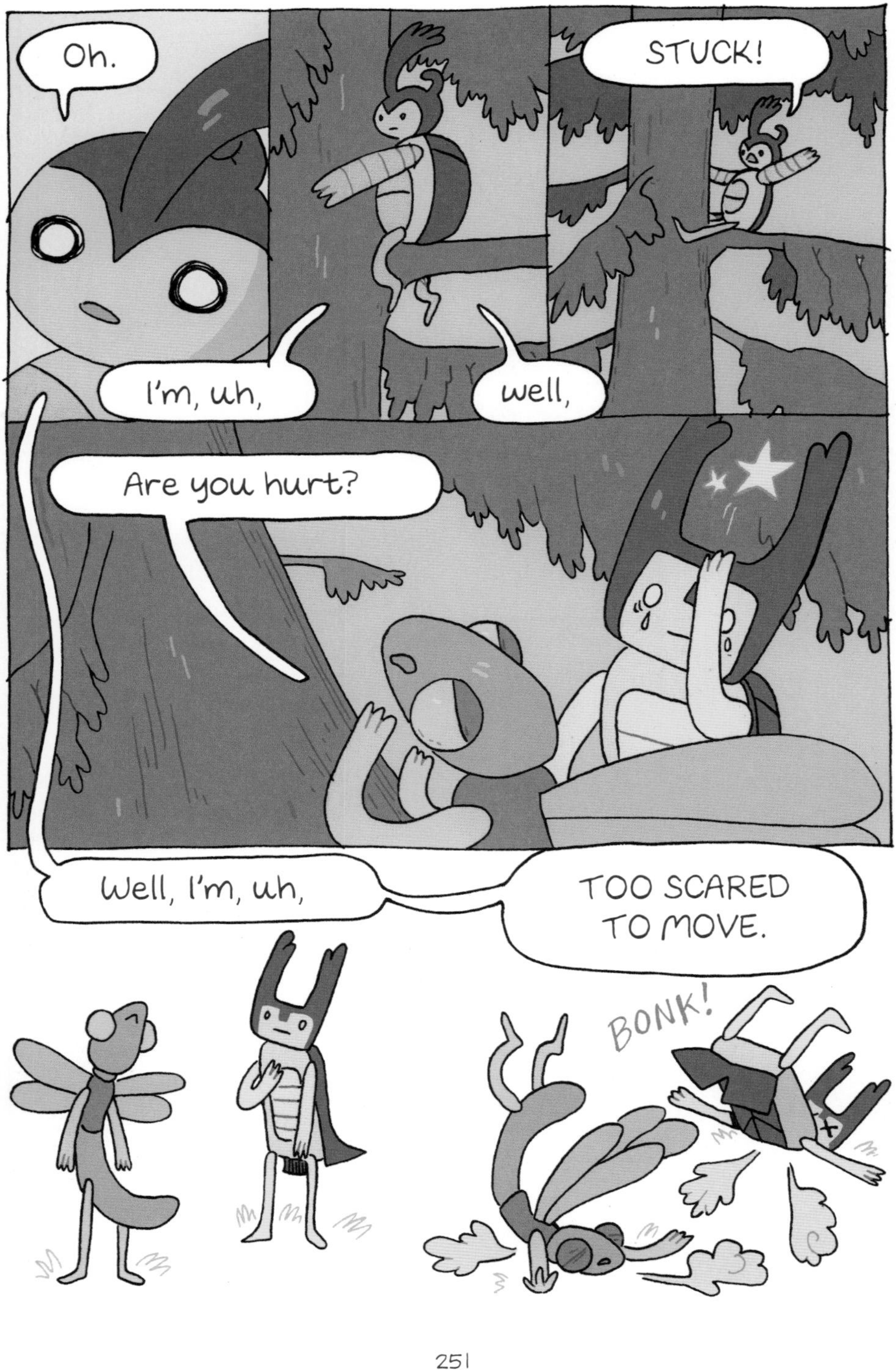
Oh.
STUCK!
I'm, uh,
well,
Are you hurt?
Well, I'm, uh,
TOO SCARED TO MOVE.
BONK!

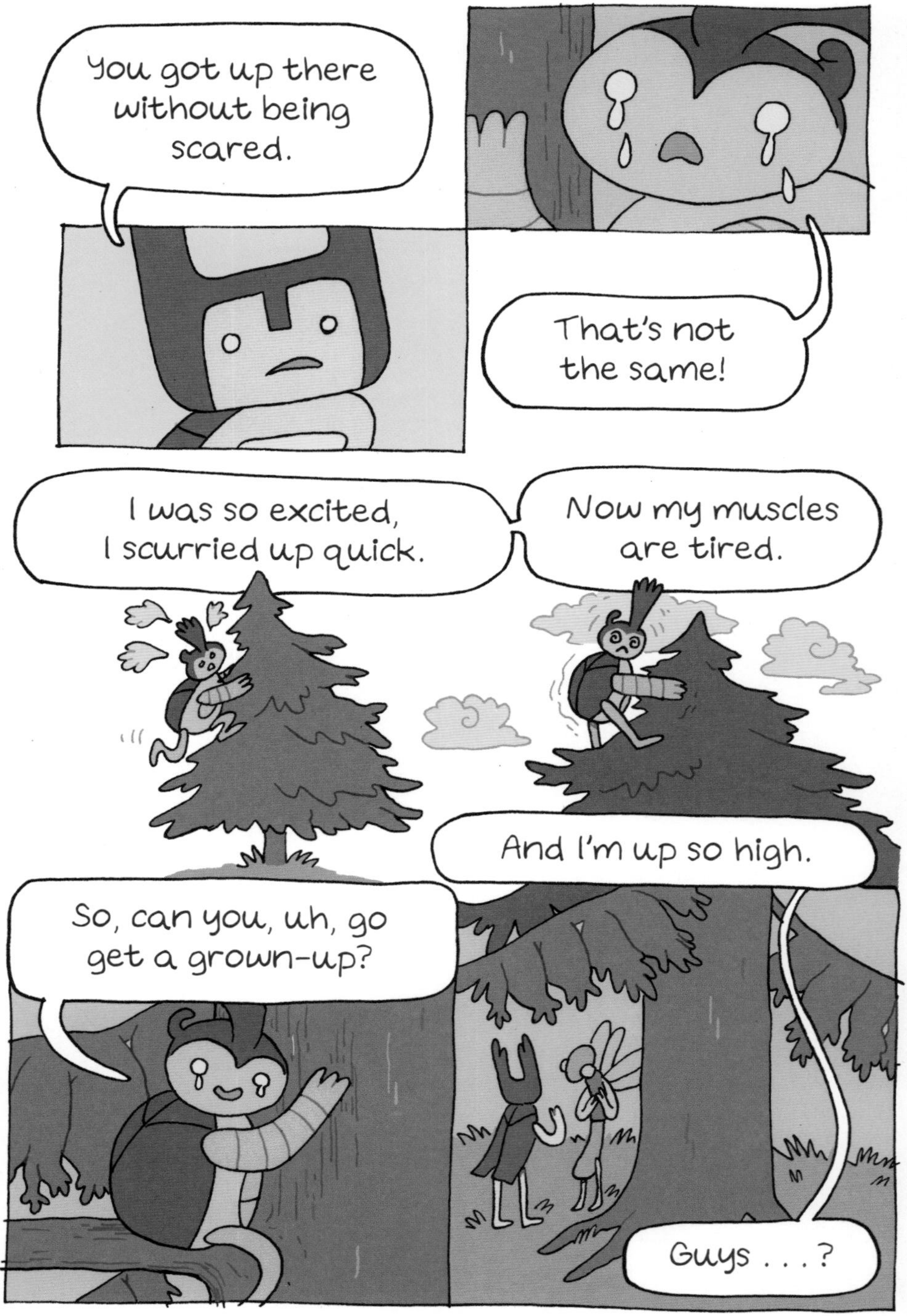
You got up there without being scared.
That's not the same!
I was so excited, I scurried up quick.
Now my muscles are tired.
And I'm up so high.
So, can you, uh, go get a grown-up?
Guys . . . ?

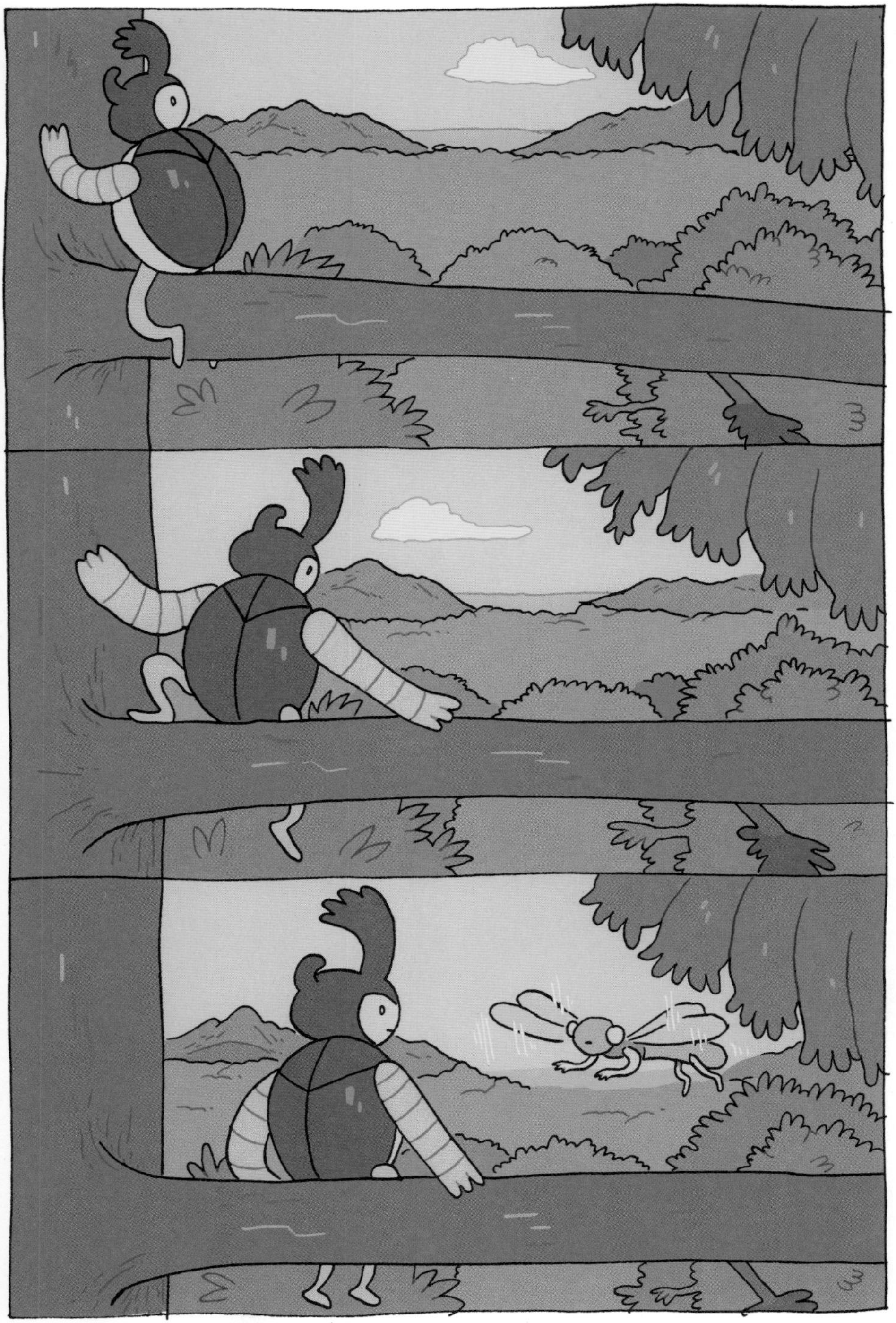

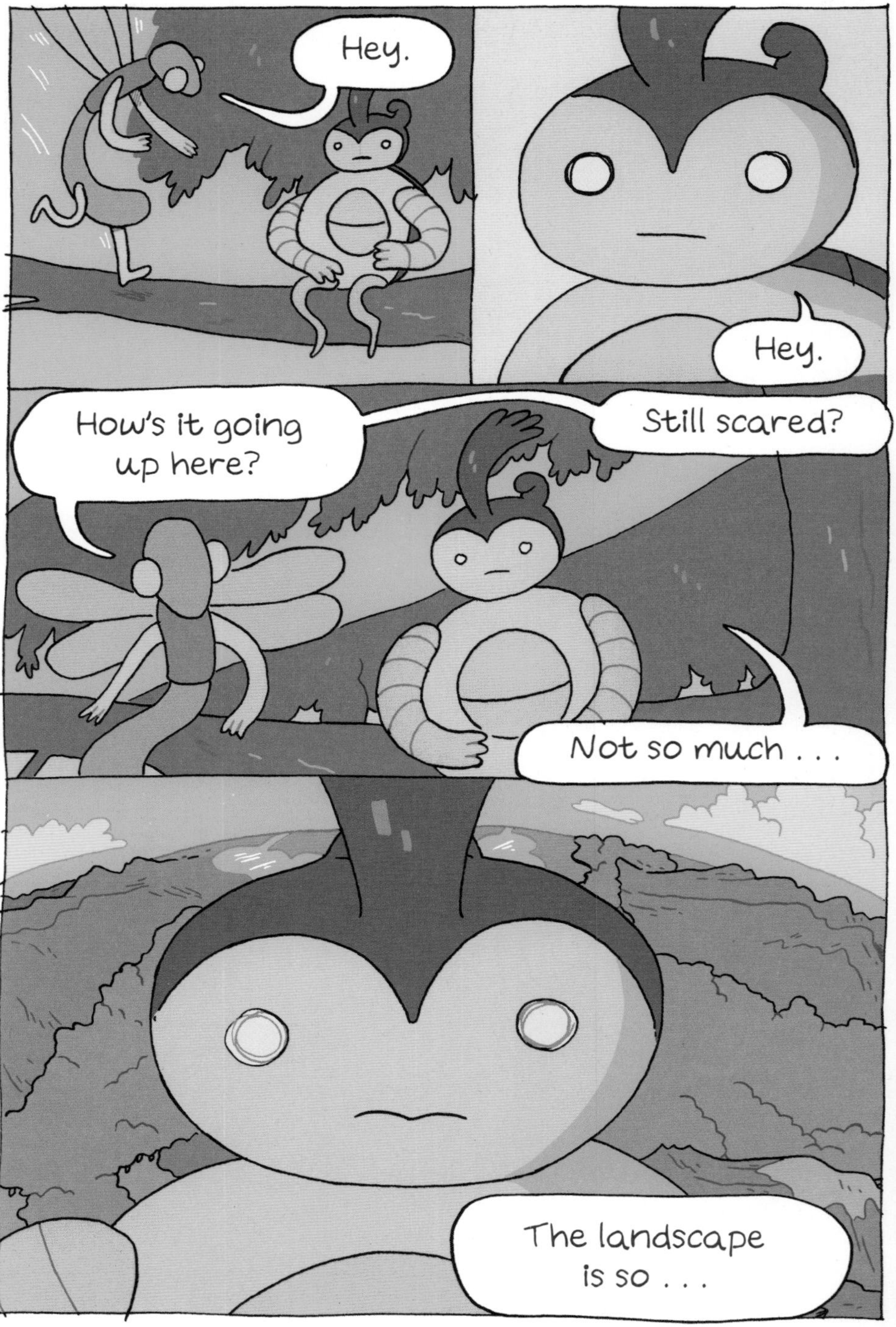
Hey.
Hey.
How's it going up here?
Still scared?
Not so much . . .
The landscape is so . . .

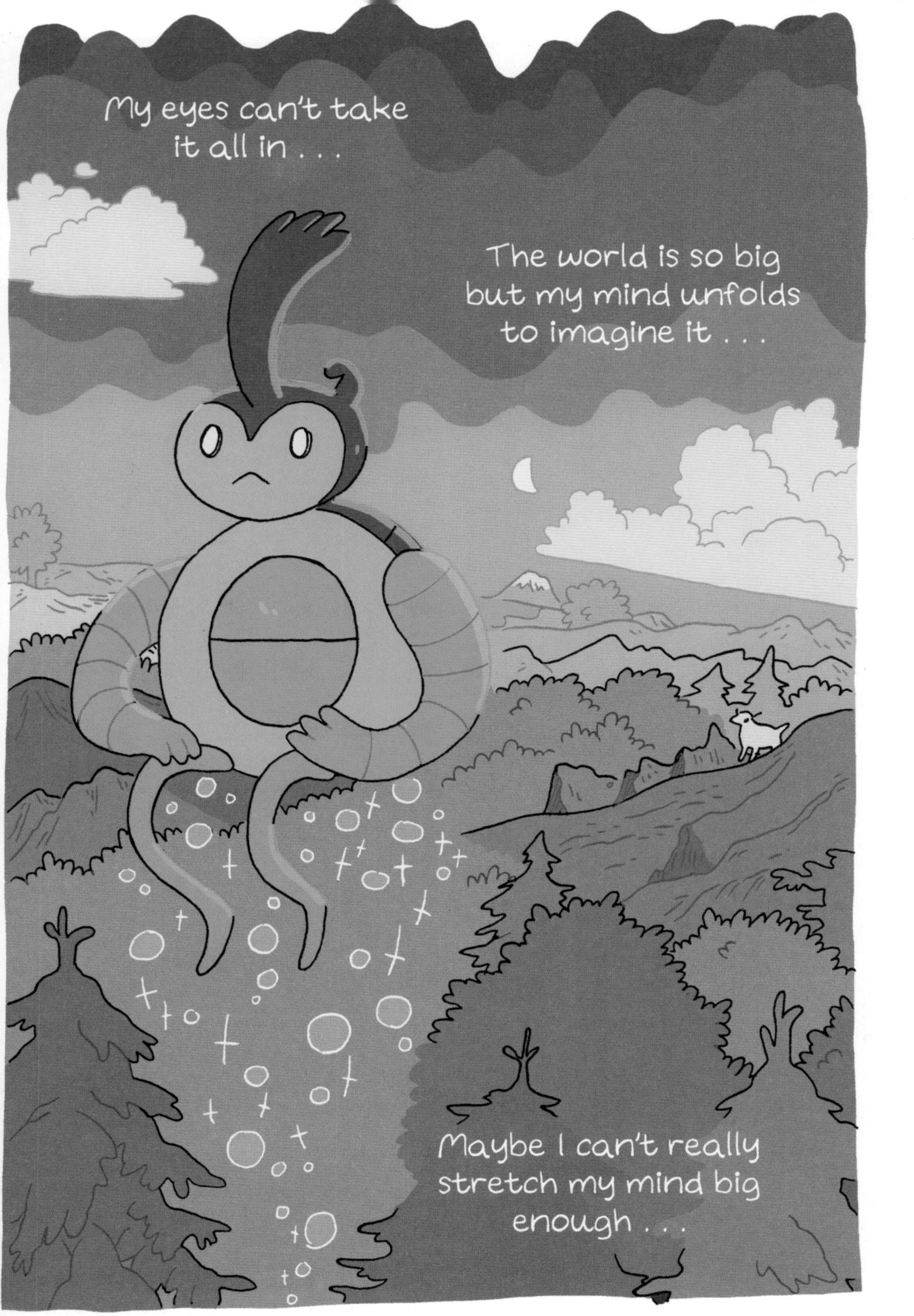
My eyes can't take it all in . . .
The world is so big but my mind unfolds to imagine it . . .
Maybe I can't really stretch my mind big enough . . .

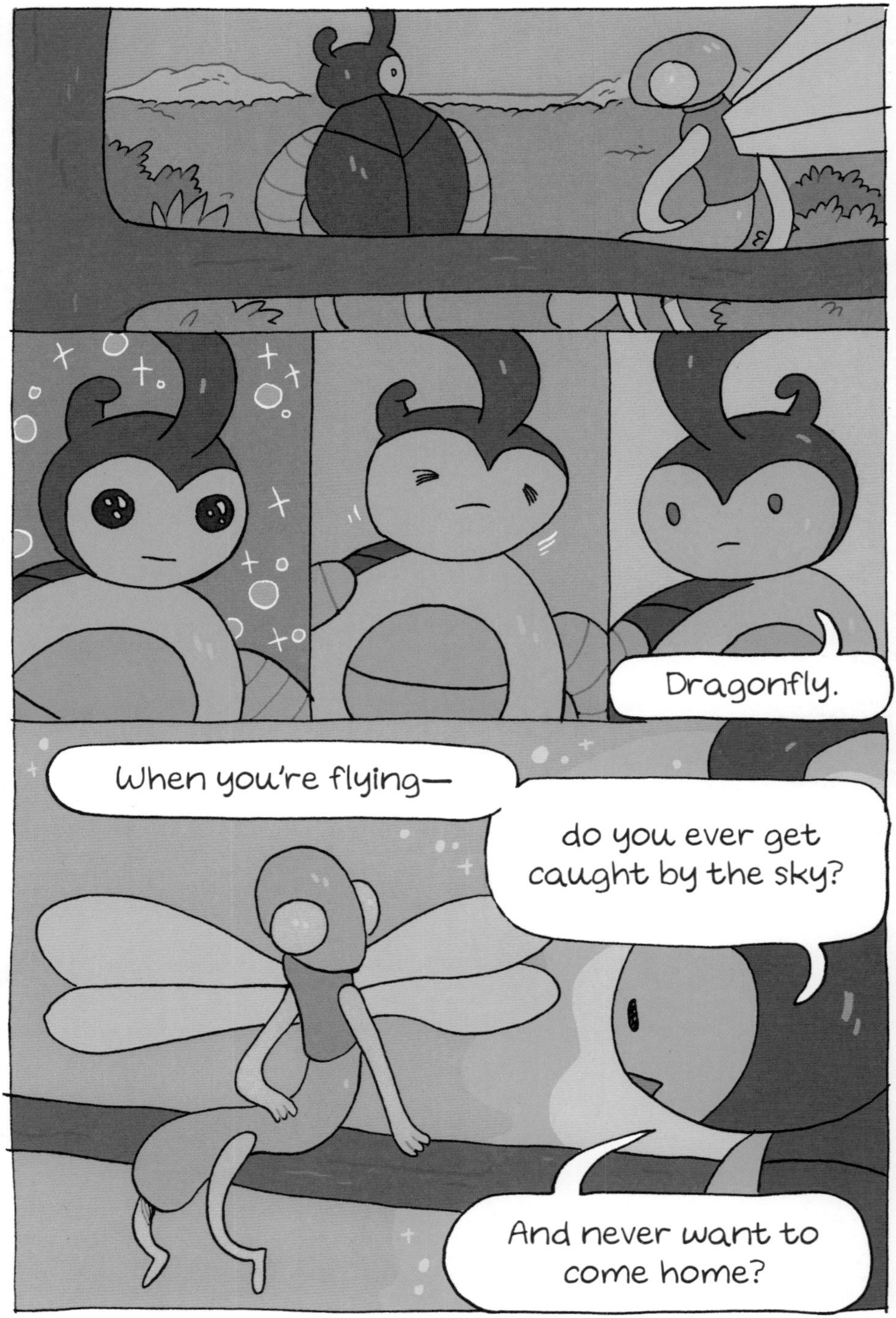
Dragonfly.
When you're flying—
do you ever get caught by the sky?
And never want to come home?

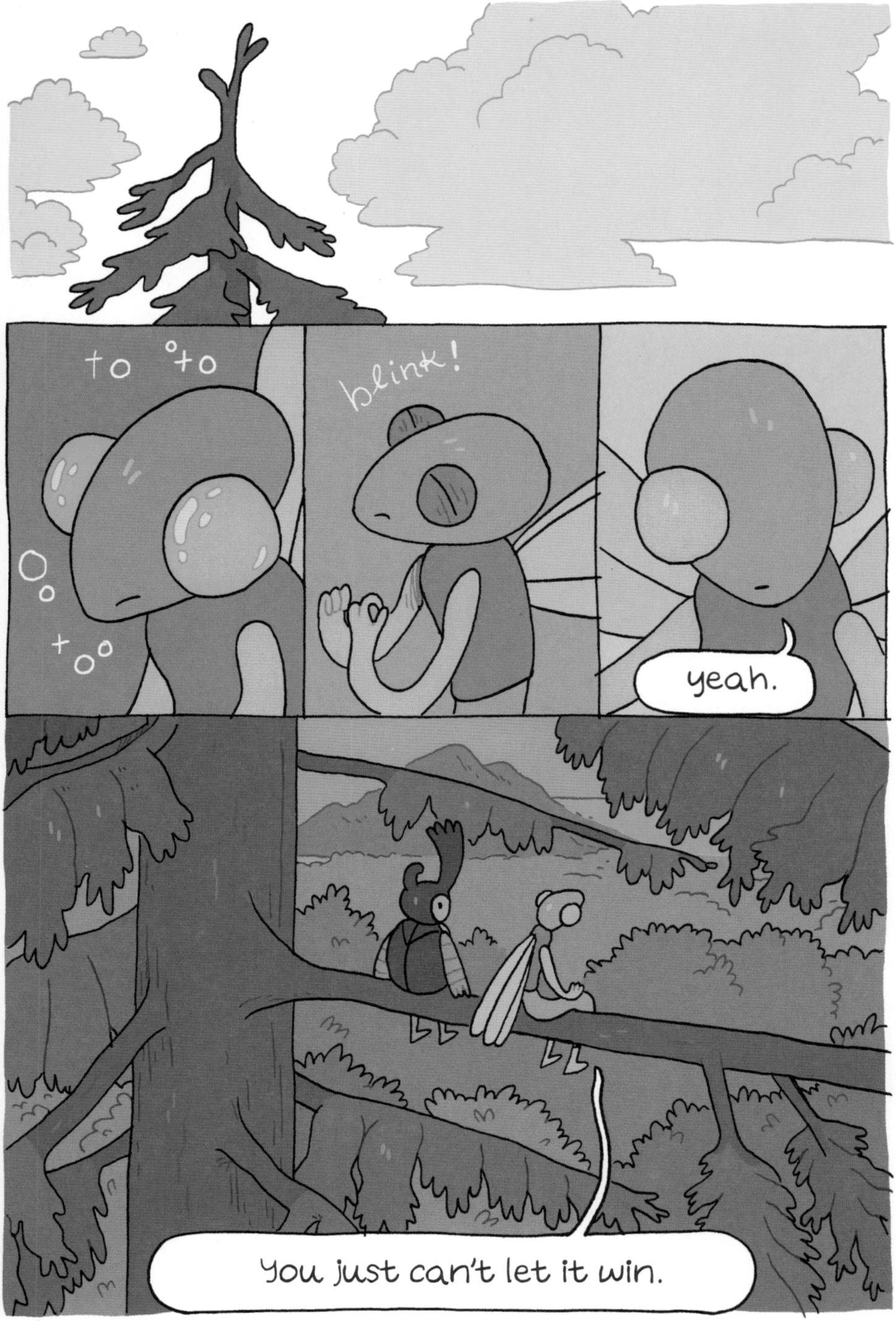
to °to
Oo
+oo
blink!
yeah.
You just can't let it win.

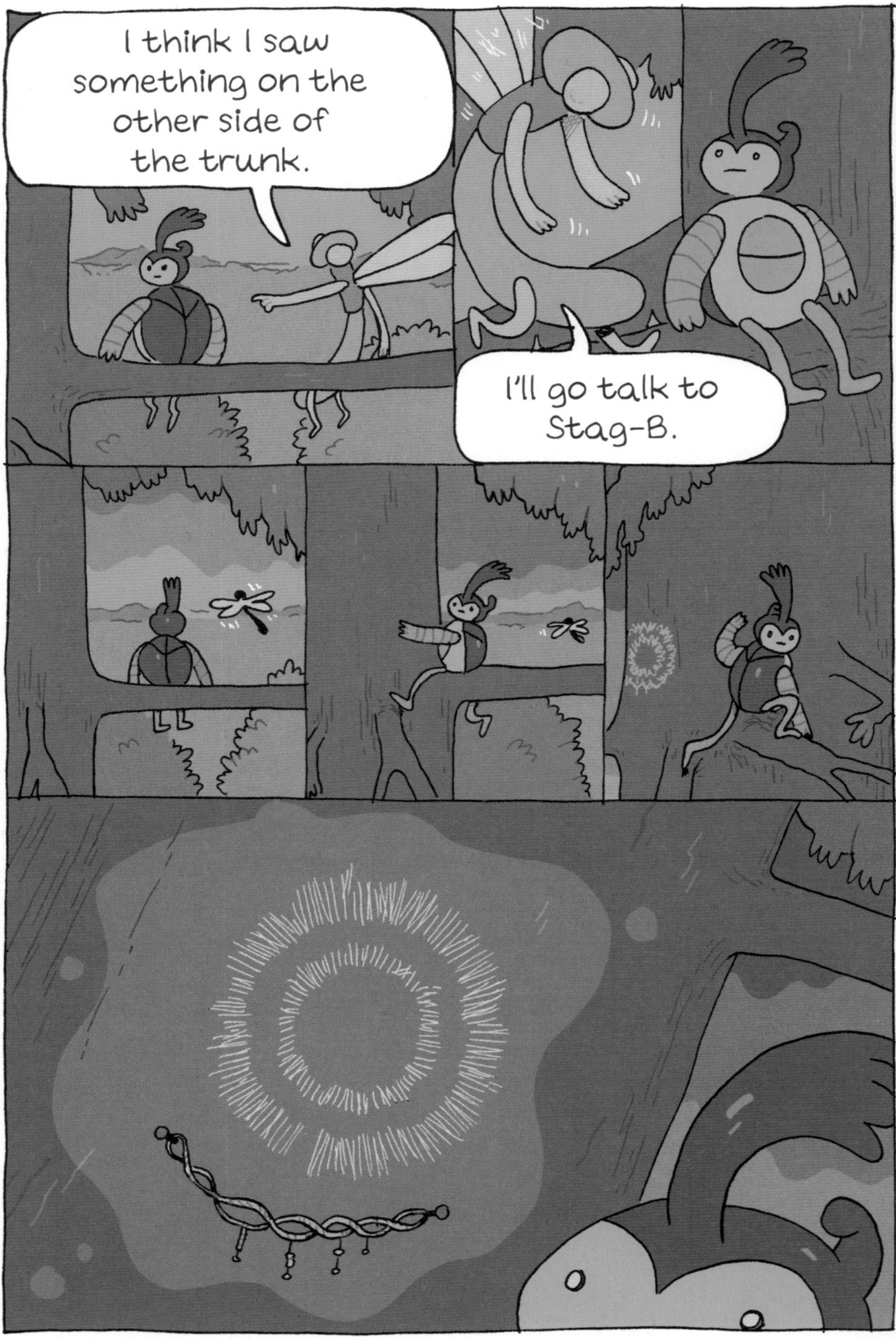
I think I saw something on the other side of the trunk.
I'll go talk to Stag-B.

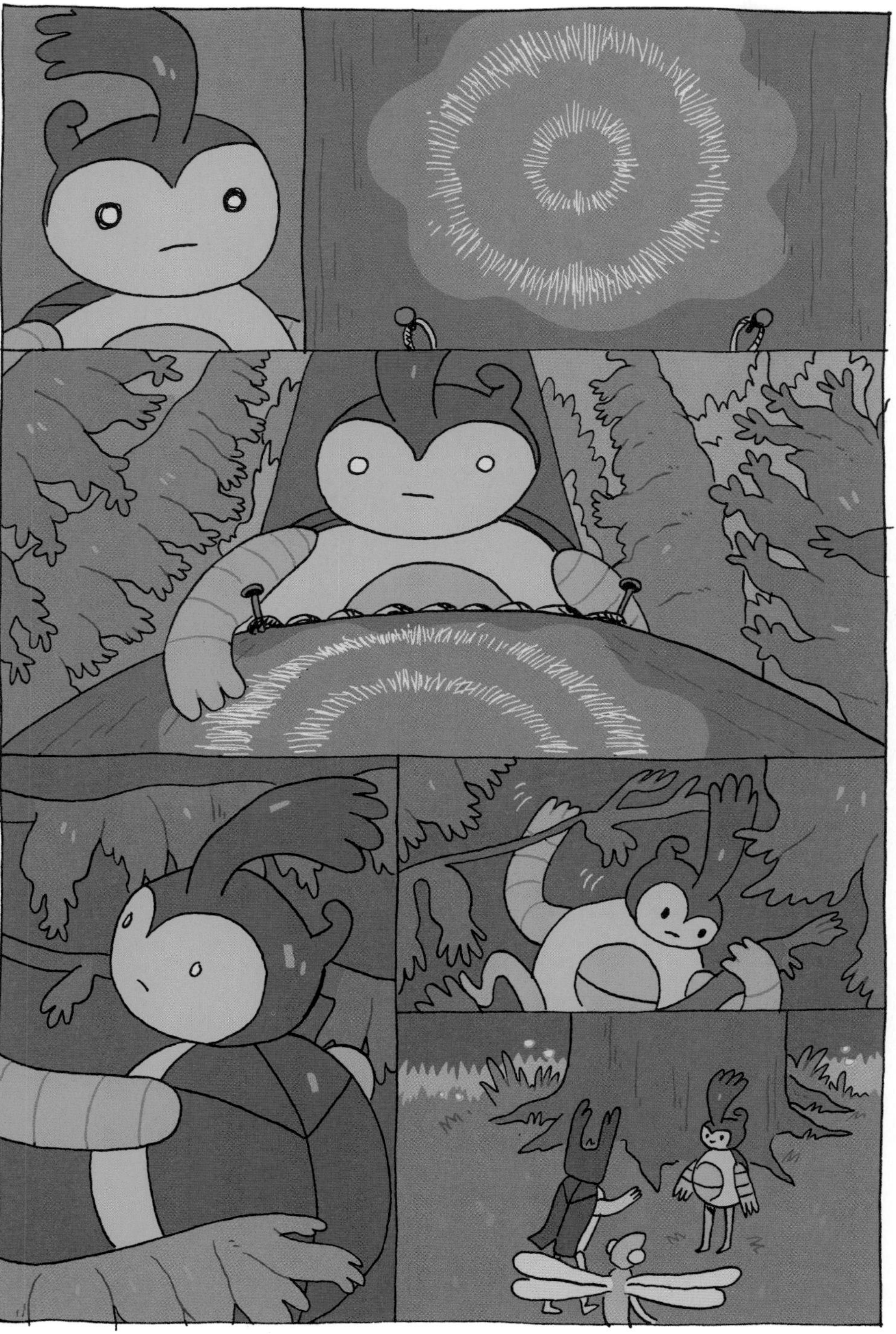

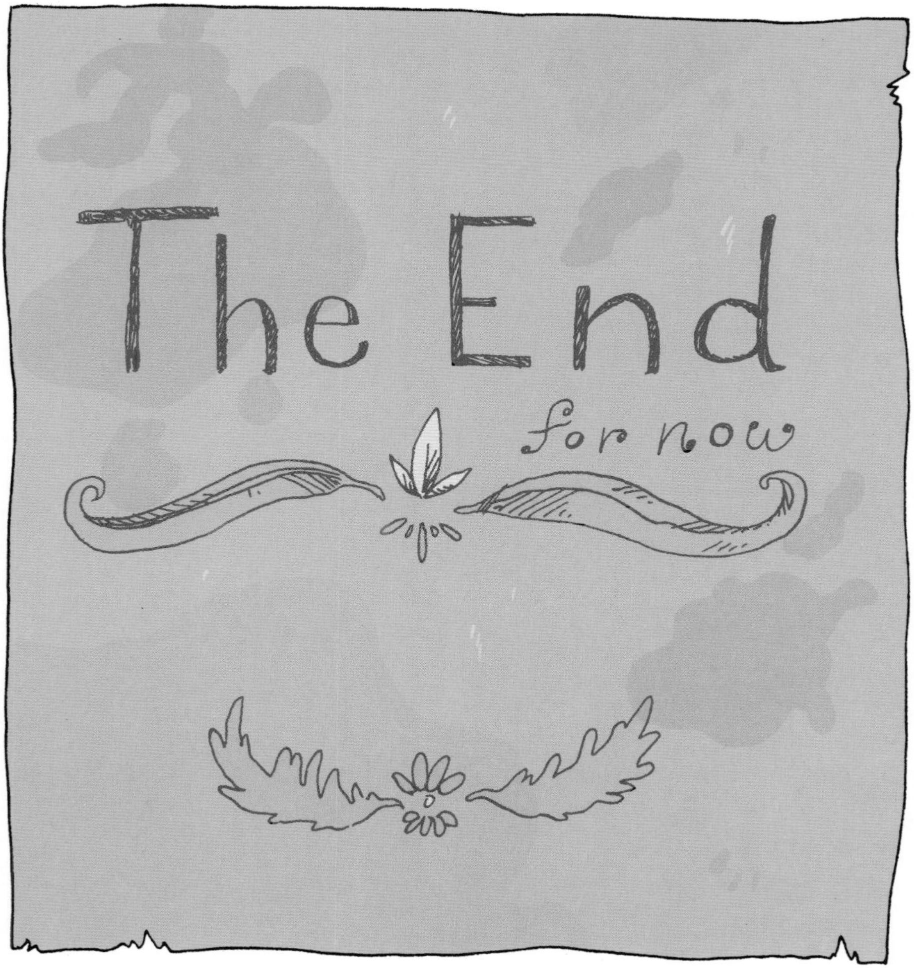
The End
for now

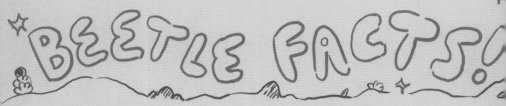

BEETLE FACTS!

There are over twelve hundred types of stag beetle and over three hundred types of rhinoceros beetle. Stag beetles and rhinoceros beetles use their horns to wrestle one another and dig into the ground. In both types of beetle, males have much larger horns than females. Although a stag beetle's mandibles look like big scary jaws, they cannot bite humans.

The largest beetle is the Hercules beetle, which is a kind of rhinoceros beetle. They can grow up to seven inches long.

A beetle's life cycle resembles that of a butterfly. They are born from eggs as larva, big white grubs that live underground and feed on rotting wood. When it's time for them to become adults, they pupate. Butterflies pupate in chrysalises aboveground, but beetles pupate underground. After their bodies develop, they emerge as adults and live aboveground. Adult beetles eat tree sap and fruit. After they mate, females burrow underground and lay eggs. Lifespans vary depending on species, but some beetles can live for two to three years.

Beetles live all over the world. What kind of beetles live near you?

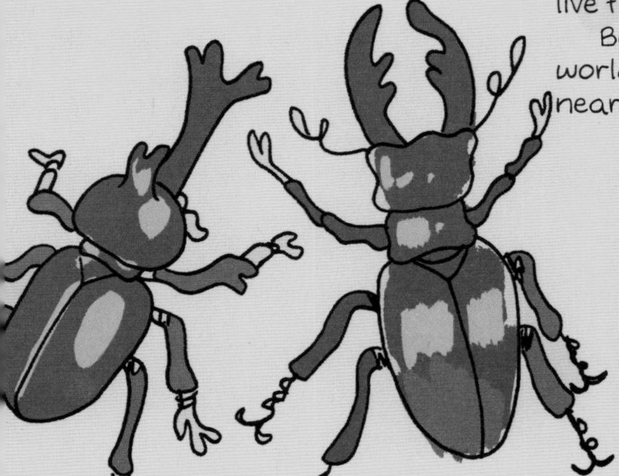

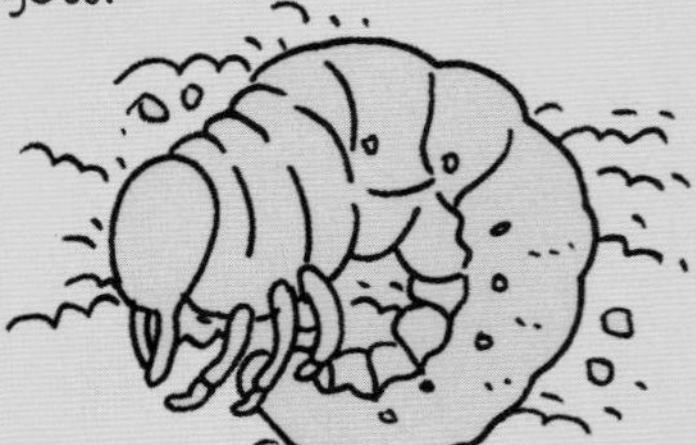

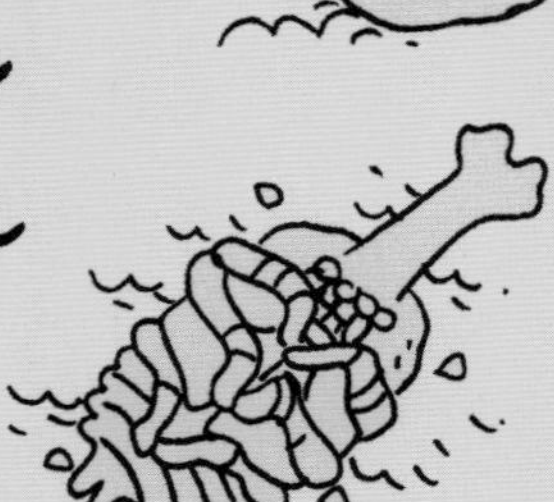

Laura Knetzger

grew up in Washington State, near Seattle. She wanted to be a cartoonist since she was eleven years old. She went to art college in New York City, and now she lives in Seattle.

She has a pet cat named Chilly. Chilly is a gray tuxedo cat. Cats are definitely Laura's favorite animal.

Laura got the idea to make Bug Boys as she was watching a documentary about bug collecting called Beetle Queen Conquers Tokyo. She drew two cute cartoon bugs as she was watching the movie, then tried to make up stories about them.

Her hobbies are reading, playing video games, and knitting. Laura's favorite food is udon noodles with tempura on top.

Bonus Comic

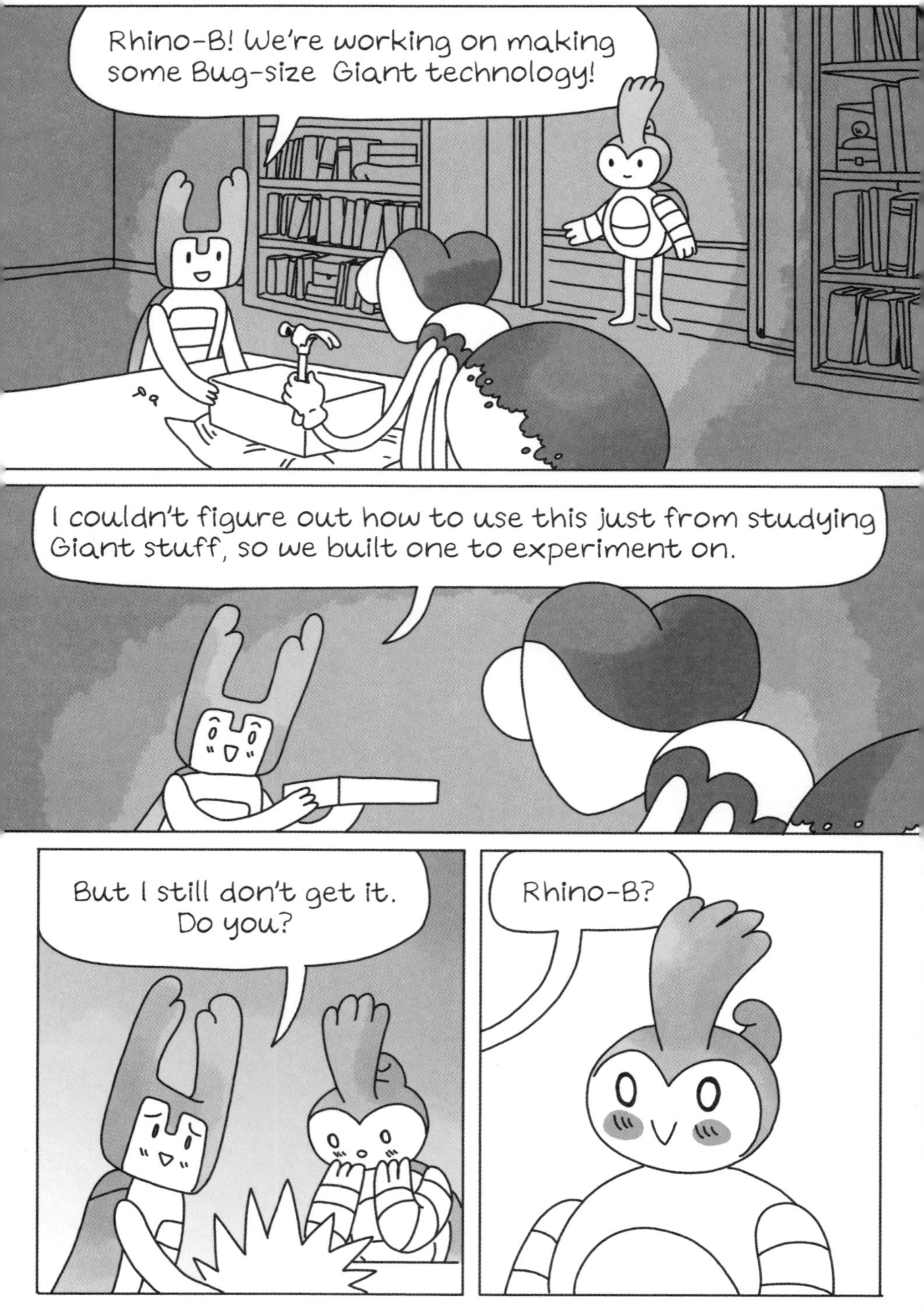
Rhino-B! We're working on making some Bug-size Giant technology!
I couldn't figure out how to use this just from studying Giant stuff, so we built one to experiment on.
But I still don't get it. Do you?
Rhino-B?

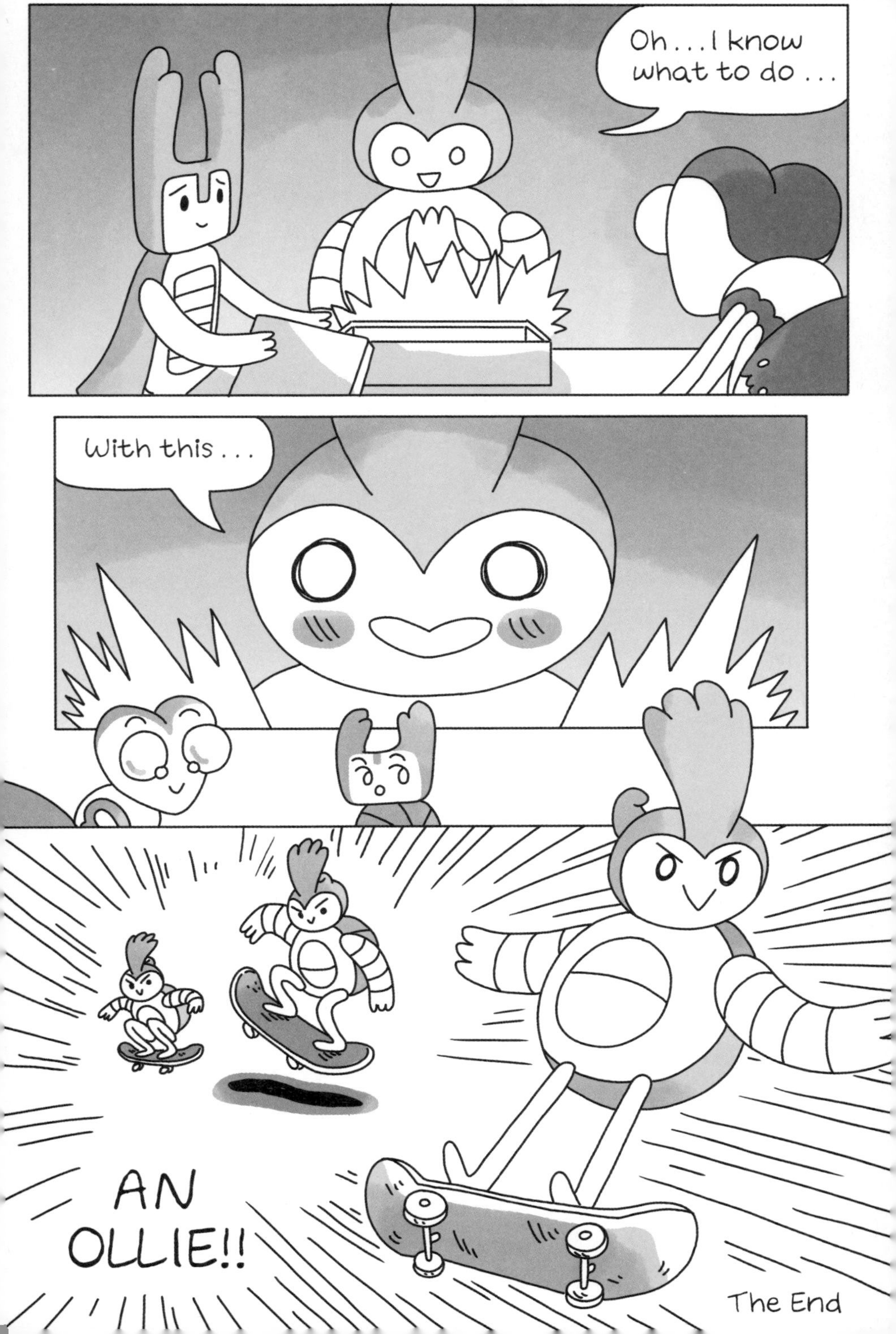
Oh . . . I know what to do . . .
With this . . .
AN OLLIE!!
The End

How to Draw Rhino-B

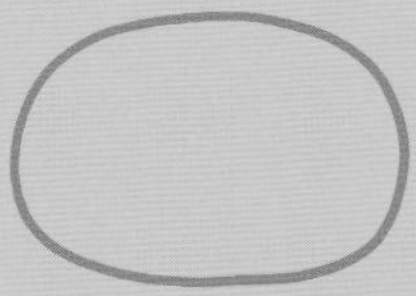

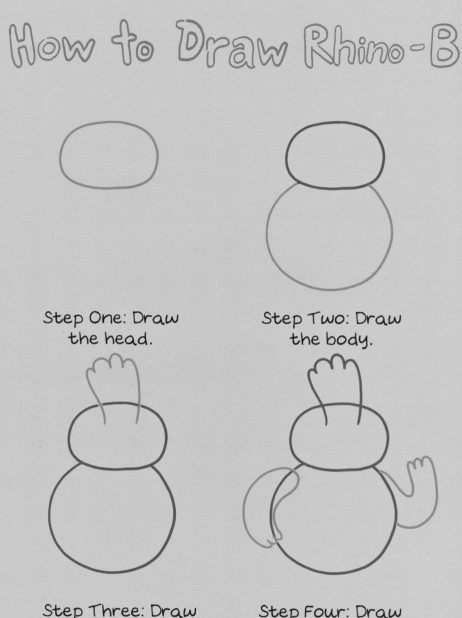

Step One: Draw the head.

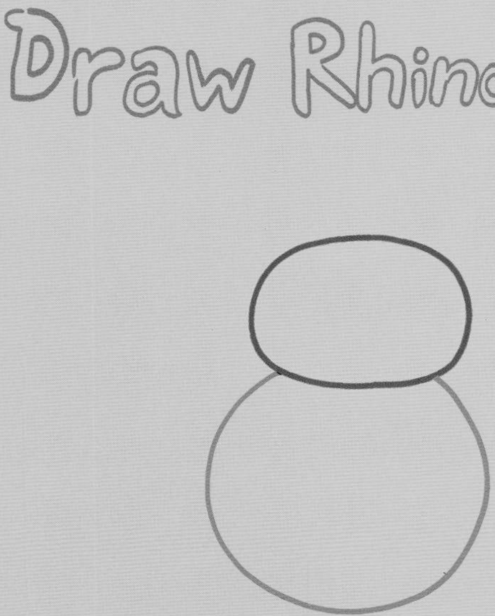

Step Two: Draw the body.

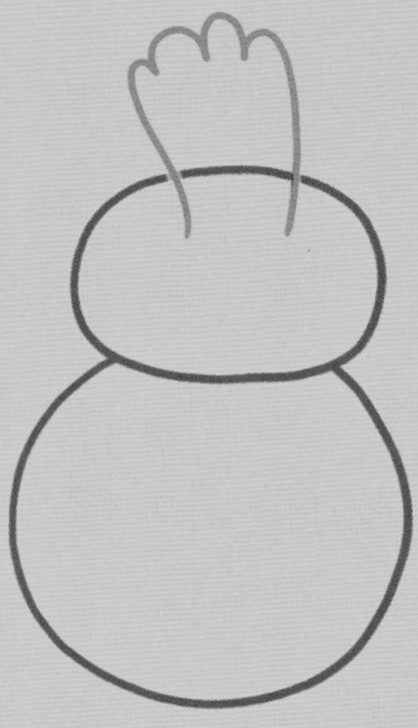

Step Three: Draw the front horn.

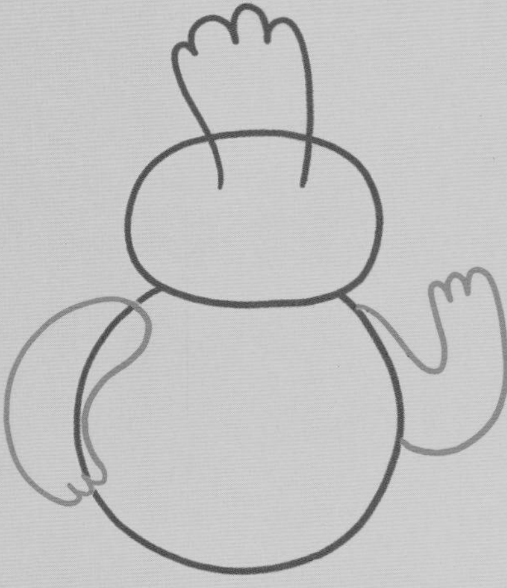

Step Four: Draw the arms.

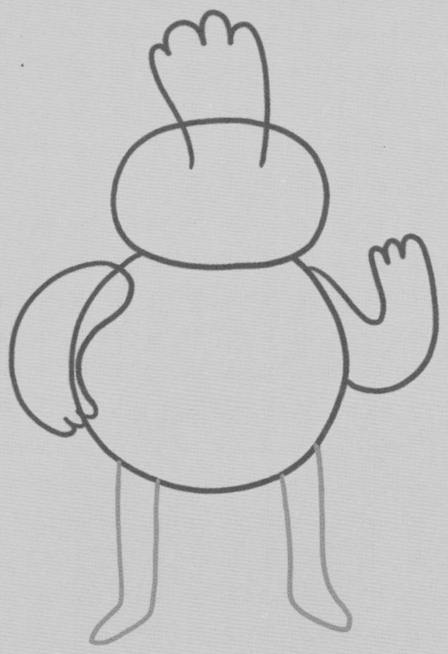

Step Five: Draw some legs.

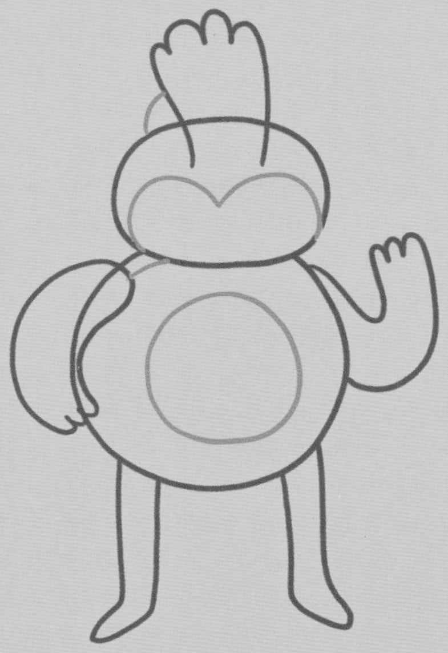

Step Six: Let's add some details.

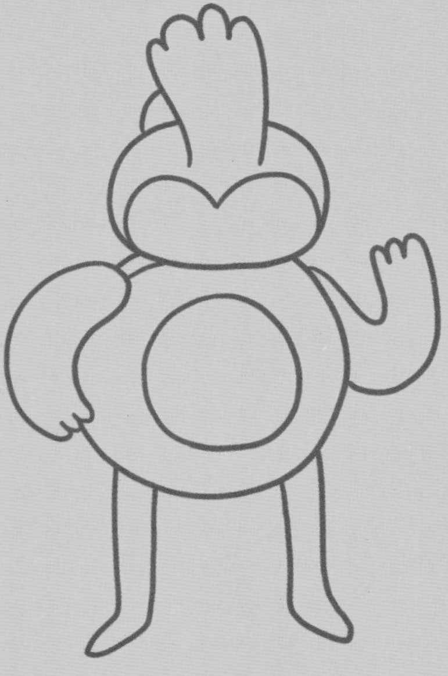

Step Seven: Erase those extra lines.

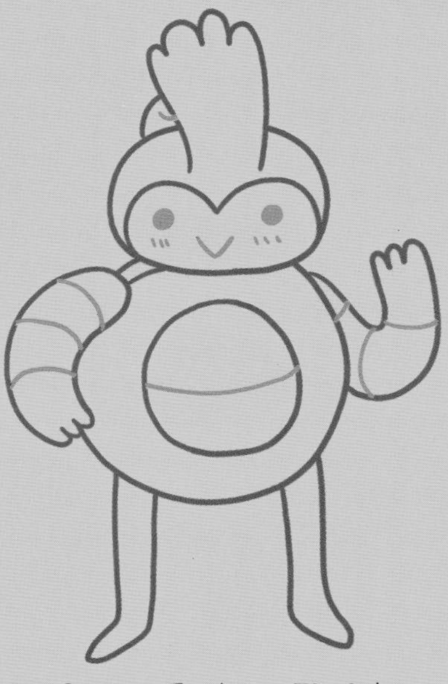

Step Eight: Finish off with a face and more details!

How to Draw Stag-B

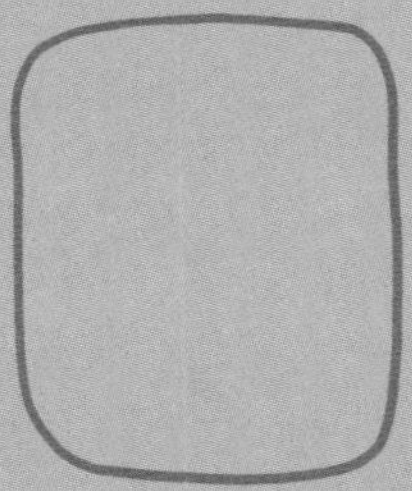

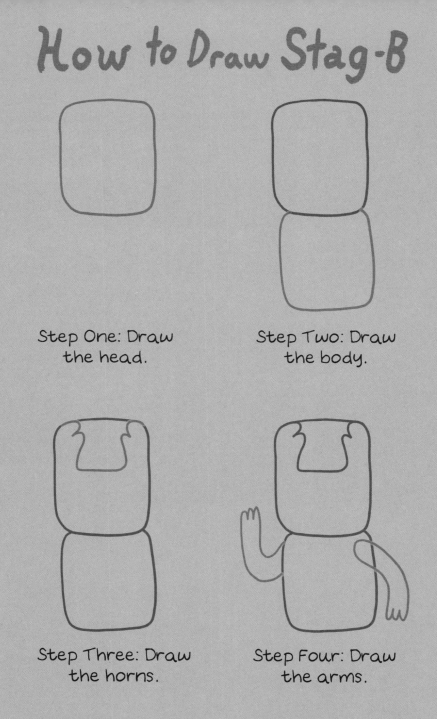

Step One: Draw
the head.

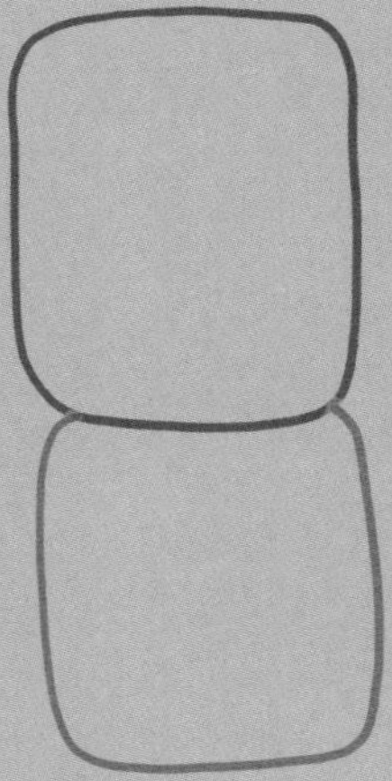

Step Two: Draw
the body.

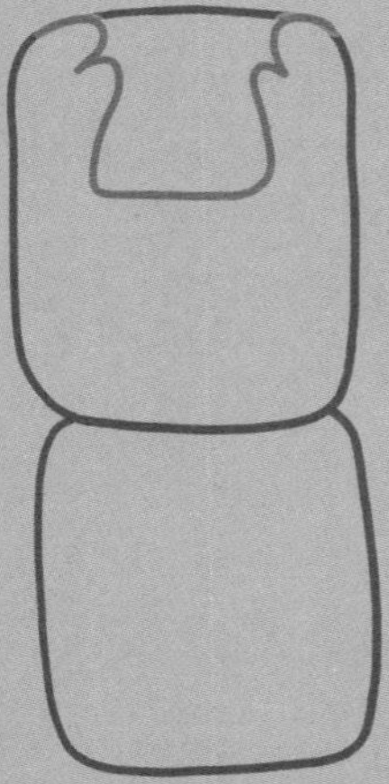

Step Three: Draw
the horns.

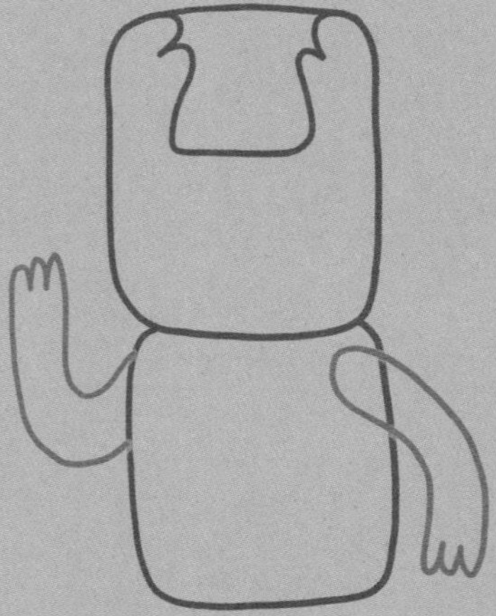

Step Four: Draw
the arms.

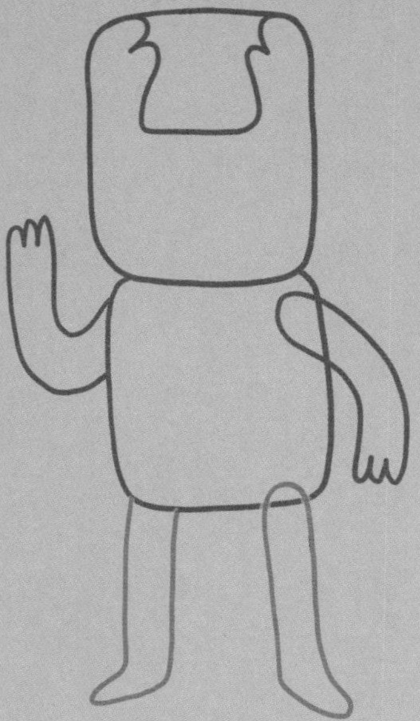

Step Five: Draw some legs.

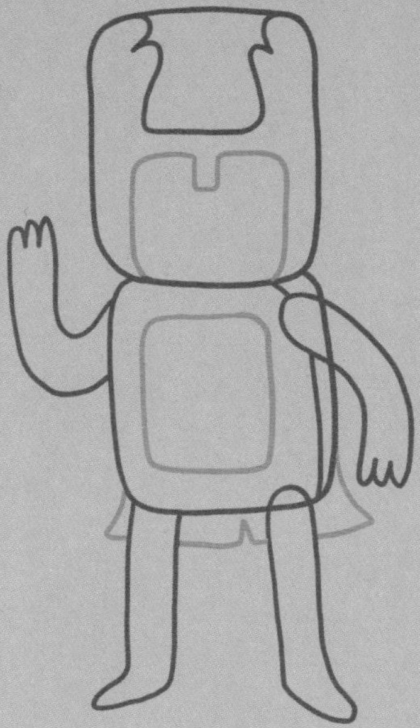

Step Six: Let's add some details.

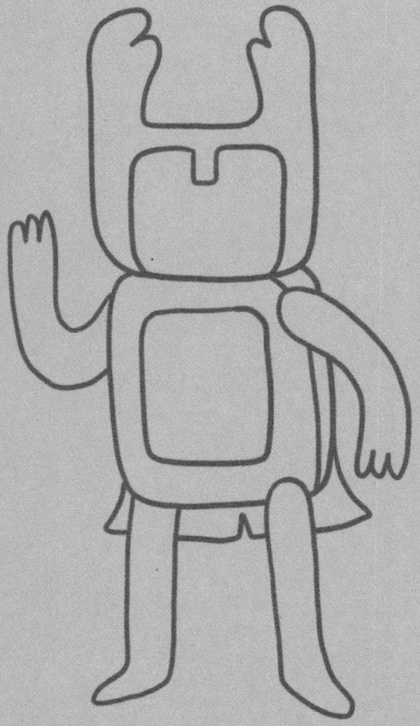

Step Seven: Erase those extra lines.

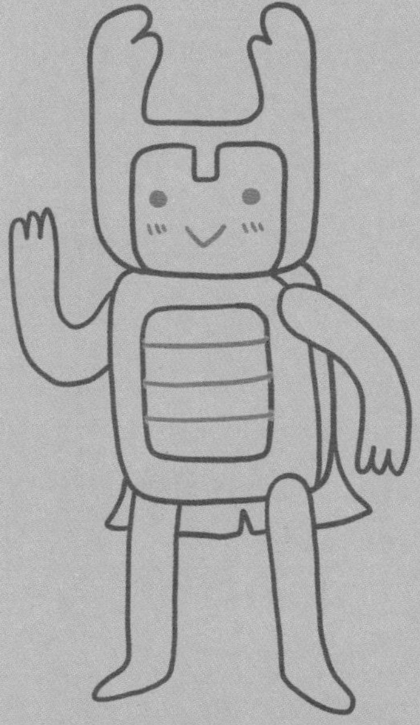

Step Eight: Finish off with a face and more details!

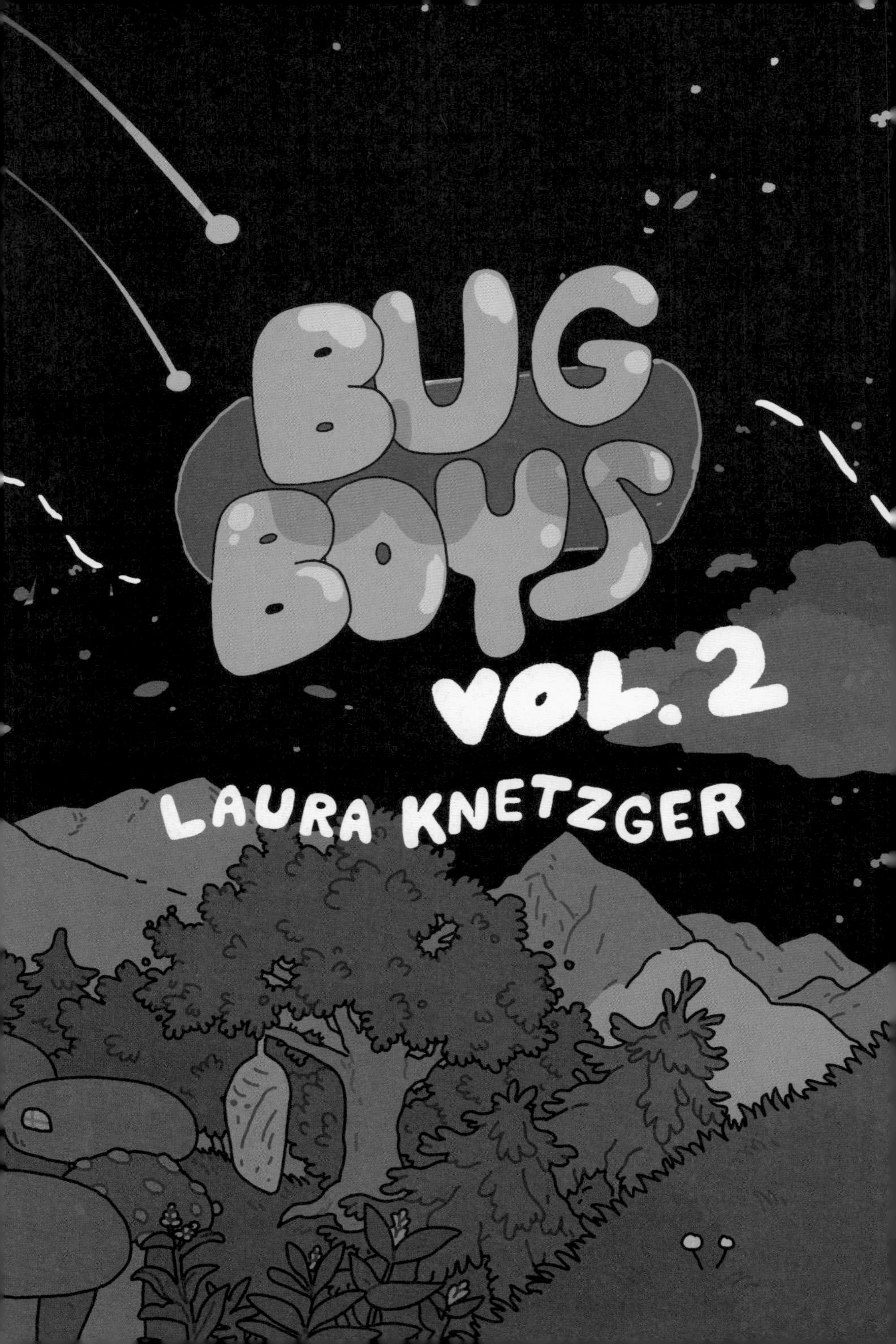
BUG BOYS
VOL. 2
LAURA KNETZGER

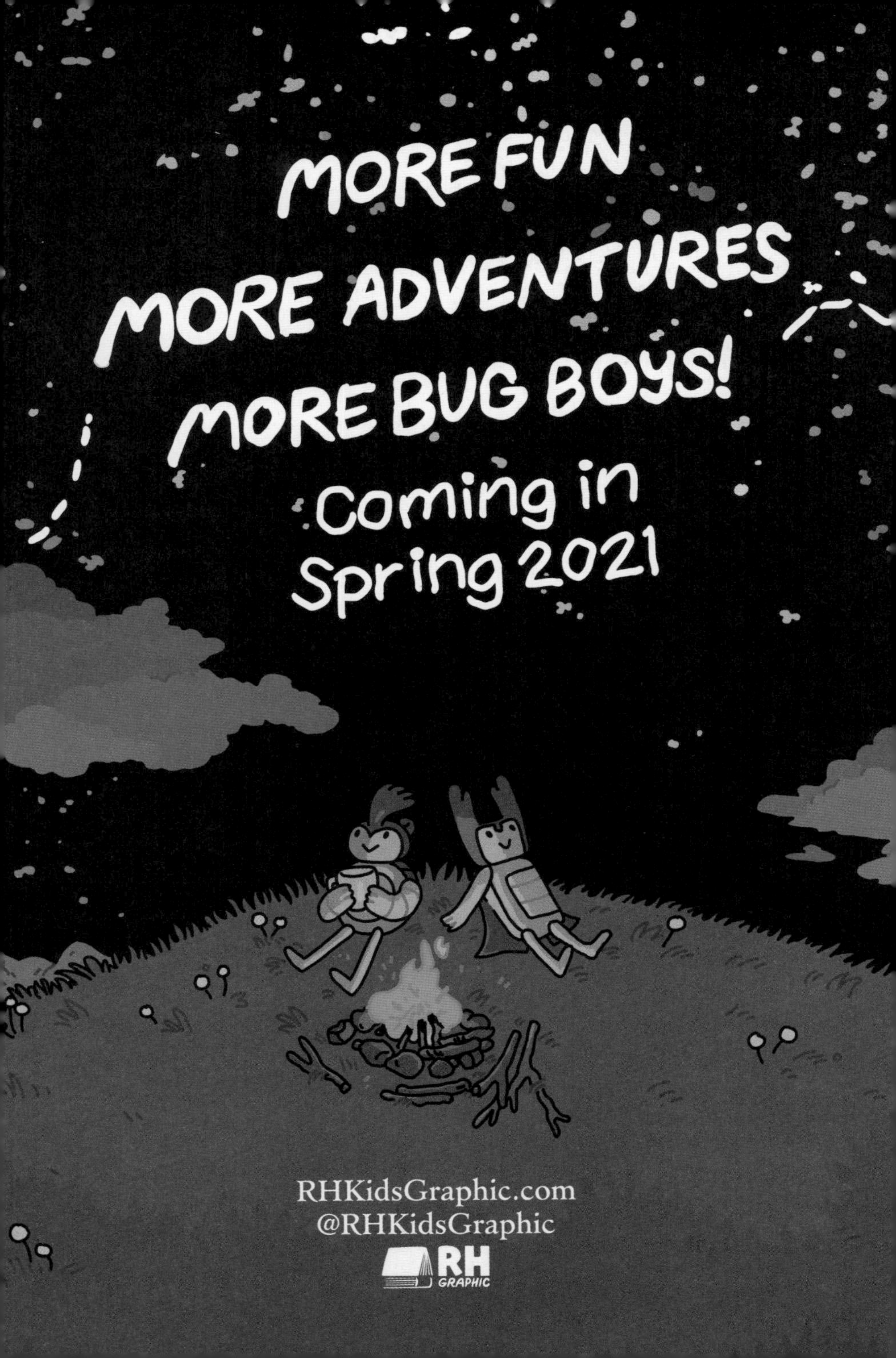
MORE FUN
MORE ADVENTURES
MORE BUG BOYS!
Coming in
Spring 2021
RHKidsGraphic.com
@RHKidsGraphic
RH GRAPHIC

RH GRAPHIC
THE DEBUT LIST

BUG BOYS
By Laura Knetzger

Bugs, friends, the world
around us – this book has
everything!
Come explore *Bug Boys*
for the fun, thoughtful
adventure of growing up
and being yourself.

Chapter Book

THE RUNAWAY PRINCESS
By Johan Troïanowski

The castle is quiet.
And dull.
And boring.
Escape on a quest for
excitement with our
runaway princess, Robin

Middle-Grade

ASTER AND THE ACCIDENTAL MAGIC
By Thom Pico & Karensac

Nothing fun ever
happens in the middle
of the country ... except
maybe ... magic?
That's just the beginning
of absolutely everything
going wrong for Aster.

Middle-Grade

WITCHLIGHT
By Jessi Zabarsky

Lelek doesn't have any
friends or family in the
world. And then she
meets Sanja. Swords,
magic, falling in love . .
these characters come
together in a journey
to heal the wounds of
the past.

Young Adult